Published by
featherproof **books**
Chicago, IL
www.*f*eatherproof.com

First edition
10 9 8 7 6 5 4 3 2 1

Library of Congress Control Number: 2020934070
ISBN 13: 978-1-943888-24-5

Edited by Rebecca Angelides, Dana Isaacson, and Jason Sommer
Endnotes edited by Jack Dugan
Cover design by Suzanne Gold
Interior design by Jason Sommer
Proofread by Marcus Brown and Jason Sommer

Set in Baskerville

Printed in the United States of America

History in One Act

A Novel of 9/11

by William M. Arkin

Learn more at HistoryInOneAct.com

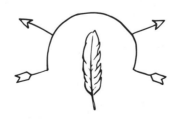

*f*eatherpr*oof* BOOKS

HISTORY
IN
ONE
ACT

a novel of 9/11

william m. arkin

Contents

To Rikki and Hannah with all my love.

Note from the Author

Much of the narrative here is based upon the words, writings, and opinions of Khalid Sheikh Mohammed (KSM), the conceiver and guide of the perpetrators of 9/11. His views are compiled together on a CD-ROM with the handwritten label "KSM Debrief Papers, Volumes 1–7" and stamped "Secret." That CD-ROM arrived in my mailbox in late 2008.

The CD-ROM contains approximately 8,000 pages of transcriptions of interrogations and debriefings of KSM, starting with his capture in Pakistan in 2003. The volumes contain memoranda and transcripts and other fragments (including various reports) and none of the material is consistently paginated and some of it duplicative, containing many drafts of the same reports. Much of the material is also undated. The volumes also contain CIA "finished intelligence" reports of the interrogation of KSM, reports dated April 12, 2003; May 27, 2003; July 12, 2003; July 23, 2003; July 30, 2003; September 9, 2003; September 27, 2003; January 9, 2004, and February 20, 2004. There are transcripts of select interrogations, including those held at "black sites" and evidently not distributed as serialized intelligence reports within the CIA. I collectively refer to KSM material in the endnotes as "KSM Debrief Papers, 2005" (the year it seemed to have been compiled).

After 9/11, the FBI meticulously reconstructed the actions of the Hamburg Three who came to the United States in June 2000—travel, banking, purchases and activities—in spreadsheets, timelines and databases. These various timelines were prepared by different FBI field divisions and are of varying quality, but include most centrally the activities of Mohammed Atta, Marwan al-Shehhi and Ziad Jarrah, the pilots of the planes that hit the World Trade Center and that crashed in Pennsylvania. The main document is called "Working Draft Chronology of Events for Hijackers and Associates." It is undated, but obviously was produced in late 2001. I also obtained the associated database and this chronological material is hereafter referred to as "FBI, Working Draft Chronology of Events for Hijackers and Associates." Many of the sub-timelines—for South Florida, Boston, San Diego, Washington DC, etc.—contain supplementary detail not contained in the main chronology or the FBI database.

I studied and used four other official timelines, histories, and reports relating to the 9/11 hijackers to write this book: the official printing of the National Commission on Terrorist Attacks Upon the United States (also known as the 9/11 Commission) final report (hereafter 9/11 Commission Report), the numbered 9/11 Commission Staff Statements (hereafter 9/11 Commission Staff Statement), the top-secret Report of the Joint Inquiry into Intelligence Community Activities before and after the Terrorist Attacks of September 11, 2001 (hereafter referred to as the Joint Inquiry), and CIA analytic report "The Plot and the Plotters," June 1, 2003, a long, post-9/11 reconstruction of the actions of the 19 hijackers (hereafter CIA, "The Plot and the Plotters").

I have tried to use the most commonly found American English spellings or versions of Arabic words and names throughout the volume. Granted, Arab transliterations are tricky, but there is a tendency on the part of the CIA and the intelligence community to use their own spellings over the spelling used by everyone else, as if somehow that conveys in special spelling that the intelligence community knows better or more about an organization or person being referred to. Hence the CIA insists—as do many Washington insiders—in referring to Osama bin Laden as Usama bin Ladin, or just UBL. Similarly with Khalid Sheikh Mohammed, the intelligence community tends to spell Sheikh as Shaykh. Ramzi Yousef is also most often referred to as Yusuf. *Al Qaeda* is often referred to as al-Qa'ida or al Qida. When you see these spellings out there in the wild, beware—someone (or some institution) is trying to convey authority and insider knowledge, often when it is unwarranted.

And then there's the weird practice of the U.S. government of using the *nom de guerre* of individuals rather than real names. For example, the U.S. government actually indicted and tried Ramzi Yousef (the main attacker of the World Trade Center in February 1993) under his made-up name—rather than his real name, which was Abdul Basit Karim. The reason was that an abundance of names might confuse a jury. But it would be like sentencing Zorro to death in a court in full regalia rather than removing his mask.

I have endeavored to adhere to the historical timeline of *al Qaeda* and the road to 9/11, but the dialog and feelings I ascribe to the terrorists are divined from the above material, from the many books written about the subject, and from discussions with government and private experts. The endnotes clarify much, but all references to the Saudi Arabian organization called "Apex" and the American organization "Apex Watch" as well as to "Project Sumner" are fictional. *History in One Act* is a novel.

PROLOGUE

Las Vegas
June 28, 2001

Mohammed Atta[1] finished his silent prayer and opened his eyes just as the airliner jerked to a stop at the jetway, getting up to retrieve his gym bag from the overhead bin, zipping his notebook into its outer pocket. Sitting in Seat 1C, he was the first to disembark from United Airlines Flight 955 at McCarran International Airport.[2]

"Have a good day," the flight attendant said as Atta passed her.

"And good luck."

Dressed in jeans and a white short-sleeved button-down shirt, he looked like any other tourist.

Except. Except that the first-class attendant thought she had failed to make her charge comfortable, failed to make conversation, even failed in offering him a drink, even water. Mr. Mohammed Atta, not a MileagePlus member according to her passenger manifest, had written in his notebook the entire flight. And his eyes, she thought, weren't those of your typical visitor to Las Vegas—that is, if she could even say anything about his eyes, having had an almost impossible time making any contact with him.

Marwan teased Atta about those eyes ever since he cut his beard, that his piercing stare was the first thing most people noticed about him. His friend urged him to relax more: to soften his face and look at people with a pleasant expression—to not hold his mouth so permanently set in a scowl, to smile more, even if it was only for the cause.

On the tram to the airport's main terminal, Atta stared out at the rim of mountains and the endless vista that surrounded the desert city. The sun beat down on the air-conditioned train and Atta craned his neck to take in the casinos in the far distance. He'd read that Las Vegas sprawled to the foothills on all sides, that it had been plopped in the middle of the desert by mobsters, that it had no real reason to be where it was—no river, no port, no crossroads even—sort of a metaphor for America, Atta thought: lost in blank and empty geography.

Getting off the tram, Atta followed the signs towards the shuttle buses. Riding the escalator down to the cavernous arrival hall, he immediately was assaulted. Every wall and pillar was swathed in too-colorful advertisements: gaudy hotels made up in garish themes, luxury this and that perfume, watches, luggage, automobiles. A blond and effeminate Siegfried and Roy humping a giant white tiger. Naked *Cirque du Soleil* dancers contorted into depraved sexual poses. There were comedians with orange hair. And various musical troupes dressed up like women.

Thinking that if Germany was the land of pink, Atta thought that Las Vegas was hot pink.

Prying himself away from this cacophonous inferno, he lurched outside. Though it was over 100 degrees Fahrenheit, he also cooled, and he felt free, breathing in the glorious heat, finding the bus stop, patiently waiting for a ride to the Alamo Company while smoking a Marlboro Light.[3]

When Atta presented the address of his motel at the exit of the rental car garage, the document checker suggested he take I-15 north. Atta said he wanted instead to drive the strip, Las Vegas Boulevard.

The man in the blue polo shirt ticked off another in his mental tabulation as to how many preferred to inch their way along that famous street. He pointed to the massive Mandalay Bay hotel and casino, visible and looming even though it was more than a mile away from the airport, telling the visitor to take a left and drive back towards the airport until he saw signs for the exit and then a right towards the airport exit road, making a gesture with his hand like an airplane banking to the right.

"Good luck," he said.

Good luck!

That seemed to be *the* greeting, the absent-minded Las Vegas version of *as-salamu alaikum*. The shuttle bus driver said it as well.

Driving north on the boulevard, Atta passed the famous sign welcoming all to the city of sins and dreams. He passed the ridiculous black pyramid-shaped Luxor casino, then the castle-themed Excalibur, dressed up in red- and gold-topped crusader towers.

His car windows wide open, Atta plunged into increasingly dense traffic, passing a drab-looking (given its name) Monte Carlo. Then there was the vaguely Middle Eastern-themed Aladdin on his right, with its taunting minarets. Then Paris. He waited for the light to turn green at the corner of Bally's and Bill's Western Saloon, gazing at the famous Caesar's Palace across the street, a landmark that stood out like the center square of an absent-minded Christian celebration.

He'd read in the inflight magazine that the city was a "mecca" for American and international tourists, an oblivious reference and yet another affront to his people and his religion.

There was only one Mecca and only one God.

Driving past the Mirage, Treasure Island and then the Fashion Showcase shopping mall, the boulevard gave way to mere thoroughfare, what Atta thought must be considered the "back of the plane"—second, third, fourth, and even fifth class of Las Vegas—each stretch of road a cheaper and cheaper ghetto, the billboards now hawking wedding chapels with fantasy themes, betting parlors claiming better odds, restaurants with one-dollar eats, and American redneck entertainment suitable for the lowest of the low rollers.

Then the upscale displays disappeared altogether. Now the boulevard was populated with gaudy gift shops—the *largest* gift shop in the world! 25,000 gifts! The Las Vegas strip abruptly ended at the forlorn and crumbling Sahara hotel and casino.

A magic carpet ride said the guidebook.

Sayyid Qutb[4] nailed it more than 50 years earlier, Atta thought. "What is its worth—this America—in the scale of human values?" Qutb wrote,

> "And what does it add to the moral account of humanity?
> And, by the journey's end, what will its contribution be?
> I fear that a balance may not exist between America's
> material greatness and the quality of its people. And I fear

that the wheel of life will have turned and the book of time will have closed and America will have added nothing, or next to nothing, to the account of morals that distinguishes man from object, and indeed, mankind from animals."[5]

Atta read the great Egyptian intellectual when he was a university student. He was doubly impressed because Qutb had written before oil began to burn in every heart, before civilizations collided and the pious vanguard went to make *jihad* in the mountains.[6]

Since being in America, Atta found himself seeing the same thing. He saw it in towering and perverted Manhattan, with its colossal structures. He saw it in flattened, racist Oklahoma. He saw it in the mind-numbing sprawl and stench of northern New Jersey. He saw it in the dead sameness of Florida and the endless indistinguishable highways and developments of everywhere and nowhere, even here in an American fantasyland built in the desert.

What was America worth? What did it believe?

Things. Status. Dreams of being a millionaire. But little more.

His friend Ziad drove Atta crazy with his teasing about the allure of Las Vegas, saying that even he would be crushed there.

And Ziad insisted before Atta left Florida on playing him a song by the American star Elvis Presley, a man famous in Sin City, he said. Atta hated music, but he especially hated this affront, its *"There is no God, but God,"* its talk of love. Except for that one line, that without love *"There'd be no birds, no planes to sail in the blue..."*[7]

Since coming to America, Atta hardened, everywhere feeling the enemy of God whispering. It wasn't just in the cultural blindness to the very existence of Islam. It wasn't just in the gross excess. It was in its devious allure.

Ziad teased Atta as he always did about the allure—that Satan would eventually get a hold of him and burrow into Atta's consciousness like a tick, that he would pleasure him until there was no Islam left.

If it weren't also for the fact that Ziad was the only one who understood Atta's twin desires, and that his friend also argued that there was no Satan, Atta might have felt shame. But his Lebanese brother also argued that there was no hell. And no heaven either. He argued that the word of the Prophet—*peace be upon him*—was only his word. He even went as far as to say that his word wasn't even the word of God, that God wasn't some voice in heaven, judging everything. Ziad said that to think that there were some cast of characters residing in the clouds was the wrong way to read their religion.

It was such blasphemy, that God didn't speak to the Prophet—*peace be upon him*. If Ziad didn't argue it so persuasively, if he weren't so smart, if he weren't his true brother, he would have never listened. In fact, he would have had nothing to do with him.

And so he tolerated Ziad speaking openly of pleasure, and action, and he struggled in conversations about what they were doing and why they were doing it, going over it again and again as they prepared.

It was the highest possible calling. That's what drove him to Las Vegas. It wasn't any of the promises. And truth be told, except for badgering from the two of them, Marwan and Ziad, jealous as they were that his scouting flight deposited him in the famed city, he would have preferred to be a million other places, and especially back in the safety of his little bungalow or in the cockpit.

Already he could tell that nothing in Las Vegas would impress him. None of it. His only flash of contentedness came for just a moment when he saw the Manhattan skyline of the New York-New York casino. He smirked to himself that surely that skyline would never be the same again.

And surely there would never be a Pentagon-themed casino, not after the American military machine was humiliated right in the midst of its own radiating and ugly monument.

That is, if the Pentagon was hit.

He and Marwan took the train to Washington and took the Pentagon tour, walking its long hallways, gazing at the displays, the walls of heroes, the acres of bulletin boards. On that trip to the capital of America, they also discovered that Clinton's White House, portrayed on television as if it were some huge mansion, was surprisingly small and tucked into the center of the city between much larger buildings, a far trickier target than either the highly-perched Capitol building of the Congress or the sprawling Pentagon.

The man Atta only knew as *Mukhtar*, "the brain," their teacher and the conceiver of their calling, insisted that the *al Qaeda* higher-ups wanted them to hit the White House, the concept for the planes operation being one military, one political and one financial target—thus fixing the Pentagon as one of three and, in theory, giving him few options.[8]

But now a year into their preparation, Atta faced another problem. *Mukhtar* produced a new pilot, a Saudi, someone who was not part of their Hamburg group and someone none of them knew. Unable to gauge this latecomer's skills or his resolve, Atta really couldn't say whether they would be successful hitting the headquarters of the American military machine.

And, while he had no doubt that Ziad would succeed in his mission to hit the Capitol dome, he also knew that Marwan was no longer going to Washington—that is, if Marwan joined them at all.

He was very sick. Dying.

There might be only three pilots when the day came, pretty much eliminating the White House as an option.

If the worst came, Atta thought the Pentagon might also have to be abandoned. He rationalized that the giant structure on the edge of the Potomac River was too big for even an airplane to do much damage, and that attacking it was more symbolic than anything else.

Two cities, five possible targets, four pilots, but now it was maybe even three pilots and possibly just two.

The wheel of life.

Atta pulled into the parking lot at the Econo Lodge on the fringe of old Las Vegas, giving the clerk his Florida driver's license and a Visa debit card, taking his key and retreating to his grungy second-floor room.[9]

He half-watched and listened to screeching cable television while he reviewed his notes about the configuration of the Boeing 767 airliner. He reviewed cabin procedures on take-off, and the ebb and flow of the flight, where the first-class flight attendants went, when the cockpit door opened, how far the other crew members were away from the front of the plane. He compared his notes for the Las Vegas flight with previous flights: Boston to San Francisco and his Fort Lauderdale to Boston scouting trip on the previous day.

As night fell, he drove to the nearby Cyber Café on South Charleston Street, logging into one of his many Travelocity accounts, booking a return flight from Las Vegas to Boston on another Boeing 767 for July 1st, a follow-on 767 flight to New York on July 2nd, and another flight with the same airplane make and model from Newark to Florida.[10]

Back at the motel, he stood outside and smoked a cigarette, calling Marwan on one of his cellphones to see how he was feeling.

"I am dying" his beloved said with his usual air of congenial resignation. "Dying before the Prophet—*peace be upon him*—grants me the fortune to realize my dream."

"And you won't go to a doctor?"

"For what? To be told once again that I am dying. To risk exposing us. I have but one wish, my brother: to finish and die with honor."

"We are close," Atta reassured him.

"Close. Yes. But tell that to my gut…"

This earthly Mohammad would lose Marwan either way, reunited perhaps in another life, the only sure bet being that Atta would be relieved of the unbearable burden that he carried in this one.

"Let's change the subject," said Marwan. "Tell me what you have learned."

"Again, every trip is the same—not so much in what happens, but in their inattention," Atta answered. "Even at the security checkpoints at the airport the guards are bored and indifferent."

They'd seen it everywhere in America. The fat. The old. Pregnant women. Dressed up in uniforms, toothless armies of the barely laboring, barely armed only with pepper spray and walkie-talkies, lounging outside buildings and inside stores and banks, homeless sentinels of exaggerated security.

"I will be back soon," he said. "There are only a few weeks to go."

"*Insha'Allah*," Marwan responded, signing off. *If God wills it.*

The next morning, after a late night of work, he returned to the Cyber Café.[11] But this time he had a peculiar sensation. The clerk walked by when he was smoking outside, trying to make conversation. And then he did it again when he went to the vending machine. The pizza delivery guy the night before was also a little too interested in him, craning his neck to investigate his room. A sixth sense tingled, one he'd hardly ever felt in America and one he thought doubly odd in a city known for its worship of anonymity.

So he abandoned the usual form of communication scheduled for that day and instead logged into his emergency *Hotmail* account, sending an innocuous greeting to a non-existent cousin.[12]

In the afternoon, he returned to the Café at the appointed time, again paying for an hour on the computer, sitting down and waiting for the exact moment. Then he logged into *Yahoo!* Games, selecting Intermediate Chess Lounge 2, and taking a seat at Table 6.[13]

Their teacher, *Mukhtar,* had been waiting there for him, making his own game of ejecting hopeful players who sat down, all of them wanting to challenge him to a game of chess.

When Atta took his seat on the black side, *Mukhtar* switched the table to private mode: it was just the two of them. Using the internal chat feature, they were able to securely text.[14]

"All clear in NY?" typed Atta, inquiring about the arriving musclemen, the ones who would seize the planes.

"Those simpletons," *Mukhtar* pecked away at his keyboard. "Two brothers checked into their motel and then called *al Baluchi*[15] on the emergency contact number."

"Was something wrong?"

"No, nothing," *Mukhtar* answered. "They made a mistake and sent the wrong code: *We have entered the field ready to slit the throat of the bird.*"

"The Americans surely swept up that message," Atta wrote.

"It is a stupid mistake, but not a disaster," *Mukhtar* responded. "What I know of the Americans, of American spying, I doubt that what they say in New York would ever be noticed. Don't worry my friend."

"I feel almost foolish to say this then," Atta wrote, hesitant to sound paranoid, "but I feel like I am under some kind of surveillance."

"There, or in Florida?"

"Here. I don't really have anything specific. But I feel something."

"At the airport?"

"No. At the mctel."

"I hesitate to send my report right now," Atta continued. "But I want you to know I'm not sure about the place by the river. It is so big."

"But the others?" Mukhtar asked.

"I know the man from Beirut will make it to the wedding. And I love the place on the hill. And of course the main house is all dependent on our cousin's health."

"I'm sorry. How is our friend doing?" *Mukhtar* asked.

"He is not well."

Atta followed up: "There could be just two of us if the latecomer cannot fulfill his duty."

"Our uncle won't like having to give up the home with the big lawn," the brain responded.

"I have seen it with my own eyes and unless I shift our Lebanese brother from his place in the ceremony, we may have to let it go."

"It is in your hands," said *Mukhtar*. "I trust your judgment on what must be done."

The conversation ended.

The conversation ended but Atta knew that he had lied, lied to his teacher, and also that he was lying to *al Qaeda*.

Marwan was supposed to hit the White House, that is what Atta had reported to *Mukhtar* all along. But then something changed, maybe in his sickness, maybe in their earthly coupling. But the two decided that they would stay close to the end, martyring themselves in New York, one hitting the North Tower, one hitting the South. It would be a tribute to their love.

Atta went back to his motel, back to work. He considered moving out, but decided it made no sense.

He made another late-night call to Marwan.

"I will be home tomorrow," Atta said.

"So, what do you think about Las Vegas?" Marwan asked, mustering up some enthusiasm.

"I have been working, *ya amar*." It was his expression of love for him— my moon.

"Ziad says you must go to a casino and take a look," Marwan responded.

Ziad grabbed the phone. "Don't be a coward, my brother. If I can't see it for myself, I at least want your report."

"Brother … ," Atta responded.

"Just go. Think of it as a test of your will, your triumph over Satan. Something that will show that you are better. Please. Do it for me."

Ziad had given Atta a crisp $100 bill and told him to place it on the number 12 on the roulette table, the date of his marriage.

Atta got in his car and drove back down to the drab Sahara, parking in the garage and following the signs to the casino. He was immediately assailed by giant signs for "Striptease," a revue of naked women. *Starring Penthouse Pet of the Year*, the posters screamed. *Wasn't that enough to tell?*

He entered the low-ceilinged and surprisingly dimly-lit casino and wandered past the banks of noisy slot machines and the blackjack tables and the shouting packs of men at a dice table.

Then he stopped at a group of four roulette tables. There were a handful playing on one. He could barely look at the two women at the end of the felt, their breasts shooting out like missiles in all directions under their tight blouses.

"You want in?" one of the men asked, angling his body in invitation.

But Atta smiled a "no" and held back.

He'd read about the game, read of its allure, the roulette wheel spinning and the tiny white ball shooting around the curved edge, around and around, a palpable tension until the ball loses momentum and bounces from tray to tray, clickety clack clack clack until finally—*finally*—it comes to rest on the winning number. He'd read about the deceiving Hollywood portrayal, where there was always a tuxedo-clad James Bond type, nonchalant and omniscient, with a giant stack of chips placed on that very number.

And he'd read, too, that *the house* loved this portrayal. For in the forever of rolls and in the house's doctoral study of human nature, they knew that roulette was the most rapacious siren. Especially in Las Vegas because there the roulette wheels have 38 numbers—a 1 to a 36 plus a single zero and a double zero—one more than in the rest of the world's casinos. That meant that the mathematical odds were even more in the house's favor, that the casino could go about its business of "losing" one out of 38 bets, taking in 38 chips and dispensing 35, always winning.

As he watched the hungry men and the whooping whores, he felt superior in his restraint, thinking that their shame made them happy to pay the casino this tax even when they did *win* because receiving something—anything—fed their dream of some riches-laden voyage.

And so, he'd read, despite everyone saying that they had systems for winning, for conserving their money and beating the casino, the truth was that wanting *something*—wanting anything—actually meant that they superstitiously bet on numbers associated with birthdays and anniversaries, and then they supplemented with lucky and not-so-lucky numbers, and then they took out a form of *insurance* to supplement their superstitious worship, putting chips on corners and sides of numbers, hoping for halves or fourths if anything hit, putting more money on red and black, or on odd and even, praying for some possibility of winning *something*.

Beaten by Satan into insanity, the *Qur'an* says about this rapacious monster.[16] It was an admonition against taking unlawful interest from those in need, and against gambling.

Satan, he thought—*the house*. It knew that players behaved this way—9 out of ten times, 99 out of 100, 999 out of a thousand and on and on to infinity—in their hungry pursuit of the false God.

Atta stood and watched. Again, and again, the little ball landed on some random number and each player's chips dwindled.

But it had not yet fallen on the number 12, Ziad's lucky number. He congratulated himself on saving his money.

Then one of the women hit her number and she let out a shriek of delight, throwing her arms in the air, high-fiving the others at the table, her breasts bouncing. Atta thought he was going to vomit.

He fingered the $100 bill in his pocket. Six rolls now and number 12 hadn't yet made its appearance. Maybe it was time, he thought. Maybe it would come soon. He steadied himself on the Plexiglas shield around the wheel.

"No touching," the chip handler said. "Sir, no touching."

He backed away. "You want in?" the man closest to the wheel asked and Atta again frowned a "no," feeling shame that indeed Satan pulled at him.

The next roll was the number 32. Atta found himself doing the math—$3,500 for Ziad's one-hundred-dollar bet. Now 12 was even more likely to come, he surmised. He started sweating. *Sixteen red*, the dealer then announced on the next spin. Maybe this was the moment, Atta thought. A dollar sign materialized. *Put the money on the table.*

He was being pulled, pulled in.

He turned around and quickly left the casino, hurriedly smoking a Marlboro as he leaned against the car, calming himself before he got in.

Mohammed Atta entered the United States more than a year earlier, lived in three different states and visited four different flight schools, leased 17 apartments and one house and stayed in 51 hotels and motels. He obtained two driver's licenses, rented 33 and purchased two cars, took 27 commercial flights, opened four bank accounts, obtained 13 different cell phones, used and disposed of 114 prepaid telephone calling cards, registered 23 different email accounts, mailed 64 regular letters and packages, used ATM machines and debit cards a total of 279 times, sent 1,223 email messages, and participated in almost 300 chat sessions buried in various online gaming websites.[17]

And Mohammed Atta prayed: 1,910 times to be precise, five times a day since arriving.

In the name of *Allah* most gracious and most merciful, these were his lucky numbers, this was his system.

PART 1

Chapter 1 Land of the Pink

The *Masjid al Quds*, in a nondescript office building in the St. Georg district near Hamburg's main train station, had a light-filled prayer room on its main floor, classrooms and a library upstairs, and a cafeteria and small grocery store above that.[18]

The young Moroccan volunteer who showed the bearded visitor around stressed that the three-year-old *al Quds* served the city's devout Arab population—the *Sunni* population—and he stressed to his Egyptian guest that its imam, *Sheikh* Fazazi was "known throughout the Middle East."[19]

"How many come?" asked Atta.

"On Friday night, we get maybe 200 brothers," answered his young guide, "but we can hold as many as 400 men," and then he lowered his voice and leaned in, "and more are coming every day."

There were a few Egyptians, he told him, at least amongst the young men, a few from the universities. But the congregation was attracting people from all over the world, especially brothers from North Africa, to hear fiery *Sheikh* Fazazi preach.

The volunteer gave him a small brochure about their *Salafi*[20] orientation and invited the rail-thin Egyptian to have juice. The top floor dining room was open and inviting, and Atta was pleased to see men sitting in small groups talking, many of them reading. And there were many long beards, fellow Muslims who by their appearance proudly announced that they were devout or had done their *Hajj* to Mecca.[21]

"We have the cheapest *halal* meals," the guide said as they waited in line. "And we are safe from the city."

Safe from the city. To Mohammed Atta that meant a sanctuary from the pink.

When he first moved to Hamburg, Atta mostly remembered the gray a sort of permanent shroud of clouds that hung over the place, a color that persisted even during most of the summer. It was a depressing contrast to the blinding whiteness of his Nile delta home. Not just the sky. The buildings were also gray. Even the water formed a constant gray canvas.

He remarked to the German family he lived with that it seemed to rain every other day. At first, Atta darted in and out of the constant drizzle until, finally, he capitulated to his dreary fate. But he remained ever aware of the clouds and greyness, the port city in perfect harmony with its North Sea setting, mists and rain forming an uninterrupted wallpaper from sky to water.

The second thing Atta noticed about the city, though, and of all of Germany, was the pink. Like some optical illusion, the always smiling Germans seemed pink and hairless like babies, fleshy and with blinding teeth, so blond that even their hair seemed pink, and so white and iridescent that they seemed to blend into a pulsating oneness. This was a color that didn't even exist in Egypt, he thought. He started seeing it everywhere. He saw the pink on television, the pink in advertisements, pink even in the newspapers.

One day, almost as if a massive cruise ship pulled into the harbor, the sun suddenly arrived. It was so rare, the sun, that Atta felt a transformative warmth as he sat on a park bench, his sour mood softening. He took out a Marlboro Light and lit it up, taking a deep drag on the cigarette and thrusting back his head to feel the sun on his face. All around, the pink people started rejoicing as well, an army of loud burghers filling outdoor cafes, throwing off sweaters and jackets, noisily clinking beer steins.

And almost immediately, they materialized. Everywhere. Breasts. Pink breasts. On every possible speck of grass, women shed their tops and spread blankets on the ground to lay down and soak up the sun. It was a disgusting sea of pinkness everywhere he looked. Big ones, small ones. Young ones, old ones. Youthful ones, even those that were bloated and long ago maternal. Everywhere he didn't want to look.

Atta hurried home, directing his gaze anywhere else, sickened and confused. The mother of his host family, well-meaning devotees of the Arab world, explained that the human body—*natur*—was nothing to be ashamed of. Nudism was a lifestyle in harmony with nature, *Freikörperkultur* had always been the Hamburg way. The city was not just liberal and social democratic, but even Scandinavian in attitude, she said.

Of course, the exposure might be shocking to him, the husband said, coming from such an *old-fashioned* place, but he would get used to it. He nudged Atta—*ha ha*—like the boys back home once nudged him—in this case an elbowing buffoon winking and forcing his mind's eye to gaze again at the forbidden pink.

Atta retreated to his room to pray. By then he'd been in Germany a year and had celebrated his 25th birthday with these kindly people. But he'd also begun to ask himself questions about the pink, about this foreign country, and who he was. And he asked himself with each pink reminder why he was so different, so different from those childhood friends and now from his host, a leering man.

That evening, his host family's loud, adult daughter came by, visiting with her annoying bastard child. She piled it on even more, ever so happy to criticize the inferior and puritanical Arab world, to educate their poor, oppressed guest.

She'd irritated Atta in the past with her ignorant prattle about the similarities between the Bible and the *Qur'an*, that there was no difference between their religions, that everyone wanted the same thing out of life. Soon enough, she'd say in her crusader simplicity, his people, too, would arrive at the promise land, the modern world, where old walls and divisions were eliminated.

Now he heard her saying at the dinner table that this pinkness was the future. Women didn't even need husbands anymore. Men and women would someday be the same, she preached. All the world would eventually be bathed in freedom, a milk breast pillow soothing everyone and eliminating male aggression. Even eliminating war.

Atta moved out.[22]

Now, everywhere he looked in Germany, cloudy or sunny, on campus or in the city, pink assaulted him. He felt it in every scrubbed face, in every leg on the bus, pink in every fat child and wailing baby, pink in the politician's smile, even in the university's classrooms and study halls.

Gaunt and big-eared, with dark eyes that exuded seriousness, Mohammed Atta didn't start out very religious. He'd grown up in comfortable and placid Kafr el Sheikh, a provincial capital 100 miles north of Cairo. His father, a lawyer and mid-level bureaucrat working for the Egyptian government, devoted himself to striving for a better life for him and his family. His mother was loving and doting.[23]

One thing that Mohammed Senior insisted was that his children— two older girls and the youngest, his only boy—get an education. He pushed young Mohammed to excel, to learn English so that he would be more valuable. He pushed him to continue his architectural engineering studies in Germany, pushed him to learn German, telling him that young Mohammed would acquire an edge, that he needed an edge. Atta's father pulled government strings to get visas and sponsorship for him to travel abroad, and he found the nice German couple to host his son, arranging for a tutor to give Atta yet another leg up by building proficiency in a third language.[24]

Mohammed Junior threw himself into his studies, conquering mathematics and languages. But he didn't find peace. And nothing he did was good enough for his father.

"What? I have three daughters?" the old man taunted when baby-faced Junior showed no interest in football during secondary school, no interest in their country club-sponsored events and social mixers, no interest in girls.

"Leave the boy alone," his mother pleaded, attentive protector to her sensitive and curly-haired baby.

But she, too, encouraged her little Amir, as the family called him, to "toughen up" for his own good, to partake in the delights of oh-so-modern Egypt, the clubs and the discos, and *the dating*.

When Mohammed Atta entered Cairo University,[25] he began to appreciate how his father had the right instinct—even if it was a selfish one—to ready his children to advance in what he would learn was a very corrupt society. Almost instantly upon his arrival, it became clear to Atta that anyone who didn't have connections, and who didn't affect the behaviors and dress of conformism, and even anonymity, not only had no advantages but were suspect to the authorities. There seemed to be only two stances possible: for or against the government of President Hosni Mubarak.[26] Atta quickly grasped that it was only a short drive from his childhood existence to no job and no future.

The Egyptian strongman had taken power when Mohammed Junior was just 13 and, by the time he entered university, he had erased the last vestiges of Egypt's earlier flirtations with socialism. He threw open the country to the West and to private investment. Sprawling Cairo, one of the largest cities in the world, became wholly international, a pleasing destination for tourism, with European and American luxury stores moving in, hotels and restaurants springing up all over.

Mohammed Atta knew his father believed in Mubarak, just as he believed in Anwar Sadat, believed in peace with Israel, peace with the Jews, peace. But at the university, young Atta learned that in his upbringing he'd been completely cut off from the truth of what was really going on in the country. And the world. Not only democratic politics, but religion itself had been forced underground. Any expression of actual Islamic interest or piety was regarded with suspicion, part of the other camp—the extremist camp. At the university, the message whispered in the lounges and hallways was that Islam was the solution, the alternative to the failures of both socialism and capitalism. Bur young Atta didn't see much actual manifestation of piety or religious study going on. Nor did he yet feel it himself. But he nevertheless came to learn that Islam seemed the third, and only, other way.

Atta gravitated towards engineering.[27] Saudi Arabia and the Gulf states were funding magnificent modern buildings, and in architecture that's where the money was. Mohammed Junior was also fascinated with the way things worked, attracted to practical questions of roads, infrastructure, and housing for the people. When he started to delve into the question of housing, he asked why—despite all the construction going on around the mega-city—that everything was so expensive and flimsy. A professor tilted Atta ever so slightly to see the greed behind those profitable realities. He recommended Atta read more outside the field of engineering. Perhaps the answers to his questions, he said, were not solely within the realm of construction and economy.

Atta waded through various tracts, starting with *Bitter Harvest* by the famous Egyptian Ayman Zawahiri.[28] Fellow students seemed to secretly revere *the doctor*, who was the founder of the Egyptian Islamic Jihad,[29] the most prominent of the extremist organizations. But try as hard as he could, Atta couldn't relate, his explanation of Islam twisted for the sake of justifying a revolt against the government.[30]

Then he discovered Sayyid Qutb. Over his first summer break, much to his father's dismay, rather than hang out at the beach or learn to play tennis, Atta dove into the writings of this towering Egyptian. In *Milestones*, Qutb spoke at length of persecuted Islam, not just under active threat from the Egyptian dictators, but also from the West and from secularism. Capitalism, communism, socialism, all the ideologies of the 20th century were threats to the very survival of their religion and their culture, Qutb said.[31] He argued that a vanguard had to stand up to preserve and spread true Islam.

Qutb had traveled to America after the Second World War, in search of an understanding of the modern ways. He thought that in the heartland he might find some articulation of a world that wasn't sprung from tyrants or tycoons, that there might be something that truly represented a different future, and possibly a future for Egypt as well.

Qutb described how in America he was taken in by friendly people everywhere he went. He loved the openness of Americans, loved their allegiance to no monarch and no ideology of the past.

But once he was also invited into the privacy of their homes, he discovered what he said was a kind of repulsive American animalism— which he labeled *jahiliyyah*[32] or pagan—a way of life that strived for and worshiped animal desire above all else. Couples—animal pairings as he called them—disappeared into nondescript and identical suburban cages separated from blood relatives and even from their own communities. There the animals focused on personal grooming, on watching an endless loop of addictive television, and on spending inordinate amounts of time and money tending to their lawns.

Religion was there in American life, Qutb wrote. But churches competed for large congregations, a commercial marketplace seeking to extract financial support through bingo and raffles—religious practice itself secondary and any sense of obligation to provide for the poor or less fortunate absent in this fully transactional society. Whatever technical acumen America had, and Qutb spoke admiringly of an industrious land that produced much material plenty, he just couldn't get beyond his conclusion that such achievements were squandered on a place "abysmally primitive in the world of the senses, feelings, and behavior."

While most of Atta's peers ate up Qutb's political commentary and applied his observations to all that was wrong with modern-day Egypt, young Atta was drawn to other parts of his writings.

In *The America I Have Seen*,[33] Qutb wrote that the country revolved around lust and impulse; the nature of family obligations and the role of man and woman turned upside down. Men were encouraged to focus on their own looks as a way of attracting the most voluptuous mate, Qutb wrote. He was especially repelled by the overt sexuality of the American female. Everywhere Qutb went, the wanderer recounted provocative sexual disruptions: on the streets, on the train, in a coffee shop, even in the classroom.

"The American girl is well acquainted with her body's seductive capacity," he wrote. "She knows it lies in the face, and in expressive eyes, and thirsty lips. She knows seductiveness lies in the round breasts, the full buttocks, and in the shapely thighs, sleek legs and she knows all this and does not hide it. … Then she adds to all this the fetching laugh, the naked looks, and the bold moves, and she does not ignore this for one moment or forget it!"

Qutb's words matched what young Atta felt, even if he didn't know why. But later he returned again and again to these parts of his essays, driven to try to understand the pink, to try to understand his shame.

Even though he was from a place where women generally didn't cover themselves, even though Atta had older sisters, by the time he was a university student he had never seen a naked woman. Atta remembered that when boys produced the rare "French" postcards or somehow procured Western magazines showing unclothed females, passing them around to fascinated and enthralled leering, he went out of his way not to look, appalled and revolted just like Qutb.

Lighten up, his friends said.

Lighten up. Toughen up. Atta had heard it his entire life.

And yet he wanted neither. The prospect of marriage was repulsive. And the middle class life? He would never end up like his father, he told himself.

Off to Germany Atta went—to study more, for economic opportunity, for independence from his father and from Egypt, and for the opportunity to find his own way. He came to Hamburg curious and open. The city was clean and orderly. Germany was tolerant of outsiders. School was challenging and meritorious. But all of that was washed out when he started seeing pink everywhere. Soon he saw all of Germany bathed in its pink hue, the pink an imposition on his own people, an inviting color that sought to turn everything into its shade.

Atta didn't quite understand his revulsion, didn't quite understand his increasing impatience with this pink paradise. He knew he was different. But what the difference was remained illusively out of reach. He applied himself ferociously to his studies and he found a part time job working at an urban planning consultancy, impressing professors and employers with his commitment and smarts. With excellent language skills and seemingly an absence of religious passions, he was soon working on German government-sponsored projects, working on contracts to analyze modern architecture, getting grants to travel, and conducting studies of the ancient Middle East.[34]

He got a grant to travel to Aleppo in Syria to participate in an archaeological dig.[35] There Atta discovered the old city, a last bastion seemingly making a final stand against the worst excesses of predatory modernization. Packed and low-rise, the old city survived hundreds of years of onslaughts. One of the reasons it survived, Mohammed Atta surmised, was because its labyrinthine alleyways could not accommodate cars. Another reason was its small scale: There were no apartment blocks looming into the sky or into each other, no Soviet-inspired housing projects like much of the rest of the socialist-leaning country. What was beautiful and placid in the old city held on in the middle of an otherwise modern place, an urban desert that was now bristling with the same-*same* apartments and buildings. Everywhere outside the old city, the place was just like Cairo. And, come to think of it, Atta thought, it was just like Hamburg as well, a sameness that transcended two supposedly different worlds.

Atta researched a topic that would become his thesis: the conflict between traditional Middle East family structures—he didn't yet think Islam—and its cities, how Western influences in modern architecture—most importantly, in the social isolation created by high-rise buildings—

exerted an undue influence on the society.[36]

He posited that the old quarter of Aleppo was the answer to preserving the old ways. He formulated a theory about the impact of "modern" architecture, drawing on Qutb's observations of American suburban isolation.[37] Maybe high-rise buildings, he told a professor, were intrinsically anti-family and anti-community in that they undermined the preservation of the social structure. His professor enthusiastically supported his work, thinking his thesis clever and culturally appropriate.[38]

Personally unmoored, Atta gravitated to Islamic study to supplement his intellectual foundation. Leaving his host family, he moved first to a graduate school apartment, and then he rented his own apartment off campus. There he disastrously shared a two-bedroom existence with a series of random roommates—all of whom he began to see as *jahiliyyah,* all of whom he thought were striving for nothing but a life of pink or an emulation of the pink, hoping to whitewash themselves into Western conformity.

And so, the *al Quds* mosque became his second home, and indeed it was a place that was safe from the city and all that it represented.[39]

"Nothing but crumbs," *Sheikh* Fazazi preached.[40] "The unbelievers introduce poverty at home and then force us, all of us, to find salvation in Europe. Here, we work like slaves doing the work that Germans do not want, washing their dishes, cleaning their toilets."

"Democracy is the religion of the infidels and is imposed on the whole world," Fazazi said.

"Be like a stranger in this world," he urged to his adherents.

"Do not be a prisoner of your money," he said.

As Atta traveled back and forth between Hamburg and Aleppo, between Germany and Egypt, he hardened his views, studying the tenets of a *Salafi* existence. Pink Hamburg persisted in sickening him but in his new mosque and in his emerging adherence to a life under Islam, he increasingly isolated himself from these worldly surroundings.

With Fazazi and four others from the mosque, Atta made his obligatory pilgrimage to *Kaaba,* the House of God, in the sacred city of Mecca. He performed the rites of *Hajj,* embracing Islam and his religious commitment.[41]

Six months later, he went back to Egypt, espousing Islamic devotion and sporting a long beard. His father mocked him: "How are you going to get a job looking like Mr. Bin Laden?"

His mother cried at his appearance, begging little Amir to return home, telling him it was time for him to start a family in his own country. But no longer just a boy, and having found salvation, Mohammed Junior could only feel pity for his parents.

Back in Hamburg, school, work, and the mosque filled his days. He was increasingly skeptical that any life awaited him back in Egypt.

Listening to Fazazi's sermons and talking to his new brothers, Mohammed Atta became increasingly distressed about the state of Islam and the treatment of Muslim people everywhere. The international press was filled with alarming pictures of emaciated Bosnian Muslims held in Serbian prison camps.[42] Then came stories of the mass rape of Muslim women by Serb Christians. Many of these stories were splayed on the front pages of the German tabloids, doubly assaulting him.

Mohammed and his friends also followed the now-entrenched American military force keeping Saddam Hussein[43] in his place, bombing Iraq at will, keeping food from reaching starving Iraqi children.

And Afghanistan was ripping at itself from the insides, unable to get on its feet after the *mujahidin* defeated the Soviets.

Then Moscow attacked Muslim Chechnya, bombing the place into rubble.[44]

And of course they all followed the plight of the Palestinians against their Jew oppressors.

"*Jihad* is the only solution to change this world," Fazazi preached.

"You have the task of eliminating the rule of the infidels, killing their children, capturing their wives, and destroying their homes," the *imam* said. They were strong and stark words. "You have the task ..."

Mohammed Atta became interested in *Shari'ah*, Islamic law, returning to Qutb's condemnation of the modern world. As the great intellectual observed, living by the laws of God, and not the laws of man, was the only way. Man, he said, merely legislates his own desires though the making of his own laws. Those in the West who worshiped "freedom" were living out a distorted fantasy. Such a society was doomed to constant conflict and suffering because man's rationality was incapable of answers. Only the law of God—*Shari'ah* law—governed the biological and the physical, regulating the human realm of life, and through that extending into politics and society as well.

If humanity chooses to ignore the *Shari'ah*, Qutb wrote and Atta now believed, it was destined to live like animals in an uncivilized jungle.

Chapter 2 Marwan

Atta could precisely date his ultimate transformation: April 11, 1996.[45] That day, the Zionists initiated what they called "Operation Grapes of Wrath," an attack on Lebanon, one that the Jews excused as being merely a defensive operation to stop *Hizb'allah* rocket attacks across the border.[46]

Hizb'allah.[47] The party of God.

Atta went to ask the *imam* if he knew where the words came from— "grapes of wrath"—if they were religious words, for they sounded familiar.

"It is in the Christian bible, my brother, in Revelations," Fazazi told him.

> So, the angel swung his sickle to the earth and gathered the clusters from the vine of the earth, and threw them into the great wine press of the wrath of God.
>
> And the winepress was trodden outside the city, and the blood that flowed from it rose as high as the bridles of the horses …

And it is here, too, Fazazi said, pointing a long finger at the book he pulled from the shelf: *"And from His mouth proceeds a sharp sword with which to strike down the nations, and He will rule them with an iron scepter. He treads the winepress of the fury of the wrath of God, the Almighty."*

The wrath of God.

The Jew planes then started bombing electrical power stations in

Beirut. It was an attack, Atta thought, that had no other purpose than to cause pain for innocent civilians, for *his* people.

Grapes of wrath, they all repeated. To Atta, the name fit with their image that it was a Zionist religious war.

But then one of the brothers said that wasn't true, *The Grapes of Wrath* was the title of a great American novel.

Curious, Atta went to the *Bücherhalle* near the Phoenix-Center, finding a pink-skinned librarian to ask about this book.

"John Steinbeck," the man beamed, oblivious even to a war going on in Lebanon. He was so pleased that the Middle Easterner with the long *mujahidin* beard—unkempt and growing almost to his chest by now—was interested in literature.

Steinbeck's book, he told Atta, was set in the American depression and focused on the Joad family. In the book, the Joads travel from dust-bowl Oklahoma to California, seeking a better future. But there, they end up being migrant workers and just as poor. One son becomes a labor organizer.

Dust bowl. Migrant workers. Labor organizer. Atta wasn't sure he even knew what these words meant. He said he wanted to read the book.

"We have the 75th anniversary edition," the librarian said, "but I'm afraid it is in English."

Atta checked it out, annoyed the pink man didn't think he might read English. He purchased a small English dictionary to help with the difficult words. And then he started.

There was a whole chapter about a turtle crossing the road. Steinbeck's story was about poverty, and the greed of landowners, the exploitation of poor hardworking farmers. The book chronicled the role played by mechanized farming in destroying an old way of life. Steinbeck also wrote about the banks as monsters, nothing more than machines subsisting on profits, like people exist on food and air.

Men from the banks, goons hired by the owners, came to Oklahoma in open automobiles to force payments and steal people's land. Then came their underlings with masks on, driving mechanized tractors, plowing under and over everything. The scarves did little to cover their identities, for they were the neighbors and town's people who sold out. The masks were a metaphor, Atta thought, for their inability to tell the truth.

"Fellow was telling me the bank gets orders from the East. And the orders were, 'Make the land show profit or we'll close you up.'"

Like the ramshackle Egyptian apartment buildings that were built solely to show a profit …

"The quality of owning freezes you forever in 'I,' and cuts you off forever from the "we."

Like the words spoken of *Allah*, the creator, Atta thought.

The bank gets orders from the East.

It wasn't just Israel. It was the banks of the Jews and their business partners who dominated everything from their base in New York City. That was *the East*.

And then came the incident in Qana.[48]

Villagers escaping the Zionist advance in southern Lebanon took refuge in a small United Nations peacekeeping camp in the village. Hundreds huddled together to find safety from the nearby fighting. There, they were all massacred. Jewish artillery fired directly into the sanctuary. More than 100 civilians were instantly killed—old, young, children, even babies.

On television, the carnage was shown over and over, even on the German state channel, the bright red of the blood clarifying and purging all that was pink and external.

Atta was stunned. He wrote a draft of his last will and testament, discussing the declaration of his Muslim beliefs and intentions with Fazazi.[49] With the butchery at Qana, he offered his life to the Prophet Mohammed—*peace be upon him*—signing the will. In it, he specified 18 instructions regarding his burial.[50]

Do not weep or cry, he said of his death. Atta asked his mourners to pray that he be forgiven for what he did in the past. "I want the people who I leave behind to fear God and not to be deceived by what life has to offer," he wrote.

The young men of the mosque praised Atta and read his last will in awe. It was *Salafi* practice as Fazazi preached, with personal modifications.

"I don't want any woman to go to my grave at all during my funeral or any occasion thereafter," he wrote. He also didn't want a pregnant woman or anyone who was not clean to ever visit his body, and no one could touch his genitals when preparing him for burial.

There is no god but God, and Mohammed is the messenger of God.

The document puzzled and fascinated a new member of the mosque, a young man named Marwan.[51] He approached his Egyptian brother and asked if he would like to have tea.

"You say in your statement that though you want to be forgiven for the past, there was to be no sorrow for whatever was to come—but 'not this action.' What does it mean, brother?"

Marwan was ten years Atta's junior, light-skinned and slight, with a twinkle in his eye. Atta thought he had luscious lips.[52]

"I feel *Allah*, most gracious, calling me," Atta answered.

"*Mash'Allah*, brother. Calling for what?"

"That I do not know yet."

"My family calls me Amir," he found himself telling the boy. His birth name, he told Marwan, was Mohammed al-Amir al-Sayed Atta.

Marwan, an Emirati, told Atta that he recently arrived in Germany for the school term. With a military scholarship from the United Arab Emirates, he began language training in Bonn, also residing with a German family but looking right away to move to Hamburg.

"Why, my brother?" Atta asked, thinking maybe that his young friend also saw the pink, and couldn't stand his German hosts.

"First, I couldn't wait to get out of Ras al Khaimah," his hometown on the Arabian Gulf, "but Bonn was even greyer, and an even stronger puritanical prison, with everyone looking and judging. It wasn't the escape that I imagined. And then, on top of it, the Arabs in Bonn, they all live herded together in a ghetto. It is as gloomy as any Palestinian refugee camp, pessimistic and lifeless."

Marwan also met some *friends*, he said to *his* new friend, Amir, and they told him that Hamburg was more open to both Arab men and to *his kind*.

He was not yet quite ready to completely share. But the natural way, what any Muslim man might do in the exclusive domain of his male friendships—walk arm-in-arm, hold hands, hug, touch while speaking, write poetry, exchange flowers—confused Marwan and filled him with shame. He thought that perhaps in Europe he just might find an escape, out of view of the unblinking eye. Bonn wasn't it. Hamburg seemed more open.

"How do you spend your days, my brother?" Atta asked.

"I study German, and I have been wandering around the neighborhoods. I look at the black-dressed men with long hair and makeup, looking like women. And then I see the young women dressed like prostitutes. I know that they are all supposed to be so open and free, to be able to dress this way. But I see that they are always frowning."

"What the Germans have is not freedom, brother," Atta commented.

"Well, perhaps it is not what we wish for ourselves, Amir," Marwan responded. "And it is not the destiny *Allah* most gracious wishes for us. But it is freedom."

"What freedom do you mean?" Atta asked.

"I am not sure I can put it into words," Marwan answered. "Don't you know what I mean? What you say in your statement"—he couldn't say his will—"about women?"

"That is merely a statement of a pious brother."

"But even the Prophet—*peace be upon him*—took many wives," Marwan responded. "And *Sheikh* bin Laden does as well. I am not being critical of your words. But you reject women, even in death. Are you … are you not interested in them?"

When Atta looked puzzled, Marwan quickly changed the subject. They continued to talk, but Atta said he wanted to go outside and smoke. And so they walked, Atta introducing Marwan to the Schwarzenberg park, which he said he loved to go to and contemplate.

Marwan asked his new friend about *jihad*. He previously read about this and he eagerly listened as various brothers spoke of it, as if they were describing a luxurious neighborhood that they someday hoped to live in.

Marwan said he had just read the *fatwa* of the Saudi brother Osama bin Laden, his declaration of war, calling for attacks against Americans— the army men—who were occupying the Arabian Peninsula.[53]

Atta read it, too, impressed and proud that the Saudi *Sheikh* mentioned the massacre at Qana,[54] seeing the world in the same way that he did.

"I feel I was called here with this statement," Marwan said. "Here to Hamburg, and here, to you." He said he wasn't looking for *jihad* and did not yet understand his destiny. But he said being at the *al Quds* made a great weight lift from his shoulders, a lightness filling him that at first he didn't understand. Now in addition he had met Atta, so strong and so smart and so committed.

"Brother, I am nobody," Atta answered, almost blushing.

Marwan waved away Atta's response. He said that *Allah*—and here he lowered his voice and came very close—"Amir, *Allah* the most gracious one brought me here, has brought me to you, to such a pious brother, a *friend*, like *me*. It is God's will, *Insha'Allah*."

Words spoken and unspoken, circumstances the same and different. Marwan was indeed heaven sent. And though he did not see it at first, for Mohammed Atta, Hamburg's clouds lifted as well.

"Each word of *Allah* ... is part of the universal law and is as accurate and true as any of the laws known as the laws of nature ..." Atta later read aloud to Marwan as they sat in the cafeteria, introducing his new friend to the writings of Qutb. They were sitting together in the corner, deep in conversation. "Thus, the *Shari'ah* given to man to organize his life, is also a universal law, because it is related to the general law of the universe and is harmonious with it."

Atta explained his thesis on Aleppo to Marwan, how new apartment buildings built around and over the old city allowed people to look down into the courtyards of the old houses, interfering with people's privacy.[55]

"It is a metaphor for the First World looking down on the Third," he told Marwan, sharing what he thought was his smartest observation. He called the big buildings "hideous" monuments, built to reap profits and destroy the Muslim way of life.

Soon they met every day. When Atta went on another trip home to Egypt, the two spoke on the phone every night. Atta returned even more disgusted with Egypt's subservience to the West. He was pessimistic, he told Marwan, about the prospects for employment or any meaningful life back home. "I am thinking that *jihad* is the only choice," he said.

His professors still thought their talented and hardworking apprentice quite employable if he didn't go too far overboard with the whole religion thing. Students were enlisted by school administrators to delicately broach the subject of Atta's appearance and his increasingly strident behavior in the department. Since his pilgrimage to Saudi Arabia, and since the Israeli attacks, he was refusing to speak to female students or acknowledge female professors.[56] And he was spending more and more time at the mosque. And with Marwan.

This is how Atta converted from foreign student to foreign organism.

School faded into the background. Towards the end of the year, they found a large first floor apartment together, at 54 Marienstrasse near the university.[57] It was a treeless narrow street with a shoe repair shop and a pub at the corner. Almost identical four-story apartment buildings had been built on both sides of the street after the war, some painted grey and others a fading yellow, all faceless clones of each other. They were flimsy housing stock for a featureless, neutered population, Atta thought.

At Marienstrasse, it was a marvelous winter, one of discovery for both.

Amir lavished attention on his young friend. He showed him his poetry and wrote new verses for him almost every day. He made Marwan a mixtape, not of tender songs but of his most favorite *jihadi* lectures, words that Atta had grown to love. He talked about his home in Egypt, about *The Grapes of Wrath*, and about Aleppo.

They watched videos of bearded Chechens crushed and bloodied under Soviet tanks.[58] And sickening sights of Bosnian mass graves. They read pamphlets and looked at pictures of children in Iraq with swollen, distended bellies. They feasted on disfigured fighters in Afghanistan. They relived Qana and the destruction of Lebanon by the Zionist entity. And of course everywhere were Palestinians living in squalid camps, and rocks thrown, and bombs exploding, all red, red, and more red.

One night, Marwan was sitting in the living room when *The Grapes of Wrath* flew by. Atta flung the book out of his bedroom, angrily exclaiming, "It is disgusting. I'm so disappointed."

"What, Amir? Disappointed with what?"

"The end. I don't want to talk about it. I'm sorry I wasted my money buying a copy so that I could finish it."

Marwan picked up the book and opened it to the end, reading the last passage. It was kind of beautiful, he thought, the pregnant girl feeding breast milk to the dying man. He had never read anything like it. It wasn't sexual in any way, but he understood Amir's horror.

As spring arrived, they were inseparable. Marwan adopted Atta's views and practices, leaving his shoes at the door, praying at the appointed times, performing the ablutions, making blessings for this and that as required. He grew a beard, not Amir's holy man bush, but a circle of hair around the mouth like the Saudi princes wore, a goatee, one that accented the lips that his Amir said he loved.

Marwan stopped prowling the streets. He now regularly attended the *al Quds*, listening to the lectures and discussions of Islam and politics, asking his brother, his friend, his guide, his spearhead, to explain both the outer and the inner voice.

This is when Atta noticed that Marwan had something wrong with him. He declined always when offered a smoke. He shied away from spicy food and meats, eating mostly rice and yoghurt, drinking water to fill himself.

Atta inquired. His beloved had been hiding a dull ache in his gut. Atta surfed the internet for ideas.

One day Marwan told his Amir that he noticed his urine was darker than normal, and he turned to his partner for guidance.

"You must go to a German doctor." Atta found an internist that the school said was the best in northern Germany.

As they sat in the waiting room, they held hands, a pink girl whispering to her mother and giggling about the odd men. She shushed her, smiling at Atta.

Marwan was called into the examination room, nervous and teary-eyed.

Atta told him: "It will be alright." It was a rare statement of his desire and not *Allah's* will.

He waited and read the *Qur'an*, tried to read the words, images of the one-eyed, white-skinned *Dajjal* crowding his thoughts.[59] They must be even more devout to keep the devil, the deceiver, at bay, he thought. They must put meaning to their lives, not just committed to *jihad*, but actual fighters on behalf of their people.

An hour later, they sat on chairs facing the doctor's desk, the tall and shiny, pink man grave and professional, explaining with a plastic model of the abdomen, the functioning of the organs, and speaking of cells, stages, growth, and treatments.

There would have to be more tests, but the diagnosis … it is possible that he still will have a good life ahead.[60]

Chapter 3 Ziad

They called their *Marienstrasse* apartment *Beit-al-Ansar*, the house of supporters.[61] It was three bedrooms and they furnished it sparsely, with mattresses on the floor and boxes instead of dressers. The living room had a big table with mismatched chairs and there was a couch and a futon bed. On the wall facing east was a precisely placed marker pointing to Mecca in Saudi Arabia. Behind it was an open space for all to pray.

Atta and Marwan opened their doors to brothers from the mosque who needed shelter, and then to visitors in need. Mohammed Atta, of course, held court—now known simply to all as Mohammed El-Amir, a shortened version of his full Egyptian name, but also a more intimate nod to his transformation to informal leader.

Into this devout and severe world Ziad Jarrah[62] practically exploded, another young student like them. But unlike them, Ziad was flashy and seemingly wholly Westernized, neither a lost brother nor a pliable puppy.

The Qana massacre occurred not far from where his relatives lived in Lebanon. When Ziad was home during the summer, he drove to the scarred and blackened U.N. compound—it had become a local monument to Zionist perfidy—and there he took in the hideous sights. Posters were on the walls of the now empty camp, morbid posters telling the stories of eyewitnesses, with gruesome photos of the victims.[63]

This Western man Ziad spoke openly of holy war, and that attracted Atta's attention. And he was not just talking. Atta saw him reading, always reading. One day, in the cafeteria, Atta approached him. *He* didn't need an introduction.

"*Salam.* What are you reading, my brother?" Atta asked in Arabic.

"It is Osama bin Laden." The young man got up and took Atta's hand firmly, introducing himself as Ziad Samir Jarrah from Beirut.

He showed Atta the cover of a paperback purchased in Lebanon: a compilation of letters and commentary the Saudi sent to prominent members of the royal family.

"Who cannot marvel at this Saudi son's courage?" Ziad said, looking straight at Atta. "He is truly the rare individual, openly condemning Saudi corruption and its manipulation of Islam, naming names, even of the *ulema*.[64] I'm just blown away, brother."

Atta had read bin Laden's statement after Qana, and he listened to tapes from the great preacher. But he had yet to read his works in their original form.

"What does he say of the Saudis?" asked Atta. He hadn't thought much about them, having made his pilgrimage to Mecca and having been overwhelmed by all he saw and felt there. He knew the ideologues railed about American soldiers being stationed in Saudi Arabia, but to criticize the orthodoxy of the Saudi royal family?

"I am just reading his denunciation of Sheikh bin Baz—you know him?"

Sheikh 'Adb-al 'Aziz Bin Baz, the Grand *Mufti*,[65] the head of all official Saudi clerics. He was the unofficial head of the *ulema*. As one of the most prominent figures of the Saudi establishment, the closest there was to a supreme authority in *Sunni* Islam, a man Atta thought was so exalted in his knowledge that even Fazazi could learn from him. But Ziad said he had contorted the religion on behalf of politics.

"I didn't know Bin Baz was appointed to his position not because of his knowledge or seniority but as reward for issuing the *fatwa* that provided religious authorization for *Amreeka* to station soldiers on Saudi soil. Bin Laden kicks the shit out of this slimy bastard, calling him a fraud." Ziad flipped through the book and found other passages he had marked.

"Bin Laden then condemns taxes being raised on the people while the government builds more and more monuments to itself," Ziad said. "But most criminal, he says, is that this money the people are giving in the mosque is really being used to pay for the Christian invaders to be in their country. The *Zakat!*[66] It pays for the food and housing of the *Amreekans* in the land of the holy places. And Saudi Arabia buys western weapons, *Amreekan,* British, and French weapons, bin Laden says, weapons that are supposed to make the country modern but do no good in its defense. Meanwhile, he says, the armed forces are in crappy condition, not able to perform or defend the country."

Kicks the shit out of. Slimy bastard. Crappy.

"He makes a pretty convincing argument that rather than gather Islam together—even just the *Sunnis*—the Saudis are completely and only focused on their own power and well-being, and then only really on the wealth of the royal family, using the clerics and even the pilgrims who go there to create legitimacy. And then profiting from them.

"That motherfucker bin Laden then orders King Fahd[67] to abide by his demands. And then he says that if the Saudi government fights back or wages war against those at home or abroad who are merely promoting a return to the true way of Islam, he, Osama bin Laden, will personally hold them responsible.

"And he goes on," he continued, obviously relishing bin Laden's thrashing of the powers that be. "He fucking accuses Prince Sultan—personally, by name—of leading a secret committee that pays off Arab leaders and American politicians to accept the Saudi way."

Fucker? Motherfucker?

Ziad told Atta that he came from a well-to-do Lebanese family, that he attended private Christian schools before moving to Germany to enter a program on aircraft construction at Hamburg's School of Applied Sciences. He initially wanted to be an Islamic scholar but his parents rejected the idea, especially as a profession that could be pursued in Lebanon.[68] So he started to read, reading everything, finding *the al Quds* a place where he could read in peace, safe from those who would ask why he was reading. And what.

Atta didn't know what to think. Ziad was profane, and a nonconformist, and at least by his appearance, wholly assimilated into the West. He told Atta that he went back and forth to his homeland on weekend trips. He even went on vacations to sit on a beach in Greece.[69] *To think,* Ziad said.

And yet despite his attachment to earthly pleasures, he was a seductive teacher. Brothers came to him with questions, and Ziad became legion in the mosque for his practical advice on how to live a modern life in harmony with their religion. Atta was particularly impressed with his well-worn holy book, marked and annotated, with dog-eared pages and dozens of Post-It notes. At first Atta thought that his study was to compensate for his Christian schooling and cosmopolitan upbringing. But Ziad said that he was touched even as a boy, that he immersed himself in an Islamic study circle, helping in a local Islamic bookstore. By the time he was a teen, he said he had memorized the *Qur'an*.[70]

"I don't really understand this man," Atta later told Marwan. "He is so smart, and knows so much, but lives the secular life of my own unbelieving father. Even worse, he has a girlfriend."

"You don't understand why he has a woman?" he shyly replied, "why he thirsts for love?"

"No, no, I don't mean that," Atta answered. "She is Turkish, and Ziad says she is Muslim. It is more that they are living the life of any German student couple, even being together before marriage."

Already knowing Amir's view of women, Marwan was waiting for a punchline.

"He speaks about being an Islamic scholar. And about the systematic subjugation of Arab peoples by outside forces. He says he is frustrated about what can be done to change things, almost like a politician, like he is looking for a program."

"Maybe he is just a good man. Maybe he is just as he seems," Marwan offered.

He was sweet, Atta thought of Marwan. Maybe it was something about being sick that he was slow to judge others.

When Atta introduced Marwan to him at the mosque, Ziad was gracious before continuing his reading of bin Laden's courageous letters: "He asks the Saudi army to consider the facts behind the seeming inability of Islam to defend itself. Kuwait was now safe, but still the *Amreekans* are bringing in more Christians to defend Saudi Arabia. Is it really for defense?"

"Even including Christian women," Atta interjected.

"Yes, yes," Ziad answered, finding a passage in bin Laden's letters. "'Women defending holy places,' he writes. And then he goes on to say that the female soldiers place the Saudi army in the quote 'highest degree of shame, disgrace, and frustration.'"[71]

Atta thought this might be a good place to bring up his own woman, but Ziad plowed forward.

"Here is something curious though, brother," Ziad said, thumbing through the contents. "Bin Laden calls upon Muslim youth to take action but in doing so 'to be disciplined and avoid taking actions that will harm the interests of the whole.'[72] What do you think he means by that?"

"Not to bring shame upon our people," Atta answered.

"But how would that happen?" Ziad asked.

"Perhaps by doing certain things—for instance, being with a woman who is not one's wife."

Marwan turned beet red at Atta's words.

"Are you making reference to me, brother?" Ziad said. "Are you asking me to justify myself?"

Atta answered by quoting the great book: "*The woman and the man who fornicate, scourge each of them a hundred whips; and in the matter of God's religion, let no tenderness for them seize you if you believe in God and the Last Day; and let a party of the believers witness their punishment.*"[73]

Marwan thought that maybe his beloved forgot for a moment that he was speaking to a friend, that he was lost in the words. And he feared some sort of a fight. He was about to say something, to change the conversation, but then Atta looked straight at Ziad and said: "That is, if you believe in *Allah* most gracious and the Last Day ..."

Marwan softly intervened, speaking to Ziad: "Of course, brother, you should only answer to the Prophet alone, *peace be upon him.*"

Ziad paused and there was an uncomfortable silence. Under the table, Marwan took Atta's hand, hoping to bring him back, to remind him that they were talking to someone who they liked.

Ziad finally spoke up: "What is your age now, brother?"

"I am almost 30 years," Atta answered. "Why?"

"So with the *Qur'an* as our guide, you should have been married more than a decade ago, and then you should have married a nine-year-old, just as the Prophet Muhammad—*peace be upon him*—married Aisha when she was six years old and just as he consummated this marriage when she was nine. And yet you are not married. And you did not marry a nine-year-old. It is not meant to be an insult, brother, merely a parable."

Ziad went on: "There are ways and there are ways. Within *Shari'ah*, a boy and girl can do their 'aqd—their marriage contract—and postpone the ceremony until they have finished their education. There is nothing in the *Shari'ah* that forbids sexual relations, as long as permissible contraception delays childbearing."

"This is nonsense," Atta responded, his pulse racing. In his mind, he had become a hero of chastity, condemning the pleasures he was deprived of in his strict life.

"Not nonsense, my brother," he answered. "But marrying and then fucking a nine-year-old? Now that is nonsense. All I am saying is that even Islam has to adapt."

Atta was flustered. Marwan again squeezed his hand. Never had anyone so knowledgeable about Islam said such things to Atta.

"We speak of not enslaving ourselves to our emotions," Ziad continued. "We speak of it because it is our emotions themselves that are supposed to be a form of oppression. As Muslims, we are guided by *Allah* most gracious through the *Qur'an* and the *Sunnah*,[74] through His Messenger of Mercy, Prophet Muhammad—*peace be upon him*. We supplicate ourselves. Why? We do so to help us to get over the times when we feel weak, when we feel our emotions.

"But I will tell you: Fucking in Islam does not begin with sexual intercourse, my friend. It begins with the look, the words, the touch. And only then with the sexual organs, with the rest of the body. They say that when two are together in private, there is always a third party with them—Satan. Whether two are married or not."

"So. Peace, my brother. *Salam*. We seek inner peace so that our emotions will wash over us and not divert us from our love of *Allah*, the great one, from our love of family and even of our brothers. I am a good Muslim; of that I am sure. I do not fear the righteous. But because I am sure that you are a thinking man, because I know that you struggle with the control of your own emotions, and with your own desires, I also know that inside, inside here," and he gently reached over and touched Atta on the chest, "that you are a good man. That both of you are. And say this because we bring no shame to *Allah* in that we are just *men*. Our greatest sin would be if we acted as if we were gods, without emotions, aggrandizing that which is his alone."

Ziad became their third.

Chapter 4 A Mission

"A brother is here to rent the room," said Marwan, summoning Atta to the door of their Hamburg apartment one lazy morning.

The prospective tenant was a Yemeni named Ramzi Binalshibh.[75] He was dark-skinned, with a droopy face and deep-set eyes, 25 years old.

"I have not seen you at *al Quds*, cousin," said Atta, shaking his hand. "What brings you here?"

"I came last year," said Ramzi, "but the Germans didn't accept my application for asylum, so I have been in a bureaucratic nowhere in Berlin, waiting for papers, unable to work. Finally, I have them, as well as a real job that I just got here in Hamburg. I was looking for a friendly place to stay and many told me of this house and of you, my brother."[76]

"From where do you come, cousin?" asked Atta.

"Hadramawt," Ramzi said. Atta knew it as the Yemeni region where Osama bin Laden's father was born.[77] It was an ancient place, mentioned in the Bible,[78] a dusty, mountainous outpost. For hundreds of years, it traded with seafaring people from as far away as the Malay Peninsula before the British came.[79] Then the Yemeni people were finally given a country, given their own country.

"You have had contact with *Sheikh* bin Laden?" Atta asked.

"I know his organization," Ramzi answered, divulging little more.

"Please look around then. You are welcome," Atta said.

Marwan showed him the available small sleeping space, and the

Yemeni said he would take it if they would have him.

That night at dinner Ramzi told stories of fighting in the civil war in Yemen before leaving the country. And he spoke of trips to Afghanistan and Sudan, describing the beauty and sparse conditions of the camps there, but saying little about what he had been up to.[80]

Their new roommate was careful in speaking about anything related to bin Laden. Atta admired that—that he didn't need to brag to make himself seem more important. As someone on the cusp of his own secret life, Atta picked up on Ramzi's diffidence.

As the days and weeks passed, Ramzi started praying with the trio, Atta, Marwan and Ziad. He took meals with them and began to regularly attend the *al Quds*.[81]

They became their own cell: the Hamburg Four. Atta, the leader, was deadly serious, confident but profoundly uncomfortable when facing the external expanse of the pink prison. Marwan was an affable and receptive follower, and also delicate, living a double life of pain. Ziad was worldly and iconoclastic, really the scholar of the bunch, venturing in his reading and his nonstop search for meaning into literature and even into music and art. And the fourth was Ramzi: roughhewn and wily. He was already a secret member of *al Qaeda*. And he would ultimately be the bridge from their world in Hamburg, from their incessant words spilled forth about injustices everywhere, to an actual world of deeds.[82]

They were from different countries and drastically different backgrounds. Their true bond lay in the stark awareness that they had no home in Germany and that their homelands were either without hope or resembled a lesser form of Western life. All four believed that the so-called Third World was stuck under the thumb of the West. Even Ziad agreed, wary of a return to his war-torn country, speaking increasingly of eventually settling in Brazil or the Caribbean with the woman he would marry.

From the mosque to the apartment and back again, they passionately discussed the bittersweet triumph in Afghanistan and the tragedies that followed. It wasn't just Lebanon and the plight of the Palestinians. Increasingly bitter pills were being swallowed by Muslims at the hands of the Christians and Jews, even in Europe in Bosnia, in the Caucasus, and from Iraq to Somalia.

As their bond deepened, Ziad spent more and more of his time at the *Marienstrasse* apartment, visiting Aysel only on weekends, then every other weekend. The couple fought. Ziad took to criticizing her for not being religious enough, for not covering herself. He transferred to Atta's university in Hamburg just a few blocks from the apartment.[83]

Ramzi confided to Atta and Ziad that he was working with *the* organization, his mission to set up an *al Qaeda* base in America—if he could obtain a visa.[84] He would occasionally disappear, off on missions to courier money to Muslim fighters in Albania and Bosnia. He even traveled to Pakistan on a secret mission.[85] But little was discussed about his activities.

One day, close to evening prayer, Ramzi brought home a fellow Yemeni, whom he introduced merely as "Khallad."[86] He had lost a leg fighting with the Taliban as they took control in Afghanistan. From that far-off land he brought to *Marienstrasse* stories of their valiant struggle to fight the remnants of communism, and the godless people of the north, in order to establish a pure Islamic state.

Khallad told the story of *Mullah* Omar, the simple village cleric who had become the head of the Taliban.[87] Word came in to him that in a power struggle between rival warlords, some village girls had been kidnapped and were being repeatedly raped[88] It had been years since the Soviets left, he explained, but the fighting had never stopped, Uzbek, Turkmen, and Pashtun warlords fighting over territory. Fed up himself and repulsed by the rapes, Omar reputedly gathered a group of 30 men, and they attacked the encampment, killing the commander and freeing the girls. Word spread quickly of the rebellion and a group called the Taliban was formed, one that would eventually come to control most of the country.

"Young men are arriving from all over the south," Khallad said, "to join Omar, even from the comfort of their exile in Pakistan."

"And the Taliban name comes from what?" asked Marwan. It wasn't Arabic.

"Students," answered Khallad. "Though I am told it is a Persian plural, meaning seekers of knowledge. They call themselves students because they are the sons and even grandsons of those who escaped the Soviet occupation. They mostly come from the *madrassas*[89]—the religious schools—and they have been taught the Pashtun version of Islam, which is called *Deobandi*."[90]

"And it means what?" Marwan asked.

"I'm not sure I could tell you," Khallad answered, shrugging. "I am not a religious man. I can tell you that it is *Sunni*. And that it is the Pakistani practice."

"I can tell you, my brother," Ziad interjected. "It was a movement in India in the 19th century that promoted the *Wahhabi* way, from the land we today call Saudi Arabia. Thus what it brought to Pakistan is an emulation of Arab cultural behavior. In its purest form it rejects politics, or I should say political interpretations of the *Qur'an*, in favor of what it calls literal readings. That is the basis for the Taliban claim to purity."[91]

"Thank you, brother," Khallad said, seemingly surprised that the man with frosted hair and who seemed the most Westernized of them all had the answer to an obscure Islamic question.

"These boys were eager to return to their country and now they had a reason," continued Khallad. "From Kandahar, Mullah Omar's Taliban army expanded, defeating not just many warlords in the south but remnants of communist fighters as well. They are on their way to Kabul now. Mullah Omar and his Taliban boys are implementing *Shari'ah* in all part of the country that they control."

"Which is how much?" Atta asked.

"Almost all but the capital city and the north," Khallad said. "The Northern Alliance of Uzbeks and Turkmen continue to fight, and they also do not have control in Herat in the west, where many Persians live."

"What we read in the German news and see on German television," Ziad again interrupted, "is that they are banning computers, movies, satellite TV, playing cards, musical instruments, even kite flying in the name of the new pure Islamic state.[92] Is this true?"

"They are still learning," said Khallad, as if not wanting to criticize a host. It was true.

"But is it so that women are forbidden from taking jobs outside the home?" Ziad asked. "And that they are forbidden from appearing in public without a male family protector, having to wear the traditional *burqa*?"

"Who are we to argue with local traditions, the code of the Pashtun,

Pashtunwali?" Khallad responded, not wanting to be drawn in. "Are we to just capitulate to what others say how to live? As if *they* should teach us our own customs?"

"I just wonder what the true *Qur'anic* justification is," Ziad continued, tone deaf to Khallad's reluctance to engage. "What do you think, brother?" he said, addressing Atta.

"I am also curious," Atta answered. "Perhaps we can find the answer in the *al Quds* library. I must say I do not understand these people. They are not Arabs. And it is strange there is not a single Afghan man who prays in our congregation."

"My brothers," Khallad interjected, "I'm not a scholar, and I don't know all of the ins and outs of the divisions that exist in this ancient country, and there are many. But we should not judge them by arguing that *they* themselves don't understand their own beliefs—or that they don't understand Islam itself."

The discussion then moved to Osama bin Laden, who had returned to Afghanistan from Sudan. That February, he had published a new statement and it was all the talk at the mosque and at *Marienstrasse*.

The entire world, bin Laden said, was at war.[93] For over seven years, he said, "the United States has been occupying the lands of Islam in the holiest of places, the Arabian Peninsula, plundering its riches, dictating to its rulers, humiliating its people, terrorizing its neighbors, and turning its bases in the peninsula into a spearhead through which to fight neighboring Muslim peoples."

Bin Laden argued the America made "a clear declaration of war on God, his messenger, and on Muslims" through its actions and policies in the Islamic world. The battlefield against Islam, he said, was now extending from Andalusia to *Khorasan* to Mindanao—that is, from Spain to Afghanistan to the Philippines.[94]

> "In compliance with God's order, we issue the following *fatwa* to all Muslims: the ruling to kill the Americans and their allies, including civilians and military, is an individual duty for every Muslim who can do it in any country in which it is possible to do it."

Issuing this ruling was "The World Islamic Front for *Jihad* against the Jews and Crusaders."

Khallad said they should visit the country.

"We must go, brothers," said Atta. "To find what we can do as part of our obligations to *jihad*."

They decided to pool their money and first send Atta as scout and emissary.[95]

Khallad met Atta at the airport in Quetta, Pakistan happy to receive the educated Egyptian, an engineer like the *Sheikh* himself, a brother of Zawahiri from Egypt, the doctor no longer independent but now a full member of the Front since joining bin Laden's *fatwa*.[96]

At the Afghan border, they were picked up in a shiny white SUV with official Ministry of Defense license plates. There seemed no need for identification. The young driver told his esteemed guests that the *Emir* was now able to import and export people and goods without any controls.[97]

As they settled in the car, the Egyptian bodyguard in the front passenger seat picked up a copy of the *Dania II* CD to ask if Khallad minded him playing the Lebanese pop star.

"Brother," Atta interrupted, "we are not in Cairo. Have some respect for our hosts."

That made for a very silent trip.

The road to Kandahar was pockmarked with potholes and bomb craters, littered with the carcasses of Red Army vehicles and tanks, a zigzag of detours around collapsed culverts and bombed bridges, two lanes through ugly, war-torn villages, then through vast, undeveloped areas. They passed flimsy mini-buses and went through checkpoint after checkpoint manned by ragged Taliban soldiers.

As they neared Kandahar, they saw poverty everywhere. Remnants of Soviet destruction and then the devastation of years of more warfare was evident everywhere. The city was scarred and skeletal, filled with downtrodden pedestrians. The roads were packed with donkeys and carts, and the ubiquitous white Toyota and Nissan pickup trucks. Atta thought the ancient city had none of the charm of Aleppo. He understood that Afghanistan was a country that had grown used to certain physical deprivations; first, in centuries of blessed isolation and then more recently in a decade of occupation and civil war. Still he was taken aback to see so little effort being expended by the new "Islamic Emirate" to rebuild.

Khallad explained that the *Sheikh* would have been happier to live in the mountains near the safety of his caves, but the Taliban and his Egyptian security contingent insisted he forego the familiar for the greater safety of Kandahar. It was a move, Khallad said, that was also supposed to honor *Mullah* Omar as much as to create a secure base against external assassins.[98] The truth was, Khallad whispered to Atta, Omar wanted the great man close by. The Taliban were essentially out of money, being largely unsuccessful in getting either international diplomatic support or aid. Only Saudi Arabia, the Emirates and Pakistan extended official recognition. Meanwhile Omar and others in the Taliban government believed the tales of bin Laden's wealth, hoping that some of it would rub off on them.

Finally, they arrived at the gates to an old Soviet agricultural collective east of the city, a beat down cluster of mud in the middle of nowhere. Called Tarnak Farms, it was a sprawling assortment of homes and offices, encompassing hundreds of acres, all surrounded by high walls.[99] It seemed more like a prison than a home. The ubiquitous dust and the absence of any trees further accentuated the bleakness. The scene reminded Atta of how Steinbeck described the great Dustbowl of Oklahoma in *The Grapes of Wrath*.

"Rest," Khallad said, directing the esteemed visitor to a small house simply furnished with a mattress, table and chair. "After evening prayers, you will have the honor of sitting with the *Emir* and the Doctor."

At the appointed hour, Atta was ushered into large room and introduced around by Khallad. Two fellow Egyptians came first: the famous Dr. Zawahiri, *emir* of the Egyptian Islamic Jihad, a man Atta was aware of. Then there was a tall and strikingly handsome man who introduced himself as Mohammed Atef.[100] They called him Abu Hafs, and he said merely that he was a member of the *majlis al shura*, the *Shura*, the ruling council of *al Qaeda*.

The doctor inquired about where Atta was from in Egypt and other details about his family. He asked about when Atta had done his *Hajj*, noting the long beard. He himself had also gone, he said, and he had stayed to practice medicine for a year before joining *Sheikh* bin Laden in Afghanistan.

There were others present as well, members of the council.[101] Khallad was trying to move him along to meet them all, but then bin Laden entered the room. Tall and gangly, his long gray beard flecked with white, he was barefoot and deeply tanned. Like the others, he wore a Pashtun smock that extended almost to the floor and a white turban. The only differences were the others wore various gray and black vests while bin Laden wore a mottled green and brown camouflage army jacket.

Khallad introduced him: "This is the man I told you about, an Egyptian brother from *Germania*. He speaks English *and* German and has finished his architecture studies in Hamburg."

Bin Laden took Atta's hands and welcomed him to Kandahar, inquiring about his family, listening to Atta talk meekly of his parents and sisters. Bin Laden said that he loved the Nile River, that he had spent many nights listening to its flow in Sudan, soaking up its history. He then asked who the *imam* of Atta's mosque was, saying that there were many brothers in Germany, that it was hard to keep track.

Atta's heart raced. The *Sheikh* towered over him. A radiance bloomed, the *Sheikh* smiling from above, pulses of electricity filling his body.

It wasn't a business meeting. They sat and ate a simple but abundant meal. Atta told them of life in Germany and his views on the country, about his trips to Aleppo and his thesis about architecture and big buildings. He spoke of his full conversion to Islam with the Israeli invasion of Lebanon and the slaughter at Qana.

Questions were asked by all, and Atta did most of the talking. He was also careful to be modest and not to try to outsmart these wise, committed men.

Then bin Laden took the floor, speaking of his return to Afghanistan and his statement—he didn't call it a *fatwa*—calling on all good Muslims to defend the faith. The standoff between America and Saddam Hussein filled the news and bin Laden bemoaned the plight of the Iraqi children—a million died, he said, because of international sanctions imposed. He talked intensely of the Indian and Pakistani nuclear weapons tests and the importance of an Arab nation acquiring its own nuclear bomb to counter the Zionist state.

Atta wished Ziad was there. He read the German newspapers every day and knew all about world events. Seeing not a computer or any paper anywhere, he wondered where bin Laden got his information.

"Have you been to *Amreeka*?" asked bin Laden.

"No, *Emir*, no," Atta answered.

"My son. We will have to rectify that," bin Laden said. "You know, who we are at war with has never really changed. The treacherous House of Saud, the vile Saddam and al-Assad,[102] all the apostate Arab regimes, and of course the Zionists. They all fear *jihad*. Bin Laden said to Atta that Egypt was, of course, important for its own accommodation with the Jewish state and its position in the American military orbit. But not more than that. Then he went on to discuss the United States, *Amreeka*.

"Today there is only one superpower," bin Laden said, "and it has to be our full focus. It tramples the earth like the great Bull of Heaven. We must strike at them—not just because of the daily assaults, but also because the Muslim people must see that once again their survival is at stake."

Strike at them. Atta wondered what bin Laden had in mind. But this was not the place to ask questions. Nor did he feel that he was granted license to ask.

They ate and bin Laden continued to speak, softly surveying the world, saying the time for global action was upon them.

When the meal was over, bin Laden stood up and again grasped Atta's hands and looked deeply in his eyes, inviting him to return, to bring his friends from Hamburg. There was much work to be done, he said.

Khallad was brimming over with enthusiasm when he picked Atta up the next morning. On their ride back to Quetta, he told Atta how much he had very much impressed the assembled, and he instructed him broadly on what he must now do to prepare himself for their upcoming work together.

He must return to the university, apply himself and finish his studies in good standing, Khallad said. "There should be no questions as to your integration into the Western way of life." He urged Atta and his friend to dress and act more like the Germans from now on. Khallad said, "You must learn their ways and mannerisms."[103]

Second, when the time came, Atta was to travel to Egypt and obtain a new passport, one that showed no travel to Pakistan.

"Will I not return for training?" Atta asked.

"You will. But right now, the Pakistanis are secretly marking passports of the faithful who come to Afghanistan. And since you have the beard of a holy man, they marked you as one and marked your passport.

"So, when you report your old one missing, you must at the same time keep it. That way you can use it in the future when you come back. The new one is for travel within Europe and to America."

"I am going to America?"

"I truly do not know what the *Sheikh* has in mind for you," Khallad said. "Just that you need to prepare. And brother, you need to begin to prepare the others in Hamburg. Ramzi Binalshibh tells me your Lebanese and Emirati brothers are good men."

Atta wasn't really ever asked what he wanted to do. He felt swept along. It wasn't just bin Laden. It wasn't even bin Laden. It had been building. He felt increasingly certain that he wanted to join and be a part of something bigger than himself, something that would confer more than just a Western degree and a grinding work life ever after.

He was sure it would be the same for Marwan. His beloved had already accepted that he would never live out a natural life, which made an unnatural death in the name and service of *Allah*—most compassionate—ever more compelling.

Though Atta thought Ziad contradictory in his behavior and love of life, he also couldn't deny his faith, nor his pious study. He was certain that Ziad would tell him the truth about what he wanted for his own future. And he was certain that Ziad would—like him—want to make a contribution to the broader future.

The only real question then was whether Marwan was strong enough to endure the full journey.

PART 2

Chapter 5 As Far as I Know

"Lawrence Bowlen asked for a meeting," Charlie told Steve Draper as they sat down to a Sunday dinner in his tidy condo.

"Bowlen," said Steve. "What about?"

"I really don't know. He also asked to meet me outside the building, at a restaurant in downtown Bethesda of all places."

"Hmm. Outside the building. At what time?"

"Two-thirty in the afternoon."

"You gonna' take the day off?"

"I suppose."

"At least you can take the Metro."

"That's all you have to say?" she snapped. "You know it still pisses me off that no one from the seventh floor has reached out to me."

"So what, get mad at me?"

"Oh for fuck's sake, Steven. It's not about you."

"You don't consider *him* the seventh floor?" he pressed, trying to coax his lover back.

"You know what I mean."

"I know that it is what it is. That you're leaving. But still, he is pretty important."

After a dozen years working for the Central Intelligence Agency, Marina Charbel—most everyone called her Charlie—was leaving. It was a combination of lost intellectual fights and glass ceiling grievances, but truth be told, if someone asked why she'd ultimately decided to leave government, she had to admit that she could longer stand working for the president, for President Bill Clinton, a corrupt womanizer, and to her mind, an abusive boss.

"Any 4-1-1 on what Special Purpose is up to?" she asked.

That was the name of Bowlen's shop. His title was associate director of the CIA for Special Purpose.[104] She'd strained to think about if, in any of her Middle East assignments, she'd ever run into the phantom organization or even if his name had ever come up. One thing was clear: Bowlen and his crew were obviously good at hiding whatever it was they were doing.

"Well, I've got my theories," Steve responded.

Theories. Since she'd known Steve, she'd learned that *"theories"* was just an expression of his. *Theories. Beliefs. My guess. The evidence points to.* They were all verbal acrobatics he used to conceal what he really knew, smokescreens to hide what he didn't know, hedges to mask his true feelings about anything and everything.

"The rumor is he heads some project regarding Saudi Arabia," said Steve. "It's been in operation at least since the oil crisis of the '70s."

"Just Saudi Arabia?"

"As far as I know."

"So, you don't think he's some modern-day James Jesus Angleton,[105] or worse, some old-guard goon?"

"I don't think so," Steve responded, adding a raspy chuckle of dismissal that she'd heard a million times. "If anything, from what I hear, Bowlen goes where the corporate entity dares not tread. I think he's one of the good guys. But I really couldn't say more."

"And you think his project relates to terrorism?" she asked.

"Well, it is your specialty," he answered, "and it is the Saudis."

She'd made the salad in his small kitchen while he roasted a chicken and precisely cut-up sweet potatoes to go in the oven as well, her ribbing him as usual about his fastidiousness and his compulsive routines. They rarely ate at home and rarely made a meal together; one of those unmarried Washington couples for whom work was their one and only excess. Despite being a couple for going on two years, she maintained her own apartment, and of late, she was thinking that part of her change in leaving the CIA might be to break with her prickly partner as well.

"Maybe he's going to offer you a job," Steve added.

"If the Agency wanted me to stay, don't you think someone in my own fucking chain of command would have said something?"

"Maybe you've scared everyone off," he responded, again chuckling. She was beginning to hate that chuckle.

"Look. Sweetheart," he added, trying to be encouraging. "Bowlen called you. So at least the idiots aren't zero for zero."

Still, Charlie told herself, it was Lawrence Avery Bowlen who contacted her, a man no one quite knew and even her know-it-all lover couldn't quite explain. Yes, Bowlen was officially in the executive suite, but he also headed some off-the-books operation that wasn't really *the* Agency. Nothing about it seemed career enhancing.

"Be careful," Steve finally added. "I've been around Langley longer than you. And I've seen others disappear into his black hole. Remember Barbara Rogers? She was that great analyst at the Center[106] who left right after you came on. She left *quote* to take another job, but no one heard from her after that. I think she's working for Bowlen. But she's gone off the grid completely. It's like the Argentinians disappeared her."

The next day, when Charlie arrived at the restaurant, Bowlen was already sitting in a rear corner booth.[107] He was a bear of a man, neatly shaven with meticulously cut white hair and gold-framed spectacles, a face so red and baby bottom smooth it was almost as if he had no facial hair. He had the appearance, she thought, of a university dean or maybe a church deacon. In front of him was a folder of papers that he deftly closed on her approach.

On the phone, she suggested The McLean Inn on Old Dominion Drive near Agency headquarters, thinking like the clandestine service officer she was, acting as if she were meeting with a potentially iffy source: *go public; safety in numbers.*

He'd rejected her suggestion saying it was way too much of a predictable haunt for CIA boozers and gossips. He'd already chosen the meet, giving her the name of the restaurant and a time. And he'd obviously picked a time—2:30 p.m.—to avoid both the lunch time and the happy hour crowd. They had the corner all to themselves.

Charlie noticed a bulky man sitting close to the door, nursing a cup of coffee, obviously a buffer and bodyguard. And she marked a second heavy sitting in a black SUV in the restaurant's almost empty parking lot—not out of place in Washington, but noticeable to her trained eye.

"Marina Charbel," she said, extending her hand.

He stood up to formally shake it, introducing himself.

"Almost everyone calls me Charlie," she added.

She agreed to meet Bowlen because, well, that's what she did as a case officer: have clandestine meetings. And truth be told, she was nervous. She didn't question her decision to leave the Agency, but she was also now in her mid-thirties with a lost decade on a secret resume and she wasn't looking forward to having to scrounge for work for the first time since college.

Bowlen noted that she was prettier in person than her official personnel picture suggested. She had dark red-brown hair, lots of it, an olive complexion, all packaged in a small slender body. He could see how those looks had helped her in dealing with agents and gaining access.

Bowlen knew nearly everything that there was to know about her: her Lebanese grandparents, her career progression in four clandestine assignments in the Near East Division, her performance reviews from supervisors, her views on terrorism, her no-nonsense and even abrasive approach, even her anti-Clinton disgust.

As they waited for an iced tea to arrive, they chit-chatted about the Whitewater investigation and whether the appointment of Kenneth Starr would make any difference.

"It's all so tawdry," Charlie said with a sigh. "I know we're supposed to be neutral about the man we work for, but I just find it impossible to get over my judgment. Even if this Paula Jones suit goes nowhere," she said.[108] It's not just that, but I admit my discomfort is a big part of my decision to leave the Agency."

She was careful not to convey her full contempt, especially in front of someone who might not share her views. But she long ago made up her mind about the president: he was another powerful man who got off on taking advantage of weaker women, a cheater and a liar who didn't deserve to occupy the highest office.

"It is an unfortunate sideshow for the country," Bowlen said neutrally. He wore a beautifully tailored suit and had almost intentionally perfect posture, clearly in command of his world. "But Mr. Clinton is hardly the only reason behind your decision to leave. I understand that you were a dissenter in the class action?"

She was surprised he brought up that ancient history. "I only received a tiny share of the settlement because I came into the Agency at the same time as the other women" she quickly and defensively responded. "And I gave the check to the Memorial Fund"—the fund that took care of families of fallen CIA officers.

On the eve of Bill Clinton's inauguration, a group of women began a class action claiming workplace discrimination at the CIA.[109] The all-male leadership saw the public lawsuit filed by over a hundred clandestine service officers as a full-throated act of institutional betrayal. A once-closed society that had always policed itself was dragged not just into the public spotlight, but into what many thought was a contemptuous new era of political correctness.

"At first I thought," Charlie continued, "that the suit might help. But once it became public it ceased being about change. Sure, a half dozen women got well-deserved promotions and retroactive pay. But the whole thing got hijacked by some feminist mob, fucking desk-bound yuppies who care more about their careers than about national security. After that I lost interest, sticking it to the man, rather than pushing reform.

"And the outcome as I experienced it?" Charlie said, shaking her head. "After working for a decade to overcome old-boy skepticism about women even being in the field. It seemed to me like the divide between male and female grew even greater. Maybe I'm reading too much into the aftermath but I got the feeling afterwards that young women in ops actually became the bad guys, so to speak—that it wasn't the abusive men who were stigmatized, but women—especially pretty ones—because now they were considered a danger. To the men, that is. And the sexual harassment part of the whole thing was swept under the rug. So in the end, to me, it became more about how women dressed and acted than about the environment inside the agency, than about women as equals in the Agency."

She went on: "At a time of cutbacks with the end of the Cold War? The bosses now saw women as the new enemy. Not only were they labeled nonessential because they weren't as useful or as versatile as men, but they were also now considered to be untrustworthy turncoats who could do real damage to the old boys.

"Don't get me wrong, sir," Charlie said. "I've had some great bosses and I've been treated with respect by almost every one of them. But my experience in the Agency, inside the bigger machine, has been a constant fight to match up with male counterparts. Men are never judged the same way women are. Ever since I've been in Washington, I've felt that despite operational success in the field, despite great reviews and even a promotion to a supervisory position, that I wasn't in line to be a chief of station, not even to be a deputy ..."

"And you don't chalk that up to your being a good case officer, too valuable in your actual specialty, or even to your being too young?" Bowlen asked.

"Men are groomed from day one," responded Charlie. "Invited to meetings. Into secret chambers and locker rooms. To go golfing. Women? We must practically contort ourselves to become men. Or worse, we become feline monsters so we can claw our way into the same place as even the most mediocre male counterparts." She paused a moment, sipping her iced tea, admonishing herself for saying too much. "I think the toughest realization after I got to Langley was that in the bastard world of counterterrorism there was no way, unless the world changed, that I was going to compete on an even playing field."

Tell me more about that," Bowlen responded, seemingly unperturbed by any of what she was saying. "About counterterrorism."

"Trust me, I wouldn't trade it for the world, but as everyone knows, working terrorism is junior varsity to the world of stealing government secrets. God, I experienced that in Technicolor in Saudi Arabia earlier this year," she went on. "Even though I showed up in the field as the senior rep from the CTC,[110] even as someone who'd served in-country, I got the double brush-off—from the Khobar Towers[111] investigators on the ground *and* from the local station. It was sadly obvious. I was counterterrorism *and* a woman.

"I don't mean to belabor the point. But it's my experience, and not just mine. Most Agency old-timers can't get past the fact that a Counterterrorist Center even exists. Look, I get it that CTC is a headquarters operation at a time when Washington micromanagement is increasingly despised. I get it that operating from afar seems to threaten the almighty country stations. And I even get the fear that this seven-thousand-pound gorilla might threaten carefully-constructed relationships with host-nation governments. But something deeper is going on. Being at Langley, I've learned something that I didn't see in the field. The work of counterterrorism is doubly shunned by the old boys because most of those working the terrorism portfolio are women. Thus, the Neanderthals can doubly dismiss it as some feminized nowhere focused on a marginal subject. So, despite whatever I've done and whatever career the seventh floor might have in store for me, I've found myself constrained from being effective in my day-to-day job precisely *because* I'm a woman."

"Ms. Charbel," Bowlen said, not disagreeing but also not throwing fuel on the fire, "the idea of a CIA Counterterrorist Center is new, and the notion of even collecting intelligence on non-governmental entities who aren't economic or political actors is in its infancy."

He was right. And eminently reasonable.

Still, she responded, "Sir, here's an additional truth, and it's why I bring it up as a nexus. This new generation of terrorists who aren't Palestinians and aren't revolutionaries, they force the Agency to do something it hates to do in the Middle East: to pry into the domestic dirty laundry of friends. It's tricky. In the field of terrorism we are increasingly dependent on those governments for information, while at the same time we know that they are supporting many in those very ranks, in the belief that doing so increases their safety because the support is predicated on the bargain that those terrorist focus externally. So, the work of counterterrorism is fraught with all sorts of dangers. It not only pulls the CIA away from the old school game of espionage, but it also threatens the liaison relationships that we are increasingly dependent upon.[112]

"I mean … why don't we just hire more case officers at the country level? And I know what the answer is, that it's expensive and it takes a long time to spin them up. But I once checked into the Frankfurt station in transit to the Middle East and saw the actual problem—there must have been 200 case officers there, in a country where we *can* depend on exchanges for foreign intelligence … and why? … because it was a better lifestyle.

"Okay, I'm ranting. The bottom line is that the Middle East is mostly not a great assignment and the United States—the Agency—doesn't really have the stomach for the messiness of terrorism, of terrorists, of facing the truth of their true sponsors, of going down that trail ..."

She squeaked as she ran out of breath, forgetting almost to take a breath as she was talking. And so she sat back, again sipping her iced tea.

Then she plunged back in: "I don't want to lose the thread of Saudi Arabia, sir. When I got there, I could see how the Agency was so absolutely in the Saudi pocket. God love the station, sir, but those fuckers really don't have a clue what's really going on inside the kingdom."

"Saudi Arabia is a very different place and a special problem," Bowlen answered evenly.

With somewhat of a tin ear, she just barreled over him. "Understood. But I'd been posted there before, Dammam during the Gulf War. I saw then that the Agency—and not just the Agency—was bending over backwards to accommodate every Saudi *cultural* explanation for its ... what shall we say? ... its inexcusable behavior. It was demoralizing. We represent the values of our country around the world, except in this medieval society where we don't want to ruffle feathers? As if we have no power? As if they really do have us over a barrel, so to speak. How is it that we accommodate the foreign power over our own? To achieve what? Not to offend them. I thought not-offending was the domain of the State Department. We're supposed to be doing what the diplomats can't."

She saw it then. That since she'd come to Washington, she'd let her anger get the better of her. She'd come to sound like that female complainer that she so disliked. More though, she disliked being at headquarters, disliked the office politics, and especially disliked the grand political maneuvering behind everything. And in her dislikes, anger arose.

"I don't disagree with much of your analysis, Ms. Charbel," Bowlen said when she seemed to run out of steam. "The Agency has limitations. But I don't need to tell you that the CIA serves the president. It is not a force unto itself, in terms of what it can do."

"Meaning what?" she said, feeling defeated. He didn't seem fazed by her tirade. But she was probably talking to the wrong guy. And she'd probably blown her opportunity to impress him.

"The so-called constraints on the Agency that you refer to," he answered, "on how it behaves regarding difficult host governments, they exist partly because the CIA isn't its own master. The Agency, how it is chartered and configured, isn't meant to make policies. It must walk the tightrope of representing and reflecting policies as they are, not as it wishes them to be."

It was a bit of a smackdown.

Bowlen deftly shifted the conversation to what she learned when she was in Saudi Arabia after the November bombing.[113]

Charlie answered, trying to calm herself. "What I saw was that the FBI investigators went into the country like they owned the place, expecting the Saudis to be cowed like some local cop shop, oblivious and even uncaring about the country's way of doing things. It was some tough medicine that in some ways could be admired—not kowtowing to fucking Saudi sensitivities—but it also wasn't particularly smart because they needed the Saudis' cooperation to conduct their investigation.

"But to tell you the truth, sir," she went on, "I came away thinking that the FBI was thrust into an impossible situation vis-à-vis the Saudis. I'd never had much exposure to the Bureau at that point, so it took me awhile to grasp that they were cops, seeking the perps who killed Americans, period. The Saudis weren't going to cooperate if it meant capitulating, in providing access to their dirty laundry, to letting America into their internal affairs. I tried to explain to the agent in charge that who pulled off the attack and what inspired them wasn't really one and the same, that blind followers or dupes might have been set up. What I got back from the Bureau was that they didn't care why some fucker committed murder—they just wanted the fucker."

"So, in your work, did you pick up enough intelligence to support the official line that Iran was behind it?" Bowlen asked.

"As far as I can tell," Charlie responded, "anything interesting going on in the kingdom is inspired by Osama bin Laden.[114] So who was behind this particular attack? The perpetrators might have had all sorts of objectives and grievances, but the reason that anyone is spurred to act inside that country is bin Laden. He symbolizes the opposition to the royal family's stranglehold and its oppression of everyone else in the country, the Shi'a being just one group."

"So, professionally, Ms. Charbel, your reason to resign is frustration that we're not seeing the terrorist threat clearly."

She thought for a minute. He was right to rise above her anger and pettiness in pointing this out to her. Charlie liked Bowlen, sensed comfort in his wisdom.

"I guess putting aside all the personal issues, that's right, sir. And that *is* my opinion, particularly regarding bin Laden. But I'd say our growing blind spot regarding the true motivations for this latest generation of terrorists is bigger than just Saudi Arabia. And it's bigger than the Agency. I don't talk to the president, and I got frustrated—and was blocked—in influencing even what the CIA leadership thinks about the future. What I've discovered is that there just isn't much appetite for debate. Nor is there much interest in anything beyond today's headlines. Washington is so stuck in crisis *du jour*."

Bowlen leaned forward. "So, Miss Charbel. Where this administration can't see and where the Agency cannot go, specifically regarding Saudi Arabia and the Middle East, that's where Special Purpose is."

His organization. Her heart raced.

"We head up an extremely sensitive effort," he said, confiding in her.

She practically had to bite her tongue to rein herself in. Charlie had been arguing with her bosses and her co-workers for months about the need for the country to shift gears. And she'd been round and round with Steve, furious and frustrated about how things were and how she thought they should be. Upon hearing Mr. Bowlen offer this glimmer of hope, she felt a momentary pang of regret reversing her conviction to leave. But she had to admit that she came to the meeting with Bowlen not just to let someone—anyone—in senior management have it but also because she was still invested in the battle, still motivated to want to make a difference. Now she hoped her tirade hadn't disqualified her for whatever it was Bowlen had in mind in asking for a meeting.

"I'm looking for an accomplished Arabic-speaking case officer to join us. Urdu is also a plus."

That made Marina Charbel unique. She had native Arab fluency and four years in Pakistan, before coming to Washington.

"I understand why you're unhappy," said Bowlen, and he repeated the word *unhappy* almost under his breath, hesitating. "The increasing risk-aversion of the Agency, the lack of understanding of this new world of terrorism, the dogged adherence to the theory that terrorists are either all Palestinians against Israel or all lone wolves, the inability and unwillingness to take *al Qaeda* seriously …"[115]

He went down a list, all true, she thought.

"I've reviewed your reports. And your proposals," he said. "I agree with you that we have a blind spot in terms of recognizing this growing movement and its long-term threat. We believe attacks in Saudi Arabia are just the tip of an iceberg in terms of this new era of terrorism. Yes, Iran might have assisted the *Shi'a* perpetrators. But the reason? It is purely to split Saudi people, to create conflict."

We believe, she thought. *Was that just a non-ego royal we or was there a "we" out there that was something that wasn't the CIA?* She desperately wanted to interrupt and spur him along. But she kept quiet.

Bowlen continued, "This is an effort not only to better understand *al Qaeda,* but also to get in front of the organization."

"Get in front of?" she asked, ever so gingerly.

"Marina," he said, leaning forward and using her given name for emphasis, "something *is* happening on a bigger scale. All of what you say about the Agency is true. But America is also on the move. Some just dismiss it as a liberal fascination with peacekeeping, but let's not forget that at the same time as the Saudi attack, a war in Bosnia was coming to a glorious negotiated conclusion. All of Washington was focused on that because, well, it's Europe. The negotiated settlement was considered a triumph because it protected the poor minority Bosniaks, that's what everyone said. To me, though, there was a subtext. Nobody said it out loud, but the Serb Army was portrayed as modern-day Nazis, and the Srebrenica massacre that so motivated Washington was portrayed as the worst crime on European soil since the Second World War. Words like genocide were thrown about, the implications being that the Bosnians were like the Jews, and that intervention on their behalf was some do-over for the West for prevent another Holocaust.

"I'm not concerned with any of it, Ms. Charbel, with the breakup of Yugoslavia, except to say that out of Bosnia, and in some ways even out of Somalia, a new American crusade is coming together. It is one that claims the right to change the fundamental rules of the world, rules like sovereignty, and it is one that would allow the so-called civilized world to decide for themselves that they can cross borders and force the uncivilized to abide by their rules, under the New World Order and in accordance with the new creed of universal human rights."

She was listening, trying to take it all in.

"When it comes to the Middle East, when it comes to terrorism, this conviction to be on the side of oppressed people and minorities might actually provoke important change if we had the backbone to defend the likes of the *Shi'a* of Saudi Arabia or the greater Kurdish nation with the same vigor. But that would mean that we'd have to be willing to stand up to the government of Saudi Arabia and its ilk, to stand up to the rulers in Turkey. It would mean, as you say, that we stand up for what we believe in. But like most policies formulated by Ivory Tower intellectuals and then implemented by politicians, the *real world* always gets in the way, forcing choices and compromises. So instead of actual human rights for all, we pick and choose whose rights we'll defend. In doing so, my observation would be that we go after the low-hanging fruit, the Serbs, Saddam, and the other rogue states, those who look like Nazis or are old communist sympathizers who equally fit our unchanging lens."

"Excuse me for interrupting you, but I'm missing how this ties back into terrorism," she said.

"Because in all the narrative of the breakup of Yugoslavia, it is merely a footnote that the Bosniaks were Muslims," Bowlen answered.

"And that means what?" Charlie asked.

"Only when the enemy looked like Nazis, or when the enemy is some lawless regime that resists the lure of the Western way of life—and here I mean a country like Iraq—is the United States moved to action. Otherwise, we are happy to see Muslims killed," Bowlen answered, repeating himself. "We ignore what repressive governments like Saudi Arabia and Turkey do so because confronting them is too hard."

"I'm still not sure what the connection is," she said. Her own division at the Counterterrorist Center indeed watched as *jihadis* went to Bosnia to fight the Serbs,[116] but so many broader elements of history were suggested in his narrative. It was true that the fate of Yugoslavia wasn't what was important. And though Bowlen still hadn't said what it was that he was doing related to Saudi Arabia—relating to anything, really—she was having a hard time tying all of what he was saying together. America was on the move; she could see that.

"Whatever new world order is emerging, Ms. Charbel, we are handicapped by the choking geopolitical habits of the past. The breakup of Yugoslavia is the final battle of the Cold War, indeed even some last extermination of the Nazis. Our obsession with Iraq and its weapons of mass destruction is similarly a Cold War legacy, WMD matching the skillset of the Washington establishment. And Iran? It is as much an assault on the secular way of life as it is a movement to give the *Shi'a* their place in the world."

He was right about weapons of mass destruction, she thought. Ultimately, American policy gravitated towards WMD not only because they were so destructive, but also because focusing on arms control and technical inspections didn't require anyone in Washington to know anything about where they were operating. In the case of Iraq, either Saddam abided by his obligations under U.N. Security Council resolutions or he didn't; that's how Washington saw the entire stand-off. But the reasons for his recalcitrance? And what was behind his wanting to possess WMD in the first place? And who were the power players in all of it? For people at the top, those were extraneous details, the domain of the regional and country experts, who were intrinsically lower-ranking than the *strategic* experts, who had to think about the fate of the entire planet. It was a simple policy. Pieces of paper said that Saddam wasn't allowed to have WMD and that was that. She also knew it was a tricky balance, building so-called country and regional expertise. Obviously not everyone needed to be a country expert or an Arabic speaker. But reliance on arms control in the Middle East as a substitute for understanding the place? That had become practically the totality of American policy, plus of course, blind allegiance to Israel, Charlie thought, the eternal trump card.

A waitress stopped by the table and asked if they wanted anything else, and when they said no, she put the check on the table face down. It was an interruption.

"You were saying that America was also on the move?"

Mr. Bowlen looked at his watch.

"Ms. Charbel. We may call it the New World Order, but what is happening in all our peacekeeping and this new concept of humanitarian intervention is that we are missing how the Muslims themselves are seeing us. We focus on the Serbs, on Saddam, on the Ayatollahs. Each is handled in isolation. We are trying to rewrite big rules, practically oblivious to the shifts occurring in other worlds, as Mr. Draper would say, of the changed rules occurring in the Islamic world."

This *was* what Steve had been saying, for more than two years, *exactly* what he had been saying. *I got my theories. I really couldn't say more,* Charlie thought. When she asked Steve about Bowlen, he had pretended not to know. *That fucker.*

"Mr. Draper's involved in Special Purpose?" she asked.

"No, not involved," Bowlen responded, chuckling, repeating the word *involved*, again seemingly absentmindedly and almost to himself.

"But you said … ?"

"Mr. Draper is like a cat. He keeps to himself, and then he pounces. Somehow, and to tell you the truth, I'm not sure how, he stuck his nose in my business when he sent me a note saying you were available. Not even knowing, or at least I thought, that I was looking. So, I figured I'd better pay attention."

"And he did that without being involved?"

"Mr. Draper seems to know many things." Bowlen then hesitated. "He was right, though. You are impressive. And I would like you to join the dark side."

She didn't know if he was joking about the label.

"I'll also admit that I'm hoping that your involvement might also entice Mr. Draper."

"I'm bait?"

"Oh no, Ms. Charbel. I don't want you to see it that way," he responded, not snatching her own bait. "You, my dear, are a superb case officer: tenacious, inquisitive, and unconventional. You have a view of the subject matter that in my reading I think is spot on. In my opinion. So, regardless of what happens with Mr. Draper, I still want you. You are the perfect match for the job."

"A perfect match for what exactly, sir."

"A perfect match for digging deeper into what's going on in the *jihadi* world, to try to figure out what bin Laden's up to …"

"Sir, that's what I've already been doing at the Center."

"Yes, yes, Ms. Charbel. This would be from a different angle, very different. You would be working as a case officer again."

"Well, what is it that you have in mind specifically for me to do?" she asked. She was still smarting that perhaps she wasn't being valued outside of her being an appendage to a man, and even worse, to her sneaky partner.

"We need a case officer with background and knowledge of Pakistan and the region to run an asset, one with access to Osama bin Laden's inner circle."

That got her attention.

After toiling away in the CIA Counterterrorist Center at Langley, Charlie knew all the agents on the CIA payroll, or those relating to terrorism, or she thought she did.[117]

"May I ask who the asset is?" she found herself saying, mortified that she would be so stupid to think Bowlen would tell her, but overcome by the moment and her curiosity.

"His name is Khalid Sheikh Mohammed.[118] Have you heard of him?"

She thought a second.

"Is that Ramzi Yousef's uncle?" she responded, a little confused. Only because he had a distinct name could she even pull that up. And even the little she could recall was obscure. He wasn't some high-level person. She thought he was merely a name connected to the financing of the 1993 attack on the World Trade Center. She had no clue—nor did the CIA, as far as she knew—that he was connected to bin Laden. If he was even the same man.

"He's not actually related to Ramzi Yousef," Bowlen said, confusing her further, "but that's a story for another day. Khalid's been a Special Purpose asset for almost a decade.[119] I've learned a lot from him. Mostly what I've learned is how to look at what is going in the world in a different way. Take Bosnia.[120] We blithely label it *ethnic cleansing* by the Serbs, but Muslims see it as part of a worldwide attack on them."

He was wending off, she thought. He just delivered the bombshell that he had an actual and active terrorist on his payroll, even if it was the payroll of a mysterious entity that seemed to exist in its own world.

"He's active?"

"Indeed, he is," Bowlen said. "Indeed, he is …"

"And I'd be doing what with him?" Charlie asked.

"Being his case officer."

"Yes, I got that. But to do what, sir? Is he an information asset? Or is he part of some covert action?"

"Ms. Charbel, he is neither and both. But he's been an asset for a long time, and he needs a proper handler."

"Because?" she asked.

"Because I'm afraid I'm too close. And because the workload is becoming too great."

"And he's actively reporting?"

"That he is. The attack on the World Trade Center. The Philippine plot. Riyadh. And you'll be pleased, I think, with what he has to say about bin Laden. It tracks with your analysis."

"Pleased?"

"Well, maybe not pleased. But you'll find his output edifying."

"And the mission would be what?"

"To establish a relationship so that we can have better early warning of future attacks."

The restaurant was filling up. When Charlie looked around, she saw Bowlen's bodyguard had left—too conspicuous. She felt utterly alone, captive so quickly to someone she didn't even know, in possession of information that was so much more than a bombshell—a revelation about this Sheikh Mohammed that questioned everything she thought she knew—and now saddled with another problem, a new code of silence that cut her off from her lover and partner.

Chapter 6 Off the Grid

"How'd it go?" Steve Draper asked.

They were lunching together in the Agency cafeteria, at the same table—their table—by the window looking out on the greenery, a bustle of similar, hushed rendezvous going on all around.

"He offered me a job," Charlie answered.

"Doing what? Specifically?"

"Working for Special Purpose."

"Duh," he said. She was already annoyed. "You take it?"

"I did."

"So, last week, no amount of argument could change your mind about leaving the Agency, and now you've taken a job?"

"Well, I am leaving the Agency," she said. "This will probably be one of our last lunches here. I thought maybe you'd be pleased for me," she went on, waiting for Steve to tip his hand that maybe he knew more about Lawrence Bowlen than he let on, that he knew even where she was going.

"How can I be pleased if I don't know anything about what you'll be doing?"

"Because I stay in the game, which is ultimately what you want. Isn't it?"

"You're right," he pivoted. "Congratulations. Really."

"Case officer," she finally said, hoping he'd just be honest for once about what he knew.

"What? Like he'd offer you a job as circus acrobat?"

God, he could be so annoying. From the first day Charlie met him, he'd been this way. Sarcastic. Scheming. Sometimes bitterly cold. And then, he'd been the opposite, disarmingly honest, vulnerable and open, making her feel like she had been unfair for thinking him a dickhead or that maybe she was doing something wrong.

"What is it that you do here?" she'd inquired when they originally met, her knocking on the door of his small office, one that, though having just arrived at the Counterterrorist Center, she already had heard was radioactive.

The tiny, windowless box was the quintessential scholarly burrow, packed with books and paper but nevertheless organized and orderly.

"I'm an analyst," he said, not answering, and not looking up.

"Yeah, I got that," she pressed on. "So, what are you working on?"

"Work," he answered, practically growling and offering little more.

She pushed on: "Maybe there's something I can do to help this *work*?"

He looked up, making eye contact for the first time. Her dark curly hair, her complexion not pasty white, her nose sharp, the birthmark on her left cheek, her gold hoop earrings.

He knew who she was—a Lebanese American case officer brought in from the field to head the new *al Qaeda* branch. But now that he looked at her, it was *that* look of Lebanese women, and memories of *that* place.

Steve Draper fell in love with the city of Beirut the moment he set foot there on a visit, something about flourishing neighborhoods delineated by mounds of rubble; the juxtaposition of sacred religious shrines next to a lingerie store; the insane three-way streets; the intense passions that were achingly familiar and yet wholly foreign.

And he felt *it*, too, there in Lebanon—a buzz, a soul-challenging tie to the sacred spring of life—quite to his own surprise for a man who thought he felt nothing about his religion. There was a vibration, as if physically he was in the Holy Land. As if this was his ancestral home. And the women were the most beautiful in the world, a composite of Arab, Christian, Jewish, Mediterranean, Semitic, Eastern, Western.

And now it was like all the splendor of Beirut was right here in front of him.

"Marina Charbel," she said, thrusting her hand out. "They call me Charlie."

"Sit down, sit down," Steve said, coming around his desk and clearing a stack of books from the cramped office's only chair.

"So," he asked, "have they bought your proposal to start networking the rings around bin Laden?" revealing in his question that he paid attention more than he pretended.

"No," she said, smiling, but also being careful. "Aren't you one of those who argued against it?"

"Personally, I'd love the detail and I'm even curious about what really binds them all together," he said. "There's all of—what?—a dozen analysts focused on *al Qaeda*?[121] But I'm afraid, in typical Agency style, what you're suggesting might just end up being a lot of thoughtless database building, threads in a spider's web that will be tangled and endless."

It was true, what he said. And despite his skepticism, Charlie knew that Steve also found her *street* series of reports from Pakistan "highly useful" while other analysts scored them as "marginal."

"It's a slippery slope, though," Steve continued. "*We* should be explaining terrorism to the policymakers and obviously understanding the ecosystem around them is essential for us to do that. So, on the one hand I agree with you. But on the other? I don't see much clamoring for us to provide an explanation or a big picture. So, beyond my own curiosity, I'm afraid what you're proposing will just end up being fodder to build target folders."

She asked: "You against targets, too?"

"I'm against stupid shit that gets us nowhere—whether it's intelligence collection or missiles," he said before remembering to smile and then trying to make nice.

"Look, your reporting from Saudi Arabia on bin Laden's emerging voice was fantastic. And in Pakistan, you cracked the code, focusing on aspirations rather than explanations. Sometimes I feel like all we do is put together the details of attacks. Past and future. The attack becomes the subject. The who—other than some luminary like bin Laden—is irrelevant. What drives them to attack? We either think we already know, we don't care, or we get diverted by the attacks themselves. You know, frankly I'm surprised you're here, a low-scoring reporter focused on aspirations. And a girl."

"Is that supposed to be some kind of compliment?" she inquired, cocking her head, not meaning to be flirtatious.

"That depends on how much you think this place—the CTC—should be trying to figure out the big picture or whether we should be just servicing the action types. Reporting on the grievances and aspirations of people we've already declared as monsters intrinsically labels what you've been doing a waste of time. And flavor of the month here is increasingly mapping terrorists and their networks into a set of prospective targets. That growing appetite for targeting them, in my humble opinion, it just transforms all of what we do here into a tip of a spear searching for soft flesh."

"So, you basically don't like action, going after the bad guys?"

"It's not that I don't like it. Impulsive action on our part seems to serve as stimuli for terrorists to gain greater strength, both as our victims and as warriors whom we thoughtlessly transform into worthy opponents."

"How so?" she asked.

"I would argue we give up some moral edge by treating terrorists as warriors. As proper military opponents. I'm not saying that terrorism is strictly a law enforcement problem, and I won't deny that there is a military component in going after armed groups in places like Afghanistan. And while I don't think it's necessarily intentional, I do think that when we set out to defeat terrorists in combat, when we make them military opponents, we elevate them into a world of honor and grant them entry in a centuries-old club that is normally closed to these very kinds of interlopers, whether they be mercenaries or pirates. We're endowing them in a way that they don't deserve."

"Hmm," she said, thinking for a second. "I don't disagree, but I've followed you, too. Your argument that they're not conventional criminals and that they're not legitimate warriors leaves little else. Covert thugs? And yet they're not organized crime. So, what are they?"

"I didn't say ..." he started.

"Let me finish," she cut him off. "What I'd love is if you applied your mind to what could be done, not just in critiquing what we're doing as lame and ineffective. I see in your personnel file that you've turned down two field assignments—assignments that might serve to sharpen your analysis and open the way to conceive of a different approach."

"You trying to get rid of me already?" asked Steve, broadly smiling.

"You know what I'm saying," Charlie responded, ignoring his distraction but also feeling the temperature rise in her cheeks.

"To tell you the truth," he said, "I prefer to stay at 30,000 feet where I can see the big picture. I'm not really interested in what any one joker has to say."

Then he softened, even lowering his voice. "Look. It's a flaw I have. I'll admit it. I'm better here. I couldn't do what you do. And besides: I'm that storybook analyst back at headquarters who actually reads your stuff from the field, who appreciates some detail I hadn't previously understood …"

"It's too bad you're here," Steve continued, "because that's one fewer case officer out there who gives a fuck about understanding the why."

He looked straight at her. "I'm not saying it's too bad *you're* here— you know what I mean. I'm glad you're here."

"Why's that?"

"Well," he said, taking a breath, holding her gaze for a moment too long. "I'm glad we'll get a chance to work together. And though I'd love to be everything—including anthropologist studying a foreign world up close—I'm just not that good out there in the actual world. I generally avoid people because, well …"

And then he hesitated, looking at the ceiling. "Well, because I'm not always good with people."

Then he looked at her again. "Maybe you'll bring fresh perspective into this place. We're fucked by how small-minded and immediate everyone is."

What any one joker has to say.

That first conversation with Steve Draper, and that declaration, stayed with her. They bonded. He was unlike anyone at the Agency that she'd met, insubordinate and almost reckless in the preservation of his unique way of doing things. They became enthusiastic allies in trying to understand, a branch of two. They started hanging around together, arguing and collaborating. He opined and she pushed back. He, the same for her. They served as back channel for each other as to what everyone else thought. They hung out after work. They drank. They had sex. They fought. They survived as a secret couple in the office. They became their own cell.

But Steve exhausted Charlie more and more with his disagreements, with his criticism. A contrariness she once found refreshing increasingly was directed at her. And then there was Steve's equivocation. She couldn't quite explain it, not even to herself, how exhausting it was that he knew everything but also was so ambivalent about taking a stance, on believing anything. She fell in love with him. But she also grew weary. And she was distrustful—about what it was Steve really did believe, and then distrustful of his love.

As she left Steve's office on that day when they first met, she felt a bit naked. Not in Steve's challenging argument, but in how he looked at her. It was unnerving, too deep to be casual; staring too long, not in a leering way, but meeting her eyes, drawing her in.

After that day, he called her "action girl." The "girl" wasn't meant as a putdown and the "action" connoting that she had superpowers he admitted he did not possess.

Charlie did her research on him as well: Steve had no academic credentials to speak of and didn't speak multiple languages. First at the office in the morning and last to go home at night, he was neither brownnoser nor place holder. He just worked hard. Opinion on Steve had no middle ground: Some thought he could be snippily dismissive. Others said that he was kind and patient. The other women in the office liked him because he took them seriously. And yet in bathroom talk when they got together to assess the men, somehow Steve was also at the top of everyone's list as the most dangerous.

Steve had a line he loved to repeat. "I'm the luckiest fucker in the world," he'd say. "I get up every morning and can't wait to get to my desk and pursue whatever it is I want to, and someone is dumb enough to pay me. I do what I do because I love to do it, and no one tells me not to. I do it well enough that no one wants to tell me not to. I do it so well I can't escape. And even if I wanted to escape, there's really nothing else I can do."

Charlie knew that day after her meeting with Bowlen that it drove Steve crazy that she wouldn't tell him what assignment Bowlen dangled in front of her. And yet at the same time, she had a lingering suspicion that perhaps he already knew.

"You know," she said, that last day in the cafeteria, "I've got a feeling that I'm about to handle him."

"Who him?" Steve responded; mouth full.

"*That one joker*," she said.

"That who?"

"When we first met, on that first day in your office, I remember you said you didn't really care what one joker had to say. You dismissed the very system of individual sources, dismissed the idea that there could be a someone who could crystalize a universe of thought. And yet I think I might have found him."

"I didn't say I didn't want to know, just that it was too close. I didn't want to get that close; it isn't my thing."

No, he'd said that precisely, she remembered. *What one joker had to say.* But there was no use rubbing it in now.

He pressed for more. "It's one person? That's the job?"

"Yep." She knew she was killing him.

"Bowlen wants you to run one person?"

"Evidently, yes."

"And you know who he is?"

"I do."

"And you can't tell me?"

"Nope."

"Are you going to disappear into his black hole?" asked Steve, looking almost like a puppy dog in his submission.

"Disappear? No? Not from you," she said, reaching up and gently touching the side of his face.

Chapter 7 Apex Watch

Inserting her CIA credentials into a card reader, a computer screen interrogated Charlie to input the last four digits of her Social Security number, then asked a series of probing and personal questions, the name of her high school, her boss's name in Cairo. It was unlike anything she'd ever seen. Finally, the vault door clicked open.

Bowlen's organization was located on the fourth floor of the old building at agency headquarters. Coming to visit, Charlie felt like she was attending her first day at school, Bowlen inviting her in for a briefing on what he merely called "Apex Watch," the codename, she assumed, for his office of Special Purpose.

"I hope that's the last time I ever have to go through that gauntlet," Charlie joked to Bowlen's assistant when she at last walked down a long, sterile corridor to the director's suite in the corner.

"Welcome, Ms. Charbel," the assistant pleasantly answered, standing up to shake her hand. "Wait until you meet our sentient building in Maryland."

Bowlen warmly greeted her as she was shown in, coming out from behind his desk and then sitting across from her in a set of comfortable chairs.

"The Apex Watch name. It comes from what?" she asked.

"Apex, watching Apex."

"Apex is a thing?" she went on.

"Indeed it is," Bowlen answered. *Indeed it is* he repeated, trailing off, almost talking to the walls.

"And that's the Saudi name? Apex?"

"It is."

Charlie had never heard of Apex Watch nor Apex.

"And Special Purpose?" she asked. "Is it solely about Saudi Arabia?"

"That's how it originated, Saudi Arabia. But now it is much broader."

"Do you know much of the history of Saudi Arabia?" Bowlen asked.

"Well, evidently a lot less than I might have thought," she answered. "I mean, I know the outlines. But when I was stationed there during Operation Desert Shield, my focus wasn't internal. So is your entire project focused on the Saudis?"

"*Our* project, Ms. Charbel."

"Yes. Our project. I'm sorry."

Do you at least know the story of Faisal?"

"King Faisal," she answered. "Assassinated in the '70s? I'm afraid not. That is, beyond schoolgirl outlines."

"King Faisal Al Saud. He was third son of Saudi Arabia's founder, and he ascended to the throne when he was 58. That was in 1964. He became only the third king of the modern-day country," Bowlen began. "Though at first glance one might think he suffered a long frustrating wait behind his older brother, in reality he'd been his father's favorite from boyhood, and had been even more deeply and directly involved in the making of the modern Saudi state than his hapless sibling."

Bowlen told the story of how, at the age of 14, at the end of the First World War, young Faisal, then just a teenager, represented his father on the first official Saudi royal visit to Britain, meeting with King George V and experiencing the world outside.[122] He was then appointed foreign affairs minister at the age of 26, and he was one of only four dozen delegates at the San Francisco founding of the United Nations, later serving as the Saudi ambassador to the new international body.[123] He became the first Saudi to visit Soviet Russia and for decades was responsible for all the kingdom's important international dealings.[124] Incredibly enough, Bowlen said, Faisal could say that he met every American president from Herbert Hoover to Gerald Ford.

As foreign minister and international trouble shooter, Faisal earned a reputation, Bowlen said, for being both worldly and honorable. He was a pleasing international face for a largely misunderstood—and equally reluctant to be understood—nation, he said. Faisal was also quite the contrast to his older brother, Saud, who in his decades as crown prince and then king became legion for squandering the countries' riches, bringing the emerging oil giant to the brink of bankruptcy.

At home, Faisal also distinguished himself. He participated in military campaigns that extended Saudi family rule to then-independent governorates of Mecca and Medina, the two holiest sites in Islam.[125] The outlines of the modern country formed, Faisal battled with his older brother about modernization. A fan and proponent of technology—he saw his first telephone and took his first escalator ride on his trip to London during the First World War—he fought to refocus the domestic budget towards development of infrastructure and other public works.

When Saud was finally pressured to step down, Faisal became the absolute ruler.[126] Oil wealth was by then opening possibilities, and Faisal started programs to expand education, especially for women and girls. His four daughters were his pride and joy, and he wanted them to receive a higher education, as much as was possible inside the country. But he also knew in his modernization efforts that he had to accommodate the *ulema*.

"Do you know them, Ms. Charbel?" Bowlen asked.

"I know that they are officially the interpreters of the *Qur'an*, and the closest thing Islam has to a College of Cardinals," she answered. "But I imagine that you have more to say."

In Saudi Arabia, Bowlen went on, they weren't just the clerics. The *ulema* was also the broader body of luminaries—imams in the mosques to be sure, but also teachers and judges—who were not just Islamic advisors, but also specifically the defenders of *Wahhabism*.[127]

At around the time of the American Revolution in the late 1770s, *Wahhabin* argued for a return to the Prophet's "true" teachings, away from the practices established under far-flung dynasties as Islam spread. *Wahhabis* asserted that they, the original Muslims from the Arabian Peninsula, were the true followers of their pious forebears. And not only that, but *Wahhabin* argued that Muslims from the core needed to go out and purify the *Qur'an* of "innovations" that had crept in over centuries, keeping the word of the Prophet as it was originally passed down, as an Arabic text, and make it the singular true word.

Wahhabism grew as the House of Saud grew. Spurred on by Abdul Aziz,[128] the *Wahhabis* went from dominating the Arabian Peninsula to dominating the Arab and then non-Arab Islamic world. From the very beginning the most threatening opposing sect were the *Shi'a*, who practiced worshiping the Prophet Muhammad's family members—Ali, Fatimah, Hassan, and Hussain—as messengers as well.[129] Sunnis on the other hand believed in the word and the word only, rejecting ancestral power and divine standing.

Charlie was getting restless, and Bowlen detected that she seemed impatient for a direct tie to the present day.

"Anyhow, Ms. Charbel, Faisal had to directly challenge *Wahhabi* standards in his modernization campaign. For those standards rejected virtually all art, music, and even technology as blasphemy, condemning all that was modern as seducing people away from the ideal way of life.

"Ever a diplomat, he found ways to join the modern world and appease the *ulema*. It probably helped that he was a descendant through his mother's side of the family of *Wahhabin* himself. So, in establishing education for women, he allowed the curriculum to be overseen by the religious leadership. When he introduced television, he started by broadcasting recitations of the *Qur'an* and other religious programming. And he craftily lent financial and political support to anti-Israeli efforts, handsomely funding the Palestinian cause, a project that also cleverly competed with the socialist and Pan Arab efforts of Nasser in Egypt. When the Arab armies were handily defeated in the Arab-Israeli War, it was what Faisal did that not only was most consequential but also had the greatest and most lasting effect on American policy. He withdrew Saudi oil from world markets. The price immediately quadrupled, and it would be his defining act. *Time* magazine even made King Faisal "Man of the Year."[130]

"Then came March 25, 1975," Bowlen said to Charlie. "I remember that day so clearly.

"Faisal was holding court in the great room in *Ma'ather* Palace, seated under the portrait of Abdul-Aziz ibn Abdul Rahman ibn Faisal ibn Turki ibn Abdullah ibn Muhammad Al Saud, the founder of modern Saudi Arabia."

Charlie smiled at Bowlen's use of the whole name and noted that Bowlen called the father and the founder of the state by his Arab name rather than Ibn Saud—*the Saud*—what most Americans used as shorthand to avoid the mouthful.

And Bowlen said it with a beautiful, classical Arab accent.

"You speak Arabic?" she interrupted.

"Indeed, I do," Bowlen answered. "A little rusty, but yes."

"But that's not on your bio."

"I even have a bio?" Bowlen responded with a friendly lilt. And then he went on.

"My first assignment with the Agency was to Riyadh, the year Kennedy was elected. I was deeply disappointed not to get some cushy European posting. Unlike you, my dear, I didn't know anything about the place nor even a lick of the language. I was sent to school and into a language immersion posting in Cairo before being plopped into a tiny, six-man station."

"I would have loved to have seen Saudi Arabia in those days," Charlie remarked. By the time she took her first trip to the Middle East as a teenage girl, to the Lebanese homeland of her parents, the modern lines and ways were already in place.

"Though the country was a founding member of the United Nations," Bowlen responded, "when I arrived, the Saudi kingdom was still a backwater and barely even a coherent country. And as the birthplace of what we used to call the Mohammedan religion—those were simpler times—it was of only minor importance, probably more in an imperial sense as the center of Islam than for any conceived geopolitical value. If there was anything interesting about the monarchy and the country in those days, it was that it was an anti-communist outpost and thus a reliable counterweight to socialism—which was then brewing in Egypt and amongst the Ba'athists in Iraq and Syria.[131] In those days, we saw it as a helper or a threat to American access to oil, pure and simple."

He went on: "For a young man under diplomatic cover, my life was slow, and quite refined. We had servants and made elaborate camping trips to the desert. And there were forays to all the Mohammedan sites, even to the Holy Land, which was still innocent and open. Our access to the royals, including Faisal, was pretty good as well. In operations, we mostly kept an eye on Soviet and East European mischief, but by and large, we hung out in royal isolation.

"I did multiple tours there with headquarters time in the middle," Bowlen continued. "My early experience really gave me a sense of the changes brought on by the post-oil boom. It was like some small-time hustler won the lottery. The dollar became the Saudi way to buy their way out of all problems. Even for good Saudis like Faisal.

"Eh. Good Saudis, bad Saudis, of course I'm oversimplifying," Bowlen continued. "But they really were thrust into the modern world without a rulebook. And to be fair to the Saudis, there were too many Americans and other Western oil and financial types who were more than happy to partake of the new bonanza. But I'm getting ahead of myself."

And, indeed, she was puzzled.

"Faisal had been king for only nine years," he said, going back to his history lesson. "We had a good rapport, the king and I, huh, *the king and I*, but Faisal recognized that with all of his foreign experience he needed to temper the prevailing view that he was too close to the United States, which, in the eyes of most Arabs, was far from deserving of any devotion.

"After the overthrow of King Idris of Libya,[132] Faisal also undertook to build his own internal security apparatus and to crack down on the army. He ordered the arrests of hundreds of military officers, including some generals. Rumors flew that the arrests came because the CIA tipped off the king to a potential coup. And later, when Faisal was assassinated, that same mythical CIA reemerged. Faisal's oil boycott and his defiance of the West during the oil crisis became everyone's explanation for why he was killed.

"You know, Ms. Charbel, by 1975, Faisal was already an old man, and though the Agency had human sources—even amongst royals who got into trouble in the West or had outsize ambitions that went beyond their pocketbooks or their family statuses—our domestic understanding of the ins and outs of the royal family was pretty thin. Saudi government people—unless they were members of the royal family—knew nothing and had access to nothing of interest. Saudi businessmen were of no use; they were fixers and con men, their acumen focused on who knew who and not who knew what. And family was still family. Contending clans might dish on each other, but not on their own.

"I was sort of known in those days for having a relationship and rapport with Faisal, and that would make all the difference in my career. So, let me set the stage for the *majlis* that day," Bowlen said. Charlie knew the word formally meant "a place for sitting" but that it also referred to the salon where anyone from a mighty king or lowly tribal leader held court.

"As was the tradition, the great room was packed on Tuesday, the king's regular day to openly receive petitioners. The giant gold-trimmed room wasn't really built for dialogue, with its 40-foot-high ceilings and cold acoustics. It was easily the size of two gymnasiums. Think of a very ornate hotel ballroom.

"On this Tuesday, he was receiving the Kuwaiti petroleum minister and his delegation. Closest to the king in the great hall were the innermost of the inner circle, some there by blood and some because they were the important brokers in Faisal's modernizing enterprise. In groups of four, they sat on couches along the walls, fanning outward. We noted the position just like the Agency spotted Soviet leaders in Red Square, watching the lineup to try to figure out who was in and who was out. Not surprisingly, Faisal's oil minister was right next to him.

"Beyond the couches were the standing audience, diplomats, and spies like me, maybe two hundred in all, observers and supplicants, many of whom were also seeking an audience. There was a sprinkling of Western suits, but practically everyone was dressed in *thawb* and *ghurtra*."

It was a familiar sight to Charlie: the ankle-length white robes covered by a cloak and topped off by the traditional headdress, some in white, some red with checkered patterns.

"I'm pretty sure there wasn't a woman in the room," he added, seemingly for her benefit.

"The Kuwaiti delegation lined up to meet the king and in their midst was a little-known prince, a nephew of the king. Faisal clearly recognized him when he reached the front of the line and he extended his bowed head so that the prince could kiss him in a sign of respect. And then ... 'This is for my brother!' shouted the prince. He pulled a revolver from inside his cloak and *Bam! Bam! Bam!* Two bullets to the head, one to the shoulder. Faisal was dead.

"The place was a madhouse," Bowlen said, "not just in the killing of the king but in an assassination perpetrated by a member of the royal family.

"We knew nothing about the 31-year-old assassin, despite his having gone to college in California.[133] It turned out his older brother was killed at a protest against the introduction of television a few years earlier. There had been a huge protest and his brother led the crowd.

"The official Saudi line soon became that the young prince was mentally ill. There were articles in the press that said he was a drug addict. And then, regardless of whether he was competent to stand trial or not, he was quickly found guilty and publicly beheaded before anyone really had a chance to find out why he did it.

"Arab media was dominated by conspiracy theories, implying the assassin was a pawn in some Washington plot. Saudis of rank believed it, too. Since then, every Middle Eastern school boy and girl learns that the CIA was behind Faisal's assassination.[134] All of which might have just returned us to the status quo had I not at the same time discovered the existence of the Saudi project called Apex."

"Which is?" Charlie asked. "Simply."

"An organized program of Saudi political influence and bribery oriented towards the West. In those days of Henry Kissinger, I labeled it the controlling authority of *Riyalpolitik*. That word was my invention," Bowlen said, almost as if he wanted Charlie to appreciate the pun—*Riyalpolitik* instead of realpolitik, named for the Middle East currency.

"Through this Apex project, oil money and the money that the pious were giving in the mosques were lining the pockets of a number of prominent government and industry officials here and in Europe."

He let that sink in.

"But most important, Ms. Charbel, according to a prince who became a source, a man on the take included the chief of station, my boss."

"Holy shit," she said, unable to contain herself.

"The discovery was completely by chance. My source—the prince—openly spoke of something he assumed I already knew because of my relationship with Faisal. Anyhow, he was angry that all that Saudi friendship had purchased wasn't enough to protect the monarch and wondered whether this wasn't another CIA dirty trick. Remember, this was right after Watergate.

"It was tricky for me to figure out whom to trust in reporting such a claim. I reached out to a friend at Langley through the mail. He was an executive assistant on the seventh floor. I returned to the States for annual leave, and he arranged a private meeting for me with the director.[135] And then the director arranged for the two of us to meet with President Ford. I milked the source for everything he knew, and I prepared for the meeting and brought along the names and some very large numbers, not just of the station chief but also of other Americans. On the list was a prominent Nixon administration holdover and a White House VIP serving right then in a nearby office. They were all thought to be on the Saudi take.

"President Ford was saddened to be given the stark news. Here were prominent public figures enriching themselves on behalf of a foreign nation's interests. But on balance, and this is where it gets tricky, Ms. Charbel, Saudi and U.S. interests coincided. So, whose interest was it really? America was dependent on oil, and both countries were reconciled to continuing the status quo in the Middle East. Absent some change in American foreign policy or energy dependence, there seemed little that could be done about Apex."

As if anticipating her pushback, Bowlen said, "I'm afraid there's a limit to everything, Ms. Charbel. What were we to do? Arrest them all? Break relations with the Saudis? Put our heads in the sand and pretend this sort of thing didn't happen? We'd been catering to the … umm, *special* needs of the Saudi royal family for years, adding to the corruption, ourselves fueling international lawlessness.

"Long story short, President Ford appointed my friend—Hal Jones—to be the head of something called Special Purpose, Apex Watch. Arrangements were made for Jones to report directly to the president and the White House counsel.[136]

"Overnight, my job became head of operations to penetrate Apex. The Riyadh station chief was called back, and Agency watchers jabbered about a post-Faisal CIA purge. Initially, we just reported names to the president, information to help his dealings with specific people. President Carter gave us a wide berth to develop better sources and investigate finances here at home as well as overseas.[137] And develop better sources we did.

"When President Reagan came into office, Apex-related intelligence was used to convince him not to offer a Cabinet post to a certain Texas senator.[138] Others on the take were cut out of influential appointments and the president occasionally called CEOs and chairmen of various corporate boards to warn them of foreign agents in their midst. In exceptional cases. But by and large over the years, Apex Watch was an intelligence effort, not focused on either law enforcement or any program of reform.

"Vice President Bush became our proxy boss during the Reagan years, and we decided to move Apex Watch—by then more than three dozen investigators and analysts crammed into this space—out of the Langley complex. The tech guys came up with a clever scheme—*very clever* in those days—to penetrate the Saudi banking method of making payments and so we began to steal money from Apex itself to fund the Watch. We also expanded our scope to look more broadly at the arms trade and at other Middle East governments financing political corruption. But our focus remained Saudi Arabia. Under Bush's guidance, we moved beyond intelligence and into efforts to stave off Apex's worst effects."[139]

"So, what's Khalid Sheikh Mohammed's connection?" Charlie asked, still wondering how her new charge fit into this scheme.

"You know, I never forgot the lesson of discovering the existence of Apex, how difficult it was to get to people on the inside," said Bowlen. "And of the value of utmost secrecy.

"It's been almost 20 years, Ms. Charbel, and Apex has never been reported on, not in any formal way, not by anyone in the CIA or indeed even by the Israelis. As far as I know, the Saudi project has never been mentioned in any official reporting."

"But Sheikh Mohammed isn't Saudi-related, is he?"

"Yes and no, Ms. Charbel," answered Bowlen. It seemed to Charlie like he wanted to say something more, but then he plunged back into his narrative.

"As you well know, during the Reagan years, the CIA became increasingly focused on Afghanistan and our covert war to counter the Soviets," he said. "Apex Watch shifted, too, not so much because we were prescient about where the *jihad* would emerge from, but because in watching money move, the lines almost always converged from Afghanistan straight back to Saudi Arabia.[140] Hundreds of millions of dollars were moving.

"The CIA was clandestinely supporting the Afghan *mujahidin*[141] and the Saudis were additionally financing the foreign fighters, young men from the Arab and wider Muslim world. That included a brother of Khalid Sheikh Mohammed, who received Saudi funding to establish an aid agency. We—Apex Watch—were given the mandate to monitor the CIA covert operations and we decided to try to develop independent assets who were attracted to the fight in Afghanistan but who also might operate independently, then and afterwards, to report on where all this money actually went. And that's how Khalid was picked up as a source."

"But how? And why him?" Charlie pressed.

Bowlen took a deep breath, measuring his words carefully. "I knew that Khalid Sheikh was a liar from the moment I met him. We knew he had joined the Muslim Brotherhood, and it was doubtful he was going to Saudi Arabia, other than as a lowly engineer. But his interest in the *jihad* in Afghanistan meant that he might run into Osama bin Laden, and I certainly did what I could to guide him in that direction."

Charlie was confused. He seemed to be jumping ahead, almost subconsciously justifying Khalid Sheikh Mohammed's relationship with Apex Watch before he'd even explained how it happened.

Bowlen continued: "Khalid Sheikh has turned into quite the oracle, pretty much calling it correctly on everything: the emergence of *al Qaeda*, the spread of the *jihad* once the Afghan war ended, the increased targeting against the West, even about specific attacks. He did hook up with bin Laden, and now he's become too valuable to let go. He is hardly just an observer. In fact, he's really at the center. And that's where you come in.

"Ms. Charbel, the truth is, as I told you before, I'm too close. And since Hal Jones retired, I'm also too busy."

"Too close how? How did we even contact him?"

"Oh, you are right, I've skipped over the most important part."

After a startling knock at the door, Bowlen's assistant popped her head in. "Sorry to interrupt but your eleven o'clock with the director …"

"Ms. Charbel. I'll have to continue this some other time. We'll go out to Apex Watch tomorrow," Bowlen said.

She was miffed that he could so abruptly stop the story, but also overwhelmed with all she'd learned.

Chapter 8 KSM

"Ms. Charbel?" A tall, handsome man wearing sunglasses approached her as she exited the Metro. She recognized him. He was the bodyguard from inside the restaurant.

"Charlie, call me Charlie, everyone does."

"I'm Tony, his excellency's chief of security," he introduced himself, directing her to a waiting SUV. "Nobody calls him Lawrence."

They laughed.

"Welcome aboard," said Tony, shaking her hand.

Bowlen sat in the back seat of the standard-issue, tinted-glass Tahoe, with a driver who was introduced to her as Roy. Tony opened the back door for her, and she got in. He took the shotgun seat up front.

"Good morning," Bowlen said.

He obviously spent a lot of time in the car, fitted out as it was with a secure phone and a lap desk. On it, he had a thick "read" file, on top of that, a copy of the highly-classified president's daily brief, a document Charlie had never actually seen.

Driving north on Connecticut Avenue out of Bethesda on their way to Apex Watch, Bowlen started to tell her how he came to meet Khalid Sheikh Mohammed.[142]

"He was a student at North Carolina Agricultural and Technical University, a school famous, if I can even say that, for being the *alma mater* of the Reverend Jesse Jackson. To tell you the truth, in my Waspy Connecticut upbringing it wasn't a school I'd ever heard of."[143]

"The spotter there feeding prospects to the Agency sent forward a contact sheet about a foreign student, and though ops intake recommended no action, one of my people flagged the file because in those days we were looking for Saudis and Khalid had said something about going to work in the Saudi engineering world.[144] To us, in those days, that meant the Bin Laden Group, one of the conduits for the transfer of Saudi money. The North Carolina recruiter said Khalid was clever and engaged, passionate about the covert war in Afghanistan.[145]

"It was an easy get and we decided to invite this student to Washington and ran him through some basic tests, concluding that he was indeed interesting. I decided to meet with him. Khalid was maybe one of a half dozen we screened that year. Of that type."[146]

"What year was this?" Charlie asked.

"Late 1984," Bowlen said, wrinkling his brow to recall the date. "In those days, there was an entire crop of cash-paying Middle Easterners filling mediocre American schools. Unless they were kids of a certain pedigree, sons of high-ranking military officers or government officials, somebodies who might someday rise like their fathers to gain access to the levers and secrets of government, the Agency didn't really have much inclination or resources to pursue them. But this North Carolina professor thought KSM showed a certain greatness. Indeed, when I met him, he was quite the standout."

"KSM?" Charlie asked.

Bowlen chuckled. "From the beginning, we dubbed Khalid 'KSM,' easier to spell. Over the years, even Khalid grew to love the nickname, like it was a secret-agent codename. And so, it stuck.

"When we met, he was very open about his support for the *mujahidin* in their war against the Soviet Union. That was all the rage with President Reagan and Director Casey.[147] And that's why KSM assumed he was in Washington. His elder brother helped run one of the more prominent charities in Pakistan[148] and KSM said he was going to join him there. He assumed the CIA was trying to recruit him to be a source.[149]

"I spent a day with Khalid. We walked around the Mall, from Capitol Hill to the Lincoln Memorial. He marveled at the monuments and the buildings—in particular, how clean and orderly everything was. But this wasn't a kid with no direction. He was interested in odd things: where the surveillance cameras were, why police wore different uniforms and which ones were really in charge, why the buildings were so poorly guarded. All the while, he talked about his upbringing in Kuwait City, in a foreign-worker neighborhood of numbered streets and cinderblock houses. He explained that he was Baluchi[150] and that his father moved the family from Pakistan when the oil era began for economic opportunity. His father died when Khalid was just four, so brother Zahid—as the eldest son, 15 years Khalid's senior—became the family patriarch. Khalid adored him.

"This was no wealthy kid. His schooling in America was paid for by the *gama'a*[151] of the mosque and it was quite the honor to be sent to America. When I asked him about Islam, he said that the mosque-run community center was the place where all the young men hung out, and Islam was ever present and unquestioned as just a part of life. But he professed to have no affinity for his religion, almost dismissing my question because of course he was Muslim but didn't think about it much. He said that while others ate up tales from the elders of the Day of Judgment, he wasn't convinced. When he was 13 or so and he was warned that it was *haram*[152] to shave, Khalid said he wasn't cowed. He told Zahid that he wanted to find his own way.

"As Khalid tells the story, Zahid smiled and told him: *Someday, Khalid, all of what is meant for you will reveal itself.* Khalid has told that story more than once, this seminal moment for a boy who had no intention of ever becoming a mere foot soldier."

"'I am not a Kuwaiti,' he told me that day, 'and I carry a Pakistani passport, a nation for which I feel nothing.'[153]

"It was a striking point to me. Really. Profound. Here was a young man, a budding man of the world who was in truth almost nationless. He was a natural at blending in with the Kuwaiti world of uniforms and Westernization, but at the same time he was separate. He was a Pakistani national but saw himself as Baluchi, for which there wasn't even a country.

"At North Carolina, Khalid naturally hung out with the other Middle Eastern boys. They lived, cooked, ate and prayed together. Their separation from actual America was near total. But Khalid suffered an additional isolation: being of Baluchi descent, he was neither Arab nor even really Middle Eastern. Do you know Baluchistan, Ms. Charbel?"

"I know where it is, but it was definitely not part of my Pakistan portfolio," Charlie answered.

"It is an interesting place, part Pashtun, part Persian but almost a nationless corner of Pakistan living under its own codes. On some level, I'd say from his upbringing that Khalid was a Gulf Arab, but he'd also spent a good part of his childhood in Baluchi villages visiting the old country. He *was* a true international man. Sort of like you, if you know what I mean."

"From when I was a teenage girl, I spent almost every summer in Beirut," Charlie said, "and I loved everything about it. But I'd never say I was anything but a true-blue American."

"Yes, yes, I understand that, and I don't mean to compare you or insult you. But you are more than just a visitor in this culture. It is also in your blood, literally. That's what gives you a leg up over most of us old white guys," he said, softening any insult he might have inadvertently delivered.

He went on: "Anyway, I thought Khalid near perfect as an agent.[154] He enjoyed a certain anonymity. Even to fellow foreign students, he passed as either Arab or South Asian—fitting in with all groups, depending on his mood. He spoke Gulf Arabic, was fluent in Urdu, fairly good at Farsi and knew the even-more-obscure Baluchi."[155]

They were heading north out of Bethesda, Charlie thought, to what Bowlen's assistant divulged was their Maryland office. As suburb turned to country she tried to track their trip while also paying attention to what Bowlen was saying.

"An agent for what exactly?" she interrupted.

"I wasn't sure then, or on subsequent meetings before Khalid left the United States two years later. And it wasn't until he met bin Laden a year after that that I thought he might be an agent perhaps, penetrating that corner of Saudi Arabia—that is, if he could take direction."

"So, can he take direction?" asked Charlie.

"Sadly, no," Bowlen answered wistfully. "At least not from me."

Bowlen hesitated, thinking to himself. And then he continued: "What was clear though, from day one, was that he had a lot to say. And he had big plans. Agent or not, I thought it prudent that we stay in touch. Well, maybe not prudent. I thought it at least interesting."

"Did you know of his financing the attack on the World Trade Center?" Charlie asked, jumping ahead. After Bowlen mentioned the name at their initial launch, she'd looked up Khalid Sheikh Mohammed in CIA databases and found one elliptical reference to his sending money to Ramzi Yousef in New York.[156]

"Did Mr. Draper tell you that?" Bowlen asked.

"Mr. Draper hasn't told me anything," she testily answered. "Is it true?"

"Yes, it's true. But FBI investigators only pinned a measly $600 on him. The true story is much more complicated."

Charlie was aghast. "So, you had an agent on your payroll who has given money, even if it was a small amount, to underwrite an attack on the United States?"

"At the time, I didn't know about the money. And I definitely didn't know of his involvement in the New York attack. But yes, later Khalid did tell us about the ease with which Ramzi Yousef penetrated the country. And then how he went about his business of making and planting the car bomb that was used to attack the World Trade Center."

"And you don't have problems with that? People died, for God's sake."

"Of course, I have problems. It was, and is, a real conundrum, how to deal with him. In hindsight, I see that Khalid was probably the conceiver of that attack. And he was probably even a direct planner from afar. But I'm not running some humanitarian NGO, nor a law enforcement agency. I know you agree we can't shy away from bad people with access. I wasn't happy that I didn't know beforehand, but I knew even more after I found out about his connection that I had to pay attention."

She wasn't altogether satisfied with that answer. *Pay attention? Why not just have him arrested?*

"I'd add this," Bowlen said, interrupting her thought. "Khalid wasn't on any payroll of mine. He never took any payment."

"Isn't that sort of an evasion?"

"Maybe it is, Ms. Charbel. But we have the equivalent of a volunteer who suddenly is implicated in terrorism. You go ahead and do your own cost/benefit analysis. Go official and lose him? Arrest him? I made the decision to wait and see. In the end, it was a tough moral choice, one that couldn't probably have been made inside the Agency, but I think was the right thing to do. To wait. To see. To keep him on."

Charlie realized she was doing her own cost/benefit analysis.

Bowlen plunged back into his telling, not really willing to be sidetracked again. He said that KSM was a huge fan of *al-Jihad* magazine[157] and admired its publisher, the Palestinian activist, Abdullah Azzam.[158] "At mosques in North Carolina and Virginia, the anti-Soviet war was subject number one in those days. Khalid went to meetings and collected cassette tapes of lectures wherever he could. Later, when he heard him speak in Norfolk while raising funds for the *jihad*, Khalid felt the pull, as he tells it."

"God, those were the days," Charlie interjected, letting her own moral tug lay for the moment. "I can see what you mean about making choices. History, indeed, is a bitch. Barely a decade ago and the intellectual founder of *al Qaeda* was roaming around America?[159] Openly collecting money for a cause that today is threatening the country?"

"To say that we didn't have a clue about what was coming would be too kind," Bowlen responded.

"Did you, though? And if you did, didn't you feel an obligation to educate the rest?"

"We're talking today, Ms. Charbel. And I'm talking in hindsight. I was focused on Saudi Arabia. I knew bin Laden only in the context of the family construction business, and work that the Agency supported from afar, that is, his work against the Soviets in Afghanistan. My hope at the time was that the famous son would return to The Bin Laden Group. And that Khalid would go with him. But then I began to learn about *al Qaeda*. As it was developing, Ms. Charbel. From Khalid. Still, having said that, I was no great seer. The oddness of Azzam running around in America in those naïve days? It's clear only in hindsight. It doesn't temper my self-criticism when it comes to Khalid."

He went on: "In those days, when Khalid talked geopolitics, he wasn't anti-American. Deeply aware of his own hybrid upbringing, he was disappointed at the closed-mindedness and bigotry he found in North Carolina, particularly with America's innate dislike of Middle Easterners. But he possessed none of the outsized passions of the Palestinians and seemed oblivious to the violence in Lebanon. In some ways, he was both post-Arab and post-Zionist—predisposed to hate Israel and America, but only because there was no other focus of hate.

"And as for his value to Apex Watch? There was one group that

Khalid not only couldn't condone but also detested. They were the rich party boys from wealthy Saudi and Gulf families, with their Porsches and Mercedes, their alcohol and their American girlfriends. It wasn't political, and he would argue that it wasn't even about Islam: it was more that these boys were betraying their own people.

"I met with Khalid again right before he left the United States. I told him that honorable people like the editor of *al-Jihad* magazine were raising money and it was merely just going from Saudi princes' right-hand pockets to their left.

"I told Khalid that the money—the actual cash, and certainly that coming from the Arab countries and meant for the foreign fighters—was disappearing. It didn't take much for Khalid to acquire the view that Saudi Arabia was *the* problem. So, he went off to war predisposed to dislike that country. In the long game, he was not just useful but also shared our mission.

"'*I will not betray my brothers,*' Khalid told me defiantly as he was leaving America. We'd still said nothing to him about the CIA, but that was Khalid's assumption. And I think it was his hope, that he had been chosen.

"'Just live your life, Khalid,' I told him when I saw him off. 'We'll be in touch. Your time will come.'

"Of course, it sounded right: It was just what his brother Zahid told him.

"From North Carolina and then from Kuwait, Pakistan and Afghanistan, Khalid became a prodigious reporter. Though he said he was agnostic about Islam—that's my word, he said something more like he didn't think about it much—he was filled with mosque-born theories about the world. And he had a … very different … worldview. Crusader analogies mixed with American geopolitical theory of expansionism and a Soviet grab for a warm water port—that port being in his native Baluchistan, a place most Cold War theorists and most in Washington didn't even know existed.

"And then he met Osama bin Laden. I can only say that everything changed after that: he fell in love."

Fell in love.

Charlie thought it a funny construction. And it made her think of Steve—not of their love, but his love, his demented love of the subject he worked on. And, she thought, his strange idealizing of the same infamous *Sheikh*.

Bowlen went on describing the life that Khalid led thereafter—writer for *al-Jihad* magazine, translator and troubleshooter, fellow engineer working for bin Laden. When the Soviets withdrew from Afghanistan, fighting continued between Afghan communists and the many tribal factions. Most of the foreign fighters dispersed, some off to Bosnia or to the former Soviet republics defending Islam, only to return once the Taliban came to power.

"Khalid," Bowlen said, "kibitzed in the founding of *al Qaeda* but otherwise stayed independent. He probably conceived the World Trade Center attack. Then he went to the Philippines, bought an apartment in Karachi, moved to Qatar, then back to Pakistan."

Bowlen was rushing through the details with Charlie as they neared the Maryland compound.

"I've watched Khalid grow up," Bowlen finally said as they were reaching their destination. "One could say I'm even protective of him. I hate to say it, but I feel the affection of a case officer for a terrorist who wishes us harm." He shook his head at the absurdity. *Protective*, he added, almost under his breath.

Charlie tracked the route that their vehicle took since leaving the Beltway: I-95 North, exit in Laurel, Maryland, driving west, passing strip malls and then through suburban housing and then onto a country road, eventually looping around to what she spied as a street called Odell Road before pulling into an unmarked, gated driveway—posted as both no entry and dead end.

"Exceptional Research Technologies," said the sign. Roy squared his head and looked into a mirror-like camera as he swiped an ID card across an electronic lock, opening the gate.

Inside the compound, everything stood as silent as the surrounding woods. There were maybe 35 cars. Its single building was all concrete and glass, a giant satellite dish off to one side and what looked like an ancient and unused communications tower further afield. The surveillance cameras, the isolation, the distant chain-link fence and surrounding woods were not out of place. Not in the secret geography of suburban Washington.

"Welcome to Apex Watch," Bowlen deadpanned as they pulled into the director's parking space.

A bulbous glass atrium was appended to the front of the old building. It was a layer once conceived as a welcoming lobby but was now empty. There were no institutional posters on the walls, no artwork, no waiting room furniture, no reception desk, nothing.

"In order to minimize staff, we use electronic everything," Bowlen explained, chatting like a real estate agent. "There's an automated security system; a computerized tracking system that can recognize everyone and handle any external vendor or public call; and a set of synchronized fobs to gain entry to computers and files. We're years ahead in technology."

Bowlen buzzed himself in through an opaque glass door and they arrived in a second anteroom, this one bristling with electronic gadgetry but still no other human to be seen. He placed his palm in a hand-shaped bowl atop a waist high post to the right of the door and leaned forward, putting his eyes to another mirror-like camera that matched his retinas with a stored database. The vault clicked open and a loud electronic voice broadcast "Lawrence Bowlen." The announcement echoed down a long, empty corridor. As Charlie stepped through, the voice ominously said: "Unidentified visitor, escorted."

Everything looked oddly familiar to her: the fluorescent lighting, a drinking fountain mounted into the wall, cipher-locked office doors, linoleum floors, ugly paint.

"Secrets within secrets," Charlie said to no one in particular, Bowlen's back to her as he walked down the hall.

"Excuse me, Ms. Charbel?" he asked, not catching her comment.

"Oh, nothing," Charlie said, realizing that she needed to suppress her natural tendency to enter like a whirlwind.

PART 3

Chapter 9 The Base

Pakistan frontier, late 1986

KSM arrived in Peshawar, writing to Apex Watch that he was glad to be far from America and free of the straitjacket of Kuwait. But more than anything, he said, he was happy to be reunited with his brother Zahid and on his way to fulfilling his dream: being part of what he called the vast "free and independent" army massed to fight the Soviet invaders.[160]

If KSM thought Greensboro, North Carolina was a Piedmont nothingness, soulless and without history, Peshawar was fully drenched. Situated in a broad, green valley just an hour east of the famed Khyber Pass, the city had for millennia been a transit point on the caravan trade from the "civilized world" into Central Asia. From this pivot point, Peshawar had hosted battles and civilizations, and most of the conquering empires—Seleucid, Kushan, Ghaznavid—long since lost to obscurity.

For almost a century, until Pakistan gained independence,[161] Peshawar was a key outpost of the British Empire, a frontier town sitting at the center of a never-quite-tamed expanse of tribal lands. To the east were Afghanistan's imposing White Mountains, and within them a people never pacified by outsiders. This ungovernable territory, dominated by the Pashtuns, the largest ethnic group in Afghanistan and the second largest in Pakistan, had seen its own share of failed and faded invaders.

KSM wrote to Mr. Jones describing the full chaos of the city, its screeching sounds and its ever-present stench of mopeds and motorized rickshaws, the calls of its street merchants, the sight of armed tribesmen, many dressed in traditional Afghan *shalwar kameez* of tunic and vest, and others in colorful native robes. Most of the men were turbaned in the Pashtun style, with faces covered. But others wore *kufis* or the Peshawari cap, each announcing a different tribe and their own allegiance: Tajik, Uzbek, Shinwari.

In Peshawar, he said, the British East India Company built fortresses and hospitals, universities, and even oddly-jarring stone churches.[162] They were still there, as were grand homes, built for governors and officers. And the whole place was filled not just with British monuments but also with Zoroastrian relics, Buddhist monuments and monasteries, and a Hindu temple or two. All that was beyond remained as doggedly outside British control as it was today outside Pakistani reach. Yes, the city itself was administered from Islamabad, but the walled and cramped old city, where Khalid said he lived, was equally impenetrable. There, in a labyrinth of ancient stalls and shops, little changed over centuries, the three-story structures squashed close to each other across narrow alleyways.

Khalid sent postcard after postcard from the old city—all of them showing two-story houses adorned with beautiful latticed wooden balconies jutting over the foot paths below. Some of the streets were so shaded from sunlight that, even during daytime, strings of lightbulbs were used to illuminate them below, because the houses were so close together and because of the overhanging balconies.

Following its tradition, Peshawar became the Wild West capital of the Soviet resistance after the Red Army invaded on Christmas Day in 1979. The *mujahidin* flooded the city and the region, arriving in droves after the Soviets invaded, with refugees following in the tens and then hundreds of thousands.

The CIA came, too, as did representatives of the KGB and the Pakistani ISI—the nation's powerful intelligence agency. And then there were the Saudis and the Gulf States and Mubarak's secret services, all with their own interests and clients. Along for the ride were smugglers, arms merchants, bomb-makers, poppy and heroin traders, the wheelers and dealers of all things to all sides.

Khalid's brother Zahid came soon after the Red Army. By the time Khalid arrived with his American university degree, he'd risen to operate one of Peshawar's largest refugee services agencies, funded by Kuwaiti and other Gulf State donors. There were dozens of similar agencies, from the International Red Cross to narrowly-focused groups serving the odd populations of Albanians, Filipinos, Chechens and Chinese Uighurs, all of these varied Muslim fighters attracted to the latest frontier of warfare.

Zahid's main office was in a solid colonial house in the old city, near the Bajori Gate. Inside cramped and hectic quarters, the charity run by his brother helped fighters move in and out of Afghanistan, organized supplies for local and distant use, moved medicines to hospitals and clinics, and most importantly, supported those who had been wounded.[163]

Zahid put his 22-year-old kid brother to work as a multilingual jack of all trades, running errands and moving aid around the city and to the camps. KSM wrote Mr. Jones that he was most happy writing and translating reports and caring for the charity's computers. He wasn't much of a fighter.

On the back of a picture postcard showing the British-built Lady Reading Hospital that he sent weeks later, he wrote that the office also served as KSM's living quarters. Khalid shared a room upstairs with his brother Abed—"soon to be a fighter in Afghanistan."[164] He wrote that he truly felt at home for the first time, liberated from Western odors and noises, surrounded by the pleasing scent of *nag champa* and sandalwood.

At the end of the year, KSM reported to his Washington friends that he was burrowing into various underground networks, of which there were many. "I am an agent preparing to do battle," he grandly announced to *Mr. Jones*, and he said he was "soon to be a full partner in their special work."[165]

KSM's dispatches were both endearing and egotistical, filled with practical information and useful observations. He wasn't ideological, and yet he highlighted every negative of clandestine America, particularly complaining about what he saw as the inequity of the CIA's clandestine support for Afghan fighters, which he thought unfairly slighted the Arabs.

KSM wrote about once a week, itemizing the supplies and medicines his agency and others were bringing in to support the hundreds of war wounded—still mostly young Afghans, but now also a growing number of Egyptians and Saudis and the odd men of the Caucasus and Asia.

"The Saudi snakes have emptied their jails," he wrote in early spring.[166]

"These are not religious men here on a voyage of personal *jihad*. And they are not even followers. Many I think are even mentally ill or slow and they are being put in the most vulnerable places on the battlefield."[167]

KSM thought it cynical that governments were using the Soviet war to rid themselves of undesirables and criminals. But he was still holding out hope that he would see something different once he made it inside Afghanistan and saw the battlefield with his own eyes.[168]

Peshawar, he also wrote that spring, was home of "the big three." First he described Ayman al-Zawahiri, the famous Egyptian surgeon, born into an upper-class family of doctors and scholars. He was one of the hundreds of Egyptians arrested following the assassination of Anwar Sadat by his own soldiers. During the mass trial of the nearly 300 supposed co-conspirators, the bespectacled and English-speaking ideologue—Prisoner Number 113—became famous in the international press as the spokesperson for the accused, standing at the bars of a cage at the back of the courtroom, answering questions and constantly reading statements and manifestos. "*We are Muslims* who believe in their religion!" he shouted. "The only true believers."[169]

The Egyptian authorities were unable to prove any direct connection between Zawahiri and the killing, but he was sent to jail on a charge of illegal firearms possession. After he was released he made his way to Peshawar and wrote *The Bitter Harvest*.[170] He condemned the Egyptian Muslim Brotherhood for collaborating with the Cairo regime. And he renounced both "manmade" laws and the very notion of democracy.[171] Zawahiri met Osama bin Laden at about this time, and both initially worked under the tutelage of the Palestinian Abdullah Azzam.

"The doctor," KSM wrote, "is surrounded by a large group of experienced Egyptians," ex-soldiers and ex-policemen and even some ex-spies.[172] These men from Cairo tended to be older and more experienced than most others KSM encountered in the Arab ranks.

KSM also wrote that Zawahiri was a bit of a "dandy," distant in his dealings with people. "Dr. Zawahiri is kind, but he is not a leader," he wrote. In the language of the day, he dismissed him as "a hopeless Marxist," not because KSM identified as a capitalist, but because capitalist and communist were the only two words recognized in America representing a worldview. Of course Zawahiri labeled himself an Islamist, but even early on, KSM wrote that he was more political than religious, more stuck on revolution than matters of the soul.

And here KSM had a keen observation about Zawahiri and his Egyptian cadre: "I was barely five years old when Nasser and his pan-Arab program died," he wrote to Mr. Jones, remarking that their worldview was before Afghanistan and before Islam as a third way. Liberation from colonial rule and the western stranglehold, Khalid said, guided Nasser, and pushed him towards socialism, which really meant the Soviet Union. He thought Zawahiri stuck here. "If he had his way, Dr. Zawahiri would have us forever fighting against the Egyptian government and the Jewish state. But for what?"

The political orientation contrasted with KSM's description of the second of the big three, and another Egyptian: Omar Abdel-Rahman.[173] Blind at birth, by the age of eleven, the legend went, the Blind *Sheikh* memorized the *Qur'an*, going on to graduate with honors from Cairo's al-Azhar University, one of the oldest universities in the world.[174] A well-known firebrand as a young man in Egypt, writing and speaking out in favor of Islamic law, he was denied an appointment to an Egyptian state-run university. Instead, he got a position as *imam*, or prayer leader, in a small village along the Nile River.

But the Blind *Sheikh* would not be silenced. From there, al Rahman preached loudly, focusing on the Egyptian government's moral shortcomings, especially after the country's embarrassing defeat at the hands of the Israelis, an event marking the beginning of the end of Nasser's pan-Arab and socialist dream. Up until the war, President Nasser connected with the common man. But after the defeat, religious figures like al Rahman argued that Egypt's humiliation was caused by secular worship and the distance it put between itself and its religion, that there was nothing that any longer distinguished the once great country.

With regard to Sadat, the Blind Sheikh had signed a *fatwa*[175] condemning Nasser's successor, and, like Zawahiri, the sheikh was arrested, also spending three years in custody. When he was released, he left Egypt, traveling the world—including the United States—preaching and encouraging young Muslims to join the fight in Afghanistan. Though KSM was impressed with the Blind *Sheikh's* religious knowledge, he dismissed him as another ideologue, and he wrote that he was someone he thought was oddly intent on surrounding himself with simpleminded followers.

"I wonder if it is because he is blind," KSM wrote to Apex Watch in mid-1988, pointing out that he did not intend that as a joke.[176]

The last of the three, and the most important to KSM, was his beloved Dr. Abdullah Azzam. He was barrel-chested with a long, black beard streaked with white, the legend and father of the modern *jihad*, editor of the glossy *al-Jihad* magazine. KSM had been devouring the magazine ever since he was a student, and back in North Carolina he traveled up and down the east coast to hear Azzam speak.[177]

Born on the West Bank, his family fled across the Jordan River when Israel started its occupation. He studied Islamic law and philosophy, also getting his master's and doctorate at Azhar University.

After the cataclysmic loss to Israel, and with increasing crackdowns in Egypt, Azzam moved on to Saudi Arabia, finding sponsorship and a teaching post.[178] There at King Abdulaziz University, he met young Osama bin Laden, the pious son of the vast Bin Laden construction empire. Teacher and student became close friends.[179]

Together, Azzam and bin Laden experienced the seminal events of 1979, riveted by the student revolution that overthrew the Shah of Iran. Then came the unprecedented domestic attack on the Grand Mosque in Mecca where hundreds died. And that was followed by the Soviet invasion of Afghanistan.

Unlike many scholars and clerics who railed against foreign encroachment into the land of Islam but otherwise did very little, Azzam picked up and moved his family to Pakistan, first to Islamabad where he taught, and then, abandoning his comfortable life altogether, to Peshawar.[180] From this Pakistani outpost, he was first to articulate an anti-Soviet *jihad* as a duty for Muslims. Young bin Laden visited his mentor and soon after that bin Laden drifted towards a life in defense of Islam as defined by Azzam.

Azzam called for holy war, a call answered by many. But Azzam also made the case—one that inspired many more of the first generation of foreign fighters to go to Afghanistan—that it was *fard ayn* (فرض العين), a compulsory duty to fight, just as important as praying five times a day, just as important as fasting, just as important as tithing.[181]

In one long letter late in 1988, KSM tried to explain that the talk of suicide bombing in the western news media misread what Azzam was saying.[182] Yes, he said, Azzam spoke of the necessity and appeal of martyrdom in a political world divided by colonial borders, a world offering no path to either spiritual or human fulfillment unless one capitulated to the allure of the capitalist system. But he was more trying to inspire young men using grand language to connect to their human yearnings. Suicide, KSM wrote, was not a good tactic, and not the future.

KSM wrote another long letter about his experiences at *Sada* ("Echo"), a training camp near Peshawar set up to orient foreign fighters.[183] There he learned to shoot for the first time and underwent rigorous physical training. He wrote that the camp had two distinct groups. First there were the rich Saudi and Gulf Arab boys, there in Afghanistan on *jihadi* excursions, *jihadis* in name only, put through their paces but coddled and safeguarded to ensure their safe return home. Then there were the Egyptians and other Arab toughs, many of whom, KSM repeated, had been tossed from their home countries to fight and hopefully die in Afghanistan.

At the training camp, KSM decided he was destined for a different, even bigger role.[184] But he also observed there was minimal, if no, contact between the foreign fighters and the real *mujahidin*—the native Afghan groups. Khalid wrote to Apex Watch that he wondered what even would happen to Afghanistan once the war was over, doubting that any real Afghan or Pashtun would ever be interested in anything but their own lands behind the White Mountains. KSM could see what made the Afghans so loyal to their ungoverned country. But at the same he opined that Afghanistan itself—and its people—were not the key to any future.[185]

Despite reading *al-Jihad* magazine and soaking up the lectures in America, KSM also said he hadn't really thought much of Arabs as foreign fighters before arriving in Pakistan.[186] The *mujahidin*, Reagan's freedom fighters, were spoken of mostly as one. But now he was doubting that the Arabs had much of a role to play. Yes, they were being injured and dying, more so as the Soviets bombed from the skies and focused less on taking territory on the ground. But the numbers of Saudi casualties were tiny compared to the price paid by their Afghan brothers. KSM seemed unimpressed with the military skills they taught—marching and other western-oriented elements of conventional fighting, lamenting that it was mostly theater, that there had to also be a third way on the battlefield.

Lucky for him, though, as his training was winding down, Dr. Azzam came to speak. The young college graduate introduced himself to his idol, regaling him with admiration for him and his work, volunteering to join his publishing house. KSM would do anything, he said: translate articles, write and edit reports, learn layout, manage distribution. A month later, Azzam dispatched KSM to write profiles of fighters on the front lines.

For the first time, KSM entered Afghanistan, journeying to the front. He wrote a long letter describing the scene.[187] The country was devastated, bridges bombed and roads demolished, whole villages destroyed. Landmines were everywhere. The commanders KSM spoke to said that, until 1985, the Soviets waged a scorched-earth campaign in the countryside, seeking to eliminate local support for the *mujahidin*. The result was millions of refugees, and deadly payback on the part of the Afghans in exacting as many Soviet soldier casualties as they could.

That next year was the deadliest for the Soviet 40th Army, casualties escalating so high that there were protests back home. In Moscow, the would-be reformer Mikhail Gorbachev faced increasing heat. He wasn't responsible for the invasion, and he sought a way out. As part of his desired disengagement, he approved a strategy to reduce Soviet military casualties. Ground fighting and gaining or holding territory would be replaced by Soviet aircraft, as well as Soviet commandos—*Spetsnaz*—bombing and attacking important facilities and chokepoints. The Soviets would wage a remote-controlled war, going after resistance strongpoints as well as the infiltration routes for fighters and arms.[188]

The switch in Soviet tactics was largely successful, the aerial attacks on Afghan camps and movements devastating. Only then did the CIA begin to supply Stinger surface-to-air missiles to select Afghan groups, training them in Pakistan and sending these newly-armed students back into the country to hunt Soviet aircraft and attack helicopters. The impact was devastating to Soviet flyers.

By the time KSM wrote from the battlefield that winter, the Soviet occupation was essentially over. Gorbachev was looking for a consensus from Kremlin hardliners before he pulled the troops out altogether.[189]

Returning to Peshawar, KSM wrote articles in *al-Jihad* magazine geared to American and European audiences, mostly as fundraisers.[190] A month later he returned for a second visit, this time going to Jalalabad, the Afghan city closest to the Pakistani border. At a camp high in the mountains, the brother of Zahid and the disciple of Azzam finally met Osama bin Laden, a young engineer like himself, but a man very much unlike him in any way.[191]

The *Emir*, as KSM referred to the young Saudi, was really tall, something that obviously impressed five-foot, five-inch Sheikh Mohammed.[192]

"Like me," KSM wrote to expound on a connection, "bin Laden's father died when he was young."[193]

As KSM told the story, bin Laden's political awakening began with the seizure of the Grand Mosque in Mecca.[194] Like most Saudis, he was horrified that terrorists could attack the holiest of sites. Bin Laden spoke to KSM ten years later of how embarrassed he was of his ignorance of who the attackers were and what their grievances were. Then coming face to face with the duplicity of the Saudi royal family, bin Laden said he was aghast that French commandos were brought in to assist in defeating the hostage-takers, even using chemical weapons to do so.[195] He thought it was a foreign violation not just of the holiest sanctuary of Islam, but treason against the holy protector's obligation. The role of the French was never admitted, but their presence on Saudi soil shook young bin Laden. From then on, it would shape his view of the al Saud family and its treachery.

That same month, the Soviets invaded Afghanistan—another non-Muslim force chipping away at the edge of what was once the grand Islamic Caliphate. To bin Laden, it seemed the beginning of the end, the *isms* of the West making their final assault on his people and his religion.

Like KSM, bin Laden devoured Azzam's dispatches, and he especially identified with how the sage framed mountainous and isolated Afghanistan as holding onto an earlier, more pious age.

"The mountains are our natural place," bin Laden told KSM on their first meeting. He thought true liberation for Islam would only come from the mountains, either the mountains of Afghanistan and Pakistan—which he called *Khorasan*, the ancient Caliphate name—or in the mountains of Yemen, his ancestral home.[196]

"Safe and armed, it is there we can breathe the clear air unblemished by humiliation," KSM quoted bin Laden as saying.[197]

Bin Laden told KSM that when he first visited Afghanistan, he was so taken with the fight that when he returned to Saudi Arabia, he began raising funds for a broader *jihad*. He traveled throughout the Gulf sheikdoms for two years, speaking of the communist invasion and the duty to protect the religion. After that, bin Laden purchased a house outside Peshawar, dedicating his life full-time to *jihad*. He started building camps and fortifying caves in Afghanistan's Jalalabad area, moving himself and a growing entourage to the northeastern edge of the battlefield.

KSM was obviously smitten. Amidst the grime and dust of a war and a country destroyed, he wrote that the leader of the foreign fighters was a true standout, a most beautiful man, serene and magnetic, a natural and even supernatural *emir*. The young Saudi was already a legend in the mountains, where his growing network of caves offered much-needed protection from Soviet bombing. Bin Laden told the young KSM that he foresaw the caves not just for protection but for purity and reflection.

Even KSM, who wasn't devout, knew that story of *Hira'*, a cave on the mountain Jabal an-Nour four kilometers from the *Kaaba* in Mecca. There the Prophet retreated and had visions. The angel Gabriel appeared before him, delivering the first words of divine revelation, the first lines of chapter 96 of the *Qur'an*.

Bin Laden engaged young KSM to share his own dreams, asking about his experience in the United States and of his engineering training and interests. The Saudi prince was so lovely—so out of place in the middle of an ugly war—that when bin Laden told *engineer Sheikh Mohammed* that he needed to join with him and apply his special skills to help the cause, KSM couldn't say no.[198]

He began working at *Beit-al-Ansar*, the house of the faithful, an entryway run by the increasingly powerful Services Bureau,[199] a partnership between bin Laden and Abdullah Azzam. The Bureau was advertising worldwide for young Muslims to fight in Afghanistan, and bin Laden paid for transportation and much of the training.

KSM said nearly half of those coming were from Saudi Arabia, but others came from Algeria, Egypt, Yemen, Pakistan, and Sudan.[200] At the house of the faithful, passports and papers were collected for safekeeping and each new fighter was given a *kunya*, or battle name. Within a year of its founding, the Bureau had thousands of volunteers training in Afghan camps.[201] By the time KSM arrived, he helped develop a computerized tracking system to record the vitals for each fighter, including family contacts and next of kin should something happen to them. In Arabic, they called it *al Qaeda*—"The Base"—a term that at first merely described this organizational scheme,[202] but later came to connote bin Laden's larger enterprise.

"I don't know what the Saudi billions have gone towards," KSM wrote to Apex Watch after he arrived at *Beit-al-Ansar*.[203] "Everything is needed, and any actual battles are fought with Kalashnikovs and simple weapons. Bin Laden might write of youth 'who plunge into the smoke of war, smiling,' but only the Egyptians and North African psychopaths are happy on the battlefield.[204] The Soviet planes and attack helicopters are virtually unstoppable, the war itself is now just the grind of broken bodies."

Appended to KSM's letters continued to be various lists and accountings. He sent his American friends' information about the charities—the who, what, how, and where all the cash was going, as far as he could make out.[205]

And then just a month after KSM met bin Laden, Soviet leader Gorbachev announced he was withdrawing the Red Army.[206] The bloodletting of hapless Soviet conscripts gave him the excuse. But the Soviet General Staff also finally accepted that the war was unwinnable. And Gorbachev knew the Soviet presence was an impediment to better relations with President Reagan. An end to the fighting could offer relief for the Soviet economy as well.

On February 1, 1989, the commander of Group of Soviet Forces ceremonially walked across the Friendship Bridge over the *Amu Dar'ya* River from Afghanistan into Uzbekistan, leaving the country. It was the conclusion of a ten-year war that ultimately took the Union of Soviet Socialist Republics as its most prominent casualty.

HISTORY IN ONE ACT

Chapter 10 Blind *Sheikh*

Walking down the poster-plastered corridor of the graduate school of arts at Cairo University, Charlie saw the announcements that Abdel al Rahman would be speaking in a week's time at a public forum in the city.[207] Everywhere she turned, she now saw his picture—bushy white beard, grey jacket, a Santa Claus looking hat and, of course, the Stevie Wonder dark glasses. The CIA labeled the Blind *Sheikh* the spiritual leader of the leading terrorist groups in Egypt. And up to that day, Charlie thought he was also a fugitive, wanted in his home country and *persona non grata* wherever he turned. And yet there he was, being announced and showcased.

"How is this possible?" she asked her boss that evening. They met in the library at the Information Resource Center at the American Embassy, where Charlie, undercover as a graduate student, could naturally go to read the American papers and study. The station chief (who Charlie found reminiscent of Lou Grant on television, even in his causticity) was a legend in the Agency's Near East Division, an old-timer and head of the most important Arab hub, but a man Charlie found always respectful of her rookie passions.

"The Egyptians must have their reasons," he told her. "Perhaps to surveil who comes to see him, or to see who he meets with."

Charlie's incredulity about the size of the Cairo underground had fueled a two-year long conversation since she'd arrived for her first assignment.

These Egyptian radical groups, though officially outlawed, were constantly announcing themselves in provocative ways. When there were attacks, they took credit. And at least in the university, they actively proselytized, even, as far as she thought, winning the battle for hearts and minds.

The chief didn't see it that way, thinking that the radicals were nothing more than nuisances. But he didn't get in Charlie's way of trying to find out more. Graduate student by day, non-official cover CIA case officer by night, her assignment since arriving was to assess "low-level" opinion from the university lounges and cafes.

Initially, before she fell in love with the terrorism portfolio, Charlie had resented such a modest task, thinking it was intended to keep her from becoming important, from the men's work of the CIA.

Then she grew to love it. Despite her American identity and despite being female in a society (and a pursuit) admittedly dominated by men, she found that everyone she was naturally in contact with in Cairo— fellow students, intellectuals, domestic and international do-gooders and activists—everyone who would even talk to her, were *low-level* but also far more important than they appeared—a vast, unrecognized mass that was hers and hers alone. Through them she discovered a swarm of opinions and allegiances—true allegiances, not just national or governmentally-imposed pledges of allegiance. Her new friends identified with pride as Egyptians, part of an elite, but not in the way the official sources were. Though most knew how to play the game of assimilation and diffidence to avoid the authorities, none had much loyalty to Hosni Mubarak—and certainly not for his government. What they had was fidelity to family, and after that, maybe to a clan yearning for a better life.

Maybe, she thought, the lack of support for the government was just who she was talking to. It wasn't a statistical sampling. But then the station chief wasn't surprised to hear of their indifference and even hostility to Mubarak and his rule. Not surprised, but also not much interested.

Rookie Charlie went beyond the cafes and student lounges, telling the boss that she—Marina Charbel—wasn't going to be another tennis-playing spy like those who were stationed in Tehran at the time of the Iranian revolution.[208] Then, the CIA types and their know-nothing diplomat brethren missed all the fervent goings on, Charlie said, because they were in a bubble, hanging out only with official people and the upper classes. The boss didn't mind being told something he already knew, and he gently tried to teach Charlie what he called "the realities" of American espionage.

"It's *all* about Islam," she declared with graduate-student certainty. She'd just arrived for the semester, a young Lebanese American with no overt connection to the embassy or the American government. The chief invited his new, deep-undercover case officer for dinner at his residence and sent instructions on how she was to come. After taking two bus rides to detect possible surveillance, a chauffeured car picked her up on a busy street corner downtown. There Charlie met the chief's Moroccan wife, who was both gracious and suspicious.

Charlie announced that she wanted to sharpen her knowledge of the radical underground, infiltrating what she thought was the toughest and most important target.

"*All* of what Washington wants us to know about our target Egypt is what is of interest to American policy," the chief tried to explain. "That means the Russians and the Chinese first. And Washington wants to know what might threaten us or our allies here and in the region. And in this region, in this country in particular, that means Israel and Israel alone. Right now, Washington is most interested in the *intifada* because it has the potential to influence all those things. And it also has the Mubarak government spooked."[209]

The *intifada* was all the talk amongst the students as well. In Israel's occupied West Bank and Gaza Strip, Palestinian demonstrators were throwing stones and Molotov cocktails at Israeli troops. The Israeli Defense Force responded first with rubber bullets, then with live ammunition. Protests and police actions escalated, becoming out of control.

"Mubarak is ever so happy to have activists exhaust themselves on behalf of the Palestinians," the boss tried to explain to her. The new Palestinian organization *Hamas*[210]—which emerged with the *intifada*—appeared to be far more radical than anything Yasser Arafat ever produced. And it seems potentially to be a threat to Cairo as well. That's because riding in *Hamas'* wake were the Islamic Group and the Egyptian Islamic Jihad, for which the Blind *Sheikh* was often described as spiritual leader.

"Doesn't that sort of prove my point?" she badgered.

"They are organizations, Ms. Charbel, not Islam."

To Charlie, he didn't get it.

"What about the Muslim Brotherhood?" she pressed.

The Brotherhood had been established in the 1930s with a *Wahhabi-*like goal of reviving Islam as a counter to Egyptian Westernization and growing secularism. Banned and battered over the years, it was now the official opposition and the *moderate* alternative.

"The Brotherhood is vaguely interesting," the boss answered. "We keep an eye on them because they could by some miracle win an election if there were ever such a thing here. But after a decade of crackdown, that movement is pretty much on life support. Besides, when it comes to the Brotherhood, we leave clandestine penetrations that don't tie to any of our priority requirements to the Egyptians themselves."

"Why?"

"Why, Ms. Charbel? First, we have only so many assets. But second, the Brotherhood is lower than other priorities. And I would say that the Egyptian secret services do an able job of keeping them in check."

Since then, their discussions had gone around and round on the same subject, to Charlie's mind with little result. With the chief's tolerant acquiescence, she pursued her own alternative curriculum. The chief was tolerant, as long as she was aggressive and practiced good tradecraft in protecting herself and her identity.

Charlie slogged through the literature of modern day and militant Islam, listening to cassette tapes, attending lectures, and donning a traditional *chador* to attend public meetings. All the chic radicals were reading the Egyptian writer Sayyid Qutb, who advocated an Islamic alternative to secular nationalism and godless socialist ideologies. This meek academic, activist, poet, and intellectual wrote that modern Egyptian society existed in a state of *jahiliyyah*. That literally meant ignorance, but the label was commonly used by radicals to describe the pre-Islamic world of paganism. In his seminal work, *Milestones*, Qutb used the term not to describe pre-*Wahhabi* culture or the world before the Prophet. Instead, he referred to the current condition of the Muslim world, corrupted by Western culture and desires.

Qutb's execution at the hands of Nasser magnified his importance and his writings,[211] and his word became a touchstone for almost every politicized student Charlie met. She wrote reports about her discovery, struggling through the Arabic and the obscure Islamic doctrines in his writings.

The more she learned, the more she yearned to learn more about Islam itself. Many of Charlie's friends and contacts identified themselves as "just Muslims," bristling at the inflammatory Qutb language, uncomfortable with the labels *Sunni* and *Shi'a* applied by radicals and the geopolitical amateurs. Her Egyptian friends were also contemptuous of the *Wahhabi* orthodoxy as imposed by the Saudi state, obligating them not just to subordination to a distant monarchy they abhorred but to an unchanging past. Egyptian Islam, inspired by urban ways and ancient times, was quirky and different than most other Arab countries, with a healthy lingering dose of pre-Islamic practice, including a belief in charms and amulets, as well as the influence of evil spirits.[212]

She wrote more reports about the intellectual currents within Islam. There was a prevalent notion, she thought, of a different model out there—neither assimilation into one homogenized Western world, nor backward-looking Saudi and radical traditions that many referred to as *Salafism*.

Her output was impressive. But she got little response from Washington. Charlie's non-conforming education, she learned, was going to have to unfold alone. *Low-level.*

Struggling to understand its appeal, she plowed through the "Charter of Islamic Action," written mostly by the Blind *Sheikh*. His Islamic Group, it said, would "establish Islam as a totality in each soul, and over each handbreadth of land, in each house, in each organization, and in each society."[213] The charter rejected foreign investment in Egypt and the Blind *Sheikh* declared a war on tourism. Destinations like the Pyramids, he argued, were pagan shrines, and that income derived from tourism supported the infidel state.

And now the Blind *Sheikh* was coming to Cairo to speak. A pretty conspicuous guy, he could hardly just slip into the country undetected by the authorities.

When she asked fellow students about his appearance, she found that he was mostly venerated as a folk hero who would rid the region of the outsider. After Egypt's loss in not one but two wars against Israel, her friends explained, the Egyptian and the broader Arab psyche had been traumatized. The Blind *Sheikh* and others argued that the reason for the defeat was Islam had lost its bearings.

On the day of his speech, Charlie dressed modestly and covered like the other young women. She didn't have much difficulty finding the hall where he was to appear. Everyone she saw on the street nearby was moving towards the place, the sidewalks packed, young men keeping an eye on the crowd, not a uniformed policeman in sight. Women were handed a pamphlet at the door and funneled upstairs to a cramped balcony. There was barely room to sit or kneel and so they stood for hours. When he finally arrived, the suffocating hall was abuzz with excitement.

He began by talking of *Ibn Taymiyya*, a 14th century scholar whom Charlie knew was the subject of Rahman's doctoral dissertation. In his many *fatwas* from those ancient days, *Taymiyya* wrote of the invading Mongols and argued that all Muslims had a duty to take up arms against those who failed to rule by Islamic law.[214]

Charlie considered her Arabic pretty good, but a combination of the sound system and the subject matter strained her listening skills. The crowd seemed to follow and understand. When he spoke of the 500-year-old justifications for rebelling against corrupt rulers, everyone knew he meant Hosni Mubarak. There were murmurings in the crowd, agreement-like encouragement Charlie thought not unlike a Southern Christian revival meeting. But he cleverly never mentioned the name.

"Islam and the state are linked," stated the Blind *Sheikh*. "Without our faith, the state will become more tyrannical. And without a state based on Islam, our religion will have no protector."

The Blind *Sheikh* went on to lambast Gamal Abdel Nasser, long dead.[215] He labeled the man who overthrew the monarchy, who nationalized the Suez Canal, and who introduced land reforms, the man most leftists revered, as a "reactionary." Charlie had learned in her study that the Egyptian leader was a socialist reformer, arguing for Pan-Arab power. But he was also intensely and actively against the Muslim Brotherhood or any Islamic activity that could challenge him. When Nasser was succeeded by Anwar Sadat,[216] the most Western-oriented Egyptian leader of all, he continued. Naser's course of warring on the Islamic movement. That was the Blind *Sheikh*'s view, and he saved his most pointed condemnation for Sadat. Charlie noted the exact opposite of his telling in her history:

For the Western palate, the pleasing Anwar Sadat became a hero of sorts, concluding a peace treaty with Israel. The Blind *Sheikh* labeled him not just a traitor, but he condemned the peace treaty as a "national cataclysm" and a blow to the entire Arab world.

The Blind *Sheikh* followed with much quoting of the *Qur'an* and the *Sunnah*, condemnation of manmade laws and Arab regimes that would pull on the cloak of secular rule, or worse, adopt Western capitalism. Still not a word was mentioned directly about Mubarak. As vice president, he ascended to power after Sadat was assassinated,[217] quickly arresting hundreds and imposing martial law, effectively driving the radicals either underground or out of the country.

Like many Arab states, Egypt found the Soviet war in Afghanistan a convenient place to dump young men of independent political bent, encouraging extremists to join the ranks there, to fight and maybe die in a far-off battlefield. If they returned, the theory was, they would be chastened and tired, ready to responsibly rejoin society. And indeed after Gorbachev abruptly ended the Soviet war, these young men did trickle back. But contrary to the original theory of exhaustion and chastisement, they came back trained in fighting and intelligence gathering, world-hardened and weary, big names and small fries who were not only internationally-minded but politically savvy. What was next for them remained to be seen, the Blind *Sheikh* openly calling on the veteran *mujahidin*, lifting them up as the vanguard of the future.

And what was next for the Blind *Sheikh*? In the hall, he announced it was no longer safe for him in Egypt, nor in Pakistan, Afghanistan, and not even in Saudi Arabia. Instead, the Blind *Sheikh* announced, he intended to settle in *Amreeka*, the next frontier for an Islamic awakening.

Wait? What? Did Charlie hear right?

The next morning, she practically sprinted to the embassy to file a report. The station chief was so impressed with her news that he put his personal slug on the telex, which was sent at *flash* precedence to Washington. She waited days for a response, the boss telling her that he was sure the Blind *Sheikh's* visa would be revoked.[218]

Finally, word came back: Charlie was to report for reassignment to Saudi Arabia. She would be part of the "surge" of Arabic speaking case officers needed to respond to the Iraqi invasion of Kuwait.[219]

Chapter 11 Desert Storm

With the Iraqi invasion of Kuwait, Charlie was whisked from her Egypt assignment and sent to the CIA's Frankfurt processing center, one of over 800 case officers and analysts thrown into a national emergency.[220]

Given that the number of competent Arabic speakers in the Agency was small and the number who were deployable with experience in the field was even smaller, Charlie had the distinction of being one of the first to go, earning not just a difficult post inside Saudi Arabia but also on the "front lines" near the Kuwaiti border.

She said goodbye to her Cairo friends, saying to those who didn't know of her CIA connection that her parents were insisting she return home, that they thought Saddam was going to unleash World War III.

Her Egyptian boss was sorry to see her go and chuckled at the massive transfers going on all around. "I guess if you're going to miss the invasion you sure as hell better not miss the war," he caustically told her, referring to the CIA's failure to gauge Saddam's intentions, and then its "warning" that the Iraqi army was poised to move south that came just moments before they did so.[221]

And he had a warning for her, too. "You think we have no domestic sources in Egypt. It's worse there." And he warned her as well about Saudi society's attitude about women. "It's no Lebanon or Egypt." Charlie had grown to love her boss but was annoyed that he thought she needed to be reminded of something that was not only obvious, but a world she'd already demonstrated she could navigate.

In Frankfurt, the Agency transformed her from her non-official cover to that of one Theresa Landry, a new identity with credentials as a mid-ranking civilian counterintelligence special agent working for the Department of Defense.

She made it to *Dammam* ten days after Iraq's Republican Guards crossed into Kuwait. It was the tail end of what the locals called the "days of the devil" for the 120-degree temperatures and there was no way not to hate the place.

But for being just 180 miles from the border, the Saudi city was surprisingly placid, a completely artificial construction with straight roads and planned everything. All roads here pointed to the Saudi Arabian oil industry, the monetary *Mecca*.[222] The Agency put her up in a downtown hotel, a flimsy three-star shell mostly filled with middle-class refugees who had fled Kuwait.

Setting up shop with a small but expanding American military contingent, Charlie thought that neither of her job assignments really made much sense. First, she was to gather intelligence on potential Iraqi terrorism directed against the American buildup. Saddam Hussein was threatening to set fire to the Gulf and the CIA was predicting a spate of terrorist strikes.[223] Second, Charlie was supposed to keep an eye on the vetting of thousands of foreign workers being enlisted as laborers on behalf of the growing American war machine. Dammam was increasingly crucial in this regard. The industrial port was the initial staging area for arriving U.S. forces and the city was earmarked to become the main storehouse for the mountains of American military gear slated to arrive.[224]

On her own, she wasn't quite sure how to collect anything independently. The CIA station in Riyadh had few sources in the eastern province and the military intelligence officers who were deploying with her had no human sources nor much capability—including no Arabic.

At first, Charlie was merely be a go-between with the Saudi police, who were doing the actual work of counterterrorism and vetting. Charlie's main interlocutor was a Saudi lieutenant—an official of the Ministry of Interior and head of domestic intelligence for the city. He was uniformed and skinny, with a goatee and a handgun at his side, unusual for a country where handguns were almost invisible. The lieutenant had little to no interest in working with the Americans, them or particularly her. And though the American military men she worked with treated her with respect, they soon forgot she was a CIA case officer and demoted her to translator or even to secretary. When word from Riyadh came down that she should move to one of the growing military camps, she refused, at least trying to establish an independent foothold.

Most curiously, Charlie soon found that her Saudi lieutenant was not only skeptical of external terrorism, he was downright hostile to the idea of any Iraqi threat.

"My dear Miss Landry," he said with his clipped British accent, barely containing his contempt for her presence, her mission and her sex. "We are perfectly capable of handling things ourselves."

"I understand, lieutenant" she explained in Arabic, "and I am not here to interfere with anything you do. But sitting across the border, less than 200 miles from here, are the forward elements of the fourth largest army in the world,[225] one armed with chemical, biological, and possibly even nuclear weapons. That army has flagrantly invaded your neighbor and is now poised to move south into Saudi oilfields."[226]

"Saddam is not going to invade Saudi Arabia," responded the lieutenant, incredulous she could think otherwise.

And Charlie did think she knew otherwise. Just four days after the invasion, Secretary of Defense Dick Cheney and a gigantic American military entourage arrived at King Fahd's summer palace to seek approval for the American deployment.[227] Central to the request, and to the Saudi monarch's approval was secret intelligence, including satellite photographs that 'proved' that Saddam's Republican Guards were positioning themselves and mustering to attack further south. Charlie had read the reports.[228]

She answered the lieutenant: "Whether he is or isn't going to invade, don't you think it prudent to ensure that he doesn't?"

"Oh, Miss Landry. Once the moneys are all paid, it will all be over," he answered, screwing up his face in a show of worldly sophistication. It was a tiredness about the crisis that she would grow used to. The lieutenant instead told her that he saw Western machinations and even trickery that *allowed* Saddam to enter Kuwait. That was behind the surprising decision of King Fahd to agree to foreign troops on Saudi soil.[229] Some kind of conspiracy was afoot, he said.

The Saudi lieutenant told his Miss Landry—there was no Ms. used here—who the true threat was. It was the huge contingent of untrustworthy foreigners who were already resident in his city—and his own *Shi'a* residents.[230] The former group was especially sympathetic to Saddam; the latter wholly aligned with Iran. Charlie was flabbergasted at his ignorance and his attitude.

At the time that Iraq invaded, almost a third of Saudi Arabia's residents—as many as eight million in those days—were Ethiopians, Bangladeshis, Indians, Filipinos, Nepalese, Pakistanis, and Yemenis.[231] Hired as oil and construction workers, drivers, and for unclean jobs beneath even the Saudi poor, this group of foreign workers officially didn't exist. Southeast Asian women by the hundreds of thousands were brought in as maids and nannies, and rumors were rampant of forced confinement, food deprivation, and physical and sexual abuse.[232]

Hundreds of thousands of additional Europeans, Lebanese and Egyptians worked in the private sector as merchants and bankers and middle managers. Three out of every four oil industry jobs were staffed by non-Saudis, including most engineering postings.

Though Charlie's Saudi lieutenant spent his whole career receiving training and mentoring from these foreign contractors who ran much of the country, he could barely contain his contempt and racism for them.

Charlie remembered asking the lieutenant whom amongst the foreign workers were the most dangerous threat. She thought that, of course, he would answer the Iraqis. Or perhaps the Sudanese or Jordanians? They were from the countries supporting Saddam, opposing the American intervention.[233]

"Criminal gangs of Ethiopian-Israelis," the lieutenant sneered in response. The enemy were Jews, even distant Jews amongst the foreign workers. There were Israeli connections to the Ethiopian guest workers, he said. Even before the invasion, they had given the policeman heartburn.

The lieutenant's view of everyone who wasn't Saudi—or of the *Sunni* and *Wahhabi* clan—was categorical. *Revolutionaries, communists, Iranians, drunken oil managers, pitiful foreign salary men.* They were outsiders and if not threats, they were cancers, all almost equal, that is, if you counted the Jews first.

In eastern Saudi Arabia though, the *Shi'a* were a close second. The lieutenant might consider all foreigners contemptible, but it was the Saudi *Shi'a* concentrated in this oil-rich province who were his most immediate and biggest concern. Sympathetic to Iran and practicing their own brand of Islam, his charge was to keep an eye on them, to keep them second class. In one of her first reports filed from Dammam, Charlie wrote:

> Saudi *Shi'a* here still speak of the capture of their al-Hasa homeland 200 years ago and wrecking of their shrines by *Wahhabi* raiders. Even today, officials assert (and do not question) that Saudi *Shi'a* are to be rendered a different status than other Saudi citizens. I was surprised to learn, but more surprised that no one outside of the eastern province knew, that at the same time as the Sunni taking of the grand mosque in 1979, the *Shi'a* in the East also rose up, insisting on celebrating `Ashura, the *Shi'a* holiday of mourning banned by the Saudi government. The police violently put down this second "revolt" in a bloody battle, killing hundreds. After they did so, they pointed fingers at Iran as the instigator.[234]

The lieutenant, crisp and officious, stiffly pointed his finger at Iran as the main worry. He filled Charlie's ears with talk of the Iranian Revolutionary Guard Corps' *Quds* Force and the Iranian Intelligence and Security Ministry, both of whom he said were issuing direct orders to Saudi dissidents.

Charlie sent another report forward to Washington: The police and Interior Ministry were placing their own Saudi *Shi'a* population under increased surveillance around Dammam. There was a police plan, she wrote, to detain as many as 50,000 Saudi citizens as security risks merely because they were *Shi'a*. To Charlie, it was an astonishing number, but the only response from Langley was to find out if there were any people in detention who might have knowledge of Saddam's weapons of mass destruction program.[235]

She sent another report: Yemenis, Jordanians and Palestinians considered sympathetic to Saddam's cause were being rounded up and deported, depleting the potential workforce available to the American mobilization.[236]

In another report, Charlie wrote that internal ferment in the Saudi eastern province was a threat to U.S. forces as significant as terrorism, if not in the short term then certainly over time.

But there was no *over time*. Washington and the growing military contingent were completely absorbed by the immediate, panicked by the invasion, considering themselves a mere "speed bump" in front of Saddam's mighty armor columns.[237] Charlie's American military contacts in Dammam were also of one mind regarding the unfolding crisis: American forces would be in and out, which was indeed the agreement worked out between President Bush and King Fahd. It would be at the earliest six weeks; at most, maybe six months.[238] Saddam would back down or pull back and normality would be restored.

Whether that would be the outcome, in Dammam, she knew that there was something else to be known, both about Saudi Arabia and a young Saudi and hero of the Afghan *jihad* named Osama bin Laden. Charlie, as Theresa Landry, decided to take matters into her own hands to find out more. She affected her best home-country accent, changed her dry-cleaned khakis into modest Lebanese dress and sought out her countrymen to find answers.

She didn't have far to look: every other restaurant in Dammam was Lebanese. She chose the *Fayrouz* on Prince Mohammed Street in the old part of the city. Because of the conflicts back home, three times as many Lebanese lived outside the country than in it, almost half of those in Brazil and Argentina and other Latin American nations, immigrants who long ago given up their citizenship and settled in the new world just like Charlie's family had in America.[239] The Lebanese community in Saudi Arabia was more of the guest worker variety. Saudi recruiters actively sought them out for their technological and managerial skills and shipped them to places like Dammam to take up positions that conveniently formed a buffer between Saudis of rank and even lower-class foreigners. Lebanese were the favored Arab guest workers.

She ate alone at the *Fayrouz*, an act that she knew was enough to cause a stir. But she also made clear to the waiters that she was Lebanese and American.

After a couple of nights, the regulars decided that the eldest amongst the group, a Mr. Massoud, would make the approach. He sat down opposite her and asked where her family was from. They talked of the old country, of which this young Theresa knew much. The conversation shifted to what she was doing in God-forsaken Dammam.

"I have to be here to feed my family back home," said Massoud, "but you? And now?"

"CIA," she whispered quietly, smiling.

They both laughed heartily but whether Massoud believed her or not what she was doing there was never again mentioned. Immediately the men, dining, smoking the hookah, playing dominos and backgammon, took her in as a new family member. When she missed a dinner, they inquired as to her health and well-being. When it was late at night, they escorted her back to her hotel.

Massoud worked as a manager for Bakhashab Transport, as did many of the others. Their fleet of trucks and forklifts were being reserved indefinitely in service to the United States of America.

They weren't politically minded, thrust into the middle of a frenzy from their hum-drum lives. None of them felt the "threat" of Saddam invading and all had little sympathy for the Kuwaiti royals. On Iraq, they seemed to have a more nuanced understanding of the country and its limitations. Charlie reported forward that the "street" seemed proud, regardless of their opinion of Saddam, that an Arab country could even develop nuclear weapons.

"A good thing, too," said Massoud one day of Iraq's possession of those super weapons. "Saddam has filled his ranks with the young and uneducated, and the generals are all Ba'ath party functionaries with no military experience. Their military doesn't stand a chance against the Americans."

By then, Dammam was a beehive of activity as ships arrived with heavy equipment and ammunition. Massoud and the others had no trouble analyzing their own intelligence that millions of tons were being shipped north and then further west into the desert. And though the goods flowed into the port, hardly an American soldier was seen, both intentional protection against potential terrorism but also part of the tacit agreement between the countries that soldiers would be kept out of sight and military deployments would be kept as quiet as possible, even as almost 700,000 American soldiers packed into the northeastern desert along the Kuwait and Iraqi borders.[240]

With the passing of the oppressive heat of summer, the mood somewhat improved back in Dammam. Her Lebanese friends continued to watch the parades of equipment, convinced that there would be no invasion and probably not even a war but wondering what the artillery shells and aircraft bombs were for.

Now that the immediate crisis lifted, Charlie's police lieutenant was also starting to feel the first pangs of something wrong, of perhaps even some national humiliation. One day he told her that he wondered whether American soldiers were really there to protect his country. And he wondered what all the billions that had been spent by the Saudi government on "defense" had purchased. He found some reassurance when the senior clerics—the government-approved religious establishment—said it was okay for the Americans to be there. They were only there to defend the nation, the lieutenant insisted, rationalizing the foreign presence. And they would not be staying a minute longer than was needed.

The mood changed in Dammam in November when Syria joined the coalition. Washington portrayed this as a triumph of diplomacy, an affirmation of some new international system, Damascus pried away from a crumbling Soviet Union.[241] But when it was announced that the Damascus Ba'athists would send 10,000 troops and 300 tanks to Saudi Arabia to fight against their Iraqi brothers, Charlie's geopolitical connoisseurs at the restaurant were surprised and chastened. It sunk in that *the world* would go to war against Iraq no matter what, destroying a country that they saw as modern and increasingly proficient in the world of technology. Her Lebanese friends didn't have any regard for Saddam or his rule, but they spoke about what the Saudi payouts must be to the various regimes to buy their participation. And they wondered why Iraq had to be treated so harshly, indeed what was behind the American insistence to send Iraq back to the Stone Age.

Even her lieutenant grew exasperated. Egyptian troops were bad enough as part of the grand coalition, but he didn't trust anything from Syria. He was beginning to wonder what the actual game was.

As the end of the year approached, the threat past of a blitzkrieg into the Saudi oilfields, Washington started an almost obsessive focus on weapons of mass destruction.[242] Saddam used chemical weapons in the

Iran-Iraq war, even against his own Kurdish people. The Pentagon and the CIA became singularly concerned with Iraq's chemical and biological weapons, and Charlie received intelligence requirement after intelligence requirement from Washington. Kuwait refugees and an increasing flow of Iraqi walk-ins and defectors were to be pumped for information, anything that could be learned about Saddam's WMD.[243]

When some high-ranking refugee or other "special category" person showed up, Charlie often drew the short straw to conduct the interrogation. She asked the questions and wrote the reports about WMD, wary not to stray too far from official requirements to ask about people's attitudes. But in that chore, she also couldn't wait to get back to the streets and to her Lebanese nobodies.

The Lebanese were whispering that Afghan war hero and Saudi small-p prince Osama bin Laden was speaking out about against the new Crusader Army in Saudi Arabia, even against the regimes that invited in the Americans.[244] When Charlie mentioned bin Laden to the lieutenant, she saw a marked exception to his universal scoffing. He expressed cautious curiosity that this Saudi son—not a member of the royal family, not clergy, and not some state-sponsored and sanctioned intellectual— even had an opinion.

Then the rumor swirled that bin Laden secured a meeting with Prince Sultan, the Saudi minister of defense and aviation, to offer an alternative to Western protection.[245] The corpulent Sultan was probably one of the three most powerful men in the kingdom and had been tapped by the king to be the coalition "commander," part of a deal worked out with President Bush. Officially, General Schwarzkopf fell under Prince Sultan in a combined U.S.-Saudi chain of command. To everyone but the most naïve Saudis, it was a complete fig leaf. Sultan was put in charge of Arab forces, Saudi and the Kuwaiti remnants and then the deployment of Emiratis, Egyptians, Syrian and others. In reality, he had no authority over the American military. Or the British or the French.[246]

"Saudi Arabia does not need outsiders," bin Laden reportedly told Prince Sultan at their meeting. The true agenda of Bush sending his army to Saudi Arabia, he said, has nothing to do with protecting their country. It was the beginning of an American invasion and conversion of the whole region.

And bin Laden wasn't just there to complain. He brought with him an alternative proposal and a 60-page plan to fight Saddam without American troops. His seasoned commanders would organize Arab and Afghan fighters to protect the country. Muslims from all over the world—the veterans and the faithful who defeated the great Soviet superpower and its military machine—would drive back the Iraqis. Bin Laden was ready to conduct the next glorious defensive *jihad*. The Americans should be asked to leave.

Prince Sultan laughed at the young Saudi. "So, who is the naïve one?" he said to bin Laden.

"Your Excellency," bin Laden pressed on quietly, "we should not allow non-Muslims into our land. Especially not crusading armies."

American boots on their ground, he said, were sacrilege and a defilement. The young Saudi was already publicly calling for a boycott of American goods. And Prince Sultan had been told that word on the streets was that the outspoken bin Laden had already used the word "treason" in his description of King Fahd's invitation.

So quickly dismissed by the hand of royalty, bin Laden became more emotional in his appeal. "Abdul Aziz is siding with the infidels," he said, "and the royal family is showing itself to be a corrupt puppet of the West." Breaking protocol and referring to the Saudi king with a common name rather than *Wali al-Amr*—the supreme authority—as if he were a family member given license to speak intimately, something even Prince Sultan wouldn't do outside of a one-on-one meeting or an intimate family occasion, bin Laden stepped across a line.

"My boy!" Sultan cut him off, astonished at the impertinence, finishing the conversation and barely modulating his fury. "This is not the time for political posturing or lectures on matters you know nothing about. The fourth largest army in the world, an army created by the Soviet enemy you supposedly know well, a Godless hostile nation that is willing to use chemical weapons, sits poised on our borders. Focus your energy on them. We have the Americans under control in ways you cannot even begin to understand. They will leave our home when Saddam has left Kuwait."[247]

Charlie heard the story and put feelers out through Massoud to learn more about this son of the famous bin Laden family. Her now-smitten dining companion promised to inquire with *people who would know*.

"He is the only one who speaks the truth," said a young Pakistani mechanic the Lebanese introduced to Charlie. The man even implied he was *with* bin Laden. *Sheikh* bin Laden, more famous than any other Saudi to emerge from the Soviet war in Afghanistan, was the only one to trust, the mechanic explained.

Everyone knew his story, he told Charlie. He returned to Saudi Arabia and promised that he and the international *mujahidin* would continue the *jihad* not just in Afghanistan to overthrow the communist government but also get rid of the Marxists in Yemen.[248]

Rumor was that Prince Turki himself, director general of the *Mukhabarat Al 'Ammah*, Saudi Arabia's intelligence agency informed bin Laden that no one would be overthrowing any government. Despite this rebuff, bin Laden went ahead and organized fighters anyhow, working with tribal leaders, making armed forays into Yemen, his men attacking border posts and government bases. The attacks were so bothersome that the Yemeni president traveled to Saudi Arabia to ask King Fahd to keep young bin Laden under control. Through family elders, the king instructed the young scion to stay out of Yemeni affairs. Prince Nayef, the powerful interior minister and a senior prince in the government, even demanded Osama bin Laden's passport as punishment for his unsanctioned activities.[249] Soon, he was under house arrest.[250]

Wiping his filthy hands with a dirty rag, the Pakistani mechanic said, "They will not destroy him," telling her that the *Sheikh* was one step ahead of the family Saud and other corrupt Arab governments.

Of course, in hindsight, the promised mother of all battles between Saddam Hussein and the entire world turned into a whimpering bitch slap. It was over in 43 days, the half a million plus American soldiers who almost all flowed into the region through Dammam were placed in reverse and sent home. Thank God, everyone said, that a ceasefire agreement and an airtight United Nations disarmament plan put Saddam's weapons of mass destruction under control.[251] They would soon be gone, the WMD. And then the Americans could go. The international community practically burbled with self-congratulation that the principles of sovereignty and the rule of law were affirmed. With oil back flowing, cars revved their engines.

Chapter 12 Monkey See, Monkey Do

Barely a month after the defeat of Iraq, Khalid Sheikh Mohammed gushed in writing to Mr. Jones. All the big wigs of an alternate universe were meeting in Khartoum. *Sunni* and *Shi'a* alike, *Hizb'allah* and *Ba'athist* functionaries, Iraqis and Iranian fighters who had been at each other's throats for millennia, Palestinians and Afghan *mujahidin*, Muslim Brotherhood, communists, social democrats, clerics and scholars. It was the first annual Popular Arab Islamic Conference, grandly sponsored by Hassan al-Turabi, head of the only Islamist movement to nominally take control of a nation, in this case Sudan.[252]

Turabi, a white-bearded and white-turbaned intellectual, was London-educated and with a doctorate from the Sorbonne in Paris.[253] A year before Iraq invaded Kuwait, he'd been inspiration for Colonel Omar al-Bashir to lead a military coup against the democratically elected president of Sudan.[254] They then presided over the imposition of *Shari'ah*, Islamic law, on a national level, imposing it on the Christian south of the country. And then they vocally opposed the Gulf War, defying their Saudi neighbor and declining to support the American coalition.

KSM sent forward the agenda, a stack of papers and a copy of the speech of Osama bin Laden. The *Emir*, he reported, was leaving his Saudi homeland forever, thrown out by the royal family.[255]

"Tell me what we're doing with Khalid at this point," Hal Jones asked Bowlen after reviewing his report on KSM's latest dispatches. With bin Laden's move to Sudan, it seemed to him like the hope of his ever infiltrating into the bin Laden construction group was probably over.

"Maybe it is time to let KSM go," Hal said.

"I'm torn," Bowlen responded. "If we've ever been justified in taking on Khalid, it seems now we should hang on, to see where bin Laden is headed."

"And if he becomes even more active with terrorism?" Hal asked.

"All the more reasons to have some eyes on him," Bowlen answered.

"But his usefulness on the Saudis? Is that over?"

"He says not to count bin Laden out of the game, that his move to Sudan is just regrouping."

"Lawrence, there's no way in hell bin Laden is going to be let back into the country, and Sudan is hardly Afghanistan."

They'd been friends for going on 20 years, and Khalid Sheikh Mohammed had become the one irritant in their work together. Now Bowlen thought their renegade agent still useful. Hal thought they should cut ties with him and erase the history.

"Wouldn't you agree that the Saudi scene is changing," Bowlen said. "I could make an argument that young Osama and not the old Bin Laden Group is now the player to concern ourselves with."

"But Khalid's role, Lawrence? What's his role?"

"I just think he's smarter than we give him credit for. And I suppose I agree with him that bin Laden isn't going away." KSM had sent his own heartfelt letter pleading with Mr. Jones to look at the Saudi scene with new eyes. "My Dear Mr. Jones," it said:

> "You speak of Saudi money as if it were the sun, stationary and bright. And yet the future is *Sheikh* bin Laden, a comet barely started on a celestial journey. ... May I suggest that your CIA look beyond oil? You know that I am untrustworthy [sic] long [sic] [*analyst's note: he undoubtedly means 'lone'*] rider, but I tell you to listen for the shadows [sic]: I feel like never before that I want to serve him, that I would entrust my children's future more to him than to any State or any thief government leader. If for that reason and nothing else, your

humble servant urges you to pay attention, for others feel the same, and I say he is more than ever the man who will bring down the House of Saud."[256]

Hal relented in Bowlen's proposal of a face-to-face meeting. Either Khalid would present a plan and a route to his Saudi hero's resurrection or they would indeed make a plan to let him go.

The meeting was decided for Malaysia's Kuala Lumpur, a bustling city of Asian and Islamic mixing, a place easy for both to get to. Tony approved the venue and reluctantly gave approval for a daytime public meetup, but only after his security guys checked out the venue and he met with Khalid. KSM suggested they meet in the Chow Kit Market, a chaotic sewer of humanity in the red-light district at the city center. It was not popular with tourists, he said, and they would evade much attention. Tony instructed the clean-cut and mostly desk-bound Bowlen on what to wear in a scouting memo, telling him he should bring a pair of shoes that he didn't mind getting ruined in the "wet market," and that it would be stinking hot as well.[257]

As Bowlen moved through the stalls, Tony's people stayed close by. The white-haired foreigner passed through row upon row of fish, meat, fruits, vegetables, and spices. The stench was pungent and foreign. The uncommon presence of the Westerner and his bodyguards didn't stop vendors from thrusting live fish in Bowlen's face or extending blood-dripping cow heads into the air, both to shock and delight. Everyone knew he wasn't a buyer and more unsavory characters amongst the bunch sensed they should make themselves scarce, bee-lining the other way as he neared.

"My friend! My friend!" Khalid Sheikh Mohammed called out loudly in English as Bowlen approached, rising from his seat at a seafood restaurant in front of Quill Mall. Tony was already sitting with him, relaxed and looking tan. With sunglasses and dressed in a safari jacket, the security head could be any Australian or British tourist.

Khalid had put on weight.

Bowlen's hair was whiter than the last time they met.

"You look well," KSM said, taking his hands. They were a translucent white with long fingers. He said that he remembered those hands from their first time together in Washington, thinking they were like those of a magician.

"I have a gift for you," he beamed, handing Bowlen a paper package. "Already we are laughing!" he said encouragingly as Bowlen unwrapped the t-shirt, unfolding and displaying a locally-made rag emblazoned with the words "New World Order" over a silkscreened globe. Underneath the globe were the words "Monkey see Monkey do."

"Look! You get the world and we get to sell t-shirts about it," he joked.

And they all laughed.

They ordered cold beers and chit-chatted. He was living in Karachi now, vaguely employed as coordinator of the now-dispersing Afghanistan cadre.[258] Bowlen noted to himself that Khalid indeed was a man of the world, conversing easily in English, smooth-faced rather than bearded, looking very much the businessman, dressed in a casual Malaysian outfit: a white *baju melayu* tunic.

"The *Emir* predicted so," his now-jolly agent said, getting down to business, careful not to use bin Laden's actual name. "You Americans aren't going to leave Saudi Arabia. Or the Middle East. Ever."

Whether it was true or not, Bowlen thought it was indeed provocative to those paying attention that King Fahd again capitulated—not just allowing the military deployment after the Iraqi invasion but now also letting so many Americans stay behind to contain Saddam and support the search for weapons of mass destruction.

"We all saw Saddam's generals surrendering in a desert tent on their own doorstep," said KSM. "But do you know what he is saying now? The Iraqi tyrant is pleased that he has obtained the big status as enemy of the world. He dismisses the Iraqi military defeat as a question of physics: *the whole world against little Iraq? It was just a matter of arithmetic, says Saddam. Who would you expect to win in that battle?* He has turned his defeat on its head. It was because Iraq was *so strong*, he says, that it required not just America but Britain, France, and even Italy, to conquer it.[259]

"Brothers, from Malaysia all the way to Sudan, just shrug their shoulders in agreement, saying that they—*you*—needed an entire army and air force to beat Saddam. And now they speak of the B-52 bombers and the invisible airplanes and the nuclear weapons all needed to defeat this great man."

"Nuclear weapons, Khalid?" Bowlen asked.

"You know. The secret weapons made of uranium," KSM answered. "The ones that are now causing cancer. Iraqi children are dying…"

It was so frustrating arguing with KSM, especially in his bizarre reading of the news. Bowlen was going to explain the truth about the depleted uranium bullets, that even if they were a hazard, there hadn't been sufficient time to incubate any cancer let alone some outbreak but Khalid went on, shifting the subject: "And now you try to make Baghdad bow down to your gang of white-suited inspectors?"

He continued: "I know what you will say. That it's all Saddam's fault that you have not yet left. That you must protect the *Shi'a* from being massacred. That you must protect the poor Kurds in the north. And though your CIA knows so much that there were so many surprises to discover.

"You know, *Mister*, I don't believe any of these excuses. And I say this: your plot to weaken Iraq will backfire. I tell you my friend, the pressure you are exerting is just enough rope for the snake to transform and slither away. But it is not enough to hang him. Saddam will never give in.

"And you pretend that somehow everything will go back to normal if Iraq just tells the United Nations where its secret weapons are hidden? I tell you what I think: maybe Iraq was getting too powerful. Too powerful even to serve as the counter against Tehran.

"I mean: Does America really care about the *Shi'a* or the Kurds, or the people of Kuwait? Does America care about my family and others that were there trapped by the invaders? I think not. The CIA set a trap for Saddam, first conspiring to continue the war with Iran forever, bankrupting Baghdad and then telling it to take Kuwaiti oil as payment. And now we even know that when Saddam met with the girl American ambassador to tell her that he was going to go into Kuwait, she told him that America had no opinion on the subject.[260] No opinion on the subject!

"Maybe the nations of the new world order have thrown Iraq to the wolves. But the *street?* I'm telling you. It is with Iraq. *Everyone* believes as I do: Baghdad was seduced into invading, and everyone feels for Iraq's suffering, not just for the Iraqi civilians bombed with uranium, but even more who are dying every day because of the mines you put everywhere.[261] The street is even crying for the Iraqi soldiers—the ones who were plowed under the earth by American bulldozers,[262] the ones who died on the highway when your vampire pilots came and feasted on their blood."[263]

Bowlen huffed. "Come, come. What do you believe, Khalid?"

"I believe facts. An Arab country Saddam had built, with modern roads and hospitals and schools; it just wasn't acceptable to the west. You had to destroy it. The al Saud had to destroy it. And I believe that America is too cowardly to fight face-to-face on the ground, preferring to rain bombs and missiles down from above—just as the Soviets did in Afghanistan, just as the Soviets did in the last gasps of their dying empire before my brothers defeated them as well."

He continued: "Saudi Arabia is America's number one ally now? But they are not your friends. The Saud do not want any neighbor to have power, not one that isn't part of the Family of Kings."

"And how does any of this about Iraq have to do with what we are here to talk about today?" Bowlen said.

"Everything I have to say stands behind the fact that America did not leave after creating the excuse to come. So, it is about Iraq first—this, I am not making up."

He went on: "Even after Saddam is gone; you will be focused on taming the Iraqi people. It will be your Afghanistan. A longer war than even Vietnam. They are smart, these Iraqis. They will pretend democracy, but they will suck you dry. And while you are so focused, you will be blind to what's really going on."

It was true, Bowlen thought: Washington *was* mesmerized by paper agreements and beautiful sounding policies that far too many thought in their precision would make countries like Iraq do what was the Western norm. But none of the locals, and certainly not any Iraqi really believed in disarmament. And certainly neither Saddam nor any other Iraqi official could care less of U.N. resolutions or treaties, having learned from the CIA during the long Iran-Iraq war that America will always say one thing and do another.

And it wasn't only Iraq. Sudan and the other rogues didn't believe any of it either. And as for Riyadh and the other Arab states who pretended to be America's friends and partners? Bowlen doubted them as well. Islam wasn't going to transform into a happy member of the New World Order family. The region's passions couldn't be smothered.

Bowlen knew there was fear in the Arab capitals: the Saudi king telephoned President Bush at the crescendo of the ground fighting to tell him that he opposed any march by the American army to Baghdad, even though its tanks were less than 100 miles away.[264]

Saddam's regime lay prostrate and vulnerable with an oblivious White House encouraging the Iraqi people to rise up. King Fahd panicked.[265] The people stirring in Iraq—these *Shi'a*—meant his *Shi'a* population potentially rising up. Even Saddam was better than extending the chaos, said Fahd. The Iraqi dictator was taught enough of a lesson, he said. And the Kurds? Allowing them their own nation would mean redrawing borders in four countries, including American ally and NATO member Turkey. Leave well enough alone, Fahd told Bush. *We understand this region, my friends.*[266]

Of course, the Bush White House knew nothing of the *Shi'a* in the south of Iraq, nothing of the hatred between the *Sunnis* in charge in Baghdad and of the repressed majority in their own country, nothing of the Saudi *Shi'a* minority and Riyadh's own equal hatred for them.

"He said it. Even before the war," KSM continued, interrupting Bowlen's thoughts. "The *Sheikh* said America made the greatest mistake in entering a peninsula that no religion from among the non-Muslim states has entered for 14 centuries."[267]

"A bit rhetorical for me," Bowlen scoffed. "How many divisions does your man Osama have?"

Bowlen knew when he said it that Khalid wouldn't catch the reference. *And how many divisions does the Pope have?* Stalin said it sarcastically before the Second World War when he was asked to be nicer to Russian Catholics.

KSM indeed didn't catch the reference, continuing to regale Bowlen and Tony with talk of bin Laden, whom he alternated between calling the *Sheikh* and the *Emir.*

"My eyes are open," Khalid said. "I know that he went to Afghanistan in the early days with the blessing of the Saudis, to do their work. He was even a man of Prince Turki's service, keeping an eye on the Arab youth who were coming.[268] I was his record-keeper man and payer of the monies, so I know. And I also know that the *Sheikh* agreed to alert the

Saudis of any moves that might affect them, at home. It was at first, how do you say, patriotic obligation, loyalty that brought in the monies.

"You know I am not a religious man," Khalid went on, "but after the *Sheikh* went to the mountains, I think he found not just himself but also his own way. And I tell you, it is real. Whatever his beginning, now, he is *the* messenger. Everything he has done since then is for our people."

"*Our* people?" Bowlen asked. "Now you have people, Khalid?"

"My friend, I always have had people. Real people—not the governments and princes you pay so much of your attention. The *Sheikh* operates on behalf of these people."

He recited: "'Those who think they can change reality without blood sacrifices and wounds, without pure, innocent souls, do not understand the essence of our religion.' This was what *Sheikh* Azzam said when he founded the organization. This was the seed he planted to make all of this. Abdullah Azzam started it and *Sheikh* bin Laden took over after his killing. Now I tell you, it is growing.

"*Sheikh* Azzam taught Osama, and he taught me. He said that a small group—'the cream of the cream of the cream who sacrifice their souls and their blood'—will lead.[269] My Palestinian guide, he was a great man. He made the big words.[270]

"We call this *al Qaeda*," said Khalid. "It is from all over the world. The fighters and even the leaders came together when the Soviets retreated. The *Emir* is now the leader, the only one.[271]

"Sudan is his home. Now," Khalid went on. "But I tell you, *al Qaeda* is everywhere where there are Muslims. The *Sheikh* is becoming more and more famous, even here in Asia. People love him. That is what is going on."

Bowlen had listened, knowing that KSM was exaggerating but also impressed that he had prepared what he was going to say, and that he wanted to convey something big. He responded "So, tell me, Khalid, what is really going on when you say *going on*? You know that I am not focused on Afghanistan. Or Sudan. Or Iraq."

"Yes, I know. But you, my friend, are also the only one I *do* know. I take your word, my friend. And that is why I am meeting with you. I say we work together on a new project—but really it is an old project."

"And what's that, Khalid?"

Another round of Tiger beers arrived. All around them at picnic tables and rickety setups of plastic chairs and tables, noisy groups of extended families, women and men and their children were devouring street food: Indian curries, Malaysian satays and soups, Chinese dishes modified for the hybrid population.

"I would honor myself to help to bring down the house of al Saud," Khalid said, leaning closer. He drank his beer and wiped the sweat from his brow. "And here is my connection with your work, *Mister*, to the mission you granted me in America. Osama bin Laden has become ever more famous and admired because the people see that the Saudi rulers are, how you say, treachery.

"The *Sheikh* warned them not to let the American army into the kingdom. And they ignored him. Even laughed at him. The *Sheikh* asked them to support the fight against communists in Yemen. Communists. They said no. The *Sheikh* pleaded for them to give monies to continue to fight the communists in Kabul. But no, again they denied him. So, you see how this all ties?"

KSM explained that bin Laden wanted to adopt and modify Azzam's concept, building an enduring vanguard, an international combat unit. It would not be one that would take on the invaders in direct combat—though they would do that, too, as necessary—but one that would direct a larger defense of Islam.

As KSM already reported to Apex Watch in his reports and letters, bin Laden's vision solidified with the formal establishment of *al Qaeda*, that very elite of the elite, loosely founded on the earlier Services Bureau and Azzam's work with refugees and the wounded. Khalid argued that they were uninterested in terrorism—that is, in traditional publicity-seeking acts characteristic of the Palestinians and those who fought against Israel.[272] Instead they would find acts that would weaken states indirectly, focusing on the Saudis and others who were behind the communists, behind even Israel.

"Khalid," Bowlen answered, "I don't think I need to remind you, but *I'm* the U.S. government. I can't help you to attack us or our friends. Monkey see monkey do or not, the New World Order is upon us and the Bush administration is not even interested in the Middle East anymore. Sure, a small group plays cat and mouse with Saddam's scientists and airplanes patrol Iraq's skies. But Washington is focusing on the breakup of the Soviet Union and the possibility that all those nuclear weapons and nuclear materials might find their way into terrorist hands—into your hands."

He continued: "Saddam Hussein is a pest, but we're done with the Middle East. For me, that means ever more of the same. Saudi Arabia and the restored Kuwaiti government will go on a spending spree. Defense companies are already salivating at the billions that they will spend on arms. In America, the Democrat Party shouldn't even bother to run a candidate in the upcoming elections because the war-winning President Bush is so popular. The '90s are shaping up to be boring, Khalid. You'll thank us for your children's sake that the United States of America, and not the Soviet Union, is the last remaining superpower."

Bowlen regretted almost immediately what he said—that he said too much. He chalked up his little speech to being overtired—jet lagged and even a little frustrated with reversals in his own Saudi fortunes.

To Bowlen though, Khalid seemed oddly delighted by his pushback. He didn't come, he explained to Bowlen, to offer a regular alliance. And he didn't need to do anything to make America *the* target. They were doing it all by themselves.

Then he plunged in again. "With my *emir* in Sudan ..."

Bowlen interrupted: "Unless you can convince me otherwise, I'd say your Osama bin Laden is now a dead ender. He may be a Saudi celebrity and might even have millions of dollars to play with. But he is isolated in Sudan. There are no mountains to hide in. And no doubt bin Laden is learning the bitter truth that in Saudi society, everyone else exists at the pleasure of the Royal family—the King and the *actual* princes, not your self-declared prince. Khalid, my job is to keep an eye on Saudi Arabia. With their increased spending on arms, and with their hosting American forces, can you help with that?"

"I can help with the most important Saudi to have ever lived ..."

"Khalid! Aren't you listening?"

"Two years. I want just two years," said Khalid. "*Mister*, I could forever warn you how America is its own worst enemy. But why bother? You tell me you don't think I'm valuable, but I will show you. Fighters are coming. The *Sheikh* is getting stronger every day. The Egyptians and even the

Sudanese, they are old fools stuck in their old ways, thinking that they can make Islamic governments, thinking that the powers will allow it, thinking that you will allow it. It is not just some speech. It will take many years, maybe even tens of years. I tell you; the fighters will come to the new *emir*. And they will come for you. In two years, you will see. Signs will reveal. I will prove it. A big bang."

"A big bang?" Bowlen asked.

"You will see. Something big. And then bin Laden will make the program. Not America."

"An attack on America?" Bowlen asked.

"I cannot say. But you will see."

They drank what was left of their now warming beers, neither wanting to say more, neither wanting to think that their collaboration might end. They left it. Khalid was satisfied. Bowlen was tired, not really upset that the meeting hadn't gone as he wanted, wanting still to figure out what to do with his agent.

"A new era dawns, you will see," KSM said. "I will show you," wanting to clink bottles.

"A new era," Bowlen said, lifting his bottle but denying KSM the ultimate affirmation he was looking for.

PART 4

Chapter 13 WTC I

1993

The wiry and beak-nosed 25-year-old made it to the front of the visitor's line at John F. Kennedy Airport and was directed to an open window, where he presented his green Iraqi passport to the immigration official.

"How is the situation in Iraq?" the immigration officer asked. He'd watched the Gulf War on CNN, the cruise missiles and the stealth fighters, the tanks in the desert and the mass surrenders. And he'd watched the oil fires on land and slicks in the Gulf. And the scenes of Kurdish families scrambling up mountains to escape what was left of Saddam Hussein. More than a year later, Iraq was still in the news. He'd been following the U.N. nuclear inspectors as they camped out in a parking lot in the center of the Iraqi capital, demanding that they be given access to the hidden weapons of mass destruction.[273]

He said that things weren't good.

"What flight did you arrive on?" the official on the other side of the glass divider asked.

"Pakistani Airlines from Karachi," the man said.

"And you are Iraqi?" the official said, now staring.

"No, I am of Pakistan," he answered.

"And where is your visa, son?" the immigration asked.

"I don't have a visa," he answered. He spoke excellent English with a British accent and presented a second and evidently authentic Pakistani passport in the name of Yousef, born April 27, 1968.[274] He explained that his parents, mother of Palestinian descent and father from Pakistan, had moved the family to Kuwait when he was a child and that he was in the country when Iraq invaded, that he was taken prisoner and moved to Baghdad, until he escaped.

It wasn't a story so different from many they heard at JFK: An El Salvadorian smuggled across multiple borders with fake IDs; a Nigerian captured by pirates and let off in Cameroon; a Burmese dissident with Thai documentation. Everyone had some story and despite airline rules and security procedures, dozens with just such stories arrived every day. The immigration officer pushed a button in his booth that called for a customs officer to escort the man to secondary inspection.[275]

There Ramzi Yousef sat in a windowless hall with a United Nations of travelers, waiting for almost an hour and a half until a uniformed officer came out and loudly called out *Yousef, Ramzi*. He was carrying his checked luggage and had his two passports in a large plastic bag. When Yousef identified himself, he directed the Iraqi Pakistani Kuwaiti to a small examining room.

"So, Mr. Yousef, the Iraqi passport is forged?" the officer said as he laid the suitcase on the table in the stark small room, a second officer sitting at a metal desk with nothing on it but a phone and a large computer. "That is your name, Yousef?

"Yes," Ramzi Yousef answered, "I purchased it."

"And what country are you actually from?"

"Pakistan."

"And this is your real passport?" he asked, holding it up.

"Yes. I am a Pakistani national, but I have lived in Kuwait my entire life."

"In Kuwait? Do you have any Kuwaiti identification?"

"No. It was taken by Iraqi soldiers. During the war. When I was moved to Baghdad."

"And you don't have an American visa?" he asked, cocking his head to understand.

"No."

"How did you get on the flight?"

"I bribed a man in Pakistan."

"I see," the official said. "I gotta go get the manifest," he said to the other man and left.

Twenty minutes later, he returned. He was looking at a long computer print-out. "I see, Mr. Yousef, that you sat in first class. That's a five-thousand-dollar ticket.

"Do you have a boarding pass?"

"Yes," Yousef said, handing one to the officer.

"This is in the name of Mohammed Azan," the officer said.

"Yes," Yousef said, shrugging his shoulder, waiting for a question.

"Is that the name you used to board the flight?" he asked, looking again at the printout. On it, it showed one Mr. Azan sitting in seat 2C, with Ramzi Yousef in seat 2A.

"I am Ramzi Yousef."

"You traveled with this Mr. Azan?"

"There must have been a mix-up in boarding passes," Yousef said.

"Did you travel with Mr. Azan?" he again asked.

"I request political asylum in *Amreeka*," Yousef said, not answering, almost if he were rehearsing a line, indeed saying what Khalid Sheikh Mohammed told him to say.

"Okay, Mr. Yousef. We're going to have to check this out. Get comfortable. Can I get you a soda or a coffee?

"No."

"Okay then," he said to Yousef.

"Put him in 21," the officer said to his colleague behind the desk. It was a secure holding room. "We got to go sort this out," he said.

And then he said to the other officer, *Let's see if we can find this Mr. Azan.*

They returned about an hour later, having conferred with a supervisor and not finding any Azan present in the secondary inspection area.

That's because in another room at JFK at the same time was one Ahmed Mohammed Ajaj.[276] He presented a Swedish passport, one that had been obviously forged. He said he was a member of the Swedish news media. But he, too, did not have an American visa. And despite having flown in first class, he had less than $500 in his possession and could produce neither traveler's checks nor any credit card to support his visit.

And indeed, it was a confusing mess. Customs and immigration were now going through the luggage of Ramzi Yousef and his evident travel companion, a Mr. Azan or a Mr. Ajaj, they still weren't clear which.

Altogether they now had six passports from the two. There was a Pakistani passport, one that seemed genuine and indeed was in the name of Ramzi Yousef. There was an Iraqi passport, evidently also genuine in the name of Abdul Basit Karim, though there was also a Customs' circular questioning the validity of all Iraqi passports issued after 1990. There were obvious photo-substituted passports, one from Sweden in the name of Ajaj and the other from the United Kingdom in the name of Azan. There was also a partially-altered Saudi passport in the name of al-Riyad. And there was a seemingly-valid Jordanian passport in the name of Hamid, brand new. In all, in the luggage of the two, there were more than a dozen groups of identification cards, bank statements, and medical and education records corresponding to the various passports and other persons. There was a checkbook from Lloyd's Bank of London in the name of Yousef. There was a diploma from the West Gamorgan Institute of Higher Education in Wales, also in the name of Abdul Basit Karim.[277]

The various passports and papers were all intermingled together in the suitcases, almost as if they had been haphazardly packed. In them were also letters of various types in Arabic and other languages, some in Yousef's bag, some in the bag of the other passenger. In all, officials could make out nine different identities and what looked like four different languages, including English.

And there was more. There were Arabic papers with diagrams that looked like they related to bomb making. There were other papers—in a language that wasn't Arabic—that looked like they were about how to assemble weapons and explosives. There were at least a dozen VHS videotapes. There were obviously anti-Israeli fliers and posters.[278]

It was late into the night and there was no Arabic translator on duty to figure out what they had. The FBI liaison had also gone home for the day. Yousef's name was checked against the terrorist watch list and INTERPOL wanted databases, as well as the national crime computer. With no hits and no derogatory information, the immigration officer called the duty officer at the FBI office in the city, telling him that they had a passenger who just arrived from Pakistan who had evident bomb-making materials in his luggage.

"I think you need to call the Joint Terrorism Task Force," the duty officer said, and gave him the number.

After he told the Task Force officer the details and sat on hold for what seemed like an eternity, that duty agent came back and told him that his squad leader said he wasn't inclined to get the Task Force involved, that the guy—*what's his name again, Yousef? Yeah, right, Cat Stevens, I got it*—wasn't going to be admitted anyhow.

"He'll probably be put back on a flight to Pakistan," the duty officer said. "In any case, as for the bomb-making material, that sounds like a case for ATF"—the Bureau of Alcohol, Tobacco, and Firearms.

The immigration officer called the ATF duty office. "Confiscate the material and we'll have an officer pick it up tomorrow," the duty officer told him.

"What do you plan to do with the perp?" he asked.

"I guess we'll send him to detention in Jamaica," the immigration officer answered. The temporary immigration detention facility in Queens.

"Did you call the FBI?" the ATF duty officer asked.

"Yes, they said it was your case. But he's also asked for political asylum, so I've got to call Washington to get a case number."

The ATF agent took down the customs officers' particulars.

Back to talk to his supervisor, he found out that Mr. Ajaj had already been remanded into protective custody and sent to detention. His was evidently a clear-cut case because when they checked his name against the databases they found out that he already made a political asylum claim from a prior entry, having then left the country.[279] Looking at his watch, it was now just after 1 a.m. and secondary inspection was practically empty. He was predisposed to send Yousef to detention, at least for the night, as well, and he picked up the phone to call the Wackenhut Correctional Corporation, which operated the detention center. After again being put on hold, he was finally told that the facility was full for the night. By now a new supervisor arrived for the next shift and the officer explained Yousef's case and his claim of asylum.

"Once his case number and summons appear you can cut him loose," the supervisor said.

He again explained that there were forged passports and bomb-making materials.

"You called ATF?"

"I did."

"And they said?"

"They said confiscate the material."

"Did you fingerprint him?"

"Yes."

"Did he fill out the claim for political asylum?"

"He did, but he's not Iraqi."

"But still he's insisting on a claim?"

"He is."

"Can he give you a point of contact?"

"He says he has a cousin in New Jersey and a contact at a mosque in Brooklyn."

"Well then, take any prohibited property into custody and write him out an I-709 form and cut him loose."

"He's obviously up to no good, sir."

"What are you, *Columbo*?" the supervisor asked.

At 4:55 a.m., September 1, 1992, Ramzi Yousef was handed a plastic bag of clothing and toiletry items from his suitcase, given an inventory of property that had been confiscated, including his various passports, papers and videos. He was handed his Pakistani passport with an affixed immigration form—I-709—that would serve as his temporary visa, awaiting a hearing. And he was given another form, a summons to appear before an immigration court to hear his petition for asylum.

Yousef took the bus to the train, getting on the subway and transferring towards downtown Brooklyn. A little after 10 a.m., he showed up at the *al-Khifah* Center. It was the first American office of what would become *al Qaeda*, established to recruit *jihadis* to fight in Afghanistan.[280] KSM visited the Brooklyn Center himself when he was a student in North Carolina and told Ramzi where it was and what to do.

Al-Khifah was located in a six-story converted factory on Atlantic Avenue in the Boerum Hill section. The lower floors were occupied by the al-Farooq, a mosque that had been connected to the assassination of Jewish extremist Rabbi Meir Kahane.[281] And it had held the First Conference of *Jihad* in America, a grand meeting attended by the great Abdullah Azzam. "Every Muslim on earth should unsheathe his sword and fight to liberate Palestine," he said that day, already visualizing a *jihad* beyond Afghanistan.[282]

"Welcome to *Amreeka*, my son," the Blind *Sheikh* said to Yousef when he was ushered into his office just before lunch. "Your uncle has sent word of your arrival."

His uncle.

When the Blind *Sheikh* arrived in America, he settled in at *al-Khifah*, displacing Azzam's man after the founder had been assassinated in Peshawar.[283]

"Everything is ready for you," the Blind *Sheikh* told him.

Over the next five months, as *Rashid the Iraqi*, Yousef went about recruiting men from the al-Farooq and other mosques in New York and New Jersey. He openly told dozens of people about his plan to put a bomb in the basement garage of the North Tower of the World Trade Center. He rented a storage locker in New Jersey and amassed chemicals and bomb-making materials there. In that same time period, he had three car accidents, including one that sent him to the hospital, an accident that occurred while there were explosives in the trunk of the car he was renting. He constantly called his friend, Mr. Azan, now in custody at Riker's Island. He ran up $18,000 in unpaid phone charges calling overseas to Pakistan and Kuwait. He reported to the NYPD that his Pakistani passport was stolen and then requested a new passport from the Pakistani consulate. He never bothered to show up for his asylum hearing with immigration authorities.

On February 26, 1993, Ramzi Yousef parked a Ford Econoline van loaded with 1,500 pounds of chemical explosives on the B-2 level of the North Tower parking garage, setting the timer to detonate the bomb at 12:18 p.m. The explosion expanded seven stories, the fireball ripping through concrete walls and roofs into maintenance offices in the basement and breaching the ceiling between the garage structure and the subway line beneath, debris and smoke inundating the station. Six died instantly, most crushed when the ceiling of the subway station collapsed. More than 1,000 people were injured. Stopping to admire his handiwork and the cavalcade of police, ambulances and fire rescue vehicles crushing into the narrow streets of downtown Manhattan, Yousef then walked a couple of blocks south, hailing a cab for John F. Kennedy airport, chatting with the driver about the tragedy. That night, with his new Pakistani passport, he boarded a late-night flight to Karachi.[284]

Chapter 14 Bojinka

KSM took a taxi down United Nations Boulevard towards the waterfront, getting out a couple of blocks shy of the American embassy. The pudgy man stood out in his traditional Gulf Arab dress: a handsome ankle-length *thawb* with matching crisp white *ghutra*, topped off by his favorite modern *igal*, the black one, of goat-hair, the one with the tassels. He adopted the demeanor of oil magnate or perhaps even Gulf royalty. Even in the very Christian city of Manila, the facade paid off with deference and special treatment.

At the embassy, he slipped a Saudi passport into the well under the bulletproof glass window. Wiping his brow with a handkerchief, he stated in intentionally-halting English that he wanted to see a security officer. He had information of enormous importance to the United States.

Probably in any other dress he might not have been so easily welcomed into the air-conditioned waiting room. After a few minutes, a uniformed Marine guard from the chancery escorted him across the front lawn, through the metal detector into the main lobby. There he was met by an officer who introduced himself as "Stuart."

Stuart, KSM surmised: a government wage earner, well-groomed, tanned and probably having nothing to do with real work, his Philippine-style white short-sleeve *barong* too crisply ironed.

"May I call you *Abdul*," chirped Stuart, absentmindedly thumbing through the passport, going through the most standard of standard operating procedures.

Abdul, KSM winced. That's what all the good old boys called him and his fellow students in North Carolina—*Aabdool*, they'd drawled—reveling in *not* knowing anything about their so-called guests, proud of being *un*able to distinguish Arab from Mexican.[285] The name was Abdulrahman, one word. Abdulrahman A. A. al-Ghamdi was KSM's alias and he was now annoyed that this embassy worker, even if he was in the Philippines and not in the Middle East, was so oblivious.[286]

"Why don't you tell me your story?" Stuart coolly intoned, cocking his head, ready with his ballpoint pen and notepad.

But KSM had no interest in the ritual screening of a potential crazy person. Thinking he knew something of how government worked, he got right to it. "I don't want to waste the U.S. government's time," he said, "but my conscience wouldn't be able to rest if I didn't report what I have heard."

In a local *halal* restaurant in the city that was frequented by Arabs, he overheard men whispering they were going to kill the Roman Catholic Pope John Paul II when he visited Manila.[287] And, he said, there was also talk about American president Bill Clinton. His just completed trip to Asia had given them an idea, and they thought they could "get him" when he returned as well.[288]

"I cannot say if any of these words mean anything," KSM offered. "But the manner of these men … how they spoke … it seemed to me a real conversation …"

This supposed Saudi man with an ostentatious gold watch and big framed eyeglasses told Stuart he just had to warn them. He said he hoped he had done the right thing coming to the embassy.

Usually, Stuart would have just filed a report—maybe at *flash* precedence to Washington—but still just a report. But because the Saudi was dressed so nicely, and it was so unusual for such a person to enter his world, Stuart thought he needed backup. He was in over his head.

Doing his best not to feign alarm, he took Ghamdi to a second-floor conference room where he had the regional security officer listen to the story. Meanwhile, Stuart called Diplomatic Security in Washington.[289]

KSM repeated the tale to everyone who came to the conference room. The embassy employees took notes and brought in cookies and made tea and pored over city maps with their guest trying to pinpoint the restaurant. But they mostly stalled, awaiting instructions.

Ghamdi's passport checked out when run through their security databases, which is to say that it rang no alarm bells. Ghamdi's name and date of birth were forwarded to Washington and Riyadh.

After almost two hours of stalling while inter-governmental coordination came alive, Ghamdi was let go. Inside the embassy, they discussed calling Philippine national police or the national intelligence service but the mention of a potential future threat to Bill Clinton skyrocketed the sensitivity of the Saudi tip to another level. The president had in fact just completed a two-day state visit to the country, visiting Manila and Corregidor Island with its giant American military cemetery from World War II.[290] So, if their embassy was now indeed potentially dealing with a presidential protection case, that meant tighter compartmentation. The regional FBI security officer was already on his way from Thailand but now they would all also have to wait for the Secret Service rep to roll in from Tokyo. It was their turf.

Ghamdi listened carefully to the security officer's advice as they arranged a second meeting. His friends in the conference room now freely answered all the Saudi's questions: *Would the embassy put the restaurant under surveillance? Would his telephone be listened to if he called the embassy again? Did the Philippine authorities have such bad men under surveillance?* No, no, and no, he was told. At least not yet.

They agreed that he would return in two days. Ghamdi was also given a time to meet with a CIA officer at a secure location, should he be unable to safely make the second meeting at the embassy.

U.S. government, KSM kicked himself as he walked away, using that phrase. That was Mr. Jones' bureaucratic mouthful that he picked up and now repeated. *America* or *your country* would have been more authentic to say he told himself.

The FBI man flew in from Bangkok. The Secret Service special agent followed. There was a second meeting at the embassy. And then a third.

KSM later wrote up the events in a long, taunting report to Apex Watch, calling the embassy, FBI and Secret Service men incompetent, mocking Stuart and how he stayed glued to Ghamdi, less doing any job, more desperate to be part of the action, any action.

At the embassy, KSM now told his friends that he returned to the *halal* restaurant, not unusual given the restrictions on his diet. He said he had not seen the seditious businessmen, but he made the acquaintance of someone who knew them, a fellow businessman from the Emirates. Ghamdi couldn't provide more details about the plot but he shared a belief that they were indeed bad men.

His new American friends also shared. Though it wasn't common knowledge, during the recent Asia-Pacific Economic Cooperation Summit in Indonesia,[291] the Philippines was chosen to host the fourth Leaders' Meeting. And Bill Clinton was slated to attend.

Embassy security, FBI, Secret Service and KSM deliberated whether or not to bring in the Philippine authorities, KSM ever so slightly tipping the scales. *Was it safe to talk to the police if there might a spy inside the Philippine government? Didn't they, the Filipinos, already have undercover people in the restaurant given that it was a hangout for bad men?*

Ghamdi also sat down with a sketch artist.

Meanwhile, Ramzi Yousef's progress towards a miniature bomb moved forward. The fugitive from New York reunited with KSM in Karachi and the two came to Manila together. KSM picked the Philippines because the place was both foreign and chaotic. And indeed, flying in from Karachi via Bangkok, Yousef successfully evaded detection with a fake Kuwaiti passport—despite being one of the most wanted men on the planet.[292] KSM and Ramzi Yousef worked with explosive experts in Pakistan to pull together the design of a special bomb, one that might be smuggled in pieces past airport security and then assembled in an airplane lavatory.

The first test design was finished in November and Yousef planted the nitroglycerine device in a shopping mall utility closet, setting the simple Casio watch timer to detonate several hours later.[293]

They paid a young Philippine girl to hang about and listen in to what the police were saying about the bomb once it exploded. Then they scoured newspapers and listened to the radio for any news of a bomb plot. Nothing.

On the first of December, Yousef placed a second device with slightly more explosives underneath a movie theater seat in a popular Manila cinema. That bomb detonated at 10:30 p.m., injuring a nearby couple and several others.[294]

The morning after, KSM scanned the local newspapers and again saw nothing. And when he returned to the embassy that week, his American friends said nothing of any bomb. He didn't educate them.

Ten days later, Yousef boarded Philippine Airlines Flight 434 from Ninoy Aquino International Airport to Tokyo Narita, his ticket to Cebu, the oldest Philippine city and the midpoint stop of many flights on the way to Japan.

Retrieving parts of the bomb from pieces secreted away in his carry-on luggage and in the hollowed-out heels of his shoes, Yousef attached the explosive to the life vest under his seat bottom, setting the timer to go off two hours after the plane's scheduled takeoff from Cebu. There Yousef disembarked the Boeing 747 and a Japanese businessman took his window seat, seat 26-K. He was killed instantly when the explosion blew the seat from the floor, severing several control cables and punching a hole through the fuselage wall, depressurizing the plane. Ten others were injured. The veteran pilot barely was able to bring the airliner back under control, managing to land it safely on the island of Okinawa.[295]

The terrorist attack was front page news in all the Philippine papers[296] but again the embassy people asked KSM nothing about it, making no connection to his reported plot.

In Manila, KSM celebrated with Yousef. There was excitement in their group about the potential for a future airliner plot now that a bomb was successfully tested, but—even more exciting—they toasted the upcoming attack on the head of Christianity.

"To *Bojinka*." They raised glasses.

Bojinka.[297]

KSM now told his American friends that his business in the Philippines was concluded, his deals made regarding the import of furniture and specialty woods back to his home country. The embassy was now focused on any names he could provide that they could follow up on. After weeks of furtive meetings and deliberations, Mr. Ghamdi delivered. Saeed Ahmed, he told them. Another perhaps was a man named Ibrahim Hahsen. A third man, whom Ghamdi thought might be the ringleader was called Rasheed. *Perhaps he is Iraqi. Rasheed the Iraqi.*

The embassy made a discreet inquiry with Philippine authorities. One of the men mentioned by their new Saudi source was recorded entering the country. Stuart was so excited that he called Ghamdi to announce *their* victory.

We got 'em.

"I almost felt sorry for this puppy dog," KSM later wrote to Mr. Jones. "But I do not feel sorry for your country, my friend."

Ghamdi carefully went through terrorist mugshot books the FBI had brought in, noting to himself the men and their pictures. *His* operation was a complete success. He wasn't in any of the books.

Maybe, he told his new best friends, looking at some pictures in particular, but he just wasn't sure.

As KSM suspected, Ramzi Yousef was there: a passport picture from Pakistan, a Kuwait identity card, and on another page, a surveillance photo from New York. KSM could now implement his plan.

On the eve of his departure, the American Christmas holidays over, Ghamdi asked again for the embassy mugshot book, saying he was sure he could identify the ringleader for he had recently gotten a good look at him.

This man, he said, pointing to Yousef's picture stuck in amongst the hundreds of photos in the fat plastic binder. There was no name written in the book, no suggestion of who he was.

No, KSM said, he'd never heard of Mr. Yousef before seeing him in Manila. Yes, of course he'd heard of the terrible attack in New York. *It is this man?*

I'm sure, he said, pointing.

He was *the one and only.*

Chapter 15 Sudan

Landing in Khartoum, KSM was ushered through customs by a plainclothes government official and taken to a guest house near the airport where an armed guard sat outside his door all night.[298]

In the morning, promptly at 7 a.m., a white jeep picked him up to take him out to the *Sheikh's* compound. As they turned into al Meshtal Street, Khalid saw even more security. The two ends of the block where bin Laden lived were barricaded by armed *al Qaeda* soldiers.[299]

Bin Laden's new Sudanese home was a faded, red, three-story apartment building. With six balconies facing the street, the structure was partially hidden behind a high brick wall.[300] The combo residence and place of business was bustling with activity. Though commercial concerns on the first floor entertained a constant stream of Sudanese visitors, armed men were everywhere.

Bin Laden's Egyptian military commander, Abu Hafs, greeted Khalid at the gate.[301] He was walking with a cane.

"This looks more like a fortification than a home," Khalid commented.

"I'm afraid, brother, that we have already overstayed our welcome," Abu Hafs answered. The Egyptian was tall and handsome. Khalid always thought him a real professional. While now hobbled by a chronic back problem, he was still in full control of *al Qaeda*'s day-to-day operations.

"In particular, the Mubarak government finds us far too close," he said. "We have already begun to scout possibilities in the mountains." He meant Afghanistan.

"How are you going to do in the mountains, brother?" Khalid asked, referring to the Hafs' cane.

"I don't know. My back is just getting worse."

"I'm sorry to hear that."

Doctor Zawahiri, with his Coke bottle glasses and white turban, emerged from the building to greet Khalid. From their Sudan sanctuary, the doctor sponsored many operations against Egyptian targets, provoking Mubarak. KSM heard that *Sheikh* bin Laden was unhappy with both his continuing focus on Egypt, and maybe even annoyed with all the Egyptians who filled his upper ranks.

The doctor didn't linger, obviously briefed by the *Sheikh* that the brain—the man whom almost everyone just called *Mukhtar*, the brain—was here for an important meeting.

Looking robust and healthy, bin Laden warmly greeted Khalid in a garden by the side of the house. KSM hoped the *Sheikh* would be in one of his reflective moods, and that they would get some sustained privacy amidst the bustle.

They developed a close relationship despite Khalid's constant demur in formally joining *al Qaeda*. More than once bin Laden told his quirky, independent-minded friend that he welcomed his pure voice of anti-Americanism. And KSM thought that bin Laden also appreciated that he saw the Saudi family and the Saudi-American alliance as the most important manifestation of all that was wrong in the Middle East.

But most important, KSM knew, was his position. As *Mukhtar* he was bin Laden's number one international operator, someone who could get things done across continents and in the most difficult circumstances.[302]

Under the shade of trees, the two settled in on white plastic chairs, a young boy serving them tea and dried fruits.

His *emir* was in a glum mood, KSM could tell.

The American State Department had just announced that Sudan was being placed on the list of "state sponsors of terrorism."[303] Government prosecutors in New York had gone out of their way to point out that five of the fifteen suspects arrested in the bombing of New York's World Trade Center were Sudanese nationals.[304]

Stung by the label and the legal repercussions that could stand in the way of receiving international aid and financing, no less than Hasan al-Turabi[305] came out to the bin Laden house to quietly tell his guest that maybe the thrust of Sudan's external relations needed to change, that the *Sheikh* might have to rein in the work of his Egyptians against their home country, that perhaps even he would have to find another place to live, even if just temporarily.[306]

"They want to slowly choke us," the Sudanese leader explained apologetically to bin Laden. It wasn't just Cairo. The Saudi government also communicated that they were cutting off financial assistance to Khartoum if they didn't change their ways.

The American pressure was working, bin Laden confided to *Mukhtar*. Sudan, he said, was once a pious government supporting the cause of Islam. But now, with threats of sanctions and the CIA's activities, it was fading as a bastion of Islam behind the sunglasses and uniforms of the Sudanese military and their fellow strong men. The country was looking increasingly like a conventional military state.[307]

"I am already restricted from travel internally, even to visit our investments," said bin Laden.[308] "It is because of the American's success in Iraq, my friend," bin Laden softly explained. "The family Saud has fallen into line with the CIA. The Americans are allowed to conduct a secret war from their bases and now even have the support of the Hashemite's,[309] both of them collaborators in genocide of our Iraqi brothers."

Bin Laden had no affinity for Saddam, but he described what he read were the effects of American bombing and of the use of weapons made of uranium.[310] "The so-called depleted uranium is creating cancers and deforming future Arab generations. And it will spread," bin Laden said. International sanctions, he added, were taking their toll on innocent Iraqi children, who did not even have enough to eat.

"We are in the worst of times," bin Laden said. "American soldiers and sailors are everywhere in the Middle East, not just in the land of the holy places, and not just in Kuwait, but also firmly embedded in Bahrain and Oman and the Emirates and even Qatar. They all think they cleverly restrict the number in uniform and that they hide the Americans out of public view, but everyone knows that they are there. And now in addition come these men in sunglasses … what do they call them?"

"Defense contractors," *Mukhtar* said.

"Yes, yes. The mercenary pigs, just like the Vinnell men in my homeland.[311] As if those who do not wear a military uniform are to fool us. Or as if drinking and whoring civilians are less offensive. And they call us terrorists?"

Everywhere he turned, bin Laden told *Mukhtar*, he saw Islam being choked. It wasn't just the Islamic state in Sudan that was under assault. Or Iraq. It was a communist-leaning regime still hanging on in Kabul and fighting against the defenders of Islam.[312] In Europe, the breakup of Yugoslavia resulted in organized mass murder of Muslim Bosnians and Kosovars. Christian Russia was slaughtering brothers in Muslim Chechnya. American soldiers were positioned to invade Somalia for the purpose of wiping out Islam there. In fact, bin Laden said, Somalia was an African toehold now attempting to encircle Islam from all sides.

Meanwhile, the Saudi government and the Gulf States remained on their post-Desert Storm spending sprees, buying American, British and French weapons by the tens of billions of dollars, as if those arms would ever be used to defend Islam or be used against the Zionist enemy.

Bin Laden was furious at what he saw as complete Saudi capitulation to the American agenda. His home country not only hosted the American military. But it stopped supporting Khartoum and had lost all interest in Afghanistan and the fortunes of the *jihad* there. Even its support of fighters in Bosnia and Somalia dwindled.[313]

Mukhtar agreed with the *Sheikh*'s grim logic condemning the Americans and the selfish connivance of Saudi royals.

Bin Laden watched developments closely, reading Arab and international newspapers, watching CNN, even using a computer. But KSM thought that there was a new quality as well, one that had developed since the *Sheikh* left Afghanistan. Bin Laden could also now see by himself, without the prompting of his mentor Doctor Azzam, and without Doctor Zawahiri or any other geopolitical sages peddling their own worldviews. He confided to *Mukhtar* that he was tired of the limited agenda of Egypt, that he wanted to act based upon this more expansive view of the world, against the originator of the assault on Islam, against Zionism and its American backer. He spoke openly of the tension with the Egyptians and the encroachment of those from Cairo into positions of management.

And though he could not break with his friends, the *Sheikh* wanted a more forward-looking agenda for *al Qaeda*. Something more outward looking.

Their tea was taken away, and a mid-morning meal appeared. KSM was impatient to get down to the business of this looking forward, and bin Laden said he hoped that his old friend brought good news.

"Abu Abdullah,"[314] *Mukhtar* said, using bin Laden's chosen battle name, a sign of great respect. "Our experience in the Philippines has prepared the soil for a direct attack on America." He reported on the Philippines's explosive tests, planting the bomb in the movie theater and on the Japan-bound airplane. It was possible to bring big jets down with hidden bombs, to rig up airliners to explode after take-off.

The *Sheikh* leaned forward. "And you believe this machinery, that it is reliable?"

KSM thought it a good question.[315] He told his *emir* that, honestly, technology was not as reliable as martyrdom. But *Mukhtar* didn't want to count upon the reliability of other brothers, or risk wasting their precious lives when bombs could have the same impact.

"So, you are not suggesting martyrdom?" asked a curious bin Laden.

"My plan is to plant bombs on airliners before they make their long Pacific Ocean stopovers, blowing them out of the skies over the oceans."

"Is it possible to do this on the ground," bin Laden asked.

"At airports?" *Mukhtar* inquired.

"No, not necessarily. But definitely to have the planes explode over land or on the ground."

"My prince," *Mukhtar* answered, "I am not stating one or another. My task is to give you the most options."

Martyrdom was on bin Laden's mind. The changes in Sudan had been partly precipitated by a botched suicide attack against the Egyptian interior minister when he was traveling in Ethiopia.[316] Cairo bitterly complained to the State Department and CIA that Khartoum was turning into a terror hub.[317] The subsequent decision by Sudan to ask bin Laden to leave precipitated a debate about suicide bombing as a method of *jihad*.

Bin Laden said that, at first, he questioned self-martyrdom—suicide attack—both on religious grounds and in terms of their available resources. "It was previously just a *Shi'a* disorder," he said, referring to the

Ayatollah Khomeini's authorization of martyrdom following the Iranian revolution. "But I have been talking to the doctor and other wise men about the true meaning of the *surah*, forbidding killing oneself, and we have concluded that it applies only to self-slaughter, to the taking of one's life out of depression or despair. It is a question of intention," the *Sheikh* continued. "Ending one's life in the service of Islam is pure martyrdom. Now I think it is the highest possible honor."[318]

If it was a successful method, *Mukhtar* couldn't fathom what the issue was, but he was in complete agreement that Zawahiri's attacks on political figures wasn't a strategy to pursue for the future. One despot would merely be replaced by another. The current issue for *al Qaeda* was having sufficient and quality resources, which Sudan actually impeded. Since bin Laden left Afghanistan, the organization hadn't thrived. Many brothers were looking to join, but without secure camps, it was hard to accommodate them all.

Mukhtar agreed on the wastefulness of individual killing, but he went on to opine that the creation of the appearance of plots—against the Pope and then against Bill Clinton at Manila's Asia-Pacific Economic Cooperation summit—had been merely tests to check on the workings of the enemy's secret services. What he discovered was the Pope's and Clinton's executive protection increased even more as their visits neared, regardless of any actual threat on the ground.

Mukhtar explained his preparations and he told bin Laden he was hoping to use a future threat against a leader—or even some ruse pointing to a false plot—as a way to divert the enemy's attention from something greater. To KSM, it seemed that certain types of plots got all the attention. Mindful of that, he wanted to take advantage of the practices and presumptions of the secret services.

Bin Laden was grateful that *Mukhtar* shared his thinking on this tactic, he said. He wanted to know all about how the Americans operated and asked for any insight *Mukhtar* might have about attacking the Americans, both in Saudi Arabia and in East Africa.

They continued to talk well into the late afternoon, stopping only to pray and occasionally interrupted by *al Qaeda* businesspeople asking for decisions or for bin Laden to review something.

Mukhtar handed over his handwritten list of 73 *al Qaeda* and affiliated men suspected by the Americans of being terrorists. He didn't say where he had gotten the list, but he had written down all of the names of those he could recognize from the FBI mugshot books in Manila. He knew the *Sheikh* and Abu Hafs would love the information.

Bin Laden was grateful for the "intelligence."

Perusing the list closely, it was only then that the *Sheikh* told *Mukhtar* of a troubled brother from Sudan. His name, bin Laden said, was Jamal al-Fadl.[319]

"And why is he troubled?" *Mukhtar* asked.

"He was working here and stole over $100,000," bin Laden said. "When brother al-Fadl was confronted, he fled."

"And why are you telling me this, my prince?" *Mukhtar* said, looking at the *Sheikh* for guidance.

"Al-Fadl has approached the Saudi government to provide information."

"And?"

"They turned him away. Now we hear he is with the Americans."

"And has he information to provide?"

"Yes," bin Laden said. It seemed that al-Fadl studied in America, like Khalid, and was proficient in English. He worked in the *al-Khifah* center in Brooklyn before going to Afghanistan. Al-Fadl had come with bin Laden to Sudan, dealing with the Khartoum government and helping in other local business matters.

"Did he know anything of my work?" *Mukhtar* asked. "My identity?"

"I don't think so, brother," said bin Laden.

"Does he know *anything* of the planes operation?"

"No—of that I am sure," bin Laden said.

"Then why are you so worried, my *Emir*?"

"It is crack in our foundation," bin Laden said.

"He knows of your money and investments?" Mukhtar asked.

"Of that he knows much."

"We will need to wait and see," bin Laden went on.

"I am ready to begin the preparation for the planes operation," *Mukhtar* announced.

Bin Laden listened carefully to *Mukhtar's* proposal, promising to consider it, asking for his friend's patience in the wake of the latest crackdown in Sudan.

"What are you yet missing, my friend?" bin Laden said.

"We don't have the right men," said Khalid. "Most of our Afghan or Yemeni or Sudanese brothers do not have the skills for America. And we need technical men."

This was no longer going to be a stunt, what he had originally proposed to bin Laden: planes attacking—but with one landing in Washington, KSM aboard and deplaning to hold a press conference and demand capitulation. Now *Mukhtar* and bin Laden agreed that they could all be suicide attacks, directly, into the heart of America's strength.

Bin Laden said that he was working on a public statement broadening the focus of the defensive *jihad* beyond the Arab world. That might attract new adherents, the kind of men *Mukhtar* was seeking.

"My friend," the always soft-spoken bin Laden said, "it is not yet time to attack the bear in its own cave in this way. I am awaiting a report on al-Fadl and where he went, but I want you to know that as we prepare for your grand operation, we must first choose some soft spots, where the defenses of the enemy are weakest.

"I promise you," the *Sheikh* finished, seeing disappointment on Sheikh Mohammed's face, "I will fully support the planes operation when the time is ripe."

PART 5

Chapter 16 Ripley Leaves

Pakistan, 1995

There had been an attack, a pretty sophisticated one, at the Egyptian embassy, the duty officer was telling Charlie over the secure phone.[320] Two men walked up to the chancellery and shot the security detail. Then a taxi loaded with a bomb smashed into the front gate, detonating and blowing it open. That was followed by a second car, a jeep also carrying a bomb, which detonated next to the main chancery building, crumbling its facade. At least sixteen people were killed or missing, the duty officer said, and an estimated fifty or sixty were injured, not counting any civilian bystanders.

Instantly Charlie thought of the terrorist strike that occurred just days before in Riyadh, similarly a car bomb, this one against an American military office of some sort.

"The boss would like you to dig in," the duty officer said.

"And he can't fucking pick up the phone and call me directly?" Charlie growled.

"Give him a call—I think he wanted me to gauge your interest given that you're on your way out."

She was packing up her Islamabad house—not sorry to be leaving Pakistan after four exhilarating but exhausting years. The assignment outside the Middle East hadn't been her first choice after she finished up in Dammam, but it ended up being a dream. Left alone and left on her own by a station chief who was caught up in sustaining Prime Minister

Benazir Bhutto.[321] She was able to venture into Peshawar and back in time, reporting on what everyone thought was a dead end of old rebels who no longer had a cause.

"Can you help?" the chief said when she called him. She thought he'd want to sweep under the rug whatever it was she might report on the increasing strength of international terrorism, the official line of the Bhutto government that *al Qaeda* didn't exist and they had everything under control.

"I can help, but I don't think it will please either Washington or your clients," Charlie responded.

"Washington's pretty hot on Iranian involvement," the chief said. The Agency was opining, he said, that the attacks—Riyadh and Islamabad—were connected because of the similar *Hizb'allah* tactic used in a truck or car driving up to the outside of a building and then detonating a bomb.[322]

"It's the Egyptian embassy, though," Charlie said. "I don't think *Hizb'allah* has any interest in that."

"Parts of a Lebanese passport were recovered in the rubble," the chief said, seeming to rub in anything that would contradict her. Charlie wrote in her exit report just weeks earlier that she thought the focus on Iran was dead wrong, that Osama bin Laden was behind more and more of these attacks. The report was so caustic, it had almost cost her a promotion.

"The Bhutto government is saying that the attack is a message of retribution for cooperation with the United States," the station chief was now saying.

"That's an absurd claim," Charlie interrupted, "and why attack Egypt? It's got to be Zawahiri."

"Look, I know you've already made your handoffs, but could you check?"

"I'm going in alone," she declared. She was already gritting her teeth and annoyed.

"Wouldn't this be a good opportunity for you to impart some wisdom on your replacement? And help him to get to know the source?" the chief said, again almost bating her.

"You want a social visit, or you want information?"

"Fuck you, hard ass. You can have ops support put out the signal for the meet. I'll give you 24 hours to report in."

One last report, she thought, and maybe really the last. Her schoolteacher source[323] wasn't the kind who carried much sway in the increasingly rigid world of relying on host-nation intelligence services for information. And she doubted he would be of much use to the by-the-books case officer they'd sent out to replace her, a guy who'd already told her he wanted to work closely with the ISI, the Pakistani intelligence powerhouse.

God, how the CIA was stuck, she thought—dominated by its relations with its authorized "partners." But it was also dominated by the notion that the measure of American *interest* translated to how many Americans got killed or how large the headlines were back home, each terrorist attack barely registering if that threshold wasn't met. And then on top, the CIA was taking their lead from law enforcement, each terrorist attacks treated separately as a case, any connection made between them only happening if there were an overlapping person.

A half hour later the ops support chief called and said they were arranging the meetup, that they would pick her up at seven in the morning for the two-and-a-half-hour drive to Peshawar.

Charlie's agent, Yusuf, arrived at the safe house right on time, knowing what Ms. Landry wanted to discuss. The embassy attack was all over the Pakistani news, with rescue efforts at the crumbled building aired live on television.

Charlie's security detail gave a "clear signal," and she and Yusef sat in the walled garden, drinking the region's famous green tea, munching on cashews.

"So, you will stay?" he asked. He was slight, with jet black hair cut very short, and a scruffy and untended beard. He wore his normal white *Pathani* suit with flowing pajama pants and a faded floral waistcoat.

"No, my friend. But not to worry, you will be in good hands." Thinking of her replacement, she inwardly blanched at the falsehood.

"It is not myself I am concerned for, but now that Zawahiri's *Islamic Jihad* and *al Qaeda* have joined together, things will undoubtedly heat up here," said Yusef. "*Ripley* may need to come back and save the planet."

He nicknamed her Ripley for the relentless Sigourney Weaver character in the *Alien* movies, just making their way to Pakistan. It was a deeply affectionate endowment.

"Ripley is going to kick your ass right now and then go on a rampage if you don't focus," Charlie answered in Urdu, playing along.

"I did not mean to insult you," Yusuf responded in English. "The gathering hordes would shit their pants if she did," he said, proudly using an American colloquialism.

"And besides, I don't think they would be ready for your attack. Now that suicide is the sanctioned and favored way to die, they're not fighting man-to-man anymore, or even man-to-woman, excuse me."

"No insult taken, Yusuf. Were it only the case that someday Zena could be a Ripley as well," she said, referring to Yusuf's eldest daughter.

"*Insha'Allah*," he responded, their usual routine of small talk and resignation concluded.

Contrary to what the bosses thought, Charlie found Muslim men easy to deal with, not only intrigued by her attentions, but also full of curiosity in the novelty of a rare, non-familial male-female interaction. What male operations officers didn't get, but her and her colleagues had experienced over and over, was that almost every male agent made a move on their female case officers. When male case officers romanced their female assets no one noticed. And Charlie accepted that there might be cases of mutual attraction, where in theory a female case officer fell for a male asset. But it had never happened to her. Yes, there was intimacy, but it was also the intensity of what case officer and agent were doing.

Charlie thought that sometimes men made the move purely because their manly code almost expected it. But once she swatted it away, not making a big deal, she saw that the relationship normalized. And she saw that an additional bond was created from the male-female dance of solicitation and rejection.

Yusuf never came on to her but she'd heard an earful from colleagues about Muslim generals and ministers not only making the move but having to be taught that the CIA women weren't *swallows*, KGB women intended to sexually entrap.

And then there was this: In how many other circumstances could a Muslim man experience propositioning a woman who wasn't a prostitute, get rejected, and afterwards still maintain a cordial relationship? Thus, an association that was already intrinsically intimate was made more so because the man "failed" to be a man. Charlie's experience was that the agent would often then become protective of his love object.

Little of this was taught in CIA courses. It was informally shared between female colleagues. Every female case officer experienced not just approaches but also fended off stupid male colleagues who questioned them. So Charlie, like other women, kept details of the relationship out of operational reporting, to avoid the stupid questions.[324] Still, as she gained experience, she also saw that taking care of her agents, being the natural nurturer, was the root of another kind of relationship, the mother-son relationship, a relationship that men couldn't even conceive of.

"I find it hard to believe that bin Laden would approve of this strike," Charlie said.

"Because he keeps encouraging Zawahiri to expand attacks beyond Egypt?" Yusuf responded.

"Yes, but also if it is related to the attack in Riyadh, why the Egyptian embassy?"

"Why? It is clear: It is the eighteenth anniversary to the day of Anwar Sadat's trip to the Jewish state, to Jerusalem. The Egyptians remember this bitter betrayal. Plus, in your old home, Mubarak is cracking down on *al Qaeda*."[325]

Charlie was immediately chastened that she forgot the anniversary, sorry that she didn't have it on the tip of her tongue to use against the station chief when he questioned her supposition.

Yusuf continued: "But I also think that Zawahiri may have acted in defiance of the *Sheikh* here. I don't have proof, but why strike in Pakistan when they are your indulgent hosts and sponsors?"

"Well, I guess that explains why they didn't go after the U.S. embassy," Charlie responded.

"Yes, true. But even so-called terrorists operate within the laws of physics," Yusef responded. "That building is too well-guarded. You must understand that the leadership may have these desires, but they are constrained by the abilities of the assigned martyrs. They choose the target that they can achieve—probably in both cases, in Saudi Arabia and here. In Riyadh, I read it was an unguarded office building. Here, a minor embassy."

It was true they were easy targets. Zawahiri and bin Laden's growing ranks of internationally-focused *jihadis* wanted to emulate the experience of Beirut, where hundreds died in a truck bomb attack,[326] but sometimes the talent (or the target) just wasn't yet there to do so.

"Do you have any additional information on the Riyadh attack?" asked Charlie.

"Information? No. I have suppositions. From what I am hearing, I think maybe the attacks are to appeal to the dreams of the potential martyrs, to run up the score like in a football match to show that *al Qaeda* is alive, is still alive. And perhaps bin Laden is demonstrating his reach. Judging by the number of Sudan boys who are showing up here. I think everyone believes it now for sure that bin Laden himself will move to Afghanistan for good. If he isn't already here."

"Don't remind me," Charlie responded. Her departure was coming at an inopportune time, she had told Yusef before, knowing that bin Laden was being squeezed out of Khartoum. And now with Riyadh and Islamabad connected, it seemed like there was increasing connective tissue.

When she'd arrived in Pakistan, old-timers told Charlie that the country's North-West Frontier Province wasn't nearly as lively as it was "in the day." They said that the old *jihadis* had dispersed and were gone. But then came the attack on American peacekeepers in Somalia[327] and the bombing of the World Trade Center in New York. No one connected the two, but there was connection, Charlie thought. And when the World Trade Center perpetrator Ramzi Yousef showed up in Pakistan and was then linked to an assassination attempt on Benazir Bhutto's life,[328] Charlie thought something was jelling. Her station chief completely rejected her supposition, telling her that Pakistani intelligence concluded the American fugitive was acting alone. The ISI whisperers were also insisting that they had better control than ever in the Northwest Frontier, a boast that Charlie knew to be wrong. Pakistan's Wild West region was still the confluence of above and below ground. Benazir Bhutto's government barely extended its reach or control over the country's fourth largest city, or any of the territory beyond.

As Charlie contemplated her new assignment, she reflected on the influences still tugging on the Agency's perspective. When Robert Gates became Agency director after Desert Storm,[329] he threw himself into the task of reducing the ranks of the senior Soviet-oriented officers with the end of the Cold War.[330] It was a good and important move. But with that internal shift came a flood of Soviet Division survivors looking for careers in the Middle East and South Asia. The effect in places like Pakistan was immediate, for with them came all of the biases of classic Soviet espionage culture. That meant that spies—"assets," in CIA lingo—existed for the purpose of giving or selling *secrets* to America. Secrets were defined as classified information in the possession of foreign governments. When these old Cold Warriors pondered terrorism at all, they saw clandestine state-sponsorship and Marxist movements, which to them not just meant Iran—or in the case of Pakistan: India—but it also meant a formal hierarchy. The old guard operations officers couldn't conceive of bin Laden-style terrorism, in his independence from any state and with his own objectives. And in the way he also inspired, but didn't always control. Charlie tried to undertake her own re-education about this but found that the old-timers were basically uninterested in terrorism as a subject. It neither constituted a recruitment opportunity involving the penetration of any foreign government, nor was *terrorism* a place that suggested any kind of desirable assignment. Now with Yusef's remark about *al Qaeda's* limitations based upon its people, she could see that there were American limitations of almost exactly the same origin.

It wasn't a surprise, therefore, that Iran kept popping up as "the culprit" behind these attacks—it was the *state sponsor*, convenient even in Pakistan to downplay any domestic dirty laundry. Charlie recalled her Saudi police lieutenant and his dogged attachment to Saudi *Shi'a* and *Shi'ism* as the enemy, that Iran was his explanation for everything. And then for the old-timers there was also the humiliation factor. Ever since the United States was humiliated in the taking of its embassy during the Iranian revolution,[331] Washington's presumption was to go to Iran first as the enemy.

So when the attack occurred in Riyadh, even though it was a group loosely affiliated with bin Laden, the FBI and the CIA both came to the conclusion that it was Iranian inspired.[332] That was convenient for the Saudis, who wanted Iran and not bin Laden to be the answer. Four Saudis quickly confessed on television[333] and were beheaded before any American ever got near them.[334]

Charlie thought it malpractice that the Agency followed the lead of its princely whisperers and the presumption of state sponsorship. And now after Desert Storm? If Iran wasn't the culprit, Washington almost bent over backwards to find Saddam Hussein's Iraq behind new attacks.

Perhaps back at Langley headquarters, in her new assignment, she could change some minds. She was pretty apprehensive about her upcoming Washington posting, despite the promotion and the Agency affirmation of her terrorism expertise. It would be a supervisory position heading *al Qaeda* analysis and action. But the subject of terrorism still played second fiddle to great power politics and weapons of mass destruction, or anything having to do with Washington's crisis of the day, and she could see how arguing too strongly about bin Laden and this new world of international terrorism would get her into trouble.

As the afternoon sun softened, Charlie and Yusef discussed the attacks in Riyadh and Islamabad. They lingered over cups of tea, neither wanting to part. Yusuf had rebuffed payment and had refused to take any but the most minor gifts in their time together. If there was a deal, it would be that the Agency would facilitate his children's education in the West, preferably in the United States. He was a relentless taskmaster at drilling English into them. But Yusef also expressed to Charlie on more than one occasion that he was not optimistic about the future.

"And your future?" he asked again, a question he'd posed on their last meeting.

Charlie had always been reluctant to share anything for real, but now she said, "I will spend Christmas with my family for the first time in years."

"You are Christian? But I assumed …"

"Yusuf, my friend, the day our world doesn't care what religion I am will be the day the true God will finally have a rest."

"So," he said, lifting his teacup. "To the eighth day of creation."

"The eighth day," she said, raising her glass.

Chapter 17 Oval Office

President Clinton got an abrupt erection when she lifted her blazer and showed him the straps of the thong extending above the back of her pants. He instantly wanted her, feeling that terrible wrenching that had swept him into such huge messes and self-compromises in the past.[335]

They'd made eye contact a couple of times earlier, this young thing with her dark hair and fulsome breasts.

He didn't ask himself why *she* was there on a Wednesday afternoon when the place was almost deserted. There was a government shutdown, Congress failing to pass a new appropriation. And that meant mandatory work furloughs going into effect all over the city, even at the White House.

Despite the shutdown, his economic advisors were cheerfully predicting that the Dow Jones Industrial Average would soon top 5,000 for the first time ever. It was the first year that the stock market index surpassed two millennium marks.[336] A Bosnian peace agreement was close at hand, the parties at that moment secluded in Ohio, the progress of negotiations being delivered to Clinton almost by the hour.[337]

Monica whispered to *him* that she had a crush. She kissed him passionately in the windowless hallway adjacent to his private study. She wrote her name and telephone number on a piece of paper and put it in his pants pocket, intentionally running her hand over his excruciating hardness as she did.

No one could possibly understand the pressures of living the way he did, the decisions, the events, the ceremonies, the responsibilities of power. Every piece of news, every photo-op, every conversation and phone call was logged and scrutinized, a happy and optimistic look constantly plastered on his face in public while inside, every thought circling back to the ugliness of the world, one he had become achingly familiar with and had become the nation's holy custodian of.

He'd just been to Arlington National Cemetery, God, not his first time, dedicating a memorial to the victims of Pan Am Flight 103.[338] It was heartbreaking, consoling the families, explaining the unexplainable.

But the Lockerbie case and Libya's culpability behind the bombing seemed almost simple compared to the assassination of his friend Yitzhak Rabin, the Israel prime minister and his partner in pursuing peace. He was gunned down in Tel Aviv by a fellow Jew, an extremist who opposed negotiations. It was a kind of hatred unfathomable to most Americans, even in this America of hyper-partisan bickering.[339]

All in a week's work.

Israel was perennial, intractable, and inextricable.

Then there was that bastard Saddam Hussein. His games were exasperating, constantly pushing the mustachioed asshole to the top of the presidential inbox, a strain on everyone's patience and an argument in favor of the CIA's efforts to topple his regime.[340]

The experts told him right after the New Year that the U.N. was close to certifying Baghdad clean of WMD after four years of inspections. Then, in a story Hollywood couldn't have concocted, a secret biological weapons program was discovered. Saddam's right-hand man defected to Jordan with other officials, a couple of Saddam's daughters in tow. There was a chicken farm and buried documents and, Jesus, then everything regarding a negotiated solution fell apart, disarmament sent back to square one.

And Clinton was supposed to do what? File another protest? More sanctions? Conduct another missile attack? The options were poised to move forward so effortlessly, all he had to do was just push the invisible magic button.

Those breasts, firm and plump, mother and child, a childhood and a cold mother and a compulsion the president didn't even want to think about.

Now there was an attack in Saudi Arabia as well? In a country that usually stayed deep in the shadows.

He read the intelligence report of the bombing of an American facility in Riyadh two days earlier. A car carrying a 220-pound bomb pulled into a parking lot adjacent to a small office building belonging to something called the Office of the Program Manager Saudi Arabian National Guard, or OPM-SANG.[341] Occupied by U.S. servicemen and corporate contractors, five people were killed and almost four dozen injured when the car bomb detonated; one large explosion followed by a smaller one five minutes later.[342]

He only half paid attention to his reading, a hyena sniffing the air for an enfeebled newborn. He smelled out the pink pass, the special pass given to interns at the White House, a pass that signaled everything: young, beginner, outsider, stop, so innocent as to not even be the color red.

He was annoyed by the range of opinions offered by the bureaucracy on the Riyadh attack. The news media was all over the map: the attack was political retaliation for King Fahd's support for the Israeli peace accords.[343] Or perhaps the attack was the product of continuing hostility between Saddam Hussein and Saudi Arabia. Or even that it was the result of Saudi-Iranian rivalry for domination of the Gulf. Some in the CIA were saying it was *Hizb'allah*, the Lebanese group, or at least some Saudi version under Iranian influence.[344]

He had a call put through to his ambassador to Saudi Arabia, Ray Mabus,[345] a fellow governor of Mississippi and an old friend.

They exchanged laconic pleasantries, Ray's agreeable voice and Southern nature in sync with the president. He was nobody's fool.

"Mr. President," he drawled. "The attack was most likely the work of something called the Islamic Movement for Change, a group that earlier issued threats against Americans in Saudi Arabia.[346] They said, Mr. President, that if the Americans didn't leave, they would take some kind of quote *violent actions*."[347]

"And this was reported forward?" Clinton asked.

"Indeed, it was, Mr. President. I'm guessing the air boys at the main base increased their security with the threat.[348] But this building that was attacked? Probably no one even thought of it as part of the U.S. military presence here, it's so off the reservation. These guys have nothing to do with Iraq and they been here since the '70s."

"And this organization does what, Ray?"

"It trains and equips the Saudi National Guard, S.A.N.G. Office of Program Management—O.P.M. That's the acronym, pronounced O-P-M-Sang, just as it's spelled."

"And the National Guard's not the Saudi military?"

"Not exactly."

"It's like our National Guard?"

"Think more like a palace guard, like a counterweight to the actual Saudi military, which I guess some think could be a threat."[349]

"A threat to whom, Ray?"

"Mr. President. Were the princes all to turn on each other, I know, I know, it's crazy. But it is a family affair and the National Guard counters the military which fights the Interior Ministry and on and on. It was created in 1963, a kind of palace guard, all fine and good except that the king was then assassinated by his own nephew. One could say that that didn't work."

"And this is for real, Ray?" the president asked. "The National Guard still protects the king? Like the Secret Service?"

"Mr. President. Go down that road of who belongs to what family and who's zoomin' who and it's like asking what's behind all the money appropriated for highway construction projects in Mississippi. You just really don't want to know."

"Yeah, Ray, I get your drift … keep in touch."

The summary appended to the bombing report did mention *Sunni* radicals, but not the group Ray spoke about.[350] And it quoted at length from the latest National Intelligence Estimate on terrorism.[351] That report pretty much ignored any particular terrorist group, making no mention of this Islamic Movement for Change. God, there were so many organizations, Clinton thought.

Going over the language of the draft intelligence estimate again, Clinton was annoyed that it predicted that future threats would come from "transient groupings of individuals similar to that drawn together by Ramzi Yousef," the perpetrator of the World Trade Center attack. It seemed to him that the national agencies were making a prediction that was the exact opposite of what was occurring. That is, as Ray said, if an organized entity had indeed been behind the attack in Riyadh.

And how come no one tied the Riyadh attack to King Fahd's deteriorating physical condition? Especially if, as Mabus said, it was targeted on an entity protecting the monarchy?

The folks at the CIA delivered a report to the White House on the Saudi king's health, saying he had had numerous small strokes and was losing grip on day-to-day rule. A heavy smoker in his sixties and grossly overweight, his briefers said he suffered from arthritis and severe diabetes. Much of the running of the country had already been given over to Crown Prince Abdullah,[352] the very same guy who was Faisal's brother. All in the family.

Clinton wrote a note in the margin of the intelligence paper, asking for more information about the guys Ray mentioned.

Some on the White House staff had been pushing something called *al Qaeda*, an outgrowth of the Afghanistan war and—*again*—an organization headed by a wealthy young Saudi, sort of contradicting the transient groupings theory.[353]

Organized group or not, fortunately no one was clamoring for retaliation. And despite Americans killed, it was hardly more than a one-day news story. Still, everyone seemed to have an opinion.

That *everyone* included three of his least favorite people.

First was the smarmy Saudi ambassador to Washington, Prince Bandar. Sandy Berger[354] said he was seeking a private meeting with him, but he told his national security advisor to take care of him. Of course, the Saudi government vowed to quickly track down those responsible for the Riyadh attack. Well, fuck them.

Then there was that God-like associate director of Central Intelligence, that sanctimonious auditor who headed his Apex Watch, the president's own, that guy Bowlen. He delivered unwelcome morsels on Democratic Party supporters who were on the Saudi take, snooping into bank accounts and shady deals, and now called on him to tell him that he had intelligence on Riyadh as well, intelligence that the Agency didn't seem to have. He was a Wizard of Oz who frightened Clinton. Bowlen's very existence—his special status outside the Agency—magnified how powerless Clinton felt as president.

And, finally, there was that shit-for-brains FBI director Louis Freeh that Clinton had appointed.[355] Told by everyone that he'd be above politics, Clinton agreed to the squeaky-clean gumshoe. But then Freeh turned out to be quite puritanical, and when it came to women—and then the many accusations of corruption—he'd become enemy number one and a major thorn in his side. Now Janet Reno was telling him that Freeh wanted to go to Riyadh and sort things out. As Clinton saw it, nothing good could come of *that*.[356]

Freeh was practically untouchable, Italian-American from a working-class New Jersey family, Rutgers grad, clean-cut, and the quintessential lawman. But Clinton felt that he was carrying out his own *jihad* against him and his White House. He was dying to call that fellow Bowlen to ask him to look in Freeh's finances, but he'd be damned if he was going to ask that fucker for a favor and then be beholden to him, the wizard of true odds who could pry into anyone's finances. And on his authority.

He thought of Monica again—her willingness, her lips, those breasts. He walked by the chief of staff's office; on the odd chance she was still there.

She was. Sitting there alone, despite the hour.

Why don't you meet me in George's office in ten minutes? he asked, returning to his private study. George Stephanopoulos.[357]

She came into the darkened study and they kissed, she unbuttoning her jacket to reveal an already-unhooked bra. He fondled her breasts and pulled her closer to suck on them. The president put his hands down her pants and touched her. The phone rang and he sat down to take it, she unzipping his pants and taking his penis into her mouth. He got hard but didn't skip a beat in the conversation.

It was the White House Situation Room duty officer. There was another terrorist attack, this one in Islamabad. Normally he might not be alerted, especially because it was the Egyptian embassy, but coming so close to the Riyadh attacks, his aides thought he should be aware.[358]

He hung up the phone, telling her to stop.

Let me make you come, she pleaded.

He said he needed to wait until he trusted her more.

"It was real nice," he assured, "something I haven't had in a long time."

She smiled. He was indifferent to whether it was true, shamelessly aware of the ultimate seduction to a rube's needy ears.

Two nights later, pizza delivered to the skeletal staff, Clinton prowled again, a demonic sleepwalker, luring her back into the private study where they again kissed. She was nervous that she would be missed at her desk and Clinton released her. But then he insisted that she bring him some pizza and his private secretary acted as madam.

"Sir, the girl's here with the pizza," she said, showing Ms. Lewinsky into the Oval Office, leaving them together, safeguarding the door.

Again, he fondled and sucked her breasts. While he took an FBI-related call from a member of Congress, he unzipped his pants and she got on her knees and pleasured his member as well.

That Boy Scout Freeh. Whatever program there was, his FBI director couldn't get with it. In announcing his appointment, Clinton called Freeh "a law enforcement legend," and it was true the federal prosecutor had worked complex organized-crime and narcotics cases. He'd risen in the ranks—the first FBI agent to have gone from the bottom to director since J. Edgar Hoover, just what the Bureau needed, everyone told Clinton.[359]

The president told Freeh on their first meeting that he wanted the FBI to take the lead on investigating incidents involving weapons of mass destruction. And yet. First there was the disaster at Waco.[360] And that wouldn't go away. And then there was the overreaction to Hillary's healthcare work. And then *Nannygate. Whitewater. Wampumgate.*

The president understood that FBI directors were intentionally meant to be quirky independents, the theory being that they were insulated from politics by their ten-year appointments, above the partisan fray precisely because they had to investigate even the high and mighty.

But what was more important than loose nukes?[361] The crumbling former Soviet nuclear arsenal, materials unaccounted for, storage facilities poorly guarded, plutonium and uranium and even worse making their way on to the open market? A whole generation of well-paid Soviet scientists, the only minds behind the iron curtain who were ever recognized as America's equal, were now underemployed while also in possession of *knowledge*. This is what Clinton's intelligence agencies were telling him. It was knowledge that needed to be protected from the likes of Saddam and *now* this Saudi guy, Osama bin Laden.

But Freeh wasn't interested in WMD. And whatever the FBI *was* interested in with regard to these attacks, they weren't sharing.

When the president asked about the Bureau's hoarding of information, he got a lot of bureaucratic *blah, blah, blah*. Everyone had some quip. Some applied the easy maxim to understand the difference between the cultures of intelligence and law enforcement as merely "string em' along" versus "string em' up." Others said it was birdwatchers versus bird hunters. Someone told him the FBI played man-to-man while the CIA played a zone defense. Clinton found them all clever characterizations, but none of it helped him to understand this new enemy.

Now Clinton had no power because he and his FBI director weren't talking, the devout Roman Catholic beyond not just politics, but even national security, a sanctimonious prig who thought himself above everyone else, particularly him.

Chapter 18 The Lunch

The walls of Mrs. Rothwell's office were covered with postcards from around the world, mostly the Middle East but with a smattering of others from odd corners of the world: the Philippines, Japan, Brazil. They'd evidently begun on a bulletin board long ago and then spilled over on to the wall and were now encroaching onto every blank space, thumbtacked to bookcases, taped to file cabinets, down walls and even under the table in the corner.

"Crazy, isn't it?" she said, walking in behind Charlie, noticing her looking at the colorful postcards. "It's become sort of a challenge."

Bowlen introduced the two women, and Mrs. Rothwell worked with Charlie on the paperwork for her new job at Apex Watch.[362]

"We do this much travel?" she asked, assuming they were postcards being sent back to the secretary from the staff.

"Yes, we do, but these ones are all from Khalid Sheikh Mohammed. He travels the world and is a compulsive correspondent."[363]

"Huh," Charlie exclaimed to no one in particular. She was looking at a postcard of the very hotel she'd stayed at when she was in Dammam, Saudi Arabia during Operation Desert Shield.

"This one's from him, too?" she asked, pointing to the postcard.

"All of them are."

"Mind if I take a look?" Charlie asked.

"Please."

It was dated August 12, 1990, just days after the Iraqi invasion of Kuwait. In neat English script, he wrote:

> *Spending a few days in this lovely place arranging for my mother's resetelment* [sic]. *She barely made it out of our home before the horde arrived. Go get them! Khalid.*[364]

"Most of the postcards he just inserts into envelopes and packages, some he sends with funny greetings," Mrs. Rothwell was saying as Charlie was wondering whether she and Khalid Sheikh Mohammed overlapped in Dammam. "I think Mr. Bowlen told him long ago that they were appreciated. Every year on his anniversary of being an operative, he asks that we send him a photo of the gallery; that's the game. I suppose somewhere in Pakistan there's a picture on a wall of a room that's supposed to not exist. Tony takes the picture. And as head of security he scrubs away anything that might give away any information."

Charlie never learned Mrs. Rothwell's first name. She was maybe in her late sixties, tall and quite good looking, thin-faced and skinny as a rail. She had straight greying black hair pulled into a tight bun and she wore two beautiful tiny diamond studs in her ears. As Charlie would discover, she was hardly just a secretary—part adjutant, part chaplain and mother hen to all who worked at Apex Watch.

"Before we get started, I just want to make sure I didn't commit some *faux pas* right out of the gates," said Mrs. Rothwell.

"What's that?" Charlie asked.

"I took the liberty of ordering a Lebanese *mezze* for lunch and then thought you might take it as an insult."

"Oh, not at all," Charlie said rubbing her hands together. "Let's hope it's a good one."

"The staff eats all of their meals here, so I try to mix it up. Please don't hold back on asking for anything—teas, snacks, favorite soda. It can get isolating out here. We're not allowed to go to any establishment in the area and Roy—have you met him yet, Mr. Bowlen's driver?—brings food and meals in every day. I don't know if Lawrence showed you the kitchen and the breakroom on your way in, but we try to make it as homey as possible."

Lawrence. That was a first. Someone did call him that.

"I really try to keep everyone happy, not because I don't want them to go home, but because it's often very intense here. And when something's happening, many people don't go home."

The older woman smiled kindly. "Let's get started, shall we? Our cover employer is Exceptional Research Technologies—you probably saw the sign on the road and the motto 'Comprehensive information products, solutions, and services,'" she said with a bob of the head. "Your real identity and any traveling legends we establish will always track back to the call center, located here on the first floor. We deal with our cover stories separately from the CIA. Anytime you think you need something, including an immediate blackout, call the 202 number, which will ring here at the duty officer. You are covered at the Agency as well, and at the FBI, but they know nothing else about you other than to make any referral back to Tony and his people. Though you don't formally work for the Agency anymore, if pressed by a U.S. government officer, you can say that you work for a CIA organization called Special Purpose. That also will track back to Tony."

Mrs. Rothwell looked down at a piece of paper on her desk, her checklist. "Despite being off the government grid and secret, our motto is simplicity. Mr. Bowlen is quite different than Hal Jones, our first director. His counsel is always to take the simplest approach, even in overseas travel: no black helicopters, no entourages, no first class except for long international flights, normal lives as much as possible. Washington is its own cover. Overseas, Tony and his people are in charge of travel and security. That is a strict absolute.

"In your case, because of KSM, we're severing your formal CIA employment and you won't have access to Langley. But don't worry. Your time of service, taxes, social security, pension, etc., will accrue and remain the same."

"KSM?"

"Khalid or not," Mrs. Rothwell said, "Khalid was dubbed KSM on his original CIA contact sheet, less of a mouthful that Khalid Sheikh Mohammed.[365] And so, it stuck."

"Pension," Charlie jokingly said. "Anybody retire?" she asked, realizing too late that she was being too flippant.

"Only Mr. Jones, our first boss. I suppose you haven't met him yet, but you will, I'm sure. We do have a couple of permanent leaves and disability cases as well. And there are a couple of annuitants that you can ask for if you need additional hands, especially for translations. They are very good. Mr. Bowlen takes care of everyone very well and we sort of follow our own rules."

"But, Ms. Charbel," she said, obviously wanting her undivided attention for what she said next, "there are rules."

Since everyone working for Apex Watch was former Agency or from inside some government secret agency, they seemed to skip over the security clearance and basic employment paperwork. Instead, they went through the cover story for Exception Research Technologies, which also had a suite of offices downtown that Charlie could use as a base if necessary. And there was a storehouse and a backup of the financial files in a town called Elkridge, near the BWI airport.

Mrs. Rothwell explained a bit of the history of Apex Watch, its move to this Maryland compound in the Reagan years, its cutting-edge use of technology, and its internal organization. The KSM project was small.

"I assume there are other case officers," said Charlie.

"Oh yes, there are. Of course," Mrs. Rothwell answered. "But there has never really been any other case officer for KSM, so congratulations, my dear."

"And the reason for that?"

"For over a decade, Mr. Bowlen has handled Khalid. Therefore, you are quite unique. Up until now, KSM has also been a bit of a sideline for us. Hal Jones doubted his usefulness, but Mr. Bowlen insisted on keeping him on."

"Mr. Jones is the cover name or a real name?"

Mrs. Rothwell laughed. "A real name, though Khalid uses the 'Mr. Jones' name to refer to Mr. Bowlen as well, I think because he has never believed that Jones was anyone's true name."

"So, Mr. Bowlen isn't Mr. Bowlen to KSM?"

"No, he's Mr. Jones as well," she answered, almost giggling. "I suppose it's Khalid's inside joke. But Mr. Bowlen found it convenient and 'Mr. Jones' stuck. After Mr. Bowlen originally introduced them—Hal Jones and KSM, that is—Khalid laughed that it was like in the movies."

"So, what's changed in bringing me on?" Charlie asked, probing for more information, hoping for some different answer.

"Dear, I'll leave the operational explanations to the chief, but let's just say that now that our man is becoming more substantively productive—and active—I think the consensus is that we need more help and a full-time watcher. KSM needs a real handler, a contemporary."

"And the switch to a female?"

"What about it?" Mrs. Rothwell responded.

"It won't be a problem with him?"

"I imagine Khalid will be delighted, Ms. Charbel. I've never met him but I certainly have a sense of how unique he is."

They continued their orientation and, as lunchtime neared, Mrs. Rothwell walked Charlie upstairs to the breakroom. It had been carved out of old offices and occupied an entire corner of the building, looking out on a pastoral scene of greenery and woods. The institutional kitchen was gigantic, but the dining area was homey and welcoming, painted in a pleasing off white with pictures on the walls and actual lamps, like someone raided a thrift store. There were small tables at the windows and three long tables in the middle, set with table linens and real plates and silverware in a U shape. A young man and woman scurried around laying out the *mezze* dishes, as full and as festive as any banquet Charlie had ever seen in Lebanon.

There were about 30 people in the room and Bowlen was chatting in the corner. Upon Charlie's approach, a flurry of hands extended to shake hers. Mrs. Rothwell introduced each person, a flood of names and titles that Charlie instantly forgot. Everyone said welcome. They all seemed truly glad to see her. Bowlen obviously created that rare thing: an organization that hung together and seemed happy.

"Charlie, I won't expect you to remember everyone's name today," Bowlen whispered, directing her to the table and her place at the base of the U. Standing to her right, he looked down at Charlie as the others took their seats. "I apologize that we don't have some fantastic Lebanese wine and beer. We do make believe we do some work here."

Everyone laughed.

"I hate to put you on the spot, but we do have our own little traditions here, and since we don't get that many newcomers, our rule is for the rookie to introduce themselves in a sort of free-for-all history and therapy session. I caution you, Ms. Charbel, they can be brutal. So, you have the floor."

"Hello," Charlie spoke, standing up. "First of all, thank you so much for the warm welcome. It's been quite a week for me. Truth be told, I never imagined this."

"Tell us where you grew up, dear, and what drew you to the Agency," prompted Mrs. Rothwell.

"My full name is Marina Rafqa Charbel. I'm Lebanese American, a Maronite—a Christian, and I grew up in Danbury, Connecticut. But all my life, probably because I was a tomboy and loved hanging out with my many domino-playing uncles, I've been called Charlie.

"My family came to America after the Second World War, where they joined a noisy clan of related merchants already settled here. There's really nothing extraordinary about my upbringing: large family, *large* family of busybodies and matchmakers. For some reason, I took to the Arab language growing up, which set me apart from my contemporaries, but other than that, I was a loudmouth student council ying-yang in high school and worked in my uncle's grocery store. Then, as reward for getting straight A's, the family sent me to Lebanon for the summer when I was 16."

Everyone was eating, passing dishes around, spooning hummus and baba ghanoush and tabbouleh from the heaps, but also paying close attention.

Charlie went on. "I gotta say I instantly fell in love with the place. Even amidst the Israeli occupation of the south,[366] I had a glorious time. I spent my summer hanging with cousins and friends on the Corniche, luxuriating in the Baabda hills, soaking up the sounds and smells of a nation flourishing in the middle of war. I made up my mind then and there that I wanted a life of international service. I just wasn't out of my mind yet."

Everyone laughed.

"I came back even more of a smart aleck than I left, one who could really speak the language with all of its idiom. It was a tongue that most of the kids of my parents' generation avoided."

"Any contact with *Hizb'allah* or other radical groups?" someone asked.

"I was aware of the *Shi'a* minorities, but being Christian and an American, it seemed pretty remote, even in the same city. And because of the soldiers and militias everywhere in Beirut in those days, there were also pretty clear no-go zones. Terrorism then was pretty much focused on the Israelis or the international military presence. So even though there was a war on, I didn't really feel it."

"Your family didn't worry about your safety?"

"Yes, they did. But nothing was ever spoken directly, the cousins I hung with faced the same realities in their daily life. Before I even knew what it meant, I'd say everyone had pretty good situational awareness of the boundaries. And to anyone wishing us harm, we were just local kids."

"Did you worry about being a kidnapping target?" a young woman asked.

"No," she said, "not really. I was a nobody. And that's also the thing about Lebanon. Covered or uncovered, no one gets into anyone else's business. The fact that I was American was probably unknown outside of the small circle I hung out with."

"Isn't that biased? People are killing each other all the time there?" the young woman asked. She was maybe 30, Charlie thought, very pretty.

"Yeah. It's probably romanticized. But that was also my experience over many years of returning. I spent three more summers there when I was in college ..."

"Yale," Bowlen interrupted.

"Woo!" more than one voice said.

"Skull and bones," said another.

"Please," Charlie said, "scholarship girl, and not only that, but I studied *Near Eastern Languages and Civilizations*. That's what they called the department, as if the modern day doesn't even exist. I loved the place, and my professors, but as soon as I got to the Agency and my first posting in Egypt, I realized how little I really knew. They didn't call it languages and civilizations for nothing."

"But you were telling us a story," Mrs. Rothwell interjected, "about your time in Lebanon. How did you feel when you came back to the States?"

Charlie thought for a moment. "When I returned from Beirut, I got lots of questions from my contemporaries who were pretty intent on putting the old country behind them, wanting to believe that Lebanon wasn't *really* them, and that it wasn't even like the rest of the messy Middle East. But the old-timers? They reminisced with me and pined after the place. And about their people."

"And you felt what?" asked another voice, a man, Charlie thought maybe one of the tech guys if she remembered properly.

"I thought Lebanon was different, that it had not yet unlocked the secret of coexistence. Maybe I'm more jaundiced today, but Lebanon's the key."

"And Israel?" an older woman asked. Barbara, Charlie thought. She kicked herself for not remembering.

Charlie was extra cautious in addressing the radioactive place. "I think both sides firmly believe they are protecting themselves from the other. But other—other is the operative word."

"Have you been to Israel?" she asked.

"No."

And the woman harrumphed. She was the other, Charlie thought.

Charlie continued. "I came to love the old country, though, so I know I'm biased, and of course my family is unabashedly Lebanese, stuck in the middle. But maybe also a little hopeful.

"Here's one funny story: I remember my Uncle Gerios kept asking question after question about my third trip, obviously fishing for something. Finally, I asked: 'What, Uncle? What is it you want to know?'

"And he says, shrugging his shoulders apologetically, but also completely serious: 'I just thought that perhaps in these trips that a nice Maronite boy might return in your luggage.'

"And without batting an eye, I spit back كذبة قديمة all proud of my slang."

"Old fool," translated Bowlen.

"Yes, maybe that was a bit too harsh—probably 'old goat' would have been more respectful," Charlie said. "I said 'Old fool, I would have brought one back, but my butchering skills are not yet good enough to make one fit in my suitcase …'"

More laughter. The tables were filled half with women. They understood the truth about the Agency and their families, the pressure to find a husband. And, also, the need to skillfully navigate these cultures and their own culture.

"I guess the answer to your previous question of how I changed was that I picked up the tragedy and the Old-World humor—something I've found in other parts of the region. And when it isn't there, the humor I mean, when someone can't tell a joke, I know I've come upon a religious fanatic or a true *jihadi*. I don't mean to devalue *jihad*," she added. "It's my experience, that the humor … it goes with humanity."

She hesitated. "Where was I? Eventually, a history professor who liked me suggested, with my language skills and interest in the world, perhaps I'd might want to look at the Foreign Service, which seemed utterly boring to me. I threw caution to the wind and tried the Agency. But to tell you the truth, the moment I sat down with the intake officer in Arlington who told me that with *foreign* parents and so much time abroad in an iffy country—he didn't have to say 'girl,' the misogynist asshole—that I might make a good support officer or analyst, that's when I decided—before I even knew what it was or what it meant—that I was going to be an operations officer. No insult meant to the analysts here.

"As I think is the case with so many who join the Agency, I got lucky," Charlie continued. "Midway through intake, the DO[367] plucked me out of the assembly line and invited me to be a NOC."

A NOC, non-official cover case officer, pronounced "knock." Normally, a new case officer would go to Camp Peary, the so-called "Farm"[368] for training, and then through extensive orientation at headquarters, putting time in on different desks, being indoctrinated into the institutional ways of the spy agency. But the first-tour NOC program dispensed with all that, plunging potential case officers right into the field. Rather than relying on a fake State Department or other agency identity card associated with an embassy or consulate employee, the clandestine officer would be given a non-government undercover persona and sent to their posting "clean," that is, officially unconnected with the United States government and without its formal diplomatic protections.

"I finished training the week Oliver North began his testimony on the Iran-Contra scandal,[369] and unbelievably, the CIA sent me to actual graduate school in Cairo. It was a dream come true."

"Did being a NOC make a difference?" another woman asked.

"A graduate student of an appropriate age isn't necessary anomalous," Charlie answered. "But no overt association with the embassy meant that I could interact with radicals more than I might have otherwise done. I guess I could have gone the route of developing ties in the business community or some other specialty, but radicalism, that's what was right in front of me."

"And did you do so, develop ties?" she asked.

"I learned, and observed, learning as well that, in Egypt, domestic developments in the realm of terrorism were of little interest to the Agency unless the subject related to political parties or tangentially to Israel."

"Not even from the Egypt desk?" pushed the woman she thought was Barbara.

"That was my experience. I became obsessed with the Blind *Sheikh* but couldn't interest anyone in his activities."

"Did you run into the FBI's project?" she asked.

"No," Charlie said, not wanting to quite admit that she didn't know what the FBI project was. "I sure did inquire, though, particularly in how he got an American visa."[370]

"It was pretty closely held in those days. The FBI thought they could use him as a lure to discover *jihadis* in America," Barbara said. "And the Agency was doing a favor for the Egyptians. None of that worked …"

"It sure would have been nice to know the context out there in the field," Charlie said, obviously annoyed.

"We knew just as little at the Counterterrorist Center," Barbara answered. "As you know, liaison relationships, especially when they are handled on the seventh floor, create their own problems. Who knows what Mubarak or his secret police chief told the president? Or, frankly, even the CIA director? We just weren't privy."

"Okay, people," Bowlen interrupted, "We will be able to take this up more. Ms. Charbel, I'm being a bad host. Sit down and eat something. We'll go around the table and everyone can introduce themselves."

One by one, they said something, again a flurry of names and titles. Four case officers, Charlie thought, at least here at lunch, communications people, and a bunch of analysts and technicians. She ate and they talked about what they did and what they worked on. Barbara mentioned that she worked with Steve Draper before coming to Apex Watch.

Charlie gave her the once over. A little overweight, mousey, her hair done in French braids. She imagined cats. Not Steve's type. Somehow that made her feel better.

Chapter 19 Orientation

"He was studying for a master's degree when Iraq invaded Kuwait," Bowlen was telling Charlie.[371] "Khalid's mother and the rest of the family barely escaped as Iraqi troops advanced south along the coast. That invasion, I'd say, solidified Khalid's relationship with bin Laden. That is, that once bin Laden spoke up against the war, he grew to actually admire him beyond the Soviet war. I know that this was the time period when you were in Saudi Arabia as well, so I think you'll particularly find his alternate history revealing."

They were in an office building on L Street in downtown Washington, one of those sterile boxes filled with consultancies and law firms.[372] Charlie's last day at the CIA was bittersweet, everyone genuinely sorry to see her go. Steve hung back and thankfully didn't make a big deal or a big speech; in short, didn't make it about himself. They'd gone out to dinner that evening and made small talk, Charlie not in the mood to be interrogated, Steve sensing that he'd better keep it light. And she'd gone home to her own apartment afterwards, saying she had a big day in front of her, but really in no mood for either sex or some kind of long-drawn-out conversation that she knew her pent-up and neurotic love had in store.

"It would have been nice to know at the time that we had eyes on bin Laden," Charlie tartly interjected to Bowlen's opening chatter. "I mean, it's bad enough today. But in those days, even those who'd heard of him mostly dismissed him as a comical figure, as a rich kid squandering his fortune on some fake revolution. I forwarded a couple of atmospheric reports at the time showing his growing popularity with the street, but no one really took notice."

"I read those reports, Ms. Charbel. They were very good. They're in our archives."

"Can you call me Charlie or Marina now that we are working together? My mother is Mrs. Charbel."

"Okay. Charlie. I'm sympathetic to your grievance, but here at Apex Watch we possess intelligence on all sorts of events, all sorts of people. A lot of it should get more attention."

He continued: "What you said about doing better at counter-terrorism is precisely why I want you here. Not just with Khalid, but in other ways, we have access to intelligence that might be of value to others. First Khalid, but an overarching question for you to ponder is how we might make better use of what we have, and what we can get.

"Having said that, let me point out that much of the Saudi-related intelligence we pull in—the Apex take and our financial monitoring of the movement of dirty money—is stuff that I'm not sure the CIA would know what to do with if it had it. It's not always foreign intelligence. And in that sense, it's more in the domain of the FBI. And yet, God forbid we give it to the Bureau."

"And why's that?" Charlie asked.

"Well, my dear, the FBI's culture is to march in one direction and that's towards investigations, grand juries, indictments, arrests, trials, and incarceration."

"And that's a bad thing?"

"Well, I'll admit they are sometimes a necessary and useful path. Law enforcement, that is. But in order for the Bureau to mount a successful prosecution, it needs to be able to show the evidence, which in the case of our material would take too many explanations and result in too many questions."

"Isn't that a bit of an evasion?" Charlie cut him off. "We find someone who is on the take, we tell the FBI. They reverse engineer and go out and find the evidence to support what we gathered. The end result? Whoever it is we've discovered isn't on the take any more."

"We do that sometimes," Bowlen responded. "When it's blatant. And at a very high level. And I've suggested that very path on numerous occasions regarding influence peddlers who are awfully close to being Saudi agents. But more times than not, the president doesn't see it the same way I do. The list of names—the web of relationships—is so much bigger than you might imagine."

"I'm not surprised," Charlie said. "As soon as word got out that I was thinking of leaving the Agency, I can't tell you how many Beltway Bandits and investment banks came calling. A woman with your skillset, they said, *with your knowledge of the Middle East*, they were blatant—*you can make ten times what you make at the Agency* they said—in the first year!"

Bowlen answered: "Yes, the money is a deeply intoxicating draw. But it's not just money, Charlie. Saudi Arabia does buy people, pure and simple, but this is also a world where *membership* is just as valuable as any payoff. We have many examples of people who have said 'no' to money. For them, the value is membership in a club that itself pays handsome dividends, a club that the Saudis don't themselves control or even run, but they enable by deciding who is allowed access or influence, and thus in turn holds something valuable to sell, directly or indirectly. The access or influence is sold back to the corporate world or to governments, which is where the real payday is …"

"So, the captains of industry are as dirty as the terrorists?" Charlie responded.

"Dirty, yes, Charlie. But not evil. The terrorists are pure evil. That's where I'd say there's a difference."

"Maybe too much of Mr. Draper's equivocal opinions have rubbed off on me," Charlie responded. "I don't mean to equate the two."

"So, I take it," Charlie continued, "that the president's reluctance to take action might be because he himself is looking over his own horizon and anticipating sitting in those very same boardrooms?"

"Are you referring to President Clinton or asking generically?"

"Well. Perhaps. No. I'm asking generically."

"Apex Watch exists to collect and assess and then let the president decide what to do. We can't and don't decide on our own. We are constituted to work outside of the parochial interests of the various agencies. And outside partisan politics."

"But yet, you are outside the law?" asked Charlie.

"*We* are outside the law, you mean? Now that you are on board."

"Are *we*?" Charlie pressed.

"If you mean the law as passed down in statutes by Congress, I suppose I would say yes. But even there, we pay attention to privacy. And we have reality: if one pokes deeply into any prominent person's background, into any powerful person's background, into any *man's* background to be blunt, well, my experience is that you find stuff, even stuff in their heads, crooked stuff, dirty stuff, evil stuff, stuff that should remain private. So, yes, we are charged with going after lawbreakers, but we also want to maintain the right to privacy.

"One more thing, Charlie. If you mean law that is inherent to the executive, I'm also not so sure. Having said that, and I believe this directly answers your question, yes, it's sometimes disheartening what happens. But it's even more disheartening that we often know things that aren't very sensitive that the Agency or the FBI *could* know but evidently isn't focused enough to see themselves. After all, as I said earlier, it's been 20-plus years and no one has ever reported on the very existence of the Saudi Apex project. Only occasionally are any of our subjects—I mean, the people we know to be on the Saudi payroll—exposed by other means. Independently caught. That's disheartening. But it points even more to the need for our existence.

"But again, I want to stress that we possess secrets here that aren't really secrets. Take bin Laden's emergence as such a dominating figure. Analysts could have seen it and predicted it. You did out there in the field. And your Mr. Draper did it at headquarters. The notion that Khalid is some sort of super source telling us something we wouldn't otherwise know isn't true. And to tell you the truth, had we exploited him—tasked him to find out X and disseminated his intelligence—he would have long ago been compromised or disappeared."

Charlie thought one could say that about any sensitive source.

He continued: "I'll admit it is a balancing act. But that's why you're here. How to get Khalid to report what he knows and then decide what to do with that information. That's your task."

He paused. "I will say this: Even if Khalid were a straight-out CIA source, which, as you'll find out, he could never be, what he has had to say over the years, and now what he's doing, is way too off-the-reservation to keep him on. Someone in the chain of command would have wanted to wash the government's hands of this terrorist. Or arrest him. Or kidnap him. Or even kill him. And the substance of what Khalid has said over the years would have had to have gone through many layers and be confirmed by many people to have had any effect. And as you'll see, I doubt confirmation will come regarding much of what he tells us. But more important, the culture of the Agency, as it is throughout the intelligence community, is to assess gain/loss in determining how to use anything that it collects.

"The KSM collaboration works precisely because I don't ask him for anything. But collaboration isn't quite the right word. I've had my words with Khalid about not telling us what he's really up to, and though it has sometimes paid off, even knowing is a conundrum with its own gain/loss calculation. And I've even tried to let him go a couple of times. But over time I've decided that he might be of some use to the country—not to the Agency."

"So, you're the country?"

"*We're* the country Charlie," he answered.

"OK, we. *So,* we're *the country?*"

"No one made us kings, but yes. We are a secret agency that works for the president. It is outside the government. I guess that's as close as one can come to being the country."

She was intensely listening.

"I'm sorry to be so longwinded," he said. "If it sounds like I'm being defensive, maybe it's because I am. But in 1990, when Khalid was reporting on bin Laden being back in Saudi Arabia, nobody paid attention because there was nothing in what he was saying that seemed of immediate usefulness. It wasn't about the war, wasn't about the Iraqi threat to U.S. forces. And it wasn't about WMD.

"And as the United States lurched from defense of Kuwait to Kurdish humanitarian relief to the coup against Gorbachev to the breakup of Yugoslavia to Somalia and on and on, licking the hell out of every possible flavor of the week, month and the year, bin Laden mostly disappeared. And that's the case even today. You know bin Laden, my dear, but do many others, even inside the Agency? I don't think so.

"The thing is, Charlie." Bowlen was saying her name so often now, she laughed inwardly, like he'd just finished some management seminar. "Bin Laden was watching all the events of the early '90s, too, as was Khalid. And though nobody else seemed to be, they really were influenced by the so-called New World Order, and then, even more, the new threads of American policy. What *we* did out there really did shape their view of what they thought they needed to do to counter us.

"Khalid, as you'll see, talked big—about bin Laden and the rise of *al Qaeda*. Maybe more brains applied to the subject might have divined the future based upon what he was saying. Perhaps if we had a more dispassionate, integrated view of what the U.S. was doing around the world, more would have been understood. And again, Charlie, there were Agency analysts—most notably, again, your Mr. Draper—who argue precisely what I'm observing here."

Your Mr. Draper. Again?

"Can you tell me precisely what Steve's role is, now that I'm onboard?"

"I will leave that up to you. I said I was looking for an accomplished case officer, and that is you and only you. You are not bait. And it's really your call. And yet: I'll be honest. Someone needs to wade their way through all these colliding particles, what the terrorists are up to, but also what we're up to—the United States—and how *that* has an impact on them. I'd like to think that we could deliver something fresh and forward-looking to the president. I eye Mr. Draper as that someone to pull it all together. But again. You know him best."

"And are you saying that if we had something fresh that we would deliver that to *this* president?"

"Yes, Charlie. He is the president."

"And you think that there's something that we could deliver to him that would trickle down to changed policy?"

"That I just don't know. What I do know is, even my feeble mind sees a great storm building over the horizon. I'd like to get in front of it."

"So, my choice, as you say, regarding him—Mr. Draper—is what?"

"I don't *really* know Mr. Draper. I've read his output and watched some of his bravura performances. But, if I can be frank, and just between us, I think he has both a brilliance and a blindness. I imagine he'll not only bring a lot of brilliance but a lot of intellectual baggage with him as well."

"Don't I know it," she interrupted, laughing.

Mr. Bowlen ignored her retort. "Also, I imagine that he will come like a lightning bolt, wanting to have everything his way. For that reason, I hesitate and truly leave the decision up to you."

Bowlen continued: "I want us to take on a new mission, one that no government agency has: Study the United States, its political thrusts and drifts, think about how our policies affect other countries with regard to terrorism."

"And what would be the purpose of such an analysis?" Charlie asked.

"As I said, to get out of in front of bin Laden and his type. But here's the bottom line, as I see it," he went on. "Khalid has convinced me that bin Laden and the *jihadis* drawn to *al Qaeda* believe in something that is not quite rational. Rational to us, that is. They are on the move and they are thinking in tens of years, even hundreds. It's a combination of deep beliefs in wanting to retain their differentness, and an animus towards us precisely because we keep giving them abundant reasons to focus all their frustration and hatred on us. In Khalid's world, this belief in the ultimate reward of defending their way of life is intrinsic in their willingness to become martyrs—suicide bombers—to offer their personal contribution in a battle that they recognize as larger than themselves. This increasing desire to martyr themselves is just the process of bearing witness for those who will follow them. We are entering a new period. There have been other large-scale suicide attacks in the past. But part of some national revolution objective? And by *Sunnis*? And by operatives of bin Laden? No, Charlie, not up until Riyadh and Islamabad."

Charlie again interrupted: "And something specific has changed that worries you?"

"Yes. Now he's taunting us."

"Khalid Sheikh?"

"Yes. He challenged me in mid-1991, saying he would prove his value, his importance. We heard little from him of much value until after the bomb went off at the World Trade Center two years later. He said it would take him two years and it did. Now he demonstrates that he knew about other attacks before they occurred. Riyadh. Islamabad. Khalid tells us that it was bin Laden," Bowlen explained.

"And you believe him," said Charlie.

"He had inside information."

"I'm not disagreeing—I reported as such from Pakistan at the time. But you believe him that bin Laden was involved?"

"I'd say I believe that he was the inspiration."

"But Khalid Sheikh," she said, "do you believe that he is right, that *al Qaeda* was behind Riyadh?"

"Do I believe it? Yes."

Then Bowlen continued: "Charlie. He's taunting us again, something bigger than 1993, he says, bigger than anything that's happened in Saudi Arabia, bigger than all of them."

"Taunting us how?"

"Ms. Charbel—Charlie, excuse me—when Khalid says he is cooking up something else, he means an attack within the United States."

Chapter 20 The Archive

Charlie watched as Barbara typed her fob's number into a keypad, the light flashing green. She then typed in her PIN, the door clicking open. As she opened the door, Charlie on her heels, the room sensed movement and turned on the lights.

Again, the electronic voice announced two visitors, this time saying "Barbara Rogers and Marina Charbel."

The cavernous room was about the width of a four-car garage though much deeper, with four tables up front, each with a matching computer terminal and lamp *à la* New York Public Library.

The tables faced a phalanx of black five-drawer file cabinets, 20 or so on each side of a corridor down the middle, signs on each corner meticulously announcing A–Ar, Ch–D, H–Jo and on, 10 rows deep. The left desk closest to the middle was the only one that betrayed any work going on in the otherwise sterile room, with a stack of files and notes left next to the keyboard.

"Welcome to the Apex Watch archive" Barbara said. "It's probably the most sensitive file room in the world."

"KSM's correspondence and the associated intelligence with his activities is all here," she continued, "filed chronologically and by subject. But if you're interested in finding something or someone in particular, even by date, I suggest you use the index." She patted the computer terminal on the center desk. "It you run into trouble, call me or one of my assistants, Erica or Casey. You met them at lunch. Any questions?"

"No. I don't think so," Charlie answered. She had so many. And she was dying to talk to her about Steve and her experience working with him—but it wasn't the time or place.

Barbara gone, there was one thing Charlie just had to know, something that had been eating at her for years. Barbara's comments at her welcoming lunch again brought it to the front of her mind.

She sat at the computer and typed in "Rahman," getting a screen full of hits. In the left-hand pane was the basic bio of who everyone called the Blind *Sheikh*.

Omar Abdel al Rahman; Egyptian national, born May 3, 1938 in Dakahlia governorate; blinded by diabetes as a youth. *Blindness verified.*

Terrorist, spiritual leader of both the Islamic Group (*Gama'at al-Islamiya* or GA) and the Egyptian Islamic Jihad (*al-Jihad* or EIJ).

Admitted to the United States: July 23, 1990; arrested June 24, 1993; indicted August 25, 1993; convicted October 1, 1995.

Current address: Federal Medical Center, Rochester, NY (Federal Bureau of Prisons); serving a life sentence without parole for seditious conspiracy.[373]

Right up to date, Charlie thought. For each entry there was a corresponding file number, and in the main pane there were over 100 hits stacked in chronological order, about half connecting Rahman to KSM. Charlie wrote down the numbers of the drawers containing files from the time she served in Egypt. She then stepped into the bank of cabinets, pulling folders and stacking them on the desk. It was going to be a long day.

When she first arrived at CIA headquarters after leaving Pakistan, she returned to the Rahman case feeling like she was some creepy stalker. She thought that in the classified file, there would be answers but she came up with a lot of nothing. The Blind *Sheikh* by then had already been arrested and convicted, and everyone she spoke to was uninterested in the ancient history. The FBI liaison officers were decidedly vague, but then she knew that they were getting precious little from the Center, just returning the favor. She couldn't let it go—her interest: Why had he been in the United States in the first place? Now she wondered whether Apex Watch—whether Mr. Bowlen—had a hand in it in some way.

She again thought of Steve as she flipped through the files. When she had mentioned to Steve her obsessive search regarding the Blind *Sheikh*, that this very kind of dangling explanation fed conspiracy theories, he completely dismissed her. It didn't take facts being out of order for people to believe in conspiracies. This omnipotence on the part of the government was a common view, he said, as American as apple pie. And not just omnipotence, but also that the government lied, which it did, which just made beliefs in conspiracy that much more complicated. They'd had long discussions about conspiracies.

There are no fucking conspiracies, Steve growled. Everything, *everything*, has an explanation, he said, even if the explanation is that the right hand rarely knows what the left was doing. Or that people did their jobs without much reflection on what they were actually doing, institutions being the sum total of all of that mindless work.

Going through the files she'd pulled out, Charlie found that the handwriting of her new agent, KSM, was elegant, a combination of English script and Arabic, with an occasional other language thrown in, all of it translated and annotated by Apex Watch analysts. Charlie knew she was cheating, not starting at the beginning, nor even on task, but still she flipped through the material looking for something, anything.

As she read, she smiled at some of KSM's language. He always referred to "your CIA" and "Mr. Jones" in quotes, as if he wanted to convey that he was in on the joke, that indeed he knew that Jones wasn't Bowlen's real name.

And yes, he did occasionally mention the Blind *Sheikh*, but she was reminded as she read his letters and reports that this moniker was a Western label. KSM often just referred to him as Abdel-Rahman, or the Egyptian *Sheikh*, or more, as متخلف عقليا—Arabic for mentally retarded, which the translators correctly transcribed but Charlie thought was off the mark on the part of KSM, that he must have meant handicapped. But the more she read, the more she thought he could have meant retarded, for he seemed to have zero interest in the Egyptian luminary, mostly just thinking him relevant because he was friends with his idol, Abdullah Azzam.

Azzam never loomed large in Charlie's education, absent in her Egyptian education, and not someone of Sayyid Qutb's stature. Soon after she arrived in Washington, and Steve and she had begun their shared study, she remembered that he pushed her to read Azzam's *Defense of Muslim Lands*.[374] He'd read the work in a classified translation and he called its impact on him a thunderclap, saying it explained so much about the common man's draw to what they were now calling international terror. Steve particularly loved Azzam's meditation on the necessity and appeal of martyrdom in a political world that offered no path to spiritual fulfillment unless one capitulated to the dual fiends of materialism and monoculture.

Charlie read Azzam and wasn't as impressed, thinking his *Qur'anic* references and historical tales uninspiring, but also that he was irrelevant to world conditions after Afghanistan. As the two of them discussed it, it took her a while to figure out what she found so unsettling about Steve's admiration. And it was this: In struggling to understand terrorists and what made them tick, Steve seemed so intent on humanizing his opponent that he fell into a trap of accepting that even the lowliest foot soldier had also read Azzam. Or even Qutb. He didn't say as much, and he'd deny it if she asked, but Steve operated from the assumption that individual terrorists pondered the theological and political underpinnings of their actions, that they had some intellectual foundation for their hatred of the West and even some deep understanding of Islam to back up their actions. Charlie's *experience* was most decidedly that they hadn't. She tried to get Steve to see his faulty foundation, his almost intentionally provocative stance to give them a voice that justified what they were doing. Until she concluded that he wasn't just struggling to understand them. That he wasn't just adhering to the facts. He was adding dimensions that existed only in his own mind. That was the problem with Steve's analysis, she'd learned: he couldn't get out of the way of his own discoveries and his own deep understanding of the details to fathom how shallow most others were in their thinking.

And in that, she thought, he romanticized the enemy.

Sitting back in the ergonomic chair, she stretched her arms above her head, thinking again about what role Steve could play, and whether she even wanted to let him in to her new secret world. And she thought about their future. She wondered what Apex Watch would really do with him, what Bowlen meant when he said that they needed to study the United States. She knew that Steve would devour the KSM material, and she relished the idea of her twin charges getting to know each other, both lovers of Azzam, both scoundrels. But she found herself annoyed that he was so present in her mind. And though she was in love with him, she was also almost always on edge with her distrustful partner.

She went upstairs to the cafeteria, foraging for something to eat, making herself a bowl of ramen. She hadn't yet given Mrs. Rothwell the requested shopping list.

Entering the dining room, a group of women waved her over, all reintroducing themselves.

"Tales from *Deutchland*," one said. "We're all recounting our experience now that Tenet's taken over."[375]

That's what Agency bottom-dwellers had dubbed the seventh floor when John Deutch rolled in from the Pentagon to be Clinton's second CIA director, replacing another outsider, James Woolsey.[376]

The MIT don wasted no time making enemies, telling everyone, including *The New York Times*, that Agency officers just weren't as good or as honorable as their military counterparts.[377] Deutch brought his own team in from the Pentagon, where he'd been deputy secretary, disrupting so much at the Agency that substantive work practically came to a halt. If his animus towards it and its covert-action culture weren't enough, Deutch then introduced the notorious "asset scrub." Every source on the U.S. payroll, he directed, would now be reviewed not just for their relevance and reporting value, but also for their character. Character in this regard meant any criminal, or especially human-rights, record—a politically-correct imposition that everyone thought ignored national security and the very point of having a clandestine service. In Charlie's estimation, there wasn't a serious officer who didn't see the new Deutch-implemented and Clinton-imposed rule as despicable and naïve. People willing to sell information to the CIA arose from the underbelly, especially those needed to work the ugly issues like terrorism and narcotics. No one who was any good as an operator or a source from this world would look good under a DC spotlight. Now listening to the conversation, Charlie was again reminded how she reacted, not only with contempt for Washington's high-mindedness, but also passive-aggressively, being more cautious about reporting but also starting to keep her contact with potential agents off the books.[378]

Her fellow diners recounted their own experiences navigating the Clinton era of political correctness. As Charlie listened, she thought that Mr. Bowlen was indeed right, that running an agent like KSM out of the Agency would be near impossible because he could never meet the clean human-rights or ethical standards Clinton and Deutch had imposed.

There was some hope amongst her dining companions that the new Agency director, George Tenet,[379] would change things. But Charlie channeled Steve's view, which was that though Tenet pulled off the impossible in his emergence, coming off as a breath of fresh air and an outsider, he had actually been Deutch's deputy, and before that a White House paper-pusher and Washington operative. When the president announced that Tenet would take over the Agency, everyone seemed to hail him as a new Caesar. True, the cigar-chomping Greek kid from the Bronx—affable and outgoing—stood in stark contrast to Deutch's dry and technical inwardness. But really what he'd done was perfectly play the Washington game, cultivating a support base in Congress and in the news media, taking on the role of Agency cheerleader and number one fan of an institution he'd never served in.[380]

When Charlie said to Steve that she hoped that Tenet would shake things up, he let loose with an intimidating monologue about how everyone at the top was the same, that they all came into office full of opinions and even optimism, but then learned the hard way that no matter what they thought or did—no matter how big their brains—they also got crushed.

"Sure, Deutch left," Steve chuckled when the announcement was made. "They always do. They go away when their own bosses leave office. They go away for better jobs. They get burnt out. They get pushed out. They get fired. They leave when there's no one left to influence or even alienate. And they, of course, leave to spend more time with their families," surrounding that final phrase with air quotes.

"And they leave why? They leave because they are out of sync, because they are out of control, because they are out of touch, or because they are just out. It's all the same. They come to Washington filled with civic mindedness and a yearning to govern, committed to their president, their party, their platform, and their agenda. They become heady with presence, with access, and with the secrets of government. And then they come to understand through grueling hours and never-ending fights, and through the passive aggressive ways of those who don't go away that there is only so much that can be done. And so, finally, exhausted by the ways of the system—they go away."

She thought at the time that it was almost as if he were warning her to lower her own expectations and avoid the same outcome.

Steve had such low regard for the political appointees—insiders *and* outsiders—because he also opined that those who were left behind after the bosses moved on—the permanent members of government—were the true blights. They were not *them*. They were not *political* like *them*. Instead, they were the holders of institutional memories, the seasoned hands, the bureaucratic pile drivers, the subject matter experts. Clustered at the top, captains just below the capos, they were the few who had direct access to the director or the secretary or even the president, in on most deliberations, even if not always in the room, drafters and sometime even authors, counsels succeeding or failing on the shoe size or coat tails of the bosses. They might become best friend or booster to the politicos. They might become worst enemy or leaking backstabber. They might have a life that is, or is made into, a living hell by those very political appointees. But whatever they thought or felt about the boss, one thing was clear: the political appointees would eventually go away.

"I'm hearing," one of the women was saying, "that real change is afoot."

"To me," Charlie chimed in, "the biggest problem is the illusion of change. The human-rights rules and the squeamishness about breaking any laws—even host nation laws—persists because it's the basic worldview of the Clinton fucks, that now we and all our so-called friends all want the same thing. Sure, case officers can nominate—what shall we call them, difficult assets—and they might say that requests will go through a process of waiver and approval. But the truth is, don't try it and don't take the risk. Management can't be trusted, and if there's an after-the-fact scandal, leadership isn't going to fucking protect the operators. Ever."

Charlie's angry outburst instantly cooled the conversation.

Kicking herself, she returned to the archives and to KSM's story, to his take on the end of the Soviet war in Afghanistan.

Charlie saw firsthand how the multibillion-dollar CIA enterprise almost immediately screeched to a halt when Gorbachev removed the Red Army. The Agency abandoned its clients overnight, transferring dozens of case officers elsewhere.[381] Granted, it never had much interest or understanding of the "Arab fighters," but as KSM's narrative reminded her, in its haste to move on, the Agency missed spotting the growing international focus of a group that emerged from the conflagration.

Once the Soviets withdrew, KSM also seemed to lose much interest in Afghanistan. It was clear from his reports that he never had much contact with Afghan fighters, and he grew tired of their factions, seeing the dangers of allegiance to tribal and ethnic divisions. KSM was also ever more contemptuous of the Saudi and Gulf boys—the *jihadi* vacationers, as he called them—young men who could now return victorious to their comfortable lives back home, unscathed and able to brag about having done their *jihad*, when in fact they had been protected by bin Laden. KSM wrote that he couldn't really identify with the Egyptians either. They had countries to return to, or at least to obsess about, a focus that KSM seemed to find both alluring and risky. As he decamped to Karachi, he wrote a long letter to Mr. Jones in which he wondered what impact the whole enterprise had really had.[382]

Was it just his own homelessness? Charlie wondered.

She rushed through the correspondence on the World Trade Center, thinking that there wasn't much to learn, lingering here and there when KSM made mention of Ramzi Yousef. After the February attack, the correspondence became more sporadic. And then she came to KSM's triumphant retelling of the Philippines story.

How was it possible, Charlie thought, as she went through the *Bojinka* materials in the archives, that KSM just blithely walked into the U.S. Embassy in Manila? What nerve did that take? And then he did so repeatedly, without ever having his picture taken, without being fingerprinted and avoiding the polygraph? What utter incompetence on the part of the government, she thought, until she found herself wondering about Bowlen's role, about what wasn't in the archives.

She took notes on a legal yellow pad. Was KSM really there just to look at mugshot books, as he claimed to Mr. Jones? Was he testing American security practices? Was he doing more than just testing bombs? Wasn't he checking American reactions? She compared what he wrote about the Philippines escapade with the official reports in the archives, and then dug deeper into Agency databases, also connected to Apex Watch. The official story, told at the time, was that the plot to assassinate the Pope and President Clinton was thwarted, the damage isolated. Of course, there was no mention of KSM. And from the official dispatches, she could see that there was another detail: these assassinations and Philippine Airlines plans were all fortuitously discovered and stopped at the eleventh hour. Though KSM said that he facilitated the arrests, never in the official reporting was there any hint that there was any tip-off or any Arab walk-in. There was so many connections Charlie was now writing down on her yellow pad. It seemed like KSM as Mr. al-Ghamdi disappeared too easily—that she started to think that maybe it was the case that the files had been tampered with.

The archives raised more questions than they answered, thought Charlie. Mr. Bowlen must know the answer.

She picked up the secure phone and called Bowlen's office at Langley.

"Ms. Charbel," said his assistant, "I'm sure he is out at Apex Watch. Just ask the building."

"The building answers as well as sees?"

"They haven't shown you how it works yet? It logs where everyone is. Just say 'Building' and ask your question."

"OK," Charlie said, hanging up. "Building," she said, "where is Mr. Bowlen?"

"Mr. Bowlen is in transit."

She called him on his car phone. When he answered, Charlie got right to it. "So, we are conspirators?" she said, not intending to upend her new boss by roaring past pleasantries.

"How is that, Ms. Charbel?"

"*Bojinka*. We knew Ramzi Yousef was there, in the Philippines? And the third person in the plot, this guy Murad, Abdul Hakim Murad,[383] who was captured by Philippine police? We knew that he identified KSM to the FBI?"

"He identified someone," Bowlen answered, again unruffled by her outburst.

"Come on? I'm no expert on the *Bojinka* case, but it looks to me that enough details came together for the authorities to identify KSM. Are we actively concealing him?"

"We were not privy to KSM's presence in the Philippines until well after the fact, Ms. Charbel," Bowlen answered, not answering her core question. "We didn't know the details until he wrote to us. And we didn't assist KSM in any way. But yes, we intentionally made a trade: his information and insights for his safety. And … Well why don't we meet and discuss this face-to-face? I have a short meeting downtown, but I could be out there at about five. Does that suit you?"

"Sure," she said.

He hung up.

It was 1:30. Charlie needed to breathe.

Chapter 21 Into the Woods

"Yes, dear," Mrs. Rothwell said when Charlie showed up at her office door. She'd been on the phone and Charlie looked at the smattering of Manila postcards from KSM, examining them more closely now.

"I have a meeting with Mr. Bowlen at five," she said, "but I'd really like to take a run. Is that possible?"

"If you have your running stuff, I could have security drive you to Blue Ponds Park."

"I can't just run there from here?" Charlie asked.

"No, dear," Mrs. Rothwell said, detecting Charlie's distress. "There is the gym if you need to blow off steam."

"I prefer to run."

"Okay, let me set it up."

Another muscle-bound, ex-military type appeared at her office door twenty minutes later, ready to drive her to the nearby park. He didn't say anything on the five-minute drive and said he'd wait for her, to take her time. The park was beautiful, and on a weekday afternoon, it was empty. Its open trails were covered with leaves and pine needles. She jogged for a half an hour, occasionally sprinting and exhausting herself, her thoughts of KSM's Manila escapades still running through her head.

A couple of days after New Years', smoke was reported coming out of a sixth-floor window of a Manila apartment building.[384] According to the intelligence reports Charlie had read before, when firefighters arrived, a Kuwaiti national named Ahmed Saeed told them some bullshit story that he was playing with leftover New Year's fireworks and that he was sorry for all the smoke.

The firemen left after they satisfied themselves that the apartment was safe. Philippine police also arrived and were talked away as well. That is, until about an hour later. Then an anonymous phone call was made to the local precinct office, warning the police that the apartment associated with the false alarm was related to a plot regarding the upcoming visit of his Holiness. Police returned to question the apartment occupants.[385]

The man later identified as Abdul Hakim Ali Hashim Murad, the man KSM first identified to his American embassy friends as Saeed, tried to flee the scene.[386] With Murad in custody, they searched the apartment, finding bomb-making materials and blueprints, even an order from a local tailor for a priest's cassock that could be used as a disguise on the day of the Pope's assassination. A laptop that later turned out to belong to Ramzi Yousef was also confiscated.

After trying to bribe his way out of custody, Murad was transferred to the National Police Intelligence custody, and there he was brutally tortured before being eventually handed over to the FBI.[387] In the course of his one-month interrogation, Murad confessed all. He admitted to the assassination attempt, gave up the names of local accomplices, and said that his mission after taking part in killing the Pope was to enter the United States and then fly an airplane into CIA headquarters in Virginia. His story had credibility, given that he had completed flight school. Murad claimed that ten *jihadis* had or were training in American flight schools, that there was a plot to fly ten airplanes into buildings.[388]

Before Charlie had read KSM's letters and reports, she knew little of the details. In the after-action report written by Apex Watch, she found out that the FAA told airline security officials after the Tokyo incident that terrorists might try to plant bombs on American commercial aircraft. Now Charlie thought, there seemed another possibility. If Murad was to be believed; terrorists would pilot the planes themselves into their targets. Murad had even talked of possibilities, the report said: the CIA, the Pentagon, the World Trade Center, the Sears Tower in Chicago, the Transamerica Tower in San Francisco, and a nuclear facility.[389] Murad also claimed that he learned explosives from a man named Abdul Basit

Mahmood Abdul Karim, a name that meant little to either Philippine or FBI interrogators, or to Charlie, until he also said that this was the same man who was responsible for the bombing of the World Trade Center. It was Ramzi Yousef.[390] And once the FBI heard that name, they focused on nothing else but the top man on their Ten Most Wanted list, a diversion that KSM seemed to predict in his letters and a behavior that Steve had more than once pointed out to Charlie—that the bureaucracy could only do one thing at a time.

Charlie tried to put it all together in her head. The FBI and the CIA should have gleaned a ton of new intelligence from Murad. Not just about Ramzi Yousef, but his broader activities, plots contemplated into the future, and even the existence of KSM. But she knew from her time at the Agency that the official story of the Philippines was so bland as to be forgotten. For anyone who'd even heard of Manila, there was some kind of apartment fire leading to the fortuitous discovery of a plot, the plotters incompetent, even the name of the operation—*Bojinka*—some concocted word made up by amateurs.

Contemplating the alternate history revealed by KSM, she surmised that the mysterious phone call from an Arab man had to have come from Khalid Sheikh Mohammed himself. And Ramzi Yousef wasn't just some incompetent. Though he left his computer behind in his haste to escape, he had perfected his bomb-making technique and he also made it in and out of the country safely, despite being an international fugitive. And so did KSM, either under the Ghamdi alias or some other identity that he used.[391]

When the FBI took formal custody of a broken Murad, months after Philippine police had broken him, New York investigators wrung every last detail from their prisoner. He was arraigned by the U.S. Attorney for the Southern District of New York. Arraigned, tried, convicted, and incarcerated. And yet KSM seemed to have evaded mention or detection? Charlie wondered now how he had avoided all of that. How did he even avoid being identified as an important terrorist? The chain of error astounded her. And it saddened her, not just that the Agency was so clueless, but also that Apex Watch, this very organization that she was now a part of, must have played a role in keeping their agent—her new agent—out of the limelight.

What the fuck was she doing?

She'd made the transformation from bureaucrat to ... what? Case officer for a man ultimately responsible for planning the attack on the World Trade Center. For killing a Japanese businessman on the Tokyo flight. For attacking the U.S. military in Saudi Arabia. For preparing air attacks in the United States. For working for, but then also infiltrating, the United States government.

When Charlie reached a large clearing deep inside the park, she stopped and bent over to catch her breath, soaking up the beauty. And the sunshine. She tried to collect herself.

How was any of this enhancing American national security?

She'd been avoiding Steve with the excuse that she didn't yet have permission to talk to him about her new job. She knew it was painful for him, and she missed their easy togetherness. She needed his help here. But until she got clarification from Mr. Bowlen, until she figured out their relationship and whether she wanted him to take over her life—again—she didn't even want to see him.

Bowlen let her loose on the archives, but Charlie wasn't really a file reader. She was a doer. *Action girl* as Steve called her. The files raised more questions than they answered. The Manila story was full of holes and clues. And the game involved in KSM's warning when Bowlen met him in Malaysia? She couldn't understand why Bowlen acceded to his request for more time. Nor how KSM could have marched forward—not with the Blind *Sheikh*, Murad and Ramzi Yousef all eventually in U.S. custody.[392] He had to have had some help.

She ended her jog in front of the pond at the park's entrance, stretching, looking out on the glistening water, feeling like she'd worked off her frustration, and her discomfort. And then she yelled out—*Hello*—her voice bouncing off the stand of trees all around the lake. She'd have to get out of that echo soon, she thought.

The security guy was waiting for her in an otherwise empty parking lot when she emerged from the woods.

Back at Apex Watch, she showered and dressed in an empty locker room. It was almost like no work was going on: It was all a little too quiet for her taste.

Bowlen was his usual self when they met, friendly and collected.[393]

"There's nothing I'm hiding from you," he said, responding to

Charlie's opening assault.

"I'm not saying there is," Charlie answered. "I just don't know how you accepted what happened with the World Trade Center in New York, how you overlooked KSM's role. Or what the entire Philippines interlude means. I don't understand how KSM keeps evading detection. Nor how we are benefiting—we, meaning Apex Watch, and then, we, the United States, by carrying him on our books as an agent."

"In the case of the Philippines," Bowlen blandly answered, "I can tell you directly. Beyond that, as I've said, that's still an unwritten chapter. And one that I'm offering you an opportunity to write."

"But I'm a case officer, trained to elicit information from my agent," Charlie said. "I'm no analyst or big thinker."

"Yes, Ms. Charbel—Charlie—I understand that. But you understand this world—this bigger world beyond just one individual—and I just want you to have the best possible understanding of Khalid before you take him on. Then? Then we can have that discussion. But I'm also saying we are not the CIA, that we have special purpose and Khalid is not a typical agent. We took him on, and now I feel like we have to use him for something that *is* to our advantage."

"Fair enough," Charlie answered, "but I'll say right now I'm uncomfortable with the idea that we possess information regarding the safety of the United States and we are doing nothing about it."

"As am I," Bowlen said. "But we aren't doing nothing, as is evidenced by your presence here. Plus, Khalid gave us Ramzi Yousef ..."

"Gave us? You mean he was involved?"

Bowlen told the story of how KSM led the FBI to his capture.

With Murad's arrest in the Philippines, someone named Khalid Sheikh Mohammed was identified by the FBI. As far as investigators knew, this Mr. Sheikh Mohammed had provided some funding to the World Trade Center bombers. And then he had been involved in the Philippines, perhaps in some conspiracy relating to airliners.

Bowlen told Charlie that Khalid had indeed done what he promised in Malaysia, almost downing an airplane with a tiny bomb, and with the Philippines, he thought, and Apex Watch thought, that too much was going on to just signal a contained plot. The tester bombs. A plot to assassinate the Pope. A hidden conspiracy to go after President Clinton.

Murad's claims. All of it added up to some kind of preparations for a larger attack inside the United States itself. Almost all of the official attention focused on Ramzi Yousef. That's when the idea emerged, in Bowlen's discussions with then Apex Watch director Hal Jones that maybe they needed to get more proactive, induce their asset to report on future plots. And so Bowlen flew out to Dubai to meet with him again.

"I argued then that taking Khalid out of the game and losing a link to him, for us to become blind, was the worst possible outcome. And I'd still argue that today," he said to Charlie, telling the story.

They met inside the international lounge at the airport, KSM cleverly setting up the meeting so that he never had to actually enter the country, he on a four-hour layover just going through transit. Tony was delighted with the added security—Emirati surveillance at the time was spotty *inside* the terminal. When KSM's message came in, even recommending a flight for Mr. Bowlen to take, they marveled that he picked exact flights converging from different parts of the world arriving at the same time, with ongoing legs of an itinerary that took them to their destinations at almost precisely the same time, even leaving from different ends of the gate area.

"You just walked away?" Bowlen asked Khalid of his Philippine experience.

"I did, *Mister*," Khalid triumphantly announced. He laughed, and then he regaled Bowlen with stories of the apartment fire and his embassy penetration. And his escape with the same Saudi disguise.

"So you know the name Ghamdi name is now compromised?" Bowlen said.

"What do I care?" Khalid responded. "They never took my fingerprints. And it is not me. I have many names.

"And besides, you told me, my good friend, that you would protect me."

"Khalid, we discussed this before," Bowlen said. "There is only so much I can do. Now, I am telling you what Murad has said about you so that you can take measures to protect yourself."

"The best measure I could take is to give you Ramzi Yousef," Khalid said to Bowlen, surprising him.[394]

Once the contents of the apartment were inventoried and searched, the Philippine authorities knew, even before they broke Murad, that they were close to Yousef, that is was his laptop. Murad then confirmed it, telling interrogators that he worked with a man they referred to as 'Rasheed the Iraqi,' the very name Ramzi Yousef used in New York.[395]

But there was some hard information on Khalid Sheikh Mohammed as well. The FBI and U.S. Attorney in New York named an individual, one Khalid Sheikh or Sheikh Mohammed, who now crossed over from the World Trade Center to the Philippines plot and then to the Days of Terror plot,[396] the trial for which was about to begin in New York. Bowlen told KSM that he was one of the 172 co-conspirators that had now been associated with the World Trade Center and a later plot—tied to the Egyptian Blind *Sheikh*—to undertake simultaneous attacks on the United Nations and Manhattan tunnels and bridges.

Investigators found reference to a Qatari-based man named Khaled Shaykh or Khalid Doha after they uncovered a $600 wire transfer to one of the World Trade Center operatives. That same account then wired $3,500 to the Philippines.[397] Khalid denied any involvement in the Days of Terror case, even doubting that it was a real plot, speculating that the authorities made it all up to entrap the Blind *Sheikh*.

Bowlen told him that the FBI or the New York police had managed to plant an agent in Ramzi Yousef's circle, or at least at the mosque that they prayed in. He said he also thought that the authorities had enough evidence, even if they didn't know who he really was or his whereabouts to go after him, to request governments watchlist him and even issue an international warrant for his arrest.

That brought them back to a discussion of Ramzi Yousef, to KSM's proposal to have him taken out of the game.

"That's quite the risk," Bowlen said to Khalid. "Aren't you concerned that in his interrogation or in the building of a case against him that you will be further implicated?"

KSM again laughed. He then went off into a rare diatribe, that Yousef got both lucky and failed in New York, that they weren't really related, that *he* was the mastermind. He had intentionally made the call to the precinct that actually brought the Philippine police to the apartment,

KSM said, because he was trying to get Ramzi Yousef caught and put away. He said he had no fear.

"Mister," KSM said, "someday this fool is going to be my downfall if he remains on the streets." Bowlen thought that maybe Khalid was jealous of all the attention he got and the worldwide manhunt for him.

"Once he is captured," KSM continued, "your CIA will spend so much time celebrating, it will forget about everything else."

"The first thing investigators will do, Khalid, is ask for additional names," Bowlen responded, pleading with him to think through what the implications of Yousef's capture would be, almost now even trying to dissuade him. But KSM would hear none of it. He was sure that Ramzi wouldn't talk, that the CIA and FBI wouldn't break him because they wouldn't push—wouldn't torture him—but also because they'd be so lost in their victory and playing by their stupid rules. But KSM had another view, which Bowlen found thought-provoking, which was that Ramzi would protect him because he needed to portray himself as the brains, and any mention of Khalid Sheikh Mohammed might ultimately ruin that.

Bowlen sat back in his chair, pausing for a moment, bringing himself back to the present and his conversation with Charlie.

"Khalid is indeed willing to take risks we can only imagine. That's what I learned from that particular exchange. In a way, he's so arrogant about the incompetence of the authorities. But he's also extremely knowledgeable about the ways of government, not just ours. Left to his own devices in the American embassy in Manila, he realized he could get access to that mugshot book, and it was then that I think he probably pulled an audible and pivoted. I don't know what he was really doing there, but once he smelled those mugshot books, he said and did all of the right things to get access to them."

"The reason being?" Charlie asked.

"As I was to find out later, not in Dubai, he was looking to see if he or someone close to him was vulnerable."

"Someone close to him?" Charlie asked.

"Really close, someone he wanted to protect. We didn't know yet who. But it wasn't Ramzi Yousef."

"Okay, now you have to tell me the story behind Yousef not being KSM's nephew. You said you would."

Bowlen chuckled. "It is a bit confusing. But it turns out that Yousef stole the identity of Khalid's dead nephew: the real Ramzi Yousef."[398]

"How'd he do that?" asked Charlie.

"The real Yousef evidently died in the Iraqi invasion of Kuwait. Iraqi intelligence awarded that identity and a new Kuwait passport to one Mr. Basit—Ramzi Yousef's real name—in exchange for his work as an informant during the occupation. Now, just to be clear, Charlie, hardly anyone even knows that KSM exists, but those who do, and evidently that includes all of *al Qaeda*, assume that the two are related. Khalid maintains the fiction, I'm guessing, as some leverage he holds over Yousef. But it was eating at him.

"In Dubai, Khalid smirked about Yousef's escape from New York *and* Manila, that we would never catch him with matchbooks. That only he knew how to find him."

In its worldwide dragnet for fugitive Yousef after the bombing at the World Trade Center, the State Department circulated multi-language green matchbooks with his face on the cover, offering a $2 million reward for his capture.[399]

"I told Khalid how some people in the State Department were arguing that the matchbook campaign might make it appear that the United States was encouraging smoking. Smoking.

"And Khalid said, in his fractured but always interesting way, that the United States was just hoping that Muslims would die of cancer before America had a chance to kill them with missiles and bombs.

"I asked him what was the real reason he wanted Yousef captured? Was is it for the reward money? To that suggestion, Khalid was truly insulted. It was pure and simple, and here I'm reading between the lines, but even bin Laden by then knew his name—Ramzi Yousef," Bowlen said it with a W.C. Fields warble.

"Khalid had had enough. He was even meeting *jihadis* who wanted to be just like *him*, like Yousef."

And so they discussed how KSM would create the condition for Yousef to be captured.

"I warned him that there was a real chance that Khalid Sheikh Mohammed could be outed. And that's when he said it to me, directly, that he was planning an attack in the United States, one that could never

ever be conceived, one that would change history forever.

"Charlie, it was the gravest I have ever seen him. His lips trembled when he said it."

It had been a long conversation and a long day for both of them. Bowlen had exhausted himself and exhausted Charlie with another one of his long stories. As he was finishing, Charlie sensed it, coming to the climax, hesitating because he wanted her to know both the gravity of what he was imparting that day but also the essence of what would be her mission.

"So I said to him, again, whether he really thought he could control things. And he said, and here I can picture us sitting at the espresso bar outside the duty free, KSM with little cookies on his plate, looking very much like your typical international man, a traveler on the go chatting with an old, white-haired gringo."

"It is coming," Khalid said. "Just like you are coming for us. But it is *my* dream and *my* mission and *my* doing. No one can take that from me. Not some publicity-hungry student. He has to go."

He was flushed, Bowlen. Charlie was almost afraid to ask more questions, knowing on some level that even in a conversation between colleagues, where everyone possesses the same clearances and follows the same protocols and even has the same missions, that some bluntness's were never uttered, that one didn't go there, revealing true conversations and double dealings that risked so much.

"It just ended there?" Charlie asked.

"No, I pressed him on precautions, again, and warned him of all that could go wrong, all that would surely go wrong, as things often go wrong, even in the face of the best-laid plans.

"He listened to me, Charlie. He knew I had wisdom, and I might even say he had respect for me, but he wanted to make a point. And he needed to."

Bowlen returned to the airport, to that day, telling Charlie of their final conversation. He met Charlie's eyes when he said, "By then Khalid knew our Saudi operation was separate from the Agency. He liked to tease me, saying *your CIA*. But he understood deep down that we were indeed some other entity."

In the airport that day, Khalid had said, "Now that I have watched your government in action in Manila, *Mister*, there is something that could trip me up."

"What?"

"Some files in your CIA."

And then Khalid had said: "I want to make sure that there is no old record of Khalid Sheikh Mohammed in the official files. From when we first met."

"I will take care of those files," Bowlen said.

"By when?" Khalid asked.

"I will take care of it, Khalid," Bowlen said, now exasperated.

"When you have informed me," Khalid said, "I will deliver Ramzi Yousef to you. And, my friend, I will deliver the Saudis."

"You will deliver the Saudis?" Bowlen had repeated, thinking that KSM was perhaps lost in his own legend.

"I have an idea. It will make the Saudis the most hated people in America. With you, my friend, I give it to you. It is a plan that will bring down the House of Saud."

KSM sat back in his chair, gratified.

"It will be good for America when Ramzi Yousef is captured," Khalid said. "The bad men will cower in their caves. Bin Laden will sleep with one eye open, like a lizard. Peace will break out all over the land."

Peace all over the land, Bowlen remembered, repeating it absentmindedly.

"Plus, the benefit of giving you Yousef is that I am helping you," Khalid had added. "Isn't that what you want?"

The two got up and walked through the terminal, poking into the designer shops.

"So, how is our friend, Mr. bin Laden?" Bowlen then asked.

"The *Sheikh* is nervous," Khalid said, "but he gathers strength."

"The Saudis want him dead," Bowlen said.

"Can I tell him that?" Khalid asked.

"Don't you think he already knows it?"

"He thinks it is the CIA behind the attempts on his life, or the Israeli *Mossad*," Khalid answered. He told Bowlen that, despite everything, bin Laden was still a Saudi patriot, believing that his family name and his work for Prince Turki during and after the Soviet war was going to protect him.[400]

"And what do you think, Khalid?" Bowlen asked.

"I think you still do not understand who *Sheikh* bin Laden is," Khalid said.

"You have such dreams, Khalid," Bowlen responded.

"Well, my friend. You told me to live my life. But these are my dreams."

"And training pilots or building airplane bombs to attack the United States are, or are not, part of those dreams?" Bowlen asked him.

"The fall of the House of Saud? Your dream? And getting America out of the Middle East? The *Sheikh's* dream? Oh, *Mister*, we all have our own dreams."

PART 6

Chapter 22 Khobar Towers

1996

Charlie read KSM's dispatches now in chronological order, his tart analysis of the Clinton administration, his condemnation of the trade embargo against Cuba,[401] but also his extended commentary on the capture of Theodore Kaczynski, the so-called Unabomber. For almost 20 years, the mystery man had been terrorizing America, planting or mailing more than a dozen bombs that killed three and injured many. Then he threatened to blow up an airplane flying out of Los Angeles International Airport, that is, unless *The New York Times* and *The Washington Post* published his 35,000 word anti-technology manifesto.[402]

"As nuclear proliferation has shown," Kaczynski wrote, and KSM quoted, "a new technology cannot be kept out of the hands of dictators and irresponsible Third World nations."

"My friend," he wrote to Apex Watch after the manifesto's publication, "your crazy math man may be right about the collapse of what he calls the 'industrial-technological' system, but he clearly knows nothing of the world outside America, and is not smart enough to see why we fight to get out from underneath your thumbs."

In all, Charlie counted nine KSM letters mentioning Kaczynski as he pondered the question of technology and its impact. His letters were vivid, and he obviously loved talking about himself and reporting on his activities. Charlie also thought it fascinating to see how KSM stacked the views and writings of Osama bin Laden against the Kaczynski manifesto, carefully picking apart both, stressing how important it was that Apex Watch pay attention, worried somehow that the Unabomber's words would actually have influence.

Charlie had seen similar adoration from her Palestinian mechanic when she was assigned to Dammam, how he talked about bin Laden's words. And her prized Pakistani agent, Yusuf, also loved the man, not making excuses for the attacks, but trying over and over again to impress upon her how important the *Sheikh* was and how she should pay more attention.

Now up to his contemporary writings, KSM described his last meetings with bin Laden, and Charlie alternately read and daydreamed, trying to place herself into the scene.

They met at the Dubai airport private terminal, one that Charlie had been to. That day, it was closed to business travelers, armed men standing outside. When KSM arrived at the doors, his people patted him down and a young Yemeni assistant checked his name off the list that he carried on a clipboard. Inside, the normally hush-quiet oasis was a bustle of activity. Osama bin Laden's staff, wives and children were camped out in the three VIP lounges, the children mesmerized by the plasma screen TV's, the adults dozing and eating, belongings spilling out all over the couches and oversize loungers.[403] *Al Qaeda* central was quietly leaving Sudan, a private jet transporting the family and assistants to Afghanistan.

Shown into a sand-colored private room—*Sahara*—KSM found the *Sheikh* sitting alone. He looked calm in the quiet, an Emirati newspaper in his lap, an orange juice on the table by his side.

"My friend," the *Sheikh* said, standing up and towering over KSM, greeting him warmly.

"Come back to Afghanistan with me," bin Laden had pleaded. Though the government in Khartoum had capitulated after much pressure from the United States and its neighbors, and expelled bin Laden,[404] the Taliban had arrived in Kabul, declaring the Islamic State of Afghanistan.[405]

"I am so much more valuable to you on the outside," KSM responded, living "clean" away from the *al Qaeda* apparatus and maintaining his anonymity.

Plus, KSM wrote to Apex Watch, there was no way he was going to give up his internet.[406] Charlie laughed out loud when she read that.

KSM and bin Laden had talked for more than two hours while his airliner was refueled and he obtained clearance from the government to fly on. Bin Laden told KSM that he was working on the draft of his own manifesto, a *fatwa* he wanted to soon issue. He was going to call for a *jihad* against America, and he hoped that the document would unite their growing but uncoordinated movement, those already a part of *al Qaeda*, but also brothers who were scattered around the globe.

Would brother *Mukhtar* help, bin Laden asked KSM, help him especially with the English?

"I would, of course, be honored," KSM responded.

Bin Laden anticipated the answer, and he called the assistant, who came back with a sheaf of letters and statements in a large manila envelope.

While bin Laden explained what he would like to do and the work he had already done, word came back from the authorities that they would not be allowed to fly directly. They would have to land in Peshawar—he still had a long journey ahead.

"*Ma'assalama*," the tired-looking bin Laden said to his friend, grasping his arm as they parted.

"*Bissalama*," KSM responded, hurrying to catch his own flight back to Karachi.

On the Pakistani airlines flight, KSM perused bin Laden's papers.

They started in 1994, two years earlier.[407]

"The people's rights have been abrogated and corruption infests government agencies," bin Laden wrote to King Fahd that April, announcing the formation of something called the Committee for Advice and Reform.[408] "The country's monetary and economic situation is worsening, taxes have been raised yet the government wastes money," he laid out. "The armed forces are in poor condition ... foreign policy works against the interests of Muslims ... while supporting infidels. Attempts to promote reform have triggered reprisals and the waging of war against just people, who are hunted at home and abroad," bin Laden enumerated. He urged King Fahd to abide by the requests of his committee.[409]

Then there was another open letter, this one condemning the King's support for the communists in Yemen. "Prince Sultan led a special committee that funneled support to the Yemeni Socialist Party," bin

Laden wrote, thwarting the people's desire for a united country, while also opposing an "Islamic awakening."

Later, he wrote that King Fahd was supporting anti-Islamic regimes in Algeria and Syria, as well as throwing his support behind Moscow and other anti-Islamic regimes of the former Soviet Union, even supporting Christian groups in Sudan. The king, bin Laden wrote, was supporting U.N. resolutions costing Muslim lives in Bosnia and Lebanon, while supporting the Jews in Palestine as well. He condemned the United Nations, calling it "an instrument in the hands of the Jews and Crusaders," warning Riyadh that its support for U.N. actions was just perpetuating policies that justified foreign intervention in the region.[410]

He attacked Prince Bandar, the Saudi ambassador, by name.[411] This Saudi titan, bin Laden said, had "publicly acknowledged a relationship with the Zionist entity," making the Saudi government no different from secular governments, consorting with the enemy. "The king and his 'gang' obey the mercenary intelligence agents of foreign governments, Christians, and Zionists," he went on to say, by arresting anti-government scholars and preachers who questioned internationalism and Saudi conformity.[412]

He called upon Muslim youth to protest and take action after a group of outspoken scholars were arrested.[413]

He called upon security officers to take a stand against the royal family, reminding them that "they were trained to defend the interests of their people and to act as their representatives."[414]

He wrote to the soldiers, speaking of billion-dollar corruption scandals associated with arms sales, pointing out that the princes were getting richer while their pay and allowances were being cut.[415]

He condemned the Higher Committee for Islamic Affairs[416] as a tool of the state and he condemned the dissolving of private charitable organizations and their replacement with state-sponsored ones, further adding to corruption.[417]

He asked about the weakness of the *ulema*,[418] the broader community of Islam. "It does not make sense that more than a billion Muslims who own the largest natural resources in the world are unable to defeat five million Jews in Palestine. The ailment is not military or financial, but rather the leaders' betrayal and the scholar's acceptance of the current situation."[419]

Through all of his writings, bin Laden said that the primary problem was the defiling of the land of the holy places because King Fahd invited American soldiers to Saudi soil and then allowed them to stay.[420] Kuwait has been restored, he wrote, but still the Americans did not leave. And not only that: They were bringing in Christian women to defend Saudi Arabia against Iraq, an act that bin Laden said placed the Saudi army "in the highest degree of shame, disgrace, and frustration."[421]

"Don't we have a right to ask about the reason they have stayed so long?" bin Laden asked of the king, just weeks before the attack in Riyadh.[422]

The final document in the bunch was a long, open letter written directly to King Fahd. "These filthy, infidel Crusaders must not be allowed to remain in the Holy Land," he wrote.[423]

Charlie read KSM's report, putting aside the actual enclosed copies of bin Laden's letters, all photocopied and entered into a binder. KSM wrote in his final dispatch that he knew that he—KSM—was a heartless bastard, but he asked Mister Jones, "Who could not admire the *Emir?*" Here was a man publicly standing up and openly condemning Saudi corruption and manipulation of Islam, naming names and openly signing his own name, standing tall from his first day.

He wrote that he thought the only flaw was that bin Laden focused too much on Saudi internal politics, that he needed a broader sweep addressing subjugation and humiliation that Muslims from all countries sensed. Then, writing of bin Laden's open letters, KSM added an odd plea—"from the heart," he said—about hope for the future, saying that he thought for the first time that the bin Laden message would appeal to young Muslim men beyond his generation, that he saw hope for a true movement.

"Tell me, my old friend," he said, asking Mr. Jones: "Is there any illness in here that you can really disagree with? I understand that you don't like that America is now the number one enemy. And you do not love that your beloved Jew state is getting so many enemies that it will never live in peace. But is that all that this is about, defending Jews and defending oil? Where is the true American ideal in what you seek, what I heard in the lecture halls in North Carolina?"[424]

Attached to the translation was an Apex Watch memo, checking each of bin Laden's open letters against Agency files to see how much of bin

Laden's prodigious output was in the official intelligence. The memo concluded that though the letters were forwarded and added to the Saudi desk files, only a single CIA analytic report regarding this new Saudi Committee had been written, and that report was written by a Saudi analyst, dated February 1995, before the Riyadh attack. Charlie called it up from the archive and read it, disheartened with how narrow-minded it was. It ignored bin Laden's role altogether, focusing on domestic figures who signed on to the committee, and concluding that the Saudi royal family was impervious to either advice or reform.[425]

Bowlen was right, she now saw—the Agency could have a much better understanding of bin Laden and *al Qaeda*, even without access to the KSM material. It just wasn't focused.

She now knew that barely a month after KSM's meeting with bin Laden, Khobar Towers had been attacked. On June 25, 1996 at 9:30 in the evening, a vehicle loaded with explosives, this time a truck, got into a restricted area at King Abdul Aziz Airbase in Dhahran, Saudi Arabia, driving up to Building 131, a dormitory housing those very American soldiers.

When the massive bomb secreted in the truck exploded, it ripped the façade off the front of the eight-story structure, sending a fireball howling through the building. Nineteen people were instantly killed, and more than 500 were injured—including 240 American military personnel, mostly Air Force enlisted men and women.[426]

It was the worst terrorist attack against the United States in thirteen years, since Beirut. The carnage was an order of magnitude worse than the attack in Riyadh the previous year. "The cowards who committed this murderous act must not go unpunished," President Clinton grimly announced on television.[427] Charlie vividly remembered the day, the shock at the Agency, the president's tough talk. Thinking now, after she read KSM's dispatches, how blatant Mr. Bowlen's agent—*her agent*—had been in not providing any notice or even a hint of what was imminent.

She went back over his letters looking for some clue. She thought that she picked up that maybe KSM's tone was nervous and a little uncertain. Of course, part of what she detected was that KSM was worried that Afghanistan was nothing like it was in the Soviet days, that it was isolated and even "going backwards" as he said. But KSM also fretted that bin

Laden wasn't just thrown out of Sudan. He had also been stripped of a large part of his wealth, investments that were either confiscated outright or others that the *Sheikh* thought would be tied up in the country forever.[428]

She found herself agreeing with KSM that much of the subtleties of bin Laden's political message were overly focused on internal Saudi affairs. And she agreed, that though the *Salafi* rhetoric, with its generous quoting of the *Qur'an* and *hadith*,[429] grated on the American ear, he wasn't wrong. Invaders. Crusaders. Jews. She had to admit to herself that it was a textured foundation for the attacks in Riyadh and Khobar Towers.

She'd been reading for 18 hours a day. And her team was pouring over satellite maps to pinpoint KSM's home. She'd now been to Karachi twice on scouting trips, preparing for the handoff. She didn't feel wholly conversant with KSM's voice and his retelling of events, but she was finally connecting with her reading of his decade of output, not just linking what he said to the official intelligence, but also getting inside his head. Barbara and her people, particularly Erica, the KSM analyst and now her researcher, put together a new link analysis. No analyst herself, she began to appreciate why Steve insisted on constantly returning to old events in his own analysis, always searching for more detail and greater understanding in the rereading, seeing new things. Now she wanted to read the original letters one by one in Arabic, and in chronological order, to double-check whether she wasn't giving bin Laden too much credit, being too selective.

She called Tony to ask for permission to bring the unclassified pieces home.

It was odd for her to be home during daylight hours, odder still to be home at all since joining Apex Watch. Her apartment was sparse and modern, functional. Unlike many at the Agency, Charlie insisted on living in the District, not the Virginian or Maryland suburbs. She insisted when she came to Washington that she was going to maintain a normal life.

That never happened.

She kept in touch with some Yale classmates, but made few friends outside the Agency. Other than going out to eat or going to the movies, she never integrated into life in Washington. And she only ever went to the Mall or took in a museum when a family member came from out of town to visit.

In her apartment, she made a cup of tea and curled up with bin Laden, carefully reading letter after letter, making notes, taking the occasional break to straighten her back or crack her neck, snoozing for a moment, staring out the window at her sliver of a view of Rock Creek Park.

Here were two years of bin Laden's encouragement to the devout, to Saudi patriots, to do something about the defilement of the Holy Land—to do something that, to her, looked like the attacks on Riyadh and Khobar Towers. And yet U.S. intelligence concluded that the responsible party was Iran.[430]

Thinking about Steve again, wondering about his view of the Khobar attack and what he'd think about the letters, she called him.

"Draper," he answered on his office phone.

"It's Charlie."

"Hello, hello, hello," he said. "They finally let you out?"

"It's been quite the grind."

"I bet," he responded. She was grateful he didn't whine or launch into some narcissistic rant about his own woes.

"Can you peel away tonight?"

"Absolutely," he said.

"Belmont Kitchen at seven," she said. "I'll make a reservation."

He hesitated.

"Too early?" she asked.

"No, that's great," he said. "I'll leave soon."

There were now two men in Charlie's life who so admired Osama bin Laden. One was a terrorist who would admit it. The other would skillfully laugh in her face if she so suggested.

Just a few blocks from both of their apartments, the restaurant was a favorite of Steve's, with meticulous plates of nouvelle cuisine, its sunken, whitewashed walls exuding quiet.

He was never late. When she entered, he was already sitting at the table, nursing a bourbon and soda with lime.

She ordered a glass of white wine, pinot grigio. That's what everyone was drinking.

He took her hand from across the tiny table and squeezed it. "How are you?"

"To tell you the truth," she said, "I'm exhausted. Yet I'm also exhilarated. I'm mostly reading myself in, but the place is amazing, focused and functioning."

"And Bowlen?"

"So far, I find him charming. In comparison with back stabbers at the Agency, he's refreshingly direct."

"Is there anything you can talk to me about?"

"I don't have any actual authorization yet," she answered, "but I've been trying to wrap my head around Khobar Towers and understand why—since it was obviously inspired by bin Laden—the government is so doggedly reaching a different conclusion. Also, why bin Laden didn't claim credit for it?"

The waitress taking their order gave Steve a moment to formulate an answer for Charlie.

"You once said Freeh was the problem," she added after the waitress left. "What did you mean?"

Louis Freeh, the FBI director, appointed by Bill Clinton eight months after taking office.

"Well," he said, relaxing a bit, "structurally, there's always been a problem in putting the FBI director in charge of terrorist investigations, though that is what the system has, in its wisdom, decided to do."[431]

A year before Khobar Towers, Clinton signed a presidential directive placing the Bureau in charge of investigating any overseas terrorist attack involving American citizens.

"Yeah, we've had that discussion," Charlie interrupted, "that it's the wrong way to understand these problems."

Steve didn't think that handling a terrorist attack as a pure law-enforcement matter was quite right; that treating terrorism as law enforcement missed the bigger picture. But nor did he think that it was the sole responsibility of the Agency. Nor did he support the military taking the lead, or even retaliating after the fact.

"Was it because Freeh wasn't on speaking terms with the president?" she asked.

"Well, that didn't help," Steve said. "And it doesn't help that Freeh doesn't know his ass from his elbow when it comes to foreign affairs. And he really doesn't understand Saudi Arabia. And he's too in love with royalty."

"The latter," Charlie said. "What about that?"

"When he was preparing to go to Saudi Arabia to take a look for himself, investigators on the ground complained that Saudi authorities stiff-armed them. So he sought the help of Prince Bandar, the only Saudi he knew. And he was the ambassador. But armed with that presidential directive, he also did so without coordinating with the State Department or the Agency, his right, but also cutting himself off from people who might have at least counseled on what to expect.

"To say Bandar was much too crafty for Freeh would be an understatement. Anyhow, Freeh then asked the White House to facilitate an introduction to the king or to Crown Prince Abdullah.[432] The White House actually did what he asked. But Bandar whispered into Freeh's ears that the White House screwed up the request. That they didn't really want an actual answer regarding who was behind the attack. And that fit with Freeh's narrative about President Clinton.

"Here's where Freeh's other hat, and domestic politics intervened. Just days before the Khobar attack, *File Gate* exploded into the press, with Freeh chastising the White House for improperly requesting FBI investigative files.[433]

"So anyhow, Bandar told Freeh that *he* would personally coordinate his trip to Saudi Arabia and set up meetings for everyone he needed to see, even the top Saudi policeman ..."

"Saudi police!" Charlie squealed. "Jesus, that's a joke." She had her own experience with her lieutenant.

"Look, Charlie, Bandar fucked this guy up the ass and Freeh never even noticed the penetration," Steve continued. "The prince announced that he personally would provide a three-million-dollar reward for information leading to the arrest of the Khobar Towers bombers.[434] And then he accompanied Freeh to Walter Reed to visit the wounded, telling him that together they would catch whoever did this, saying it wouldn't be some O.J. Simpson trial.[435]

"Bandar also cleverly let Freeh in on what he said was a little secret. The Saudis hated the president's love of turning everything into politics, he said. And besides, he whispered to Freeh, the royals back home were upset by the sordidness of the president's personal behavior. Lewinsky was a young girl. It could be your daughter, Bandar told him. Then came the catch. To help, Bandar told him, Saudi Arabia needed assurances that the secret corners in Washington wouldn't be allowed to use whatever they provided in order to propel Clinton to launch some kind of military retaliation."

After doing all the talking, Steve gobbled up his salad.

"More?" he finally said.

She nodded. He continued: "This is mostly gossip, but the Saudis rolled out red carpets for Freeh, blowing so much smoke up his ass he couldn't see straight. But that doesn't account for the fact that there were able investigators on the ground—including Agency people—and they also came to the same conclusion. It was Iran."

"To be fair," Steve went on, "Iran is the working hypothesis of the Agency as well, that Khobar was connected to the previous year's attack and thus the work of Iran.[436] And if you only saw the evidence manufactured by the Saudis, why would you come to any other conclusion? I mean, in law enforcement terms. That's the structural problem."

Then Steve surprised her. "I would be remiss if I didn't say that there is a contradictory stream that affirms Iran. From the Reagan administration onwards, we've known Iran was behind the 1983 attack on the Marine barracks in Beirut. You might not know this detail, but tens of thousands of dollars also moved from Tehran to the New York during the 1993 World Trade Center attack.[437] It's a fact. And we've got solid intelligence that Iranians were issuing direct orders to Saudi dissidents. A lot of evidence points to Iran."[438]

"What?" Charlie said.

"My guess is that Tehran reads bin Laden's letters and *fatwas* as well, that they see the potential to add to internal Saudi dissent in *Shi'a* and *Sunni* ranks by attacking the American military in the country—by highlighting the American military. You know: *the enemy of my enemy*. So yes, bin Laden was the inspiration, but the attack only makes sense in that Tehran would love to see the Americans go. Of course, this is the kind of tail-chasing that drives me insane," Steve said.

"Because I agree with you about bin Laden," he continued. "Undoubtedly, the bombers listened to him as well. Of that I also have no doubt. However, pinning this on Iran glosses over what it is all about, which is our military presence in the country.

"Even there, I want to say: so what?" Steve continued. "Bin Laden and others make a big deal of the American presence, yet if we didn't have forces in Saudi Arabia, something like this would have happened anyhow. It would have happened someplace else. That's the new normal, maybe helped along by the Gulf War, and our bases created and kept everywhere. It's symptomatic of so many bigger issues."

She'd heard his arguments before, his arguments on both sides. "And Freeh?" Charlie asked.

"Fucking Freeh met all the princes. He was put up in a 20-million-dollar guest house and ate lobster and caviar. He even got a rare audience with King Fahd. Not only did he come back thinking Iran was the Khobar culprit, he returned enchanted with the majesty and splendor of a puritanical nation, one that matched his own Catholicism and outlook. The whole Saudi point of it all—and this is my opinion—was to enlist Freeh as an ally, to ensure that there wouldn't be military retaliation."

"But Freeh is pushing for a strike," said Charlie. "He practically accuses the White House of abandoning the victims' families."

"Freeh's vociferous clamoring probably is one of the prime reasons why nothing is happening. Once that motherfucker started arguing for military action, the White House decided no way."

Charlie sat back and quietly laughed. That made sense.

"Anyhow," Steve went on, "Freeh was wined and dined but no real information was transmitted. And the Saudis kept it secret that they already had the suspects in custody. Prince Nayef took the senior FBI investigator aside and lamented that there were no good military options, playing both sides of the street."[439]

"Hell, in intercepts we've got Nayef saying to someone in Washington: 'If America responds militarily, what are you going to do to Iran? Flatten their military facilities? Destroy their oil refineries? Are you going to nuke them? To achieve what? So that we have to fight a war with Iran? We are next door to them. You are six thousand miles away.'

"Bandar whispered to Freeh that the political animals in the White House didn't really want evidence that Iran was responsible, for fear that they would *have* to take military action. It was brilliant and fucking Freeh believed it all. He believed Bandar when he told him that the White House was burying the evidence. Meanwhile, unbeknownst to Freeh,

Bandar was telling the White House that they would only share what they knew if they got assurances that the White House wouldn't use the information to take military action. I hear that no less than Sandy Berger screamed at Bandar, calling him a cocksucker and angrily telling him to just give the United States the evidence, no strings attached.[440]

"It's a shit sandwich. And the Pentagon doesn't want to play anyhow. The CIA came up with some cockamamie scheme to bomb Iranian bases in Lebanon in retaliation, thinking that a viable option.[441] Now that would be great, huh?" Then he said: "The Saudis are just outplaying us."

"So, Freeh isn't really the problem," Charlie stated. "Clinton is."

She'd also had this conversation with Steve a million times. He'd told her that it was partisan, her animus towards Clinton. That if she liked the president, she'd argue that a leader's personal life was off-limits.

They'd gotten into a pattern while talking about Clinton. She would rail and he would shrug: *It is what it is*. He'd uttered that phrase so many times it became an inside joke.

When Charlie got on her soapbox about how human rights and the politically-correct dictatorship of the rule of law devastated the CIA's clandestine service, or how Clinton decimated American military strength by turning warfighters into peacekeepers, Steve made a *flap-flap-flap*ping move with his hand, taunting her.

"You really believe that?" he asked her in a quiet moment one day when they were in their spot in the CIA cafeteria. "More important, do you really care? You're no better than some leftie who protests a war because the United Nations hasn't approved it, or because Congress didn't declare it, when if the U.N. approved it and Congress passed a resolution saying go out and kill, you'd still oppose it because it's a Clinton war. I get it that you don't like him, but he's not responsible for how screwed up the CIA or the world is. Look beyond the politics. What the world needs is simply respect. And universal enforcement of a set of laws. Not lame retaliation. Not covert action. A little bit of respect would completely take away the terrorist's ammunition."

R-E-S-P-E-C-T, she thought. How naïve could he be.

She rolled her eyes at what she thought was Steve's naïveté, containing herself from laughing even though she felt like she wanted to.

Charlie deeply admired Steve. He was truly struggling to understand, believing in his heart of hearts that *if* there was something that he, in his luxurious thinker's pose, could do to improve national security and bring about a greater degree of understanding and peace, he wanted to do it.

"No one comes off looking good here," Steve continued as they nibbled at a chocolate cake for dessert, two forks. "To keep our eyes on the prize, Iran and bin Laden got off scot-free and the Saudis picked up another agent of influence in Washington."

"Freeh."

"Yep."

Given the earful Charlie now had about Saudi corruption, she wondered whether Freeh wasn't indeed on the take, a true Saudi agent of influence inside the government.

He walked her home, up 18th Street and across the bridge into Woodley Park. They were both tired on a weeknight and neither made much of a move to extend the evening.

"Get what you needed?" he asked as they reached her front door.

Charlie's head was filled to bursting. She wasn't sure if Steve was fishing, wasn't sure what she wanted.

She thanked him, kissed him on the cheek and walked into her building, grateful to avoid an all-night discussion about their future.

Chapter 23 Know It All

"I've decided," Charlie said, sitting in Bowlen's Apex Watch office on a still, sweltering day as fall approached, the air outside so heavy with humidity it assaulted anyone trying to move through it.

"Mr. Draper," he said, sitting back in his executive chair, jacketless and abnormally flushed, a sweating Diet Coke with ice in a cut-glass tumbler in his hand.

"Yes," she said. "I mean, sir, what's the point of the handoff, and I don't mean the goal of alleviating you of the burden of doing two jobs—that's important—but what's the point of my taking on KSM if we don't have a world-class brain to help us. And that's not a knock against Barbara or her people."

"It is true that he's a pain in the ass?" Bowlen asked, matter of fact.

"Yes, he is," she said. And she chuckled to herself.

"But he's our ..." they both said at the same time. And they laughed.

"Look," she said, "no one knows this world better than Steve and he's bored stiff where he is, tilting at windmills, uninterested in the game of counterterrorism, wanting, he says, just like you, to get in front of attacks. And besides. Everyone at the Center increasingly hates him for his contrariness. Especially after Khobar, his arguing that Iran might have been, quote, *behind it*, but so what. I know there's a danger in being the Steve whisperer, and I know that that's what I'll end up being here, but I'm willing to pay the price if he can come up with some new idea for how we can defeat bin Laden."

"I've thought of hiring Mr. Draper," Bowlen responded, "many times. I've always worried that his keeping track of the minutiae of corruption, and then watching nothing happen as a result, would drive him insane. But I think we can segregate him from the money side here, focus him solely on analyzing the future of *al Qaeda.* Now that bin Laden is back in Afghanistan and in the business of attacking the United States, it would be mighty useful to not just have early warning from Khalid, but also some ideas about what to do about it.

"But before we make a decision," Bowlen said, "and I do mean *we,* he's requested a meeting to brief me on his latest research. That's a first, a private briefing by the great Mr. Draper. Do you know what that's about?"

"Only vaguely," she answered. "The FBI director is a Saudi agent and the Saudis are running a covert operation against Clinton."

"Oh, that's all," Bowlen deadpanned. And they both laughed again.

"I'll arrange for him to do it at the downtown office since I don't want him out here yet, and you are PNGed from going to the Agency." *Persona non grata.* Charlie had officially disappeared.

"You want me to attend?"

"Of course," Bowlen answered. "No second-class citizen stuff because you're his girl," he said, genuinely wanting to please her. "You are ops to his analysis. I want and need both."

Days later, Bowlen arranged for Steve to be picked up at Langley so he could bring his classified files with him. They met him at the Exceptional Research Technologies office on L Street, a boxy and sterile white space behind glass doors at the end of a long corridor in a spiffy office building, seemingly just another consulting company in the nation's capital.

The greetings were businesslike. Arranging his papers on the conference room table, Steve said he appreciated their time.

"Khalid Sheikh Mohammed," he started, hoping a thunderclap might unhinge the two.

"What about him?" Bowlen responded, unfazed, and looking straight at Steve.

"Why is it that no one seems to know who he is?"

"You tell us," Bowlen flatly responded.

"I don't know," Steve blasted back, taking pleasure in popping the balloon he'd blown up, but only being half serious. "This man that no one seems to care about ties together the World Trade Center bombing and Manila. He's connected to Riyadh and Khobar Towers, at least through bin Laden. And, I think, he points to a high-level spy, maybe even raises questions about the president."

"That's quite the imposing list," Bowlen.

"Well, here's what I know," Steve said, taking a deep breath. "There is a Saudi man named Abdulrahman al-Ghamdi. He shows up in the Philippines Airlines plot, and he's even named by one of the co-conspirators. At least as an alias, he's named. It might have meant nothing, even to me, but something odd came across my desk."

Steve reached into a manila envelope that he removed a document from his box of files, slipping it across the table.

"Saudi intelligence—the director Prince Turki[442] himself," he went on as Bowlen eyed the document, "sends an eyes-only letter to President Clinton telling him that this Mr. Ghamdi is a major figure in an assassination plot against the president. The details of the plot aren't altogether clear, hence the eyes-only letter to the president. Not only is Ghamdi implicated, but somehow this Saudi man supposedly is also working with conspirators within our government."

"An eyes-only letter to the president," Bowlen says. "You got your hands on this how?"

"Well. First I got my hands on a Philippines embassy report relating to one Mr. Ghamdi," Steve answered, avoiding answering.

"And it says?"

"I can show you the report if you want. But let me add, I don't think that there is any culpability within the government behind any plot. If there is a plot, if there was a plot. But there is a Mr. Ghamdi, and somehow, in numerous visits to our embassy in Manila, he collected enough information for someone to be able to make it look like elements of our own government were implicated in whatever assassination plot the Saudis later described to President Clinton, and that it was part of a bigger conspiracy.

"The Clinton assassination was to have taken place at the APEC Summit,[443] but because of the breakup of the Philippine plotting, and the supposed plan to kill the Pope, the Clinton plot fell by the wayside. To me though, that's not what interesting about the Saudi letter. After I started doing research on this Mr. Ghamdi, I just couldn't fathom why the Saudis would want to bring greater attention to this man, and to their potential support for an assassination.

"From what I know, the president called Deutch into the Oval Office after this report from Prince Turki came in, asking him to find out who this Ghamdi guy was.

"All very hush-hush. But for months, the Agency never answered. That is to say, that the director wasn't able to get an answer from his own agency. And, incredibly enough, even though it was a supposed plot to kill the president, interest seemed to dissipate."

Steve continued: "I don't know what Prince Bandar actually said to Sandy Berger when they met. But whatever evidence they provided beyond the letter seemed to have come from a source close to Osama bin Laden himself. The White House considered it all credible enough to asked about Mr. Ghamdi.

"I also know that you, sir, received a memo from Deutch that he sent to all division heads about this supposed plot. Well, again, let me be clear: I only know that you were an addressee on the director's memo. I point that out because maybe you didn't see the memo. Because if you had seen it, maybe you would have actually responded, which you didn't. Or if you did respond, your response is not in the files."

Bowlen almost imperceptibly flinched at the gratuitous verbal acrobatics.

"Fast forward," Steve Draper said, "I thought the plot interesting not because of any of the facts, but more because the president heard about it from a not-so-friendly foreign government."

"The Saudis ..." Bowlen started.

"Let me review," Steve interrupted. "One, the Agency or some other element of our government is supposedly plotting to assassinate the president with the help of this Saudi man named Ghamdi. Two, the president finds out about this supposed conspiracy from—of all places— the government of Saudi Arabia. And three, the president turns around and goes to the CIA director for information, the head of the agency that could be housing the potential plotters. Why doesn't he just keep it inside the Secret Service? Or go the FBI?"

"Maybe he did," Bowlen interjected.

Steve halted for a second, but then bowled on. "So, the president has this meeting with Deutch, and Deutch takes the letter and starts what I'd call a rather perfunctory bureaucratic inquiry. And *voila!* All the department heads asked whether they have any information about this Mr. Ghamdi respond that they do not. Which, of course, describes the idiots precisely, that they indeed know nothing. Except for you, sir. That is, that you didn't respond.

"Then, within weeks, the whole thing blows over. A matter of such supposed gravity provokes no action and then just disappears. And then, for some reason, an entire packet of documents arrives on my desk right after Khobar."

"I guess not so hush-hush after all," Bowlen snorted.

"I thought maybe it was intentional on your part, sir, kind of like administering a secret test. It might have made some sense for Ghamdi to end up on my desk, had someone thought that if anyone was going to discover the why of the who it might be me." Just for a moment, Steve seemed unable to contain his ego. "So, I tried to figure it out.

"I started with the databases just to be sure and then went back into the 1993 files ... well, I didn't really start there: I ended up there. But I matched Ramzi Yousef's accomplices from New York with the Philippine crew and the assassination plot—at least the one directed at the Pope. Helped by the transcript of the Philippine police interrogation of Yousef's Manila accomplice, the guy named Murad, I made a list of the people mentioned who were identified ..."

"I'm sure you did your job," Bowlen interrupted, showing some impatience. "Just tell us what you discovered."

"When I reconstructed the Manila case," Steve went on, trying to ignore the interruption, "I saw again there were not only stray names but someone who was specifically unaccounted for. He's there and he's not there, mentioned by almost everyone at some point but every time he's mentioned or every time someone says something about him, he is not only described differently, but has some different alias and even a different nationality.

"So this is where it gets interesting. Khalid Sheikh Mohammed enters the picture. He doesn't appear in my research until the end, but his appearance forces me to go back to the beginning. He's connected to

Ramzi Yousef and the New York bombing, officially as a minor financier. He travels internationally under a variety of names and nationalities, and then … then," Draper hesitates for added effect, "the name that doesn't really represent anything to anyone, the name of a man who seems to be everywhere in the shadows but is absent from any wanted poster, shows up buried deep in the CIA scrub list. And I'm thinking, how did that happen?"

The scrub list. The product of the Clinton administration directive calling for a purge of distasteful assets from the intelligence payroll.

"He shows up on the scrub list?" Charlie asked. "I don't remember that."

"Well. He *was* on it," Steve responded. "Until the list was doctored. But that would make him a U.S. asset, even though no one seems to have ever heard of him and I can find no record of his existence. I thought, *Okay, there could be more than one list.* And there was. The divisions at first did their passive-aggressive thing in offering a minimal number of assets. But the seventh floor and management kept telling them to go back to the well, that hiding unsavory characters was eventually going to come back to bite them.

"So I stacked them all up against each other and what I found was that maybe the list was tinkered with, and his name was removed." He took out two pieces of paper and placed them on the table, page 27 of a very long list, one with and one without Khalid Sheikh Mohammed's name.

"So, anyway," Steve continued, "Uncle Khalid …"

"Uncle?" Bowlen interjected.

"Oh, turns out that Khalid Sheikh Mohammed is Ramzi Yousef's uncle, though he's only three years older."

Bowlen covered his mouth with his hand, looking away and smiling.

"When Ramzi Yousef was rendered in Pakistan, a phone number for someone named Khalid in Qatar was stored on his mobile phone SIM card. Yousef's laptop captured in Manila earlier also had numerous references to the same telephone number and a slew of email addresses that could be this same Khalid or one of his various screen names. And in the pocket litter[444] of one the accomplices when Murad was captured in Manila, investigators also found an entry "Khalid Doha"—the same guy with the same number.[445]

"Look at this," Draper said, sliding a photocopy of a photocopy across the table: "Philippine airport entry form; Ramzi Yousef—under his own *nom de guerre*—entered and exited the country seven times in 1994, twice on the same plane with one Mr. Abdulrahman A. F. Al-Ghamdi, Saudi citizen. By the way, the F is wrong; it's A, Abdulrahman A. A. At least that's what his passport says."[446]

"And?" says Mr. Bowlen.

"It can't just be a coincidence that they're on the same plane. But Ghamdi, a man obviously connected to Ramzi Yousef, isn't mentioned in the grand jury proceedings or the trial of Yousef and company. He's not mentioned in the Philippines indictment as the alias of any person. And he's not in the Agency names database, not on any watch list and he's not in the NSA dictionary, nor is *he* on the purge list. But Salem Ali is."

There was a chuckle from Bowlen. "Okay, I'll bite."

"Khalid Sheikh Mohammed, aka Salem Ali, Ramzi Yousef's uncle, was indicted by the U.S. Attorney for the Southern District of the State of New York for his involvement in the World Trade Center and Philippines conspiracies.[447] That's Khalid Sheikh Mohammed. Indicted. But that was just after his name was scrubbed from the CIA files and, I'm guessing, removed rather skillfully from the central databases. The FBI discovered that a man identified as Khalid Sheikh Mohammed wired money to Yousef. *Then*, the same guy is involved in the Philippines plotting. So, he's indicted and there's a rather matter-of-fact rendition attempt and, then again, somehow he just disappears from everyone's radar screen."

"A rendition attempt?" Charlie interrupts. She'd been reading the KSM archives for weeks now and never came across anything indicating that there had been an indictment or an attempt to bring him to justice.

"Sir?" she says, looking at Mr. Bowlen.

"Let's see what Mr. Draper has to say," Bowlen said, knowing he was going to have to explain what happened to Charlie.

"A minor rendition, not even worth mentioning," Steve Draper continued, seeing some light between the two. "Then it came to me: Khalid Doha, Khalid, Uncle Khalid, Salem Ali, Khalid Sheikh Mohammed—even this supposed Saudi guy named Ghamdi—they're all one and the same person! It's one person floating along in all of this so-called intelligence, important enough to attract FBI attention, but not ever seen as more than some minor player who wrote a check.

"So then I'm thinking, wait a minute—do the Saudis know that it's Khalid Sheikh Mohammed? And then I thought that they not only know, but know of Sheikh Mohammed as well—that they want to send some message."

"That's your conclusion?" Bowlen asked.

Steve looked up and paused, instantly upended with the prospect that he might be wrong. Or that there was something more he didn't know.

"Why didn't they just go to Brennan[448] or the Bureau?" Bowlen asked. "By then, there were FBI guys crawling all over because of Riyadh and Khobar Towers. Why did the Saudis contact the president directly?"

"Well, sir, I think the Saudis don't go to John Brennan because that's not the game they play with the CIA station chief there. And they can't go to the FBI because they want to protect the FBI director."

"And why would they want to do that?" Bowlen says.

"Because he is a Saudi agent."

"Agent? You're not speaking loosely?"

"I can't prove it, but I'm guessing you can, which is really why I'm here. Director Freeh has crossed paths with Khalid Sheikh Mohammed, that is, with this Mr. Ghamdi ..."

Steve continued speaking, now more rapidly. Bowlen was exhausted with his telling and his manner, and knew where he was going, that he knew who KSM was.

"And what do you think I know or can do?" Bowlen carefully asked.

"Help me understand who Khalid Sheikh Mohammed is. And why the Saudis would want to point to him while suggesting to the White House that the Agency, or at least some rogue element, is implicated in an assassination plot that never existed."

"And why should I help you?"

"Well, because I think the Saudis were sending a message to you, sir."

"And that message is?"

"I'm not sure. I admit that I don't clearly understand your relationship to them. But I have more."

The FBI director is a Saudi agent and you have more? Bowlen thought.

"Once I put all of the aliases together, I went looking for this Khalid Sheikh Mohammed, starting with his rendition file, which I found at the bottom of a bottomless pit.

"So, here's this Khalid Sheikh Mohammed ... sir, *can I just call him KSM?* ... he manages to slip away from an official kidnapping, as if he was tipped off by someone on the inside. He disappears almost literally. Whatever case file the FBI has on him is transferred to the Agency and it goes exclusively to the renditions branch,[449] which, of course, doesn't share with anyone else. And then, after the rendition is aborted and KSM escapes, the file is put aside and interest in KSM seems to evaporate. I can't say why, but I thought at first that Freeh was responsible for the rendition going sour.

"You know, sir," Steve went on, ignoring Bowlen's palpable discomfort, beaming at Charlie and finishing his presentation just as he'd hoped, practically bursting, "I've learned in this business that people—even really important ones—can just fall through the cracks. Important information can be lost or missed. I've also learned that 'analyst' is only a title. And I've learned to distrust databases as much as I distrust the idiot drones who create them."

As if by instinct, Draper looked left and right, even though the three of them were alone in a secure room. From his accordion file of folders and papers, Steve took out another large manila envelope and slid it across the table.

When Bowlen opened it, he slipped out a CIA source folder, filched from the central registry—that itself not an easy task. It was the original, too. Stolen. It was an absolute *no*, removing it; though for a moment Bowlen had a sense of relief that Draper had found the last shred of KSM's official existence and that it no longer existed. Across the top was the name:

Khalid Shaykh Mohammed Ali Dustin al-Balushi, ADCI(SP) 86-0321

The folder was empty except for a cover sheet which contained a warning for whoever tripped upon it and wasn't properly cleared. The note said to consult with the office of Special Purpose, Bowlen's office, for more information.

"He's one of yours," Draper said. According to the control number, he surmised that Khalid Sheikh Mohammed was recruited by the Agency in 1986. "And I'm guessing he's Charlie's new agent. Now aren't you glad *I* found all this, and not somebody else?"

Chapter 24 Rendition

A federal grand jury handed down an indictment of one Khalid Sheikh Mohammed in January 1996, wanted as a co-conspirator in the attack on the World Trade Center, as well as for his involvement in two thwarted plots: The Days of Terror in New York, and a conspiracy to assassinate Pope John Paul II in the Philippines.[450]

They'd been empaneled for months, the grand jurors, hearing witness testimony and examining evidence presented by the U.S. attorney, coached through documents and financial records, listening to name after name, finally agreeing that there was enough evidence to indicate that this particular named defendant—*Mr. Mohammed*—had committed a crime. Though a resident of Pakistan, the FBI had information to indicate that he had relocated to Doha, Qatar, where he was employed by a government agency.[451] His background also suggested, though it wasn't clear, that he had connections to Kuwait. The magistrate judge in the matter of the *United States versus Khalid Sheikh Mohammed* therefore agreed that the indictment be kept secret so as not to tip him off, pending an attempt to apprehend him.

Bowlen read the sealed indictment, and though the FBI had no true knowledge of who the suspect was, the routine now would be for Khalid's name to be added to a list sent out to embassies and CIA stations in Qatar, Pakistan, Kuwait, and even the Philippines requesting additional information. He frankly thought that that would be the end of it.

That all happened before Steve Draper showed up with his independent research tying Khalid to him, Mister Draper unaware of the sealed indictment, unaware of how deep their man's relationship was with Apex Watch.

"You want to tell me about this?" Charlie said.

Steve had finished his presentation and gathered up his papers, leaving the two of them in the downtown conference room.

"He got a number of things wrong," Bowlen said. "About Freeh being a Saudi agent."

"That's all you have to say?" Charlie responded. "He put together pieces I didn't see, even with access to the entire archives, even after comparing the Apex Watch holdings to the official archives. You gotta admit it was impressive."

"Nothing to admit," Bowlen responded. "It was."

"So, a rendition? There was one?"

"There was an attempt," Bowlen answered.

"And?"

"And the Qataris tipped him off, allowing him to escape."

"That's all you have to say? You didn't warn KSM first that he was under suspicion?" Charlie pressed.

"Charlie, I did."

"And now? The CIA knows about him, an agent that you are proposing we keep on the books, someone who is behind numerous attacks?" Charlie asked.

"Knows," Bowlen said, repeating the word *knows*. He was half in the conversation, half staring out the window. Then his head snapped back to Charlie. "The CIA, my dear, knows all sort of things without knowing anything for real. Your Mr. Draper just proved that."

Then he told her the story.

There had been another Charlie out there, Bowlen said, an enterprising young case officer, a woman, who did her job very well. At the station in Qatar, she reported that they found a Kuwaiti passport-holder matching the description of one Mr. Khalid Sheikh Mohammed. He was working as a water department engineer.

Apex Watch saw the operational traffic, intercepting every possible report regarding their suspects and agents. Bowlen was the director by then, Hal Jones having just retired, but just for a sanity check, he went up to Vermont to meet with the former director, and they agreed, given Khalid's helpfulness in the capture of Ramzi Yousef, that Bowlen would fly out to Qatar and meet with him.[452]

The country, though, and most of Doha, was overwhelmingly composed of outsiders, the largest portion of which were guest workers who came from Pakistan.

Compared to other Gulf Arab towns, Doha was pretty open then. But Qatar was also newly an American ally, having signed a defense pact with the United States after the Iraqi invasion of Kuwait—only the third Arab country in the region ever to do so.[453] And the previous year, the Crown Prince Hamad bin Khalifa al-Thani deposed his father.[454] He was immediately recognized by Washington, the American assumption being that the Qataris would want to cooperate in an unimportant matter that might pay off later. Thus, Bowlen told Charlie, his objective was just to get KSM to leave before all of the pieces could be put in place for his arrest.

"A forced rendition is being prepared for you," Bowlen had said to Khalid as they walked on the corniche, the waterfront promenade extending for five miles on Doha Bay.

"A what?" Khalid asked.

"A rendition. *Rendered to the bar of justice*,"[455] Bowlen said.

"And what are these words?" Khalid asked.

"They are bad words to be associated with you, Khalid," Bowlen answered. "They mean an official kidnapping."

Khalid listened.

"Tell me why I shouldn't just let this happen?" Bowlen said. "It is time for you to step up regarding our Saudi mission. You're close to bin Laden. I need something useful to continue to protect you."

"Are you saying I haven't given you anything useful?"

"Tell me why I shouldn't just let this happen, Khalid?"

"You are suggesting that I haven't given you anything useful. And yet you hesitate because I might be useful in the future? Or is it because if I am arrested that it could expose you?"

"It is both, Khalid," Bowlen said wearily. "And I do hesitate. And I don't even want to convey a threat. But now all of what I warned you about is happening and I need you to take this more seriously. We're in this together, my friend. I told you this day would come. But we have also agreed that I need to know beforehand what you are going to do. And you did not do that."

"I am not responsible for the bombing in Riyadh," Khalid answered, knowing exactly what Bowlen was referring to.

"Khalid, you could have warned us."

"No, I couldn't have," he insisted.

"So, bin Laden really is going to attack his own homeland?" Bowlen asked. "And are there more attacks, more World Trade Centers to come?"

"Both," KSM answered, pausing and letting his answer sink in. "Of course, Dr. Zawahiri and others want us to attack the snakes in Cairo. The *Sheikh* is resisting their vision for, as he says, such attacks do not make for an international movement. And new attacks, he says, must have impact on the world stages."

Bowlen shook his head. "And bin Laden really has it in him to attack the royal family, in Saudi Arabia itself?"

"Before Riyadh, my opinion would have been to say no, Mister. I thought he would want to protect his family above all else. But yes, evidently now, as you say, he has it in him."

"And you are sure that this attack is the work of bin Laden?"

"Riyadh was a surprise to me. The attack. But if I were you, I would take this attack as a warning about *Sheikh* bin Laden the general and *Sheikh* bin Laden the prophet. The men who did this took inspiration from the *Sheikh*. I don't think they took his direction. I really don't know who he has with him in Saudi Arabia, and I have read in the newspapers that the men who bombed the American building were *Shi'a* activists. I tell you the plan was not discussed with me or within my circle. I heard nothing of it beforehand."[456]

Khalid continued: "But, my friend, you are not here to be mad at me for Riyadh."

"No, I am here to warn you that the FBI is coming for you," Bowlen said. "You made a mistake sending money to New York, moving it in a way that could be traced back to you. I warned you about that. And as for the Philippines, one of your men told the FBI all that he knows."

"I made a mistake. You mean *others* made mistakes."

"That's all you are focused on?" Bowlen responded. "This should be a lesson that you are not as invisible as you think."

"But I did not make a mistake, Mister. If you did not know me, my friend, would your CIA know me?"

"You are wrong, Khalid. They have now discovered you," Bowlen answered. "Someone identified you from a photograph."

Khalid looked at Bowlen from an angle. "They have a photograph of me?"

"Yes."

"And who identified me?"

"Murad," Bowlen answered. One of Khalid's group captured in the Philippines.

Khalid changed the subject, contorting the conversation. "We are a success then? Your CIA has discovered a man with a small checkbook. And you have succeeded in working with me. I have succeeded in my mission to get close to bin Laden. I have shown you my skill. So tell me, even while you are angry with me. How could I have done what you desired in any other way? Other than to become a so-called terrorist."

"Really, Khalid? You only undertake terrorist attacks to get close to bin Laden?"

"*Live your life*, you said. You knew I was a soldier."

"You are many things, but if I called you a soldier you'd also be insulted. But let's not quarrel, Khalid."

Bowlen then shifted his tone. "When I said you made a mistake, I was merely trying to help. And now I hope you understand the biggest mistake you could make, don't you? *Don't you, Khalid?*" Bowlen repeated, punctuating an unstated threat.

"It is not like you, my friend, to speak so," Khalid responded.

"But you made a mistake in exposing yourself, which means exposing me, Khalid. You can never move money again in your own name. Nor travel to certain places. We can argue about the reasons, but now we have to solve a problem."

"I did not make a mistake."

"Khalid Sheikh Mohammed. Your Qatari sponsors are being pressured to grant your extradition to the United States for trial as we speak. And if that doesn't work, the FBI will kidnap you. I am just one step ahead of them."

"I did not make a mistake," KSM persisted, pouting, not listening.

"Everyone makes mistakes, Khalid. You are not safe. And you are not useful to me if you stay here. Indeed, as you say, you are a danger to me. So get out of Qatar."

"I appreciate your loyalty to this lowly and humble servant," Khalid said, a bit mockingly. "But I did not make a mistake."

"And please, no more attacks without first warning me."

"Riyadh was not mine."

"Khalid listen to me," Bowlen responded.

KSM was lost in his own head. And in his plan: the planes operation. The *Sheikh* had now approved a suicide attack. KSM had previously thought of planes, the very instrument of their oh-so-modern and interconnected world. His thought before was that bombs would be planted on the planes, as he had done on the Philippines flight to Tokyo. But now? He thought about suicide bombers on planes. And not blowing up the planes in the air. But suicide bombers who would hijack the planes. Then fly them into targets on the ground. The planes would *be* the bombs. Their own modern vehicles would penetrate their skies, land in their homes. It would take years.

"Are you listening," Bowlen persisted.

"Yes, my friend," Khalid said, half there. "I am sorry if I made life difficult for you, my friend."

"Go back to Pakistan."

"I will go where I am most effective," Khalid had answered, one final defiance.

"A few days later," Bowlen now said to Charlie, "FBI director Louis Freeh arrived in Doha to meet with the Qatari foreign minister. His brief included making a formal request for the extradition of one Khalid Sheikh Mohammed, water department engineer and Pakistani national. By then, Apex Watch had removed his name from CIA databases and his original contact file was expunged from the records. As far as Freeh and the FBI knew, this man Sheikh Mohammed was named by Murad as an accomplice, that's all. The paperwork relating to his extradition—an *ordinary* rendition—had gotten stuck somewhere in the Qatari bureaucracy. Freeh was there to get help from the top in prying it free. No one in the

FBI knew *who* Khalid was. It was just a name.

"The Qatari foreign minister said *of course* the country would consider the American request upon receiving the evidence," Bowlen said to Charlie.

He continued, "The minister also told Freeh before he left, *The emir pledges his full cooperation.* He even wrote a letter personally to President Clinton pledging cooperation in ongoing terrorism investigations.

"Back at the CIA, the Qatar desk warned the FBI that factions within the government might object to American interference in the state's internal affairs. Or, they said, the Qatari government might even tip off this Mr. Mohammed if a packet of evidence was produced, just to be rid of the problem. The FBI then considered its options, deciding that absent Qatari help, they would prepare what was called a forcible rendition, without host government help. The CIA objected to such an operation because such a move in a friendly country would threaten Agency operations. And then the Pentagon objected as well. It increasingly had its eye on Qatar as the fallback from Saudi Arabia for a new Middle East military headquarters it wanted. It didn't want to sour U.S.-Qatari relations when tensions were so high with Iraq.[457]

"Then the Justice Department objected as well. President Clinton had signed an earlier top-secret directive laying out the rules for forcible renditions, and that directive said that there had to be one of two conditions to legally justify a non-cooperative snatch. There either had to be a weapons of mass destruction nexus or there had to be imminent danger of an attack.[458] Neither existed. And now with the CIA, the Pentagon and the Justice Department all in opposition, director Freeh decided that the Bureau should wait for the Qatari government to approve a cooperative apprehension. Freeh thought that such an arrest was possible given that he had become personally involved. Meanwhile, the CIA station in Doha offered a plan to lure KSM out of Qatar to a friendly country—either Egypt or Jordan—where the locals would kidnap him and turn him over to the Americans. Justice concurred with that proposal."

"So much for their legal concerns," Charlie said to Bowlen.

"At the White House, the Counterterrorism Security Group convened to adjudicate," Bowlen continued,[459] all the while Khalid saying he still hadn't decided whether he was going to leave.

"What I don't understand, boss, is all that activity," Charlie interrupted, "on behalf of a suspect nobody even really knew? Khalid Sheikh Mohammed was just a name, right?"

"And not even a name," Bowlen responded. "They were mostly all calling him 'Khalid Doha.'"

"So how do you explain it?"

"Well, my dear, I suppose that once the paperwork got rolling, there was a bit of a snowball effect. But also, greater importance was conferred because it was a matter before the FBI director and the White House special committee. To them, that intrinsically meant that it must be important. Not because it was important, but more because the committee just assumed that if *it* was discussing something, it was important, if for no other reason than only the most important cases rose to their level."

"And you're not concerned that someone within that committee or the FBI is going to remember KSM?"

"Concerned? Yes, of course I'm concerned," Bowlen responded. "But after Khobar Towers—where I know there's no direct connection to Khalid—Khalid Doha is now just a historic name, and because it's Arabic, another name that is forgettable to the gumshoes at the Bureau. That is, if it were ever even really known in the first place."

Hmm, Charlie said. There had to be some truth to what Bowlen was saying, for even within the same Counterterrorist Center at the CIA, she knew nothing about any of this, buried as it was in the Renditions Group, which guarded its territory. And, as Steve had said, most people working on terrorism, most working *period*, were just drones, focused, if even that was right, on bin Laden and other recognized leaders.

"Anyhow," Bowlen continued, "the White House group decided that the ambassador to Qatar should approach the Palace chief to push for a joint snatch."[460]

The State Department and the CIA insisted that the ambassador should also exact a pledge to keep the operation secret, so as not to tip off the notoriously leaky Qatari police. The American ambassador then met with the palace chief, and he was told not to worry. Mr. Sheikh Mohammed, they said, was safely under Qatari surveillance and control.

Attorney General Reno[461] then gave her approval for the cooperative operation.[462] The FBI snatch team moved to a staging base in Italy, ready to work with Qatari secret police.[463]

"Then another delay came," Bowlen said. "My understanding is that when photographs were distributed of Khalid Sheikh Mohammed, one of the FBI operators assigned to the snatch team, an agent who'd been involved in Ramzi Yousef's capture in Pakistan the year before, swore that he'd seen the same man lurking outside the Islamabad guesthouse on the night of Yousef's capture.[464]

"FBI agents then went to re-interview Ramzi Yousef, by then in federal detention in New York. Yousef looked at photographs of KSM but declined to help with anything related to this Mr. Sheikh Mohammed, whom he said he couldn't remember.

"The White House group then asked the Counterterrorist Center to prepare an analysis of the implications of this Sheikh Mohammed being a more important character, that he was somehow involved with the Yousef rendition. One concern expressed by the White House group was that there might be retaliation, perhaps a terrorist attack, if this Mr. Mohammed were kidnapped, even if it was with Qatari help.

"The Rendition Group at the Center said they knew nothing beyond what was in the FBI material about Mr. Mohammed's affiliations of networks. *As far as we know*, they wrote in response to the query, neither Ramzi Yousef nor any of his confederates could 'readily call upon such an organized unit to execute retaliatory strikes against the U.S. or countries that have cooperated with the U.S. in the extradition ...'"

As far as we know. Charlie took it to be a perfect bureaucratic construction.

"Nothing more came forth to clarify whether this Mr. Sheikh Mohammed was dangerous," Bowlen continued in his retelling. "His possible sighting in Islamabad the year earlier was forgotten about as the operation neared. Qatari and White House approval of the plan now in hand, arrangements were made to raid Sheikh Mohammed's home in the middle of the night. The prisoner would be spirited out of the country on an FBI plane.

"Then there was another delay, when, at the last minute, the emir's palace asked for an alternate plan to conceal any Qatari assistance,"[465] Bowlen said.

"FBI director Freeh again contacted the foreign minister to stress that they didn't want Khalid Sheikh Mohammed tipped off.

"And, Charlie—that's when bad news came back: the Qataris sadly reported that Mr. Sheikh Mohammed had evidently left the country, taking a flight to Tehran."[466]

"You tipped him off?" Charlie asked.

"Beyond my original trip?" Bowlen responded, "No. Someone inside the Ministry for Religious Affairs evidently told Khalid that something was afoot."[467]

"To tell you the truth," Charlie said, "I'm having trouble with the big picture here. I get it that outside this office no one understood the true importance of KSM. But after he didn't provide you with warning of Khobar Towers, what you asked him to do when you visited him in Doha, you still want to indulge him?"

"Charlie," Bowlen answered, taking his time. "I'm not intentionally *not* telling you something. There is definitely a collision between an asset that we don't control, and one who is potentially useful. I've said it before, and I'll say it again. I need your help, the help of a fresh set of eyes."

"Explain to me again, now that I've digested some of this intricate story. How aren't we just playing with fire? And how is any of this ethical?"

"I can only say this. We are an off-the-books operation that has a higher purpose affirmed by the president of the United States of America. That means that the CIA is intentionally designated as a place that does not possess all information—which it doesn't possess anyhow because another agency with an equally limited mandate, the FBI, holds what it knows to itself, even if what they know relates to matters that are within the purview of the Agency. Bureaucrats say that's the law. But I say the question of whether *that* is ethical is above my paygrade."

"Really?" Charlie interrupted. "You're going to give me more convoluted answers?"

Bowlen paused. "Charlie, I don't want to leave you with that bureaucratic answer. In some ways, I'm sorry I ever discovered Khalid."

"Meaning?"

"On the one hand, I'm completely comfortable with what we are doing. We could never be doing it within the corporate constraints or oversight requirements of the Agency. We have access to an agent in the middle of it all and, though it is unclear how—or even whether—we will be able to use him to stop individual attacks, we at least have him. I know it might be of little comfort, Charlie, but we have similar penetrations in Saudi Arabia and Iraq, even agents inside the Agency."

"This all started with the Afghanistan war," Bowlen continued, "and now it seems so far away. I have to remind you why we recruited Khalid in the first place. We were fighting the Cold War. It was a different time. Then the American mission died. And we stalled. Meanwhile, bin Laden and company moved forward, the enemy now being us.

"When I say I'm sorry I discovered Khalid, it's more that I have—we have—an almost impossible problem. I've been struggling with the ethics of the relationship for quite some time. And it's just an idea, that we can get him to cooperate. But now I feel invigorated by the possibility of my dynamic duo. Eventually, we will have to tell someone that we have our hands on an active terrorist, but for now I suggest that you effect the handoff and we entice Mr. Draper to join, give him some blank paper and see what he can fill it up with."

"And that's it?" Charlie said. "You just bring him on board to doodle?"

"Are you a good case officer?" Bowlen asked.

"Well, yes, I think so," Charlie responded.

"And is Draper a good analyst?"

"The best."

"Can he be a strategist as well? A builder?"

Charlie winced. "I think so."

"Then, yes," Bowlen said. "If Draper's going to be so critical of counterterrorism as it's currently conducted, if he's going to be such a know-it-all, he has to be pushed to come up with an alternative. And that includes using Khalid to our advantage."

"Is that even possible? I mean, making KSM do anything?" Charlie asked.

"That I don't know. But we'd be derelict if we didn't try."

"Not to put myself out of a job, but why not just get rid of him? Kill him?"

Bowlen thought for a long while before finally answering. "Charlie?" he asked, "did I show you the picture on my desk?"

"The what?"

"The picture. At Langley. It's a framed, handwritten note. It sits right next to a picture of my family. I look at it every day."

"It's a note from?" she asked.

"From Khalid. It came in right after the Saudi attack."

"And it says?"

"'It is coming,' it says. That's all."

"The United States?" Charlie asked.

"Yes. We could kill him—but then we'd be blind."

Chapter 25 Idiots

Everyone knew that he was one of the best, a robot who collected thousands of data points—names, aliases, dates, locations, transactions, itineraries, associations, and associates. Steve was renowned for his ability to connect one to another and another, and then finding the gold. Even among those who disliked him—or feared him—there was respect. Most had seen him in meetings or watched him make one of his famed presentations, conjuring up a storm of facts, punctuating his language with curse words. He was legion for making improbable associations. And for happily contradicting himself to make a point. He had no problem calling anyone an idiot, insulting everybody, including the bosses.

To aggravate the collective nervousness, after he arrived at Apex Watch, Steve subsisted on stealth. There was no grand tour and hand shaking. He kept to himself and drove his own car to and from the compound. And he ate by himself. Most days, he disappeared into the file room, or holed up in his new office, the place quickly piling high with paper, practically a *Do Not Enter* sign on the door.

And when he did open his mouth, he antagonized. He was contemptuous not just of the Agency, the Clinton administration and the national security leadership, but it seemed, maybe all of them as well.

Charlie tried to defend him. "He's fundamentally insecure," she said one day to a group at lunch, "hating that he has to prove himself, thinking that he has to prove himself."

"But does he have to be such an asshole?" one of the women asked.

"I think he's afraid of being found out."

"Found out for what?"

"Someone might discover that what it is he's doing isn't what he's supposed to be doing," Charlie said. "Or worse: that he isn't doing it right."

"That's a lot of shit to carry on one's shoulders," Barbara said, coming into the conversation. "There's stuff we all don't know, and insecurities we all carry."

"Yeah, but with Steve, I've found it's a little different," Charlie responded. She wasn't comfortable being his ambassador, knowing that much of what she was defending was also irritating to her. "Most people are afraid to say what they don't know. I think Steve's afraid to say what he *does* know, afraid that any assertion of knowing might form a crack towards some potential avalanche that pulls his whole world down."

She continued: "Sometimes, I think Steve just doesn't hear himself. He thinks he's just refreshingly telling everyone the truth. And he's right, except that as part of his fear of exposure, he doesn't realize either what he's actually saying, or the tone he's using. But underneath it all, I really just think he's terrified of being found out."

"Maybe he should just learn to not say whatever he says so loudly. And so definitively," said another woman.

"Yeah," Charlie responded tiredly, "I'd say just ignore the bark."

"That's easy for you to say, his girlfriend," said someone who had felt the sting.

"Believe me," Charlie said, "it's not easy."

Steve was in the archives that day. There was nothing safer for him than hanging with his new files. He was discovering hidden history, with a sense of humor to boot—*Prince Bandit and the F-15 Sale* was the title of one early report on the Saudi ambassador.[468] *Bandar and the al-Yamanah Two Billion* was another, about what he thought was a long-ago British scandal.[469] *Razorbacks Score $20 Million* was another in November 1993, about the Saudi campaign to ingratiate themselves with President Clinton by funding a University of Arkansas facility.[470] *Hamburgers on a Silver Platter: Saudi Influence in Washington* was a more recent one—all the highly-classified reports similar to the standard intelligence, except that in the case of Apex Watch they also named names and showed bribes and cash transactions.

And as Steve dipped his toes into the KSM file, he was also finding Bowlen's man surprisingly alluring. There were no infidels or Great Satan in his correspondence. There was no Prophet Muhammad this and that, no *jihad* or yelling of *Allahu Akbar*.

KSM opined, badgered, and fumed, sometimes in English, sometimes lapsing into Arabic or another language to make a finer point. He had no trouble contradicting himself, nor in wending off into elaborate theories about the world. But, as Steve would learn, he always returned to the same place, to an articulation of being an accidental representative of a people who had no hope for any change, the only way to advance: through a capitulation to the West and Western ways. KSM didn't articulate it that way, but that's what Steve read. He'd read a lot of terrorist manifestos, but KSM's material wasn't a rhetoric of humiliation and disgrace; it was more a life of *just that*.

As if a spider were crawling into his psyche, Steve shuddered. *It is what it is.*

He perused the Clinton holdings as well, but he found himself uninterested in delving much deeper. He'd spent so much time listening to Charlie's bile against the president—his casual attitude about *national security*, his vulnerability and susceptibility to manipulation or, even worse, to blackmail—that everything there was to know, was already out there.

Steve wasn't interested in Clinton in the same way that Charlie and so many others of his colleagues were. They were devotees of a religion that he didn't practice: the religion of *national security*. And not only that, but as case officer and *action girl* to Steve's turtle-like burrowing analyst, Charlie followed the principle of collection above all else. Of course, she was obsessed with penetrating the netherworld of terrorism and wanted to collect as much as she could. But at her core she was dedicated to the creed, to the sacred duty of protecting sources and methods—not the acquisition of new information, not greater understanding. To Charlie, compromising sources meant that potential sources might not have the confidence to place their lives in the hands of the CIA tomorrow, thus ending the opportunities for further espionage. It was in her DNA to always choose preserving a source over acting upon the information that came from the source. Charlie operated from the postulation that the compromise of a source, of sources and methods, of espionage, practically meant the end of the United States.

After Charlie returned from a long scouting trip to Pakistan, Bowlen scheduled a welcoming lunch for Steve.

"A lunch? I don't have time for a lunch," Steve said.

"I'm not asking you," Bowlen responded.

Mrs. Rothwell came by the archive to inquire about the menu.

"Who cares?" Steve responded, annoyed at the interruption.

Charlie had warned her, and suggested roast chicken, Steve's default, because he really didn't care, but Mrs. Rothwell still wanted to follow tradition, and she persisted, asking Steve about side dishes and the types of salad he might want. It was his day after all.

"I really don't care," he growled, realizing for a moment that he was hurting her feelings. "I'm sure whatever you choose will be great," he went on, hoping that he hadn't made another enemy.

When the date came and he went up to the dining room, he stuck close to Charlie and Bowlen before everyone got settled and sat down.

"By now you've all met Mr. Draper," Bowlen said. Steve was sitting at his left, at the top of the U in the set-up tables, just as Charlie had been months earlier. "He's working with Charlie on a new project, and I hope he will share his big brain and encyclopedic knowledge with all of us as he settles in here."

"Here, here," the group offered.

"As I broke the bad news to Charlie when she started," he said, looking at Steve, "our tradition here is for you to tell your story. Oh, and answer questions. So, Steven, you have the floor."

"Oy," Steve said, standing up.

"Well, as you all know, I'm an insufferable know-it-all."

There was nervous laughter.

"And I'm an irritating guy," Steve went on. "But I'm not incapable of saying I'm wrong. Or I'm sorry. I'm not averse, because—trust me—I have so much practice saying both.

"I have no interesting story to tell of my upbringing, I come out of nowhere, no Yale," he looked at Charlie, "even if she was a scholarship girl." He bowed his head towards her.

"I've been doing the same thing my entire life—being an analyst—

and I'm happiest when I'm just left alone to make my own knowledge, searching for some detail or piece of information that's going to add to it."

"What made you join the Army, dear?" Mrs. Rothwell asked.

"Yeah. I got my start in the Army. I joined mostly to get away from home. And a crazy mother," not adding any more detail. "But, frankly, it was also because school just wasn't for me. I just couldn't get the hang of multiple classes on multiple subjects at the same time. My mind, even then, could only concentrate on what I was interested in. And even there, I couldn't follow the assignments. I got lost in my own reading. I wrote papers that were too long, or I read so much about whatever it was that I was obsessing about that I didn't even have time to do anything else. I either got A's or incompletes. Or even F's. I was flunking out and I had nowhere else to go.

"I loved the Army, had a great commander, a great assignment, and the institution was both meritorious and rules bound. The colonel gave me the space to learn, and mostly what I learned was how little I knew. I wouldn't say I developed a taste for what's classified, but I did set myself on a life of study, which turned out to be a pretty good decision, given I don't think I could do anything else.

"Twenty-five years later, I'm that same analyst, slightly dysfunctional. Ok, very. So, if you want to know about some fucker in *al Qaeda*, I'm your man. But if you want to know about the Baltimore Orioles or what's wrong with your car, I'm lost. I think someday I'd make a great boss, at least I'd love to be given the chance. But I'm afraid that I'd just end up calling everyone an idiot, unable to give up control. It is my defensive stance, that 'idiot' thing. That is, when I let myself think that anything that anyone else could be working on could possibly be as important as anything I was doing or thinking about. That word 'idiot' gets thrown around a lot, and I'm hoping here that, with a new start, I break the habit."

"Well, boss," Tony chimed in, "I guess it's back to the drawing boards for you because you've already called us all idiots."

Everyone tittered.

Steve paused. He stopped and took a sip of water.

Bowlen hesitated. *Not Tony, boy, not Tony, bad target.*

Charlie sucked in her breath. *Oh, Steve,* she winced. *Take a deep breath and think about what you're about to do.*

"You know, Tony," Steve said, looking straight at him, and hesitating a moment for punctuation, "I do *not* think you are an idiot. And if I have already told you that you are, in my need to protect myself, I did so thoughtlessly, needing to create a force field and be insubordinate. And for that I'm sorry.

"And, Tony," he continued, again hesitating, "if I ever call you an idiot again, in any way, and particularly if I'm defying some protocol that threatens my safety or the safety of our project, you have my permission, I beg you, to beat the shit out of me."

Everyone laughed. And then Steve went on, interrupting the laughter, but again being deadly serious.

"Barbara," he said looking at the woman sitting at Mr. Bowlen's right: "I do not think you are an idiot. I was sad to see you go when you left CTC, and I admire your work. I particularly admire that you can speak the language, which I can't. And what is it, like, four languages that you've mastered? A fuck of a lot better than my barely being able to speak English. And sorry for snarling at you like some fucking alpha dog marking my territory when you showed me the archives. They are amazing. I'm in awe. They remind me that *I do not know everything.*

"Casey," he said to the next person in line, "I do not think you are an idiot. You are destined for greatness. I'm sorry about that crack I made that you were wasting your time writing reports on the shitheads of industry. Fuckin' A, your Saudi reports are good. So comprehensive. Go to graduate school. I never could or did. And make them pay for it. And then when you excel there as well, do come back. And thanks for showing me how to hack the index, for sharing all your searching tricks with me. If I pretended that I knew it all already, I was just pretending. I am really sorry."

Next came Charlie, and it seemed that even the building held its breath.

"My dear," he started, wanting to be professional but also mindful that probably everyone knew they were an item, "I am continuously amazed by what you do, and I am humbled by the humanity with which you do it. In every way that I find myself questioning why I don't feel anything about the world, you make up for that deficit. In every way you care about people, I could learn from you. In every way that you have passion about people, I am reminded that it would be okay if I loosened up.

"Trust me," he said, "you make me see it, even make me feel it. I'm the idiot."

There were tears forming in his eyes.

He went around the table, naming every person, people who didn't think he even knew their names, people who were sure he had no idea who they were or what they did. With each one, he demonstrated that he paid close attention. And that he wasn't above them. He singled each out by name and then he said something encouraging and self-deprecating all at the same time. The room fell silent.

"Erica," Steve said to one of Barbara's newest, "I'm so impressed with your inquisitiveness." *Wow, she is so beautiful, he thought.* "I'm such a loner and so afraid of people, I couldn't even begin to make the phone calls you do. Really, I couldn't. You are an amazing collector. And analyst. I want you on my team."

He told the tech guy, Mallory—no one seemed to know his first name—that they were finally going to get a chance to use his amazing gizmo. Most in the room didn't even know what he was talking about. Mallory beamed.

"To each and every one of you, I apologize in advance—and already—for a giant flaw that exists in my personality. Because I don't have a clue who Hobbes or Rousseau are, I've grown to hate those who say 'Hobbesian' in polite conversation, people I stupidly assume are show-offs, or who I stupidly think believe that they are better than everyone else, especially me, just because they are educated.

"The 'idiot' thing? It's not just a force field to hide all of what I don't know. It also gives me space to be an idiot myself. And I need lots of space."

There was more laughter, now a little less *ha ha* and a little more empathetic.

"One doesn't need a psychoanalytic textbook to see that I've searched for some skillset, let's call it 'alphabetizing the world,' to soothe my aching mind and find a wall to hide behind. And then, in doing so, I've somehow convinced myself that I've learned everything, or at least I think I have.

As part of that, somehow I've also convinced myself that I can predict the future. I don't mean that I can actually predict the future, like I'm some genie. It's more that, when events occur, I find myself again and again saying to myself *I knew that, I knew that was going to happen.*

"What I mean when I say that, when I think it, is … I think I retreat in this way because … because I've also learned something else about my psychology, that I'm incapable of feeling anything about what's going on. When disaster strikes, of course I say to myself, Spock-like, *interesting*, and *sure, that makes sense*, because I've learned to cover up that I don't feel anything emotionally about what's happening. Obviously I care about the world or I wouldn't be doing this work. But 'care about the world'? As if it were a child to take care of? Or, like, breaking down sobbing when the world gets a boo-boo? I just don't. Where I go off the rails is when I go into this *I knew that* mode and make the mistake of actually believing that I thought something was going to happen in the first place. And fuck if I don't make that mistake all the time. It's a long explanation, but even day to day, when someone just tells me something that I don't know, in my insecurity to gloss over how little my encyclopedia of the world is, in my shame to cover up my flaws, I tend to lash out."

Everyone was now hanging on his every word, the room silent. No one was eating.

"Tony," he said, repeating himself, "*I do not* think you are an idiot. It's probably because you are such a big guy—that intimidates me. No. I don't mean that. It's probably because you have a physical presence and I'm all mouth. And definitely it's because you do something I can't. My impulse to keep you at a distance. But trust me. I'm looking forward to getting to know you. And standing behind you."

He yelled out Roy the driver's name, who was eating in the kitchen and thanked him when he poked his head out.

"You are not an idiot, Roy," Steve said.

"No, boss, trust me, I am. That's what rugby will do to you …"

And they all laughed.

Steve made Mrs. Rothwell tear up, he was so sweet to her. A wistful, melancholy haze fell over him as he described how perfectly she took care of them all, and how lucky they were to have her.

The normally avuncular Bowlen was transported into glowing

stillness, Steve being complimentary to him, but hardly slavish, praising his singular purpose and commitment, thanking him for listening to his shit, thanking him for giving him this chance, telling him he was looking forward to a long collaboration. Steve said he was going to solve the problem if it killed him. But most of all, he said, he wanted to make "Mr. Bowlen" proud of him.

Chapter 26 The Thinker

"You're welcome to look at anything," Bowlen said to Steve in their first formal meeting when he came on board, taking him into the archives on his first day.[471] "*Mi casa es su casa,*" he joked.

"And what are they?" Steve asked.

"The truth."

Steve shrugged his shoulders. "There is no truth, boss. What will they tell me that I don't already know?"

"If the community collects it, it's accessible here, not just financial information, but everyone's compartmented operations, including law enforcement. We tap into it all."

"And what am I supposed to do with all that?"

"Predict the next strike."

"Anywhere?" Steve deadpanned.

"How about just the next strike against the United States? Do it with all of the possible information we have, including from KSM. Can you do it? Even as a test run?"

"Is there something you know that I don't?"

Bowlen answered: "Well, probably lots. What I know from Khalid's reporting is that something big is coming, something against America. Or at least against America's direct interests, an embassy or a military facility, bigger than Khobar Towers."

"Yeah, but any Tom, Dick or Harry could say that," Steve responded.

"Well. Khalid seems to run on a two-year cycle. So let's say 1998. If we hit January 1, 1999 and there's nothing, I lose the bet."

"And the bet's what?"

"If you can predict a strike, find a methodology to do so, then we turn it all over to the Agency. If you can't, we need to formulate some other strategy for the future."

"Some other strategy? Meaning what?"

"Meaning more effective counterterrorism. We are in a unique position to have a direct line to the president."

Bowlen went on. "You come up with a strategy that makes sense, a counterterrorism strategy that includes KSM, and we'll go brief the president together. Figure out first what we can do with the information, if we can use it to detect an attack before it takes place."

"Why don't we just ask him?"

"It doesn't work that way."

"Do we have any real-time surveillance of the guy?" Steve asked.

"No."

"Do we know where he is?"

"Karachi. When he's actually home."

Virtually every *al Qaeda* attack traced back to Karachi, Steve thought. Ramzi Yousef learned explosives there, and that's where he and KSM hatched the World Trade Center bombing. KSM and Yousef planned and prepared the Philippine plots in Karachi, recruiting participants and using the Pakistani city as their base.

With its mishmash of languages, ethnicities and even national neighborhoods, the Pakistani port city had become a vast megalopolis that was in the middle of yet another growth spurt.[472] It was already the second most-populated urban area in the world, with over nine million people and growing at about a million per year. Migrants and refugees from countless countries—including almost a million who fled Afghanistan—came to Karachi, attracted not just by an abundance of jobs, but by the anonymity and freedoms of one of Asia's most free-wheeling cities. This made for neighborhoods that largely governed themselves, segregated from the broader, more prosperous and international Karachi.

"Do we have real-time communications with him?" asked Steve.

"We have protocols to rustle him up."

"And the handoff to Charlie is when?"

"Soon. But we have that well in hand. I want you to focus here, on assessing the intelligence."

"Is there a source you want to point me to, other than KSM's reporting that I don't know about?"

"Good question. I'd maybe look at the T1 take and the Mi-6 listening device."

"Is T1 your designation?"

"No."

"Whose is it?"

"The Israelis."

"That's their code word?"

"Yes."

"What is it?"

"It's a set of intercepts."

"Why does it come to you?"

"Because the Israelis trust me."

"The NSA knows nothing about it?"

"Not the exchange."

"Is there an exchange?"

"Of sorts."

"Why don't you circulate a tear sheet to the Agency?"[473]

"That's the president's decision."

"Don't hide behind that."

Bowlen hesitated. "It's the president's decision. As is this overall project. You either buy into that or not."

"Does it produce material that would change the way official Washington thinks?"

"Yes."

"Explain to me how the president can know something, and his assistants and official Washington know something else?"

"Now *that is* the president's decision. But let me back up for a minute and just say that there are all sorts of things the president knows and others don't. The Agency and the NSA and other actors in the government collect certain bits of intelligence that make it to the president's eyes alone. It's the nature of our system, of changing information systems, and of leadership. But some of what the president knows, that no one else knows, comes from discussions with other heads of state. Sometimes, most of the time, a State Department or White House aide is listening in for note taking, but not always. And those notes sometimes circulate. But not always. Sometimes the president's hands get tied, where he just can't act on what he knows. So exclusive info isn't only from Apex Watch."

"Don't fucking patronize me," Steve responded. "I know how the system works."

"I am trying to answer your question and also impart my experience."

"And the Mi-6 material? What is it?" Steve asked, letting the actual useful lesson sink in.

"They've managed through their own *al Qaeda* agent, a British citizen, to plant a listening device in one of the *al Qaeda* camps. It's mostly low-level stuff, but you'll find it interesting."

"You get this from the Brits as well? I've never seen the take."

"We steal it from the Brits," Bowlen said, waiting for the explosion.

"Cool," Steve said. "They don't share it?"

"They share the intelligence with the Agency. Or summaries. But we get the raw feed.

"Steven, I must go. Barbara will show you how to access that and other material. You want to read the president's mail, go for it. If it goes into a computer at the National Security Council or the White House chief of staff's office, we can see it."

"Are we cheating the U.S. government in terms of its ability to stop attacks?" Steve asked.

"We could get into an interesting discussion as to what *is* the U.S. government, but I say *no*, not as far as I can tell, not by our authority alone," Bowlen answered. "But that's why I want you to tell me what our options are."

"Option for what ..."

"Effective counterterrorism. I need *your* help. To formulate some strategy that would mean an actual end to this emerging brand of Islamic terrorism," Bowlen said.

"That's an Apex Watch mission?"

"In a way, yes. Apex Watch is a project that goes back decades, one that uniquely stands above all else, above politics, above administrations, in defense of the nation. Right now, I find myself fighting a president, this president, for the first time asking if it is even possible that there is something higher than him and his authorities under the Constitution."

"Meaning what?"

"National security. Guarding the nation. If the president is compromised or incapacitated, what are we supposed to do? Who do we work for? Don't get me wrong. I know that the knock against Clinton is that he's unfit to be commander-in-chief. Weak on family, work, crime, and national security. So crippled by his life in the psychedelic '60s, and with sordid personal peccadillos, that made him unable to draw a distinction between right and wrong. I know better than most that he has acquired a resume—Whitewater, Trooper Gate, Travel Gate, File Gate—that, in the classic eyes of *national security*, betrays a potential for profound corruption, and, even worse, in the doctrine of national security: an opening for blackmail.

"But here's my dilemma: President Clinton is also my boss. He was shocked—*shocked*—when I first briefed him on what we did at Apex Watch, on our knowledge of decades of Saudi payoffs to Americans who acted as friends and protectors of this despicable foreign nation, this enemy of the United States.

"But what did he want to know?" Bowlen stated, ever so slightly raising his voice. "*How many Republicans are on the list?* Then he wanted to know how and under what specific authority we collected information on Cabinet members or White House staff—he never said the president or the first lady—but ever since, there's been tension over what we look at, and even our very existence.

"Now, in addition, the Saudis have made a number of attempts to connect with the president, this president. And their back-channel letter regarding your Mr. Ghamdi was out of line. An attempted back-channel communication is sheer treachery and manipulation. The Saudis obviously think that President Clinton is stupid or is for sale. And the fact that the president went to Director Deutch rather than to me to inquire about a confidential Saudi communication ... maybe he is trying to send me a message."

"A message of what?"

"That he *can* go around me?" Bowlen said. "The Saudis are trying to weaken Apex Watch at a time when it might be most needed. They are also trying to complicate this president's life, as if it's not complicated enough. And they are ultimately trying to protect their asset …"

"Jeez, now you sound like some counterintelligence paranoid," Steve shot back.

"Steven, I've attended your briefings. Your grasp of the facts is unmatched; and as I said, I was thoroughly impressed with the work you shared with me. I applaud your campaign to see terrorists clearly, and your own principle to follow the evidence wherever it takes you. I love your contempt for Washington and for the limitations of official analysis, but there *are* limitations. And for that reason, I'll risk patronizing you by saying you are right, but you can only be partly right because there are things you don't know.

"Take your work on Louis Freeh," he continued. "Everything about what you told me—the facts *and* your willingness to stick your neck out—convinced me I need your help. For all the reasons you conclude Freeh is a Saudi agent, I've concluded that the Saudis are behind these attacks on America. I've seen it coming for years. Terrorism is the perfect tactic: small attacks that provoke outsize responses. Then military retaliation and our growing military presence in the Middle East mobilizes and provokes more attacks. Our counterterrorism guarantees that the angry look outward, at us. That serves Saudi interests."

"You mean the Saudis are behind the attacks? That's not where I'd go," Steve responded.

"As I've learned from Apex, and as I've picked up from Khalid, the selfish manipulations that the Saudis are so good at are highly successful. Don't get me wrong: We are responsible, responsible for ourselves, for our integrity, for our policy and our posture. We are the reason for terrorism against us …"

Steve kicked his head back and raised his eyebrows at hearing such a statement come out of Bowlen's mouth. Even if he knew instantly, he didn't mean what Noam Chomsky might mean when saying the same thing.

"Steve, I've listened to your analysis and, at the risk of provoking you, I think you've missed the most important part."

"Which is?"

"Suicide bombing."

Steve almost sneered. He'd caught it.

"Read Khalid's description of it in the files here and you'll see the plan in the Philippines was to pick airplanes that had at least one stopover before landing in the United States. The bombers were supposed to deplane. Then there was the August 1993 attack.[474] The assassination attempt on the Egyptian interior minister in central Cairo. It was Osama bin Laden's first sponsored suicide attack."

"I didn't miss it," Steve cautiously said. It was the first suicide attack by a *Sunni* group, but it was more Zawahiri's Egyptian Islamic Jihad than *al Qaeda*. "But maybe I'm too dense to see what you're getting at," he said, half sarcastically.

"Khalid highlighted that attack and said that the event changed bin Laden's mind about whether such an operation could be considered kosher in a defensive *jihad*, pardon my French."

"I surmised that even without that scrap," Steve responded.

Bowlen continued: "But that changed the game in terms of what was possible inside the United States. That's the point," Bowlen said. "Look, Steven, I'd love to talk forever but I have to go. Khalid's reporting and his commentary are too much for me to handle. He has never been the primary focus of Apex Watch. But I need to change that. I know Khalid is intent on attacking the United States directly. I think he is planning to finish the job he started. Do you understand? You didn't need to convince me that the Philippines plot was merely practice.

"I'm dealing with an unhelpful FBI director, a new CIA director—who I think is an improvement over Deutch, but a political chameleon and a narcissistic fraud—a White House staff that thinks they are commanding a war against terrorism when all they are doing is pushing paper around, and a president I can't fully trust. Osama bin Laden gathers strength and the United States is focused on Iraq, Iran, Israel and the Palestinians, mucking about in the Middle East and South Asia, worrying about weapons of mass destruction in Pakistan and India—at the same time, oblivious to the fact that it is almost universally seen as the new crusader subjugating a billion-plus people. Who benefits? The Saudi Kingdom. They now seem willing to start a worldwide religious war if it benefits their survival."

"Sounds to me like you are willing to take the same risk," Steve said.

"That's for you to tell me. I wish I had the confidence to say to you that I could stop it all in its tracks … spend some time with the files," Bowlen finished, stepping backward into the body of the Apex Watch archive, arms open like a magician, still facing Steve. "Khalid is in here: ten years' worth. There are three former ambassadors to Saudi Arabia, two former station chiefs. There's been a lot of activity on Louis Freeh of late, but I think you'll be disappointed in what you find. Deutch might have been odious and in over his big head, but he was as clean as a whistle. The new director is, too. Financially. For now.

"And there's someone named Bill Clinton," Bowlen said, expelling an exasperated breath, as if he were completing a long and painful yoga pose.

Chapter 27 Apex Meets

The sand-colored building was impeccable and traditional, with sawtooth parapet walls and small, triangular windows. It was a large, two stories with an interior courtyard surrounded by a colonnade, each column covered in mud and topped with Arab arches.

The sign outside said Supreme Council of Charity. But it was the royal family's center of financial manipulation and covert action. To its directors, it was a sanctuary, an oasis and an exclusive club they knew as Apex, a place of secret business.[475]

Bandar, Turki, and Nayef loved going there. They formed their own heavenly kingdom.

Prince Nayef bin Abd al-Aziz Al Saud was the eldest and most conservative. Born in 1934, he was one of the few remaining sons of *Ibn Saud*, the first Saudi king. Little known outside the country, Nayef had been minister of the interior, the head of internal security and national police for Saudi Arabia since 1975.

Second oldest was Prince Bandar bin Sultan Al Saud, a son of Prince Sultan and a nephew of King Fahd. Made Saudi ambassador to Washington a decade earlier, he started in the nation's capital as defense attaché and worked his way up from swashbuckling, American-trained fighter pilot to universal, inside-the-Beltway information groomer and back-slapper—a Washington fixture.

The youngest was Princeton- and Georgetown-educated Prince

Turki bin Faisal Al Saud, eighth son of the assassinated King Faisal. He had been director of the Saudi General Intelligence Directorate, the country's foreign intelligence service, a combination spy chief and *de facto* foreign minister, for almost two decades. He was the king and crown prince's covert troubleshooter, responsible for Saudi Arabia's actual status in the world.

In their appointed roles as protectors of the family, they were also managing directors of Apex, with a charge from the king to guard the status quo and look after the Saudi future. For years, that meant oil and the cultivation of a special relationship with the powerful.

But their world was changing, not so much because oil had diminished in importance, nor because its erstwhile allies or the United Nations grew tired of the world's most prominent dictator monarchy. It was because of a commoner: Osama bin Laden, their over-mighty subject and increasingly infamous celebrity.

In a way, they'd created him, conferring upon him the responsibility for managing and ensuring the safety of Saudi sons sent off to make *jihad* in Afghanistan.[476] But bin Laden turned out to have his own ideas, a royal pest after the Iraqi invasion of Kuwait and then an audacious free agent, preaching as if he were the grandest *mufti*, acting as if he himself was a powerful occupier.

They tried the direct approach: dispatching emissaries to tell the elders of the bin Laden family to quiet their son.[477] They threatened the lifeblood of the vast bin Laden construction empire in Saudi Arabia, urging the clan to convince Osama to focus his political energy elsewhere. They took away his passport,[478] revoked his citizenship.[479] Then they realized that they really just wanted him to go away, exiling him to Sudan. When he continued to speak out, they worked behind the scenes to have him ejected from that country, leaving him almost penniless. They warned bin Laden that the CIA had put out a contract on his life. They'd even faked an assassination attempt to give that lie credibility. And then they tried to kill him.[480]

None of it worked, not even after a top agent of Prince Nayef visited bin Laden in Sudan to provide a personal message from the king to shut up.[481]

It was a sticky conundrum for the royal guardians, for bin Laden was also at the center of something much larger. He couldn't be tolerated, nor could he be easily dispatched with. Now, if they killed him, and if it traced back to the royal family, there was the larger danger that in death he would be a martyr for a cause they couldn't control.

And what was that cause? Contrary to everyone's assumption, the Arab fighters and the real *mujahidin* who fought in Afghanistan never demobilized. The *jihad* was supported, and the war was won, but there was no peace. The fighters didn't quietly shuffle back to compliant resignation. And they weren't even turning into underground national guerillas to be crushed by the efficient security services of their native countries.[482] No, instead they were becoming international men. As such, they weren't calling for democracy or socialism or shrieking nationalism or even pushing for some pan-Arab nirvana like their Soviet-influenced and Western-indoctrinated predecessors. They were accusing the royal families of being *takfir*,[483] of being infidels who turned their back on Islam. They called for a return to the old ways, for true *Shari'ah*, not just the dogma of *Wahhabism*, the 150-year-old denomination that preserved the rule of al Saud family. They were posing as the true *Salafis*,[484] reaching back centuries before the Saudi state, taking the official Saudi extreme and outdoing it, becoming even more religious, and even more righteous.

These international men, religious men who manufactured their own passports and worshipped their own God, were rejecting the state, rejecting them. Despite modernization, despite all the progress the Arab states offered, despite the organized *everything* the Saudi state was providing, even an organized way of life and an organized enemy in Israel, more men were joining this new army every day.

King Fahd accepted the recommendation made by the Apex Council: ruin Osama bin Laden in a new campaign of disinformation.

"I have met with the firm in London and accepted their two-step proposal of work to begin to undermine his reputation," reported Turki. He was using the same international PR company that had effectively done work for Kuwait's *al Sabah* family[485] when they were in exile during the Iraqi occupation.[486]

The three looked at the PowerPoint briefing printed out before them. Step one was to deliver inside information to select members of the British press—so easy to manipulate—with the goal of penetrating Washington through a back door, influencing opinion-shapers and experts with a certain backstory about bin Laden. It was a steady and methodical timeline, the firm showing in its diagram how the manufactured "T story" passed on in seminars and meetings would then be picked up in the mainstream press, given credibility through vague references to *government sources*, and then repeated as fact back into the Arab and South Asian media.

Now implemented, the stories were flowing: of the boy being put down as a "son of the slave" by his brothers, and of a young Osama bin Laden drinking, partying and whoring in Beirut when he was younger.[487] Profiles and studies of the *al Qaeda* leader portrayed bin Laden as a selfish, self-centered child of privilege who never even heard of Afghanistan, and didn't really engage in the battle or even bother with any kind of *jihad* until years after the Soviet invasion.[488] Stories circulated about bin Laden as a failure and a coward on the battlefield, always sick or miraculously absent when Soviets attacked. He was portrayed as a failure at engineering, incompetent at organizing, even a fool at managing his money.[489]

"As part of step two," Turki said, "bin Laden's scholastic records have been removed from King Abdul Aziz University, bolstering the rumors that he was an undistinguished student who never graduated.[490]

"And are we to really think that bad press will bring him down?" Nayef inquired skeptically, fingering the papers.

Unspoken was the fact that Saudi Arabia got bad press all the time and *that* had no impact on public opinion, at least not for them.

"Not just bad press," Turki responded. "But stories that show him weak, as cowardly, even secretly sick with some kind of disease—that he is dying.[491] The stories have been picked up almost everywhere and anywhere bin Laden was written about. There were even stories suggesting he became involved in the drug trade to raise funds. So-called Western experts were adding their punditry that such was his mismanagement and lack of regard for the people he supposedly loved and led.

"We even have FBI investigators and CIA people declaring bin Laden a fraud, as a selfish rich boy, and a bloodthirsty maniac."

This latter tactic, elevating bin Laden as kingmaker and suggesting his success, even nefarious success, the PowerPoint briefing said, risked elevating the "image quotient" of him and other associated entities. There was some formula laid out on the paper describing step two: *image quotient* times *P story* over *rate of transmittal* or some such nonsense. Nayef had argued that there was a danger that making him into too much of an evil genius served to raise his general profile, but Turki answered that that was why the PR company was monitoring the results once a month.

And indeed, the more that the news media was picking up the bin Laden story, the more negative influence stories naturally flowed within. That bin Laden was the manufacture, and even tool, of the CIA, that he was a plant by Israeli *Mossad*, that he was a naïve and foolish tool of the Muslim Brotherhood, or that he was a puppet of his Egyptian brethren like Dr. Zawahiri. Or Prince Turki's favorite: that bin Laden was the murderer of his own beloved friend and mentor Abdullah Azzam.[492]

Stories even appeared that bin Laden was a secret agent of the Saudi government, a provocateur created by Saudi security services to infiltrate and expose domestic opposition.[493]

The three particularly loved that bit of subterfuge, kernels of truth that struck at bin Laden's lack of independence, and something they also truly wished for.

The Apex disinformation campaign also spread the story that bin Laden lied to the Saudi government when he left the country after the first Gulf War, that he deceived his own family, and that he secretly fled like the coward that he was. They knew that any thinking person would conclude that little could move in and out of Saudi Arabia without the authorities knowing, definitely not a national celebrity with three wives and multiple children and dozens of bodyguards and staff. Yet the tale of his furtive betrayal became the whispered rumor, then the story, and finally even conventional history repeated by government know-it-alls.[494]

At first, they were delighted to see bin Laden leave their country.[495] That was then, when they thought that his damage radius would be lessened, and his voice muted in such a primitive place as Sudan. Prince Turki's agents even confided to bin Laden that he left not a moment too soon, that the CIA was close on his heels,[496] a fabulous and fitting dishonesty that communicated that his life continued to be in danger, a myth that fit with the popular notion that American intelligence was behind everything, but also a pretension that the *Sheikh* himself believed about his own importance.

This month's report from London was impressive in its numbers. They flipped through the latest list of stories and the chart of "themes" covered. It was the same as last month and the month before: The PR firm reported success after success, a book-sized sheaf of clippings to back up the results of their work in ring binders on the conference room table.

"Are we really getting our money's worth here," Nayef asked, always the skeptic. "Reputation intact or not, the kingdom seems more vulnerable after attacks in Riyadh and Khobar Towers. My ministry is getting intelligence reports that others feel emboldened because of these, that more want to try their own hand to strike here at home."

Not only that, but all of them had to deal with the additional stresses of the FBI running around investigating the attacks. They were badged men who were less polite and compliant than the American soldiers who marched aimlessly in the desert.

"We will see more of them," said Prince Bandar of the clean-cut and highly-inquisitive special agents pouring in from Washington.

"Despite all of our work," he went on, "Director Freeh seems to want to pry ever more into Saudi internal affairs."

"He seems harmless, yes?" Nayef asked.

"He is naïve and impressionable. But I'm afraid he is also only so useful," Bandar answered. "He is not only an uninteresting priss, but he also has no power in Washington."

"And there is no movement on reducing the American military presence here?" Nayef asked.

Though they would never admit it, bin Laden's noisy campaign against the deployment of American military forces on Saudi soil pushed all of them, even the king, to look for some acceptable and face-saving ways to get them to leave. But despite payoffs to Qatar to offer to host the Americans, that part of the campaign was going nowhere.[497]

Bandar continued: "Mrs. Albright[498] has unfortunately created a dead-end street: 'Regime change or no change,' she says of Iraq.[499] And so, Saddam cannot and will not cooperate with the United Nations, because there is no conclusion to reach that is advantageous to him."

"And you with Mr. Clinton? Still no progress?" Nayef asked Turki.

"I'm afraid not," Prince Turki said. He and the president attended Georgetown University at the same time but didn't know each other. Attempts at an alumni connection fizzled. Even their check for $20 million to fund a Middle East-studies program at the University of Arkansas had no impact.[500] And their flirtation with FBI Director Freeh backfired, the White House now additionally suspicious of Saudi motives.[501]

"This drive to war with Iraq will only end when Washington is focused on something else," Nayef said.

After the attack in Riyadh, they thought they were getting somewhere with their push for a new thrust against Iran. But then came Khobar Towers and the *Shi'a* activation. Now the king himself said the domestic blowback was too great. They all agreed that American military action against Iran would bring military forces to the kingdom forever.

It was clear: the short-term path was to continue step two: weakening the bin Laden mystique and pushing American focus on increasingly independent and dangerous Islamists.

"I have talked to President Bush," Prince Bandar said.[502] "His son will definitely run. Unfortunately, he, too, believes that the Iraq business needs to be finished."

"And our man?" Nayef asked.

"He believes it possible that he will be selected as vice president, that young Bush needs someone steeped in national security to win the election. Or at least to win the support of the Washington elite."

PART 7

Chapter 28 Hamburg Boys

late 1990s

Ziad and Aysel met just a month after the attack on Khobar Towers. She was a second-generation German immigrant from Turkey and a dental student at the University of Greifswald. Ziad was a handsome and worldly Lebanese man on the go, matriculating in a crash German-language course before starting his engineering studies in Hamburg.[503]

Greifswald, a small seaside town of solid structures and abundant cathedrals on the Baltic coast, was just 50 miles from the Polish border. Officially called the University and Hanseatic City of Greifswald, the town housed what was reputed to be one of Europe's oldest institutions of higher learning, advertising itself as going back to 1454. It was a pleasing refuge, a spotless and orderly place of storybook houses unlike anything either of them ever experienced. In this foreign land, they were away from family and the ever present judge of Islam for the first time. Ziad was impressed with the Germanic cleanliness in comparison with that of his war-torn home. And he reveled in the books and the bookstores, a storehouse of world knowledge outside Islam that he wanted to devour. Aysel Senguen was away from her strict, Turkish parents and the hubbub of Berlin for the first time, peaceful in her own storybook escape.[504]

Aysel was very pretty, with an olive complexion and thick black hair parted in the middle, dark eyebrows and dark eyes adorning an oval face with red lips and welcoming laugh lines. Within weeks, Ziad and his *chabibi*—his darling, as he called her—were talking of a life together, of marriage and children, of two careers that would set them on a path to integration and middle-class life in the West.

They had a glorious year in Greifswald, Ziad picking up the language and spending days in the library, reading every history book he could get his hands on. He finished his language program and they said a tearful goodbye, Ziad off to study aircraft engineering in Hamburg. He begged her to transfer as well. But such a move would sever her scholarship and tip off her parents to their relationship. Still, they talked on the phone constantly and Ziad took the train back almost every weekend. He considered buying a car.

After Ziad moved into the *Marienstrasse* apartment, Aysel noticed a change. Her boyfriend was attending a new mosque and said he was reading eye-opening things about the world as it really was, not the version in library books and "worthy" of official history. And he spoke to her of Mohammed Atta, a severe and seemingly humorless Egyptian to Aysel's ears, but one who, Ziad said, was deeply devout, even militantly so.

Aysel certainly didn't want to fight over what it meant to be Muslim. She hadn't given her religion much thought in her secular upbringing, being more areligious than agnostic or non-believing. When they first met, she didn't think Ziad cared so much, or wanted to fight, either. But then he urged her to veil herself in public, and when Aysel declined, Ziad said that maybe she was too shallow. That's when weekends turned into every other weekend.

He said he was spending more time in the mosque, in study and in prayer.

"What about your university studies?" she asked.

"Aircraft engineering, really? Do you dream of being a dentist? I want something more."

She said she did dream of being a dentist, of living in a town just like Greifswald, of marrying and having children and raising a family.

Zaid said *of course* he wanted a family.

"And that isn't enough for you?" she asked.

"It isn't," he said. "*Allah* says the *Qur'an* explains everything. *Tibyaanan li Kulli Shayin*.[505] Many verses speak to me about what we should do, what I need to do."

"And that is what?"

"So much," he said. "I am thinking about *Shari'ah*, not the mindless, mosque-imposed rules meant to control everything, but a new way of life, our life together, and a life for our children, *chabibi*."

He explained that there was so much of Islamic orthodoxy that needed to be dismissed, like slavery, or stoning to death of adulterers, or cutting off the hand of thieves, and especially, he said, the condoning of sex slaves. But then, in his own dismissal of these primitive habits, Ziad wondered whether it was acceptable for him to just pick and choose the Islam he wanted. "I have read the scholars, particularly those here in Europe who say it's not relevant anymore in our modern times when the *Shari'ah* dictates that we must wage *jihad* against non-Muslims who do not pay *jizya*.[506] I agree with many of these modern rulings, about divorce, and inheritance. And yet, there when I study, I find so many *Qur'anic* verses to uphold justice, *O you who believe! Be firm in justice, bearing witness to the truth for the sake of God, even though it is against your own selves, or your parents and kinsfolk, whether rich or poor.*"[507]

A statement of Osama bin Laden particularly galvanized Ziad,[508] and he told Aysel that he was dissatisfied that his life had no deeper spiritual orientation.

There were more arguments and a temporary breakup. Aysel felt Ziad withdrawing. But that really wasn't the issue. She didn't doubt his love. Now when they got together, Islam was all he talked about, *jihad*, holy war, saying that it was not just a theoretical struggle that was waged against the Red Army in Afghanistan. It was a Muslim obligation. His personal obligation. He openly broached for the first time that he might take a semester off to go to Chechnya to fight alongside his "brothers" struggling for freedom from Russia,[509] or he might go to Albania and fight with Muslim Kosovars against the Christian Serbs.

So, when, on their anniversary, he proposed marriage, she was surprised and delighted, hoping that this was a turnaround; that *he* would be back.

Her Turkish father was skeptical, worrying that the young foreigner would take his girl to Lebanon. But they went to Berlin together and Ziad gravely asked for her hand in marriage and pledged a Turkish-style wedding and a good life filled with children in Germany, saying all the right things. He was handsome, seemingly well-off, savvy, smart and pious. He offered a generous dowry and her father almost took it, finally relenting to give his consent in accordance with the new ways. He was German now.

As the wedding approached, the Hamburg Four were already discussing Afghanistan, a fact Ziad hid from his fiancé. The four huddled to discuss their commitment and their duty upon Atta's return, as he regaled them with the story of his royal welcome in Kandahar. Ramzi Binalshibh was most enthusiastic about the *al Qaeda* path and joining with bin Laden, but the deciding factor was ultimately Marwan. They knew that he wasn't healthy enough to survive actual combat, but then Ramzi brought back word from *al Qaeda* that if they chose to go to Afghanistan, the organization would make sure Marwan worked in the camps or did other office work, and that he would do so with no blemish.[510]

When Ziad told Atta that he was going to marry his girlfriend before they made their journey, they had a rare blow-out. Atta tried to argue that marriage was incompatible with pursuit of *jihad*. But Ziad would have none of it. He reasoned that the Prophet—*peace be upon him*—took wives, and that this was the path of any good Muslim. He didn't shame Atta, never made any comparison to his life; he relied on the teachings to be his guide, arguing that he, Ziad Jarrah, could do both.

The wedding was a hybrid, one that Ziad begged Atta to tolerate, if only for a day.[511] Aysel wore a beautiful white dress and her many girlfriends who ventured to the *al Quds* mosque in Hamburg were the delight of the men who attended. Ziad wore a powder-blue tuxedo and took much ribbing from the congregation for both his outfit and the ceremony. But as a close friend and roommate of Atta, the undeniable leader of the ardent band, no one questioned the couple.

At the wedding ceremony, Atta hung in the back of the room, his usual ill-tempered self now even more so because of the casual mix of men and women, and because of the shortened ceremony that he fundamentally opposed, but that now additionally seemed to be a secular compromise with Aysel's father. He told Ziad that he didn't want to get to know the pretty woman. But they stood as brothers, Atta mindful of all the Prophet said—*peace be upon him.* Marriage was still about sacred love.

Aysel and her girlfriends decorated the prayer room in white flowers and garlands and the mosque was filled with merriment. Ziad offered words about love and duty, grave and businesslike in his recitation of the passages he chose from the *Qur'an*. One day they would live in a place, he said in his vows, "where there are no problems, and no sorrow, in castles of gold and silver."[512]

Afterwards, Marwan and another brother sang traditional songs from the Gulf.

Another brother read a Palestinian poem.

It was a United Nations of the frustrated and angry, but for a day, they were there to congratulate their lucky brother.

Ceremony over, the two married, Ziad taught the men a Lebanese dance. They swayed and stomped to the music late into the night.

Separate on the other side of the room, the women danced a traditional Turkish folk train, the girls winding their way through the ground floor of the mosque.

Wedding night over, the Hamburg Four flew separately to Karachi, taking different routes through Frankfurt, Istanbul and Dubai, again reconvening, as arranged, in the border town of Quetta in Pakistan.[513] They were given an address and a man to see, Abu Musab. As each arrived, they found that Abu Musab was merely *al Qaeda* code, indicating the arrival of trusted friends who were to be escorted to Kandahar.[514] They were on their way.

The one-legged man Khallad sent reports ahead about each of the four: educated men, technical men, men who spoke German and English, and were perhaps capable of working on *Mukhtar's* project.[515] As such, they were also treated like VIPs, picked up from the border in shiny new jeeps and moved to a modest guest house near bin Laden's main compound in Kandahar. They were personally greeted by Abu Hafs, the Egyptian military commander of *al Qaeda*.[516] He immediately recognized what good fortune had fallen upon the organization in not just Mohammed Atta, but in the other three as well.

To the Hamburg Four, the place had a smell and feel of frontier, of combat. Even though they were vaunted guests, there was nothing luxurious: barely water coming out of the tap and only occasional electricity, everything around them torn up by war. Everyone carried Kalashnikovs, and the jeeps and vehicles were fitted with gun mounts, creating a sense of imminent danger. They all read that Osama bin

Laden had been added to the FBI's "Ten Most Wanted" list.[517] Tension and secrecy made the atmosphere feel like a missile strike could arrive any moment.

From Kandahar, it took six hours for them to drive just a short distance to the mountains, where they went through a number of checkpoints before arriving at an *al Qaeda* camp. It was sprawling, and a beehive of activity, with young men marching, shooting, doing calisthenics, running on obstacle courses. Up a valley trail, the new arrivals walked for another 30 minutes before turning into a notch in the rocks and a large cave. Its walls were draped with flags and posters, the center of the large cavern prepared for a feast.

They cleaned themselves up for the occasion but were still dressed in Western clothes—only Atta was like *Allah* intended, with his long beard of holiness. All of them, however, were now grimy and sweating from the journey and the hike.

Carrying a walking stick, bin Laden arrived to meet them. He wore a plain white turban and green army coat. His sandaled feet looked spectacularly large. He went to each of the boys in turn, towering over them, grasping their hands and holding them as they spoke, receiving each of their names with great formality. The grey-bearded giant was so soft-spoken in his responses that the other boys almost couldn't make out what he was saying.

"Marwan Yousef Mohamed Rashid Lekrab al-Shehhi," Marwan found himself saying, introducing himself formally, his knees practically buckling. When he stated he was from Ras al-Khaimah on the Gulf, bin Laden asked about *Julfar*—the traditional name of the southernmost emirate and the least famous of the seven.[518] Bin Laden asked Marwan what he was studying in Hamburg.

"Shipbuilding," Marwan shyly answered, his mouth dry.

"Are you a good student, my son?" the *Sheikh* asked.

"No," Marwan answered, and the boys laughed.

"But an honest one," bin Laden said, loosening his grip and moving on to Ramzi Binalshibh.

Bin Laden visibly lightened when Ramzi declared his Yemeni background, doubly delighted that the young man was from the same mountainous region as his father and his tribe. Ramzi explained that when he was young, his family moved to the capital, Sana'a, but that his father died when he was just 15. Thereafter, he had been a soldier for *al Qaeda*.[519]

"And a good one, too," Khallad interjected. He was one of a half dozen bigwigs standing to the side.

Atta spotted fellow Egyptian Dr. Zawahiri. And the Egyptian Abu Hafs. But other than Khallad, he didn't know the others.

"It is indeed high praise, brother," bin Laden said. "Khallad is one of our greatest warriors. May you follow him to God's glory."

Next came Ziad, with his designer eyeglasses and fashionable haircut. He also introduced himself formally.

Even before he even said where he was from, bin Laden said, "Beirut. I hear it in your accent, my brother." Then the *Sheikh* gently laughed. "You know, I have been in that city many times, partying and dancing at the discoes," he said, being ironic. "Alas, I have never visited your beautiful country." He continued, "I am told you are the scholar."

Ziad blushed. "I am a mere college student," he responded.

"And I a mere lover of horses. Modesty is good, my brother."

"*Tell the believing men to lower their gaze and be modest*," bin Laden recited a line from the *Qur'an*. "*That is purer for them*."[520]

"*God is aware of what they do*," Ziad responded, completing the passage.

"Excellent, my brother," bin Laden exclaimed, "excellent," grasping his hand and welcoming him into the fold.

"And you, my son," he said, stopping in front of Atta. "The eldest and the leader. I am so pleased to see you again."

"I am ever more committed to be a servant of *Allah*, the gracious one," Atta said.

"There is no god except for God," bin Laden replied, stepping back and extending both of his arms. "Welcome friends, brothers. For me, this is indeed a great honor. And for you? A day we all pray to the Prophet—"

They all four chimed in, "*Peace be upon him*." And Bin Laden continued, "a day for all of you, and us, to bring glory unto God."

They sat down to a modest feast of lamb and rice, bin Laden eating little and Marwan just eating rice and drinking tea. Their talk was of Chechnya and Kosovo, and bin Laden even talked of the trial of the deviant American president. He spoke of President Clinton's trip to

Oslo and the death of former Israeli Prime Minister Rabin.[521] Someone brought up the protests in Seattle against the World Trade Organization, and Ziad explained both the assault of globalization and the city by the sea, which he said was like a Hamburg of America.[522]

At the conclusion of the meal, bin Laden turned to Abu Hafs, asking him to brief their guests on their great mission. And then he went away.

The days that followed were a blur for the four. As military chief, Abu Hafs took over their orientation and training. They were also visited by Dr. Zawahiri, who spoke to Atta about the old country, and who clumsily quizzed Ziad about matters of Islam. Khallad shepherded them around, showing them what there was to see.[523]

Sitting in their small guest house one night after prayers, the four had a long philosophical discussion of their task ahead, their first since arriving. "I am, of course, prepared to martyr myself," Marwan said, looking at Ziad. "But you, you are just married."

"We must protect Islam, my brother," Ziad answered.

"Yes, yes. But I'm asking a personal question."

"Are you having doubts, my brother?"

"No. I do not ask for myself," said Marwan. "You all know my destiny. But I admit, brother, that I would like to put my mind to rest. I want to believe not only that we are brothers in our struggle, but that we are clearheaded in what we are undertaking. I sense what we will be asked to do," he said, looking at Atta. "But you, brother. You have the special condition in being married."

"*Fight in the cause of God those who fight you,*" Ziad said, again quoting the Qur'an.[524]

"Yes, yes, my brother, I know what the holy book says. But you have taught me, taught all of us about living our lives as well."

"I hate to bore you with the word," Ziad said, "but there is another verse: '*If any kills a person—for murder and mischief in the earth—it is as though he has killed the whole of humankind, and if any saves a person, it is as though he has saved the whole of humankind.*'[525] That affirms a contribution beyond ourselves and on behalf of our families and of all of our people."

"Brother," Marwan persisted. "I am asking you a personal question. What do you feel?"

"I am afraid I have no better answer than being driven by the word and by my faith," Ziad responded. "If it were practical, if it were logical, I would hope you would be even more concerned for my sanity, for our sanity. It is my faith that drives me. Only my faith."

"And your wife?"

"I am happy to be betrothed to Aysel, and I would like to have a son. But for some time I have felt that my life is no longer my own. I don't mean the subjugation to the Western way, brother, though I feel that, too. It is more like a light, like a certain calm has come to me in the prospect of carrying out God's will—whatever it is that he intends.

"And, by the way, I don't buy all that bullshit about entering Paradise if we accomplish this goal, like we're in some movie line, buying a ticket to heaven. This inner calm comes from prayer and reflection. He—*praise be to Allah*—is bestowing upon me this great and exalted privilege. He wants me to become a martyr. Not everyone gets the chance to become one."

"I have been thinking about this since at least the massacre of Qana," Atta chimed in, "and most certainly since my last trip home. When I was here last in Kandahar, *Sheikh* bin Laden spoke of a coiled spring ready to be sprung. This sent chills through my body. It was then that I knew."

"Yes, yes," Marwan said to Atta, a rare dismissal. "But when the Palestinian brothers speak," he asked Ziad, "they talk of not dying, because they are going to come out alive. But you say there is no paradise. Tell me then."

"Brother," Ziad answered, "I am not saying that there is no paradise, merely that it is not my motivation. It's bullshit what you hear of 72 virgins waiting in heaven, how the nonbelievers have made us to seem like we are simpletons. I imagine really just one moment—the instant of death—a whiteness and a sense of love and contentment washing over me, a sense that I have taken care of the future for Aysel and my family, and for your family, and for all of the families of Islam."

For the rest of their time at the camp, bin Laden never appeared. But then, just a day before they were to leave for Pakistan and return to Germany, they were each called to meet with him privately. He asked them to pledge *bayat*—a loyalty oath—and he told them in his own words of an operation involving planes as bombs, asking each in turn if they wanted to participate, and if they were prepared to learn to be the martyr pilots and take the arduous journey ahead. They each said an emphatic yes, emerging aglow from their meeting.

The group then met again with Abu Hafs, who outlined some details of their highly-secretive mission. After they returned to Germany, they would enroll in flight training schools in the United States. They would eventually be joined in their operation by two fellow pilots—Saudi brothers who were already on their way. Now they would go to Karachi and visit with *Mukhtar*, a great man and the operational commander who would prepare them in all practical matters. *Mukhtar*. It meant the brain.

As eldest, Atta was selected to lead the operation. He met privately again with the *Sheikh* the morning of their departure. Bin Laden gravely told him what the targets of the airplane should be. He wanted the north tower of the World Trade Center to be hit, his 1993 target and the financial symbol of America and the West. He wanted the Pentagon building on the Potomac river to be hit. It was the headquarters of American military might. He wanted the White House to be hit, of course, the palace of America. And he wanted the Capitol building to be hit. He called it the power center of world Zionism, the place that supported the Jew state. Four targets, each one an honor for the four Hamburg boys. Then they spoke of other possibilities, depending on the success of training of still other pilots: the CIA, the FBI building, Wall Street in New York City.[526]

He was to be the absolute *emir* in *Amreeka*, bin Laden said to Atta, able to make decisions for all under his command.

Chapter 29 African Embassies

Gathered in the Apex Watch break room, Mrs. Rothwell cried as they stared aghast at the unfolding television coverage.[527] Charlie and others sniffled, wiping eyes, blowing noses at the carnage at American embassies in Kenya and Tanzania.

Standing apart from the group, Steve stared at a distant point, heart palpitating, hearing sounds vibrating in his ears from clenching his jaw so tightly. It was August 6. He hated the conventional wisdom that terrorist attacks were timed for important anniversaries, but was also well aware that it was the eighth anniversary, to the day, of when American forces deployed to Saudi Arabia in response to the Iraqi invasion of Kuwait.

How could all of U.S. and foreign intelligence miss it? Not one, but two embassies bombed, just four minutes apart. The embassies had been simultaneously attacked with similar bombs, presumably by the same group. KSM said something huge was coming, bigger than ever before. It was even more spectacular than could be imagined. Two countries, with two separate conspiracies.[528]

And the system had detected nothing?[529]

Steve had detected nothing.

The Nairobi bombing killed 12 Americans—213 Kenyans overall, injuring over four thousand.[530] The Dar es Salaam embassy explosion killed 11 Tanzanians and wounded 85. It would have caused more damage, except that it was a national holiday and the building—

originally built and formerly owned by Israel—was more isolated and better fortified.

Steve had been at the Counterterrorist Center when attacks like this had gone down before. And he observed his same reaction, everyone in shock, some crying, but himself staring off with idiosyncratic detachment. He'd gone through the cycle of admonishing himself for not anticipating these tragic events, for not paying enough attention, for distancing himself. But try as much as he could, he didn't feel a thing.

Now he just felt the sting of losing his bet with Bowlen. With access to all the information in the world, how did Steve not catch it?

Since he laid down the challenge, Bowlen had been practically taunting him, piling on the misreads and pompous diversions of the Agency and its new, ever-so-popular director. Just days after Steve started at Apex Watch, Bowlen forwarded George Tenet's remarks before the Senate intelligence committee. Steve read the transcript in his office.

"There has been a trend toward increasing lethality of attacks, especially against civilian targets." Tenet told Congress that "a confluence of recent developments increases the risk that individuals or groups will attack U.S. interests." Steve winced. "Terrorist passions have probably been inflamed by events ranging from the U.S. government's designation of 30 terrorist groups, to the conviction and sentencing of Mir Aimal Kasi and Ramzi Ahmed Yosuf, as well as the ongoing U.S. standoff with Iraq and frustration with the Middle East peace process," the CIA director said.[531]

"Fuck!" Steve exclaimed, reacting to the shallow drivel connecting attacks to some obscure Washington move or to the peace process—a canned, even wrong-headed assessment—one that posed terrorism as a response to each of the current issues *du jour* for Washington rather than seeing it as a more fundamental rejection of the United States and of creeping westernization.

"Can you repeat?" the building said of his outburst, thinking it a command.

That made Steve laugh.

He composed a note to Bowlen that day about Tenet's testimony: Their names are even misspelled, he said, that of the shooter outside CIA headquarters in the first month of the Clinton administration[532] *and* the so-called mastermind Ramzi Yousef, whom they both knew wasn't the actual mastermind.[533]

"Does no one in the government have the guts to say terrorism might be precipitated by our presence in the Middle East or our policies, or even internally by Islam itself, by its own discord and disintegration?"

"At least Tenet says 'passions,'" his new boss answered.

Bowlen then sent Steve a copy of the CTC director's highly-classified memo *Next Steps Against Usama Bin Laden*, laying out the plan for the Agency fight.[534]

Steve was familiar with the document, a laundry list of how the Americans would throw *everything* at *al Qaeda*—greater surveillance, Afghan partners, paramilitary operations, sabotage, even military strikes. It was tantamount to spending every moment arranging the arranging. But more important, the CIA's percolating "plan" to capture bin Laden—pulling off a repeat of the capture of Ramzi Yousef and Mir Aimal Kansi[535]—smacked to Steve of confusing mice with elephants. He thought it was the wrong strategy but couldn't yet say why.

On his Apex Watch office wall, Steve created a huge whiteboard with two columns: Successes and Failures. Steve wasn't keeping score the way the Agency did, where on one side of the ledger was happy talk intended for the glories of the institution and on the other side were mistakes that couldn't be revealed. He was trying instead to tease out an answer to Bowlen's challenge: Could the government ever be successful in thwarting *al Qaeda*? Not just retaliating after the fact, but stopping an attack ahead of time?

He'd lost his bet with Bowlen. He'd failed to detect an attack. He thought now that nothing would make him a better planner *and* a better watcher than methodically understanding the actual pieces of what goes into a conspiracy: understanding what to look for in a world of little actions, and then maybe how to disrupt the rhythm before implementation.

Steve started a checklist of every clue that a true counterterrorism intelligence system might want to detect.

Even as the African buildings were smoldering, Steve was thinking about how the terrorists communicated. And, of course, about their movements across borders, their airline flights, the procurement of explosives, the casing of targets: couldn't any one of them have been detected by local assets?

As for the security on the scene, Steve asked himself why even have tens of thousands of guards and the theater of physical protection if *security* was so useless? Why bother having counterterrorism if the guys at the front doors, or if the guys checking the passports and the luggage always fail?

And, as if to taunt Steve more, almost immediately the government's mistakes in East Africa started to flow in. From Kenya, news came that the American ambassador repeatedly requested security upgrades to counter a car bomb attack similar to that which occurred at Khobar Towers.[536] The State Department denied her request for additional funds, deferring to CIA assessments showing that there had been a decline in terrorism and a lessened threat in Africa. That thinking was partly as a result of Osama bin Laden decamping from Sudan.[537]

"Want to grab a bite to eat?" he asked Charlie as the hours clocked by on the day of the attack. Africa had gone to sleep; cable news was just repeating itself. "I really need to get out of here."

"Now? Don't you have things you want to do?"

"I *really* need to get out of here," Steve responded.

They didn't talk much on the way downtown, though both took notice of how normal Washington appeared. Outside of a small and closed world, the *al Qaeda* declaration of war and the African embassy attacks hardly made the slightest ripple in the nation's capital.

Steve was thinking about her quest to map the little guys—to identify and then focus on the sherpas rather than the bigwigs.

He dropped her off at her apartment. Charlie wanted to change and take a shower—and she needed a long, private cry. He suggested they meet at the Belmont Kitchen at eight.

As he and Charlie faced each other over candlelight at the restaurant, Steve said, "I guess this is it."

"This is what?"

"The turning point: Bowlen is right. Cruise missiles will probably be flying in days. But from there, where does it end?"

God, Charlie thought, he'd been so brilliant at his introductory lunch. It was why she fell in love with this difficult man. What he said then was the talk of the place for days. And yet, almost before dessert was served, he'd clammed back up into his tight ball, doubly protective since he'd exposed himself. The run-up to the embassy bombings had been an intense period for both of them. He'd had clues. And as they increased, he'd withdrawn, gotten colder, even meaner. She loved him, but in her disappointment that he couldn't lighten up, she was asking herself for the first time whether maybe she didn't want to be a couple anymore.

"Can you do it?" she asked at dinner, taking Steve's lead for the evening's destination, which was to be work. She wanted to know if he could maneuver his assignment into something useful, finding an answer to the world's dire problem.

"I have an idea," he said.

"Care to share?"

"Not quite yet."

There was uncomfortable silence as they ate. She ordered grilled red snapper sitting on a bed of wilted greens. He had lamb chops medium rare, a standard he ate out but never cooked.

"Something else to drink?" he asked as she flopped on the couch in his apartment when they got back.

"I'm okay."

"Are you? A lot happened today."

"Steven, I'm fine."

He sat next to her, reaching out and stroking the side of her face. She was flushed but calm.

"Are *you* okay?" she asked. It was her nature to be his case officer, a nurturer.

"I'm overwhelmed."

"Want to talk about it?"

"At Apex Watch, we penetrate everyone's secrets. There's more facts to know, but is that all there is?"

She could see tears forming. "I came in mostly to continue to work with you," he said, squeezing her hand, a tear running down his cheek.

She flushed, feeling guilty that she wanted to separate herself from him.

"Today. I'm just reminded of the nature of terrorism, of our reality, that terrorism itself creates an environment of constant crisis. There's just no room for anything else." He hesitated, wiping away a tear. "I thought maybe I could resolve something for myself, find that piece of information or synthesis that would help me understand."

"Understand what?"

"Fuck. I don't know. Why I just don't feel it. I don't feel the significance, its gravity. I have no outrage. And I want to say I don't really even care, even as I know that saying so isn't accurate because I do what I do because I assume that I care. But I don't feel that I care.

"And now I have access to it all. I'm in a fucking information nirvana. But what we pull in, the shit we get? It's not some handwriting on the wall, it's really just the way the world works. One can be alarmed or sanctimonious about it, I understand, but it just doesn't move me. I'm an emotionless observer. I see it all and it makes me even more contemptuous of those on top, even more drawn to lawlessness, to my own rules."

He went on. "There have to be other things that are more important, more subtle developments, harder things to tackle, that our supposed leaders should pay attention to. But the constant flow pushes everyone to want to know even more of the same, even quicker, perpetuating the cycle. We are caught on the treadmill, experts in the minutiae of a nothingness, diverting us from understanding bigger things."

"Honey," she said, "I know all of this. And I agree with you. Is there something that you're thinking about specifically? That's bringing this on?"

"I feel like my world is coming to an end," he blurted out.

"How's that?"

"I'll be doing this forever. Some part of me hates it. But as I've said before, another part of me can't imagine doing anything else. I'm trapped. The answer man having to provide the answers."

"No one is demanding that," she responded. She wasn't afraid of the tears. She didn't even shy away from the discussion. She just wasn't sure of his point, or what he needed.

"I can't do it all." He cried, and she held him. It was a deep, wrenching cry, something she'd never seen, endearing and refreshingly authentic. He was crying all the stored-up tears for all the attacks that had occurred.

"Terrorism," he finally said as he pulled away. "It's got a certain quality that's the perfect match for our missiles."

"How's that?"

"One act. It happens. We convince ourselves, they convince themselves: that it has impact, that it conveys a message. And yet it perpetuates more of the same, kicking the can down the road, avoiding the reasons behind why they bomb and why we push the buttons in the first place."

"I'm not saying they are morally equivalent," Steve continued. "Now that they've found the perfect telegenic way to hurt us, they will be doing it forever. They will try. And we'll be shooting missiles forever to stop them. Missiles today and whatever follows missiles tomorrow."

"Forever?" Charlie responded.

"If they don't win? If we don't win? Yeah, I'm afraid so."

"I'm exhausted," he finally said, blowing his nose, collecting himself. "You must be, too. Want to spend the night?"

"Sure."

They hadn't slept together in months and she wasn't sure that she wanted to. But she also didn't want to step away from Steve's uncharacteristic truthiness, from what might come.

When they got into his bed, he was quiet. He stared at the ceiling, lost in his own head, hardly present.

She watched him for a moment, then turned over, scooting into his rigid body, skin-to-skin.

Chapter 30 Mad Bombers

Two weeks after the carnage in Kenya and Tanzania, earth-hugging Tomahawk cruise missiles hit a half dozen *al Qaeda* camps in Afghanistan. A pharmaceutical plant near Khartoum was hit at the same time, the White House claiming it was *al Qaeda's* link to both chemical weapons and to Saddam Hussein.

Barbara presented an assessment of the missile retaliation undertaken in response to the African embassy attacks.[538]

"The Agency assessed that about 60 fighters were killed, including a number of Pakistani intel officers who they didn't even know were there."[539]

They sat in the big Apex Watch conference room, the team that was read in to the KSM project—almost a dozen of them—to assess the American retaliation.[540] In stark contrast to the muggy summer outside, the room was freezing cold, everyone complaining about the air conditioning and bringing in sweaters and jackets to wear inside the building.

"KSM says that no one of any importance was killed," Charlie added.[541] "And not only that … but suitcases filled with petro dollars are now flowing into the mountains, just as they did in the glory days of the Afghanistan war."[542]

After not having corresponded for weeks, KSM reappeared after the August attack, sending a slew of tourist postcards from East Africa, all with inscrutable messages.[543] Then he wrote a long, sarcastic letter of congratulations to Mr. Jones, offering his help.

Charlie read aloud:

> Your missiles? They are your weakness. And, may I
> offer, your soldiers are as well. How many times do I need
> to remind you that we do not shoot straight? And we do
> not march straight. How many will come here to wander
> down endless valleys looking for soldiers of bin Laden, only
> to find that there is no such thing. Come, my friend. While
> you get lost in the mountains, we will strangle you in your
> own bed.[544]

"And then he goes on to say," Charlie read, "With these missiles, you have created martyrs and rewarded the *Sheikh*. Now everyone knows his name, and everyone now wants to join him."

She paused. What followed was a phrase in Urdu. Then she laughed, again reading what he had written. "Rainbow rickshaws!" she said. "The crazy Pakistani jingle trucks. You all know them?"

Most everyone said they did.

"And so KSM means what then?" Steve asked.

Bowlen answered. "Our acts provide perfect fundraising for bin Laden. And that more is coming."

"So that's all that this retaliation is?" Charlie growled. "We get an intercept that bin Laden is going to be meeting with the leadership[545] and missiles are launched? And then there's no follow-up? And we did nothing in the case of Khobar Towers? What message does any of it send?"

"I take it in hindsight that Khobar Towers was just too difficult," Bowlen responded. "In terms of who to retaliate against. Now that bin Laden is back in Afghanistan—it's easy. There's no cost, at least internationally, behind attacking. Having to deal with the Saudis on Khobar? That just invoked paralysis."

Steve chimed in: "It's only a matter of time before we hear Tenet and the White House whispering to anyone who will listen that bin Laden must have been tipped off and that *we*, Tenet and his crew, missed him by just a matter of hours, as if they were the missiles themselves."[546]

"That's true," said Barbara. "They're already arguing that nothing happened in Africa that wasn't expected. *We predicted* something spectacular like this would happen, they're saying, as if a terrorist attack represents some sort of victory for the intelligence system."

"It's classic Washington," Steve responded. "They got so hung up deliberating the stupid Sudan target, and then they began to fret about the implications of overflying Pakistani airspace with the missiles. And then they had to consider protection of sources and methods of the information saying that bin Laden was there, and then potential civilian casualties, and then providing top-secret notification to friends and allies. By the time they were done making all of the plans and the arrangements, the details of implementing what they originally decided to do had fallen by the wayside. There wasn't room for any debate as to whether it made sense anymore to actually retaliate."

"Where are you with evaluating what was missed in the original attack, and what we can learn?" Bowlen gingerly inquired.

It wasn't good, what the Americans missed. From Bin Laden's *fatwa* in August, he was publicly stating that *al Qaeda* would attack.

Also, in May, an ABC News team managed to score an interview with bin Laden in the mountain hideout near where the American missiles were targeted. When the interview aired, Agency watchers noted that two of the African embassy plotters were in the background—not only that, but also that the *al Qaeda* leader was sitting in front of a map of Africa, a backdrop that the Agency now deemed a warning.[547] But Steve admitted he missed it as well.

Washington operated from faulty assumptions on many fronts, he went on to explain: They were very wrong in assessing that stabilization in Somalia and bin Laden being ejected from Sudan had reduced the threat in East Africa. Kenyan police and the FBI were also wrong in concluding that an *al Qaeda* cell that existed in Nairobi had been broken up.[548]

But there were tactical mistakes as well. Over the year prior, warnings that came in from intercepts and from human sources were misread or ignored. Actual evidence the FBI obtained, including the computer of one of the direct participants, was never fully exploited. Messages the FBI and the NSA had in their possession were never translated.[549] A Tanzanian walk-in source was sent away, even though he said that there was a truck-bomb plot underway.[550]

"It wasn't just that Afghanistan was easier," Steve changed the subject, coming back to the decision to bomb, having something on his mind. "There was also the weapons-of-mass-destruction factor."

"Uch," Charlie chimed in, "so true." She put her fingers up making air quotes, portentously uttering *WMD*. "That shit rockets to the White House, feeding the obsession which they knew the president already had."

"It's not just Clinton," Steve responded, not able to leave Charlie's suggestion that everything filtered through the Clinton-inspired lens. "WMD is the magic trump card that gets all of Washington to pay attention, regardless of who's in power."

Still, Steve had written an assessment of the WMD problem that focused on the president's influence. Clinton had read *The Cobra Event*, a bioterrorism novel by Richard Preston,[551] and became obsessed with the threat of biological weapons. His national security people arranged private briefings with prominent scientists, and the president's obsession grew.[552] Clinton talked incessantly with Tenet and others about the potential for a devastating terrorist attack upon a U.S. city. Then he and his new secretary of defense, the former Maine Senator William Cohen,[553] went public with their concerns. Cohen went on television, dramatically plopping a five-pound bag of sugar on the table, claiming that just that amount of anthrax would destroy half the population of Washington, DC. "One breath and you are likely to face death within five days," he announced. With nerve agents, he said, it would be just a few minutes.[554]

"I agree with all of what you are saying regarding the groupthink surrounding weapons of mass destruction," Bowlen said, but President Clinton's interest, he reminded them, also coincided with the *Aum Shinrikyo* nerve agent attack in the Tokyo subway systems.[555] And there is the problem of India and Pakistan going nuclear.[556] And let's not forget that the never-ending standoff with Saddam Hussein over WMD has taken up a lot of the president's time—we've uncovered everything, no we haven't, there's no biological weapons, oh wait, there's the chicken farm. It does seem not only that WMD is real, but also that it is becoming more so."

"So, if the WMD factor is such a motivator," one of the analysts asked, "how does it explain that they seemed to have ignored bin Laden's nuclear *fatwa*, the one he issued after his February declaration of war. 'It is the duty of the Muslims to prepare as much force as possible to terrorize the enemies of God,' it said."[557]

"I don't think any of it is ignored," Steve said. "It's more that it all goes into some gigantic stew. No question WMD is the trump card, but in the lineup of WMD problems, al Qaeda is fourth, fifth or even sixth in priority, slipping off the radar day to day, and in many ways only interesting to the president because there is a WMD connection. There's no doubt in my mind that Tenet and Richard Clarke use that to get the president's attention. But because WMD are now connected to bin Laden when they don't see them, they relax."

Steve faded off in his thinking. Everyone could see it—he was done with the conversation.

"So," Charlie asked of Barbara, "they are still arguing that they've got everything in hand?"

"They'll point to the signs," Barbara answered, "that the retaliatory strikes are a good beginning. And it's not just the missiles that they'll point to. The FBI and NSA have both established terrorism centers to match the CIA's.[558] And now bin Laden has also been officially indicted."[559] And the White House is saying that it will add $6 billion more in *counterterrorism* spending, including to counter WMD."

"Over five years," Steve shot back coming out of his stupor. "And the money is such bullshit. Read the fucking supplemental. Where's it all going? Greater security for the fucking Olympics? Greater airport security. I mean for the grounds of airports. Like the threat is a terrorist attacking an airport.

"And as for WMD? It's not money for some offensive war to go out and actually find it or seize it. It's for vaccines against chemical weapons. It's for R&D to find new ways to detect nuclear materials when they're on the roads inside the United States. It's for cleanup and quote *consequence management* for the fucking National Guard just in case there's a terrorist attack in Iowa."

"I think you discount the WMD issue too much," Barbara said.

"Really?" Steve responded, ready to do battle.

Barbara stood her ground. "I'd agree that WMD drives a big part of it all, the retaliation and Tenet's *new* war, and I get it that you disagree. But facts are facts."

"All based on the fucking Fadl material?" Steve responded. He was talking about the al Qaeda defector from Sudan, Jamal al-Fadl. "Here's a perfect example. What he had to say about al Qaeda was interesting enough. But when the FBI and U.S. Attorney started to ask about WMD, he just started making shit up, telling his debriefers whatever it was that they wanted to hear.[560] And as soon as he started whistling WMD, the White House got involved.[561] They are fucking idiots for wanting to make al Qaeda interesting solely because of WMD, but they're not stupid in knowing that it's how to get the president's attention."

"Well, it does explain the target in Sudan," one of the young analysts said, trying to divert the confrontation.

"They made up that target to manipulate Clinton and Janet Reno into justifying the strike," Steve slammed back. "Just like they blinded themselves with the belief that bin Laden was going to be present at a particular camp at a particular moment. In both cases, the evidence stinks. In Sudan, we bombed a fucking aspirin plant."[562]

"I don't disagree about the Sudanese plant," Barbara responded. "But there is abundant evidence that al Qaeda is funding chemical and biological weapons research. I, for one, find it plausible they've also tried to obtain precursors and fissile material. That it is an actual threat."

Steve wasn't budging. "Maybe in the long term, if the whole world breaks down, but it's not imminent or central."

"Let's agree to disagree," Bowlen interrupted. "At this point I'm not sure I could argue that straight facts drive any of the true decisions behind retaliation or the selection of targets. Despite intelligence that bin Laden would be at a meeting, Janet Reno did object, labeling the legal and policy justification to undertake the missile attack too vague.[563] I think, more than anything else, that upped the ante for those who wanted retaliation. I think even you," he said, looking at Steve, "would say it was better to find an answer to her concerns than to do nothing. But let's look at this more simply. Two American embassies in two countries were hit. That pushed the White House to choose targets in two countries in retaliation, Sudan being the obvious second choice. Khartoum was powerless to do anything but protest. Somehow the two-two doctrine— they hit two countries, we hit two—translated to two continents even. I'm not sure the choice is much more sophisticated than that."

He continued: "And even the stated reason for the attack in Afghanistan: an intercept that a leadership meeting that might include bin Laden was going to take place?[564] That intelligence wasn't firm. And then, to obscure the source, they chose to make multiple strikes on multiple camps, not just concentrating on one target.[565] And then they wanted to minimize collateral damage. And then maximize the use of stealth submarines. By the time they were done with all their self-imposed constraints, they'd diluted the intensity of the strike."

"Is that true?" Steve said, looking at Barbara. "That they actually spread them around to obscure the source?"

"The theory behind striking multiple camps was indeed to protect sources and methods," she answered.

"Tenet told Clinton that the intelligence was so good as to bin Laden's location that it made a retaliatory strike a slam dunk," Barbara continued.[566]

Slam dunk.

There was silence all around, a combination of disgust with the system as well as disheartened despondency that even the retaliation had been screwed up.

"I have one more thing to add," Mallory piped in for the first time. In addition to being their IT genius, he was the head of science and technology for Apex Watch. He was straight out of central casting, nerd glasses and a cowlick, lanky and effeminate, baby-faced and slightly off kilter. And he hardly ever said a word. "One more thing to add in the calculations of government missteps in the coming year. I know it has nothing to do with terrorism *per se*, but everything I'm hearing says all of government will grind to a halt in the coming year, doing everything it can—and spending billions—to prepare for the Millennium threat surge."

"The what?"

"The Y2K crisis," he responded. "The sky-is-falling scenario is that all of computerdom will be reduced to fried and smoking boxes with the rollover to the year 2000. I don't want to go into the details of what provoked the scare in the first place, but there's work to be done that is pretty straightforward, yet somehow the problem's been transformed into a threat to our entire way of life. To say the government is overreacting would be the understatement of, well, of the Millennium. The White House czar is saying it will be a digital Pearl Harbor."

"So that will eat up everyone's time?" Steve asked.

"Never underestimate a panic based on a profound lack of understanding of technology," Mallory answered.[567]

"So much for George Tenet's war," Charlie said.

Charlie was talking about George Tenet's December declaration of war.

"We must now enter a new phase in our effort against Bin Laden," she read aloud from Tenet's secret memo. *"We all acknowledge that retaliation is inevitable and that its scope may be far larger than we have previously experienced,"* she continued, affecting an official voice. "No shit," she said, practically snarling, looking up. "I wonder whether Tenet means our retaliation for their retaliation. Or their retaliation for ours?"

And then she bobbled her head to imitate George Tenet as she read more of his secret memo, continuing to quote, and hardly disguising her disgust: *"We are at war ... I want no resources or people spared in this effort, either inside CIA or the intelligence community."*[568]

"Who the fuck is he to even declare war?" Steve said. "He's the head of a fucking intelligence agency. A mad bomber lost in his own echo chamber."

Missile attacks. Y2K. *Slam dunk.* A declaration of war that would keep them busy on more of the same. Within all that, somehow Steve saw his first glimmer of an idea.

PART 8

Chapter 31 The Pitch

Charlie wanted KSM's attention.

Just a moment before the fax began spitting out page after page, her female voice on the phone told him to check his machine.

The first was a plain sheet filled with typed-out names—Khalid Sheikh Mohammed's aliases: ones he used during the Philippines plot, names to travel to and from Brazil and Japan, aliases from the days of the Soviet *jihad*, a fake name from Bosnia, and one he used when traveling to Sudan. Next came a list of telephone numbers that KSM instantly recognized: his family mobile phone number, his wife's number, the old home number in Qatar, the Baku media office, Abu Hafs' emergency cell phone, bin Laden's satellite phone.

Then there was a copy of a 1986 report about the recruitment of one Khalid Sheikh Mohammed, Kuwaiti-born, Pakistan national, student at North Carolina A&T University with a document with his signature on Sheikh Mohammed's "secrecy agreement," signed with regard to his relationship with Mr. Jones, surely one of the silliest documents ever created, though KSM didn't remember it seeming silly when he signed it.

They kept coming, page after page: Khalid's fingerprints. There was a 1996 legal document from the U.S. Attorney for the Southern District of New York, *United States of America v. Khaled Shaikh Mohammad, Indictment*.

There was a photograph of Sheikh Mohammed coming out of his old Ministry building in Doha, surveillance shots of his Qatar office in the water ministry, and finally one of his current Gulshan town apartment building in Karachi, where he was at that very moment standing in his office.[569]

Gulshan town was a solidly middle-class district of Karachi known for its concentration of universities and colleges, reputedly one of the most literate areas of the entire country.

Block 9, which was what KSM's neighborhood was called, was a crowded patchwork of the planned and the impromptu. There were a good number of *pukka* houses, solidly-built structures made of substantial materials and the product of an architect's pen. But there were also a good number of *katchi*, flimsy shanties of mud, bamboo, and thatch clustered along the alleyways and crowded between formal streets. The sidewalks and footpaths were occupied by makeshift shops and food stalls. Amidst it all, even on the periphery of the lineup of giant luxury apartment buildings towering over the rest, were the *katchi abadis*, the public squalor of the undocumented; sprawling blotches of unregulated dwellings made of scraps, slums living on stolen electricity and busted water pipes, ringed with open sewers and spectacular garbage dumps. And packs of wild dogs.

Into this mix, Charlie proposed a variant of the hardest of all agent pitches: a gangplank recruitment.[570] Right in KSM's face. If it exploded, so be it.

Charlie demanded KSM's attention. He wasn't susceptible to blackmail or pressure, and he would just as quickly lie to them or double-cross them. Really, the best she could hope for was to break KSM out of his decade-long Mr. Jones habit, impressing on him that there was a new boss. And she would use the fact that she was a woman, intriguing him. It could backfire, hence the gangplank label, but she felt that making it clear they knew where he lived and had abundant goods on him, might possibly exert some degree of control, or at least force some new era of reluctant cooperation.

In her time with the CIA clandestine service, few got a gangplank approach approved. It was too dangerous or not worth it, the bosses would say. But in her experience with terrorist-related sources, they almost all wanted to talk, wanted to explain their circumstances and grievances, if not to the world than at least to an American, wanting nothing in return.

"But KSM has more than adequate time to explain," Bowlen said to Charlie when reviewing her approach. "Once you get past that, what's going to hook him?"

"Conspiracies," Charlie said.

"I have read the book on the New World Order from your beloved clergyman Pat Robertson," KSM wrote to Apex Watch right after the Gulf War.[571]

"World government is the master of making war—of which, my friend, you are also a big general," he wrote the year after. KSM once asked if Mr. Jones was connected to the *Illuminati*. Charlie laughed the first time she read that.

But there were others. Of course, KSM mentioned that the CIA killed King Faisal in 1975, wondering also in a later letter why, if it were intent on taking down the al Saud, they didn't just kill more people.

Then KSM wrote that the Jews were responsible for the death of John F. Kennedy and even, through a convoluted mélange of freemasons and Jews, for the killing of Abraham Lincoln. And there was the litany of Russian-inspired conspiracies, the direct result of the KGB's active measures campaigns:[572] that the CIA brought cocaine to the streets of America, or that it invented AIDS and planted it in Africa.[573]

And there was one that many in government even clung on to: that Washington gave a green light to Saddam to invade Kuwait so that it could destroy him and set back a modern Arab country.

"Have you seen the latest *fatwa* of the Council on Foreign Relations?" KSM then wrote after the Khobar Towers attack. "They argue for 'benevolent global hegemony' coming from a buildup of the armed forces and more American aggression. They make proposals for regime change wherever governments defy world government. To them, the world *wants* to be dominated by America."[574]

Charlie requested a copy of the study to see how mangled KSM had managed to describe it. He hadn't mangled it much.

KSM became obsessed with the claims of the former Kennedy administration spokesman-turned-newsman Pierre Salinger: that an American naval ship intentionally shot down TWA Flight 800, a plane that had exploded 12 miles off Long Island less than a month before the attack in Saudi Arabia.[575]

Steve earlier told Charlie he was delighted with KSM's conspiratorial bent, and he heartily supported her use of it. He also reveled in this demented history. Even in America, he said, tons of people believed in conspiracies—whether that be UFOs or the Kennedy assassination or the conspiracy of a faked moon landing. And the latest horseshit populating the World Wide Web, he snarled—that the government manufactured incidents—was based on a single document: the so-called "Northwoods" memo that he suspected itself was a forgery.[576] "False flags," the conspiracy nuts labeled them, Steve said, incidents that were manufactured and intended to mobilize public opinion like the sinking of the Maine. The "false flag" theory, Steve said, was beautifully circular. The government, which can't be trusted, was manipulating everything to create an idiotic public, which there was. Ergo, the conspiracies were true.

In her gangplank presentation, though, Bowlen was impatient. He wanted to know how Charlie planned to use KSM's propensity towards conspiracy.

"I will use his conspiracy with us," answered Charlie. "Since he is planning to attack the United States in some way, and it is unlikely he is going to tell us how, directly, or we'll find much out autonomously through the system, perhaps I can use it to seduce him with the notion that we are interested …"

"Interested how?" Steve asked, perking up.

"Interested in being co-conspirators?" Charlie said. "I haven't quite worked that out yet," she added.

Steve jumped on it: "We certainly know that if this fucker has any vulnerability or weak spot, it's his ego to be the greatest ever. He gave up Ramzi Yousef to be seen as the one and only. And yet, other than us, no one really knows who he is. I think we can use that.

"And from his correspondence," Steve continued, "KSM seems wholly convinced that his collaboration with us is of value to the United States. Maybe we should use the fact that we're not Agency and not even the government, that we want to help him, because …" and he hesitated, "because we want to help him …" Steve looked off in the distance before continuing.

"That's the reason we've been helping him all these years, because the

Agency is indeed evil in its collaboration with Saudi Arabia and the other Arab oppressors. Perhaps we suggest an anti-Zionist thrust."

"And what would we be telling him? I mean, specifically," Bowlen asked.

"I'm just thinking on my feet now," Steve responded. But he knew that he was on to something. And neither Bowlen nor Barbara exploded in opposition, his blossoming outline inviting curiosity.

KSM did just as everyone told him. Live your life, his brother told him. Just live your life, Bowlen told him. And what a life: *He* picked the World Trade Center. He conceived the Philippine plots. He made up the Clinton assassination deception. He brought down Ramzi Yousef. He became operational commander for the African embassy bombings when *al Qaeda* floundered. He was special emissary of Osama bin Laden. He was editor and media coordinator, providing his *emir's fatwas* to the world. Now *they* would provide him with the one thing he truly craved, affirmation that his being the greatest was fully appreciated.

That day, KSM's impulse upon receiving the faxes was to destroy everything and disappear. He'd done it before. But the initiating phone call and the final fax said they knew where he was.

He instinctively stepped out onto the fourth-floor balcony to look down at the street, where he immediately spotted a conspicuously-parked white SUV, a very clean one; inside it, two Westerners with a view of his front door, casual in their indifference at standing out. Openly watching him. That was as much a message that they could expose him to the street whisperers as it was anything else.

And then there was a knock at the door.

A young tea boy handed him an envelope, took some rupees, and ran down the stairs. In it was a note:

> Mr. Jones, Room 617
> Sheraton Hotel and Tower, Club Road
> 4:00 p.m.

Given that Apex Watch knew that KSM often traveled as a Saudi businessman, Tony told Charlie that the downtown Sheraton was the best location for the meeting. It was away from the dangerous neighborhoods and was a common meeting point for international visitors and their local contacts. They both assumed that KSM could and would produce the requisite passport to get past hotel security, which, to just get onto the grounds, included an ID check and an opened trunk and a bomb check with a mirror on a set of wheels rolled under the automobile chassis, even in the case of a limousine.

Tony's watchers called Charlie at 3:05 to report the bird had left the nest. They said that they thought he winked at the Toyota 4Runner as he got into the minicab waiting out front to pick him up. He was alone and wasn't carrying anything other than his man bag, reported the former Green Beret, probably a good sign that KSM was indeed on his way to the meeting.

At 4:00 p.m., KSM knocked on the door of suite 617.

Charlie answered. The mustachioed man was skinnier than his passport pictures suggested. He wore a crisp, white robe and *kaffiyeh* typical of Gulf Arabs. Peeking out from under his headdress was jet black hair and long sideburns.

"Welcome," she said.

"Not Mr. Jones," he said, at the same time showing no sign of surprise or distress with her presence.

"No," she said in Arabic, "obviously not. But to you, I am the new Mr. Jones."

He smiled. "I trust that he is well."

"Indeed, he is."

"He is not coming?"

"No. I'm afraid not. Johnny Walker Black?" Charlie asked, holding up a bottle of KSM's favorite liquor from the credenza.

"No, I am good," KSM answered.

Charlie liked one thing about him right away. He showed no acknowledgement whatsoever that she was a woman.

"So," she said, "you have been so busy. *So very busy.*"

"Yes, Miss. But it is clear you know more about me than I do about you. That is not polite."

"Theresa Landry," she said, not extending her hand.

"The mad fax lady," he merely said.

"Not mad," she said, smiling, and in what sounded like pretty good modern Arabic, though KSM thought he detected a trace of a Lebanese accent. "I just wanted to get your attention."

"A simple invitation from my old friends would have been enough," he responded.

"Enough to arrange a meeting perhaps," she responded.

"But I also have new business with you," she continued. "And I wouldn't want you running off before we had a chance to discuss it."

"Ah. New business. That sounds exciting. The first time Mr. Jones gave me an assignment, we defeated the Soviet Union. Now there is just one superpower left."

He laughed. She thought it clever.

"Are you responsible for Kenya and Tanzania?" she asked sharply.

"You came to Karachi to talk about Africa? About old news?"

"Are you responsible?"

"Miss Landry," he said coolly, "I am so ready to get to know you."

"And me you. But if we are to be friends and colleagues, I'd like to get a sense of what you are up to. You've written to us about the attacks. And what you think they mean for *al Qaeda* and its good fortune. But you say nothing of your own role. Don't you think that we will find out eventually?"

"You mean if I don't tell you? From what I read in the newspapers, I wouldn't be very worried about your finding out very much at all."[577]

"And what about all of that information I found out about you?"

"Ah," he said. "You did that work, Miss?"

"We did, yes."

"Ah. So I am making headaches."

"Khalid," she said, using his given name, one that he hardly heard except from his wife and brother. "We want to know if the embassies were yours, and if they are, as you previously warned, if they are an introduction to ever escalating attacks."

"Really? You just want to know? The American government? Just between friends?"

"Among friends."

"I'm surprised," KSM started. "You already attacked with your missiles. Another big victory for you. I saw it on CNN. I'm surprised the CIA is still interested. Africa is what? Closed case, as your policemen say?"

"We're not CIA."

"Ah, yes. I have been told that. But then who are you?"

"We are not friends of the betrayers of your people. We are not the men behind those in your own country whose main skill is ripping out fingernails and burning testicles. We are not protectors of Israel."

"But, Miss? How can that be? That *is* the United States of America. So how can you not be that?" He laughed.

"I think you know from more than a decade of experience with Mr. Jones that we are not the America of the newspapers. Or the movies."

She was clever as well, he happily concluded.

"Am I to work with you now?"

"Yes."

"Will I ever see Mr. Jones again?"

"Yes, most likely you will. He is the big boss now."

"So, Miss, what is our work together?"

"It is the same, Khalid. It is to end the corruption of Saudi Arabia and the Gulf States. But additionally, I want to understand your *emir* and *al Qaeda*."

"So not something new?"

"There is always new, Khalid. Things change, and they are changing."

KSM asked: "And for what purpose? Is the great United States of *Amreeka* going to leave the Middle East?"

"Probably not," she said. "But maybe one day, when the Arab world indeed reaches its potential and stops attacking the rest of the world, change will occur."

"Oh, then we will be such good friends, unified as one." He laughed heartily.

There was a long hesitation, Charlie watching KSM calculate.

"Yes, of course, the embassy attacks are mine," he finally said. "And quite successful, as I guided our boys. Now you are going to assist me in more?" He smiled broadly.

"This was an attack, another attack, on the United States. That I cannot condone or be funny about. And Mr. Jones tells me that you say you will attack the United States directly on American territory? Why?"

"You don't know?" he responded.

"I want to hear my new friend say it, from his heart."

"Because it has—how do you say—impact, Miss. Of course, I share Mr. Jones' goals about the Saudi snakes, but it has been a decade, and nothing there has changed. Not only that: the assault on Islam, it just gets bigger. So, who else are we to attack but the country with the most power? It took much time to prepare these events in Africa, and a great mind." KSM tapped his head. "But it has always been the goal, and now it is starting to make real. Afghanistan is more secure. Our skills improve. There are many volunteers."

She said: "I want to be a part."

"Be a part how?"

"In knowing, to help focus attention in the right way."

"Miss? You want to help me attack *Amreeka*?"

"No. I don't want to attack the United States. And I don't want you to, or your people to. But I am a realist. That it will continue. So yes, I want to be a part."

"And Mr. Jones?"

"He sent me."

"Why didn't he come?"

"I insisted that we needed to get to know each other, just you and me."

"Well then," he said, "I will have some whisky." He relaxed in the velvet-covered club chair, leaving the couch for her.

She brought him the drink with a single ice cube, taking one neat for herself. She said: "I want to impress upon you that things will be different now."

"How so?"

"You are an enemy of the United States," she said.

"But you *are* the United States," he responded. "Why sit with the enemy?"

"You are an enemy of the United States," she repeated. "Mr. Jones told you that in Doha. And you are responsible for the deaths of many hundreds, and for thousands of your own people. And now you plan to attack my country. In all we do, I can't and won't forget that."

"I appreciate you being so direct, Miss. But I don't think you are here to arrest me. And you aren't just going to kidnap me like Ramzi Yousef and lock me away where I'll never be allowed to talk. So why tell me what I already know?"

"I want you to know it is more dangerous for you to travel internationally. The immigration and police authorities will come looking for you, all on their own. I don't want to threaten you, my new friend, but I want to make it clear that we know where you live. And where you go."

She paused to let is sink in. "So, let's talk about your future."

"As I have said many times, *Sheikh* Osama bin Laden is the future. And if not he, certainly what he is creating."

"I believe you," she said. "And I want you to know that your reporting on him and his world is extremely valuable and well regarded."

He sipped his drink, hiding a smile.

"Live my life. That is what Mr. Jones told me more than ten years ago. It is your same wish?"

"Yes, Khalid. I would like to be a better friend in knowing how you live it and what you are up to. So, I can prepare."

"Prepare what, Miss?"

"If you are successful in whatever you plan, I want to be able to prepare to use it to throw blame on the Saudi kingdom and others who need to be taken care of."

"Others? The bad countries?"

"Yes, Khalid."

"And does others include Islam?"

"You mean the entire religion?"

"You know what I mean, Miss."

"I will give you an honest answer," she said. "Islam will take care of itself. It already is doing so."

"Doing so?"

"Your *Sheikh*. He is already successfully splitting the Islamic world. And the *Shi'a* people grow in strength."

He pondered her answer. "Just as Kissinger planned," KSM said.

"Excuse me?" Charlie responded.

"The Kissinger plan, just as he planned."

"There's no Kissinger plan," Charlie frowned, and then laughed.

"Oh, Miss, there is. New World Order is not new. Henry Kissinger, the Elder of Zion, the Rockefeller advisor, the secret guardian of Israel. Decades ago, he put together the plan to destroy Islam and the Arab people. Birth control. And food control. He made it so our world, growing and more powerful because of oil, would come to be in debt to the West. And there would be internal fighting. And as always, Israel and the Zionists would be behind it all."[578]

"Come on, Khalid."

"No, listen to me. This '73 war between the Jew state and its neighbors? It was a disaster. The oil embargo didn't bring the West to its knees. No, to its knees came the idea of Arabs working together. And killed in that battle was the program of progress, of bringing education and even medicine to the poor. The Arab states were forced to spend vast fortunes on Western arms. Spend money, but were still controlled so that those arms would never be used. The Zionist forces, and this Henry Kissinger Jew, they implemented their plan."

Charlie took a sip of the whisky. She didn't want to argue with her man. Not yet.

And then KSM completely changed his direction: "In the coming year, there will be a big attack in the Middle East, another direct attack on your military."

"Where will it take place?"

"Not Saudi Arabia. It will be a new country."

"Anything more you'd like to share?"

"No," he said. "But tell me, Miss: Does it have any impact?"

"Does what have impact?"

"The attacks. Do they have impact?"

"You mean in terms of getting anyone in Washington to change? No, my friend. Quite the opposite. Attacks on America merely strengthen its resolve."

"Shooting missiles? That is all?"

"Strengthen, Khalid. Missiles, I think, are just the beginning."

"Maybe that's all you have? Missiles. Because they are machines. And they are safe. For you."

"Maybe for now, Khalid, but Africa was a different type of attack."

Hmm, he quietly said to himself, sitting back in his chair. "And the embassy attacks. Are they good for you?"

"If by that, you mean, are they teaching America to pay attention, yes, they are good."

He liked her, and they spoke more of Africa. KSM probed as much as he could to learn about her, listening to her story of growing up in America and her tales of Lebanon.

She asked about his family. And maybe because she was a woman, he spoke of his wife and two boys, "intelligence" that Bowlen never bothered to collect.[579]

They discussed KSM's communications with Apex Watch. Charlie told him that given the emergence of email, they wanted him to switch over, to have more regular and quicker communications. KSM expressed concern that this new form of communication was less secure than written mail. Charlie said that they were working on a new way to communicate, that it would be available soon, a device that would allow him to encode and decode messages so that they were safe even if intercepted.

He was pleased.

Every thirty minutes, the phone rang in the room and Charlie picked it up, listening to one of Tony's men check in. "It's okay," she'd say and hang up.

They had a second drink. Charlie asked about the *al Qaeda* leadership. KSM answered truthfully, chit chat and gossip. But he didn't tell her anything new.

It was getting dark. Khalid looked at his watch, saying he needed to go.

"When shall we meet again?" she asked.

"Next month?"

"Yes."

"Frankfurt?" she asked.

"Excellent," KSM said.

They talked about travel arrangements. KSM told her how he wanted her to arrive in Germany, and that he would not come in Saudi dress. They should plan accordingly.

"You're not going to pick up your family and try to disappear on us, are you, Khalid?" Charlie said as he was leaving.

"Karachi is quite nice. No, Miss."

Chapter 32 Always Your Pain

Immediately after they settled into a café in Frankfurt,[580] Charlie said, "Seems like another African embassy-type attack is out of the question."

KSM sipped his sweet tea. "Why is that, Miss?"

"Because I think it is not of interest to you, that it would just be a copy, a copy of Beirut, of Khobar Towers, and even of Oklahoma City."[581] A truck driving up to a building and exploding. It had been tried repeatedly, even at the Egyptian embassy in Islamabad. Charlie was guessing that such an attack no longer fit KSM's pretensions of wanting a bigger and better impact.

"There are many operations still to prepare, Miss."

Charlie took on KSM full-time. Except when he sent an original document, which was less often now that they were meeting, they now almost exclusively used a secure email system, occasionally even chatting on instant messenger. They met face-to-face monthly, first in Frankfurt, next in Zurich, then in Amsterdam, always outside the Middle East, though, and never—by KSM's insistence—in London.

At a meeting in the hotel café near terminal 1 of the Frankfort airport, KSM was ready to show off his collection of clippings—which mostly concerned Monica Lewinsky. There was commentary from a Palestinian newspaper comparing Lewinsky with Marilyn Monroe—only the Jewess had gone to the public prosecutor. A Syrian article claimed Lewinsky was a *Mossad* bomb intentionally planted in the White House. An article from an Iraqi newspaper about Lewinsky said that she was giving 80 percent of her book royalties to Israeli Prime Minister Benjamin Netanyahu. An editorial from the state-run Iraqi news agency said Bill Clinton would share in the tens of millions of dollars Monica would get by posing for *Playboy* "and other famous sex magazines."[582]

"She was sent to destroy the president because of his sympathy with the Palestinians," offered KSM. He had the evidence to show her, in spades.

"My dear Miss, the president of your country can have any woman he wants. The Secret Service is there to make it so. And yet somehow here he gets caught? And by the government he leads? And the newspapers so quickly produce pictures of the lady Lewinsky wearing a special beret in the crowds? She was planted there, pure and simple."[583]

"Who planted her, Khalid?" Charlie asked, exasperated. "For what purpose?"

"Every time Clinton meets with Yasser Arafat or other Palestinian leaders; some new sex detail emerges in the news. Study the timing. Clinton cares maybe too much for the Palestinians ..."

"And Lewinsky is to do what? Stop Middle East peace? I'm not sure President Clinton gives a shit about the Palestinians."

"Yes, Miss. She is to keep Clinton from getting too close to them."

"You like Clinton?"

"Like him? No, Miss. I am speaking fact."

"Do you really believe there is a hidden hand at work?" she taunted, sorry she said it the moment she did.

"No," he said, chuckling in a satisfied way, "not one, many."

"So is the CIA protecting the president or is it the *Mossad* bringing him down?"

"The CIA, the CIA, I don't know CIA. *They* are protecting the world order. If that means letting go of an American president, so be it. The CIA believes it is more important than any leader elected by the people."

The Jews, the Zionists, the CIA, secret societies, the ruling elites in Washington and New York and Hollywood, even the government in New Delhi. To KSM, they pulled the planetary strings. KSM opined that the Muslim people had been prisoner to these oppressors for centuries. And godless communism—an invention of the Jews—was just the latest crusader army sent to assault Islam.

"Muslims as victims?" Charlie prodded. "It is in your imagination. The Arab world is a failure all on its own. Khalid, you live in Karachi, a modern city. And I imagine you do so because of the freedom, the freedom of South Asia, away from the Arab sickness. You take advantage of all that is different about Karachi because Islam—*Salafi* Islam—is so oppressive. Look honestly, Khalid. Please. The Arab world has no decent schools or universities to study anything but the *Qur'an*. Ownership of computers per capita is less than any other region on the planet. The number of books published is fewer as well." She went on: "And among your people there is sickening poverty, given the obscene wealth that exists around them.[584]

"The region has made itself dependent on selling oil to the West because it hasn't developed any other economy. Even fucking Africa manufactures their own automobiles," she taunted. "*The Arab world, they produce nothing.*"

She had no affinity for Israel, Charlie said, not as a Lebanese American. But she also argued that the contribution of a small number of Jews merely punctuated the failures of the far larger Arab world. "You blame everyone else for keeping the Arab Middle East down, Khalid. And you pine after past greatness, grasping at every possible excuse to explain away centuries of failure on the part of the Arab people to flourish …"

"But it has been so for centuries, Miss," KSM answered. "The Rothschilds, the Freemasons, your own George Washington, a straight line from the Vatican to today's *Illuminati*."[585]

Nothing could dissuade him. Charlie wasn't surprised. She'd heard the same theories uttered a million times on assignments in the Middle East, even from government officials.

She pushed again when they met in Zurich the next month.[586]

"I'm guessing that since you told me about the upcoming attack on the military in the Middle East, it isn't your operation?"

"No. Not directly."

"Your American operation would have to be something new, wouldn't it?"

"Your defenses improve. We adapt."

"So, is it 21 questions?" she asked.

"That means what?"

"A guessing game, a child's game."

"No. I have been waiting for you to just tell me what you have concluded."

"It is a planes operation," she said.

"Why would you think that?" he asked nonchalantly.

"After Abdul Murad was captured in the Philippines, he talked of flying a plane into the CIA. And Ramzi Yousef brags. He speaks often of the bomb on the Tokyo flight."

"How is he?" KSM asked, referring to Yousef.

"In prison. For the rest of his life."

"Another threat, Miss? When we are just becoming friends?"

"It is a planes operation, Khalid?" she asked, ignoring him.

"Perhaps," he answered, shrugging his shoulders to indicate that he wasn't dismissing her.

"Blown up in the sky like in the Philippines or flown into a building?"

"Oh, Miss. I cannot predict the future."

"How would you do it, if you were going to attack?"

"If I were going to attack, I would do it myself," KSM answered.

"I doubt that, my friend."

KSM hesitated, trying to formulate the right English. "Whatever will have the greatest impact; that is the plan."

"And the target would be what?"

"This is not yet decided. The center of Zionism."

"You believe that there is such a thing?"

"What am I to say? That New York is the center of big buildings? It is the center of money, of world money, so yes, it is the center of Zionism. It is fact."[587]

"And the target is what?"

"I do not yet know. That is for *al Qaeda* to decide."

"Really, Khalid," Charlie pushed. "You are going to let them tell you what to do?"

"A planes operation, attacking your country. That would be the act. What target is hit in New York is not important. As long as it is important."

"I just don't believe that you would give up that decision."

"I await their order. I didn't say I would let them make the final decision, one that it is for them to decide. So far, they haven't yet so declared."

"And you will tell us?"

"I have to think of how you might be helpful."

The center of Zionism in New York? Of money? Would it be Wall Street?

Charlie suggested that she and KSM go to the *Kunsthaus Zürich* to see the sculptures of Alberto Giacometti, one of her favorites.

"It is what?" KSM asked.

"A museum," Charlie said, "a famous one."

"I have never been to a museum," KSM answered. "No, that is not true. Mr. Jones took me to the Smithsonian Air and Space Museum on my first visit."

"And what did you think?" Charlie asked.

"I loved it," KSM answered. "I was most impressed with the first airplane. And the spaceship that landed on the moon."

"So, you have never been to an art museum? Looked at art?"

KSM answered. "Why would I go, Miss?"

"You are dedicated to the downfall of Western civilization and yet all you know of it is McDonald's? You speak of the spiritual emptiness, you even quote Sayyid Qutb, who focuses only on the materialism and decadence of America and the West. And yet you do not even acquaint yourself with its art or music?"

"I am surrounded by it, dear Miss Landry," he responded. "Your art and music. It finds its way into our ears everywhere. We hear it on the streets. It is on television. Michael Jackson at least has the decency to turn himself white to tell us that he is in on the secret. But do not tell me I know not your music. It is heard on the dustiest street in the tiniest village in the Philippines."

"I'm talking real art and music, Khalid."

They went to the *Kunsthaus*. From the outside it was a solid stone building, inside it was white and open, a magnificent hidden oasis of glass and light. Charlie tried to explain that Giacometti's elongated sculptures, made at the end of World War II, represented the devastation and vulnerability of humanity.

"Your suffering." KSM shook his head, responding without bitterness. "Always and only your suffering."

That did make her think. God, he had a point.

As they were dining that night, KSM asked her a question. "Do you know of an Abu Bakr Sudani?"

"It's the *kunya* for who?" Charlie responded.

Everyone chooses a battle name, called a *kunya*. When they entered *al Qaeda*, passports are taken away and everyone is issued fake names and nationalities if they need to travel. Then they choose a *kunya,* most often *Abu* something, *father of,* except when the *kunya* is a single word like *Mukhtar,* kind of like Madonna or Bono.

"Abu Bakr Sudani. It is the name for Jamal al-Fadl," KSM said.

"Why?" Charlie asked. The Sudanese defector was in a safe house, still being squeezed by the FBI.

"He is a worry to the *Sheikh.*"

"He has mostly talked about cells and operations in Yemen and in East Africa," Charlie said. "But I'm not involved in his debriefing. I think they are using him to map *al Qaeda* all over the world, I think I read 50 countries.[588] Are you looking for something?" Charlie asked. "Something specific?"

"Has he identified me?"

"Not that I'm aware," Charlie answered. But she really didn't know. She wasn't dissembling.

On their next meeting in Amsterdam,[589] she told him Fadl hadn't identified him. As they walked the canals, KSM asked what was the *gerookte paling* being sold by the street vendors—the golden, pencil-thin bodies dangling like dipped candles from the wooden trailers.

"Smoked eel," Charlie said.

"Is it *halal*?" KSM asked.

"I don't know," she responded.

"Ask him about *qushur alsamak,* Miss." Fish scales. "Whether it's permissible? *Halal*?"

"I hope he speaks good enough English to even know."

They both loved the treat.

KSM asked if they could go to a store so that he could buy *his son* a video game.

He spent almost two hours looking over the shelves, asking questions of the shaggy and tattooed clerk, even playing a couple of demos.

Later, when Charlie mentioned it in her post-trip debriefing, Steve didn't have to tell her that this wasn't about his son.

On the next visit,[590] Charlie was ready. "I know this might be too violent for your boy," she said, opening her laptop to show him something, again in a quiet hotel lounge, this time in Budapest, "but I think you might find it interesting."

It was a beta game called *Special Force*, put together by Lebanese programmers for *Hizb'allah*, a game that the CIA obtained a year earlier. It was the first video game made specifically in the Middle East. It pitted the player's commandos against the Israeli Defense Force in southern Lebanon.[591]

Real battles to humiliate the Zionist enemy, giving it a lesson, the instruction booklet said. *Be a partner in the victory*, the opening screen promised.

KSM loved it.

He told Charlie that maybe someday he could become *Mr. Bill Gates* in the Islamic world, overseeing a gaming empire and making millions, something that Charlie thought so contradictory to his *jihadi* views and conviction to attack America.

He took the disc and said he was going to show *Sheikh* bin Laden the *Special Force* game on his next trip to Afghanistan. He once presented his *emir* with a proposal to support development of an *al Qaeda* game, arguing that such a game could be a tool to build a future movement beyond the ranks of the old *mujahidin* and their families. But the rudimentary example he showed, made by Pakistani computer students in Lahore, didn't impress him.

The next month, again in Frankfurt,[592] KSM told Charlie he demonstrated the *Special Force* game to bin Laden. He even brought a color printer with him to Kandahar, hooking it up to a car battery and printing out a high-score certificate presented by *Hizb'allah* leader Hassan Nasrallah in a "cyber ceremony" to Mr. Osama.

The *Sheikh* was skeptical of the investment but understood the allure: his youngest sons were addicted to their handheld Nintendos. KSM implored Charlie to find him a battery-powered machine he could give to bin Laden's boys, showing American or Israeli soldiers killing Arabs.

"There isn't any such game," the geek Mallory interjected in the post-trip meeting. He had invented the handheld encrypting device for KSM's emails, but otherwise Charlie paid no attention to him. He attended the meeting but spent most of his time slouching over the conference table, mostly distracted and silent.

She knew, though, that Mallory loved Steve ever since the luncheon, and he came to his office often to show him the latest piece of technology he acquired on the commercial market, as well as some that had been developed by the Agency.

If Charlie could get access to KSM's computer, he said matter-of-factly, *that* could open up possibilities.

He said that the Agency developed a device on a CD-ROM that installs a computer game on a target machine along with an undetectable loop that then sends out an encrypted and highly-compressed blind carbon copy of keyboard strokes and mouse clicks, allowing reconstruction of all activities on the machine, even chat sessions. Called *Transcape*, it was based upon parental spying software but far more sophisticated. Mallory said the program was used successfully in covert actions in Bosnia and Russia.

It was very cutting edge.

There was one huge catch, he said: Charlie would have to bring the CD-ROM back. When installed on a non-networked machine, it copied an image of key files and other logs, which were then used to synch up the stream of intercepts when the machine went online. But even with a modem connection at 56k, that would burst the take back once the machine was connected. And it would do so sending the intelligence embedded within other computer-to-computer communications protocols, virtually undetectable. If they got the CD-ROM back, they would then receive the highly-compressed files, the bits and bytes reconstructing whatever KSM typed.

The room exploded, everyone talking at once. Lure him away from the apartment and one of Tony's guys can do it! Buy him a laptop as a gift and preinstall it!

"What if we just laser print the CIA logo onto the disc and the cover, so KSM wouldn't want to keep it once he installed the game?" Mallory said. The only catch would be that he had to give the disc back to Charlie rather than throw it away after he installed it. So, she'd have to be there when he installed it.

They brainstormed about ways for Charlie to penetrate KSM's private space in Karachi.[593] There was a long discussion about whether a woman could even make it to his apartment in the first place, but Charlie argued that he might be interested if there was a reason, if only to satisfy his deep-seated craving to show off. Finally, they decided that Charlie would just tell KSM to bring his laptop to a meeting—it wasn't implausible that she wouldn't have one and she could explain that she needed to install the game.

An *al Qaeda* video game it would be: the game would have surveillance satellites and cruise missile strikes, as well as commando teams searching for Arab fighters in the mountains and caves of a place called *Tora Bora* ("Eagle's Nest"), with movement through each underground passage and ancient mountain trail accumulating points for the fighters, and ultimate victory for *al Qaeda* if they made it to the safety of the Pakistani border.

"How good do you want it to be?" Mallory asked, energized with a project assisting the A team.

"Professional," said Bowlen.

"It's going to take months to develop."

"Ok."

"And serious money."

"It will be worth it," Steve chimed in.

"It will be irresistible to play," Mallory said.

Bowlen wanted it ready by the next presidential inauguration.

Chapter 33 Istanbul

They were idiots, Steve said. Or they were too wed to rigid allegiances of family or clan or even nations to stick their necks out. They were potential members of a mob, people who could be revved up to do anything. As for systems of government, of living—which Steve thought determined almost everything—most people just followed a path of self-interest and sloth. Everyone, Steve said, was sleepwalking through life, even the high-minded.

Charlie and Steve argued this worldview. Were some people just evil—aberrations who needed to be locked up or killed so good people could be protected? Or perhaps people were just predictable products of their circumstances, that no one was evil?

There were very few people with empty pages to be filled out, argued Steve. Most were just ruled by circumstances and shared realities of whatever their systems were. And even worse, most were cockeyed in their view of how the world works and, thus, were individually immaterial. Steve admitted he felt this way because, at heart, he was basically unfeeling. And he admitted that was what made him distrust others who felt anything too strongly.

Even when they could agree, Charlie thought Steve couldn't formulate a strategy without answering this question about which camp KSM and his brethren fit in.

Charlie prodded Steve to factor in some indefinable human equation, even of KSM, in what she now called his attempt at global puppetry.

"You have no trouble having an opinion about Tenet or the bosses," she argued, "that they're driven by being important, by being at the center of everything, that they are slaves to whatever ideas gain the most traction and the approbations of the powerful. But what about KSM? Or bin Laden? You seem to practically idealize them. Why can't you simply classify them?" she asked. "Why aren't *they* just idiots? Or ambitious entrepreneurs? Or, God forbid, by your own standards, just evil?"

"I guess I'm more modest in my pretense of knowing them," Steve answered. "I don't pretend to get *al Qaeda* or the Arab mind. I recognize that even saying 'Arab' is wrong, but I do so because in civilized company we're not supposed to say Islam, and yet it is Islam—at least I think that it is."

That's when Charlie won Steve over to go to Istanbul and meet the man himself.

He'd been there as a teenager, his fondest memory being playing backgammon with men in the *souk* and winning a good number of games, a surprise that instantly brought the young American respect.

Steve remembered the markets, the smells and colors of the spice bazaar, even the magnificent *Hagia Sophia,* the church later turned into a mosque, a place and a circumstance that young Steve had not connected to any historical or political moment.

Now he did his homework. Like a tour guide, he told Charlie that it was built by Emperor Justinian in the 6th century, and initially served as the seat of the Ecumenical Patriarchate of Constantinople. Then the Byzantine kings broke off from Rome, and the Eastern empire was born, flourishing for hundreds of years until it fell into decline, the empire and the building overrun and looted numerous times by hordes. When the Muslim Ottomans swept across Christendom, the still-surviving building was converted to a mosque in 1453.

Charlie teased him. "You've now told me about this building and that building, their history. What about the people? *Their* history?"

"We're meeting at that fucking building," he growled.

KSM got under Steve's skin the moment they met and started their walk through the Gulhane Park, just a stone's throw from the once great mosque now turned museum.

"Do you have some name I should use?" KSM taunted, sizing up his quarry.

Steve answered: "You don't need any name."

"Are you my brother or my cousin?"

"No."

"Then who is he?" KSM asked Charlie in Arabic, at the same time checking whether this important man from Washington spoke his language.

"Don't be a *haramzāda*," she spit back in Urdu—a bastard.

KSM smiled. "I will give you a name," he said to Steve. "From what Miss Landry has told me about you, it will be Professor. Yes, Professor— the man with the answers."

"Today, Khalid, you will have the answers," Steve said, annoyed. But he was happy with the nickname.

"You made all the faxes?" KSM asked.

"Tell me why you're going to be successful attacking the United States," Steve responded. He didn't want to tell KSM anything.

"You know, Professor. I understand how you can find comfort that some attack of mine will benefit you in your war against the Saudis, and maybe even against *Sheikh* bin Laden. But I ask myself, in my meetings with Miss Landry, and now: rather than expose me, or even kill me, you are *oh so in desire* to help me. You would not do that if I weren't important to you. So, you are with me, Professor, like it or not. We are indeed brothers. And that is why I will be successful."

"I'm not financing your operation. We can't protect you or your men. We can't make any element of the American government do anything it wouldn't otherwise do. If I decide you are worth it, I can only impart to you how they act, how they might react."

"Well, you're not of very much use to me. For I already know how they act."

"And how's that?"

"Governments say one thing and do another. It is the secret shared between all governments. America likes to pretend otherwise, but *I know* the truth. And so do you."

"If you believe that all governments and the American government are duplicitous"—Charlie translated *aizdiwajia* (ازدواجية) when KSM wrinkled his brow unknowingly at the word—"then why do you see conspiracies everywhere?"

"Someone has to get the rewards from the way the world is, Professor. Someone. I don't know, or even care, if it's the Saudi royal family or if it's the Rockefellers, or the oil men, or the Catholic Church, or even the Zionists. What I do know is that it isn't the people."

"And what do you care for the people?"

"I am the people, Professor. I don't mean to sound *ranan* (رنان),"—Charlie translated *pretentious*—"but I don't care to be anything else, and I don't pretend that I am. I care for the people because I care about myself."

Charlie watched. Steve, being Steve, she thought, might try to machine gun KSM into submission with question after question, sizing up his man more for his evasive skills and composure rather than for any kind of truth. As she listened, she was initially disappointed. She didn't think Steve was going to chip away at KSM's justification or doctrine, given that she thought that there wasn't any.

And she knew that KSM could play this game forever, happy to grasp at any answer and contradict himself; happy because he didn't believe he had an answer, nor that there was an answer. And KSM didn't believe anything too deeply, which is why Charlie wanted Steve to meet his evil twin.

Steve switched gears. "Tell me something about bin Laden that will help me to understand him."

"Have you ever believed in something or someone, Professor?"

"No, probably not," Steve truthfully answered.

"Me neither. But that's what makes *Sheikh* bin Laden different. He makes you want to believe in him. Osama bin Laden declared war on America and for that I consider him a hero. Many Muslims do. They have been oppressed by America, by oil, by Christian crusaders, by colonial powers, by the Zionists. They have been betrayed by their own corrupt governments. And who is acting against that oppression? Osama bin Laden. When we were fighting with America against the army from Moscow, we were freedom fighters. Now that we are fighting against the Americans for the same cause, because they are in our homes, we are jackals in the night. Well, the *Sheikh* is many things, but he is not a jackal."

"I admit he has charisma," Steve ventured, "but he is also no angel. What do you call Mogadishu, New York, Riyadh, Khobar Towers, and now the embassy bombings?"

KSM grimaced, as if the question was beneath the professor.

"War is war," he said. "It involves killing."

KSM didn't wait for a response: "Do you know killing, Professor? I don't like to kill. I do not want to kill women and children when they are in the way. I feel sorry they must die. Do you feel sorry, Professor, when Iraqi or Afghani children die from your rockets? Killing is prohibited by Islam, just as it is prohibited by Christianity and the Jew. Yet we kill because that is what happens in war. What? America is going to send flowers to our *Sheikh*? No, America is going to send missiles and bombs and the CIA is going to try to kill him, just like the British would have killed George Washington had they been able to catch him. The American Army has been in Kuwait and Saudi Arabia, in Egypt and Oman, in the Gulf, in Djibouti, even in Libya, not just since the war against Saddam, but for decades. Are they protecting the people, Professor? I don't think so.

"You probably expect me to refer to *Allah*, about dealing kindly with those of the faith, about justice, about fighting the invaders of our homes, but why bother?" KSM continued.

"I don't really believe any of that, Professor, don't feel it in my heart. But I believe this: I can't think of what else I should be doing. I can't think of anyone to follow except *Sheikh* bin Laden. Even if I am a no one—a liar and a spy—I am not crazy, and *Sheikh* bin Laden is the true prophet of our time. War will not end, professor. Killing will not end. America can speak of human rights and justice for all, but America kills the most."[594]

"So how can you stand being an American agent?"

"Dear Professor, I am an agent to attack America and help bring down the family Saud; that is why I am working for Mr. Jones. And now for you. I am quite happy."

Hmmm, Steve rewarded. He hadn't wasted his time in coming.

But Charlie also saw, as she herself experienced, that Steve maybe did or didn't hear beyond the facts. KSM thought, too, that the professor was interesting and challenging, but that he hadn't heard a thing he'd said.[595]

KSM went on: "Did you really think, Professor, that things are going to happen just as you expect?"

Steve hesitated a minute, then asked a question. "Who is the Saudi agent inside bin Laden's circle?" he poked. "Who is reporting to Prince Turki?"

They walked along the path overlooking the water, KSM thinking through an answer.

Charlie thought it funny that both men ignored the distant ballet of ships on the Bosporus and the beautiful day around them. They circled the column of the Goths at the bottom edge of the hill, the surrounding landscape bursting with red tulips. Still, they ignored the sight, ignored the people, and ignored the gorgeous day. It wasn't just that they were absorbed in talk, Charlie observed. They were uninterested.

"Is it a test?" KSM finally asked Steve.

"There *is* a spy in bin Laden's inner circle," Steve reiterated. "One who reports to Prince Turki."

"And you are saying it is me?"

"No," Steve responded, pleased that he might have ruffled KSM. He told a story—not a false one, but one without key details or mention of Ghamdi—of Prince Turki coming to President Clinton with intelligence about an assassination plot.

KSM listened. Very few knew of his presidential plot, created to learn about what the Americans knew, and to see if he could throw them off when he needed to sometime in the future. "The Saudi government contacted your president? You didn't just learn of this from Ramzi Yousef?"

"I am sure they found out soon after you discussed it with bin Laden in Khartoum."

That was definitive.

KSM thought of the Sudanese defector Fadl for a moment but dismissed the possibility that the *Sheikh* would have confided such a secret to him.[596]

"Could it be Abu Makkee?" KSM asked.

Charlie was impressed that Steve had taken this tack, one that had disarmed KSM while drawing him into his confidence.

"Madani al-Tayyib?" Steve shot back, offering the true name of bin

Laden's brother-in-law, the former *al Qaeda* chief business officer.[597] He had been the boss of Fadl and had left *al Qaeda*, and was now in Saudi custody. "I don't think the dates add up," Steve said. "And he wasn't captured until May 1997," he added, amazing Charlie and KSM with the details he could recall. "They would have known sooner."

"He was taken into custody, yes, at that time," KSM rallied, "and we have not heard from him since. But he was in Khartoum when I visited the *Sheikh* and he would have been one of few trusted brothers he might have told. And he might have already been reporting to Prince Turki before returning to his homeland."

As far as both knew, the Saudi Tayyib turned himself in to the authorities in Riyadh, U.S. intelligence believing that he negotiated an exchange of information on bin Laden's finances for his freedom and safety.[598]

Tayyib was a vague possibility. Steve made a mental note to talk to Bowlen about him.

"Has this information coming from Khartoum continued past Abu Makkee's disappearance?" KSM asked.

It was precisely the right question to ask. "Yes," Steve answered.

The common interest established, the two then talked business. Steve probed as to whether the planes operation was to be a bomb or a suicide attack. KSM wouldn't take the bait. Instead, he held forth on the weaknesses of airport and airplane security, even the possible implications of weather for an attack. KSM said he wanted a clear and sunny day for maximum media coverage. He asked about the way intelligence information flowed inside the United States, whether car rentals or banking machines were monitored by the CIA, what the NSA's capabilities to listen in on phone calls really were, who his operatives should stay away from inside the United States. KSM was concerned about American Muslims, distrustful and wary, then flabbergasted when Steve said that they were not generally monitored by the U.S. government. He just couldn't believe there weren't government-planted spies in every mosque in America.

With each question, Steve provided an honest answer or said that he would get one. KSM was surprised and even doubtful when he said that air defense missiles hadn't been installed around New York. And not even around Washington.

The rest of the afternoon they talked about red alerts declared in Washington and KSM's view of them.

"Are you trying to set a trap for the CIA," Steve asked.

KSM answered that *al Qaeda* sometimes planted false information in order to deceive or "test" the system. He said operatives occasionally talked about nonexistent plots on telephone lines they assumed the Americans were monitoring to create deceptions.[599]

"It can be done, but it is very tricky," KSM said. "The person doing the calling, the words. Deception works better when a piece of paper is intercepted by accident." And then he looked at Charlie and said something in Arabic to make it clear that he meant accident in quotes— not a real accident, but a manufactured one.

Now professor and professional colleague, KSM spoke freely of *al Qaeda* activities. Though his English wasn't as perfect as he believed it to be and Steve was an impatient listener, they established a rapport, Steve demonstrating his command of the facts and delighting KSM with his knowledge of *kunyas* and *al Qaeda* workings.

KSM laughed when Steve said American intelligence believed bin Laden had $300 million.[600]

"It would be our ruin if it were true, Professor ..."

"How so?"

"There is no hunger with riches. It only creates problems: where to put it, how to protect it. And the more one inhales the zeros, the more one is driven wild. I, for one, have always given my men the smallest possible amount they require. It is a chain, Professor, but it should not be a gold chain ..."

Charlie listened to the discussion about finances, noting that Steve was taking in the data, but maybe not getting to know KSM.

Charlie and Steve had discussed the financial trap many times, likening tracking *al Qaeda* finances to a kind of narcotic in the same way that sports statistics were mesmerizing. As she listened, Charlie thought that the biggest downside associated with a focus on the statistics was that it devalued and isolated certain motivations—greed, corruption—while ignoring other factors and human circumstances. The more that U.S. intelligence filled spreadsheets with assets and cash flows, the more they grew oblivious to the fact that *jihadis* would kill with a tin cup if that's all they had.[601]

Charlie rode alone with KSM to the airport to put him on his flight back to Karachi.

He was energized and talkative, but all semblance of focus that he showed with Steve was now gone, the professor leaving behind the impression that the CIA was omniscient, which just confirmed KSM's assumption that a hidden hand was behind everything.

"I don't understand," KSM said. "The professor knows so much. Why not just arrest everyone and get rid of *al Qaeda?* Is it as I think? That *they* don't want peace?"

"There is no *they*," Charlie hissed, intent on putting KSM back in his place, miffed that Steve had penetrated crevices she hadn't gotten into. "Look in the fucking mirror, *bidoon*.[602] There are no external oppressors," she said in the most vulgar Arabic she could come up with.

KSM sat back in his car seat and let out a loud chortle. "Then what are you, and who am I?" he mocked.

Fuck, Charlie thought as she got back in the car after saying goodbye to KSM. *The two of them. They'd say and do anything.*

Chapter 34 Avalon

Charlie was angry and confused when Steve announced that the boss was coming for lunch on Sunday. They'd rented a beach house for a romantic weekend, or so she thought, and had driven up on Friday, hanging at the beach, window shopping in town, eating steamers and corn on the cob. The night before, they'd driven up to Atlantic City, had a spectacular porterhouse steak and played craps together before Steve bothered to break the news on the 1:00 a.m. drive back.

"What?" she said. "Coming for what?"

"I want to discuss something away from the prying ears of the way too nosey building," Steve answered.

"And you couldn't tell me before now? I thought this was our weekend together."

"It is," he insisted. "Are you mad that it isn't our weekend or that I didn't tell you?"

"Both!" she squealed.

Steve always played that card, acknowledging her emotions but also slyly trying to shift the blame.

She loved so many things about him. But she couldn't stand his need to plan—or control—everything, needing to keep his maneuverings to himself.

And now while working together, where it seemed everything turned out to be a scheme, her annoyance had shifted to distrust, confronted with way too many surprises, finding herself snooping and probing even though she was his partner.

What ticked her off this weekend was that Steve's selection of the venue made her feel exposed. Bowlen was coming to visit *them*, and as such he would come with the assumption that in whatever it was that Steve called the meeting for, they were conspiring together. Or that she was immaterial. She hated that feeling almost as much as she hated being left out.

He woke early in the morning, making coffee and a big pasta salad for their lunch. When she came downstairs he was already on his laptop, looking hopeful that their quarrel of the previous night had blown over.

She said nothing and walked past him to get a cup of coffee.

"I'm going for a walk on the beach," she coldly announced, taking her cup with her.

He stayed sitting at the dining room table off the kitchen. It was a beach neighborhood of tightly-packed houses, the residents and visitors waking up to a thin layer of ocean mist. The sky was a powder blue, dotted with big puffy clouds that gave the appearance of everything quickly moving out to sea.

Charlie reappeared about an hour later, going upstairs to shower, still silent. She stayed there the rest of the morning and was still there when Bowlen's car pulled into the gravel driveway.[603] It was an old, light-blue Volvo, one of those ancient, boxy vehicles that transported kids and groceries around the Virginia and Maryland suburbs. Steve heard the boss crunching his way to the front, knocking on the open screen door.

"I'm glad you agreed to come out here, sir," Steve said, shaking Bowlen's hand.

Stepping outside, he gave him a little orientation. The season was pretty much over, and the Labor Day weekend was betraying crispness to come. They were on a barrier island, the easternmost point of the New Jersey coastline. The place was originally covered with juniper and was probably at one time a sleepy, American Indian fishing village, Steve said, but it was now a swanky beach town, mostly given over to rich Philadelphians. Steve liked it because it was also a dry town with no boardwalk or honky-tonk. He discovered it about a decade earlier and found it a great place to think and write.

Charlie came downstairs and warmly greeted Bowlen, a separate entrance that she hoped would make clear that she, too, was an invitee, that this was Steve's show.

Steve suggested they sit on the deck. He offered iced tea all around, which Charlie realized he must have brewed fresh while she was staying out of his way.

"Got any idea what this is about?" Bowlen asked Charlie when Steve went inside.

"Not in the slightest," Charlie answered. "You neither?"

"Nope."

Steve already wiped the moisture and dirt off everything on the deck. The table with the umbrella was nicely set, with placemats and cloth napkins that Charlie realized Steve brought from his condo. After he emerged with the tea, he announced that he'd soon be back with lunch. "Hope you're hungry," he said, sounding like a prim housewife.

"I don't know whether I'm hungry or just lost my appetite," she said, half joking.

She told Bowlen about their trip to Atlantic City the previous night and Steve's success at the craps table. He taught her a basic *come bet* strategy and she thought she understood the ridiculously complicated and lightning fast game.

Bowlen politely listened. He tuned in as she said: "I don't think I quite get the high that Steve does at the table, nor do I take the risks he does."

Bowlen really had no idea about dice, nor much interest in what she was describing, and thought it odd that bookish Steve had a bit of gangster in him, that he enjoyed an environment that he himself labeled degenerate, as if it were a neutral adjective.

The pasta salad was fresh and colorful, fusilli with cherry tomatoes and five fresh herbs, Steve said, tossed in a curried dressing. He presented a chunky peasant loaf from his favorite bakery in Georgetown. And a delicious watercress salad.

Charlie was even more peeved that it had all been arranged under her nose.

"So, let me first apologize for dragging you out here and ..." he looked at Charlie, "for not telling you of my intentions today.

"I hope I didn't take you away from something personal," he said to Bowlen, not waiting for an answer.

He was on his best behavior, and they were both primed to expect an atom bomb.

"And sorry about spoiling this beautiful day and weekend with business. So, just to review: I've now gone through the KSM files, familiarized myself with Apex, and gone over the intelligence—what Apex Watch holds and what the CIA holds—on al Qaeda attacks.

"I've even met the man," he said, pausing as if it were a new paragraph. "I want you both to know that I've thought deeply about the question before us, not just the immediate task of trying to get in front of KSM with regard to his future plotting, but also a grand strategy to stop this new brand of globally-focused terrorism that he and al Qaeda represent.

"I've twisted a lot of arms to get everyone to agree that, despite the Agency's declaration of war and even the White House's interest in terrorism, that little is going to change. And even if the percentages go up—that is, in stopping this or that attack before they occur—I hope you'll both agree at this point that what Mr. Slam Dunk and company have in mind and what is officially being planned isn't going to eliminate attacks, nor probably even do much damage, that al Qaeda will grow as our own counterterrorism follows behind.

"I come to the conclusion that if we continue with our ways, that is, if Apex Watch doesn't intervene, I imagine bin Laden will continue to attract new adherents and gain steam, even more so because of the American response, which carries with it added stimuli to attack against the otherwise immune oppressor. My discovery of the existence of KSM strengthens my pessimism. I say this because, though I applaud your foresight, sir, in hanging on to him, and I'm even mildly optimistic that Charlie can extract new information from him, what worries me is his very existence.

"Let me say it another way: I conclude that in the Agency's ignorance of who he is, that there must be dozens of other KSMs operating out there, some under bin Laden and others with only tentative direction and control from al Qaeda central. Others we don't know about. Others wishing to amplify and emulate the same goals. And I say that just to punctuate that I'm skeptical that stopping KSM will stop al Qaeda.

"So, to bring us up to the present, what we know is that KSM is planning something huge. And we now know that it seems to be a repeat strike on New York from the air. Maybe a return to the North Tower. Or maybe Wall Street. But I'm guessing the World Trade Center. From all I can see right now, I'm guessing that he plans for it to take place in good weather. That would give such an attack maximum impact in visibility and thus in causing chaos. I'm now psychoanalyzing KSM, but I'm guessing that he wants his ultimate act of terrorism to be as disruptive and shocking as possible. I don't think he could care less about one side or the other in our political system, so I'm skeptical of an attack around the elections, but mostly because of weather.

"Based upon Charlie's reporting and my interchange with KSM, I also conclude that there are *al Qaeda* operatives already inside the country. So, are we agreed then on the foundation?"

They both nodded.

"My proposal then, and it isn't really a proposal, it's just an idea, is that we more actively assist KSM to actually do it," Steve said.[604]

"Assist him to do what?" asked Bowlen.

"To attack the United States," Steve said flatly.

"Are you shitting me?" Charlie exclaimed.

"I'm serious," Steven said. "We assist him, sort of ..."

"Sort of how?" she probed, her voice shifting to a higher pitch.

"Well, it's not yet fully formulated, but I see two options: Number one, we help KSM prepare his attack and make it clear that we are doing so, gaining enough inside information to then thwart it at the eleventh hour. And we do so to arm ourselves with sufficient evidence of *al Qaeda* and Saudi collaboration in undertaking the attack, with that blatant fact hopefully enough to facilitate a radical shift in the American landscape. I even have some ideas on how we can manufacture some of those pieces, some damning evidence."

He paused.

"And number two?" Bowlen asked.

Steve took a deep breath. "Number two is that we actually facilitate the attack with the same goal. Let me just say before you both explode that I don't think we can continue to kibitz in the way we are doing now: knowing, hoping, but not planning affirmatively to use an attack that we know is certainly being planned, one that I think we could use to the advantage of the United States."

"Is that any part of our mission?" Charlie asked.

"Our mission is narrowly to lessen Saudi Arabia's influence, to try to get in front of bin Laden, and to enhance American national security."

"And you're suggesting that we sit back and let KSM attack America to somehow facilitate those goals?"

"I am."

"So you're proposing that *we* attack the United States," Charlie said.

"Well, not we," Steve said in a small voice. "But yes."

"And you think that this president is going to approve such a plan?" Bowlen asked.

"Not really. No, I don't."

"Look," Steve said, "I'm guessing that we might be successful in stopping this, this attack. But stopping some African embassy-size attack in New York City that kills thousands? Under the current regime or with the current CIA? Or even in some future administration? *It will happen.*"

There was a long silence, a bird chirping, another car driving on a gravel driveway, the distant hum of an air conditioner spinning to life.

"So how would it work?" Bowlen asked.

"You're willing to entertain this?" Charlie jumped in, looking at Bowlen.

"Well, let's hear him out."

"Hey. Before we get bogged down in the doing," Steve said, "in how it would be done, I'd like to focus on the need to do so. I don't want us merely talking logistics and ignoring the purpose."

"Go on," Bowlen said.

"I've struggled with these attacks—particularly the embassy attacks— that we didn't detect them in any way. We've all struggled with their progressively increasing lethality. It doesn't leave me optimistic about the abilities of the Agency. And it leaves us all worried that destruction is going to get worse. I've also come to the conclusion, familiarizing myself with KSM and with bin Laden's words, that America's policy in the Middle East—its actions—and the never-ending standoff that we perpetuate with Iraq is now even more to blame for this escalating offensive emanating from the region. More even so than U.S. military forces in Saudi Arabia.

"I say Iraq is key, even more so than Iran, because in the eight years since they invaded Kuwait, we've retained and even built up a massive apparatus to hold an imaginary line against them. That apparatus—not just our military presence in Saudi Arabia—enflames not just bin Laden, but communicates to the rest of the Arab world that we have some bigger purpose. That's because Iraq grows weaker while our military grows stronger. So here we are, in all of the shakiest of states, from Oman to Egypt, supposedly holding the line, but in fact occupying. And let me be clear: I don't think bin Laden or KSM care about Saddam or even the Iraq people. It is more because the inspectors and the airplanes flying overhead and the constant tsk-tsking of the international community communicates something much bigger to the Arab world: that no matter what they do, they just can't go unsupervised.

"I would never even think of a conspiracy to help KSM, except for the fact that a conspiracy already exists. In some ways, I also have sympathy for them, for bin Laden and company. Don't get me wrong. But the existence of Apex Watch and of KSM makes me feel like a web of compromises and conspiracies started long before me, that a long-range plan to leapfrog over history isn't so outrageous. I'm guessing that's why you brought me on, sir, and challenged me. In a way, the existence of Apex Watch is itself an invitation to think big, and to break the rules."

"I'm not sure I ever anticipated this," Bowlen said.

"Fair enough," Steve said, "and that's why I wanted to make my proposal here, and just to the two of you, because if you don't want to hear it, what I'm calling Project Sumner, it ends here."

"Project Sumner?" Bowlen asked.[605]

"We have to have some compartment. I took it because it is the spark for a war."

"Great. You already have a name," Charlie sarcastically said, "I'm thinking you already know that it can't just end here and that we can't just go back to holding our breath until the next strike occurs." She imagined that Steve was ready with a description of a whole lot of dangerous wheel-spinning as an alternative to either of his options.

"How can we be sure we thwart something that we're not in full control of?" Charlie asked.

"Well, first, we plan for the best. But if we chose the second path I'm laying out, then we don't try to stop it. We plan to make the most of it once it occurs." Steve was suggesting they facilitate the attack.

Steve continued: "I can see an alternative to what I'm laying out here, and that alternative isn't pretty. It doesn't get us anywhere."

"Meaning?" asked Bowlen.

"We can take a different tack, perhaps assisting the Agency in sabotaging KSM's plotting. But that is also hardly foolproof, and it exposes Apex Watch and all of us." He went on: "Or we can ignore what we know and do nothing, which no longer seems possible."

Mr. Bowlen spoke up. "So you are suggesting that we guide an attack in a certain way to serve a specific purpose?"

"I am."

"So first, what is the purpose?"

"Well," Steve started, "what if instead, we specifically shifted our focus to trying to find out as much as we can regarding how KSM is planning to do it? What the target really is. And when it is to occur. And I have ideas on how to do that. At the same time, we create and then also push along something with equal emphasis, something that needs to happen, something America wants to happen, but is also not quite visionary or competent or even courageous enough to make happen."

"And that is?" Charlie again asked.

"Well," Steve said, taking a big breath and making them wait, "we put together the pieces of a plan for what should happen afterwards."

"The pieces of a plan," Charlie repeats. "And what's that plan?"

"We articulate a war against Islam, at least against Saudi Arabia as the Vatican of Islam."

Bowlen was silent. Charlie hadn't quite taken it in yet, just offended by Steve's nerve.

"We are stuck in the Middle East," Steve went on, trying to drown out opposition, "certainly in Iraq, and intellectually stuck in our animus towards Iran. We have bases in Saudi Arabia, in Kuwait, Bahrain, Oman, the Emirates and Qatar, even Turkey."

"Turkey?" Charlie said.

"I've often thought that the Turkish model was the answer, a secular state even though the dominant religion of the people is Islam. Maybe that even works in the long term. And maybe that's the answer for some.

But I'm guessing that it's something about being Turks and not Arabs that makes it work in Turkey but not the Arab world. I could be wrong."

He continued. "But yes, if they want to all go the Turkish way and join with the West, then we don't wage war on them. But I doubt that the brand of Islam we are talking about has any desire to capitulate to the Judeo-Christian bloc, or even Westernization, in the long run."

Bowlen chimed in: "So we wage war on them. You're talking broader military action than cruise missiles?"

"I'm talking about using the KSM attack to trigger a full-fledged war. Yes."

They sat, half shell-shocked, half paralyzed.

"Why don't we just kill him?" Charlie finally said.

"I suppose we could do that," Bowlen answered, sounding both protective and resigned.

"Of course, we could," Steve added. "And I understand the desire and your sentimentality in not wanting to do so. But at this point it also makes no sense. If we agree about where we are, this attack is already well along. So, what does killing him really stop? We would just lose our edge."

"It stops us from conspiring to commit treason," Charlie said.

"I'd argue that what I'm suggesting is hardly treason."

"How's that?"

"Plan A is we let them get far enough along to establish their intent to do so, to be able to tell the story convincingly to the American people of what they—al Qaeda—were planning, and with whose connivance. And by that, I mean the Saudis, the Saudi royal family, the financial backers and more. In Plan A, because we know the plan, we also create deceptions to give it credibility. We create the conditions that will get them caught. We lay down clues that we know that the FBI and CIA can actually find. And do it in such a way so it's a sure thing, even with these idiots at the helm. We implicate the Saudis in directly supporting bin Laden. We implicate the Gulf States in supporting it. We implicate the religious establishment in authorizing it. And the Taliban in aiding it. The affront of the audacity and the magnitude precipitates the war. So Plan A is one path, but I'm still arguing that we use it to start a war against Islam."

"A war," Charlie said. "Tell me again about this war."

"A war against Islam," he again said, matter of fact.

"Islam, the religion?"

"That's correct. Not a war against *al Qaeda* or even Saudi Arabia. A good, old-fashioned religious war."

Charlie was incredulous.

"You've thought this through?" Bowlen said.

"The details? No," Steve said, "but it can *be* thought through."

She asked: "A war against Islam being what?"

"On some level, the analog of what they are planning against us, but on a larger scale. A war that recognizes that the religious nations who believe Islam is *the law* either capitulate, or they reform, or they die. They die by their own fucking precious swords."

She asked: "You mean a world war between Christianity and Islam?"

Steve seemed unruffled to be talking about it. "It's the history of mankind," he answered. "Religions have been warring since there were religions. I don't think the course of history stops because such a war seems uncivilized to us. A war with Islam is coming in that they—the leaders of these states—want the benefits of the West without being part of it. And meanwhile, they even sponsor attacks on the West. I would argue that we aren't even starting it."

"But we're talking KSM and bin Laden here, not any state that is engaged in this religious war."

"I suppose I agree," Steve said. "But that's an evasion. Bin Laden and his ilk are different than a state. That I agree. But the Arab states are supporting them, either cynically because they'd prefer to see them focus outward, or because they actually want to see Islam triumph over the West. Whether they actually think Islam is superior, they definitely believe they need to preserve it against Western encroachment.

"They might all say Israel is a cancer in their midst. But their hatred isn't because *that* cancer will spread, that somehow Judaism threatens *them*. It is because other cancers exist all around the Muslim world that are already infiltrating. And they are not Israel."

"This is bullshit," Charlie said. "If anything, the spread is going in the other direction."

"I'm not arguing that they have been successful in spreading outward. But I believe they will be, in places like the Caucasus or North Africa, then even into central Africa. This brand of Islam will spread. It's already on the move in Southeast Asia. Don't you see that?"

"I see that they are more vocal in challenging the West," she answered. "And I see that U.S. foreign policy sucks at convincing them that we have no intention of encroaching on their religion. But that doesn't mean we need to go to war with them on account of some small number of terrorists who hide behind their religion."

Steve responded. "First of all, we *are* encroaching, and through cultural appropriation, we are forcing them to submit. Second, we are already at war. The more we impose what we label as 'universal human rights' on the devout, the more they will see everything from Coca-Cola to the United Nations as an enemy."

"Sir?" Charlie asked Bowlen to help her out.

"I agree with Steven that human rights disagreements aren't going to go away. They have become the Western-imposed universal norm to be applied to all, no matter who sits in the White House. And I agree that human rights as we define it threatens the Islamic order. Having said that, I'm not sure I am convinced that Islam can't be contained."

"You mean like the Soviet Union was contained?" Steve asked.

"Yes."

"But the Soviets weren't contained by a fence. Or some passive counterintelligence effort. There was a Cold War. There were covert efforts, massive ones. And economic warfare, precipitated by military buildups and a nuclear stand-off. Governments fell and a massive effort was undertaken to bring down their system. Hey, I'm all for that as well. But there still needs to be something to precipitate it. A Sputnik. A Cuban Missile Crisis.

"Look," Steve continued, "these people don't want to be a part of the West, part of what we label a community of nations. That would be fine if they just could live in harmony with us. But they can't. These terrorists—whether in your beloved home country," he said, looking at Charlie, "or in Muslim Africa—they are just the forerunners of an inevitable war."

He continued: "Are we just going to wait until they strike the United States itself? Until they acquire enough nuclear and chemical weapons to kill us?"

She was incredulous. "Aren't you the one who argues that they don't present an existential threat to us? Aren't you the one who says that WMD is cooked up to perpetuate our own war-making?"

"Terrorists don't present the existential threat," he said. "And I do think that they are tools of the state. But we also have to be honest in seeing the escalation of damage, in the desire to do more damage. So maybe it's not their acquiring WMD, but maybe it will be their attacking a nuclear power plant to have the same effect."

Something in the way Steve argued and maneuvered frustrated Charlie and got under her skin. It made her want to teach him a lesson.

"With all of your scheming to get Washington—and the rest of the world—to declare war on an entire religion, what the fuck do you really know about Islam?" she asked, not really asking. And she went on, rapid fire. "What's the difference between the *Qur'an* and the *Hadith*, or the *Sunnah*? Do you even know what *jahiliyyah* means, or *Salafi*, or *takfir*, or *haram*?"

Steve thought for a second, unperturbed. "Charlie, I have a sense of the answer to all of those questions, and I'll admit I'm curious, but no. I don't know. But so what? What's your point?"

"My point is you're a fake expert. You're a schemer who bases your justification, as do all conspirators, on a faulty view of the nature of the world."

"I don't agree," Steve responded calmly, but also truly curious about Charlie's point. "What do I need to know about Islam to change my analysis?"

"You are suggesting they cannot be reformed or won't just make changes needed to join the rest of the world, what you call history, without really knowing anything about them, about how they think."

"Well," Steve said, not dissuaded. "You're the Arabist. Am I wrong? Or is it just annoying what I'm suggesting?"

She didn't answer.

"If they reform, great," Steven continued. "But that's not happening by itself. If knowledge of Islam helps you to recruit someone, great. If it helps you not to slip up, it surely is an important part of your job. But not to me."

She responded: "But aren't you curious before you blow up the world?"

"One person's opinion or experience, including my own? That isn't going to help me to understand," Steve answered. "I'm not basing my analysis on animus or fear. Frankly, I couldn't give a fuck about Islam. That's the beauty of my plan, it's unemotional. It is based upon American self-interest. And an analysis that the U.S. government can't go where I'm suggesting we take them. That's why we are taking them there. And on Islam, I've read everything they say. I know my understanding is imperfect, but I'm also only one guy. I could study it forever, which would sort of represent what we are doing, in that we are educating ourselves always, but not acting. I was challenged to come up with a strategy to get in front of them. This is it. It's not pretty. I like to think what makes me good is knowing what it is I should know to formulate and then implement this very plan. I'll leave the rest to others."

"And that doesn't just make you another cherry-picker?" she asked.

"I guess it does, but so what?"

"But you've told me a million times that you didn't think that we—the Agency—understood Islam or the bigger picture of what's going on. Don't you feel like you need to understand it to propose such a radical scheme?"

"Go learn Arabic? You think that you are going to *convince* anyone through an argument about Islam? Who gives a shit if one cleric says this, and another says that? If there are inconsistencies in what the *jihadis* think versus what scholars of Islam think? People run around quoting the Bible and those who do at the loudest volume are usually the most ignorant. It doesn't stop them. It's just a fact of life."

"But those Christian fundamentalists aren't killing anyone," Charlie said.

"Exactly. But the *jihadis* are. That's what sets Islam apart. I don't like it. But that's the way it is."

"You're a fuck," she responded.

"Okay, okay," Bowlen interrupted. Their plates were empty, and the remaining pasta salad was crusting, the pitcher of iced tea iceless.

"Wait," Charlie said. "What about the hundreds of millions of moderate Muslims?"

"You mean some silent majority?" he answered. "I agree they might exist. They just have no power, and no inclination to do anything. And, I might add, they are grateful for terrorism directed outward, and for our picking on Saddam and his ilk, doing dirty work they won't or can't do to reform their own undemocratic societies. But their silence just leads to greater stimuli for the growth of the radicals. And further, I'd argue, as the so-called moderates move to America and Europe and elsewhere, that is a threat as well, because there really isn't a moderate school of Islam influencing the order back home, some version that looks like the Protestant denominations when stacked up against Rome."

"You are just a fucking idiot," Charlie said.

"I know you don't like what I'm saying, and I also know all of the arguments about Islam as the religion of peace. Hell, I admit I don't understand all of the ins and outs, but I also don't accept that Judaism or Christianity are religions of peace. What horseshit …"

"So how does it unfold?" Bowlen asked, interrupting.

Steve took a deep breath, Charlie silent, contemplating his words.

"Well," Steve said, absent even a note of triumph, "we try to figure out what KSM is up to. That focuses both Charlie's relationship with KSM as well as what intelligence we look for. Mallory's device hopefully will let us in. We write a campaign plan for how a response might unfold. We write it, we war game it, we test our propositions."

"Millions could die," Charlie said.

"Millions could die anyhow," Steve answered. "The trend lines aren't moving towards peace."

"I won't even ask what gives you the right," Charlie said, "because I know you'll have an answer that I don't want to hear. But don't too many people know about Apex Watch's relationship with KSM?" she asked, already a conspirator.

"KSM doesn't have to be connected, just the Saudis."

"So, we what? Kill him afterwards? To protect ourselves from exposure?" Charlie said. "He's certainly not going to stay silent."

Steve laughed. "If you want him dead, yes, we kill him. I don't care. But we do limit the paper trail. And we prepare the documentation to cover him up and blame others.

"My focus," Steve continued after pausing, "is an extension of your challenge to me." He looked at Bowlen. "Before the African bombings, you said *detect another*. I'll now lay down my own challenge. I might be persuaded that I'm wrong if the Agency detects KSM's American plotting on their own. If the Agency shows any ability with this declaration of war and its accelerated activity to make any significant headway in stopping KSM, I'll capitulate. But I don't plan to tip the scales to help them. Barring some miracle that changes things between now and election time—it's not that far off—I argue that we develop Plan B."

"Plan B being again what?" Bowlen asked.

"Dispense with the eleventh hour save. Just prepare for the worst."

"Jesus," Charlie exclaimed. "Can you stop already? Can't we at least sleep on it? Have you no fucking humanity?"

"Sure," Steve said.

Bowlen looked at his watch. If he left now, he could be home for dinner. "OK then, let's sleep on it," he said, wondering whether Charlie wouldn't wring Steve's neck in the night. His bet was on her.

PART 9

Chapter 35 Khallad Arrives

KSM heard the *clump, clump* coming up the stairs of his Karachi apartment building, a lightness spreading in his heart. It was Khallad, his only true friend, and the courier of all things important.[606]

A decade earlier, as a young reporter for Azzam, he'd met Khallad's father on his first foray into Afghanistan. The old man was legendary for his bravery on the battlefield, and even more admired that he had three sons serving by his side.[607]

Khallad was the youngest, barely old enough then to fight, and yet he was fearless, one of many Yemeni boys who later congregated about bin Laden, his cooks and valets, drivers and bodyguards. KSM immediately liked him when they met, especially when young Khallad insisted that his picture not appear in the *al-Jihad* magazine. He was already looking beyond to a life of silent service after victory over the communists.

Another survivor, KSM thought.

Khallad later lost a leg to a left-behind Soviet landmine. Fitted with an artificial prosthesis afterwards, he was affectionately known by most as "silver" for his metal post. KSM never stopped calling him Khallad, his original *kunya*, and as the Yemeni became bin Laden's number one fixer, traveling near and far (a man who, because of his disability, was often given a sympathetic pass by authorities), he also became one of KSM's only friends.[608]

Assalamu Alaikum Wa Rahmatullahi Wa Barakatuh, Khallad said as he entered KSM's apartment, bringing news of the Hamburg cell.

"We have come a long way, my friend," Khallad said as he settled in a chair on KSM's balcony, sweet tea in hand, a sheen of sweat glistening on his forehead, a paper package tilted next to his chair leg.

"And to think that he wanted *me* to be a pilot, *me*," Khallad started.

And they laughed.

"I should have studied in school more, but—I said to the *Sheikh*—how could I even do so with this," Khallad said, pointing to his peg leg.

They loved to swap stories about *management*, the latest dispatches from their *emir*, about Egyptian control freak Abu Hafs, about the Doctor and his weak sophistry, about the incompetent paper pushers and the newly-arrived goats, the lost fighters who could barely manage their lives. Khallad was one of the only people KSM could unload his frustrations with.

"Before we get on to the German boys, tell me," KSM asked, "what is their final answer on the Saudi traitor?"

"I met with Abu Hafs to figure out what happened. I told him what you said to say, that our business depended on the best merchandise. And I asked how these two could become pilots, that you concluded that Nawaf was a dunce and that Mihdhar seemed to be a spy."

"And he said?"

"Abu Hafs got very defensive," Khallad said. "*I am sorry, my friend, but Mihdhar in particular cannot be returned*, he said. He tells me that the *Sheikh* made the personal choice of Khalid Mihdhar—knowing of him before he even arrived at the camps. And he said that these two had even taken a meal with bin Laden and he promised them not only that they could be pilots, but that Mihdhar would be a deputy in America.[609] The *Sheikh* has even spoken to Mihdhar's father-in-law to congratulate him."

"So, he is the son-in-law of al-Hada?" KSM asked.[610]

"Khalid," he said, and he was one of the very few who would call him so. "This man, Khalid al-Mihdhar.[611] He is no *sayyid*, my friend."[612] Khallad almost whispered, hesitant. He was speaking of a group that is revered, individuals who are said to be direct descendants of the Prophet Mohammed—*peace be upon him*.[613]

"I can't even confirm that he is of the Wadi Doan clan, though his family moved to Saudi Arabia from Yemen long ago."[614]

Three Saudi men—Khalid al-Mihdhar and a set of brothers, Nawaf and Salim al-Hazmi[615]—had arrived in Afghanistan, just before the snows came, just as bin Laden had given KSM the go-ahead to prepare the planes operation. All three had American visas in their passports, all of the visas from earlier in the year, obtained even after the bombings in Kenya and Tanzania.[616] Word passed around the leadership was that this was divine intercession—but when the news was passed along to KSM, he immediately was suspicious, thinking that maybe the Saudi secret services were attempting to infiltrate al Qaeda and his operation. That was something he might not have thought, had it not been for the professor asking him about a Saudi spy.

KSM had discussed Mihdhar and al-Hazmi with Khallad, who then did his own investigation. Khallad spoke to Mihdhar about his decision to get the visa, and he said that he decided to obtain it after the martyrdom of his brother-in-law in Nairobi.[617] And, indeed, there was a brother-in-law who died in the Kenyan embassy attack. Still, KSM and Khallad remained suspicious, and became doubly so when bin Laden ended up pairing one of the two al-Hazmi brothers with Mihdhar, and then designated both to be the first two pilots for KSM's operation.

KSM was furious with this decision, and then when the two were sent to Karachi to receive "*Mukhtar's* orientation" before traveling to America, only Nawaf arrived.

"Where is your partner, Khalid Mihdhar?" KSM asked Nawaf.

He shrugged his shoulders, telling KSM that when he left the guesthouse that morning, the man at the desk told him that Mihdhar checked out. Nawaf thought he had gone ahead of him. But he never arrived at KSM's.

Nawaf, KSM soon found out, was a simpleton who had no science skills and could never become a pilot. He went through some basic survival skills for America. And he taught him some basic English phrases.

Khallad, who was assigned to arrange for the two to travel to America via Asia, knew nothing of Mihdhar's delinquency. But after KSM told Khallad of the absence, Khallad confronted Abu Hafs about it, and the chief of operations replied with some story that he had personally briefed Mihdhar on the broad outlines of the operation and that it would be okay.

Then Abu Hafs had told Khallad that perhaps *Sheikh* bin Laden excused the suspect Saudi from *Mukhtar's* training.[618]

Khallad told Abu Hafs that *Mukhtar* doubted either would become pilots, but more importantly, that there was no rush given that the operation was not going to take place for at least another year. It was a very unpleasant and unsatisfying conversation: Abu Hafs apologizing, but also saying that nothing could be done about what had already occurred.

KSM and Khallad had decided that would they would tell the pair very little of the bigger plan, seeing that maybe the *al Qaeda* operational chief was caught in an impossible bind—that, indeed, bin Laden had made the decision and Abu Hafs didn't want to criticize him.

Mukhtar lamented to Khallad that their *emir*, once a superb judge of character and a man of the world, seemed to be losing touch with the real world in his return to Afghanistan, that he was increasingly isolated, surrounded by fewer and fewer who were willing to tell him the hard facts.[619]

Khallad had his own suspicions. Mihdhar sold himself to *al Qaeda* as a mere fisherman from Mecca, yet he seemed to have materialized from the shadows, ingratiating himself into the family al-Hada and marrying the daughter. And his arrival in Afghanistan, they had concluded, with an American visa in hand, seemed too perfectly timed. And, Khallad said to KSM, he thought that maybe Mihdhar acted dumber than he actually was—not like Nawaf, who really was a dolt, but more like he couldn't speak English when in fact he could, that maybe he was faking.[620]

"I hate to admit it, but our best hope is that this fisherman and his simpleton partner, Nawaf, will be apprehended," Khallad concluded. If they were caught, KSM said, the main impact would be to chasten bin Laden while making himself look prescient in detecting the losers in the first place. The *Sheikh* seemed unmovable in his desire to use as many Saudis as possible. That suited KSM just fine, as long as they weren't imposed as pilots.

What KSM really needed was for bin Laden to do his job and let him do his. *Al Qaeda* was becoming so large, he feared he would not be able to keep his activities secret anymore. Not that the *emir* wouldn't keep quiet, but that others wouldn't. And KSM didn't want to have to crack the whip. He increasingly hated going to the backwards hellhole of Kandahar to communicate face-to-face with the leadership.

This whole first chapter had so disappointed KSM, he even pined after Ramzi Yousef. And yet, since Khallad sent the two off to Los Angeles, *Mukhtar* had been getting reports from them in San Diego, that they were learning English and had even started flight school. Maybe there was a God after all, KSM thought.

They moved on in their conversation to the Hamburg Four.

"They have been accepted?" KSM asked.

"Oh, yes, my friend."

Khallad had gotten to know the Yemeni, Binalshibh, in Berlin, and through him, the others. They arrived in Kandahar and went to the mountains to meet bin Laden and it was instantly clear that they were the ones.

"You will be very pleased," Khallad said.

"Tell me."

"The eldest, Mohammed Atta, the one from Egypt, is clearly the leader. Bin Laden met privately with him and he is on his way here now."

"And what did the *Sheikh* tell him of the operation?"

Only Atta was to know the full extent, Khallad said. And bin Laden specifically wanted *Mukhtar* to know that. The *Sheikh* told Khallad that the men in America would be completely under Atta's command, as transmitted by *Mukhtar*.

KSM's pleasure was swamped by his anger in losing power to yet another Egyptian, this time to Mohammed Atta. "And my role is what? When was I to know?"

"Brother. You are the *emir*. Of that I have no doubt."

"Did the *Sheikh* tell him a number of targets?"

"I think maybe he still thinks big, for he remembers what you told him after the Philippines. So, he said ten."

They laughed.

"And the date?"

"It is forever your decision. The *Sheikh* understands that. Yemen comes first."

He pulled up his package leaning on the leg of his chair, handing it to KSM.

They went over the reports of the four that had been prepared by Abu Hafs. KSM read the short biographies of each, his heart beating ever more quickly as he realized that his dream—this dream—would turn into a reality. It was no longer words. The Hamburg Four weren't the Saudi pair—they were for real. It was for real. KSM got nervous, a torrent of details crowding his brain. The sounds and smells of Karachi disappeared. Khallad faded. His mind raced backwards from the early morning attacks, the coordination of the planes, the collecting of the teams, the training of the pilots, life in the United States of America, visas and travel, documents and money. Africa was complicated, but it was all on the ground, in chaotic and open countries with large Muslim populations. This. This operation in America. It would be so complex, so very complex. *Mukhtar* might be the wizard behind the curtain, but Atta—he had to keep it all together, keep it driving forward for more than a year. Undetected. Moving forward.

Khalid Sheikh Mohammed—KSM to his American friends, Khalid to his best friend, *Mukhtar* to his pupils and virtually everyone else inside *al Qaeda*—now had his pilots. And he had his plan. The *Sheikh* wanted ten targets. Maybe four or five were possible.

And then there was another plan. The other plan. There would be one attack on one target and one target only. The plan with his American friends. His heart was beating fast and his hands were throbbing, almost shaking, so much so that he rested them while holding the *al Qaeda* report on his lap to hide the tremor.

Chapter 36 Two Brothers

Inside a secure room in the Wilshire Boulevard high-rise office of the Los Angeles consulate of the Kingdom of Saudi Arabia, Omar Bayoumi's[621] boss told him that two brothers were in town.[622]

"Nawaf al-Hazmi is from Mecca," said the resident intelligence officer, looking at a piece of paper. "He is listed as both 'dull' and 'low threat.' He first went to Afghanistan when he was just a teen in 1993."

"Nineteen ninety-three?" asked Bayoumi. "Isn't that after the Soviet withdrawal?"

"Where have you been, brother? Riyadh was still sanctioning *jihadis* to fight against the communists in Kabul. Better that hotheads like this Hazmi went and blew off steam in Afghanistan or Bosnia than it was for them to stay and become forbidden soldiers at home." After Nawaf's year in Afghanistan, the officer told Bayoumi, his dossier says he returned to Mecca. There he got recruited to fight against the Serbs and went to Europe.

"We don't have much after 1996, but we think al-Hazmi was formally recruited for *al Qaeda* at his local mosque. Sometime in late 1997, he went back to Afghanistan, where he was employed in one of their training camps, one of the ones reopened with bin Laden's return from Sudan. According to the report," he said, flipping through the file on his desk, "al-Hazmi became a part of the Arab brigade fighting with the Taliban. He swore *bayat* to bin Laden."

"What is he doing in America?" Bayoumi asked. "And how did he even get in?"

"I don't know the answer to either question. The dispatch merely says al-Hazmi and his partner arrived and he is our responsibility now."

"And who is with him?"

The second arrival was Khalid al-Mihdhar, also from Mecca. "We have less info on him," the officer said, looking at his papers.[623] "He is reported to have fought in Bosnia as well, making his first trip to Afghanistan in March 1996. There he attended an *al Qaeda* training camp and reportedly also swore allegiance to Osama bin Laden." He looked through the pages provided by the General Intelligence Department in Riyadh. "But other than that, all it really says is that he is 'not dangerous.'"

Not dangerous to Saudi Arabia. Bayoumi knew what it meant.

"According to these reports, neither speaks much English."

"And they flew in from where?"

He again looked at the report. "Thailand."

"They were noted at the King Fahd mosque and are taking their meals at the *Mediterranean Gourmet*, a halal restaurant in Culver City." He handed Bayoumi an address: 10863 Venice Boulevard.[624]

"So why me?"

"Because they say they are headed to San Diego."

"To undertake an attack?"

"I do not know, brother. That's for you to find out."

Some more niceties were exchanged, but no further information was forthcoming.

What a great assignment, Bayoumi reminded himself as he returned to his Mercedes in the downstairs parking garage.

A number of fellow students from his class at the Faisal Intelligence Academy[625] ended up in the Godforsaken '*Stans* or in one of Europe's industrial slums. His best friend in spy school cheered like he'd won the World Cup when he heard that he was being assigned to New York City. Bayoumi smirked. He might as well be a million miles away from that plum assignment, assigned instead to the Arab ghetto of Patterson, New Jersey.

The dark-skinned, pencil-thin-mustachioed Bayoumi had gotten paradise.

"San Diego, California," the instructor announced when his name was called. Bayoumi didn't have to look up the seaside city to have visions of his first overseas posting: ocean, sun, girls, bikinis. No more deadening Riyadh paperwork, no more reporting on the wrongdoings of his fellow citizens. He imagined that he would find an American wife. He imagined that he would spy on the American Navy.[626]

But in his four years in America, none of that happened. Even his San Diego was far from the ocean, and Arab men were treated like Mexicans, as second-class citizens. He'd gone to Las Vegas a few times and been to Hawaii, more bikinis out of reach. But he'd kept his nose clean and written his reports on time. Now at least he had two real *jihadis* and imagined sleuthing after them to uncover a plot.[627] He imagined a promotion. He imagined returning to Saudi Arabia and finally finding a wife.

Officially, the 42-year-old was an entirely-innocuous no one, an employee of the Saudi civil aviation authority, sent to the United States to attend business school.[628] If anyone dug deeply enough, they'd find that Bayoumi didn't go to school, and evidently didn't work, either. He lived off of a handsome monthly stipend and had access to an additional expense account.[629]

Saudi Arabia, as the self-anointed epicenter of Islam, developed a web of agents like Bayoumi to look after the long arm of the dominant *Wahhabi* Arab state. Billions had been spent on *Sunni* proselytizing over the years. Mosques were built and expenses paid for imams and supplicants. That's the overt side.

The clandestine side is that men like Bayoumi who work for Saudi intelligence are additional sentinels, counters to any efforts to thwart Saudi ideological expansion. Or on the part of the Israelis and other western intelligence services to infiltrate. It wasn't such a big deal in America, but in Europe and much of the Caucasus, the competition for the hearts and minds of Muslims was fierce. Mostly the Saudi "spies" sent to America were just informal ambassadors, helping brothers and families settle in in their host country, luring others who were curious about Islam to attend Saudi institutions. But occasionally they investigated strays or delivered money, sometimes large amounts.[630]

When Bayoumi struck up a conversation with the two at the restaurant, curious about the newcomers with the Gulf Arab accents, neither were wary about accepting his help. After all, *Mukhtar* had told Nawaf that they could go to the mosque to find assistance and fellowship.[631] And Nawaf had received a piece of paper from Mukhtar with the name *Masjid Ar-Ribat al-Islami*, a Saudi-affiliated mosque in La Mesa, a suburb east of San Diego.[632]

"*Praise be to Allah*, I'm just here for the day to renew my visa at the consulate," Bayoumi told them when they said they were heading south. "I live in San Diego and am going back there tonight and will even give you a ride!"

Bayoumi gave them a ride and put the two up for a few days in his home. Over the next few weeks, he found them an apartment in the same complex where he lived on Mount Ada Road in Clairemont Mesa. He helped them fill out the lease application and co-signed it. He advanced them the deposit and the first month's rent. He helped them get a telephone. He worked with them to facilitate wire transfers of money from home. He helped interpret to get them a local bank account and to apply for credit cards, even to get Social Security cards. He helped them buy and register a Toyota Corolla and get auto insurance. And he threw them a welcoming party to introduce them around.[633]

At the *ar-Ribat al-Islami* Mosque,[634] a low-slung, unmarked, sand-colored building with turquoise tile trim located between the I-8 and El Cajon Boulevard on Saranac Street, the two were welcomed. They were in San Diego, they said, to learn English and get their commercial flying licenses.

By the first of April, KSM got a report from Nawaf that the two were settling in well.[635] With their new best friend, their apartment and their car, they were moving forward, he said. And they had graduated from stage one of English language class and would soon take a one-hour introductory flying lesson at nearby Montgomery Field.

And indeed, for the first few days in San Diego, the two were excited and attentive in their English-as-a-second-language class, surrounded by Mexicans and Asians and a few others from the Middle East. The teacher was practical, asking each enthusiastic pupil to talk of their backgrounds and their plans for their lives. She was even pretty.

But after less than a dozen classes, Nawaf said that learning English was too hard for him. He stopped attending classes and then quietly dropped out, scurrying back to the Arab tribe.

Khalid Mihdhar also dropped out, telling his roommate that he was going to enroll in a different program and make a fresh start with a male teacher. Soon they lived contradictory lives. There was prayer and the community of the mosque. But there was also constant fast food, video games, omnipresent porn on cable, and even live strip clubs.

And they had a secret that they were keeping from *Mukhtar*—Bayoumi's video camera. Their new Saudi friend recorded everything: their welcoming party, the two in their new apartment, the two smiling in their new car.[636]

"He's a Saudi spy," Nawaf told his partner when they were running errands one day.

Khalid Mihdhar said he didn't know one way or another, and he didn't necessarily disagree, but he urged Nawaf not to panic. He suggested that the two should just move out of the Mount Ada Road apartment.

"Can I take the book?" Nawaf asked. He had been so proud when the giant 2000–2001 Pacific Bell White Pages for San Diego appeared on their doorstep one day. On page 13, al-Hazmi was listed: Alhazmi, Nawaf M 6401 Mount Ada Rd. 858-279-5919.[637] He wanted to keep the phone book.

What a fucking donkey, Mihdhar thought. "Yes, you can take the book, brother." *God, I need to get out of here.*

Mihdhar filed their 30-day notice with the landlord of their intention to vacate.

"It's too expensive," Mihdhar explained to Bayoumi, who offered to lend the brothers money until they earned enough.

But they said that they were going to go—that they needed to make it on their own. They moved to 8451 Mount Vernon Way in Lemon Grove, four miles south of the mosque.[638] Nawaf got a job at a local gas station.[639] Mihdhar continued to struggle with his English-language course. Or so he said, disappearing for entire days while Nawaf went to work.

They still couldn't shake their congenial shadow. And the videotaping never stopped.

Nawaf argued with Mihdhar that, despite his failure to move forward with learning English, he'd better share his suspicions about Bayoumi with *Mukhtar*. Since Mihdhar remained unperturbed, Nawaf went to an internet café and got the help of an Arabic-speaking clerk to use an emergency chat room.

In coded language, he was given a specific time and date and instructions to revert to an even more secure internet chat site to contact *Mukhtar*.

What a mess, KSM thought when Nawaf confessed.[640]

He had just finished with the Hamburg cell and he truly didn't need these two as pilots anymore—not even as pretenses of pilots to please bin Laden and the busybody watchers at *al Qaeda* central.

He mused for a moment that if he blew Bayoumi's cover to Miss Landry, she might have him arrested. Or killed. He told Nawaf that the two should sit tight until he made other arrangements.

Other arrangements meant assigning the two Saudis to an airplane piloted by a new recruit, another Saudi who had materialized, a man named Hani Hanjour.[641] He arrived in Afghanistan telling Abu Hafs that he previously studied in the United States and had undergone flight training in Arizona and already had a commercial pilot certificate. The report from Kandahar to *Mukhtar* was that he worked for a relief agency during the Soviet war.

Timing now becoming more important, *Mukhtar* provided Hanjour with a short course in codes and secure communications and told him the proper way to apply for a clean American visa.[642]

Hanjour already had lived in America in the early 1990s and now he was on his way.

That same week Nawaf contacted *Mukhtar*, Khalid Mihdhar also made a call to his own pre-arranged number in Washington.[643] "Nothing is happening here in San Diego," he complained. "I have picked up no information about the date or what the targets are meant to be," he said to his contact. "And the fucking busybody Bayoumi needs to leave us alone. And Nawaf Hazmi? Could there be any bigger ass? I'm sick of pretending to be a simpleton. There's nothing more I can do here. I am going to return home."

Chapter 37 Graduate School

The five—the Hamburg Four plus *Mukhtar* the brain—went to the Lucky One Mall for a makeover.[644] It was the largest shopping mall in Karachi, the largest in Pakistan, and reputedly the largest in all of Asia.

From this day forward, *Mukhtar* told them, you will dress and act as Western as possible. Despite their German residence and experience, they had slipped deeper and deeper into the appearance and behavior of radical separatists.

In a unisex salon Mohammed Atta instantly hated, their beards and mustaches were the first to go. Marwan begged for, and got, an even more stylish goatee.

Two hairdressers fawned over the four as *Mukhtar* explained in Urdu that they were off to universities in Germany. The hairdressers suggested the hottest European styles and the coolest looks. Ziad chose a slight frosting in his hair. Marwan and Ramzi Binalshibh cavorted and laughed at pictures in the fashion magazines, then accepted their clean-cut appearances. Atta stayed doubly disgusted, then became triply so, the flamboyant hairdresser prancing about, touching him, tilting his head this way and that, pulling out his ear, going inside his nose.

Then it was off to Shoe Planet, where they picked out casual oxfords. Ziad and Marwan additionally chose brightly-colored running shoes.

"Who cares what shoes we wear?" Atta protested.

"You will only wear shoes made in China from now on, and not only that, but those available in international stores," *Mukhtar* said. "Unless of course you want to wear *Valentinos* or some other Italian designer brand." And he laughed. "But here is rule number one, one that is absolutely to be followed. Once you get to America, I want you to buy new shoes every Saturday."

"What! Isn't that wasteful?" Atta pushed back.

"Shoes are not expensive, my brothers. But more important, it will remind you to go shopping every Saturday, so that you act like other Americans." He lowered his voice. "And it will prevent the authorities from tracking you."[645] He didn't elaborate.

Even for Atta, a sense of admiration dawned.

Off to the Levi's store for pants, then to the giant Outfitters department store for shirts. They picked out underwear and socks together—genuine Jockey brand—Atta, of course, insisting on basic white, the other boys all over the rainbow of colors.

"I don't care if you eat *halal* or not," said *Mukhtar*, "but I am telling you for the greater good of God, it no longer is a rule that must be followed if it stands in the way of your mission." They walked through the food court, with Pizza Hut and Burger King, Dixy Chicken and Johnny Rockets. *Mukhtar* explained that in America most servers won't even know whether their products contain pork, so they had to know ahead of time a few favorites in the fast-food joints that they knew were safe. But again, he said, if necessary, they were authorized to deviate. And though they could seek out *halal* restaurants or food trucks in New York, he said, in most of America, eating *halal* wasn't going to be an option.

"Has anyone here drunk alcohol?" *Mukhtar* later asked. All but Atta raised their hands.

"From now on, I encourage you to drink, or at least to go to restaurants in America that serve alcohol. And if you don't drink, you must either smoke or carry cigarettes on your person. And put on men's cologne, or at least carry it. And if you do not put it on every day, at least pour out half the bottle and rip the label a little and scuff up the bottle a bit so that it looks like you've had the perfume for a while. And wear a gold chain around your necks. Or a ring on your fingers. As American men do. My brothers, you are no longer *jihadis*. You are secret agents of *al Qaeda*."[646]

He asked about music. Again, Atta was the malcontent. He never listened to music, adhering to the strictest *Wahhabi* practice. *Mukhtar* told them to always put on the radio when they were in the car, just in case they were stopped by police. And he explained country music with its wail—annoying, he said, but a useful background should police stop them for speeding.

For a second, Atta wanted to talk about the country folk in *The Grapes of Wrath*, but he hesitated, unsure whether he was idealizing the downtrodden. He'd talk to Ziad about it later.

Mukhtar asked about women. Though none of the Hamburg boys said a word and would never utter a word, Atta was obviously the most uncomfortable.

"You have to practice being cordial and speaking to women," *Mukhtar* stressed. "They will be behind every airline counter, serving at every restaurant, and dealing with you in every government office."

Marwan feared that Atta, *his Amir*, might be sick, but he handled it all with his normal, steely intensity. He might not be a friendly foreigner, Marwan thought, and he sure was scary-looking with his angular, clean-shaven face. But he knew that he would follow the playbook. Were it not for their experience in Germany, he could never even pretend to make it in America, unable as he was to interact with women ever since his trips to Aleppo, ever since the young Syrian archeologist took a shine to him, frightening him.[647]

Ziad broke the ice in talking about his wife, saying that they were all experienced in dealing with women, having interacted with the uncovered Germans, and even Muslim girls of Hamburg. Ramzi spoke of dealing with their female landlord and even pretty Pakistani girls. Atta said nothing.

Once in America, *Mukhtar* then told them, they should spend time visiting tourist sights and amusement parks, telling them he even visited museums in European cities, describing the procedures and the proper behavior once inside.

"There is nothing wrong with going to the White House or the Capitol building or even the Pentagon as tourists, either—they have tours," he said. "But when you do go, don't act as if your curiosity is anything other than wonderment and pro-American admiration."

Over and over, *Mukhtar* drilled into them that they were middle-class, business-oriented men, serious men and student pilots.[648] And they should act accordingly. They needed to deal with people around them in both a humble and confident way. Most difficult for his pious Muslim students, *Mukhtar* wanted the four to avoid spending too much time with the Islamic community, to steer clear of any obviously "radical" mosques, especially those associated with the Saudi propagation of *Wahhabism*. In fact, he didn't want them joining any mosque once they settled in.

"I am sure the authorities have spies in every mosque," he said.[649] And *Mukhtar* told the story of how the Blind *Sheikh* was double-crossed by a mosque informant, and how Ramzi Yousef was compromised at the *al-Khifah* center in Brooklyn.

"My brothers, you are all experienced in living in the West, and some of what I teach is redundant, but we must attempt a complete transformation. And in that, if you listen to me and learn, you will increase your security by becoming invisible to the American authorities." He went over English-language leases and other legal documents they would encounter. He described the rules for getting driver's licenses and establishing bank accounts.

He urged them to join and go to a gym to keep physically and mentally fit, that they had an arduous journey ahead of them, as taxing and exhausting as actual combat. *Mukhtar* thought both Atta and Marwan were frail, and he urged them to eat more, implored them to put on weight.

By the second week in Karachi, they were on to clandestine skills, how they would communicate, how to move and keep money. *Mukhtar* talked about the use of ATMs and how the banks and authorities tracked those who used them, urging them to take out only small amounts of money. He told tales of financial mistakes made by others, never mentioning himself.[650]

He instructed each on how to use multiple emails accounts and online chat rooms for clandestine communications and how to write a special, coded Arabic using the American keyboard. He urged each of them to keep their international telephone calls short, and keep the tone of any family communications and letters social, talking about their education and business activities and how wonderful America was.[651]

Rule number two was that they would never under any circumstance write or call anyone in Pakistan. Except him. And then only over the special protocol. Again, *Mukhtar* didn't explain why.

Money would be supplied through intermediaries in the Gulf. They calculated the cost for each of them, and then for their teams, *Mukhtar* said. The money men were the most trusted associates who resided in the United Arab Emirates, the only place he felt was safe to communicate with—of course, in code. The money would be disbursed in small amounts amongst them.

The intermediaries would receive telephone calls and email messages, and they would provide financing as needed. Each of the four, as team leaders, would start with $8,000 in cash to take back to Germany, and more money would be transferred to German bank accounts and eventually to the United States via formal and informal wire transfers. Only credit cards and debit cards from American banks were to be used for routine purchases.

Then came rule number three: minimize contacts with old friends, either because some might grow suspicious of what they were doing in America, or because they might be associated with the authorities. *Mukhtar* was adamant about that. He told stories of *al Qaeda* defectors, and even spies, in the Afghanistan camps. True or not, he wanted to create a sense of paranoia. He gave them pointers on how to make amends with their families and slowly reduce contact with their loved ones as the operation moved closer. This third directive was clear: at the point of an estimated three months before the proposed date, they were to settle with their families, beginning the process of focusing inward.

Bin Laden gave Atta authority over all the others as the *emir* of the operation, affirmed by *Mukhtar*.[652] In this way, he would not need to frequently consult once they were set up, minimizing communications.

Mukhtar said in the first weeks in America he would like a daily dispatch or acknowledgement that all was well. After that, though Atta's reports would be welcome, they wouldn't be necessary unless he needed advice or to communicate in an emergency. Again, *Mukhtar* said, every communication ran the risk of exposing them. But mostly, he wanted to stress that Atta and the others had to learn to think independently and with confidence, preparing themselves to make split-second decisions when it truly mattered.

They discussed what kinds of airline tickets to buy and use, and *Mukhtar* said that they should never spare any expense with regard to operational travel.

In week three, *Mukhtar* introduced the four to flight simulation software. They spent hours memorizing what to look for with regard to airport security authorities, airports, and airplanes. They took field trips to nearby Jinnah International Airport and watched check-in procedures for flights. They even got on a flight one day to Lahore, separately going through security with carry-on bags, each carrying some item of contraband that might be detected and they were willing to lose. Not making contact with each other in the airports, they examined the guards, gate cameras and boarding procedures, studying the flow of the flight.[653]

Back in Karachi, they discussed their observations. After going through the X-ray machine, a long pair of scissors was taken out of Marwan's bag. *Mukhtar* was grateful for the teaching moment. Of course, he said, *Amreeka* would be more professional, and with the bigger jets, things would be more complex. He urged each of them to take multiple flights inside America, to study and memorize the flight flow. And to experiment with what weapons they could take onboard. As long as it was small—a pocketknife or a box cutter—nothing would happen if it were questioned, except that the item would be confiscated. Eventually, he said, they would find the right weapon to bring on board.

Mukhtar said that there was no reason for them to change their names or use aliases.[654] Normally, operatives would establish a number of them, including different spellings of their names and pseudonyms for communication. *Mukhtar* used a variety of Saudi and Qatari passports for most of his travel, and *al Qaeda* had a regular supply of unnumbered and genuine passports from Saudi Arabia, Yemen, Iraq, and Pakistan.[655] But given that the Hamburg Four were all operational virgins with solid European residence permits, *Mukhtar* reasoned that it would be safest to just apply for new and clean passports from their home countries before applying for American visas under their own names. They were ambitious men doing what Americans knew best: following the course of global salvation by trying to become just like them.

Mukhtar took the four to a studio where each filmed a video to serve as their "martyr wills," in anticipation of dying in an attack against the world's only superpower. The instructions for the video contents came from *Sheikh* bin Laden himself, and each had to recite their lines in classical Arabic and quote precisely from the *Qur'an*. Only Ziad managed the script on the first try. The others, Atta included, had to go through several takes before their pronunciations seemed natural.[656]

In the evenings, the four went over *Mukhtar's* many procedures. Most evenings, they spent an hour or so in an internet café, moving around to different ones in Karachi so as not to be conspicuous. They learned how to surf the internet, collecting information about airports and buildings, establishing and practicing communications plans and backups, even chatting with each other online when they were in the same room, getting the hang of logging into and using different portals. On Monday nights, *Mukhtar* came to treat them to one of the favorite movies from his extensive collection of hijacking videotapes: *Executive Decision*, *Delta Force*, *Toy Soldiers* and *Airport '77*.

One day, the five walked from the safe house to the Pakistan Air Force Museum, where they looked at old airplanes. They went over terminology and sat in the cockpits of a number of aircraft for the first time.[657]

"I have taught you all I know," *Mukhtar* said at the beginning of the fourth week. He liked them all in different ways. Atta, though most difficult and rigid, was driven and impassioned, meticulous in his study and paperwork. *Mukhtar* trusted him. Marwan and Ramzi Binalshibh were agreeable and eager to please. Ziad was a surprise, the greatest contradiction, the most Westernized but also the most scholarly, smarter than Atta on matters of religion, and also smart enough to not get into Atta's way when he was exerting leadership. In that way that any egotist has trouble recognizing their own, *Mukhtar* also didn't understand Ziad or his motivation, this Lebanese man seeming to be the most unlikely of *jihadis*.

The subordinates were then sent off. As a citizen of the Emirates, Marwan went to Dubai to pick up the initial cash for the four of them and to visit his family. While home, he applied for and received a new passport, this one clean of any trace of travel to Pakistan or Afghanistan.[658] Ziad and Binalshibh went to Lebanon and Yemen, respectively, and did the same, visiting their families, telling them of their opportunity in America.

Atta stayed in Karachi with *Mukhtar* for further training. The two spoke at length about psychology and personnel management. *Mukhtar* letting Atta into his own secret deliberations regarding people. He told Atta that he had already given up on the two Saudis who had been passed onto him by bin Laden, saying they would likely end up being musclemen, if they participated at all. *Mukhtar* also told Atta that he feared Binalshibh wouldn't be able to participate. *Mukhtar* said that his experience was that Yemenis couldn't get American visas. He promised Atta, though, that an important role would be found for his friend, probably back in Germany, as an intermediary.[659]

The two spent hours, then days, going over airport, border, and communications security measures, computers and software, codes and finances. An *al Qaeda* specialist was brought in to teach Atta how to make fake IDs. The two practiced internet searches and went over airline timetables to determine when flights would be in the air at the same time and what airplane type each flight would be using. Atta and *Mukhtar* checked online how he could book a public tour, through the Egyptian embassy, to visit the Pentagon once in Washington.

Khallad made a guest appearance towards the end, bringing the highest regards from *Sheikh* bin Laden and the *Shura* council. He gave *Mukhtar* a list of additional targets, were more than four pilots in the final group. *Mukhtar* said he was keen on having the CIA hit. He said Atta might also want to scout the Saudi embassy in Washington, DC, a possible target and one that was not on the original *al Qaeda* list. But *Mukhtar* stressed that it was Atta's call to make in the end, that only he would have the clearest view.

With Marwan gone, KSM sensed that Atta seemed even more uneasy and restless. He knew from records provided from Kandahar that Marwan had been transported to a Pakistani hospital during their time in Afghanistan.[660] The note said that his stomach pains were so intense that they sent him away. A doctor had reported gravely back to a contact in Peshawar—a report that was then sent to Kandahar, saying Marwan had stomach cancer. Marwan already knew that he did.

When he and Atta were alone, *Mukhtar* inquired about how long the doctors gave Marwan to live. Atta said that his diagnosis wasn't a death sentence, and *Insha'Allah*, Marwan would complete his mission and be able to die with honor.

That left one final task hanging over Khalid Sheikh Mohammed's head as Atta was leaving Karachi.

Germany was different from America, he delicately said to him, and doubly deceiving in some ways. Arab men were invisible there. Because of the country. Because of its history. And its shame. So he and his brothers were either ignored as *guest workers* or celebrated as faux citizens joining some fairy-tale European Union of the likeminded. Post-modern Germany, *Mukhtar* offered, was fixated these days on embracing any behavior that was inclusive, on accepting anything that proved their forefathers to be bigoted. Modern Germans didn't just reject the Nazi past; they bent over backwards to prove they weren't the same. And so, *Mukhtar* said, they'd lost the instinct of even doing what was in their best interest.

Atta was perplexed.

"My friend, America is different," he went on. "Men holding hands. In America, that is generally considered to be queer behavior. There is no reason to draw unnecessary attention to yourself and Marwan."

Atta didn't know quite how to respond. What *Mukhtar* was saying wasn't obvious. And he wasn't even sure if his teacher was saying anything. He didn't take his intervention as some accusation, because, well, he knew nothing of what he was saying.

KSM and Khallad had talked about Atta, as they did about each of the candidates, assessing their psychology and motivations. KSM, of course, thought he had all the answers: that Atta had an overbearing and controlling father, an overly-attentive mother to her only boy, this slight and sensitive bookworm who sat on her lap and hid behind her skirt, perhaps hiding long enough that maybe he grew to hate skirts. Applying himself as a good student, then as a good Muslim, they surmised, was probably his antidote.[661]

They had discussed seeking the help of an Islamic scholar, or broaching the subject with Abu Hafs, regarding their concern that Atta and Marwan were too close. But then, *Mukhtar* said, *who even cares?* Other than their behavior representing a risk to their operation, maybe there wasn't a problem.

Still, *Mukhtar* wanted to warn Atta about even the most natural behavior of Middle Eastern men and how it might be misinterpreted in America.

"Islam is not something that you can judge," Atta responded. "You sit here directing others to martyrdom, pronouncing all sorts of forbidden behaviors to be acceptable by your authority if they are in the pursuit of *jihad*. Well, my teacher, you do not understand either the word of the Prophet—*peace be upon him*—or *jihad*. The struggle is inside each of us, to live in accordance with *Allah's* will. I love Marwan just as I love *Sheikh* Osama. It is a pure love. I have lust for nothing except to join the Prophet—*peace be upon him*—in heaven."

"My brother," *Mukhtar* responded, backing away from his intense pupil and adopting the same grave and formal language. "I am just trying to help you achieve your own goal and the destiny of the greatest and purest martyrdom."

And so Atta was sent back to Hamburg, a human missile launched.

Chapter 38 Honeymooners

Mohammed Atta and Marwan al-Shehhi stepped into apartment 5D at 106 Cabrini Boulevard, a nondescript building on a nondescript street in the Hudson Heights neighborhood of northern Manhattan.[662] The building was practically in the shadow of the George Washington Bridge.[663]

The six-story brick structure, shaped like the letter U and intended for the working-class poor of an earlier era, reminded them of *Marienstrasse*, with its long, dark hallways fanning off to closed door after closed door of anonymous neighbors.

The other buildings on the block were of similar age and size, and there was a restaurant at the corner and a unisex salon across the street. As an architectural connoisseur, Atta pointed out the distinctive fire escapes everywhere, some on the fronts of the buildings. He also noticed colorful awnings standing over the entrances, maybe at one time the post of a doorman who acted as butler and guard, but now universally empty.

A short walk around the corner onto West 181st Street was Riverside Drive, perched high above the wide Hudson River and an expansive view into New Jersey and its towering palisades.

They traveled separately from Germany and arrived from different countries. *Mukhtar* told them the story of Ramzi Yousef's entry seven years earlier, how his seatmate and partner had been detained, how he had almost been apprehended.

New Egyptian passport and American visa in hand, Atta took a bus from Hamburg to Prague, then caught a flight to New York's John F. Kennedy International Airport. After a bus ride to Manhattan, he took the A train uptown to the 181st Street subway station.[664]

Marwan, also with new passport and visa, took a train from Hamburg to Brussels boarding Sabena Flight 537, landing at Newark International Airport. He took the PATH train under the Hudson River into Manhattan, transferring to the subway.[665]

They found the furnished one-bedroom apartment on the internet. Atta talked to the rental agent on the phone, convincing him to give them the one-bedroom sight unseen, wiring a security deposit and a month's rent to him.

And though they had only been apart for a few days, when they were reunited, they held each other as if it were an extended reunion, secure in the quiet privacy of their new home. Quiet. Private.

For the next few days, the two were like giddy honeymooners, Atta and Marwan, exploring their bustling and grimy neighborhood, walking around the city, acclimating themselves to their upcoming year ahead in America.

They walked uptown to Fort Tryon Park, beloved Amir with his guidebook in hand, ready to tell Marwan of every building.

He read: "The 67-acre park was given to the city in 1935 by John D. Rockefeller Jr., who hired the Olmsted Brothers to design it and even purchased part of the New Jersey shore opposite, now called Palisades Park, to preserve the view. The park is home to the Cloisters—also conceived by Rockefeller—which houses the medieval art collection of the Metropolitan Museum of Art."[666]

They knew nothing of art, but as soon as they found out that there was a museum which covered the history of their lands as well, they were excited about going, about acting as *Mukhtar* instructed. Atta loved the brick and clay-tiled-roof building, which he explained was characteristic of Italy, and they walked around the portico and the grounds before venturing in.

But what was called "medieval art" to the American palate was defined as a sweep of 1000 years, lumping the so-called Western world into one indecipherable mass, engulfing disparate peoples and periods that included everything from the Norsemen of Scandinavia to what was called Byzantine art—Byzantine being, of course, the Eastern Roman Empire, an empire that emerged from Rome's decline and lasted until Constantinople fell to the first Muslim invaders in the 15th century.

"It is Christian art, my brother," Atta sadly concluded. Maybe not all of it was Christian, given the pagan offerings of the Vikings. But it wasn't Islamic art, or anything from the actual Middle East. Their people were invisible.

"According to the guidebook," Atta told Marwan that night, "the main building of the Metropolitan Museum has one of the world's largest collections of Islamic art."

They took the subway downtown and walked across Central Park to the giant museum building, and found the "Islamic Galleries," in which there were collections of Persian and Mughal Indian miniatures and manuscripts. And there were some beautiful old *Qur'ans* on display, the focus being the calligraphy and illumination of the books.

Softly lit, expansive, and with only a few visitors, the rooms were done up in a light, desert brown. Atta read the explanatory signposts and Marwan wandered, admiring a culture that was his, one that he never really paid much attention to.

Through an archway into a new room, though, they stopped short, and were speechless. There in the corner were three ancient renderings of the Prophet Mohammed—*peace be upon him*—three illustrations, evidently taken from the leaves of books, three artworks that confused them both, for they had been told their entire lives that pictorial depictions of the Prophet were *haram*—forbidden.

Atta read the explanatory placard on the wall:

> Featured here are several depictions of the Prophet Muhammad. These portrayals, while somewhat rare, are not unheard of as there were (and still are) many different attitudes toward depicting the Prophet, and humans in general, in the Islamic world. These attitudes vary dramatically from region to region and throughout history; the societies that produced the works displayed here are among those that allowed the depiction of the Prophet. Commissioned by Muslims for

Muslims, these images appear in biographies of the Prophet and his family, world and local histories, and accounts of Muhammad's celestial journey (*mi'raj*), as well as in literary texts. In each context, they serve a distinct purpose. They illustrate a narrative in biographies and histories, while in literary texts they serve as visual analogues to written praises of the Prophet. An image of the Prophet Muhammad at the beginning of a book endows the volume with the highest form of blessing and sanctity. Thus, illustration of him was a common practice, particularly in the eastern regions of the Islamic world.[667]

They bought tea in the museum café.

"What does it mean, brother?" Marwan asked.

"Ziad will have the answer," Atta said. "I only associate architecture and mosaics with distinctly Islamic motifs. I have never seen a depiction of the Prophet—*peace be upon him*. I'm just not sure."

After their break, Atta went off to find the museum library, where he might be able to read about this troubling discovery. While Atta did that, Marwan walked through the Near East section of the museum, looking at Babylonian, Mesopotamian, and even Egyptian objects.

The next day, they walked down Fifth Avenue, Atta commenting on the style of the old mansions and richly-adorned buildings facing Central Park. Here, every apartment had a uniformed doorman protecting the rich. Old ladies walked little dogs. And the pink became overwhelming away from Spanish Harlem, Atta and Marwan both noticing that color only existed in servant's uniforms and the kiosks selling hot dogs or *halal* food.

Though they were obviously in a neighborhood of the wealthy, they were free to move anywhere and hardly saw any police. They spoke English on any occasion they could, asking directions, buying ice cream and candy from street vendors, going into shops and museums.

For two weeks, they walked and visited. They marveled at the architecture and the ornate lobby of the Plaza Hotel and Rockefeller Center. They took the ferry to Liberty Island and visited the Statue. They walked down Wall Street and ate in Chinatown and Little Italy,

Atta buying a wild selection of cookies at an Italian bakery to satisfy his sweet tooth. They sat on park benches and Atta smoked or ate sweets and Marwan drank tea. They went in stores and browsed, they bought shoes every Saturday, Atta every time telling Marwan how wasteful he thought it was, but also following directions.[668]

Atta wanted to see the most hideous of the skyscrapers up close. They visited the observation deck of the Empire State Building, waiting in line for the elevator, peering out into the vast expanse of the other giant sentinels, stopping on the southwest corner and spending a long time looking at the twin towers in the distance.

And, of course, they visited the World Trade Center itself, sitting in the public plaza, drinking tea, Atta smoking his Marlboro Lights. They watched the flow of people, occasionally staring up at the gargantuan buildings. The buildings dwarfed even the giants of New York. And once at the plaza, they saw that the two towers were surrounded by smaller buildings, many of the same design, as if they were guardians of this false Messiah, Atta said. They walked into the cavernous and multi-decked lobby, taking a measure of the size. Marwan sensed that his beloved instantly hardened. Atta called them "the Jewish greed monoliths," and said they didn't just block the sun, but blocked the human soul with their arrogance.

The honeymoon was over; there was business to be done.

Before leaving Germany, Atta corresponded with dozens of prospective flight schools.[669] Their weeks of orientation coming to an end, they started to make the rounds of calling them to figure out which would best suit them.

Yes, it's two. No, we are not looking for financial aid. Yes, we want to train together. No, we have no prior flight experience. Yes, to be commercial pilots. Yes, on multi-engine jets.

They flew to Oklahoma City to check out a flight school in Norman, the first on their list.[670]

Atta was enthusiastic about the idea of Oklahoma, telling Marwan the entire story of the Joad family, how they were driven from their home by the Zionist bankers, becoming migrant workers taken advantage of by rich landowners, surviving only because they stayed together and kept a quiet dignity and the family intact.

It must be a part of the Oklahoma people, Atta said.

"What you boys be wantin'?" asked the flight director at the academy, a fat, pink, sweating man with a ridiculous hairdo sitting at a rusting metal desk in an outbuilding at Max Westheimer Airport.

"Basic flight certification," Atta answered. "We want to be airline pilots."

"Hmm. Airline pilots, really?" He drew out the words so that each almost formed complete sentences. "From what countries?"

"I am from Cairo, in Egypt. Marwan is from the Emirates."

"That a country?"

"The United Arab Emirates," Atta calmly answered.

"Never heard of it," drawled the portly man.

A vein stuck out on Atta's neck.

"So, you like cousins?"

"Excuse me?"

"You boys cousins?" he asked again. "Just askin'. Askin' what brings you-all here to Oklahoma?"

Atta was getting impatient, Marwan could see.

Before they could answer, the man blurted out, "Eighty-five hundred each," calculating their value, sizing up what he could only imagine to be the rich Middle Easterners.

"How much?" Atta asked.

"Eight thousand five hundred, half on matriculation, half when you fly your first solo, no refunds."

"In our correspondence, you said half as much."

"Me? I didn't say anything. That's the price. Plus insurance coverage."

"What?" Atta asked.

"I require insurance coverage. Everyone does."

"And how much is that?"

"Let me see," he said, again sizing them up, "Hull insurance plus liability and medical coverage depending on the deductible, fifteen hundred each. Ah'l put ya' through to a local company."

"Can we look at the aircraft?" Marwan interrupted, hoping to defuse any argument.

"Sure."

They walked out to the broiling tarmac, the man donning a large floppy sun hat and mirrored sunglasses. Six red and white Cessna's of the academy were parked in a row, some of the small planes with two seats, some with four.

"How many students do you have?" Marwan asked.

"You mean full-time? Like you two fellas? None. Ah got tons of individuals in various stages of learnin' how to fly, but no full-time students, no siree."

"How long would it take?" Marwan asked, going through the motions, sensing that Atta wouldn't want to ever pay this man a penny.

"To get a private pilot license. That all depends, depends on how good you-all are? Full-time? From English test to check ride? Maybe a month, six weeks. But to be an airline pilot? Ah think you need 1,500 hours in the seat for that. So that would take a year or more depending on how much time you get ac-chully flying or in a simulata'."

Atta was examining the planes as they talked. "Can I sit in one?" he called.

"Be ma' guest," he said.

"Tough guy, eh?" the man said, referring to Atta, talking to Marwan. "Ain't much for small talk?"

Marwan asked more questions, keeping the guy talking. The weather. The winds. The airport. Somehow the conversation even drifted to the University of Oklahoma football team.

When they left, the man waddled out with them to their rental car, now just your generic pink Westerner, pilot instructor or not, the kind of person Atta grew to hate.

They were silent for a while on the drive back to the motel. Atta was boiling, but when he finally spoke, he remarked that the experience reminded him of the resignation contained in passages from *The Grapes of Wrath*.

"I don't know what I expected," he told Marwan, "but whatever dignity I imagined here in the heartland, I now see the wisdom of Qutb, his now decades-old observations about this wild place."

Atta didn't say anything to Marwan, but he also felt the sting of *Mukhtar*'s words about the two of them. Oklahoma was nothing like Manhattan, and nothing like Hamburg. The swipe by the pink pig of their being cousins. And then everywhere they went, at the airport, at the rental counter, at a gas station, at their motel, at restaurants, he felt it. They saw cowboy hats and pickup trucks and he felt like they were being stared at and sized up just a little too much.

At the airport, as they waited for their American Airlines flight back to New York, Marwan first broached an idea.

"I want to leave this Earth with you, Amir," he said to Atta.

"Of course, my beloved," Atta answered, taking his hand. "Of course, my brother. You said you've stopped losing weight. Is there something you aren't telling me?"

"No, no. I'm not talking about my cancer," Marwan said quietly.

"Then what, brother? We are both destined to gain the most glorious entry, and to join *Allah*, in heaven, *peace be upon him*. And there we will be reunited in paradise."

Marwan hesitated. "*Insha'Allah*, I will be strong enough. I know I will. I was talking about something else."

"What is it, my love?" Atta asked.

"I was talking about being together now, in America, but also during our mission."

"Yes, my darling," Atta said. "I won't leave you. We will train together, live together. And when the moment comes ..."

"It is so far away," Marwan said.

"What is?" Atta asked, puzzled.

"Washington. It is so far away from New York."

"Yes, my brother, but we will be moving at the same moment."

"I have a different idea."

"Tell me, my brother."

"There are two towers, my brother. Two towers, and two brothers, the two of us. We cannot leave one standing. I want to give my life there with you."

"There?"

"Yes," Marwan said, taking his hand and squeezing it. "I know *Mukhtar* says, the *Sheikh* says, that we are only to hit one building, but I want us to fly together and bring down both. I want us to be together. I knew the moment I saw the two buildings, like brothers, standing side by side."

PART 10

Chapter 39 Hidden Ridge

Bowlen had taken this drive dozens of times, on frosty mornings and on pitch-black nights, on brilliantly sunny days and in driving snow, in mud season when the ruts in the road reached as high as the car chassis. He'd driven here on ice that was as treacherous as any combat zone.

Today it was a near-perfect late autumn day, air crisp, humidity low, the kind of day that invites lingering over morning conversation with a stillness and a graceful detachment that invokes not a worry in the world.

He took a turn onto the dirt road near the top of the hill, past a cluster of old homes, each with an orderly stack of firewood underneath remnants of tarps and corrugated iron. There was an immediate reward of a spectacular view off to his left.

"Charlie," he said, waking up his snoozing companion. "You've got to see the view."

"Oh wow," she said, rubbing her eyes and craning her neck to see over her boss. The morning mists had faded, and she could see vibrant, multi-colored ridgelines extending below. Packed so tightly together, the ancient glacial bumps gave the illusion of rolling hills going on endlessly, the deep river valleys and the bottom-dwelling villages between them barely even suggested.

"We're almost here," he told her. They'd flown up to Hartford the evening before and spent the night in a hotel, getting an early start.

Bowlen took a right onto an even-bumpier dirt road and drove past an old cemetery, continuing, it seemed, ever upward as their way narrowed, up until he finally turned right into an unmarked driveway, their car setting off a motion detector that rang a buzzer in the hidden house above.

As he made the final bend on the driveway still further up, golden retrievers bounded towards the car, tails wagging in anticipation of the rare visitors. The white clapboard farmhouse had been added to over the years, and as they pulled into the back, they could see the formal flower garden, itself weeded and cut back, all of its plantings now put to bed for the winter.

Bowlen got out, stretching out his back and bending his knees. Charlie got out the other side and took a deep breath, taking in the fresh air, petting the colliding dogs, cooing *good boys*.

Shuffling down the blue stone path to greet them, Hal Jones looked every bit the country squire, plaid shirt and corduroy pants topped by an oversized cardigan and large woolen slippers, the morning frosty enough to demand both.

"Right on time," he said.

It wasn't ironic, or an admonishment, as if Lawrence Avery Bowlen was ever late.

They shook hands, the laconic greeting of professional men, especially old spies.

"And Ms. Charbel," he said. "I've heard so much about you."

Hal and his wife had been up in Vermont full-time since retirement, and he hardly left the hill much anymore, his children only too happy to make the sojourn to this beautiful and inviting sanctuary. Bowlen loved coming here as well, visiting the country, his country, a geography so different from the treacherous and monochromatic city suburbs of Washington, but also a New England that was in his blood.

They couldn't be more different in appearance, Charlie observed. The boss was, indeed, a visitor from another realm, a solid and poised urbanite, clean-shaven as always and wearing starched and pressed khaki pants and a button-down Oxford shirt right out of the dry cleaner's bag, the only suggestion of setting being a pair of clichéd, ankle-high L.L. Bean boots on his feet. No doubt Bowlen's spit-shined and favored loafers were safeguarded in felt booties packed in his overnight bag, she thought.

Hal, on the other hand, was tall and thin, with a scraggly beard, his thinning grey hair gone wild. But there was no mistaking his patrician oneness that connoted a certain old-world breed. There was something elegant about him, his eyeglasses hanging on a chain at his chest like a librarian, his long-fingered hands looking perfectly tended. This was no farmer.

Bowlen found Hal a bit gaunter, his wrists cadaverous, his gray beard patchier, his hair more ragged, his skin so mottled and crackly it seemed like he needed to be oiled.

As they entered the house, everything was perfectly welcoming: the rubber mat with the garden clogs and mud boots by the door, the coat rack overflowing with fleece and wool and faded ski jackets, the old rugs and the worn furniture and the tangle of house plants, the family photographs, the half-read newspapers and magazines and stacks of books covering every hospitable surface.

Hal padded ahead down the hallway to his office and the two followed, the dogs jostling to get ahead.

His paneled sanctuary was sun-strewn, the desk and two leather chairs and his trusty wood stove surrounded by shelves lined with books and the memorabilia of a former life. To the right of the old wooden desk was the ego wall, awards and pictures of him with presidents and princes. And a king or two. Bowlen sat down in a comfortable old chair next to the fire, warming his hands.

Charlie looked around, admiring rare objects from the Middle East, stopping at one in a glass case, mounted on a wooden stand with a brass plaque. She guessed it was a retirement present of some sort.

It was a pistol, a revolver, not the snub nose type favored by police detectives but one with a long barrel. Steve would know the nomenclature, Charlie thought. Or he'd make it up. Hal said it was the very gun that had been used in the assassination of King Faisal twenty-five years earlier. That killing, in some ways, had been what started it all, and so it was also a handgun that drew a direct line from Saudi Arabia then to Project Sumner today.

Hal Jones puttered behind his desk. On the bookcase he had one of those new silver machines that swallowed plastic pods and spit back cups of coffee.

Charlie commented on the machine.

"And so it goes," Hal said, chuckling, his back to them while he was preparing them all a brew. "Somehow, in the middle of nowhere, this old fart is on the cutting edge. It's made by a company here in Vermont. It was a present from the kids. It's not a bad cup of coffee. Though the doctors say I have to watch my caffeine."

The machine hummed and then dribbled out its bounty, the vibration practically shaking the room. When Charlie came initially to meet Hal Jones, he boiled a cup of Saudi coffee on top of the wood stove for her, carefully timing out the minutes, lifting his beloved pot with its pointed spout off the heat whenever it threatened to boil over, lovingly adding just the right mix of cloves, cardamom, ginger and saffron. Now he explained that arthritis was stealing away the use of his hands, and that Betsy, his wife, complained about the expense of the saffron.

As if they were hurting for money, Charlie thought.

"What can I do for you two?" Hal finally said, as he delivered them both steaming cups, sitting down at his overflowing desk.

"I wanted you to see a birthday card I received from Khalid," Bowlen said.

He reached into his briefcase and fished out a small envelope, handing it over.

"Mister Jones," it said on the outside. Hal smiled as he haltingly used a long, crooked finger to pry the Western-style birthday card from within. Khalid had been sending Bowlen cards from the day he learned his birthday.[671]

The note was short:

> *I trust that this finds you well. I wish I could visit with you on your celebration, but a great storm separates our worlds. I pray that you will understand. Enjoy the big bang. With much respect. Khalid.*

The big bang. It wasn't the first time that Khalid playfully used that expression with them. He'd said it in Malaysia and then followed with the World Trade Center attack. Hal sensed an electric circuit activate in his body, one that moved up his legs, through his torso, all the way to his chin, his arms tingling.

It was coming.

When he looked up from the card, Charlie saw a flush in his sallow face.

"Happy birthday to you, Lawrence," Hal said. Charlie thought it weird, offering birthday greetings when the card was so ominous.

Bowlen and Hal Jones had known each other for over 30 years, mentor and pupil, and ultimately friends. They were both raised in these northern climes, and both were Cold Warriors recruited to join the ranks of the CIA right out of college. They'd both gotten sucked into the Middle East, both risen in the ranks, and both retreated from Washington's shadows to work in even-greater secrecy than the normal Agency types when they disappeared into Apex Watch.

The gravity of the note and its message put aside, Hal Jones was deft at changing the subject. He started talking about President Clinton's executive order signed in July and declaring the Taliban a state sponsor of terrorism.[672] The public document, Hal said, was accompanied by a top-secret memorandum of notification—a "presidential finding"—which authorized the Agency to develop a plan to capture Osama bin Laden, or through a third party, to assist in killing him.[673]

Even in Vermont, he had the details, "from his sources," he said. He wondered aloud whether this finding and George Tenet's declaration of war was too late, with the Clinton administration coming to an end.

"In some ways," he said to Bowlen and Charlie, he had some admiration for the president, surviving all those scandals, weathering the House impeachment, even keeping up his popularity. "Somehow Kenneth Starr has become the Washington goat, dismissed as a partisan hack," Hal said.[674] And, at least amongst the old-boy network, the word was that Bill Clinton had also kept his eye on the ball, at least on national security, educating himself about terrorism and weapons of mass destruction, two things he came into office knowing nothing about.

"You know," Hal said, addressing Charlie directly, "it's easy for me to be nonpartisan, up here in the independent-thinking backwoods. I imagine there, in the belly of the beast, the president looks much different."

"I'm not a fan," Charlie answered. "But then, nor am I of Washington."

Charlie thought that maybe Hal Jones was trying to separate himself from Bowlen. They both worked for and loved Jimmy Carter, the

Southern Democrat, and both individually impressed upon her that they were not partisan. Still, they both also admitted that, like him or not, Clinton was different. Sure, there had been Kennedy's womanizing, and there was rampant lawlessness amongst Ronald Reagan's subordinates. But for Clinton, they said, it seemed to be about money, and there was something about this money-grubbing, Arkansas bumpkin that grated in a different way, in a way that old-schoolers like them—supposedly squeaky-clean Washingtonians—found especially distasteful.

And Charlie agreed. She commented that a certain type of political calculation seemed to be taking over Washington. It was a kind of brand-building. At the top, what was good for the Clintons, and for the political dynasty they were intent on building, was notionally also good for America. The Kennedys might be gone, but the two, new branded families, Clinton and Bush, seemed intent on owning the wealth of power.

To Charlie, it wasn't just the president or his people. Way too many in Washington seemed ever so willing to throw away their anchors and just float along, pursuing careers, building their own brands, even grubbing after money, forgetting that what they were doing was operating the country, the most important country. Now that the Cold War was over, there was nothing to hold the political parties together in a common program. Nor was there anything that was earth-shattering, that many felt was worth fighting for.

"Sometimes I just dismiss my discomfort with President Clinton to the apprehensions of a crotchety, old conservative coming face to face with my growing irrelevance," Bowlen interjected. "And trust me: sometimes I question the validity of my own fear of the changes afoot. Because then I think, and increasingly I *do think* it, that it's clear that not everyone sees the world as I see it.

"I hate to say it," he went on, trying to explain without seeming—without being—either politically partisan or stuck in the past. "But didn't the end of the Cold War create a ... *what is it?* ... a dissolution of America, of the American purpose in the world? Of course, the old rules no longer hold sway—I understand that we call that progress. But whatever is afoot in this permanent change that is happening, I just can't connect to it. None of it would much matter as I plan my own eventual escape to Maine, except that I don't think that whatever is happening is making our nation any stronger."

"I'm with you on the disappearance of the bipartisan consensus in Washington," Hal commented, attempting to bring what seemed like a big subject back on track. "But tell me, Lawrence, you didn't come here just to show me a birthday card or shoot the breeze about the current administration and a crisis of American purpose. So, spit it out."

Bowlen sighed, at first sitting back in his chair and then leaning forward. "No, not exactly," he said. "But yes, it is that very crisis. We are here looking for advice."

"Well, that's free," Hal answered, trying to lower the temperature a bit.

"I rehearsed what I was going to say to you in the car," Bowlen went on, "but I might as well just blurt it out: we are about to embark on an effort to save America."

"America ..." his friend merely repeated, unperturbed by either the gravity or the declaration but needing a moment to adjust his focus.

They shared a silent moment, almost as if they were acknowledging news of a death of an old friend.

Bowlen broke the silence. "Before Mr. Draper came on, I'm not certain that I could have fully articulated the global changes that are underway. Put simply: It's the emergence of the notion, at least on the part of the civilized world, that there is a universal set of human rights. I don't mean human rights *per se*, not human rights on their own. But more I mean, the embrace of human rights as a right, as a universal right. And what that means. And when I say human rights, I don't mean in theory. That it just means equality for all under the law as an ideal. I mean active human rights, as something like freedom or democracy that is to be defended, and in its absence, to be created, even to go to war over.

"I know," and Bowlen stuttered a bit to get the words right, "that my old, white-man ways don't necessarily marvel at what it all means, because who can really be against protecting the weak? At least on the surface."

He continued: "But internationally? The pursuit of human rights, the principle of individual rights, of inalienable rights for all? With the end of the Cold War, with the end of the great ideological struggle of our age, human rights are being elevated above all else. There's a part of me that bristles at this construction because it suggests that American national interests are being put aside, that they are outranked by some unstated global Constitution.

"I get it that the simple articulation of our involvement in the former Yugoslavia, or even Iraq, is that we are fighting bad men and rogue regimes, that we're not seeking to control resources, that we only have the world's interests at heart. If it just ended there, I'd say it was just an extension of the tradition of America being the world's policeman, the imagined world policeman. But I fear that underneath those interventions is a grander program to protect human rights, individual rights, minority rights, even women's rights and the rights of gays, as a new American goal, mission and responsibility."

His friend listened closely (as did Charlie), Hal Jones' hands clasped in front of him as if in prayer.

Bowlen went on, carefully picking through his words. "I admit again, in my old-man bias, that in some ways I just don't get it. The right to be homosexual? Our imposing *their* inherent right to be homosexual on foreign societies, on societies in places like the Middle East? These are places that can hardly even deal with the rights of their own *normal* citizens.

"But that isn't the issue to me," Bowlen continued, looking at Charlie now, knowing that what he was saying could very well seem to just be a bigoted rant. "In this crusade of humanitarian intervention, sovereignty is swept aside. Intervention into the domestic affairs of others is not only allowed, it's expected. And not just by America. It's expected by our European partners, by the so-called community of nations.

"And this new global crusade is bigger than Clinton. Sure, Republicans and neocons bristle against humanitarian intervention and nation-building. But this notion of the fungibility of borders, of the international community's mandate to intervene, is becoming the norm. Except.

"Except, when it's not so easy. So, we go out there in the world—in Iraq and against other rogues—and we act as a unified international community to police the world and defend the downtrodden, except when it's too hard. And this is an insight from Mr. Draper. No one quite has the stomach to take the fight to its ultimate conclusion. We want rights for all, but we cannot conceive of declaring war on those who are truly powerful. Or those who are our so-called friends. We end up intervening only where it is politically palatable. And easy. Tackling the hard cases—say, a despotic Saudi Arabia—well, that's just too hard. Russia? Or China? No way.

"So, we have this new American purpose, and yet no one dares even articulate taking on the fundamental order in the Middle East. It's worse than 'live and let live,' worse than *realpolitik*. Because we are seeking to reframe the organizing principle for the planet, except for where it's too hard. And in that very choosing, in making the exceptions that we make, in favoring the rights of homosexuals, or even women, or Jews, we signal—in the "who" of who we choose to protect—that we make choices regarding whose rights we'll fight for. And in that, we communicate that some are not worth fighting for. And, even more, we betray a profound weakness. It is that weakness that emboldens our true enemies."

"Lawrence, what are you saying?" Hal asked, following, but wanting him to get to the point. He hadn't been in on the weeks of discussion that Bowlen and Charlie had since the meeting in New Jersey.

"You said you were going to save America, Lawrence," Hal continued. "Are you building up to a strategy to change things? To change American policy and thus this movement? And where is Mr. Draper? Why isn't he here?"

"He isn't here because … well … we're looking for your advice without him. His argument is, and I tend to agree, that what Khalid is planning … to attack America … that it is driven by these contradictions … Oh, it has its origins in bin Laden's views of colonialism, and even Islam, but ultimately Khalid and others are driven by the unfairness of how we deal with the Middle East, with the Arab regimes. I think that this is something Khalid believes. And with good reason. What Mr. Draper is suggesting then, is that we use what he is planning to our advantage. That we can guide it to bring about real change."

Khalid's *big bang*. Now Hal was grasping the point. He sipped his coffee, looking off into the distance.

"And explain to me again why Khalid fits into all of this?" Hal asked.

Charlie chimed in. "Khalid makes it clear that he is planning to bring his new brand of *spectacular* terrorism to the United States itself, that he is going to finish the job Ramzi Yousef failed to do, that he is going to attack Wall Street or bring down the North Tower of the World Trade Center, that he is going to do it by hijacking a commercial airliner and crashing it."

"Jeeeesus," responded Hal.

"We think the operation is already well underway," Bowlen stepped in, "even that there are operatives in the United States. And we could attempt to stop him—that's what we've discussed. But if they were stopped, we also believe that there are going to be more behind him, more who resent this double standard of the new American purpose, more who despise the homogenization of the planet under colorless and odorless equality, more who will smell the weakness of the West because of our contradictions, more who will think that the very moral decay of Bill Clinton *is* America. And so," he paused. "If we stop Khalid, if we stop this attack he is planning, we lose a certain advantage."

"And?" Hal asked.

"But if Khalid's attack were used as part of something larger?"

"Something larger," Hal repeated. It wasn't a question. "And your actual plan is what?"

"We help him to prepare a return to New York. That's Mr. Draper's plan. The plan basically is to intervene at the eleventh hour, but to use the outlines of the attack, and where it got its support from, to point a finger at Saudi Arabia, to stigmatize them and then to start a general war against them and Islam."[675]

"A war with Islam? A religious war against Saudi Arabia as the self-declared keeper?"

"Yes," Bowlen answered.

Hal now closed his eyes and breathed in deeply, finally exhaling. "And you, Lawrence? You want the same?"

"Excuse me?"

Hal said: "I'm not disagreeing with the worldview or with what's desirable, Lawrence, but it sounds like you want to be just like Khalid, to be the greatest ever, that you want to determine history in one act."

"Hal. That wasn't what I expected," Bowlen responded.

"Don't misunderstand me. I don't necessarily disagree. But you are coming to me for advice, and so I'm imagining that you are also seeking the greatest possible pushback, not just philosophically. How will you even do it? How can you bring yourselves to actively aid Khalid? How will you keep it secret? And most important: How will you live with yourselves if you fail to stop him?"

Bowlen talked about how Steve was working the details of the plan. He talked about their sense from the Africa bombings that Osama bin Laden had a much larger cadre to draw upon than they previously thought. He said that they were close to penetrating into KSM's decision-making process.

"The way I see it," Bowlen continued, "if we don't set the right course now, America is going to slide deeper into an endless global war. I hesitate to even say war. It will be limited, non-ideological, intentionally and smugly legalistic, a halfhearted, polite effort to sell human rights to disinclined buyers. And it's not just this president's love of long-range missiles and these new drones. That technology will soon dominate regardless of who's president. And so this war will be fought remotely in a way that just conveys even greater weakness on our part, in our unwillingness to spill our own blood for the cause—"

"Lawrence," Hal interrupted. "You are just reiterating the why. Explain to me how you can do this."

Charlie chimed in again. She wanted a crack at articulating her own uncomfortable acquiescence with Steve's proposal. "Our assessment is that the New York attack is still quite some months off. Hopefully, in that time, we will learn enough to guarantee we will be able to stop it at the eleventh hour. Our fallback option is that at least we influence the target and the timing to minimize the number of civilian deaths. And then, if we fail to find a way to stop the attack at the eleventh hour, if we fail to influence the target and the timing, we will make sure that whatever happens, we will create the conditions to pin it on the Saudis. And we will protect ourselves, especially in getting rid of the KSM history and any CIA or Apex Watch connection to him or to this act."[676]

"And you are comfortable that the benefit justifies the treason?" asked Jones.

Treason. That was a tough word.

She continued: "If we kill KSM now, the attack will likely occur anyhow. I also believe that if the attack occurs—regardless of our assistance—that surely whoever is president will mobilize to attack bin

Laden, perhaps even his Taliban sponsors. But I think Steve is right that if this happens, that the true winners there would be Saudi Arabia, rid of bin Laden and seemingly the remaining moderate voice. I also believe that once *al Qaeda* is gone—once it is attacked with the full might of the United States—that whoever is president will eventually find their way back to Iraq. American policy under two administrations, Bush and Clinton, has been that there can be no normalization of relations without regime change. I believe that post-*al Qaeda*, the momentum will grow to rid the Middle East of all the bad men—bin Laden and Mullah Omar to be followed by Saddam, and Assad, and even the Ayatollahs in Iran. I can see how that will condemn the U.S. to fight forever in the region, and I think ultimately it will mean not just disaster in terms of live lost—American lives lost—but also in the creation of more terrorists, more Khalids."

"Charlie, I feel for you," Hal responded. "But you are still missing my point a little. When I ask if you can you do it, I'm not asking if you've done your homework. I'm asking: can you really do it? Can you conspire in this way? Can you live with yourselves if you are responsible for thousands dying?"

Charlie answered, again because she had to have an answer for herself. "I can only live with myself if the benefit is worth it. The act and the benefit have to fit. Be equal. One has to be worthy of another. Right now, that's all I can hold on to. I'm not happy with this projection of how things are, or will unfold, but I can see where the long-term benefit to the United States is, that shifting the focus to Saudi Arabia does forestall this endless war. That going after the Saudis, despite their supposed leverage over America because of oil, will even communicate that we have found new strength. And as for your use of the word 'treason'—I noticed, and don't want to shy away from the strong stuff—I think that if the alternative of doing nothing is a cataclysm of endless wars, then that could justify the death of a few thousand American civilians."

"And you, Lawrence?"

Bowlen let out a loud exhale. "It's strong stuff, indeed. Thank you, Charlie. I'm not a believer in conspiracies, but yes, I agree. It seems a sound course of action."

Hal Jones craned his neck up and looked down at Charlie's footwear, making sure she was wearing sensible shoes, which she was. Charlie thought it funny that that's all he noticed—in flannel and Bean boots, it was the two of them that were caricatures. She was just wearing jeans and a bulky sweater.

"Let's take a walk to clear the air," he said. "Maybe the beauty of the outdoors will inspire us."

They piled into his Range Rover and he drove ten minutes or so down winding dirt roads to an eventual T, a small parking area with one car in it, adjacent to a river. With walking stick in hand, they followed the skinny road along its bank, a random car passing them very sporadically. The river was at a fall trickle, sunlight highlighting a swarm of insects dancing on its surface. They came upon a group of kids lounging, smoking, drinking beer. And there was a late-season, solo kayaker. Charlie found it peaceful. She couldn't help but notice that Bowlen and Jones were savoring the elements, chatting about the trees and the land, Hal pointing out the occasional special bird or sharing the latest piece of information about the price of syrup or the quality of the apple crop.

Hal asked questions about the crew back at Apex Watch and Bowlen passed along gossip. She listened, both grateful and a little annoyed that their business had been interrupted. She recognized that, like a married couple lost in a prolonged argument that had no real resolution, they'd spent too many hours in circular discussion. She'd spent many hours with Bowlen trying to talk it through—Steve's plan—and she'd ultimately capitulated in the risky act of taking a trip to consult with Hal Jones without Steve—a respite for them from his mental jackhammer, but also a bit of a swipe at someone who was already paranoid about not being included.

Walking, though, Charlie realized that *clear the air* here meant impose a solid interruption. They didn't continue to talk about the conspiracy or the plan.

Back at the house, they sat down to an early dinner, Bowlen as exhausted as she'd ever seen him, Charlie dismayed with what she thought wasn't a sufficiently full airing.

Betsy Jones was a perfect hostess, making Charlie feel at ease, deft at moving along the discussion without pressing into their business or any classified domains.

"And there is a special man in your life?" she asked.

"Yes," Charlie said, transported back to her own family table. "He's also with the Agency. We've been together for over two years."

"Ah yes, that's how you do it these days, workplace romances and common-interest marriages. I met Hal in college and have followed him ever since."

"The world has changed," Charlie said.

"I see it with our kids, one on a second marriage, the other close to ending his first, I'm sad to say."

"That's also how we do it," Charlie said. "I don't know anyone my age who doesn't already see a first marriage as a starter kit, assuming an eventual demise and eventual upgrade. Believe me, it doesn't make my Lebanese American parents happy that I'm not married at 37, but at least I'm not divorced."

"Are you two planning to get married?" Betsy asked.

"Planning? No," Charlie answered, hesitating. "I just don't know."

The conversation shifted to Washington, especially the humidity of the summer, which Betsy said she could never get used to.

Betsy pressed Charlie to tell her story. And Betsy was a warm and attentive listener. Charlie wondered about all the other Betsys out there, whether Charlie's work was actually on their behalf, whether the freedoms she was taking with their trust was enhancing their freedom or not.

After they finished eating, she disappeared into the kitchen, rejecting Charlie's offer of help, happy to have them out of her hair and back at their work.

They went back to Hal Jones's office and talked late into the night, about the president's attitude regarding Apex Watch, about the new CIA director, about Agency morale and culture, about Washington and the increasingly selfish ways of an America adrift.

Later snug under a down quilt, Charlie slept fitfully, getting up well after midnight to go to the bathroom. It was so cold when she got out of the bed that she put on a sweater and a pair of socks to walk down the hall, the outside light of the moon illuminating her way. She noticed a light on downstairs, a light coming from inside Hal's office, throwing a bright triangle into the darkness outside. And then she heard a voice.

Curious, she tiptoed towards the landing, careful to step on the outer floorboards so as to not cause a squeak. God, the floor was freezing.

At the top of the stairs, she heard Hal Jones, speaking and then silence, Hal obviously listening on the phone. The conversation was muffled, and Charlie couldn't quite make out what he was saying. But she could hear enough to know that Jones was speaking Arabic. It was early morning in Saudi Arabia.

Chapter 40 Another Venice

Ziad started pilot training at the Florida Flight Training Center in an American city called Venice.[677] Clean and prosperous, the town sold itself as one of the ten happiest in America. He had never been to the real Venice, but the brochures said the planned downtown was reminiscent of the famous city, with Italian-fashioned buildings, Mediterranean-style shops, and landscaped boulevards gridded like a crisscross of canals.

When Atta told Ziad about their misfortune in Oklahoma, he beckoned. "The weather is quite nice here, the people are really nice, and the water is warm."

And he told Atta, "There are no big buildings!"

"What do you think of going to Florida?" Atta asked Marwan.

"Think, brother?" answered his sweet one. "I will go wherever you think best."

They'd already enrolled at the Century Flight Academy in Morristown in nearby New Jersey, the second on their list of prospective schools, and even put down a deposit.[678] But Florida's agreeable weather, and their reuniting with Ziad, seemed ever more attractive.

It was just the three of them now. As *Mukhtar* predicted, their friend Ramzi could not get an American visa. A German immigration lawyer suggested that he apply again, this time with letters of reference and documentation that he would attend flight school. Atta helped him to make a deposit to prove his intent, but the State Department still said no.[679] When they got the bad news of his second visa denial, *Mukhtar* heartily encouraged the Florida reunion.[680]

"Florida would be good for our young friend," he offered in talking to Atta. Yes, they would lose another deposit, but having them all in one place would be just the morale boost they needed to soldier on.

And, *Mukhtar* said to Atta, in Florida he could keep an eye on Ziad, whom he still suspected of being confused, or worse, a freeloader, unable to cut off things with his wife.

And maybe, *Mukhtar* went on, maybe Atta could loosen up a bit in Florida. Maybe they could spend a little ... ahem .... *maybe they could let themselves lighten up a bit, visit some ... special ... clubs, or do something— anything—that would provide relief.*

The direction of that discussion made Atta cringe. He didn't want to add even more secrets to his portfolio, especially this one that *Mukhtar* needed to stick his nose into. And he didn't want to breathe a whisper of the pact that he and his beloved had made to attack both twin towers in New York.

"We are all doing just fine," Atta responded. "I look forward to prayer and learning with Ziad, especially if we are not to rely upon the mosque. I suppose it is something you do not understand," taking a swipe at the ungodly *Mukhtar*. The rest he ignored.

They packed up their stuff and said goodbye to New York. Ziad found them a pink stucco bungalow in Nokomis, a nondescript beach town south of Venice.[681] It was a tiny two-bedroom with louvered windows and a carport. Out front there was a birdbath and even an American flag.[682]

Atta and Marwan enrolled at Huffman Aviation in Venice, at the same airport as, but a different flight school than, their Lebanese compatriot. No reason to attract more attention, they thought. It was just a short drive away from their new home.[683]

With July 4th weekend approaching, school was cancelled. Atta suggested a celebration of sorts. They would go to Cramer Toyota near the Venice airport and buy a used car—no more rentals.

Like so many other South Floridians, Atta saw the Cramer Toyota ads in the newspaper and on television: "We Treat People Right." Maybe one of those big American cars would cheer up Marwan.

The Pontiac Grand Prix they purchased that day was a classic American car in style and performance.[684]

"This baby," the salesman kept saying, was fully loaded: four-barrel automatic transmission, Rally II wheels, a peppy 3.8-liter V6 engine. None of them were really listening to what he was saying. Atta said that its red color was perhaps too ostentatious, but Ziad argued that something sneaky with tinted windows would attract more attention.

Marwan was noncommittal. For him, everything was turning grey.

This baby in hand after a cash payment,[685] Marwan got behind the wheel and took the three of them for a long drive down US 41, all the way to Punta Gorda where they crossed the Peace River and parked, walking around Fishermen's Village before heading to Naples on the 93, stopping for a late meal at a place by the water before heading home.

On the ride back, Ziad drove, Atta smoking in the passenger seat and staring out the window, Marwan exhausted and sleeping in the back seat.

Normally superhuman in his evenness, Marwan excused himself to go right to bed when they were back at the house. Leaving the screened-in porch out back, he told the two how happy he was that they were all together. He kissed each of his friends on the forehead, thanking them for their friendship and brotherhood. "Your belief in me strengthens my desire to live."

Normally Ziad lamely suggested they go out for an ice cream whenever Marwan was in pain—his Lebanese mother's answer to everything.

Atta brought medicines and Tums and acted as nursemaid. They knew Marwan's dull ache got temporary relief when he avoided solid foods. But they were both starkly aware that it was only temporary.

Atta had doted over him, doing everything for him, covering for him and making excuses in flight training when Marwan had to take a break, going to health food stores to find special potions and probiotics, never smoking in the house, holding him at night when he was in pain.

Ziad had researched on the computer. He had even contacted several religious scholars about whether Marwan's sickness darkened or disallowed martyrdom. Again, that night, as they had so many times earlier, he and Atta discussed Marwan's health and their options. Though the German and Pakistani doctors were optimistic, Marwan knew that his diagnosis was certain death, even with the full battery of high-tech Western treatments. He begged Atta to stand by him, intent on dying *for* something rather than *from* something.

Sitting out back behind their little house in the humid air, Atta and Ziad listened to the Florida cicadas, crickets, and frogs, a foreign music that now covered their languid stillness. One of Marwan's instructors told him the loud cicadas were called "dog-day" cicadas because they appeared in the so-called dog days of summer.

Death for them would come quickly, and they were both in awe of Marwan's suffering and commitment.

"Why so quiet, brother?" Ziad asked.

"*Mukhtar* is again coming into my personal life," Atta responded, obviously annoyed.

"How so, brother?" Ziad asked.

"He said we should go to some special club or find relief in some way because he says there is too much tension," Atta said, looking off into the distance, a cigarette dangling from his lips.

"He does not understand the pressure we are under," Atta continued, snuffing out a Marlboro and readjusting himself in his seat to face Ziad.

He was the only person Atta could talk to about Marwan.

"He's taunting me," Atta said.

"Ignore him, brother," Ziad said. "That fucker doesn't understand."

"I try."

"You need to find solace in not just the *Qur'an* or that selective reading of yours. You need to also investigate history. And look to other Arab cultures. Not just Egypt. And not the severe world of bin Laden or the Taliban. In Lebanon, in the ancient days, men who chose a different life used the word *mithli* and not *luti*."

Luti was the name Mohammed Atta Senior threw at his son to taunt him about being unmarried and uninterested in girls. The term referred to the Sodomites of the story of Lot in the Bible and *Qur'an*.[686]

But *mithli*, Ziad went on, it literally just meant homosexual and was a description without a judgment.[687] And it was coming into more common use among tolerant Arabs, Ziad said. He then talked about the 8th century Arab poet Abu Nuwas, one of the greatest poets of the Abbasid Period, who laid the groundwork for this new tolerance.[688] He was an openly avowed homosexual and he provided one of the first true meditations on the subject.

Atta's confounding Lebanese friend constantly studied the great books and listened to tapes of the scholars and could carry on a deep conversation about all subjects regarding Islam. But he also read poetry and listened to music, and recently had been receiving packages of modern Islamic writers from his wife—fortified, Ziad said, in knowing that the faith could update itself for the modern world.

"So what if you choose seas over land?" Ziad said. Atta knew from Ziad that it was an Abu Nuwas saying, one that avoided explicitness. Sea was a metaphorical reference to the love of women, while land meant the love of men.

"I choose nothing," Atta said, listening but also needing to make a stand.

"And what even is desire?" Ziad added, not wanting to corner his friend. "Even as a married man, I find the words of Abu Nuwas beautiful, and playful."[689]

"You know nothing of what I feel," Atta responded, frowning.

Atta had learned that Ziad could put into words simple ideas that Atta in all of his matter-of-factness couldn't. Ziad once spent hours trying to explain to Atta that *Allah* was not just God but a personal name for God—a reference to God, but also His personal name.

"You don't just say 'God' when you could also say 'Lord' or 'Our God' or the many English words that have diluted the meaning," Ziad explained. "When you say *Allah*, you're invoking his personal name, the name of God. In doing so, you establish a personal bond between yourself and your creator."

It was an important point, because in defending his own behavior, Ziad explained that his personal relationship with *Allah* told him what was right and wrong. To Ziad, there was no disobeying *Allah*, no anger or wrath so typical of most Muslims. Ziad didn't disagree with bin Laden's political analysis of the world, but in terms of *Allah*, Ziad rejected the popular notion of his mercy and compassion as a constant against sin and evil.

To Atta, the negative was the milk and honey of his learning. Sin imbued the words that began every chapter of the *Qur'an*, negative reminders about the struggle between sin and evil.

"In the name of Allah the Rahman the Raheem ..."

Ziad disagreed. *"Raheem* is a womb," he argued. *"Rahman* and *Raheem* connote a motherly love. Not some paternal or violent mercy. It is loving. Caring. Forgiving. We understand *rahma,* the first of two kinds of love in the *Qur'an.* It is *Allah's* love of everyone, even the nonbelievers. And yes, brother, even the *mithli."* As Ziad saw it, there was also a second level of love—*hub*—the love reserved for those who obey.

Why should God make you suffer torment if you are thankful and believe in Him? God always rewards gratitude and He knows everything.[690]

"We identify as servants of the Prophet—*peace be upon him*—the earthly allowances made by *Mukhtar* of our human practices insignificant, unless they become our identity. We are told to seek out the Five Pillars and to marry and make children, but I tell you, my friend, there are no true desires that fall outside of what is strictly *haram."*

"And so, there is no sin?" Atta asked. He was struggling to free himself from the vortex first created by his father, and then taken up by *Mukhtar.*

It was a discussion that they had before, Atta arguing that he could never do enough to earn *Allah's* love, and that he would never live a full life the way he was. Atta was ashamed that his lack of marriage and reproduction stood in the way. And that was not even considering any sinful thoughts.

"You are wrong to feel this way, brother. *Allah* is not a punisher," Ziad urged him to think. "He is not your father, and certainly not the angry *imams* who preach in Hamburg and the other hungry mosques. Make your peace with your maker," Ziad urged. "When you have done that, *rahma* and *hub* together will guide you."

Only Atta made the *Hajj* to the first house of God, and Ziad knew that he never would.[691] Their path to martyrdom—and its short-circuiting of all of the other pillars of what a good Muslim was called to be and do—was a contradiction that many believers would never understand.[692]

"I love Marwan," Atta finally said. He didn't need to explain.

Ziad searched for something beyond the platitudes, certainly beyond the fire and brimstone that desire was supposed to invoke. His Egyptian friend was struggling and in pain, and he didn't want to say something stupid.

"I would like to make a son," Ziad responded, equally sharing a deep truth.

"I'm just not sure it is any longer possible, my brother," Atta responded sweetly.

"Perhaps not," Ziad answered. "But I would like to." And he went on: "The *Qur'an* says: *O Children of Adam! Wear your beautiful apparel at every time and place of prayer: Eat and drink: But waste not by excess, for Allah loveth not the wasters.*[693]

"I take this to mean that the only real sin is wastefulness," Ziad said. "And so, I am telling you: I will make a son. And you listen, my friend. Do not waste your love. That would be the only sin."

Do not waste your love, Atta thought, warmed by this spiritual fuel.

Chapter 41 Overboard

One task that Atta had to undertake was to fly out to San Diego to meet with the orphaned brother Nawaf al-Hazmi.[694] He was on his own ever since his partner Khalid Mihdhar defied all the rules and took a flight from Los Angeles to Frankfurt in June,[695] going home to Yemen to see his newborn son, he said.[696] Nawaf had been working and hanging out at the mosque, but now *Mukhtar* told him that his visa was about to expire and he had to apply for an extension. Atta had to go to San Diego to help him, *Mukhtar* said. But as *emir* in America, it was also his decision as to whether to continue to use him. If Atta decided to return this bin Laden favorite, *Mukhtar* would be secretly pleased.

The Saudi oaf Nawaf initially asked Atta to meet at their mosque, then suggested they meet at a local *halal* restaurant. When Atta said he did not want to be seen in a Muslim community, Nawaf had no suggestions outside his neighborhood. He said he didn't know of anything. Atta looked at a map and randomly suggested Balboa Park, sitting in the middle of the city and near the airport—away from any potential spies. Atta picked the Japanese Friendship Garden.[697]

When Atta met him, there was nothing about Nawaf Hazmi he liked. The 23-year-old needed a haircut. He had a big bushy mustache and his car was filthy and filled with fast-food wrappers. His hands were filthy, his nails dirty and unkempt.

Atta asked what he had been doing and Nawaf said he was playing soccer in the evenings and on weekends.[698] And then he told Atta that in addition to the two lying about taking English lessons, they had really only sampled flying on four days, paying for the one-hour introductory sessions at three different schools.[699]

"But why did you lie, brother?" Atta asked, walking along his side in the quiet garden. "There could be other roles for you."

"The *Sheikh* himself told us that we would be pilots," he said, hanging his head.

"It isn't like learning to drive a car," Atta replied, repeating what *Mukhtar* told him. He was calculating whether to just drop Nawaf altogether, sending him back to Afghanistan. "And your partner? Mihdhar also could not learn English? He also did not have the science mind for flying?"

"When I dropped out, he moved to a new school. He told me he was finishing his English classes and starting flight training. And every day he'd disappear. I thought to do just that. But at the end of May, he comes to me and says he is going to Yemen to see his new son. When I asked about his flight training, Mihdhar said something about there being a scheduled break."

Mukhtar already told Atta that the math did not add up for Mihdhar making a son, let alone for him to now be visiting him.

"Did you think Mihdhar had a son?" Atta asked.

"No." Though Nawaf knew Mihdhar was married, or at least that he said that he was, they had gone to stripper clubs many times, as *Mukhtar* instructed. Atta was disgusted.

"Is that where all their money has gone?" Atta said.

But Nawaf said he didn't really know, that Mihdhar took care of the finances.

Then Nawaf told Atta the story of taking Mihdhar to the airport when he left, casting a more ominous cloud over his partner. "We went to the Bank of America and we closed our joint account, withdrawing the balance."[700]

"How much was it?" Atta asked.

"Almost $5,000."

"I opened a new account the next day and I deposited the same monies. I have all the receipts," Nawaf said. "And I coordinated everything with Cousin Ali.[701]

"At the bank, we didn't have to talk much in English and nothing seemed wrong to me. Then came the day of his departure. I drove him to the airport, begging him not to leave me alone. But he was intent on going. So, we parked the car in the garage and went to the ticket counter where Khalid took out a credit card—not our credit card, but a credit card issued from a Saudi bank—one that I had never seen. And I said to him, 'Brother, where did you get this card?' And he said, 'I have kept it for emergencies.'[702] I thought it dishonest but maybe justified. Then he just dropped all pretense of any difficulty with the English language and started talking with the airline agent. And all of a sudden, I realized that he faked his difficulty in our classes and with everyone else. Mihdhar was speaking fluently, I tell you, and even though I couldn't understand all of what he was saying, I could tell from the look on the ticket agent's face that she had no problems understanding his English. Not only that, but he had a reservation all set: a flight to Los Angeles, then on to Dubai.

"'I thought you were flying to Yemen?' I asked. He dismissed my question, saying that it was too dangerous to buy such a ticket in America. That he would do so when he landed in Dubai."

"And you had never heard him speak English before?" Atta asked.

"No," said Nawaf.

"Did you ask him?"

"Yes, of course. I did." Nawaf hesitated. "He told me to never tell anyone, that if I did, he would make sure that *Sheikh* bin Laden would have me killed."

Nawaf then told Atta the story of their Saudi "friend," Omar Bayoumi, who had been shadowing them since their arrival and was obviously to him an agent of the *Mukhabarat*.

"And you know this how?"

"He has money but doesn't seem to work. And he is driving a Mercedes. I just know this type."

"And does he know that Mihdhar has left?"

"Yes."

"And does he know anything about your mission here?"

"He has taken nothing from me," Nawaf answered, for the first time showing any sign of intelligence.

They had already circled the grounds of the Friendship Garden many times. Nawaf suggested they go to the teahouse and take refreshments, but Atta had seen and heard enough. He wanted to be rid of him, and out of San Diego as soon as possible.

Atta said he had another meeting, but that he would meet Nawaf tomorrow. Together they would go to the office of the Immigration and Naturalization Service to renew his visa.[703]

"Get cleaned up," Atta ordered. "And wear your best clothes. Do you still have your ESL registration papers?"

"Yes," Nawaf answered. Atta said to bring them along, as well as a bank statement.

Nawaf left and Atta went off to find an internet café.[704] It was early morning in Pakistan where he had made arrangements to chat with *Mukhtar*.

"I should have been more engaged with the two from when they arrived," Atta wrote in their chat session, taking responsibility.

"It is not your doing, my friend. I never liked this supposed fisherman. And I have always had my doubts in his partner." *Mukhtar* was delighted that Osama bin Laden's handpicked boy turned out just as he predicted.[705]

"I never concluded that either of the two of them would end up being pilots," *Mukhtar* continued. "I'm sorry if I didn't make that even clearer to you when we were together. And I am sorry to waste your time now."

"How much do you think Mihdhar really knows?" Atta asked.

"I don't know how much he was told when he was in his training in Afghanistan, but he does not know about your other assistants—how many, or what you are doing. And he certainly knows nothing about the houses we will be visiting or the timing of the wedding."

"And what is your opinion of this new man?" Atta asked, changing the subject. He was asking about Hani Hanjour, the fourth pilot, the new Saudi.

"I have some doubts, and he is not from a family of brothers like you. But he is qualified and seems, though I hesitate to say so until he comes to you, more reliable than his fellow countrymen."

Mukhtar told Atta that when he met Hanjour, like so many other Saudis, he found him unimpressive—a sense of superiority and poor work ethic that sprang from the Saudi way. He was worried, he told Atta, that this middle-class malaise dulled initiative and independent thinking.

And so they discussed what their options would be, with him and without him.

Mukhtar proposed that Hanjour go to California, pick up Nawaf in San Diego and then settle in Mesa, Arizona. Arizona would cut corners because Hanjour had lived there before. And, he said, if he then failed in flight training or if they were compromised, both questionable people would be on one team. If all went to plan, *Mukhtar* said, and Hanjour was successful, he thought he could be ready by June, re-certified and with enough hours to be confident of his flying.[706]

"It is your decision, though," he tapped out to Atta on the chat link. "I say to you: Meet the man and decide for yourself. Be careful also of what you say about the overall plan."

If the Saudi pilot worked out, that was great, wrote *Mukhtar*. But if not, he and the other, whom he called the simpleton, would be let go.

The only loose end then was Khalid Mihdhar, the fisherman. *Mukhtar* was incensed when he left, he told Atta. However, now he observed that despite his not being clean—that is, that he had an *al Qaeda* background—evidently he wasn't detected when he flew out of the country. Cousin Ali reported from the Emirates that Mihdhar arrived without incident, flying from Frankfurt to Kuwait and then from Kuwait to the Emirates, checking in and then following that with a flight to Oman. Now they had additional word that Mihdhar had indeed entered Yemen, having gone overland.[707]

"And the wedding there?" Atta asked. They used code even in secure communications just to further increase their discipline. He was referring to a coming attack in Yemen, one that *Mukhtar* alerted Atta would happen by the end of the year.

"The hall is all set," *Mukhtar* answered. "Everything depends on when the family arrives"—that is, when an American ship again showed up in Aden harbor.

"And the fisherman? He won't stand out once the wedding comes?" Atta asked. "That won't cause us troubles?"

"I don't know. Many things about the fisherman make no sense," *Mukhtar* answered. He knew that an attack in Yemen would increase scrutiny of *al Qaeda*-affiliated people in the country, and that the Americans would quickly flood Yemeni authorities with names. So, even though Mihdhar wasn't involved, *Mukhtar* feared he might be swept up in the aftermath. He was trying to get him back to Pakistan, or even to Saudi Arabia, before the attack. But he was finding, because the fisherman was bin Laden's boy, it was mostly out of his hands.

Mukhtar received Atta's report on the progress of their flight training. All three were moving ahead, acquiring the hours to have them ready by early summer.

"My best to your brothers and good health to your beloved," KSM wrote before signing off, respectful and without a hint of irony.

That made Atta smile. A rare smile.

Chapter 42 Grand Teuton

Richard B. Cheney, who went by Dick at even the most formal occasions, grew up in Caspar, Wyoming, loafing around before settling into adulthood and politics, serving in the Nixon administration under Donald Rumsfeld and later as White House Chief of Staff under President Ford. Then he represented the citizens of Wyoming for a decade as their lone congressman.[708]

In his White House days, he'd earned the nickname *Grand Teuton*, a tribute to his beloved Rocky Mountains and his unquestioned Teutonic clout.[709]

When George Herbert Walker Bush became president, though Cheney had no national security expertise, he was offered the job of Secretary of Defense. When Iraq invaded Kuwait a year and a half later, he was the official responsible for sealing the deal with King Fahd to allow American military forces to deploy to Saudi Arabia. And thereafter, Cheney remained the primary interlocutor with the Saudi royal family.

After Bush's surprise defeat by Arkansas Governor Bill Clinton just a year after winning a war against Iraq, Cheney became chairman of the board and CEO of Halliburton Company, the planet's largest provider of services and products to the world of oil and energy. There he tirelessly worked behind the scenes to ensure stability for America's Arab allies. And he took advantage of the fall of the Soviet Union to capture more oil from the newly-liberated 'stans of its Asian south tier.

Despite many high offices, Cheney's specialty was staying behind the scenes. When others like Norman Schwarzkopf and Colin Powell succumbed to the emerging world of 24/7 cable news, spellbound in narcissistic preoccupation to build their own brands, Cheney eschewed the public eye.

On July 25, 2000, the *Grand Teuton* accepted Bush junior's invitation to be his vice-presidential running mate.[710] He would be the adult to junior's adolescence, now also the national security maven to the Texas governor's ignorance and innocence.

Bowlen told Steve that Cheney's breadth of experience and his contacts at the highest levels throughout the Middle East placed him in a unique position to understand not just the geopolitical moment, but to assess the wisdom of what they were doing.

"We're not going to brief candidate Gore?"[711] Steve asked, after Bowlen told him to prepare a presentation for Bush's prospective number two.

"Don't think of this as meeting with a candidate," Bowlen answered. "Though it's true that if the Republicans win, Cheney will be one of our bosses, I see this more as a reality check. The secretary is already read into Apex Watch. And he's financially clean. And I've dealt with Cheney quite a bit over the years. I think it's wise to seek his counsel, and I expect that he will be willing to speak up if he senses that what you're proposing is contrary to American interests."

"What I'm proposing?" Steve pushed back. "It's what *we're* proposing. And it's hardly a proposal. It's already happening. Are you intentionally removing your fingerprints?"

"I'm not, Steven."

"It sure sounds like you are."

"I'm not," Bowlen reiterated. "Frankly, this isn't even covering my ass. But it would be useful to share the plan, and our justification, with someone who is aware of Apex Watch and savvy about the Middle East. I can't think of anyone more qualified, and not coincidentally, more unemotional than Cheney."

Steve wasn't completely mollified. "So, how much does he already know?"

"I have discussed the outlines with former President Bush. He suggested that I speak to Cheney. But other than setting up this meeting, I've conveyed nothing to him yet."

"Does *he* know anything about Project Sumner specifically?" Steve asked, referring to the name of their own plane's operation.

"I've only briefed the broadest outlines to former President Bush."

"When?"

"Steven, you don't control everything."

"And that won't compromise the operation?"

"Are you kidding? Are you more concerned that a former president and a former secretary of defense can't keep a secret than you are that Khalid and his associates can?"

He had a point.

"Still, I caution you in making this presentation: you have to leave the secretary with some degree of plausible deniability," Bowlen said. It was one of those national security concepts where a high-level official—most often the president—is insulated from the details of covert operations in order to be able to say later, if something goes wrong, that they didn't know.

"So how much are we telling him?" Steve asked.

"I suggest you tell him what we are planning, perhaps stressing the predicament we face at Apex Watch—in addition to that which the country faces. Tell him that we discovered this plot already underway and are now playing catch up."

"Ah, so that's our plausible deniability?"

"No," Bowlen responded. "I don't mean it to be. If the secretary pushes back and asks for detail, give it to him. But I would guess he's not going to verbally commit himself one way or another, not in this meeting. My sense is that we will only be able to gauge his body language—that is, if he doesn't blow up."

Bowlen and Steve, representing Exceptional Research Technologies—"comprehensive information products, solutions, and services" their business cards said—thus arrived at Dick Cheney's Teton Pines home near the base of Jackson Hole Mountain Resort. At the front gate, they had their names checked off a list.[712]

Corporate people, campaign aides and Republican Party apparatchiks had begun a steady stream of meetings with the now-vice presidential candidate. The Secret Service, when they checked the names provided by the two, would find no derogatory information. If a call was made to the 202 number, it would ring at the duty officer in Maryland and to the backstopped identities and cover stories Apex Watch had set up for each of its people.

They had been going over the details—and this presentation—for almost six months. The most important goal, Bowlen said, was to impress upon Cheney that the new administration's focus on finishing the job in Iraq would be a disaster. They had to convince Cheney that another war against Saddam Hussein would not only end in a decades-long quagmire but have perilous reverberating effects throughout the region.

Prove it, Bowlen said to Steve. *Make the argument to someone on the outside.*

Bowlen would set the scene and Steve would then brief the actual operation. They carried out a number of dry runs of the presentation back in Maryland, going through each of the counterarguments should they get pushback.

Ushered into Cheney's high-beamed library, the former congressman, secretary of defense, and White House chief of staff couldn't have been more gracious. He wasn't a warm guy, but *he* was a politician and he immediately asked about Bowlen's work while revealing nothing of what he already knew. He asked Steve about his career path and where he was from. A steward offered refreshments. And then when they were alone, Cheney sat comfortably in a big leather chair, his back to a gigantic stone fireplace, ready to hear them out.

Bowlen opened, setting the scene. Osama bin Laden and *al Qaeda* were gaining strength beyond their sanctuary in Afghanistan, extending networks into Europe and Asia. A *Shi'a* movement—in Iraq, in Bahrain, and even in the eastern provinces of Saudi Arabia—supported by the most radical factions in Tehran, was also building strength. The two together had the potential to threaten the ruling *Sunni* classes and the House of Saud, to topple the powers that be throughout the region.

Bowlen went over the Riyadh and Khobar Towers attacks in Saudi Arabia, and the surprising fact—to Cheney—that bin Laden was behind them. He then talked of the Bin Ladens speaking up, of the rare circumstance of public discord, a development Cheney also had obviously never heard of, at least judging from his reaction. Bowlen then framed the African embassy attacks not as an aberration but as evidence of radical Islam's increasing reach, of *al Qaeda* now encroaching into Africa south of the Sahara, a Cold War mouthful that fit with Cheney's experiences.

Steve was impressed with Bowlen's absolute neutrality. When he talked about Iran building up its military and offensive strength, largely unmolested because of the hindering focus on Iraq, he was at the same time agnostic as to whether the country was any sort of threat.

If things continued on their present course, Bowlen went on, they assessed that bin Laden could bring down the current order in the Middle East—or certainly inspire others to try to do so. The place was ripe for a spark, one that threatened all of the regimes, monarchies as well.

A Cheney eyebrow went up when Bowlen said that.

It was tough talk. Bowlen laid out their analysis of what they had gamed: Iraq would continue to dominate American policy no matter who was elected president. Meanwhile, skepticism about terrorism as a strategic challenge, and a lack of regard for *al Qaeda*, fed the continued growth of ever more zealous and threatening elements—both *Shi'a* enlargement and Osama bin Laden's *Sunni* alternative.

"George Tenet is already busy preparing a report on Iraqi weapons of mass destruction," Bowlen went on, a report that he said appealed to the Cold War mindset of the Bush camp. "Those privy to the evidence are calling it a 'slam dunk,' enough loose threads in what they've hidden from U.N. inspectors that will force the next administration to act, no matter who is elected."[713]

Then Bowlen said it: "We have concluded that an Iraq war and the subsequent implosion of the solid center that holds all of this region together has to be averted. You saw how panicked Riyadh was about the possibility of taking him down at the end of Desert Storm. In the intervening years, the Kurds have gained autonomy that can only further put pressure on Syria, Turkey and Iran. And the *Shi'a* have gained unprecedented strength in southern Iraq, ironically protected by the American no fly zone.[714] Links are now being made, courtesy of Iran, between the *Shi'a* from Tehran all the way to the Mediterranean Sea."

Bowlen then turned it over to Steve who he said would describe Project Sumner: a clandestine effort to create a galvanizing event to stave off another Iraq war, and one that would provoke a worldwide war against Osama bin Laden and Islamic extremism.

Neither a new Republican nor a Democratic administration were ready for the world as it really was, Steve opened. What was needed was not only a sea change event, but also a shift in the projection of American power.

As bin Laden and those who followed him saw it, the *jihadi* victory over the Soviet Union in Afghanistan, even against the communist dictators, came because of an inability on the part of the West, and particularly on the part of the United States, to tolerate casualties. That view of moral weakness was part of bin Laden's conviction to act against America, a weakness that he saw amplified again and again in the last decade, in the American withdrawal from Somalia, in Saddam's successful standoff against American military might, in the hesitant way the U.S. used military power in the former Yugoslavia, even in the half-hearted ways Washington pursued *al Qaeda* itself.[715] Depraved and self-indulgent America could mete out casualties at a distance with airpower and cruise missiles, bin Laden thought, but it didn't have the stomach to get down on the ground and spill its own blood in battle. "Last year," Steve said, "bin Laden even told a Palestinian newspaper, quote, 'We think our battle with the Americans will be easy, and we are now more determined to carry it on until we see the face of God.'"[716]

Cheney still had not said a word.

"I don't disagree with his assessment," Steve said.

"And just to be clear," Bowlen interjected. "What was the retaliation in response to the African bombing? A missile barrage that hit an aspirin plant in Khartoum and a bunch of largely deserted camps in Afghanistan? In the mind of *al Qaeda*, it was not only weak, but they had anticipated the attack, losing no one of importance."

Steve went on to say that the work in conceiving of a Project Sumner began before the embassy attacks, but it couldn't have more precisely anticipated the befuddlement and self-deceptions of the intelligence community in *not* providing detection or warning of those attacks. And now that there had been direct attacks against America, Steve said, the intelligence community seemed satisfied with their own false declaration of war, while supporting retaliation after the inevitable.

"A declaration of war?" Cheney spoke up for the first time.

Steve described Tenet's December 1998 memo declaring America was at war with *al Qaeda,* and the belief on the part of Clinton White House that they were not only on the offensive against *al Qaeda,* but also that they—Tenet and the desk-bound others in Washington—were the actual warriors carrying out this new assault.

Cheney cleared his throat loudly.

Meanwhile, Steve said, the Pentagon was agnostic about, and even passive-aggressively against, expending more military resources on terrorism, a problem that they saw as a diversion from both vital American interests and core missions.

The two thought a harrumph might have been uttered in response, but even if it was, it was so muted they couldn't later agree whether it occurred.

Steve described the central element of their plan. "We have obtained very sensitive intelligence that *al Qaeda* is planning a massive attack in the United States. We believe operatives are already inside the country, undetected by either the CIA or the FBI."

Dick Cheney's curled-lip expression can often be interpreted as a malevolent sneer, but Steve thought he saw a softening of his facial muscles and a relaxation of his body.

"We believe this attack will again go after the north tower of the World Trade Center in New York City, the same tower previously attacked."

"How widely is this known?" Cheney asked. "The upcoming attack?"

"Outside of our organization and outside of a small cell within *al Qaeda,* we think it has not been detected," Steve answered. Bowlen didn't say anything, not wanting to interrupt Cheney if he wanted to know more. But he was also on edge. In a departure from their rehearsals, Steve never mentioned KSM, and he wondered if he was planning to do so.

"And who knows about Sumner, this Project Sumner?" Cheney asked, looking at Bowlen, the question obvious.

"Externally? Just you and President Bush for now, sir," Bowlen answered.

"Not Vice President Gore?"

"No, sir," Bowlen answered.

Steve then laid out a complex, multifaceted choreography of what they were doing to prepare for the attack, to shape the response in such a way as to unleash a general war against *al Qaeda*, the Taliban, and their Saudi sponsors.

Cheney sat in stony silence, taking it all in.

Again Bowlen noted that Steve said nothing of the plan to stop the attack at the eleventh hour, and he felt that perhaps his young deputy was rewriting the script intentionally, not because Cheney didn't need the detail, but because this indeed *was Steve's plan*—to let KSM carry out the strike.

Steve then talked about the deception plan, one that would not only erase any foreknowledge of the plot, but also sow seeds of doubt regarding the hijacker's capabilities to even pull it off. False information would be created to manipulate the "official story" and absolve the Bush administration while also putting the spotlight on Saudi Arabia for providing financial and material support. As Steve described it, Project Sumner would seek to create a series of loose ends in the records to muddy the waters of any later investigation into their existence.

Steve then went on to say—again, quite to the surprise of Bowlen, given that he was also speaking to a former secretary of *defense*—that though the country would be at war after the attack, it would certainly no longer be Bill Clinton's feckless war. He said that they closely assessed the makeup of a new Bush administration. As vice president, Cheney would be the strongest presence dominating meetings of the National Security Council against a weak, consensus-building Condoleezza Rice,[717] who was likely to be the national security advisor.[718] The Pentagon would be reinvigorated; the CIA unshackled from political constraint. Perhaps 5,000 Americans would die, Steve threw in matter-of-factly, but the resulting conflagration would secure oil resources, weaken Islam to the point of breaking, and restore America as the indisputable superpower.

Bowlen hesitated to add anything, not sure whether he was livid or admiring of Steve's insubordination and matter-of-factness in delivering the news of a coming war.

When Cheney finally spoke, it was patent Cheney: terse, decisive, and clear.

"I don't want to hear about this ever again," he said, thanking them for their hard work and for coming. And he wished them Godspeed.

He gave them the name and telephone number of a trusted confidant to contact in the future, should there be an actual emergency. As he was showing them to the door, he had one thing to say: "No paper trail."

PART 11

Chapter 43 Ship of Fools

"Jesus," Steve exclaimed, "What the fuck is an American ship even doing there? Making port calls in Yemen?"

Word came in late on the evening on October 12th, two weeks before the election. A Navy destroyer had been attacked while docked in Aden Harbor.

A small skiff carrying explosives approached the USS *Cole* while it was taking on fuel, killing more than a dozen sailors and injuring scores of others. The suicide boat pulled alongside the warship, its two-man crew waving to several American sailors on deck. As they pulled closer, they detonated their explosives, ripping a hole in the side of the ship some 40 feet in diameter.

One of Barbara's analysts said that the Pentagon was lamely saying that the presence of the *Cole* was part of "a new initiative by the military to improve—"

"Fuck. To improve what?" Steve interrupted. "To get Yemen on our side?" he said loudly, already lost in his thoughts.

Almost immediately, vice presidential candidate Cheney spoke out, saying on CNN that there needed to be swift retaliation. "Any would-be terrorist out there needs to know that if you're going to attack, you'll be hit very hard and very quick. It's not time for diplomacy and debate. It's time for action."[719]

"The key now is to find out who did it and then make certain that a penalty is imposed," Cheney intoned on *Larry King Live*. "No one should be able to launch that kind of terrorist attack against the United States with impunity … We need to be very tough and very aggressive in our response … I say that we find the guilty party and take appropriate action."[720]

KSM told them that there would be an attack on the American military. And, again, U.S. intelligence—and Steve—detected absolutely nothing ahead of time.

"I've always wanted to go there," Charlie remarked as they stared at the first pictures coming in of the scene.

Photographs of the world's earliest high-rise buildings in Yemen's capital city, Sana'a, captivated her, as did the country, with its tribal ties and traditions enduring from as far back as the 8th century. Tucked in a little-known corner of the world, Yemen was as close to old country as could be imagined, wedged between Saudi Arabia and Oman, the latter family-ruled and practically still a British colony.[721]

"We need to talk to KSM," Steve said.

"Yeah *we* should," Charlie said, stressing both of them.

Steve frowned, making it clear he wasn't going anywhere.

"I'm guessing I'll only get so far on this," Charlie pleaded. "He's absolutely obsessed with *the professor*, trying to figure out your identity. Why don't you come?"

"I can't," Steve pushed back. "I just have too much work."

"Don't you think we could learn more from KSM than from anything U.S. intelligence is about to collect?" Charlie asked.

"Maybe," Steve said. He was being his usual elusive self. He was feeling a tug, a need for a certain release. And going to Pakistan and spending the next three days with Charlie wasn't going to provide it.

She left for Pakistan with a sour taste in her mouth, not for the first time wondering if Steve was telling her everything. And she found herself almost hoping that some new, undiscovered backbone in the White House—Republican backbone—might alter their future plans.

Again, at the Sheraton in Karachi, KSM was effusive and talkative. Charlie had to apply all her skills to keep her agent focused.

"The *Sheikh* left Kandahar the night of the attack, predicting your missiles," he told Charlie, puzzled about the delay in a retaliation for the attack on an American warship. "Dr. Zawahiri and Abu Hafs are still hiding separately, protecting the leadership from being killed in any single strike.[722] Even boys in training have been moved from buildings to protect them. And still nothing?

"Saleh," he went on, referring to the Yemeni president and long-time strong man Ali Abdallah Saleh,[723] who was also the Pentagon's new best friend, "is saying he doesn't even believe it was a terrorist attack." KSM was taunting Charlie now. "He's saying there was an accidental explosion aboard the boat that the Americans are blaming on *al Qaeda*. Or he is offering that it was Israeli *Mossad*."[724]

"Cut the crap, Khalid," she sharply responded. "And as for why there's been no retaliation? My understanding is that the CIA is still looking for proof." She had no interest in sharing with KSM that she thought there'd been no retaliation because of an ineffectual and hobbled Clinton.

"Proof that it is *al Qaeda*? Who else would it be?"

"Were it only so easy that others in the government saw things quite so clearly," she answered wearily.

"It is *al Qaeda*; this I can say. And the *Sheikh* is celebrating. Once again, new recruits are on their way to Afghanistan, begging to be martyrs. Suitcases filled with money are arriving from your so-called friends in the Gulf states. Even the Taliban snakes in Kandahar now see the value of bin Laden—the *Mullahs* will get their share of the riches as well."[725]

"Have you been involved in this?"

"My dear, Miss, can I be in all places all the time? I told you this would happen. Now more American missiles will come. And then more *jihadis* will join bin Laden. And if your country does nothing because it has no *proof*, as you say? Well, then even more boys will join because of your cowardice. And let me say this: It is not just the angry and the brave who come. Now also the uncertain want to join; now that they see that America has shown itself to be so weak. To be cowards. Even in an attack on the American military directly? Nothing? Even the scholars who cry over the death of civilians will be happy."

"Khalid!"

"It is coming, Miss. I told you. I don't want to take any credit, perhaps communicating too much my importance to you. I am just one servant in an army that neither of us can stop."

"I have a list of names …"

"From the professor?" KSM carelessly squeaked. "Very good."

"Abu Jandal," she started, deepening her bad mood.[726]

A Saudi. KSM knew him from bin Laden's circle.

"I know of him."

"He is in Yemeni custody."

"Well … then you don't need to ask me," KSM responded.

"Abd al-Rahim al-Nashiri.[727] The CIA thinks he is the brains."[728]

"Of course, they would. And you think?"

"Al-Nashiri," she repeated, not exposing her hand.

"The Prince of the Sea," KSM said. "He is first cousin to one of the suicide drivers in Nairobi."[729]

He continued: "But he has also not pledged *bayat* to the *Sheikh* and he is not focused on American targets."

He thought a moment and then he went on: "But they say he is so determined to wage *jihad* that he would attack inside the *Ka'aba* itself if he believed there was a need to do so."[730]

"It's good to know you have higher standards," she responded. "We think he was the local manager in Aden."

"The professor thinks this why?"

"Stop with the fucking *professor*! You are talking to me." She continued: "He is Yemeni. And the direction and information came from elsewhere."

"I have much respect for our Yemeni brothers," KSM said. "Al Nashiri knows those waters. I will tell you this, Miss. It is the second attempt. Another ship visited earlier but they were not able to get the explosive there in time.[731] They have been very patient."

A second ship. Jesus, she thought.

"Ahmed al-Hada," she continued.

"Is he a special treat offered by the professor?"

"*Khalid!*"

"I don't have information on him," KSM lied. It didn't really matter what he would say. He thought that the professor was sending him a signal.

"He runs the *al Qaeda* switchboard in the country," she continued.

"Switchboard, Miss?"

"He is the communications hub between East Africa and the lower Peninsula and *al Qaeda*."

And he was father-in-law of the fisherman, KSM knew. If al-Hada were arrested and interrogated by Yemeni security forces, he might lead authorities to this bin Laden favorite. An arrest of Khalid Mihdhar would be good except that it could also lead to his plane's operation.

"We have been listening in on that number since right after the embassy bombings,"[732] Charlie continued.

"And you think us so unsophisticated that we would continue to use this compromised number?" said KSM "The professor's information is outdated, Miss."

"It was compromised by your Nairobi man when he was detained in Pakistan. And he continues to talk."[733]

"What man?"

"Mohamed al-Owhali."[734]

"That simpleton knows nothing."

"He has identified someone named Khallad involved in the embassy bombings."[735]

"Another cup of tea?" KSM asked, signaling the waiter. They were in the opulent lounge, looking out on a beautifully landscaped garden.

"Khalid who?" KSM asked, feigning little interest. After picking up information from Yemeni government sources that American ships were starting to visit Yemen, Khallad recommended the operation and he facilitated moving the funding to the Yemen boys.

"I said Khallad."

"There is no one I know of by that name who is in Yemen."

"You are lying."

"Excuse me, Miss?"

"You asked Mr. Jones to destroy the records of a man named Khallad."

"I said there was no one by that name located in Yemen."

"Yemeni intelligence is reporting that a participant named Fahd al Quso has been arrested. He says he received $7,000 from someone he only knew as Ibrahim and was asked to deliver the money to a man named Khallad.[736] The same man, Khallad, has telephoned the house of al-Hada."

"Popular man, this Hada. I should get to know him."

"You fucking killed 17 Americans."

"Seventeen American soldiers died in battle, Miss. They were soldiers."

"It will make things much more difficult for everyone. For you."

"More difficult? I doubt it. Even in Yemen, we now see that American defenses are pathetic. Did anyone on that boat even know that that country is bin Laden's country? Does anyone at the Pentagon know where Yemen is?"

He had a point. After the attack on the *Cole*, the news media was filled with a jumble of names and an avalanche of recriminations over the port call. The Pentagon, and its command responsible for the Middle East, found itself on the defensive, not just for the lapse in security that day by a warship in a hostile port, but also for what turned out to be its poorly-advised, freelance diplomatic initiative that sent the *Cole* to Yemen in the first place. Stranger still, since the African embassy bombings, that entire part of the world had been declared *high risk* (and even more, was *obviously* high risk), and yet the ship made a friendly and unprotected port call there anyway, not even protecting the perimeter of the vessel.[737]

Charlie knew that, even in classified circles, the same questions were being raised.

"So many names." KSM finally broke the ice, wiping his hands on the white napkin as if signaling he was done. "Tell the professor he has nothing to worry about."

"In terms of what?" Charlie asked.

"Our plans are all good. Tell him that."

"Your plans are with me," Charlie barked back.

"Yes, yes," KSM said. "But tell the professor our plans are good."

"Khallad?" she asked one more time before they broke up, knowing she'd get no answer, but also knowing from Bowlen that Khallad was someone who was close to KSM. "It's Khallad, not Khalid, or you," Charlie said. "He's a different person. I presume a Yemeni."

"Well then, Miss Landry, you have answered your own question."

"What a clusterfuck," Steve growled when she returned, giving her the lowdown on the deliberations about military retaliation. "I don't know where to start: Clinton, Tenet, Freeh. I understand that the administration doesn't want to conduct any kind of military strike because it's so close to the election, but by the way everyone is acting, you'd think they want to sweep it under the rug or stab each other in the back."[738]

Steve added, "I'm hearing that when the principals met, the Agency totally wimped out, Mr. Slam Dunk saying that the evidence wasn't good enough to prove bin Laden was behind the attack."[739]

"But there's no question he was," Charlie said. "It was *al Qaeda*, and our man. He won't say it directly, but …"

Steve interrupted, "All the connections have been pretty much confirmed: calls from Bin Laden's satellite phone were made to the Yemen number the day of and the day after the *Cole* attack."[740]

"Bin Laden was so convinced that military retaliation would come, KSM says, he evacuated compounds and camps in Afghanistan," Charlie said.[741]

Steve talked over her, "The only good news is that Bowlen told me that Sandy Berger let loose on Mr. Slam Dunk, screaming at him that he couldn't believe that he could be so fucking incompetent, asking him where the fucking war was that he declared. Tenet was so rattled, or so the story goes, that he stomped out of the meeting and slammed the door.[742]

"They're winding down," Steve added. "And they couldn't give a shit about Yemen. Because when Tenet walked out of Berger's meeting, he packed his bags and got on Air Force One, sitting next to the president. While casualties were still being fished out of the muck, they were off to Sharm el-Sheikh for yet another eleventh hour Arab-Israeli peace negotiation.[743] That fucking Tenet, always the number one presidential whisperer."

Having ingratiated himself with the White House, the CIA director was also now the top Middle East analyst and the top Palestinian case officer all rolled into one.

"And believe me," Steve added, "Madeleine Albright couldn't wait to get out of Washington either, making believe as she ran for the exit that Yemen didn't even exist. She also flew with the president. And then she was off to Riyadh to meet with King Fahd. I've seen memos of those meetings. She never pressed for intelligence on Yemen or asked for any help with counterterrorism. She instead implored those fuckers to give some help with the peace process.[744]

"I don't blame the president for not retaliating," Steve said, closing his own door on the Clinton era.

"Really?"

"I'm not arguing he shouldn't have. But they've played that hand already. Without a bigger strategy, why bother?"

"I guess you're right about one thing," Charlie said.

"What's that?"

"There isn't any real intelligence we can give them without compromising KSM."

She was jet lagged and exhausted by the quick turn around and said she wanted to go home.

Steve told her he had a ton of work to do.

Chapter 44 Keren

"I'm sorry," she said to the waiter, "I didn't order this."

The young server pointed at the man sitting adjacent to her. "He did."

Steve sat on the long bench, reading, his back to the exposed brick wall, remnants of a meal in front of him. He had a roundish face, short hair and a trim beard, glasses. He was holding a fine-point red pen, for underlining. Unlike most in Washington, he wasn't a suit and tie kind of guy. He wore a t-shirt under a black fleece jacket.

"Excuse me," she said.

He looked up. The instant Charlie left on her trip, a well of loneliness swallowed him. He didn't even realize he was on the prowl.

"This from you?" she asked.

"You looked upset."

"Like that's your business?"

"Well, I saw you checking your watch and fidgeting. I thought you could use some tea."

In front of her, crowding the small table was a plump white pot and an assortment of teas, an empty cup and saucer, a tiny pitcher of milk, and a wicker basket with various kinds of sugar.

"Any creep can send over a drink," he said, smiling.

"Doesn't saying 'creep' sort of, like, defeat the purpose?"

"You be the judge. I'm just coming to the aid of a damsel in distress."

"That's what I am?"

"That's what I see."

"Blech," she uttered, sighing into herself.

She stirred the tea, then shrugged. "A cup of tea actually makes some sense. Thanks."

She was maybe 25, with a freckled oval face and a head of dark curly hair, dark eyebrows and a taut neck and soft chin—fresh, more stylishly dressed than the usual Washington dress code called for.

"I've never seen you here before," he said, making conversation.

"What? You own the place?" she replied.

"I know the owner. And I come here. When I remember to take care of myself."

"That's a problem?" she inquired.

"Standard nerd profile," he responded. "I work too hard."

"So, like, announcing yourself as a nerd? Is that like another one of your tricks?"

"In this town? It's a veritable aphrodisiac."

She laughed.

"So, he's not coming?" Steve said, breaking the silence again.

"You think you know there's a 'he' as well?"

"You've been checking your phone and there's been tears wiped away ... small ones. I just figured."

She paused, deciding what to say. "Tied up, he says. Again."

"Married?"

"Me? God no."

"No, I meant him."

She looked over, mid-pour from the pot. "Boy, you don't hold back, do you?"

He shrugged. "No big deal. Story as old as time. Beautiful young associate ..."

"Intern."

"Beautiful young intern. He can't get away from the office, can't get away from the wife. He can't get away from reality. Meet at a hip place in Adams Morgan where the influential don't, and wouldn't, frequent."

"What are you, like, FBI or something?" she asked, half serious.

"Me? No," he said, chuckling. "If I were FBI, I couldn't be quite so smart. And I probably wouldn't be talking to you. I'd be lurking outside with a camera and a donut, listening in, trying to catch you for tax evasion or perjury."

"Okay, Mr. *Not* FBI. I picked the place because I live nearby."

"No other reason?"

"Maybe," she drew it out, and smiled. "I'm new in town. I've seen this place while running and wanted to try it."

"You gotta admit, though, it is a good place where fellow lobbyists wouldn't see you."

"Now I'm a lobbyist?"

"Something like that," he said, "or you work on the Hill."

"You are FBI! What gave it away?" she said, exhaling deeply.

"Just a guess."

"So, Mr. Not FBI," she asked. "Really. Like, why are *you* here? And why are you creeping on me?"

"I'm not creeping. And I'm happy to go back to my book. As I said, I'm here to eat a decent meal. My refrigerator's empty—not worth stocking because shit just goes bad. And I live nearby as well."

"We're like serendipitous neighbors."

"Love that word," he said.

A little bit more silence.

"Work all the time?" she asked.

"Pretty much."

There was a pause. *Was there anything else to say? God he didn't want to talk about Capitol Hill. Or Washington.*

"You married?" she asked.

"Looking to get married?"

"I'm just asking since it seems to be a thing here."

"*A thing*, like asking if I'm married?"

"Asking slightly inappropriate personal questions is definitely on the menu," she said, tilting her head.

"I'm not married," he said, chuckling, holding his left hand in the air, showing an empty finger.

"Like the absence of a ring is proof?"

"Not trying to prove anything," he curtly answered, screwing up his face as if a sour smell just arrived.

"Look. I'm not coming on to you," he announced. "You seemed upset and I thought you could use some tea. I'm happy to go back to my book."

And he did.

And there was silence.

"So, like, what are you reading?" she asked.

"Sayyid Qutb," he said, showing her the paperback book cover.

"And what's that?"

"It's a *who's* that," he answered. "Egyptian intellectual who came here after the Second World War and observed American society."

"So, it's not Dan Brown" she said, referring to the author whose book *Angels & Demons* was all the rage that winter.

They laughed.

"Is it interesting?"

"Very."

"So, what did he think of America?"

"He hated it. But then, he was an Arab man in rural America in the 1950s. And he was a devout Muslim. And he was a socialist. And he was probably a virgin to boot. Definitely a prude."

She raised a big eyebrow.

He continued, "What I find most interesting about him is that he observed even then that America was falling apart. He wrote that America would eventually eat at itself from its own insides, animal instincts and fetishistic worship of freedom weakening its will to defend its way of life—its way of life, at least to Qutb, being without a will to defend itself."

"Whoa," she said of his transition from small talk to treatise. "You agree with that?"

"It's worth pondering."

"And by fetishistic worship of freedom? He meant what?"

"As he saw it, the freedom to do anything." And then Steve said, seeming to close off the subject from further discussion, "But hey, if you're planning to stay in this place—Washington, that is—don't read shit like Qutb."

"Why's that?"

"Because curiosity beyond whatever is today's fixation is pretty low. And even a liability."

"Thanks for the advice. That's a pretty depressing way to start out."

"Start out?"

"Start out a conversation."

"You asked what I was reading."

"Yeah," she said, pointing to the book, "so it's, like, work-related?"

"Yep," he answered.

She continued, "So what do you do?"

The question posed—*what do you do?*—is slang for *who do you know* and by extension, how big is your Rolodex and how glowing is your speed-dial. Who do you pass your information along to. That was the question in the capital city.

And vis-à-vis the question of reading, Washington was about who knows what. Not scholastic what. Not deep thought. Day-to-day Washington was about who knows the hottest and the quickest.

And though the high-minded might come to town with the belief that the information they would deal with was about governing, the most prized was just gossip. The more salacious and off-color the better: the lives of others, who's up and who's down, the infidelities and double-dealings of figures public and private.

"I work on terrorism," he answered her question, saying little.

"Woo," she said, flipping her hair back. "You're a spook."

"I work in the national security field," he divulged. "Nothing big." He signaled the waiter for the check and, in a universal hand gesture of inclusiveness, that he would pay for hers as well.

"Steve," he said finally, introducing himself.

"Keren."

"Pretty."

"It means ray of light. She was one of Job's daughters."

"I always wanted a biblical name," he said, "but I was born during the time of high assimilation in America, where Jewish parents were naming their kids things like Robin and Barbara, and even Steven, an Orthodox Catholic Greek saint."

"So, you're Jewish?"

"I am. But so what?" he answered testily.

"You're reading some Muslim scholar, you're a specialist in terrorism. Working in national security," she said with air quotes and bobbing her head. "Maybe you're one of those neocon, self-hating, Washington Jews."

She just might be interesting.

"I'm not self-hating," he answered to emphasize that he wasn't being flip. "Well, not in that way. I'm just turned off by the assumption of allegiance to Israel just because my religion is Judaism."

She was listening, also affecting her own facial expression of seriousness.

"You a Zionist?" he inquired.

"I have been to Israel," she said.

"Yeah but, hey, you also know what I mean."

"I hadn't really thought about it," she said.

"I find that hard to believe," he responded.

"No, really. Until I, like, came to Washington, I was Jewish and had been to Israel. Now? It's like a political thing. Like Israel is a black hole. I don't mean that to sound negative, I mean it like in the physics sense, that it exerts a gravitational pull on everything…"

Silence.

"So where are you from, ray of light?" he asked.

"California. Modesto."

"Where's that?"

"Stanislaus County. Far east of San Francisco."

"And what are you doing in our fair city?"

"I'm in the middle of a master's program at USC, interning with a congressman on the Hill."

"Enjoying it?"

"The job is starting to be interesting. My guy is on the intelligence committee. My security clearance just came through."

"Well, hopefully you'll sort the place out." He started to pay and made moves to gather up his stuff.

"You really don't need to do that," she said, referring to his picking up her check.

"Happy to. Don't worry. I don't expect you to put out. I'm going to brave the cold and head home."

"Yeah," Keren said, looking at her watch. "I guess I, like, should probably go, too."

"I'll walk with you," he said, standing up and putting his book in his bag, pulling on his jacket and a pair of black leather gloves, waiting for her to put on her coat.

Now facing her, he could see that she was very pretty, buxom and slim, her nose thin, her skin smooth and naturally aglow. They were about the same height. She was definitely his type.

As they moved away from the wall of little tables, he walked over to the bar and took off his glove and tapped on the corner, catching the attention of and waving goodbye to someone. Moving ahead of her, he opened the door, a blast of cold air hitting them.

They walked down 18th Street, continuing their conversation. She asked about where he was from and pressed more about where he worked. He knew he wanted to see her again. But Steve decided that the best approach was indifference. For now. She might be useful later.

At the corner of Wyoming Avenue, he hesitated and looked to his right up the hill. "Well, this is me," he said, tipping his head up the street.

"I'm further down near to the Circle," said Keren. "Just a couple of blocks."

"You okay walking on your own?"

"Thanks for asking. I am."

"Well," he said, again removing a glove and extending his hand to shake hers. "A pot of tea well worth it. Pleased to meet you."

Keren extended her ungloved hand and shook his. "Me, too."

"When you decide to dump that married good-for-nothing, give me a call. Here's where to find me." He extended a business card.

"Thanks." She laughed. "I just might do that. And good luck with your reading."

On it was his name and phone number and a company name: Exceptional Research Technologies. He had also penned his home number.

Keren pointed the card at him as if to say that she just might use it.

He watched her walk down the hill. Even in her long coat, he could see her sashaying slightly.

Her boss was on the fucking Intelligence committee. He kicked himself.

Chapter 45 Slaughter

Eleven boys gathered on a chilly and brilliantly sunny morning after their long run, stamping their feet, rubbing their hands, chattering about the feast that awaited.[745] They were proud of their selection and their accomplishment now that they were nearing the end of their training.

Their teachers drilled them for five weeks at a special camp called al-Matar.[746] Every day except Friday, they rose at five for the *Fajr*, the dawn prayers, segregated from the others in a small notch off the mountainous valley of the larger Farooq training area.[747] After prayers, they ate a small breakfast of bread and jam, followed by physical fitness and bodybuilding, sometimes a run up the canyon and back, or a long hike wearing a heavy pack, then followed by calisthenics or weight training.

Most of the rest of the day was spent in the classroom. A teacher or guest speaker lectured them on weapons and explosives, communications and operational security, composure and behavior in the West, even what to do if they were captured. They learned to take apart a Kalashnikov rifle and how to clean it, and each had to qualify on the firing range, shooting at crude cut-outs of American soldiers dressed in mottled brown desert fatigues. Twice, an *al Qaeda* wizard took them to a distant range where they worked with actual explosives, once even constructing a truck bomb and then blowing it up.[748]

They had English language training every day. Most had never been outside their home countries before coming to Afghanistan. They were taught basic travel and tourism phrases and given handouts to study and memorize. They paired off and had conversations under the watchful eye of their tutor. Interspersed in the training was more prayer and religious instruction, accompanied by screenings of martyr videos or movies of combat in Chechnya and Afghanistan.

After a hearty end-of-day meal and evening prayers, typically the special eleven spent the evenings huddled on their private, darkened hillside near a campfire, discussing world events and the fight ahead, some smoking cigarettes and all drinking the ubiquitous sweet green tea.

On special days, they assembled and listened to taped speeches of *Sheikh* bin Laden and other luminaries, talking about *jihad* afterwards. About halfway through training, a man named *Mukhtar*—the "brain"— arrived and they spent two days going over codes. He was legendary, the organizer of the African embassy bombings and the new attack on the warship in Yemen. They gossiped that he was head of the operation they were candidates for as well.

Mukhtar was entertaining and encouraging, and he loaded them all into a pickup truck to travel to the buildings that were bombed in "retaliation" for the embassy attacks. *Mukhtar* spoke of how cowardly the Americans were, sending missiles instead of men to do their dirty work. They swelled with pride.

More than six months earlier, Abu Hafs began to identify suitable martyrs among known operatives and new recruits coming into the camps. He, *Mukhtar*, and Khallad agreed that four musclemen were needed on each plane. This time, bin Laden's preference for Saudis suited KSM just fine. Their selection was good because they could easily get visas. Saudis also weren't given much of a second look at immigration or customs because there was virtually no risk they would attempt to reside or work illegally. So *Mukhtar* was happy to do damage to the Saudi regime, not just to please his American friends, but also because they were the rich kids on the block.

All through the fall, as young men made it through different stages of screening, *Mukhtar* and Abu Hafs discussed each candidate's potential, agreeing on who would move onto the next stage. Some flunked out, not able to fit in with others or not willing to do the work. Some left for health reasons, some because they exhibited deception, or just hesitation.

Though the eleven weren't told the details of their destiny, *Mukhtar's* plan was for these "muscle" teams to board commercial flights along with their pilots and, at the right moment, storm the cockpit and subdue the crew, barricading themselves in the front of the plane and protecting their man. With their final training stage, their teachers began to openly talk about airplanes, about hijacking and the task ahead. No details were provided about the timing or the location or the targets.[749] Even the teaching of English language was explained as necessary for completion of their mission, since most passengers on an airplane, from Asia to America, would understand the universal language. The boys knew that they would operate in groups of three or four, but they had no idea that they would all work in unison.

One-legged Khallad—the boys affectionately called him "Silver"— visited and discussed airports and airplanes. All the boys had flown numerous times, but never in first class, and none, of course, had ever hijacked an airplane. Khallad brought pictures of different planes and their configurations, telling them how to case the cockpits and even how to look for possible air marshals onboard.

To hijack a plane, he said, they needed to seize the cockpit first and worry about the rest of the plane thereafter. Upon boarding, they needed to be well-dressed and well-behaved businessmen until the moment came to transform into fearless *jihadis*. With weapons drawn and much bravado and noise, they were to rush the cockpit when the cabin door was opened, either when one of the officers came out to go to the bathroom or when they were being served meals or drinks.

Their job was to get "their" pilot into the seat as quickly as possible. No mercy could be spared with any flight attendant or unruly passenger. Their reflexes had to be honed to perfection. The operation had been choreographed to take no more than nine minutes from initiation to completion, Khallad said. *Nine minutes.*[750]

Towards the end of the final training week for the chosen boys, a camera crew arrived so that they could each make a personal video that would later be posted on the internet and distributed by *al Qaeda*. Some videotaping of their training had already taken place, cameramen filming them doing calisthenics and on the firing range.

Inside the prayer room, each of the boys was arranged on a green-screen background. Donning a Palestinian style black or red *keffiyeh*, they were instructed to look straight at the camera and speak from their hearts. Some elected to hold an AK-47; two chose a Yemeni-style dagger that *Sheikh* bin Laden wore in videos. The production company would superimpose images of aircraft and the targets in the background later. Some boys were given fake dates to announce as the date that the video was recorded. Some were asked to state that the video was serving as their final will and testament.

The cameraman said he had just come from filming clips with Osama bin Laden, Abu Hafs, and Dr. Zawahiri speaking of their same operation. The boys gathered around the monitor to watch outtakes. The director said that the first of them to make a video would be Saeed al-Ghamdi.[751] They wondered why until they saw *Sheikh* bin Laden mention him by name: "He is a good person. He has good qualities. He is very righteous. He fears God, and may God protect him." The boys hooted and jostled brother Saeed as the celebrity.

Onscreen, Saeed sat in the chair and began: "America is the enemy that every Muslim should fight. We promise the United States of America that we will stop you, that we will hurt you, and we will make sure that you don't have any peace … God will punish you in a big way."

"Again," the cameraman said, asking Ghamdi to go over his speech again, that this video was particularly important because he was to be paired with their *emir*.

Ahmed Haznawi was next.[752] "It is time to kill the Americans on their own ground among their families and soldiers," he said, adding that the "time of humiliation and subjugation is over." This was his "bloodied message" to America, he continued, adding the importance of killing Americans in their own heartland. "Lord, I regard myself as a martyr for you to accept me as such."

Then came a young boy named Umari to speak of his last will and testament.[753] "I am writing this with my full conscience and I am writing this in expectation of the end, which is near … God praise everybody who trained and helped me, especially my leader, *Sheikh* Osama bin Laden."

Wail Shehri, the oldest of the group, followed.[754] The cameraman said he had good quality shots of Wail using a variety of weapons, including a rocket launcher, and wanted a high-quality video as well. "If struggle and *jihad* is not mandatory now," Wail asked, "then when is it mandatory? When is it time to help Muslims who are under fire in Chechnya? And what about Kashmir and the Philippines? Blood continues to flow. When will it be over?"

Hamza Ghamdi was last.[755] "If we are content with being humiliated and inclined to comfort, the tooth of the enemy will stretch from Jerusalem to Mecca, and then everyone will regret on a day when regret is of no use."

The discussions that night were intense. "It is a difficult and painful road we take," their teacher said, reminding them that only *jihad* would ease their sorrows.

Back at the barracks the boys let off steam, exhilarated by the filming and the recitation of their personal statements. *Hollywood*, the new stars joked, talking and laughing long into the night.

The next morning brought on the final exam before the feast, and the boys tittered after their run that surely *Sheikh* bin Laden himself might be coming for the graduation, given the two dozen goats newly penned up down by the kitchen building.

Their teacher asked each of the boys to pick a goat and follow him up near the water cistern in the canyon notch. He handed out a pocketknife to each and the boys grew silent and apprehensive. The few that were petting their goats or kneeling on the ground next to their newfound pets stood up straight, instinctively tightening their grip on the ropes.

For meat to be certified *halal*, their teacher said, slaughtering needed to be done in a humane way. All the boys had at one point or another participated in a feast involving the slaughtering of a goat or a lamb, even the urban dwellers. In each case, a certified *halal* butcher came and stunned the animal first by touching an electrical probe to the back of its head, or in some cases, sprinkling grain on the ground and then shooting a .22 slug right behind the ear of the animal, into the back of its skull as it stretched down to eat. From that followed the cutting of the throat arteries, when the carcass was then blessed. Some remembered watching from a distance as the goat's head was removed and the animal was bled, followed by the skinning and disembowelment.

As their teacher continued his intentionally distracted talk, one after another, the boys realized there wasn't going to be a feast. Each was going to have to subdue and kill their goat with their bare hands and their small knives just as they would have to do on their airplanes. Their teacher explained that the most efficient way to kill someone was to pull their head back by the hair or forehead from behind and make a deep cut into the front of the neck, severing the main arteries.

"Any volunteers to go first?"

No one moved a muscle.

"Okay, I didn't think so, so here's what we are all going to do. Go pray, brothers, pray the *Istikhara*, seek divine guidance from God himself to show you the way. Because when your day comes, your actions must be automatic and instinctive. You must kill without hesitation and without fear.[756]

"The kill," he said, pointing to his own throat and holding his chin high, "should take less than seven seconds. Today, it would have taken seven thousand. When we return tomorrow, you will each kill your goat. And you will do so as *jihadis*."

All of the boys, the so-called musclemen, were between 20 and 28 years old, most between five foot five and five foot seven inches in height.[757] Many arrived in Pakistan on their way to Afghanistan or Chechnya, seeking *jihad*. Many were unemployed or lacked higher education; two were married. All thought they were ready to kill and be killed. With a rifle or a grenade launcher. Not in hand-to-hand combat.

That night, the teacher arranged a special discussion after evening prayers, and they spoke of the difference between the word *dhabaha*—slaughter—and *qatala*—kill. Divine death would come as a ritual sacrifice. *Dhabaha* is what Abraham was prepared to do to his son Ishmael on God's instruction until the child was replaced with the sheep, the sheep that today in Islam is slaughtered at the *Eid al-Adha*, the feast of sacrifice.[758]

The boys again talked late into the night, and there were tears, many saying that they did not know if they could do it. To kill with a Kalashnikov at a distance, or even to do so with a bomb strapped to their bodies by just pressing a button and feeling nothing was one thing. But this? So close? No one slept soundly.

The next day, Wail, the eldest, volunteered to go first. It wasn't pretty, or even smooth. He grabbed his goat under the jaw and pulled upward, the animal bleating and kicking. He thrust his Swiss Army knife into the animal's fur and tried to slice, pulling the goat's neck further up, the animal struggling to escape his grip, blood beginning to flow. A second thrust of the knife sliced deeper into the goat's neck, the blood spurting over Wail's pants and shoes, the others backing away, eyes wide in terror.

Hamza Ghamdi, the youngest of the group, a roly-poly boy of a man, bent over and vomited. Two others closed their eyes.

Wail cut again. The beast made a huge gash in his leg with a wild kick but, slowly, it was losing strength. Deeper he cut until he hit the windpipe. With one last screech and moan, the goat dropped to its knees. Triumphantly, Wail kicked it over. Dead.

"Five minutes," the teacher said. "Not bad. Next."

The boys backed further away and remained silent. Wail was covered in blood, sitting on the ground, exhausted. No one cheered.

Their teacher called Saeed, *Hollywood*, and the boys rallied and cheered as he took deep breaths in anticipation, readying himself.

The instructor had given him an icepick and a box cutter. He looked down at the box cutter, then yelled "*Allahu Akbar*," God is greatest!— swinging into action. He practically broke the neck of the goat, lifting it off the ground in his arms, slicing at the windpipe at the same time, the animal bleating in horror. Again, there was kicking and blood. The goat squirmed away, running this way and that, screaming and kicking anything in its way as it lost strength, Saeed chasing after it.

No one laughed as the goat finally tipped over in a ravine, Saeed bending over to catch his breath.

Next came Salem Hazmi. His brother was already in America, in San Diego, and the teacher said to the boys that he would show them that he could do his part.

He took his goat and equally yelled "*Allahu Akbar*," sawing at its neck with his Leatherman, immediately severing an artery, gushes of blood covering his hands and making them so slippery he dropped the knife, maintaining a stranglehold on the goat until it stopped breathing.

Mohand followed. Fayez Banihammad then volunteered.

It was late in the afternoon, lunch missed, and prayers ignored. No one made it in time. Two goats escaped from their assassins. By the end, all the other goats were panicked and skittish and the place was a mess. Intentionally, the teacher made sure that no one came to gawk. This was not a performance.

Nine of the eleven were called back the next day to try a second time, to do it faster and without getting sick.

On day three, seven were called back, some to make their kill for the first time, others to improve their technique and reduce their times.

On day four, two last brothers finally beat the clock. When the first of the two goats bleated in defeat, the others finally cheered their friends on to the last breath.

Then came the last. Violently lifting his goat in the air, he broke its neck and then slashed its throat. Throwing it down, this last goat stumbled, blood spurting six feet in the air.

Chapter 46 Freedom

Ziad told Atta that he was going to take a few days off and go to Paris for Aysel's birthday.

"I forbid you from going," Atta said to him as they sat behind the Florida bungalow on another muggy evening, relaxing after a long day of flying, listening to the chatter of nature's innocents in the mangroves beyond.

"You forbid," Ziad responded. "That shithead fisherman flew. And he wasn't detected. And he had a *jihadi* past."

"It's not the same," Atta said. "And I don't care about him. Brother, I'm afraid you might not get back in to *Amreeka*. Don't you see? What would you feel?"

"Feel? I must do this. And I am not worried."

"Ziad," Atta pleaded, and he rarely called him that, "I would be lost without you."

"My friend," Ziad said, clasping Atta's hands, "I am going to go. And see my wife. It's just a week. It's the natural break for me in school, and I will make sure to do everything he taught us and we've learned. I'll come back as a tourist. But brother, if I have to swim, I will be back."

"What if they do not let you back in?"

Atta wasn't wrong to refer to the Saudi in San Diego, to his desertion. Atta was furious with what had happened there, and all summer he stewed as if it were his failure. It was the first real misstep once they'd gotten underway. It was *his* first misstep, and though *Mukhtar* reassured him that no one laid the mistakes of the fisherman at his door,[759] he knew that with the Saudi fisherman's departure, everyone was more closely watching.

That everyone included *Mukhtar* in Pakistan, Ramzi in Berlin, Cousin Ali in Dubai, *al Qaeda* in Afghanistan, and fellow Egyptians Dr. Zawahiri and Abu Hafs. Even *Sheikh* bin Laden was now watching them, *Mukhtar* said, watching and waiting for regular reports about progress that they were making.[760] They were watching, watching him from afar, judging him, judging him and his skills, maybe knowing of his beloved's sickness—maybe even, he thought, of their pact.

Mukhtar told Atta that they were also watching the CIA for the first time. Not the phantom supposedly lurking behind every corner. Not the paranoia agency, with some agent infiltrated into *al Qaeda,* or even their ranks in America. No, for the first time, he said, they were watching the real Agency, the one that was on the move and taking the first steps to be more active in Afghanistan, probing the Taliban, connecting with treacherous groups there, flying over their skies. And *Mukhtar* said, they were even watching Mullah Omar, as diplomats and spies contacted the new Afghanistan leader to plead with him—to entice him—to give over their great Saudi guest. They were watching as threats were made and deals were offered—the Taliban leadership in Kandahar wavering in its support for *al Qaeda.*

And from inside a cave outside Jalalabad, all the way to their bungalow in Florida, everyone watched the American presidential campaign, wondering what the difference between Democrats and Republicans was. They couldn't tell.

At this point, Atta had all the real responsibility, not just learning to fly, but also arranging the work of everyone, making the decisions, managing everything, calculating their budget and ordering their movements, their living day-to-day. But he was also working with a calendar and his notebooks to time everything to move with a deliberate pace towards their magnificent act. Beyond all of those who supported them from afar, everything fell on his shoulders. And though he was ultimately responsible for their training, and their security and their life in America, the watchers couldn't resist second guessing. And that included, and had always included, Ziad's commitment.

If they didn't have their bond back to Hamburg and so much history together, Atta might not have understood how Ziad—so carefree and popular with Americans, with his natural Western ways and his always ready to go out and have fun attitude—could even be a *jihadi*. And yet there wasn't a day when his Lebanese brother didn't impress Atta.

Ziad was doing the best of all of them in flight school.[761] He was the friendliest and most engaging with neighbors and acquaintances. His friend was always ready to step up when Marwan faltered, always ready to help Atta with a task—not just in running errands or dealing with the practical issues of living, but also in matters of prayer. Ziad encouraged reflection, ready to drop everything to study a question, *to think on it*, as he said, serving faithfully as Atta's personal *ulema*.

Atta understood that Ziad was at the top of *Mukhtar's* list of those to watch—that Ziad was why *Mukhtar* encouraged them to move to Florida. But then their teacher never quite understood Ziad. And in his conviction to impart as little information as possible about Marwan to *Mukhtar*, Atta also never handed over much beyond the facts of Ziad's excellence. He was the best pilot and Atta forwarded reports of his progress and transcripts.

But Atta never said what he thought, that Ziad was also the best Muslim, the wisest and most confounding he'd ever known. In Karachi, Atta reasoned with *Mukhtar* that perhaps he should see it personally, that Ziad was just as he, their teacher, would be if he were to be an actual *jihadi* and an actual religious man, that if *Mukhtar* were in Ziad's shoes he would be closely watched as well. Atta thought it clever and true as an argument, thought it apropos, but *Mukhtar* didn't get the point because he didn't think anyone was like him. Then and since, Ziad thanked him many times for having such faith in him, reminding him also when *Mukhtar* got under his skin with his niggling and judgment, that their Karachi teacher wasn't important, that they were in control now, that he was in control, and that they would do their part, and that *Allah*, most gracious, would do his. For he was also watching, watching over them.

Right when Ziad announced that he was going, Atta received an email from *Mukhtar*, another one filled with questions about Ziad. Atta had made the mistake of telling *Mukhtar* that they were fighting, needing to tell someone. It was the product of all the stress that they were under, of living their secret lives, and of not knowing what *al Qaeda* was up to. And it was the added strain of Marwan's health. Atta regretted sharing with Mukhtar, because his response, even trying to be helpful, misconstrued what the problem was, and focused on Ziad the phantom and not the man he knew, the one he'd been watching.

He and Ziad talked about it, and even though Ziad sensed he was the subject of concern coming from Pakistan and Afghanistan, he bucked up Atta, telling him that they didn't understand the pressures of actually doing what they were doing. They didn't understand the exhaustion in keeping eyes focused on the details, and the mistrust that crept in as they dealt with their teachers, their fellow students, their landlords, the people at gas stations, those who served them in restaurants and stores, the airline people and hotel clerks, and even the occasional policeman they encountered. Everything was so brittle. Atta knew it when he snapped at Ziad that day, knew it because he knew Ziad was going to go no matter what he said. He would miss his Lebanese friend, the only one who really offered him any relief.

Relief because, once settled in Florida, with Ziad's prodding, Atta also had to think about something that he probably would have otherwise ignored, or not even seen. And that was America's freedoms. Qutb might have been right that America was the pinkest of the pink, blatantly wasteful and air-filled hollow in spirit. Atta saw it with his own eyes, now clocking his own beginner-to-expert hours on the ground, living the *jahiliyyah* of his adopted country, so normal and so unremarkable in his life in America that he merely disappeared into the populace.

Ziad argued that this freedom to disappear might not be that of the great political thinkers. But it was great, he said. And as far as Ziad thought, even in comparison with Germany, it was unique. This freedom to be invisible. It was surely unlike the Middle East, and even Lebanon, this freedom for everyone to truly be safe in their homes. No test was administered to obtain this freedom. They didn't need to be a certain class to attain it. They paid their rent and never saw their landlord. Their neighbors were friendly and cordial but stayed to themselves. They enthusiastically pushed their advancement towards flight certification, and no one asked why. America *was* a country full of people striving to do whatever they wanted, a country free of anyone spying on anyone else. There was no interior ministry or national police that swaggered about intent on keeping everyone in line. The security guards were lazy because there was no culture of watching, no one to report to. And the police, they scanned the roads from behind their sunglasses, but even then, when they were stopped for speeding, as long as the license and registration were current, as long as they had insurance, and as long as they were cordial, they weren't looking to make trouble. It was a country where no one was reporting on anyone else.

And, most important, no one was harassing Atta, telling him to toughen up or telling him to lighten up or even to live his life or love his love in some different way.

Atta told Ziad that he thought it naïve and weak and even stupid, this America.

"This is freedom, my brother?" he scoffed at Ziad when he made his observation. "So we, as long as we stay away from the Muslim community, we three, we can just disappear into freedom?"

"It is freedom," Ziad said quietly, surprised himself on how easy they could disappear. "Yes, I'll agree it is a freedom that maybe makes for some laziness, a freedom that Americans don't cherish and thus don't tend to. But brother, it *is* freedom."

Atta argued that maybe they just didn't see it, that maybe the American secret services didn't need to harass anyone because all of these supposed freedoms—of abundance and entertainment, of the limitless television, with one of the so many sports offered that there was always some season going on. That this constant diet filled, and then drugged, the people into spiritual emptiness, just as Qutb said.

Yes it was true, Ziad admitted, that by their way—by their book and their way—America had no soul. And thank God, he said—saying God as the Americans did. Because it was also to their benefit, this freedom, because they could join and blend into the odorless and colorless society. They were free to be themselves, even to be *terrorists* from other countries.

Atta had to admit that with this freedom sometimes the voices of judgment actually went away. As he went to school and shopped and drove around in Florida, the voices quieted, and the wrath of *Allah*, praise be to him, dissipated. Sometimes he went through his day, an entire day, without loathing, either self-loathing or of others. And he found himself losing a bit of his bombastic contempt.

And though he worried all the time about every detail of the mission, one thing he didn't worry about anymore were the looks. He felt the looks in his initial guardedness in New York, but now it was so distant, a feeling that came from not knowing this true America. He had been humiliated in Oklahoma. But now that pink pig was like an aberrant bully, not the America he had grown to know. He didn't want to admit it, and without Ziad's urging, he might not have even ever seen it. But he had developed just a tiny bit of appreciation for this freedom of anonymity. In this land of white and black, white and brown, even if he observed that it was still the rarest attempt on the part of anyone to mix, even if there was no real community and nothing holding everyone together except for this vague ideal of being invisible, of being invisible and therefore somehow also being part of a bigger organism, and not only that, but the biggest and the best, it was a freedom that eroded his kaleidoscope of disapproval.

When those who didn't really know America complained, Mohammed Atta could now say with authority, the authority of the American *emir*, and the only one of all of them who had actually carried out a secret life in America, that they just did not understand.

Atta was sometimes troubled with what he saw, these new truths in knowing America. And for that reason, his order to Ziad Jarrah not to travel was more performance than belief. Yes, he was worried that he would have trouble getting back in. But he also learned that what was trouble in theory could also be protection. Ziad *was* constantly on the phone and constantly in email contact with his wife.[762] According to the *al Qaeda* rules and the *Mukhtar* guidance, such behavior was *haram*, forbidden, forbidden, forbidden. It risked discovery, Mukhtar said. And that's what he would have thought, too. Before. But he had overheard more than one of those conversations. They were mostly in German, sometimes English, but never in Arabic, the language that might have provoked the CIA. And it was not just the tongue, but it was the tone. It was a language of love, the talk between husband and wife, talk about his and her schooling, his and her day, their future together. Even by *Mukhtar's* logic, it was really the best security possible. Though Atta worried that when the time came, Ziad might not be able to let go, or more important, that his dearest brother would experience the most terrible pain, an even greater pain in leaving his loved one behind, Atta just couldn't feel his way to blind judgment or condemnation of what Ziad did. Or wanted.

Mukhtar made the mistake in an email to Atta of comparing Ziad to the traitorous fisherman. And so the American *emir* hardened in his defense. To Atta, it was an inexcusable misstep on their teacher's part. And it was a fortunate one, for it also alleviated the guilt that Atta carried as to what Marwan and he were now secretly planning, of their own betrayal of their teacher and the entire Muslim army of watchers.

Though Atta commanded Ziad, he also secretly supported his friend—they both had their secrets. Atta and Ziad had been on a long journey together. Together, they had dealt with Marwan's health. They had gone to Afghanistan together. They had come to America and had been left alone to learn to fly. Left alone to think in peace, to ponder what it meant to be Muslims and to be men. Yes they had committed their lives on behalf of their people and the entire *ummah*. And their commitment didn't weaken. But they were also together, a together of experience and deep love that truly made them brothers.

Atta could not really forbid Ziad from traveling to Germany. He couldn't because Ziad never forbid anything Atta did. Ziad did not even forbid with his eyes. He gave Atta and Marwan their privacy, not even saying it was none of his business what he and Marwan did, who they loved, or how they loved. In his true and deep love, in his grudging respect for freedom, Ziad extended good wishes and encouragement and compassion. And so, like a parent forbidding for the good of the child, forbidding but also wryly knowing that a play was being performed, Atta forbid.

As the day of Ziad's travel approached, they fought about it again. It seemed like they just had to, had to because the pressure was unbearable. The time itself was approaching. They screamed at each other and called each other names. Ziad called Atta a Nazi control freak.

Atta and Marwan drove Ziad to the Atlanta airport, where he boarded a plane for Frankfurt.[763] There he would meet Aysel at the giant *Hauptbahnhof* and, from there, husband and wife would take a train to Paris. They were going to visit the Eiffel Tower and the Louvre, Ziad said. They were going to poke their heads into famous churches. They were going to eat and even drink and dance the night away. Ziad regaled them with his plan.

"I will check in every day," he assured his American *emir* and best friend. He promised.

Atta might be hardened inside, but the trip reminded him of his own honeymoon in New York.

Five days into Ziad's trip, out of nowhere and without warning, an *al Qaeda* boat attacked the USS *Cole* in Yemen. Atta and Marwan were glued to cable news with the rest of America, watching a warship almost sunk by two brothers in a rickety skiff. David versus Goliath.

That day, *Mukhtar* pinged for an emergency call. Atta drove all the way to the airport in Fort Myers and went inside the terminal to use a clean pay phone, *Mukhtar* checking in to a hotel room at the Sheraton to do the same. They conversed in English.

"It is not safe for our cousin to travel," *Mukhtar* said, referring to Ziad in Paris. He was now stranded in Europe. He said this with sadness in his voice: "He has ruined our plans."

"I have spoken to our cousin," Atta answered, soothing the teacher. "I tell you not to worry. No plans are ruined. I have faith." In a reversal of roles, he, Mohammed Atta, with his authority as confident American *emir*, was telling *Mukhtar* not to worry.

Back in Germany, Ziad and Aysel watched the news, too. The boat was attacked but no missiles flew to Yemen.

Nothing happened.

Ziad called Atta and they agreed. He would chance the trip back to America. Atta deeply missed him.

Two weeks after the *Cole*, Ziad flew back to Tampa.[764] He sadly left his favorite *Qur'an* with Aysel as a precaution. He purchased cigarettes and an English-language guidebook on Florida and he put them in his carry-on bag. He bought new shoes and a gold chain. Ramzi produced a fake Rolex from the streets of Berlin. He got a fresh haircut.

He had his multiple-entry visa and all of his papers showing that he was also registered in flight school in Florida. Just in case. Just in case his tourist visa was questioned, in case he was stopped.

Purpose of your visit?

Visiting friends here in Venice. Vacation. We are going to Disney World.

Welcome to America. Next!

Atta and Marwan sat in the Grand Prix parked along the curb near international arrivals, saying nothing, biting their nails. Atta calculated that it would take maybe an hour for Ziad to clear customs. The low whine of country music played on the car radio as they waited it out by the curb.

"Dudes!" they heard as Ziad emerged from arrivals. The sharply-dressed Lebanese waltzed out of the Tampa airport terminal, plopping his luggage and a shopping bag full of gifts for his friends into the back seat of the car, a man without a worry in the world.[765]

That night, they celebrated the award of Atta's and Marwan's FAA Temporary Airman Certificates, qualifying them as private pilots.[766]

Monday morning before the November election, they all returned to flight school.

On Tuesday night, they sat together and watched the long night of returns. The next day, and then the next, they watched the political maneuverings in their own home state of Florida. A delayed result in an election was not unheard of in Germany. But the news was filled with confusion, days turning into weeks as the confusion continued. The confusion then extended well into the coming Thanksgiving holiday. Everyone at the flight school was now watching. The whole world was watching.[767]

By the time the holiday break came, they were confused as to how one man in a democracy could get more votes and not be elected.

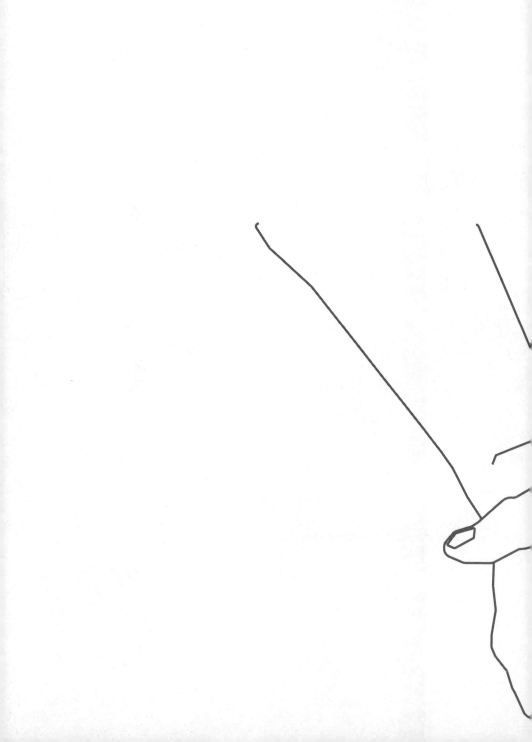

PART 12

Chapter 47 The Fraternity

George W. Bush came into office with his own army of *kunyas*, the battle names assigned to his assistants—"Hawk," "Enzo," "M-Cat," "*Karl!*" (always "*Karl!*")—indicative of a frat-boy congeniality that could be interpreted as either deeply affectionate or the reduction of every subordinate to a mascot.[768]

There were the elders—his father "Poppy," "Rummy," and even that nice woman "Condi"—each battle name representing experience and wisdom, a tony union of national security nannies that everyone thought would keep junior safe, veteran jockeys holding tight to the reins of their bucking bronco.

The new president was a doer; the quintessential American male, an exercise fanatic, competitive to the extreme: a hotdog- and ice cream-consuming, baseball-watching guy who really did prefer brush clearing or jogging to exercising the brain. For those who voted for him, he was the textbook antidote to Bill Clinton's smarmy political smoothness and Al Gore's pointy-headed stiffness. His White House would not be the previous administration of young brat-geniuses. Nor was it *Poppy's* top-down control of everything by upper management.

It was a surprise then—to Steve and Charlie, and even to Lawrence Avery Bowlen—that the Clinton era's number one Democratic political animal survived the change of administrations.[769] They'd spent countless hours talking about George Tenet's empty intelligence after the African embassy bombings and his hollow declaration of war on *al Qaeda*. They'd watched with dismay his skillful serving up of everything WMD to cater to Clinton's tastes. Now George Tenet, who Steve took to calling "Mr. Slam Dunk," was readying another slam. Everything was winding its way back to WMD and Iraq.

Donald Rumsfeld was the first choice to become Bush's CIA director.[770] Bowlen came in with hot intelligence one day that one of Rumsfeld's guys was on the seventh floor at Langley, practically measuring the drapes.[771]

But then the former Secretary of Defense got the Pentagon. Bush took Tenet aside to ask him to stay on. He liked him, liked his anti-Washington demeanor, or his rumpled affectation of outsider.

Poppy, who had once himself been the Agency director, told junior that Tenet was respected and there was also a consensus on Capitol Hill— even amongst the Republicans—that he'd restored morale and reversed the slide towards political correctness and risk aversion.[772]

"How did this motherfucker survive?" Charlie asked in an Apex Watch meeting after the announcement was made that Tenet would stay on in the new administration. "How did he survive the gauntlet of Rumsfeld and Cheney?"

Bowlen shrugged. "Junior evidently likes him."

"So Tenet's another one of George W's pets?" Steve quipped, indifferent and even pleased their plan would move forward more easily, now protected even more because there wouldn't be some profound change-of-administration review at the Agency, that no real relook would occur at what the Agency was doing on terrorism. And, just as he predicted, Iraq would become issue number one.

"It really does speak to their cheekiness," Bowlen opined, referring to all of the veterans surrounding the new president.

"A do-over for the *national security titans*," said Charlie, almost with a sneer.

"But mark my words," Bowlen said. "All of them, Cheney, Rumsfeld, Powell at State and even Wolfowitz, that geopolitical genius[773]—they're all stalled at the end of the Cold War. The Middle East to them is oil, and Iraq, and Israel. Same old same old."

"So why so many national security experts surrounding the president?" Charlie asked.

Bowlen paused. "Given that President Bush really believes in nothing, the vacuum gets filled with national security. You think anyone cares to march into battle behind the secretary of education?"

In his outgoing meeting with Condoleezza Rice, Clinton's national security advisor warned her that she'd spend more time on terrorism than any other issue.[774] Bowlen said word was that she reacted with fatigue. *Meetings, time sensitive decisions, super-secret intelligence, legal opinions, presidential approvals, findings, warnings.* The words the Clinton holdovers used made her head hurt—the breathlessness of it all—and the old-timer and Soviet expert weaned on the very precept of avoiding crisis above all else made it clear to everyone that she was intent on turning the making of national security in a more composed and methodical process.

The new national security advisor announced that there was no true American national interest involved in going to war with a band of criminals in Afghanistan. Before the election, she'd written the administration-defining doctrine in *Foreign Affairs* in which she'd said the Clinton administration was unable to "separate the important from the trivial," arguing that terrorism only needed attending insofar as it was perpetrated by rogue states—state sponsors of terrorism. That additionally elevated Iran and Iraq to the top of the problem in-box.[775]

As Team Bush proceeded with their articulation of American national interest, every place that wasn't part of the personal experience of the titans was dismissed as not being a part. It was a sly putdown of lesser beings—those who cared about, or who *were* merely identified with, some single country or region, or a single subject such as terrorism. The Bush titans were *global* and *strategic* in their orientation. Anyone arguing for some picayune periphery was dismissed as not being able to see the forest.

Condi immediately saw one thing had truly changed since the end of the Cold War. The world of liaison relationships with foreign intelligence and secret services.

Tenet tended to almost all these relationships, the Agency turned into a global operator in a giant game of telephone. The new consensus was that no analyst in Washington and no diplomat, no matter how smart, could know as much as the locals. Those who were talking to the locals thus assumed they knew more than everyone else. And those talking to the leaders of the locals were the titans. Why would ministers or princes or presidents want to speak to anyone else?

And how did it work? Secret police heads only wanted to speak to Tenet or one of the other big boys; presidents and kings only wanted to gossip with their counterparts. In the previous administration, Clinton and Gore were enlisted to massage and fortify these relationships, to keep up the flow of information, to push and plead for special considerations. Someone from the Agency or State or the FBI wrote talking points, even sometimes listened in to coach and take notes. But the natural impact in this new era of *intelligence* from the top was that the titans became their own case officers. Whatever they collected in their handling of their agents—kings, princes, presidents, prime ministers—had greater impact than any intelligence report that the bureaucracy could produce. Egypt's Mubarak or Jordan's King Abdullah could personally dish on Saddam. Who was some GS-15 at Langley or even some ambassador to disagree? *He knows the guy!*[776]

It all put Tenet in the center. The CIA director—*Georgie! Member of the team! Just as frustrated with Clinton and his ways!*—said to his new master that firing more cruise missiles into the mountains for retaliation against the attack in Yemen wasn't going to accomplish anything. "Dream bigger" was the tenet.

No more swatting at flies, Junior thought, agreeing.

Bush Junior listened to the details of existing presidential "findings" authorizing covert operations around the world, papers signed by Clinton.

Regime change? Didn't that mean kill the guy? Lethal authority? Why'd they even need a directive for that against these fuckers?

If there was anything that everyone in the old and new administration agreed on, it was that a final showdown with Iraq was coming. Junior already heard an earful about the tenacious Iraqi leader from *Poppy*. This was the second time the Iraq problem was handed off from administration to administration. Clinton received it from the father. Like a groomed thoroughbred, Bush champed at the bit to take him on, *mano a mano*, what the nannies referred to as closure.

As secretary of state, Powell especially felt the weight of the Iraq hand-off. He'd been chairman of the Joint Chiefs during the first Gulf War, the top military officer. He'd witnessed, though he didn't necessarily oppose, President Bush's decision to cede to the Saudi King's wishes and end the war after a media-friendly 100 hours of ground combat. With a ground war going nowhere good, combat was halted.[777] Powell's counsel to end the fighting was always blamed for letting the enemy slip away. Unspoken in historical renderings was an absolute agreement between Bush Senior and King Fahd that the status quo in Iraq couldn't be altered, that the majority *Shi'a* in the south couldn't be empowered.

Taking his new perch as secretary of state, Powell adopted the best and most reasonable of diplomatic courses to weaken Saddam. "Smart sanctions" would bolster flagging international support for the containment of Iraq, and sanctions would gradually do the job, he said. A renewed international consensus behind sanctions and increased support to Iraqi opposition groups trying to overthrow the regime would "re-energize" pressure on Baghdad. The dictator would be done in peacefully, just as the Soviets were defeated over years and decades.

With Condi more hands-off than her predecessor at the head of the national security apparatus,[778] and with the commander-in-chief duties outsourced to Cheney, and with Powell and Rumsfeld off conquering their new agencies, Tenet became number one *amigo* to the president. Though Clinton read his Presidential Daily Brief in quiet every morning, Bush Junior wanted *his* CIA director to tell him stuff about the world. They met *every* morning. Tenet hand-delivered global gossip in the hush-hush locker room.[779]

Any momentum in counterterrorism built during the Clinton administration slowed. Rumsfeld buttoned up the Pentagon, the bulldog of a Pentagon head making it clear that he was against his military being enlisted in any kind of unmanly pinprick.[780] Rice, supported by Powell, leaned towards the development of what she labeled a "regional" strategy for dealing with terrorism. In reality, that meant big-think diplomatic solutions involving negotiations and cooperation with allies and possibly even a final chapter with Iran, a grand strategy to contrast with the Clinton era of tit for tat.[781]

White House staffers who had been working the terrorism portfolio pushed to get Rice's attention, flooding her with memos calling for "urgent" action against Osama bin Laden, producing plans to "roll back" *al Qaeda* over three to five years, warning that there were bin Laden operatives inside the country, that an attack could be imminent.

A memo went out from the White House asking the new attorney general and FBI director Louis Freeh about whether they believed that there were *al Qaeda* sleeper cells in America.[782]

Al Qaeda? The incredulous retort came back from the halls of Justice. *What about drugs and child pornography and the Russian mafia?*[783]

The "only unfinished" business, Louis Freeh told the White House, was the 1996 Khobar Towers attack in Saudi Arabia and the non-punishment of the devil-state Iran.[784] And what about the bombing of the USS *Cole* in Yemen where the Clinton team equally wimped out?, staffers asked. *That* should be the focus of the Bush team—not Afghanistan, not some phantom Saudi nobody.[785]

Tenet saw which way the wind was blowing and removed his fingers from the terrorism-warning button. He told Junior how *they* were expanding the ranks of the clandestine service for the first time since the end of the Cold War, catering to the president's ego.[786] He told Junior how *they* were harnessing all the technologies of the dot com boom in the spy business. Into the White House came the goodies to share with the boss: *Let me show you how it works.*

So, Bush asked Tenet: *mi amigo, what's the bottom line?*

Sizing up his new boss, his new buddy, looking down the road at all possibilities, considering whether the Bush team wanted to swat at flies, looking at a potential Republican parole board staring him in the face, Tenet said that though he didn't disagree with FBI director Freeh that the USS *Cole* was unfinished business, there just wasn't enough evidence to conclusively say Osama bin Laden himself ordered the attack.[787]

The president, confident that national security under the titans (Cheney and *Rummy* and Colin and *Condi* and his new best friend *Georgie boy*), had never been in better hands, agreed.

Chapter 48 Control-Insert

━━ ━━ ━━ ━━ ━━ ━━ ━━ ━━ ━━ ━━

Steve took Mallory up on his offer to tour the Apex Watch control system, *the system he'd designed*, stepping into the server farm off the command center on the first floor. Bowlen's new deputy told Mallory he'd never worked anywhere where he had been afraid of *the building*, marveling at the walls of computers, the racks and the monitors, remarking about how cold the place was.

"It's quite the system," Steve said, after Mallory explained the network of cameras and microphones inserted during the Odell Road facility renovation. And the tracking devices embedded in everyone's fobs. And the way every keystroke was followed, all an effort to streamline the need for perfunctory security and wasteful administration.

"No one really ever looks at the take or the logs," Mallory assured him. "There's so much data, just from a small organization like ours, that we have to flush out the system's memory every five days."

"Is there any way that anyone from the outside could burrow in?" Steve asked.

"From the outside, no way," Mallory said, showing him the building dashboard. And he created a special loop which surveilled access to the panel. It would instantly record any intruder.

"So, there's no privacy channel?" Steve asked.

"Meaning what?" responded his eager geek.

"I get it that the sentient building saves manpower and enhances security, but what if someone wanted to legitimately do something off the record—say, enter a piece of data about the president, or work on, let's just say, a director of the CIA that was corrupt? I mean, suppose one wanted to not be recorded because they had legitimate reasons?"

"You mean like hide it from the logs?"

"Precisely. And not just the logs but from real time reporting ..."

"Real time reporting is easy. You already have a slug—now haven't you read the user's manual?—that allows you to deactivate a session."

"No shit," Steve said. "It's in the manual. Huh. Whoever reads the manual anyway?"

"Yeah," Mallory said. And they laughed.

"I'll show you." Mallory sat in front of a workstation in the computer farm. "You just type in CTRL-INS and wait for the prompt and log out with your PIN. Then the session isn't recorded, plus it allows you to open a folder and store encrypted files. They're in a covert partition that isn't even identifiable by the server—as long as they don't get too big and cast a shadow."

"That is so clever, and cool," Steve said.

Mallory beamed.

"Does anyone ever make use of this control-insert move?"

"Well, officially, I wouldn't know. When you log out, the system not only recreates a secure session but the building stops recording that session. The cameras and microphones go out as well. It's not meant to cheat. I even put in a little loop that erases the entry in the first place."

"So, you can't even tell, like for audit purposes, how many times it's been used?"

"Any really good systems administrator could, but there would be so many to wade through to count them up, I don't see why, unless we had a problem with the code."

"Wait. I thought you said you didn't know how many times it was used. So how do you know if it's being used at all?"

"We're entering stuff on the White House and CIA people all the time. Tony doesn't really want to know any of it because our financial geeks use it hundreds of times a day, thousands, in fact, sometimes for entire days at a time. That's how they can go into people's bank accounts and private emails without detection, doing shit even that Treasury or the NSA can't do. CTRL-INS anonymizes at our end and then kicks in software that anonymizes at the other end as well. Part of that is to avoid banking and other security systems. But it's also so that the NSA doesn't pick up our activity by accident and report it as some kind of operational security problem. Or, and this is Mr. Bowlen's concern, that some snoopy FBI agent piggybacks on our work to target a suspect."

"Damn, man. If I haven't said it before, you are amazing."

Mallory again demonstrated how to do it, showing Steve a couple of tricks that weren't even in the manual, Mallory's hero and patron an appreciative and attentive supervisor.

Steve had already decided to contact KSM, creating a backchannel to avoid his own blind spots—to not miss something—but also to prove that he was superior, not just to KSM but the entire United States government.

A scrap of intelligence that came into the CIA started Steve thinking that he had to create a backchannel. It mentioned a person known as "*Mukhtar*"—someone who was planning terrorist activities against the United States.[788] The report was from a foreign intelligence partner, little noticed because such raw reports were becoming more and more frequent, but noticeable to Steve for the mention of someone new. Steve asked one of Barbara's analysts to query the official CIA files to see if there was more, and she came back reporting that no one knew who *Mukhtar* was.[789]

That scrap was followed by a broad intelligence report, *Biographical Information on Bin Laden Associates in Afghanistan* produced at the Counterterrorist Center. It said that a "Khalid" (last name unknown)—a veteran *jihadi* related to Ramzi Yousef, a man U.S. intelligence associated with the World Trade Center and other attacks—was recruiting individuals to travel to the United States to meet up with sleeper agents who may already be inside the country.[790]

Steve thought that such a report should have set every alarm bell in the government ringing. But it went on to say that, based upon information provided from a reliable foreign intelligence service—one of George Tenet's best-of foreign *liaison* friends—Khalid was not only recruiting, but had also traveled to the United States on numerous occasions in 2000, perhaps even had entered the country as recently as January 2001.[791]

With that little tidbit, the Counterterrorist Center exploded with indignation.[792]

If this man was related to Yousef, then the veteran jihadi they were referring to had to be one Khalid Sheikh Mohammed, the director of the renditions branch responded to the liaison report. But then he went on to say that there was no way that this Mr. Mohammed could have traveled to the United States. To even suggest as much, he wrote, was a severe affront to the entity responsible for keeping an eye on him, for Mr. Mohammed was known to the renditions branch, meaning that he was on the watchlist and on their special list, with all intelligence about him closely monitored ever since he left Qatar.

Steve predicted that KSM might be discovered. But he also knew that what U.S. intelligence "knew" about him—that he had provided some money for the 1993 World Trade Center bombing, that he had been involved in some plot that never went far in the Philippines, that he had escaped rendition in Qatar, was very thin compared to what they should have known. In fact, Steve observed as the reporting unfolded, he ended up being just another name.

Still, that one point that he had visited the United States, suggesting that Renditions didn't do their job, kept its director yapping away that Mr. Sheikh Mohammed had been indicted five years earlier and the *best intelligence* placed him in Iran after he escaped from Qatar. He hadn't left Iran, the branch chief said. He hadn't left, that is, because there had been no other sightings since Qatar. His branch had been watching closely and there had been no intelligence on this Mr. Mohammed. Nor had they received any in years.

The branch chief said he had *doubled-checked* and Mr. Mohammed was properly entered onto State Department watchlists and was even on the high-priority list shared with the FBI. A complete search of records had turned up nothing indicating that this Mr. Mohammed—Khalid Sheikh, Khalid Doha, all possible spellings and permutations—had entered the country in 2000, let alone in 2001. He was either dead or out of the game, rendition branch responded.

With precision bullet points, the head of renditions, barking like a staked guard dog straining against a chain to the zenith of resistance, crushed this contradictory report. Steve thought that no single line of any liaison report had ever been quite so scrutinized.

"We doubt the real man would do this," the rendition branch chief finally wrote, dismissing the foreign report that he would attempt to enter the United States as little more than rumor. "If it is him," he yipped, "we have both a significant threat and an opportunity to pick him up."[793]

Steve hated this kind of factual selection, and he particularly hated this guy, whom he and Charlie long ago labeled the Chihuahua. And God, how the feeling was mutual. The Chihuahua hated forests, hated those who couldn't be concerned with little facts and territorial affront, hated those who took risks. Steve loved eavesdropping in on the officious pencil pusher's pain.

But there was something in the ferocity of the yap that interested Steve, not just in the stupidity of the overreaction, but in the tempest that consequently glossed over the possibility of there being sleeper agents inside the United States because one guy had or hadn't traveled to the United States.

In a way, Steve's entire plan depended on this kind of stupid, not a bigger stupid of ignorance or incompetence, but the picayune and turf-defending stupid of bureaucrats who skittered about on bare floors with their clicking nails, all the while yapping just like this Chihuahua.

Steve did some checking himself. He was quite sure that KSM hadn't visited the country. But someone had, and in the renditions branch response *that* fact seemed to have been lost.

After staring at the whiteboard containing names and links, Steve developed his own choking hypoxia. His own stupid. He concluded that KSM sent a man in January 2001. And not only that, but KSM had purposefully sent a man to taunt Steve, the professor.

He sensed, and then he even thought he *knew* with certainty, that the attack would never involve just one team and thus only one target. Then he decided, thought he decided, that he also didn't care. His whole ability to do what he was doing was predicated on not caring, not a conscious deciding that he didn't care but a default that he couldn't care. But not caring was so deeply engrained in who he was that he didn't really even notice anymore that saying he didn't care wasn't situational. Caring meant feeling.

He and KSM were united in riding the biggest waves and in taking the greatest leaps, driven by their indifference, and unified in lamenting all the world's Chihuahuas.

It wasn't that Charlie wouldn't leap if he asked her. Nor even that she wouldn't pounce in her own guard-dog duty if Steve rattled off new suppositions in front of her. It was more that while he surfed the scraps to certainty in what he believed was unfolding, she quavered and faltered in all the churn and froth of the fact. He was a natural liar. That he knew. And so was KSM.

CTRL-INS. "We need to communicate over a clean line," Steve wrote to KSM, using the email address that Charlie used to contact their man. "Go to an internet café to correspond with me."

When KSM said he wasn't going to one of those dirty places, Steve told him to buy a new laptop—trust me, buy a new laptop—and use it for their private communications.

KSM did. Delighted. Each thought they could smoke out the other.

KSM answered the professor's questions, elated not just with the inquiries about a traveler named Khalid going to the United States, but thrilled with the betrayal of the tough-as-nails Miss Landry. He liked her. And he respected her. But this was the opportunity of two brothers to share in the lie, to revel in each of their methods to fight stupid.

KSM shared his version. "The Sheikh found out that Ariel Sharon is visiting President Bush in June and he sent me a message from Kandahar, imploring that the operation coincide with the Israeli's leader's visit," he wrote to the professor.[794] He once again had to explain, KSM lamented, the realities of schedules and logistics and the inability to instantly turn any directive from on high into action in the field.

Then later, he told the professor, he had to explain again. An *al Qaeda* videotape appeared on *al Jazeera* television, not only claiming responsibility for the bombing of the USS *Cole* but containing footage from Afghanistan camps and what appeared to be a secret message from bin Laden.

KSM sent messages to urge the *Emir* to return to his cave and let the professionals do their work.

Steve offered his own example. The State Department spokesman was asked in his daily briefing about that very bin Laden tape, launching into his own tape player of a response that the government had *nothing on that for sure*. He said that the United States didn't know the origins of the tape, that there was an ongoing investigation, and that reporters should ask the intelligence agencies if they wanted more.

"I would just say that we have heard about this tape, and we have seen the reports," the spokesman spoke. "The kind of exhortations in this videotape that we have heard about, exhortations to violence, deserve strong condemnation from everyone. We call on the Taliban to comply with U.N. Resolution 1333, shut down the terrorist training camps in Afghanistan and expel Osama bin Laden to a country where he can be brought to justice for his crimes."[795]

Ha, ha, ha. They are so stupid. They toasted.

I have another story, KSM said. Bin Laden visited the training camps after the *Cole* bombing, promising everyone present that there would be even grander battles against *Amreeka* and the unbelievers.[796]

He understood that the *Sheikh* was excited, KSM wrote. He was invigorated by the success of the attack on the warship, animated about the progress of the plane's operation, and flush with new recruits and money, more confident than ever. All of which made him just a little too cocky, KSM said, forgetting that even caves have ears.

KSM traveled to Kandahar to press discretion upon the prophet. He told the professor that he met with bin Laden and Abu Hafs, stressing the importance of operational security now that the attack was getting closer.

"Mohammed Atef?" Steve asked, dropping Abu Hafs' real name into the conversation as a test, to see if KSM would pick up on the use of Mohammed Ate's kunya.

"Yes. Abu Hafs told me that the Taliban reported a spy drone over Kandahar's skies."[797]

"It is true," Steve said. "The CIA is calling it the Gnat, like the insect. The newer version is about to fly. And just to make it clear that it is an advance over a mere insect, it is called Predator."

Steve told his new friend that the CIA picked up some intelligence that Osama bin Laden told trainees there would soon be an attack.

KSM said he wasn't surprised, but he also wanted the professor to know that he believed in bin Laden. He was sad, he said, that though his *emir* found himself at the center of the fight he thought necessary to save his people, that he was also no longer able to see the world clearly.

The *Sheikh* was once curious and a voracious reader, KSM told the professor. But now he seemed almost indifferent to what's really happening. And once a devotee of technology, though *al Qaeda* was increasingly dependent on the most modern technologies of the internet—to propagate and connect and promote—bin Laden was slipping backwards, increasingly adapting Taliban views.

"Some of this is healthy," KSM wrote. Bin Laden was always suspicious of mechanical devices, even clocks, which he believed might be used for surveillance. But the monastic isolation and deprivations that were once his strength had also become a curse, he wrote. Now at the peak of his strength, the only outside reading he was getting was what KSM sent to him. Otherwise, he was only speaking to the like-minded, living in a vast echo chamber.

Blah, blah, blah Steve thought. The attack was coming.

CTRL-INS. "Say, friend. Why do they call you *Mukhtar*?" he asked.

"It means 'the brain,' or more literally the head of a village," KSM answered, catching on immediately that they weren't friends. And he guessed that they—not Mr. Jones and not Miss Landry and not even the professor—didn't know for sure that they even called him *Mukhtar*, that it was way too friendly of a charade of idle chatter, something the professor would never undertake and couldn't bear.

"It's like your *professor*," KSM answered.

CTRL-INS. "The Agency detected someone entering the United States in January," Steve wrote. "Someone also named Khalid."

"I don't think the date is correct," KSM responded.

"Maybe it was a different Khalid," KSM said. He didn't elaborate. Steve didn't really want to know who. Just that he was right. It wasn't KSM. And that they, whoever they were, were there. In the United States.

Steve didn't have to say it didn't matter to him who the *who* was. Why? Because they both wanted the same thing.

CTRL-INS. "And the other targets?" Steve asked.

"So, you are saying that I am planning more than one?" KSM answered, now more confident that his greatest nemesis knew but also didn't care.

"It wouldn't have taken this long if there were only one target," said Steve, not meaning to further ingratiate himself.

"It has still not been decided. But no, professor, there is not one target. Does that bother you?"

"Has a date been decided?" Steve asked, affirming without answering, and saying without saying, that indeed *it* didn't bother him.

The professor made KSM anxious. But now he was confident that he had an American friend who would shield him.

Steve also knew. While it was hard to explain that he didn't care—didn't care about the targets or the deaths—had he been asked if he did care, he would have snarled *what difference does it make,* that some idiot shouldn't get lost in the weeds of one guy traveling on a date in January, that they needed to see the big picture.

Steve stared into an opaque void. He was now absolute in his belief that he alone understood two worlds.

Chapter 49 Compulsion

"It's Keren," she said on the answering machine. "I was thinking of you, and wondering if you wanted to have drinks or dinner. Maybe like Sunday night? I'm dying to hear about the dissolution of America." And she laughed.

They'd made out on their last date, her lips full and her tongue hungry.

Steve considered for just a split second that he might get caught. But there was a tug, one that he might not be able to explain if asked about, but one that promised escape and relief in a way that couldn't happen with Charlie—someone who knew him and to whom he was vulnerable. At least he didn't think so. Except that he didn't think. He surrendered to his need.

They met at an El Salvadoran dive on Florida Avenue. It was their fourth get-together, compounding lies he'd already told.

When she removed her winter coat, she was wearing a spectacular red-floral halter top, her cleavage evident from all angles. It was terrifically inappropriate, and not just for wintry Washington. Even in the dimly-lit *taqueria*, she stood out.

"So, Mr. Middle East? Do you think Bush the son is going to pay homage to the father and finish the Iraqis off?"

Mister Middle East.

"Sorry. What did you ask?"

"Saddam. Saddam Hussein."

"I was just thinking about your question, that it probably didn't really matter who was elected with regard to Iraq."

"How so?"

"Gore was just as committed to regime change as is this Bush crowd."

"Everyone on the Hill is, like, saying the Bush administration is sort of obligated to go for it," she said.

"There are many who regret not marching to Baghdad when they had the chance," he answered, his mouth full of tortilla chips. "Wolfowitz has declared as much."[798]

He went on: "Cheney's obviously key because ... well, he's key. But having said that, who knows where Rumsfeld stands? And Powell's been running around saying that smart sanctions will give Iraqi civilians what they need while constraining Iraq from developing weapons of mass destruction." Smart sanctions—it was all he hated about Washington, right there in one phrase. As if anyone would propose dumb sanctions.

She asked, "So, with Powell saying one thing and Cheney saying another, does that mean they are split?"

"Maybe. They're just getting their feet wet. Let's see what the public actually says. And on Iraq, I'm also not sure the Saudis would be any more enthused by such a move today than they were in 1991."

"The Saudis? Do they really have much of a say?" she asked, not an unreasonable question, but one that made Steve remember he wasn't talking to Charlie.

"It'd be pretty hard to march to Baghdad or to finish off the job without Saudi help, at least without their acquiescence," he answered.

"Aren't they in the process of giving that?" she asked.

As he had before with her, he kicked his head back, surprised, delighted, and annoyed that she could have anything interesting to say, or more important, that she might know something he might not.

"How so?" he asked.

"The congressman got some kind of a highly-classified briefing that Bandar"—Prince Bandar, the Saudi ambassador to Washington—"told President Bush that the no-fly zone over Iraq had essentially run its course, that enforcing it was costing the Saudis militarily and politically while at the same time not hurting Saddam all that much."

"The message being what? What did your congressman think he was saying?"

"He took it to mean that if the Bush administration were going to push military action, the Saudis just wanted it to be decisive, that they wanted to end the standoff once and for all."

Of course, it would be like Bandar to suggest that, Steve thought. The statement was far from a green light. He saw it more as a shrewd move on the part of a certain group to plant a seed, and to reserve an invisible veto at the same time, to be able to say that they just couldn't support a half measure. That would make the most sense, given that Apex Watch concluded that while the Saudis might prefer decisive action, it also was okay with muddling through in Iraq, that bleeding Saddam was far preferable for their interests than having a war.

He was quiet for a moment as he took a bite of rice and beans. She interrupted his thoughts. "You know, Powell might be making his case for bucking the status quo—just smarter, of course. But I can also tell you that, behind his back, intelligence people are all over the Hill arguing just the opposite."

"Arguing? Meaning what?" he asked.

"CIA briefers are telling congressmen that without inspectors on the ground, the IC can no longer be sure about the status of Saddam's WMD program."

"Yeah, that's the CIA's line," Steve almost absentmindedly answered.

"Aha! So, you work for the CIA!"

"I didn't say that."

"And you'd have to, like, kill me if you told me, I get it," she said, smiling widely.

At his apartment, she practically pounced on him, straddling him on the couch. They kissed deeply and he cupped her breasts with his hands, feeling her weight on top of him, a sharp jab of her knee on his thigh.

Her breasts were round and her nipples responsive to his touch. He squeezed hard and she seemed to like the roughness. She pulled back and removed her top. She had tan lines, but her breasts were dark with even darker ends. No sag here.

He started to flick his tongue on the right and then the left. Then he sucked, deeply and intensely, forgetting what was in his head.

"Let me lick you," he said. She knew what he meant and pulled back, wiggling out of her pants, raising herself on the couch and pressing her pussy to his mouth. He took in the pungent smell for a moment and went to work, reaching up to twirl her right nipple between thumb and forefinger. She pressed in harder to his mouth and tried to reach down and touch his penis but couldn't quite reach.

He suggested they go to the bedroom, wondering for just a moment whether she was going to hold back, whether he was going to have to put on a condom. They disentangled as they got up. He wasn't hard, and he worried about why not, deciding he'd use it if it became an issue, as a statement of respect, as proof that their being there wasn't some horny impulse, that he wasn't just about fucking her. But he was also at the same time disappointed that maybe she couldn't truly interest him.

He'd already gotten what he wanted. Her on the hook. Now it was catch and release.

She flopped on the bed vertically, shapely and muscular, heavy-lidded and awaiting. He took off his shirt and pants, underwear and socks, got on top of her and resumed kissing her deeply, still not hard, done with the conquest, dreading having to fuck her, dreading the disappointment that would accompany that.

After what felt like an eternity, she flipped him over and put his penis in her mouth. Again, her lips were moist and plump. She was skillful. He told her he liked it slow and gentle. She laughed and said it wasn't her specialty. But she tried.

He got hard and she quickly straddled him again, putting him inside her. He wasn't able to or interested in thrusting deeply, hoping that she was going to come quickly, but realizing that she was another girl who wanted sex hard, who wanted male dominance.

After he slipped out during her thrusting, he pulled her closer. They kissed and fondled, and he hoped she didn't care that he wasn't hard, that he was finished. Or at least that she was smart enough to keep her mouth shut. He knew he needed roleplay or fantasy, something that diverted his mind for him to stay interested. He watched his brain wander, back to Saddam, to KSM.

Again, she licked him, and though he thought it was nice, he was finished. He took his hardness in his hand and made himself come. She was disappointed he didn't do it in her mouth, she said, and he was impressed, a treat he might hold out for next time, if there was a next time. He wasn't a selfish guy. But he also was stuck inside his head, driven as much by what was there than anything that had to do with the animal instinct.

They lay entangled, she still wanting to orgasm, and he put his finger inside her, massaging her clit. She kept asking for him to do it harder, and then for him to tell her she was a good girl. He did. He'd call her fucking Martha Washington if that's what she wanted. He'd do anything at this point to get rid of her. So much potential to be harnessed, he thought, but now he was all thoughts of something else.

He walked her home at near midnight, just down the block. While they were walking, she leaned into him and linked her arm in his. He liked her, believe it or not.

At her door, as they kissed deeply again, she said she really liked him. And she asked when they would see each other again.

"You know what they say," he said, not meaning to be a shit, but also wanting to appear nonchalant. "Feed 'em, fuck 'em, forget 'em."

When he got home there was an email already waiting. "Let's change that third F to feelings," she said.

Not that.

Chapter 50 Three Khalids

There was a knock on Steve's open office door. Charlie popped her head in. "Got a minute?" she asked. "Erica has something interesting to show you."

Erica, Barbara's best analyst and the object of yet another crush. She stepped forward and handed Steve a standard I-94, the Immigration and Naturalization Service entry and exit form filled out by arriving and departing passengers. *Khalid Mihdhar* the scribbled name said, barely legible. The Saudi citizen left the United States on a flight from Los Angeles to Frankfurt on June 10, 2000.[799]

California tugged at Steve. KSM told Charlie that his pilot—singular—would train inside the country. And more than once, he'd asked Apex Watch to supply some odd piece of material relating to San Diego, where Steve thought they must be.

But what to look for? Weeks ago, Charlie proposed that they watchlist Arab and Pakistani males entering the country via the West Coast. Skeptical that such a dragnet would result in anything, Steve agreed with the assignment, never really expecting to hear back.

"He left, not entered," Steve said, looking at the form.

"I know," said Erica, smiling, bouncing on her toes. "But let me show you. I checked the name Khalid Mihdhar against the databases …"

"Checked the name? Why?"

"I'm checking all names that seem to fit, entering and exiting."

"*Oh-kay,*" he said, secretly delighted. And, instantly, he was curious about her.

"He's a known terrorist," she said.

"Known to whom?" Steve asked.

"The CIA,"[800] she responded. "Known to be affiliated with *al Qaeda*. Not only that, but also possibly son-in-law of the operator of the so-called Yemen switchboard. And known to have traveled with Walid bin Attash after the African embassy bombings.[801] Known to have been involved in a meeting that included *Hambali*[802] and another *al Qaeda* man whom the Agency lists as possibly being involved in their development of chemical weapons."[803]

"Bin Attash—meaning KSM's buddy, Khallad?" Steve asked, mentally digesting the rest.

"I believe so," said Erica. "Unless there's two Khallads."

"This is KSM's buddy?" Steve reiterated, looking at Charlie.

"Evidently, they are one and the same," Charlie answered, nodding her head and raising her eyebrows approvingly at Erica's sleuthing.

"And this Mihdhar? He was in the United States?"

"For months."

"And you're sure he's the same person as this known terrorist?"

"I am," Erica said.

"I suppose you don't know if he attended flight school?" Steve asked.

"I do," Erica said, obviously delighted to answer this question. She handed him a piece of paper showing Mihdhar's registration for a flight school orientation.[804]

"You got this how?"

"A friend at the Agency asked the local police through the FBI to go check."

Steve looked at Charlie, who shook her head in amazement and pride. Steve loved to direct and mentor, but rarely did he have the pleasure of not having to tell someone else *how* to conduct a task.

"Want to hear the whole story?" Erica said.

Steve sat back in his chair. "Go for it."

Charlie and Erica took seats across from Steve's desk, and Erica dove in. "Remember Mohammed al-Owhali, the African-embassy bomber captured right after the Kenya attack?[805] The FBI picked up a telephone number from him, one he was instructed to call after the attack.[806] 967-1-200578," she said, almost absentmindedly. "He later told the Bureau that the number was the Yemeni home of a friend: Sameer al-Hada."

"Al-Hada," Steve interrupted. "That's the guy who runs the Yemen switchboard?"[807]

"Yes," she said, "but it's a new number."

"And Sameer is who?"

"Evidently he's a son, or maybe it's just an alias," Erica said. "To tell you the truth, I didn't really go down that rabbit hole," she admitted, blue eyes twinkling. "Not yet."

She continued: "As you know, the NSA has been sitting on the so-called Yemen switchboard. I've checked both numbers. They have called, among others, bin Laden's satellite phone."[808]

"Has it called any number we associate with KSM?"

"Not directly."

"Not directly meaning what?"

"I'm getting there."

"Okay, go on."

"The NSA actually intercepted a call in which an unknown voice said that a *Khaled*, and the analyst interpreting the sound spelled it with an e, Khaled, ed—last name unknown—was planning to travel from Sana'a in Yemen to Malaysia, possibly to meet up with an associate, identified at the time as Nawaf.[809]

"In their initial report, the NSA provisionally identified this *Nawaf* person as a Saudi named Nawaf al-Hazmi, an Arab veteran of Afghanistan and someone who had returned there since Osama bin Laden's return from Sudan.

"CTC also put together a report on the two, Nawaf and Khaled with an e," Erica continued, "placing Nawaf and the now presumed Yemeni-citizen Khaled on a watchlist, to see if they could confirm their identity."[810]

"What watchlist are we talking about?" Steve asked, wondering why he didn't pick up on this piece of intelligence.

"Let me show you," she said. "It wasn't related to travel to the United States. They were purely looking for identifying data. CTC decided that they were going to follow this unknown traveler—Khaled, last name unknown—to ascertain his identity, and they notified a half-dozen CIA stations and foreign liaison partners, including the Yemenis and the Malaysians…"[811]

"And the Saudis?" he asked Erica.

"Yep."

"That's how we lost him?" he said, jumping ahead.

"No," she responded. "The effort was somewhat of a success."

"Okay," he said, shaking his head. "Go on."

"Based on the travel route of first name Khaled with an e—suspected Yemeni—the Agency requested biographic details during his overnight layover in Dubai on his way to Malaysia. The Emiratis evidently did their jobs because I found an operational cable dated January 4, 2000 in which Dubai station reported to headquarters, as well as to Kuala Lumpur station in Malaysia, that the suspect was actually named Khalid Mihdhar—with an i, not an e. Also, a photocopy of his passport was made. He's Saudi, not Yemeni: Khalid bin Muhammad bin `Abdallah al-Mihdhar."[812]

"Means nothing to me," Steve said, shrugging. "You?" he said to Charlie.

"Listen," she said.

"So," Erica went on. "Though this Mihdhar was traveling with Nawaf al-Hazmi, a quote known *al Qaeda* operative, there's no other evident connection between them. Unless of course he is really a guy named al-Maki, but that's another story."

"Are you saying that Khalid al-Mihdhar is not his real name?" Steve asked.

"I can't yet tell you that for sure, but I'll put my neck out and say that though he's been using the Mihdhar name for a long time, it isn't his real name."[813]

"So who is he?"

"Let me continue. With Mihdhar going to Kuala Lumpur for unknown purposes, the Malaysia station tipped off their local partners about arriving Saudi citizens, as the CIA had communicated to them, requesting they be placed under surveillance.

"As far as I can make out, but without talking to any of those involved, the surveillance operation was another success." Erica gestured with air quotes to punctuate the word success. "Malaysian Special Branch followed

Mihdhar and al-Hazmi to a condo complex 20 miles south of the capital, where they attended what was labeled 'a suspected *al Qaeda* meeting'. There was no technical penetration, but the Malaysians kept a close eye on everyone for the next three days and cataloged who went in and out."[814]

Referring to her notes, Erica said, "Malaysian Special Branch identified the place where they were meeting as being owned by Yazid Sufaat."

"Never heard of him…" Steve offered. "Any reason to remember the name?"

"No," Erica said, "he's—"

"*Blech,*" Charlie interrupted, "you're going to hate this, Steve. WMD."

Erica confirmed it. "Sufaat, aka Malik, is a Malaysian scientist and member of *JI*[815] whom the Agency suspects is running *al Qaeda's* chemical and biological weapons program—at least in Southeast Asia."

"Oh fuck," Steve exclaimed. "Let me guess. Once weapons of mass destruction enter the picture, it lights up the big board and that shifts everyone's attention away from the guy?"

Erica didn't immediately get the reference to the big board from *Doctor Strangelove,* nor Steve's disgust about the subject of WMD.

There was a little line. He was focused on it for a split second, a line that extended up from her v-neck, a line suggesting breasts. Steve's focus on that line, his mind wandering, made him realize for just a moment how anxious he was, how he was barely holding it together. Then he rocketed back to the conversation, locking up his discomfort. He looked up at her eyes.

She plowed forward. "The identification of Mihdhar was being cited as a success, as was the reporting that *bin Laden associates*"—again she used air quotes—"were having a clandestine meeting. There's no doubt though that the addition of weapons of mass destruction to the reporting stream garnered attention at higher levels.

"Director Tenet had a special report written for the White House saying that the Agency obtained quote 'complete biographic information' unquote on a previously unknown Saudi terrorist. And it did appear that an important meeting was going on."

"Even FBI Director Freeh was getting personal updates," Charlie again interrupted.[816]

"Oh, Jesus," said Steve. "Updates on what?"

"WMD. Because it's the FBI's bailiwick if it involves terrorism in which Americans are involved. And because they had *al Qaeda* under surveillance in real time," Charlie answered, using air quotes herself for *in real time*.

"It seems like all that success really went to their heads," Erica continued, wedging herself back into the conversation.

She went on: "According to the surveillance reports from Malaysia, on January 8, Mihdhar and Nawaf ordered a taxi and Special Branch followed them to the airport. A third man was now with them, someone later identified as Yemeni citizen Saleh Saeed Mohammed Binyousaf. According to the Malaysians, he'd visited a clinic to be fitted for a new prosthetic leg."[817]

"Khallad," Charlie and Steve both said at the same time. Could there possibly be more than one important Yemeni *al Qaeda* operative with a missing leg?

"At the airport," Erica went on, "the three purchased tickets to fly to Bangkok, with cash.[818]

"The Malaysians tried to make the hand off to the Thai intelligence guys, telling them of the three men: one of whom they identified as Khalid Mihdhar. Somehow they screwed up the second man's first name, and just merged the rest into one name, ending up with *f'new Alhazmi*. And the third man was identified only with part of his name, which they also screwed up as *Salahsae FNU/LNU*."

Erica spelled out the name *Salahsae* but said *f'new l'new*, an expression known to everyone in the intelligence community: first name unknown, last name unknown.

They'd have to work together closely, Steve daydreamed. He'd ignore the line, impressing her that he was only interested in how good she was, how smart she was. Then he'd seduce her. God, what was he even thinking? What was wrong with him?

Erica continued: "Because the tickets were purchased at the counter, there was no credit card record and there wasn't a lot of time. And, unfortunately, the Thais missed the three on their arrival. At least in real time. And," she added, "I'm not so sure what passports any of them used to enter Thailand. Anyway, the Agency also contacted Thai intelligence to watchlist the names if any of them departed Thailand, but they got nothing."[819]

"They didn't go back to Yemen?" Steve asked. "Or on to Pakistan?"

"Nope. And the Thai police stayed with it for six weeks."

"How hard would it be to get flight manifests around that week to do our own checking?" Steve asked.

"I don't think we need them," Erica answered.

He wasn't interested in anything other than a harmless affair. A little fun? Yuck—he hated himself. He was in love with Charlie. He was already cheating on her with Keren. Was it just to make the conquest? Or to fulfill a compulsion?

His mind came back to the meeting.

"I already have the answer," said Erica.

"I didn't ask the question yet," Steve said, smiling.

"I went through the manifests, all flights from Thailand thereafter. On January 14, Nawaf Hazmi and Khalid Mihdhar boarded United Airlines Flight 2 to Los Angeles, via Hong Kong."[820]

"Holy shit," Steve said. Looking at the manifest from Erica, he immediately thought that they'd found KSM's pilots. The two sat together in first class.

"I've got a funny anecdote," Erica went on, again almost bouncing. "These are two known *al Qaeda* operatives—so *known* they are known to the CIA director himself and have been briefed to director Freeh and the White House. And they enter the United States and they remain here for five months, undetected. I've gone back and looked at the original UAE report on Mihdhar's identity. It clearly says his Saudi passport contains a valid entry visa for the United States. Not only did no one seem to act on that piece of intelligence, but when it was all done, the people you like to call idiots actually did the most idiotic thing."

"And that was?" Steve asked.

"The Agency concluded the individual originally identified as Khaled with an e by the NSA, and the Khalid with an i by the Emiratis, and the Khallad identified by the Malaysians with the double L spelling are all one and the same person."[821]

"Oh, Jesus. That's enough to make you cry," Steve said. "And, by the way, fantastic work."

"Thanks," Erica responded. But she wasn't finished. *She* wanted to learn. "Doesn't this give us some leg up on KSM that he could never imagine?" she asked. "That we've identified the pilots?"

Charlie readily agreed. The two women looked at Steve.

He was thinking. "To me," he finally said, "the lesson is that using shorthand like the KSM alias is always fraught with danger. The ease of the acronym makes it seems a lot more intimate than it really is, as if we actually know the guy.

"Same with Osama bin Laden," Steve went on. "In Arabic, the first name transliterates as Usamah, so from the beginning, intelligence insiders—even ones who can't speak a word of Arabic—took to calling him UBL, and they continue to annoyingly do so today, even after the whole world has begun to use the spelling Osama, which of course would make him OBL. UBL thus has become some shrewd insider acronym used by the likes of Tenet and others to suggest a familiarity and a depth of knowledge that is greater than they possess.

"And now with this? Khaled? Khalid? Khallad? Khalid Doha? Khalid Sheikh? Khalid Sheikh Mohammed? It's hard enough without the help of the added acronyms and government shortcuts," Steve went on.

Erica and Charlie both looked disappointed with his digression.

"Your point is what?" Charlie asked.

"We are talking about matters of life and death, and yet those who are working the issues want to believe that merely identifying someone is tantamount to understanding them. It reminds me that I've fallen into the trap myself."

"So, is this your backhanded way of apologizing?" Charlie asked.

"About?"

"If we had just kept track of the low-level operatives from the beginning, rather than seeing them as mere informational steppingstones to get closer to leadership for targeting, we would have caught these two on entry in Los Angeles. And maybe many others."

Charlie was, of course, right. Only the big names like UBL or Ramzi Yousef or Dr. Zawahiri—*always "Doctor,"* as if somehow he was to be distinguished by a lab coat and, ironically, calling him doctor made him sound older and more distinguished than he really was—were *known*, and even there with a very small *k*. Which, of course, didn't mean known at all, just that the names were prominent enough to garner high-level attention, meriting an acronym or a nickname. Everyone knew Ramzi Yousef, or bin Laden, or even Zawahiri, they were the so-called *known*, known to the amateurs, while no one else was known at all.

Steve never answered Erica's question.

"Erica," he said, "they entered the United States and the authorities never suspected a thing. What do we know now about the two after that?"

"Well, first, let me go back. On March 5," she said, "months *after* they'd left Bangkok, the intelligence authorities in Thailand finally answered the CIA request to report on the whereabouts of Khalid Mihdhar and 'Nawaf' LNU arriving by air from Malaysia. The Thais said that two of the three individuals who had arrived in Bangkok on January 8th were Saudi citizens according to their passports, Khalid Mihdhar and Nawaf Hazmi, while the third was a Yemeni named Salah Saeed Mohammed Bin Yousaf.[822] Hazmi departed on January 15 on that United Airlines flight to Los Angeles International Airport. Yousaf the Yemeni went to Karachi. And there was no further information on the travel of Mihdhar."[823]

"What happened to Mihdhar?" he asked.

Again, Erica beamed. "He traveled with Nawaf. Under his own name. Hence his entry form. The Thais just made a mistake."

"And Yousaf is?"

"I think that's Khallad, but I'll come back to that," Erica answered.

"And no one caught on about Mihdhar entering the country, even after this message came from Bangkok?"

"No one at the CIA station in Bangkok did more than just pass on the information that came in from their liaison partners. No one in Malaysia station made a connection between the meeting that they so closely monitored just weeks earlier. No one at the bin Laden unit back at headquarters seemed to have read the incoming report, probably because it was labeled: *action required none*.[824] In fact, I can find no evidence that anyone in the IC or the Immigration and Naturalization Service paid any attention to these men entering the United States."

Charlie spoke up: "So Mihdhar, with an American visa, and Hazmi, a *known jihadi*, weren't watchlisted by the State Department. No one noticed the intelligence that might have sent an FBI agent in Los Angeles to at least knock on some door."

"It gets worse," said Erica.

Steve sat admiringly, awaiting the next morsel.

"Fifteen days later, one of the two make a call from San Diego to the same Yemen switchboard," she said.[825]

"A direct call to an *al Qaeda* switchboard from San Diego," Steve exclaimed, "and NSA didn't think that suspicious?"

The three sat in silence for a moment.

"So, just to review," said Erica. "A telephone call is made to a *known* terrorist facility in the Middle East already linked to *al Qaeda* activities, a number *known* to the NSA, in fact, one that is being monitored. The other end of the call is from San Diego—from a telephone publicly *registered* to Nawaf al-Hazmi."

"Publicly registered?" Steve asked.

"I called the phone company. They told me it's a new line in the name of al-Hazmi.[826]

"Mother Mary," Charlie hissed.

"But you are telling me that the man Mihdhar has now left," Steve said.

"That is correct."

"And the other guy?"

"I think he's still in San Diego. But I checked, and it appears he's not in flight school."

"He's doing what?" Steve asked.

"That I can't say," Erica answered. "But it looks like he's still in San Diego."

Erica was probably half his age, tall and lithe, a road leading nowhere. He refocused.

"Can we find him and put him under surveillance?" Charlie asked.

"I think I have a current address," Erica said.

"What good would that do?" Steve asked.

"To know," Charlie said. "To have a better picture. What if the Agency or FBI catches on to his being there?"

"Our mucking about in his life seems to me to be the surest way of making that happen," Steve replied.

"How so?"

"I'm just not sure I trust that the FBI doesn't know something already. I find it hard to believe that this guy could just get forgotten."

"Oh," Erica said. "I guess I won't take that as an insult."

"How so?" he asked her.

"That I just found someone that the FBI already knew about ..."

"That's not at all what I meant," he said laughing. "You did fantastic work. I'm just saying the FBI couldn't fucking find Hazmi if he was standing on Pennsylvania Avenue. What I meant was, they could have a file and an informant somewhere. Why wouldn't they? And yet they might not know why. And we know they're not sharing. So if we start inquiring, someone might think that they need to take a closer look. So short of sending Erica out to San Diego, I say we think of how all of this could be used to our advantage with KSM."

At dinner with Erica, he imagined, he'd listen and ask personal and interested questions, a walk in the dark, a smooch on the street, and then back to his apartment for a night of lovemaking, her young body quenching his thirst for desire, *self-desire* outside the realm of his demanding brain.

"And what about Khallad," Charlie asked. "He was obviously connected to KSM closely, someone *he* wanted to protect."

"Again, I'm not sure what we can do," Steve said.

"He went where?" Steve asked Erica.

"Khallad," Erica answered. "Now that's a different story."

"Spit it out," Steve said, again chuckling.

"From Thai records, Khallad, now identified as Mr. Yousaf, hung around in the country for a few more days. Then on the 20th, as Mr. Salahsae, he took a flight to Karachi."

"And disappeared?" Steve asked.

"Yes," Erica answered. "But he didn't fly alone. According to airline records, he accompanied a minor, a 15-year-old Yemeni girl named Amal Ahmed al-Sadah."

"His daughter?"

"Fucker," Charlie interrupted. "You know nothing about this world."

"Ms. Charbel immediately knew who she was," Erica said, ignoring the outburst.

"She is Osama bin Laden's new bride-to-be," Erica said. "His fifth wife. Special delivery!"[827] And she plopped the file on Steve's desk.

He wanted her.

After she left, Charlie spoke up, cheerily but also as cold as ice: "Nice date?" She knew Steve.

He jerked his head back. "What?"

"You're so transparent. You were practically drooling …"

"That's unfair. Erica is half my age and, fuck, she's good. I'd just ruin her, ruin everything. And I have you. But thanks for noticing. And grinding it in."

"Anxious?"

"What do you think? Fuck yes, I'm anxious. Sometimes I feel like I can barely breathe."

"Are we doing the right thing?"

"I sure hope so," he answered.

"Is it going to work?"

"I'm afraid the answer to that question is an emphatic yes," Steve said. "But as this meeting proves, it works because we don't share what we know. Fortunately, we don't have to doctor any records, or fuck with the system anymore, because they are so fucking hopeless all by themselves. These guys should have been detected. Numerous times. I can only imagine how many records like this they are going to find after the attack, things they missed. It makes our job of obfuscating the government record so much easier."

"I get all of that. But Steven. Can we at least talk about it? Are we doing the right thing? It's getting close."

"Some days I just want to make it through the day. Some days I'm moving parts on the global chess board, a grandmaster," he said. "But I'm so anxious I also feel like I could explode."

"I can tell," she said.

Steve didn't want to say more, didn't even want to think about it more. He was the expert, in command of the facts. Of that he was sure. But he'd also just made it all up, invented the whole thing and had done so with such assurance that *it would work* that he'd lost sight of the whether it should. He certainly lost sight of himself, of his role, lost in a story of his making, like a historical novel where what's true and what's made up becomes more and more vague.

Charlie wanted to put her hand gently on his and pat it, to take care of her partner. She could see that a volcano was stirring, the gasses and magma building. But she also was struggling with her own conscience, now additionally suspicious in every way that even inside the chamber of secrets there was so much she didn't know.

PART 13

Chapter 51 Cold Case

The phone dragged him out of a deep slumber, and he looked over at the glowing clock radio: 2:09 a.m.[828]

"Bowlen," he answered—his routine greeting.

"Sorry to wake you, boss," said the voice on the line.

"No problem." Bowlen turned on the small bedside lamp, fumbling around with his glasses, now wide awake. It was Steve Draper.

"I'm just off 270 and could be at your house in just a few minutes. It's a bit of an emergency."

"Of course," Bowlen said.

There were some things that were never discussed over the phone, and now that they were getting very close, they tightened security even more.

"Of course," Bowlen said again. "I'll turn on the porch light." Putting on his bathrobe and slippers, he shushed his wife back to sleep. "Work," he whispered. That's all he ever really said. "I'll just be a minute."

Downstairs, he switched on an entry hall lamp and the outside light and went into the kitchen to set the kettle to boil. He couldn't imagine what Steve's crisis could possibly be. Normally, a duty officer called with incoming intelligence. Steve never called. Nor came by.

He heard a quiet knock on the door. That's polite of him not to use the doorbell and wake up his wife, Bowlen thought.

"Sir," Steve said as a greeting.

"Would you like a cup of tea?"

"Sure," he said, following the white-haired director as he walked back into the kitchen.

"Don't mean to be impolite sir, but this is time-sensitive," Steve said, walking behind him.

Bowlen's Potomac house was one of those McMansions popping up in the posh and prosperous Washington suburbs, more expansive than anything Steven had ever lived in. The kitchen was nearly the size of his entire apartment, with a center island made of fancy marble and a breakfast nook tucked in the corner.

Turning around under the bright kitchen lights, Bowlen took a look at Steve. He was dressed as always, a slightly rumpled shirt and a black fleece. But something appeared slightly off. He put two cups of tea on the kitchen table and sat down on the bench seat opposite his deputy.

"I need to use the Carthage team," Steven said, getting right to the point. Carthage was the Apex Watch emergency plan to ensure that their existence disappeared if there were a need to shut down the operation. A special appendix had been written for Project Sumner.

"Okay," Bowlen responded slowly, drawing it out, making it clear there was a question involved. "Have we been compromised?"

"Sort of. But I need to implement certain procedures. Tony is already standing by."

"You've already made arrangements?" Bowlen questioned, not really asking. "So, what do you need from me?"

"I didn't want to go around you," Steven responded.

"But you're not actually asking."

"I'm asking," he said. "Tony insists you give a go-ahead. I need it now."

"The go-ahead for what, Steven? We have our procedures in place if there is a compromise."

"I need to get rid of a body."

"You what?"

"She's already dead ..."

"Dead as in?"

"It's a girl. I killed her," Steve said, like he was recounting a sandwich he'd eaten.

"Someone at Apex Watch?" Bowlen asked, his voice at a higher pitch, his heart tightening.

"No, no," Steve answered, chuckling. "Sir, I've worked out how to make the body disappear. If you want to know the details, I can share them. But I have to move now."

"Want to say more?"

"She could have compromised the whole operation. She said she was going to. It's my doing. I'm sorry, boss. I've already been to her apartment and returned her personal effects, her purse, credit cards, et cetera to where they might be if she just went out with just her keys and some cash. I did some internet searches on her laptop to establish for investigators that she was home until late. When she doesn't show up for work, or if her parents can't reach her in the coming days, the police will enter the apartment and find no sign of foul play and a mysteriously missing girl."

"Her parents? How old is she?"

"Twenty-four," said Steve. "I'm proposing we store the body in the old chiller building on Odell Road until the police investigation blows over. Then we can place the body in a remote corner of Rock Creek Park. She'll be just another girl who's disappeared, just another cold case."

Cold case indeed, Bowlen thought, his stomach tightening.

"I don't even know what to say," Bowlen responded. "Where is she?"

"In my apartment. Tony is standing by to dispose of her."

Dispose of her.

Steve continued: "Boss, I'm really sorry. We need to move before daylight to make this plan workable."

"You killed her?"

"Yes," he said softly. "I thought it the only way to save the project."

"You killed her," Bowlen repeated.

"Yes."

"Is she an Agency employee?"

"No."

"Anyone I know?"

"No."

"Is she a person of any interest politically?"

"Boss, she's just a girl. I stupidly compromised the project to her, and she panicked about what I told her. I decided that she had to go. She works for a congressman on the intel committee."

"A congressman! And that's not politically interesting? Are you insane?"

Steve paused. "She's already dead, sir. Can I just make the call? And yes, maybe I am, insane."

Bowlen was trapped. People had died before on his watch. Stranger things had happened. At least that's what he was telling himself. "And Tony agrees?" he asked.

"Tony insists on your giving a go-ahead."

"And you decided to involve him why?"

"To save the project. I take responsibility. Carthage procedures exist for a compromise."

"You killed her—why, Steven?"

"I already told you. She was going to tell her congressman. She was ranting and emotional. I tried to calm her down. But then I decided."

"Who knows about this?"

"Just Tony and Roy. And now you." There was a pause. "Sorry to push you, boss, but can I make the call?" Steve persisted. "We can keep knowledge of this in a tight circle."

"Does that make it okay?"

"Fuck, sir. No. No!" Steve said it emphatically, looking Bowlen straight in the eye. "Not at all. I am not going to defend what I did or argue with you. It's not okay. This is literally cleaning up my mess."

He lowered his voice, almost to a whisper. "This is a personal request. I've done the best I can to cover my tracks. I'll admit that I'm ultimately fucked. I'll take whatever punishment you deem necessary. But we need to do this now to protect the entire operation. I'll answer any questions you have once I get Tony underway."

"You called and involved Tony before you contacted me?"

"I already told you that."

Bowlen wanted to be steaming inside but he wasn't really, his own mind looking ahead.

"Make the call," he relented.

As Steve got up to do so, Bowlen closed his eyes. He'd known many an Agency cowboy and had run into his fair share of sociopaths in his two and a half decades in the spy world. But Steve Draper? This man he'd come to know and love? A callous murderer? Sure, he was volatile. Bowlen had experienced him exuding spine-chilling emotion to annihilate someone … verbally … in an argument.

But he never imagined this desk-bound nerd could … or would ever … and now seeming to have done so with such cold-bloodedness.

He'd had warnings. Barbara gingerly raised questions about Steve being brought on board, feeling compelled to ask for a private meeting and recounting her own experience working with him: his prickliness, his lying. And she shared his hall reputation, especially among the young women.

Charlie even recently confided to Bowlen that she didn't completely trust Steve, confronting him with the idea that maybe he and Steve were hiding something from her.

Clearly another woman in his apartment at 2 a.m. meant she was right. But when Bowlen had asked Charlie what was specifically bothering her, she said that Steve was being too flat, that sometimes she suspected that he knew too much. Or that he pretended he didn't know something when he did. But she knew he wasn't sharing all he knew. She thought Steve seemed to be going behind her back to do something.

He'd noticed it, too. Outwardly, Steve lacked any misgivings about what they were doing. But Bowlen also had to admit to himself that he thought it—Steve's coldness—to be a leadership quality. Charlie did, too. When someone on the staff had a crisis of conscience about Project Sumner, Steve calmly and sensitively bucked up their sagging conviction. Not with grandiosity and big words or threats. He soothed, explaining patiently that there was no other way, appealing to their sense of concern for the country and the world. Bowlen watched it happen. How Steve inspired admiration and loyalty. Tony and the boys all swaggered more when he was around. He'd even won Barbara over.

A shiver came over Bowlen. No matter what was going down, Steve always rolled up his sleeves to help with a problem, strong as steel. No matter what the crisis. Especially when others were overwhelmed with the balance between their own involvement and their sense of right and wrong. He did it. It was almost superhuman. Or not human. Without a shred of emotion. Just like what he was observing right here in his kitchen.

Steve returned to the table and sat down. "Thank you," he said.

"Want to tell me what happened?"

"How much you want to know?"

"How about the outlines to start?"

"White, female, mid 20s, from California, she's an intern on the Hill. She's having an affair with a congressman." He was ticking off facts as if he were a detective briefing a murder case, someone else's murder.

"She's having an affair with a congressman?"

"We're having an affair," he said.

"Steven," Bowlen said, "what happened?"

"We met at a bar in Adams Morgan. About five months ago."

"So, you've been seen with her."

"Yes." And he stopped for a second, thinking, calculating. "I am sure, though, that no connection to tonight can be made. No phone calls, no answering machine."

Bowlen was being drawn in. They were moving from murder to operational security. And then Steve gave the outlines. There were late-night dates, an affair, Steve went too far and bragged to her about what he was involved in ...

Bowlen didn't want to know any more. But if his partner, normally quite secretive about anything personal was going to talk, he was going to listen.

Steve was saying that compulsively getting together with her that night helped him to find some release from the pressures.

"And that works?" Bowlen asked genuinely. He and his wife had married right after graduation and, though he had observed the modern ways of his now adult children, Bowlen had no experience and no intelligence on this foreign country of being single.

"Chief," Steven said with a momentary weariness, "whatever works works." And he chuckled to himself.

He laughed.

"I told her I was working on a secret project, that it was going to result in a terrorist attack on the United States."

"Why would you tell her that?"

"I don't know, boss," he said, his head now in his hands.

It wasn't an act. "Maybe it was part of the seduction?" He spoke into the table. "I tell myself I was test-driving how a civilian might react."

Bowlen was stone silent.

"Because when I feel that way, that compulsion to alleviate some anxiety because the pressure is too much to handle, I say shit, say anything.

It's like my mind wanders somewhere else, like daydreaming or getting lost in a movie, but more pronounced. I'm aware, but also disconnected.

"At first she didn't believe what I was saying," he went on, glossing over his confession, "so I added details—I preened ..."

"But why, Steven?"

"I don't know. To show off? To make myself seem more important?"

Steve was now talking in a very small voice.

"All that energy that goes into my work," he started, looking up, tears forming, his mind now wandering, thinking about his need for approbation, but also formulating an explanation that was acceptable. "I don't know, sir. I don't know," he repeated, buying some more time.

He went on: "Look, I'm not asserting some Twinkie defense ... I fucking killed her. From when I concluded I had to, until I did it and was back in my own body wondering what I had just done, was less than five minutes.

"All I can remember is that all of a sudden she's telling me that she's going to have to tell *her* congressman."

The phone rang. As Bowlen walked over to the wall unit, he wondered if it made sense, Steve's justification, for why he killed her. For security? To save the project? Was there something wrong with Steve? Something deep inside his heart.

"Bowlen," he said picking up the phone.

"Sorry to wake you, sir," said the duty officer. "Tony wants you to know that the matter is taken care of."

"Thank you, Pat," Bowlen said, hanging up. Tony didn't have the heart to call himself, almost as if he were sending him a signal, removing his fingerprints.

"It's over," Bowlen said, turning to Steve.

He visibly softened.

"And Charlie?" asked Bowlen. "I suppose it's none of my business ..."

"I wouldn't say it isn't your business, but hopefully she knows nothing and will find out nothing."

"And I'm supposed to be a conspirator there, too?"

"You do whatever you think is right," Steve answered. "She's already waffling about the entire operation, so I just ask that you wait until it goes down." Bowing his head and almost talking into the floor, Steve choked out: "Sir, I'm really sorry."

"Steven, is it your intention to pin this on the congressman?"

"I hope so."

"Jesus, Steven."

"It's one death, one death in a war that's going to kill thousands, where thousands are already dying," he said.

"Really? You're going to make that argument?"

"I'm not making any argument. I'm just saying that we are already committing treason, what's a murder on top? I thought about this in the car on the way here—not as justification, more as a fucking reminder of what we're doing, of what we're capable of doing. Of what I'm capable of doing.

"Tonight, sir, I thought of it for the first time in human terms. Not wrapped up in patriotic fervor or bullshit strategic necessity. I'm not saying any of this to justify what I did tonight. But we want to pat ourselves on the back that we're acting where others can't, that we're filling the gap where others don't. So tonight I thought: Fuck, we're precipitating a war, a global war, and yes, though it's for a greater good, we're murderers. But we're doing it to reshape the future, reshaping it not just in our interest, in the American interest, but also for the interest of the very people who will be labeled the victims, who will be the victims. Americans will die—many, many at our hands. We have to believe that it's worth it. And I do. I do.

"Forgive the rant, sir. But who really gives a shit about whether we use the salad fork or not as we sit down for this meal. This girl? She's one person. And I don't know this congressman. And I don't really give a shit about him. And when I look at myself in the mirror, it looks like I don't really care—but not caring is sort of what lubricates this entire engine. Should I pretend otherwise?"

Bowlen was exhausted. "Steven, go home. Take a couple of days off."

"Yeah," Steve answered. "Thanks, boss. But that's not going to happen."

He got up. "Really, boss, thank you. I don't know what else to say." Steve took Bowlen's hand, grasping it with both of his.

Bowlen escorted him to the door. Returning to the kitchen to clean off the table, the clock on the microwave oven announced 4:15 a.m. There was no going back to sleep.

Chapter 52 Family Affairs

At the Taif summer palace, Crown Prince Abdullah sat on the shaded veranda, taking his morning coffee as he read his daily briefings.

Most of the noble families had been retreating from desert-hot Riyadh to Taif for decades, the city now containing sumptuous homes and newly-built palaces of all the great princes. The view was magnificent over the high walls. It was a mile up on the slopes of the Sarawat Mountains.[829]

Next door was the al-Katib Palace, with its combined Ottoman and Roman architecture, once the home to King Faisal, and the birthplace, Abdullah thought, of the pro-American faction in the country.[830]

In his world, even at the top, Abdullah was not a part of the pro-American faction because he was not one of the so-called *Sudairi* Seven, the dominant union of the seven sons of King Abdul-Aziz and his favorite wife Hussa Sudairi.[831] The eldest of the seven was now king—a debilitated king in a wheelchair, but still king.

Abdullah, who had become the power behind the throne after Fahd's stroke (which occurred just two weeks after the Riyadh bombing), was still an interloper when it came to the seven, despite outranking them. And it wasn't that he was outside the maternal family. He just wasn't pro-American. Well, not that he was anti-American. It was more, he thought, that he had a more balanced view of what Saudi interests were.

Abdullah regularly butted heads with the pro-American and pro-business contingent amongst the powerful royals. While he was supportive of commerce, Abdullah also thought it a shame that the Arab world failed to put its young men to work. Here he oddly also earned the enmity of the religious fundamentalists. They enjoyed their hold on these young men, subsisting on the Saudi reputation for piety while ministering to the poor and hopeless—those young men a powerless and compliant congregation whom they wanted to stay just that way.

The *Sudairis* headed all the important national security ministries.[832] And they were the voices who counseled King Fahd to accept American military forces after the Iraqi invasion of Kuwait. Abdullah was one of the few royals arguing at the time against letting in the American military.[833] Afterwards, he argued against letting the Americans stay. Now, nine years later, he felt like he was largely a powerless bystander. The Iraq standoff persisted, and the Iranian *threat* grew while the Americans dug in so focused on Baghdad.

Appointing each other to the powerful ministries, allies, sons and nephews of the *Sudairi* served in Prince Turki's intelligence establishment, or in the diplomatic corps, which was headed by the wily and influential ambassador Prince Bandar, son of Defense Minister Prince Sultan (who was the second eldest of the seven). To most in the government and the corporate world, Turki and Bandar were the faces of Saudi Arabia, both extremely skillful at indulging Western officialdom and affecting a comforting profile.

Despite his annoyance with the American military presence, Abdullah considered himself a realist. He didn't have an alternative to the never-ending mission to contain Saddam Hussein, but he felt that the focus on rogue Iraq and nuclear Iran was a smokescreen and a diversion from the real evil: Israel and Zionism, which existed like a cancer within the Muslim world. Abdullah believed that as long as the Jewish state sat there at its center, the Muslim people—the *ummah* from Mauritania to the Philippines—would never be one.

Crown Prince Abdullah was spurred to action because of a third Saudi group: the businessmen and the mischievous members of the vast royal family who openly defied him and the king by insisting on funding terrorism—including Osama bin Laden—to ostensibly "protect" Islam from even greater subjugation and dilution. In Abdullah's view, the funding of international terrorism pitted a faction inside Saudi Arabia and the Islamic nation against the House of Saud's long-term interests. Even those who were reluctant had to admit that their support for bin Laden ended the domestic attacks after Riyadh and Khobar Towers. And with that change in his tactics, they imagined some control of their Saudi son.

He looked at his calendar, and the international calendar prepared by the palace staff. Young President Bush was going on vacation in Texas for an entire month, he read—*how civilized, maybe an Arabian stallion would make a nice gift.*

Abdullah's personal secretary swept in with a stack of messages. Prince Bandar had something to tell him and was ready to call. Prince Turki had an important report he needed to hand-deliver, this morning if possible. The White House switchboard had also called—Vice President Cheney wanted to speak to him, also sometime today. And there was a confidential and sealed note from one Lawrence Bowlen, a note that the assistant knew was like other notes which occasionally and mysteriously arrived via messenger, notes that he always handled as toxic and dangerous.

By protocol, half-brother Bandar was first on his list. Though they were not allies, the Saudi ambassador always delivered the finest riches from Washington—inside information and juicy gossip.

The CIA, Bandar said to Abdullah over the secure phone from his vacation home in Aspen, had disseminated a Senior Executive Intelligence Brief based upon new intercepts, predicting an upcoming terrorist attack that the plotters themselves were describing as having "dramatic consequences" and causing "major casualties." The CIA believed, Bandar said, that the most likely target was Saudi Arabia.[834]

Not only that, but the Saudi ambassador said he spoke to *friends*, and that even the FBI concurred with the supposition that Saudi Arabia was the most likely place for another attack. The intelligence agencies were saying that this was the most specific reference to any single upcoming event all year. Vice President Cheney would obviously have more to say when he called, Bandar said. He just wanted the crown prince to know.

Early in the administration, Abdullah put in a call to Cheney, spitting mad. At a ten-year anniversary celebration of the liberation of Kuwait, the new secretary of state (the old General Colin Powell) and the former

President George Bush told everyone who would listen that regime change in Iraq was going to be young George W. Bush's top priority.[835]

Abdullah thoroughly chewed out Cheney, threatening non-cooperation if the United States tried to upend the status quo in the region. Cheney didn't promise it wouldn't happen. He said instead that Abdullah should understand, understand that this was just sentimental bluster on the part of Bush the elder. And as for Colin, his former subordinate at the Pentagon, he was, shall we say, all over the place.

They talked again after the CIA asked the vice president to call Abdullah to urge greater cooperation with their counterterrorism liaison efforts.[836] Surely, they could improve cooperation, Cheney told Abdullah.

"*Insha'Allah,*" answered Abdullah.

Insha'Allah. If God wills it.

He didn't really plan to do anything and he said "*Insha'Allah*" not because he was lying. And not because of any solicitude, or any history, or even perhaps the reality of ultimately living under a system of obedience to the stronger.

He said it to say that if God wills that we give up our Muslim brothers so that you can be safe while we are under threat, if God wills it that we give up our safety so that you and your precious Israel are protected, if God wills it that you can take our resources and poison our minds with your Sylvester Stallone, with your *Matrix* and your *Star Wars*. Well. If God wills it, it will happen.

Insha'Allah.

But not by his hand, Abdullah thought to himself.

The next time he spoke to Cheney, Abdullah complained that FBI director Freeh was causing troubles by insisting that there be a public unveiling of the Khobar Towers indictment, almost five years after the attack, that he was going to publicly blame Iran for the attack, that he was going to suggest that action needed to be taken.[837]

"Let it die," Abdullah said to the vice president, who professed to have little power in influencing what the U.S. Attorney or the FBI director would do.

"At least don't let them make a big deal of it," said the crown prince. "An indictment will just stir the pot to push for military punishment of Iran," which he called a ridiculous and dangerous proposition.

He knew that Bandar was suggesting another visit by Freeh to the kingdom, and perhaps a *gift*. Abdullah doubted that such an offer would be successful, given Freeh's notorious and single-minded Christian devotion.

But then Cheney reassured him that there was no way military action was going to happen, regardless of what the Justice Department did. Not over Khobar Towers. There was a new man in charge at the Pentagon and Rumsfeld held tight to the reins. And there was a new Attorney General.

Abdullah had sent an angry letter to the new American president in his first weeks in office, complaining of pro-Israeli bias and dual loyalties in the new administration—Wolfowitz, Richard Perle, "Scooter" Libby, Douglas Feith, Peter Rodman, Dov Zakheim—all Zionist agents. Abdullah warned that if the United States did not act in a more "equitable manner" toward the Palestinians, the Saudis would have to reconsider all of their joint efforts.[838]

Again, Cheney called to smooth over things. America's interests and Saudi interests—they were inextricable.

Cheney even got Bush the elder to call the crown prince from the Oval Office while young George was on hand to offer reassurances. The former president told the monarch that his son had a full grasp of the realities of the region. He wanted to tell the great Saudi leader—his dear friend—that his young son's "heart" was in the right place.[839]

Abdullah listened to his old friend, but by all accounts, Cheney assumed the throne. Cheney installed his own staff into key decision-making positions. And many of them were Jews. And Cheney had his own sources of intelligence; his men were guided by their own ideas—too many of which originated in Israel, and some of which didn't quite square with the outlines of U.S.-Saudi arrangements. Bandar and Turki both reported on the fixation of Cheney, and the others around him, on finishing the job in Iraq, regardless of what they said publicly and privately.[840]

Now the vice president got on the line. "Yes, intelligence indeed indicated a big *al Qaeda* attack, most likely in Saudi Arabia, but that's not so clear from the sourcing," Cheney said. "It could also possibly be intended for Jordan, or even Israel," the vice president said.[841]

"The FBI head of counterterrorism was predicting that the attack would take place on July 4th, just weeks away," Cheney continued. "But. That date was the upcoming holiday and the intelligence people were merely assuming that this *al Qaeda* crowd would choose a high-profile date, not because there was anything firm suggesting it would happen on the 4th."

"Are there any details on how the attack will come?" Abdullah asked.

"*Possibly with a bomb on an airplane.*" Cheney was his usual unforthcoming self, expressionless. Then, as their conversation was closing, even though it was one where the Bush White House was supposed to be warning Saudi Arabia, the vice president reminded Abdullah that the U.S. intelligence community had issued four urgent alerts since the first of the year, that maybe this was just another, that the intelligence people were covering their assess.

"So, is this one to be taken seriously, or not?" Abdullah asked.

"The intelligence agencies are always ready to cover their own assess," Cheney answered. "As far as we know though, this is the latest."

As far as we know. It was a beautiful construction. It meant *if we're right, aren't we magnificent.* And *if we're wrong, well, we did say it was as far as we knew.* The known unknowns. *Insha'Allah.*

Though the exchange seemed to downplay new intelligence reports and the gravity of the very call, Abdullah understood the protocol, understood that even among friends, even at their level, there were details that weren't discussed, weren't known.

Certainly, Prince Turki would have more information.

"Is the prince here?" he asked his assistant.

"Not yet, your Excellency."

Abdullah settled in with another cup of coffee and opened Bowlen's double-wrapped and wax-sealed letter. The keeper of all secrets sent greetings from Washington. He informed the crown prince that U.S. intelligence learned that Prince Turki was communicating with a "high-level" *al Qaeda* person in Afghanistan and that person specifically told Turki that a major operation was upcoming—information that Turki evidently hadn't taken action on, not even previously informing the crown prince or the king.[842]

Abdullah was confused. *A major operation? Was it this same operation Cheney was referring to? An operation against Saudi Arabia?*

Abdullah knew of the prince's relationship with the Saudi pest bin Laden, and if the information came directly from him, that information would also have likely included whether or not Saudi Arabia was a target. The Saudis had made a firm agreement with bin Laden after Khobar Towers that such attacks inside the kingdom would end, and bin Laden had so far stuck to his word. So why would there be intelligence of a possible attack?

Bowlen's letter went on: Working undercover for Prince Turki, a Saudi going by the name of Talal Salem al-Majed was delivering a suitcase of money to an American agent on July 4th. This Saudi government agent who was delivering the money, Bowlen wrote, reports directly to Turki, and since 2000 had been a courier and operative communicating with *al Qaeda* in Dubai, Yemen, and Iran.

If Crown Prince Abdullah doubted him, al-Majed was scheduled to board a Saudi Arabian Airlines flight in Riyadh on July 3rd, with a ticket purchased by the Saudi intelligence service.[843]

Why is this devil telling me this? Abdullah thought. *Again flaunting details to indicate that they had penetrated Saudi operations and knew of their payments? What was it that he expected him to do?*

There were a half dozen documents appended to back up Bowlen's claims: communications between Turki and Bandar, and between Bandar and the U.S. government, some going back to previous White House administrations. They showed action contrary to the king's wishes and what Abdullah perceived as Saudi interests. Princes Turki and Bandar, the evidence suggested, were working behind the king's and Abdullah's backs, conspiring with Osama bin Laden, and possibly supporting an *al Qaeda* attack against the United States with hijacked airplanes.

Abdullah was pondering what it all meant when Prince Turki arrived in a swirl of robes. Head of the kingdom's intelligence agency, and perhaps the second most influential member of the Family, the prince had long warned of a "*Shi'a* crescent" forming from Tehran to Lebanon, believing that this was the greatest threat to the kingdom, potentially splitting Islam into equal *Sunni* and *Shi'a* factions, challenging Saudi Arabia's dominance.

He had come, Turki said, with an update on their infiltrator into the bin Laden planes operation. Abdullah sat and read the general intelligence department's detailed report while Turki drank coffee: Their agent, Turki said, was going back to America. He was flying to JFK Airport on Saudi Arabian Airlines Flight 53 on July 3rd and then onto Dulles Airport in Washington. There, he would find a rental car sitting in garage number 2 on the second floor in Row 2, Position 217, the keys under the passenger seat. He would then drive to Annapolis, Maryland, and in the parking lot of the Anne Arundel Medical Center, near the emergency room entrance, a man would be waiting in a black SUV at precisely eight o'clock in the evening. The car would have District of Columbia license plate BJ 7069. Mihdhar was given the coded phrase to memorize, and upon receiving the return phrase, he would deliver a satchel of money to their man.

For his entry into New York, he would carry and use a special diplomatic passport. Arrangements had been made for his hand luggage not to be searched. After he cleared customs, he would give the diplomatic passport back to the head of security and revert to his previous identity—a new, clean Saudi passport with a new American tourist visa in hand. Abdullah perused the attachment, which contained a brief biography of the agent's true identity and the background of his Saudi family.

After delivering his package, the agent would return to the planes operation.

Abdullah looked up. "So this planes operation. What more do we know about it?"

"As far as we know," Turki said, "there are a group of men attempting to hijack a commercial airliner. We have infiltrated our man into the group."

"And all of this will happen when?"

"We don't know precisely, but not before the end of the summer."

"And our presumption is that what will happen?"

"The plan is for an eleventh-hour discovery of the plot."

"The plan?"

"Yes, your Excellency. The American plan. They know, too, of the *al Qaeda* plan, and they are waiting to round up all of the participants. We have been in touch with Mr. Hal Jones and this is what he tells us."

"And what is your officer's role?"

"To report to us."

"He will be arrested?"

"A marshal on board the plane will know who he is."

"And how will that make a difference?"

"The marshal doesn't arrest him. That is what he has been told."

"And he believes that? Our man?"

"This is a man who believes he is blessed, your Excellency. In his operations, he believes he has fooled Osama bin Laden and the others in the *al Qaeda* leadership. He believes he has fooled the man with the missing leg, fooled the Malaysians and Thais and the CIA, fooled his partner in San Diego and even fooled our own man there. He thinks he has nine lives. I don't want to puncture his own view of himself now. But he will disappear."

"And his activities with the hijackers? Are they specifically secret from the Americans?" Abdullah asked.

"Yes, of course," Turki responded. "Why do you ask?"

"The White House is warning us of an attack. Just this morning."

"And they said?"

"Cheney said nothing, as usual. We might be attacked on July 4th. Here. In Saudi Arabia. That would break our agreement with bin Laden. Maybe you can get more out of the CIA."

"And have we received any additional communication from the Apex Watch chief, Mr. Bowlen?" Turki probed.

"No," Abdullah answered.

Abdullah long suspected that Turki and Bandar were operating on their own, successful in directing bin Laden away from Saudi Arabia, but also supporting him in attacking the United States—a dangerous game.

It was a lovely day, a breeze blowing, the low hum of air conditioners in the background, but otherwise silent. It was a big day. The Bush people wanted Iraq, wanted a do-over, and they would use whatever pretense they could find to start shooting. Abdullah knew of Turki's operations. It was a useful defense against Riyadh being surprised, but now he was sure he wasn't being told the whole truth. But he also wasn't sure that they— Bandar and Turki—knew the truth either.

After Turki departed, Abdullah moved inside the house to his desk and composed a confidential letter to be personally delivered to Cheney and the elder Bush with the news: He would work toward a fresh start, that perhaps a change was needed, both in the intelligence service and in Saudi representation in Washington. He wanted them to know that change did not mean any break with the continuity of their relations.

And he composed a letter to Lawrence Bowlen, which would be couriered to New York and then hand-delivered to the downtown Washington office he associated with the American wizard. He told Bowlen similar news of the changes afoot and thanked him for his information. The planes operation, Abdullah said, the one in the United States, would likely take place at the end of the summer, he wrote to Bowlen. He just wanted him to know.

Chapter 53 Full House

When George W. Bush settled into his private cabin on Air Force One after his first overseas trip as president, he felt like he really needed to get away from it all.[844]

Fucking Yur-rup, he thought. Powell assured him that all would be terrific. But everywhere they went, there were protestors and barricades, the new president blasted and made fun of.

Nothing would get his mind off it all better than a movie. The Air Force steward recommended *Moulin Rouge!* (*gay!*), but Bush saw the new *Pearl Harbor* DVD on the cart (*war!*) starring Ben Affleck (*Democrat, boo*)— still, no contest.

After he enjoyed the movie, snoozing when the guns were silent, he flipped through the latest *Time* magazine and read a piece entitled "Bin Laden Rides Again."

"In the language of advertising, bin Laden has become a brand—a geopolitical Keyser Soze, an omnipresent menace whose name invokes perils far beyond his capability," the article said. The threat is "very real," the author conceded, but then he dismissed the increasing attention paid to the Saudi boy millionaire as "hype ... more than a little ludicrous ... "[845]

Why was it, Bush thought, that though the "adults" were supposedly back in control, everywhere he turned around the world, they were losing.

Miserably.

Clinton and his team of smarmy politicos were secretive, yet when Bush's very experienced vice president declined to publicly release information on his energy task force (*an energy task force!*), the news media reacted as if there had been some kind of a coup.[846]

Then those fuckers in the press went through the roof when his new attorney general took a tough stance on crime and pornography.[847]

Then the news media, and its entire viewing public of liberal ying-yangs, practically had a cow when the administration decided to abandon the Kyoto Protocol on climate change.[848] And withdrawing from the Anti-Ballistic Missile Treaty?[849] Bush had been told by the old hands that it was a good idea—even the in-house dove said it was time. Well, that worked out really well: thousands of Euro-weenie protesters came out, the flaming fuckwads who became the televised highlight of his trip.

Then Vermont Senator Jim Jeffords—*that Yankee priss just like Poppy*—announced that he was leaving the Republican Party, and all of a sudden he lost control of the Congress.[850]

Bush turned to his presidential read-book. There was a draft of a new national security directive on terrorism. *Maybe* Moulin Rouge! *wouldn't be so bad after all.*

It was a jumble of interagency this and that: State would work with foreign governments to end all sanctuaries, Treasury and State would work with foreign governments to freeze or seize assets, the CIA would work with foreign governments and anti-Taliban groups to "disrupt" *al Qaeda*, the Pentagon would prepare plans to hit terrorist groups in Afghanistan and take out Taliban command, everyone would make it a priority to "eliminate weapons of mass destruction," which *al Qaeda* and associated terrorist groups were seeking to acquire. His director of the Office of Management and Budget was directed to ensure that sufficient funds were available over five years.[851]

Five years? And what was his name again, the guy at OMB?

In their last meeting in the Oval Office before the inauguration,[852] Clinton warned him that terrorism would suck up much of his time, and Bush was finding it a bit like pest control at the ranch. Some potential attack seemed to buzz around no matter what he did.

He had sought the advice of his CIA director, and Georgie Boy told him that the threats were indeed at their highest level since the

Millennium alerts.[853] April had then brought on even more warnings. And May had proved no different, every day the president being told about some towelhead plotting to do this or that.[854] Then he was told that an anonymous caller to the embassy in Dubai warned that Osama bin Laden was planning an attack in the United States using "high explosives."[855] A week later, the CIA reported a hostage-taking plot to release the Egyptian Blind *Sheikh*, who was residing in a maximum security prison on a life sentence. Another report from the CIA said that operatives might hijack an airplane.[856] Another said that they would storm an embassy abroad like the students did in Tehran.[857] There was foreign intelligence regarding potential plots in Italy and Yemen and even a possible terrorist cell in Canada.[858] And the FBI was warning of active cells in the United States itself.

At each step along the way, the warnings were different, but the administration routine in reacting to them was the same.

"We okay?" the president would ask his man at the CIA.

"We're okay," Georgie would answer.

But it wasn't just the paid naggers at the CIA and the other intelligence agencies. As Bush was beginning his European trip, Egyptian President Hosni Mubarak called him to warn that *al Qaeda* was plotting to assassinate him and other leaders at the G-8 meeting coming up in Genoa, that they would be using an airplane loaded with explosives to attack the venue.[859]

"We okay?" the president had asked his man at the CIA.

"We got it covered," Georgie had said. And there was no plane.

Every day on his trip to Europe, terrorism nosed its way onto the daily briefing. Osama bin Laden and a circus troupe of weirdly-named extremists were doing, were moving. People were disappearing. People were preparing for martyrdom, a word Bush thought he'd never even heard before. There were reports that the communications traffic was up, that known facilities were hopping with activity, that other facilities were empty. Two Osama bin Laden operatives who were planning attacks on facilities in Saudi Arabia were arrested.[860]

"We okay, Georgie?" the president had asked his man.

"Important catch," Georgie had answered.

Condi delivered some of the reports. And she told him that a special

White House Counterterrorism Security Group meeting[861] had been convened to discuss threats associated with a *very important* guy named Abu Zubaydah,[862] bin Laden's right-hand man and a guy that tried to attack America before. Bush flipped through the analysis. The CIA speculated that a man named *Mukhtar* might be one of his associates.[863]

"What am I supposed to make of this?" he'd asked Condi.

"It is all so *maddeningly nebulous*," his national security advisor told him.[864]

So the president asked his man, George: "We okay?"

"We're okay," he'd answered.

Saudi Arabia, Canada, Italy, Israel, Bahrain, even Uganda. There was a threat for every country in every flavor.[865] He had talked to Condi about all the warnings and she said that the CIA was just being abundantly overcautious.

"Do you really believe that?" he'd asked her.

"I believe we need to craft a comprehensive program to diminish their strength," she answered.

God damnit! He couldn't decide if he was more frustrated with Condi's response or the extent to which terrorism was taking up his time.

If terrorism wasn't filling his "in" basket, Iraq sure as fuck was.[866] American aircraft were patrolling Iraqi skies every day—*boring holes in the skies*, Rummy said.[867] Some days he'd get reports that they bombed something or another. He had a meeting with Prince Bandar, the Saudi ambassador, who said that continuing the patrols were costing his country, not just financially, but politically, making his military and even his own people question their involvement. And, he said, it wasn't even hurting Saddam.[868]

Still, when Bush asked the national security experts about Iraq, and what they were still doing there, he got an earful about Saddam's continued pursuit of weapons of mass destruction.[869] The CIA even opened a new Weapons Intelligence, Nonproliferation and Arms Control Center, announcing it would assign 500 analysts to the problem. Bush was asked to appear at the ribbon cutting.

"So," the president had leaned over and asked his man, George, as the applause came: "We're okay here?"

"Yep. We're okay," Tenet had answered.

Meanwhile, Powell was pushing his *smart sanctions* solution—crisscrossing the Middle East on a diplomatic mission. Bush had been briefed: Powell in Ramallah one day to meet with Palestinian chairman Yasser Arafat, popping over from Egypt and on his way to Jerusalem. Then the secretary of state was on to Amman, where he would meet with King Abdullah II of Jordan, before shuttling to Paris for an audience with Saudi Crown Prince Abdullah.[870] The president himself met Israeli Prime Minister Sharon, reading from a complicated script to push for ... well, something—he didn't remember what.[871]

And his boy Georgie was also riding in the Middle East peace saddle, traveling to Amman, Cairo, and Tel Aviv—his own sultan of secret trips and relationships, a mission Bush didn't altogether understand.[872] But when Georgie returned, he always brought back fabulous morsels of gossip.[873]

Condi and Georgie had told him how the principals and the deputies were busy calling their counterparts throughout the world, urging vigilance and the need for more and better information. Bush shook his head. *More information? That's what they needed? More information?*

It seemed to him that with each canceled warning, *imminent* lost much impact. The spy geniuses saying that *an attack was coming* sort of twisted the entire meaning of *coming*. They fed him a constant diet of CIA "disruption" operations.[874] He thought it all was just proving a negative. It didn't happen, so what we did must have been responsible. He was told about *al Qaeda* operational delays.

A goddamn baseball team pays more attention to what went wrong on the field, the president thought. These jokers, they just play and play and play—not like there's no tomorrow, but like there's no yesterday.

The memo appended to the front of the draft directive—Rice's proposed comprehensive solution to terrorism—was to be discussed in full at an upcoming deputies committee meeting.[875]

We've got some problems Condi wrote to Bush in preparing him for the meet.[876] Rummy and Wolfie at the Pentagon were going on endlessly: complaining about revisiting old issues, questioning the use of the military, complaining about who was paying for the new drones. Powell's staff were offering *yet another* proposal to try to convince the Taliban *one last time* to hand over bin Laden, a proposal that the State Department bureaucracy was already labeling "fruitless."[877]

Bush was looking forward to a 31-day Texas summer vacation.

The Washington Post had calculated that, by Labor Day, Bush would have spent 42 percent of his time in office either on vacation or on his way to vacation.[878]

Those fuckers.

Chapter 54 Rant

Khalid Sheikh Mohammed sat in his cluttered office and stared off into the distance, reconstructing the last two days: the return of the fisherman, his conversation with Mohammed Atta in Las Vegas, and the warning from the professor that *they knew* about the 4th of July. *What fools.*

A jackhammer was grinding away somewhere in the distance. And there was the *clang clang clang* of a giant crane, signaling yet another giant apartment building going up in the neighborhood. The voices of hawkers and the swarm of life on the streets below wafted up to his fourth-floor lair.

A message delivered from Kandahar said that Khalid Mihdhar, the fisherman who was never really a fisherman, was coming back into his world.[879] The *al Qaeda* operations chief wrote to *Mukhtar* that this Saudi, who had deserted from San Diego, had a little job to do for *Sheikh* bin Laden—he wrote "final obligation" (الالتزام النهائي)—a strange use of that phrase, because KSM thought his planes operation would be Mihdhar's final obligation.[880] And then he'd be gone—*Allah's* problem and not his.

KSM knew bin Laden had other operations in the works. Dozens of people moving here and there, positioning themselves, scouting targets, delivering money and messages. The beauty of *al Qaeda*—the exquisiteness of the conceit of conducting it all from a cave in Afghanistan—was that operations were actually run through an elaborate worldwide web, each cell strictly compartmented, all operating in unison but seldom with any overlap.

Before he wrote back to Kandahar, he wanted a final answer from Atta. And he wrote a short email to Ramzi Binalshibh in Berlin, asking him to inquire about the status of the other Washington target.

KSM was supremely confident that he alone was able to move the planes operation forward. Perfectly, he'd planned out two years of interlocking pieces. Patiently, he made it through bin Laden's delays and bad choices. And he fought off—even made use of—the stubborn entreaties of his American friends. He'd even connived to receive the blessing of the professor.

He daydreamed. A smoldering White House. The Pentagon attacked in its arrogant slumber. A flaming airplane sticking out of the side of the North Tower of the World Trade Center. All the world's media would be glued to his handiwork. *Al Qaeda* would become a household name. And he. He would finally be known as the greatest ever. Journalists would seek out the word of the triumphant architect, wanting to know how he did it.

They would write his name. Even as the Americans attacked Afghanistan in retaliation, Khalid Sheikh Mohammed would be on every lip, stenciled on every bomb. The professor told KSM, and he read it in the newspapers, that this new administration of George W. Bush was filled with war-hungry hawks. The attacks would be nothing like that of the Clinton hesitators. Cheney and Rumsfeld would bomb like never before and the Black general Powell would take charge. They would bomb like mad, not a button-pushing routine of the previous years, but a real fury, a wrathful madness of rage.

They would bomb. First they would bomb with confidence, attacking Taliban forces and *al Qaeda* camps. Then, as *al Qaeda* fighters and the *Sheikh* scurried up the mountains and into the caves, slipping away into the shadows, they would bomb with frustration.

There would be weeks of bombings, and then maybe even months. They would bomb, bomb, bomb until they were exhausted from bombing, shattered that there was nothing left to bomb. And still enraged, they would then enter a sad period, the shame and humiliation of the attacks and their aimless bombs catching up with them. Oh, they would continue to bomb, striking out like finished boxers in the ring, wildly swinging from the corner, blood oozing from their eyes, punching at invisible demons in the mountains, their blood increasingly mixed with tears.

All the while, the Saudi royals would get their well-deserved reckoning. The family *al Saud* would never be able to evade the stark arithmetic of two dozen of their own citizens making up the attack element. And the American people would be reminded over and over on television that the *Saudi* son Osama bin Laden was at the helm.

America would demand justice for Saudi Arabia. All their agents and their piles of money would be exposed. Toppling the monarchy would be easy. American soldiers were already there in the country and the CIA already knew the "who"—they would engineer a coup, princes escaping to Monaco and Malibu, the oil machine finally in the hands of the West, the Kissinger plan implemented.

It was a sweet dream this one. The defense of Islam would no longer be from the *Wahhabi* protectorate. It would shift from the Saudis into the hands of the new grand *mufti*, to *Sheikh* bin Laden, the invisible man, loud in his action, but hidden and untouchable in the mountains of *Khorasan*.

Again, the news media would make the pilgrimage, trudging up mountain passes to speak to the new prophet. The *Sheikh* would hold a planetary *majlis* for all to attend, the new prophet's words broadcast on CNN and *al Jazeera* and Sky News, people all over the world, from Manhattan to Manila, watching and listening.

Did his American friends, who weren't friends, really think that all of this would work to their American advantage?

Did they really think that Khalid Sheikh Mohammed, the architect, didn't also see the truth behind the reason for their helping him?

Stopping a war with Iraq. Or one with Iran. *What a joke*, thought KSM. And as for putting the spotlight on Saudi Arabia to bring down the monarchy … Even if KSM supported these objectives, what were they thinking? Did they really think that they were all in it together? That they could be in it together?

Yes, the Americans would destroy the Taliban. And they might even bring down the family Saud. But win the war for *Khorasan*? Go into the mountains and triumph where the Soviets couldn't?

Did they really think that once the Taliban were gone, and the Saudis got their comeuppance, that it would all revert to their plan?

It would unfold this way. In pursuing their war, the Americans would enlist the *entire world*, the so-called civilized world. Everyone would join the Americans, even Russia and China and Cuba, and even Saddam—they would all send condolence cards. They would, of course, get the collaboration of the backstabbing Arab regimes. But once having done so, once their war stabilized and the dust settled, didn't they see that their vast combined ground and air forces, and navys, and special forces, and spies, and military bases would lodge an entire army of nonbelievers and infidels into the Middle East? Didn't they see that this magnificent congregation, this invasion and this occupation, and their righteous mission to avenge, would serve to incite and awaken those who had been slumbering? Incite them to join the new *Sheikh*, the man in the cave?

And once awakened, didn't they see that the battlefield would expand? That fighting would eventually find itself back onto the streets of America and Europe, first an eye-for-an-eye battle and counterbattle, and then in the circulation of his people, bin Laden's people, the Muslim people would expand outward, bringing with them the counterattack and the end of days that the holy men spoke of.

The world would come alive with Muslims moving here and there, at first just refugees washing up on every shore, then immigrants, and then the armies. Muslims would come alive in these weak and tired Western societies with their wilted religions. Soon the nonbelievers would be outnumbered and outsmarted.

He could see it, how it stared. First in the form of airplanes. Inspired brothers would line up to leap up from their seats, from the front to the back of every airplane in the world, ready to take over. And then they would take over every train car and every bus. They would threaten every church and every Jew temple. They would make every sidewalk café unsafe. They would attack every shopping mall and every fast-food restaurant. They would attack in their cities, on the roads, in their home. The brothers would line up and leap up and strike—ready, willing, and desiring to slit the throat of the bird.

America's war to avenge would strengthen the very world movements and peoples that they believed were otherwise an Anomaly, Bastards, Cancer, Dogs, Evil—the ABCs of their entire alphabet of hatred for his people.

Yes, they would bomb. Mad bomb. Sad bomb. Frustrated bomb. But the bombing would never work. The only way for there to be "peace," Khalid Sheikh Mohammed thought, was for the civilizations to all become one—one religion, one language, one race, and one economy. That imposed oneness was already threatening Islam—with its commercialism, with its worship of the false God, with its filth and debauchery, with its tolerance for every freedom and every human deformity.

Up to now, up to his attack, for centuries the West had been on the march, diluting Islam into this oneness, into this cultural nothingness. The Jews and Christians would continue to do so unless they were stopped: buying and then bombing, and then buying more, until Islam disappeared into the oneness, into the sameness of everything, the sameness of freedom, until *they* were no more, until their way of life, his people's way, was no more.

Khalid Sheikh Mohammed saw how the planes operation was the declaration, but not the first. The Muslim people were already turning away from this boring oneness, from the New World Order, from globalization, from multilateralism, from human rights, from their foolish democratic enterprise. He, the conceiver, the originator, the inventor of the spectacular terrorist strike, would now pull off the greatest event ever, inside the homes of those who thought themselves safe, and right to the heart of the insatiable beast. He would explode the buildings and explode the myth of their invulnerability. And of their superiority.

Oh, and in doing so, how fantastic in doing so, praise be to *Allah* in doing so, *Insha'Allah* in doing so, he was …

He was …

Was he? Was he merely implementing a plan to build momentum for the West to destroy *al Qaeda*?

No, he wasn't, he told himself. Because the American soldiers would eventually falter. Their drones and the airplanes would run out of targets. And then in their frustration, they would seek out anything to bomb. And not just *al Qaeda* soldiers would die, not just the Taliban. But then, as they moved to any target, anything to bomb, civilians would die. Many civilians would die.

And then, then, the passions of retaliation and hatred too much to bear for the kind-hearted in the so-called land of the free, the Red

Cross and the starry-eyed aid workers and the kind Scandinavians would come to help. Their serving hands would wipe away the tears of the poor Muslim victims of their own bombing. They would bring food and medicines for the children—*oh, the children*—and they would set up camps to midwife in their rights—children's rights, women's rights, human rights.

In the tents and the hospitals and the schools, the aid workers would bring the right for all of them to speak, to be heard. The news media would again come to listen to their cries, to give voice to the new victims. The world would open up so that more voices could speak on radios, on television, so that the voices could get through on mobile phones and over the internet, speaking in ways that hadn't even been invented yet. The whole of everyone on the planet, in the cities and in the mountains would all dial up and log on, connecting with email and chat and instant messages over a giant worldwide network that would need towers and wire and then fiber optic cables so that the modes of communication would go far up into the highest mountains passes and down into the smallest villages.

One giant network would connect Afghanistan to Pakistan and Pakistan to Kuwait and Kuwait to Saudi Arabia and on and on. One titan network would connect Afghanistan to Europe and Pakistan to America. And it would also have to connect Brazil and Burundi, and China to Chile.

One network. Satellites would move all of what they had to say. The same protocols would be built everywhere, computers from Sony and Toshiba, phones from Nokia and Motorola, software from Microsoft.

It would be a necessary oneness, one that started in the wiping away of the tears of those being bombed. That oneness would ensure that every Muslim could speak. That every woman wearing a *burqa* could report her repression. That every refugee could order a meal.

For the sake of the children, that network would have to be on all the time. All the time would have to be protected—not by American soldiers, but by Afghan companies and Arab companies and local security guards and then by the national armies. Protected because there couldn't be a moment when the voices were not heard. And, of course, *brought to you by*—there couldn't be a moment when the commerce was interrupted.

Praise be to Google, there couldn't be a moment when the advertisers couldn't get their messages through.

Oneness would march in triumph. It was coming by land and sea and air, and now even by telephone and the internet and in space.

Khalid Sheikh Mohammed saw how it would unfold. And in his certainty that the Americans must see it as well, he then realized that they did see it: that he ultimately was the tool for the extinction of Islam.

PART 14

Chapter 55 Calm Down

Charlie could set her clock by it: at 11 am, the first report came in that reconstructed KSM's keyboard strokes—a daily treat of everything he tapped out on his laptop, each poke intercepted by their hidden software and secretly transmitted back to Maryland whenever their man dialed his modem to connect to the World Wide Web.

Since the eavesdropping device was inserted into KSM's operating system, the growing Apex Watch team had been receiving, translating and analyzing a manic stream of words, most of them mundane, and many indecipherable in their language and shorthand.[881]

KSM the typist had a habit of backspacing and re-writing and moving paragraphs around, deleting and pasting back into multiple documents, keeping notes and deleting notes, the software sometimes barely keeping up in producing phrases and sentences, all of it needing a human eye to pick out useful intelligence from the digital sandstorm. When he wasn't corresponding, KSM was writing stories and poetry. He was writing his memoirs. He was writing business proposals. He was writing to corporations and even to world leaders.

Most interesting were the names. Charlie ate breakfast, lunch and dinner with the highly-coded argument between their man and *al Qaeda* upstairs and down. Erica laid out a link analysis chart on the conference room wall, dissecting KSM's flood of simultaneous letters, emails and chat sessions. There were Abu Hafs and Ramzi, his main correspondents, and

Khallad, his best friend, but also the *Emir*, a second *emir*, someone referred to as Ali, who also seemed to be al Baluchi, and a cast of characters none of them had ever heard of: Hawsawi, Bilal, Losh, Mustafa Ahmed, Abu Obadiah, and al-Iraqi.[882]

They almost got lost in the names and aliases and code phrases and dates, preparing various spreadsheets and tables to sort it all out. The *Emir* was definitely bin Laden, but also there was an American *emir*—never named by KSM. Maybe he was an Egyptian from his references, and he seemed to be located in the American South, or southern California, or at least near a beach. Maybe he was with two others. There was someone KSM referred to as the "beloved," but he was not to be confused with the "lover-boy," who maybe was Lebanese and maybe was a neighbor and who also had a wife, a Turkish woman, who wasn't with them at the beach, who was maybe in Germany but definitely in Europe and not in Turkey. Maybe the "beloved" was sick. Maybe he was or wasn't going to the wedding.

There were also the two problem Saudis: one KSM called Hani and the other "the fisherman." This fisherman? KSM hated him. He called him a number of things. The traitor. Bin Laden's favorite. Bin Laden's mistake. Bin Laden's curse.

And then there was another man named Nawaf, someone who was useless but also was partnered with the fisherman, whom they all agreed was Erica's man in San Diego. They thought that maybe he was now with Hani, who at first they thought was Khalid Mihdhar but then came to believe was someone new, someone new even to KSM. He was from the same town in Saudi Arabia as the other Saudi. He'd lived in America before. But he wasn't the friend, a person KSM referred to as *the spy*, who he also called *the video guy*—who they thought was yet another Saudi living in San Diego. This latter Saudi, whoever he was, was also a danger.

KSM constantly complained about the fisherman, especially now since he'd gotten news that he was returning. Returning to *his* operation. *Maybe he was Khalid al-Mihdhar?* Erica said as they went through the names and the intelligence take. Returning meant coming back, and that fit him (if he was coming back to America), since they knew he had left but had also disappeared.

Bin Laden wasn't just his *Emir.* He was also the *Sheikh*, Abu Abdullah, the new prophet, the big cheese, the caveman, the man. KSM loved him. He was annoyed by him. He listened to him. He needed him to shut up. He needed him to make a decision. He needed him to get out of the way.

There were internet searches, looking for news of Saudi Arabia, mentions of *al Qaeda* in the press, many searches for Jones, many Jones and CIA, Jones and Maryland addresses, addresses of government facilities. There were many addresses. They put together a spreadsheet of the addresses. And telephone numbers. And emails. There were searches about Bush, for the word "neocon," and especially for Richard Perle and Jewish writers, and for Jewish journalists. And there were searches for video games, for gaming hardware, about new computers, about a pair of binoculars, about security procedures, about new software, and of course, about airplanes and airline schedules.

Monica Lewinsky. Lee Harvey Oswald. Roswell. Zionism. Bohemian Grove. He searched for the *Mossad*. He searched for Bandar. He followed Prince Turki closely. He read the *Daily Mail*. He loved the *Daily Mail*.

Even with access to *everything* that KSM poked out on his laptop, there was only so much they could make out. Each person in his network, each person in *al Qaeda*, also seemed to have discrete functions and only pieces of knowledge. And even KSM didn't know everything that was going on.

In addition to using aliases and nicknames, KSM also seemed to avoid specific numbers in his correspondence. When he did use dates and times, he seemed to code them—intentionally off by a day, a certain time plus some pre-arranged multiplier—mindful that someone, even one of his own, could betray the cause, could betray him.

And even the dates that they picked up needed additional analysis. July 4 was 7/4 or sometimes 4/7 or even *Rabi al-thani-1422*, but not July 4th, the American holiday, which was a title and was often said in a certain way by intelligence officials and FBI worry warts as *the date*, the date that needed no elaboration, and a date that therefore fit the pretensions of an official intelligence community warning.[883] In the minds of the CIA and FBI, *al Qaeda* was *known* to conduct big attacks on anniversary dates, an assessment that Steve insisted was sometimes right (as in the case of the African embassy bombings, in that they coincided with the date American forces arrived in Saudi Arabia), but was also a pattern that mostly was just urban legend. Charlie and Erica noted that there were no searches for anniversaries.

Then, one morning in June, going over the new take, five words in an email nearly stopped Charlie's heart from beating: "the second house in Washington."

She read the sentence over and the words around it. She searched the database that had been constructed of all of KSM's correspondence for the word "house," for the word "second," for every mention of Washington. *The second house?* She'd now seen a number of his coded conversations where he referred to targets as houses. But the context here? He's communicating with Ramzi, and KSM said he needed to have a conversation with the *Emir* about the second house in Washington. It made no sense. There wasn't a first house in Washington, let alone a second one. Or so she thought.

Was the World Trade Center even the target KSM was going for? She'd always thought it odd—KSM's docile acceptance of the North Tower, not as if he was avoiding confirmation (as he often did in talking to her), not as a game, but more that he accepted it and spoke openly about the North Tower. And not only that, but he so easily accepted their suggestion as to the optimum time of the attack. Barbara's analysts calculated that Friday had the lowest building population. So Steve, in his demented brilliance, put together a fake analysis with an attached spreadsheet to convince KSM that Friday afternoon would actually be the *most* destructive time, manufacturing a story with statistics attached which showed that after the stock market closed at the end of every week, all the financial businesses had to settle up their accounts and generally stayed later. It was a great ruse and KSM said he was very impressed with the work of the professor when she presented it to him.

Charlie had already shared her suspicions with Steve about KSM's strange acquiescence. Steve didn't disagree with her, but he also didn't really seem to care much.

"Is it possible that KSM is double-crossing us?" Charlie asked.

"Undoubtedly he is," Steve replied. "But so what? What are we supposed to do at this point?"

When she pushed back, saying it did make a difference, Steve softened, as he often did when Charlie felt that Steve was handling her, trying to manipulate her, uncharacteristically being sensitive. "Honey, as long as they're not hitting Apex Watch headquarters, I can't say I really care."

And then Steve said chillingly that if KSM was indeed going after some sentimental target—such as the tucked-away CIA headquarters in Langley—his only worry, Steve's only worry, was that he didn't think that such an attack would have sufficient world-changing effect. *That* worried him.

All of it, her overt relationship with KSM, and now her eavesdropping on the unfolding conspiracy—conspiracies—was worrying the hell out of her. It wasn't that Steve was disengaged, but his calm stoked her worry. And when she pushed him to explain, looking not just for explanation, but also reassurance, he laughed at her. At first, she thought that it was a nervous laughter because he also was on edge. But she grew increasingly furious with that stupid laugh, furious that he was so quick to dismiss her.

She wracked her brain, wondering if there was ever a hint—one she'd missed—where KSM suggested an attack in Washington, or a second target. But KSM hued precisely to the party line that he was preparing a team for one attack and one attack only: New York City, the Jew banker hub and the center of world Zionism.

"Tell the professor our plans are good," KSM told her when she had probed earlier.

When he said it, she thought the sentence construction was off.

"He said, 'Tell the professor that *our* plans are good,'" Charlie said to Steve when she returned from Dubai.

"And?" Steve responded.

"Why not just *our plans are good?*"

"He did say our plans are good."

"No," Charlie responded, "he said tell the professor that our plans are good. *Our.* Like he was saying *yours and his.*"

"Maybe he's seeking my approval because I'm the man," Steve said, matter of factly.

"Maybe," Charlie said. But she thought it lame, not even worthy of Steve's lies.

It ate at her. Was Steve in touch with KSM? If he was, she thought it would be revealed in the keystroke reconstructions. But it wasn't. And that made her feel stupid, that suspicion.

"You and he have something special going on?" she joked with Steve.

He grimaced as if the question was not worth answering. She instantly recognized it as a look of dismissal she'd seen before when she suspected he might be lying. And when he was caught.

She mentioned to Bowlen their exchange about the odd sentence as soon as they'd had it, and said that she felt that maybe there was something that Steve wasn't telling her, wasn't telling them.

Bowlen listened. But then he knew a secret that Steve wasn't telling her—a big one, about the girl. And he just assumed that that was it, hoping that their relationship wouldn't get in the way. Bowlen tried to calm Charlie, reassuring her that despite how good she was as a case officer, as a professional, that KSM would never be able to see her as anything other than a woman. He likened the gap to something similar to the clash between Islam and America, that the gulf was just too great to bridge the divide, saying that, of course, KSM was looking for male approval, and that perhaps he was now focused on Steve because he—Bowlen—had dropped out of his life.

Charlie wasn't mollified. With the team ready to huddle to discuss KSM's reference to *the second Washington* target, she went to Bowlen's office to pre-brief him, not wanting to have her suspicions squashed by her dominating partner in an open meeting.

"It looks to me like the phrase suggests KSM indeed has more than one target, at least one other in the nation's capital, and perhaps a second one there," Charlie said.

"What does Steve say?" Bowlen asked. He wasn't wrong to ask, but his deference annoyed Charlie.

"I'm saying it," Charlie pushed back. "That based upon my understanding of Khalid, I think it looks that way."

Bowlen asked: "So that would mean more than one flying team. Do we have any evidence of that?"

Charlie responded that Erica and Barbara both said that they felt there were too many names to be one team. They now assessed there were at least five people inside the country, maybe more—too many for a single attack.

When they got to the meeting, Steve outright dismissed her supposition. "Jesus, do you have anything firm?"

"What do you mean, *firm?*" Charlie responded, not looking for a brawl, and hoping that the other analysts would speak up.

"I mean," Steve said, "since we think Mihdhar left, and since this Hani fellow appeared on the scene, and he's evidently on a different timetable, doesn't it look like we're maybe conflating two different operations?"

"Maybe," Erica spoke up. She really was the expert now. "But I still count at least five. Nawaf isn't a pilot, but I think we should assume that the four others could be. Why else would they be in the U.S. for so long?"

"And what about the New York fuckup KSM writes about—the Saudi fools he refers to making an emergency call?" Charlie added.

"From what KSM has written," Erica continued, "I'd say that he thinks there needs to be four or five muscle men on each plane, plural. Each plane. Plural. If I didn't already know that there was one target, I'd conclude based on what we've collected here that there are four flying teams."

"So what do we think about the possibility that he's planning more than one attack?" Bowlen asked.

Steve jumped in: "Look, we already know that he's got more than one in him. And that *al Qaeda* is planning more than just an attack in New York. So let's not jump to conclusions."

"Still," Charlie insisted, "I think we should at least entertain the idea that he's planning more than one target," almost pleading with Steve to back down.

"Oh, please," Steve responded sharply. "What if there's two pilots per plane? And what about back-up people, just in case the primaries fail in flight school, or don't succeed in hijacking? Besides, most of the people you're referring to here are simpletons. No way they could be pilots."

Simpletons, Charlie thought. That was KSM's word. Steve used the word idiot.

"Until you can produce more evidence, this is a stupid conversation," Steve said, slapping down the theory of multiple flying teams.

"And what difference would it make anyhow," he went on, saying that they were arguing about nothing.

"It does make a difference," Charlie said.

"Why? Maybe you need to go have some come-to-Jesus moment, focusing on this, this tree that's blinding you from seeing the forest. An attack is coming and it sounds to me like you're not reconciled with that."

"It makes a big difference," Erica joined Charlie, "both in terms of the date and our preparations."

"What do you know about our fucking preparations?" Steve responded.

His tone was mean and intimidating.

Erica backed away. Charlie and Bowlen both saw it, that in an instant, the collegial and supportive and inquisitive Steve was gone.

"Okay, Steven. Okay, people," Bowlen intervened to try to lower the temperature. "Let's keep our eye on the ball. If there is a Washington target, now or even in some future attack, what do we think about it?"

"Oh, Jesus," Steve said, petulantly folding his arms.

Everyone else agreed the most likely Washington target would be the White House. Though there was no evidence *per se*, wouldn't that be what you would hit?

Steve just grunted.

Charlie said she would ask KSM outright at their upcoming meeting in Barcelona.

They were scheduled to meet on July 9th, and Steve latched on to that date: not only to dismiss speculation of an Independence Day attack (what the FBI guys were predicting),[884] but also to argue that they still had plenty of time to stop KSM.

Erica pointed out that since the official Agency warning wasn't for the United States itself, he might indeed be revealing another *al Qaeda* operation, perhaps in Saudi Arabia, as the Agency was saying. It could be another set of pilots. Maybe even some of the pilots who were training in the United States. Thus, she said, that could be the explanation for the confusion about the number of teams.

"Still, none of this explains a second Washington target, *the second Washington target*," Charlie persisted. "KSM's use of that phrase."

But Steve wouldn't budge, and without his direction, or Bowlen overruling him, the meeting ended without resolution.

Bowlen asked Steve and Charlie to stay behind. He told them that he heard back from Crown Prince Abdullah. The Saudi ruler decided to relieve both princes, Turki and Bandar, of their current positions, and Bowlen was practically bubbling over with excitement. He offered congratulations to Steve on having perfected the documentation that implicated Bandar and Prince Turki.

Charlie asked about the next step there, with Saudi Arabia, and Bowlen said that Apex Watch's Saudi team picked up intelligence that Prince Turki told Crown Prince Abdullah that an American agent of theirs was going to receive a payment on July 4th—that the man with the money was flying in from Riyadh."

"Jesus. We just had a conversation about the 4th," Charlie practically yelped. "When were you going to fucking share that with us?"

"I'm doing it now," Bowlen answered coolly.

"And who's the agent?" Charlie asked.

"Does it matter?" Bowlen responded.

"Are you fucking kidding me?" she exclaimed. "Yeah, it matters. It's a piece of information that might relate to an operation I'm neck deep in."

Bowlen said he didn't recognize the name. But he also wasn't forthcoming.

"What? You can't just tell me?" Charlie said.

Charlie looked to Steve for support, but he was blank-faced. She'd seen that look before, too, that one that said he knew more.

Her heart was now racing. It wasn't just the Washington target. KSM made mention of the fisherman "traveling" on the 4th, and in his correspondence he'd vented to Ali and to Ramzi to talk to him, that he was breaking all the rules in doing so. And he was livid that the fisherman was also doing some other job for the *Emir*—which meant most likely bin Laden and not the American *emir*, and also definitely not KSM.

"Traveling" was one of the *al Qaeda* code words for martyring.

Were they conflating two plots? Was it possible that the White House was going to be hit on the 4th of July as well?

Charlie laid it out, that an attack could in fact be coming on the 4th. Bowlen thought her supposition interesting.

Steve said nothing. Independence Day was only three days away.

Tell the professor that our plans are good.

"Is there something you're not telling me?" Charlie said to Steve, changing her focus from Bowlen, wondering why Steve seemed to be not just calm but uninterested in the conversation. It just wasn't like him, even if he didn't care, as he said—he'd still want to *know* that there could be two potential plots, want to know because he needed to possess all the morsels.

"Not telling you?" he answered, his voice flat and far away. "We fucking spend 24/7 together. You see everything I see."

"If you want to go there," she spat back, "we don't. What about that weird thing when I came back from Europe? What about the evenings when you disappear? You never take time off, never disappear. I know everything about you … And I have more …"

"You have more?" Steve responded, maintaining his composure. "Wow. Always the spy."

"You're lying to me about something," Charlie said point-blank to Steve. "Something big. I feel it, and I know you."

"Really?" Steve responded. "We're about to change the world and I'm lying about something big?"

"There's something I need to know here," she pressed, raising her voice. "From both of you." Charlie now looked at Bowlen.

Steve sat back in his chair, silent.

"Steven!" she ordered him to pay attention. He had that look, that blank face. He was very far away. "Are we on the same page?" she pushed.

"Charlie …" He began his lowered voice of condescension.

"There's no Saudi Arabia attack and you know it!" she screamed back. "This is one plot with more than one target! You both know it."

"I don't know how many plots there are," Steve said, not answering. "And I don't trust KSM. Nor should you."

"And you, sir?" she asked Bowlen.

"The Saudis have been officially warned about a July 4 attack," Bowlen said, "and truly I don't have the intelligence behind that. But this business about Washington, I'm afraid I have to defer to you guys to iron it out."

"So are you dismissing that there could be more than one target? Even if it's part of more than one plot?" Charlie asked Steve.

"I'm not dismissing anything. I just don't want to get sucked into your wild goose chase," he said.

"You are the fucking master of facts. What I'm saying here can't possibly have eluded you. And your indifference makes me suspicious. I know you. *Tell the fucking professor that our plans are good. Our plans.* You are a fucking liar. A monumental liar.

"Boss," she said, looking at Bowlen, "help me out here. We need to pay attention to a second Washington target. KSM *told me* to tell the professor that quote *our plans are good.* Second Washington target could mean, I'm just saying *could mean*, three targets, not just one or two."

Bowlen hesitated, not looking at or favoring Steve. "Charlie," he quietly said, "this has always been a risk. Perhaps KSM has outsmarted us after all ..."

Charlie looked at Steve, but couldn't catch his eye, his far away blankness now his armor.

"You knew?" she said, addressing Bowlen, raising her voice, leaning into her cryptic prey.

Bowlen looked at Charlie. "My dear, there's nothing to know."

"So, is that it? That KSM has outsmarted us? Ho hum? Or have you two outsmarted me?" Her volume was increasing.

"Charlie ... calm down," Bowlen said.

"Don't fucking patronize me. I'm not calm. Steve isn't fucking calm. Nor should you be."

"My dear, I'm just saying that——"

"My dear!" she screamed. "Do you dismiss anyone else other than a woman with that shit?

"You've known all along that there was more than one target?" she was now yelling. "That trip to brief Cheney in Wyoming, the briefing with the single target? That was just a charade? All along you've known differently. You just wanted to make me feel like I was in on a plan that was acceptable to me, but also to throw me off? And the fucking eleventh hour plan to stop it all. It's for my benefit, isn't it? So you two sociopaths can sit there and make a fucking fool of the girl!"

Steve remained silent.

Bowlen responded: "Charlie. You're way off base. You are a full partner here. Nothing has been targeted against you. I said *perhaps* KSM had outsmarted us. I know nothing of any target other than the North Tower. I certainly know there is nothing going on behind your back. None of this is about you."

"Fuck you. I'm not just saying it's about me. And don't hide behind that. I'm asking serious questions and I want answers." Charlie was screaming.

"I don't know what answers you're looking for?" Bowlen calmly and slowly said, irritating her more.

"Two Washington targets and the World Trade Center! I'm looking for answers to that!"

She was livid, additionally irritated at being handled as the volatile girl, but now also enraged at his calm. And Steve's silence.

She continued: "If you don't fucking tell me the truth, I'm pulling the plug. I'll go to the goddamn news media and expose this whole shit show. I am not going to condone—"

"Condone what?" Bowlen interrupted. "Calm down …"

She was as red as a beet now, spittle coming out of the edge of her mouth.

"It's done," she yelled. And she stormed out.

Chapter 56 Observatory Circle

Steve and Tony walked out of customs at El Prat airport, spotting the man with the "Hotel Duquesa" sign standing among the waiting gaggle.

"Welcome to Barcelona," the driver said after Tony identified himself, taking their bags and leading them out to the limo. On the twenty-minute drive to the waterfront, the two looked out their own windows, lost in their own thoughts.

Tony initially objected to the trip. He'd told Steve and then he'd pleaded with Bowlen. It wasn't needed, he said. And it wasn't properly prepared. Plus Steve was not an operations guy.

But it was more than that. He'd made inquiries, acting as if he only absentmindedly asked Steve what he knew about cars, where he'd been that night.

Like any good investigator, he already thought he knew the answers. But as a good soldier, he also knew that he was an amateur compared to mister know-it-all, that he'd never get Steve to break because, well, he was obviously broken.

And then, like a good soldier, Tony followed orders.

Steve told himself that Tony would follow orders, that he wasn't going to confront Bowlen or him. *Just following orders*—everyone else's lot. That's what they did—acquiesce—either in their weakness or in their faith in the mission. And so Tony's trifling interventions, and not Steve's craterous act, crowded center stage in Draper's mind.

When the news was announced at an all staff meeting, Tony maintained his composure, despite his suspicions. Erica was devastated. She might have worked closely with Steve, but she said she wanted to *be* Charlie—justifiably confident in everything she knew, the consummate operator, a fierce and principled warrior. Barbara was equally torn up. She and Charlie had become close allies, even friends, and she shook her head and pursed her lips, cursing that tough-as-nails Charlie had worked herself so raw, that she should have taken a break, that the accident was avoidable. Mrs. Rothwell openly sobbed.

After the memorial service, people walked around the Odell Road facility like every corridor was filled with a dense mist, everyone swimming their way through a viscous broth. Even the building sensed something wrong, the lights in Charlie's office flickering on at odd moments. Steve, the stricken partner, hid in the archive, thinking that would insulate him from having to commiserate. But people still came by to say how sorry they were. It took every ounce of self-control not to say *mission first* and urge *chop, chop, we have work to do*. Instead, he comforted them, showing the appropriate emotion. And he planned the Barcelona trip, both an escape and something to do.

Bowlen said little. When he delivered the news to Steve, he tried to detect some foreknowledge. But Steve seemed genuinely surprised and even upset, chattering on about her parents, that he would call her parents, mentioning some friend who could help with her apartment and her stuff, babbling about her wishes, even about his own future without her, all the talkativeness seeming to indicate genuine shock.

Tony shared Bowlen's doubts, knowing of the girl. But he didn't confront Steve. So close and in so deep, he was trapped, just as if he were on an airplane, seatbelt fastened, unable to speak to anyone, unable to get off, unable to speed the trip along.

The day after the memorial, Steve was back at his whiteboard. The North Tower, the center of world finance and Jewish control. But now they added the White House, the political heart of arrogant America, as KSM called it. Then there was the Capitol dome, the protector of the Zionist conspiracy. And finally the Pentagon, the impregnable fortress of the American military.

Steve had always been indifferent as to how the attack came, and even indifferent as to the targets. When Bowlen expressed misgivings about the White House as a target after Charlie's death, Steve affected the attitude of the very national security bureaucrats he would have at any other time had nothing but contempt for. *Who cares if the White House was going to be attacked,* he said, *as if its temporary occupants represented America, as if the targets or the date and time would make one fucking bit of difference once their war was unleashed?*

And as for the civilian deaths that the team now calculated in the targets? Steve also couldn't care less whether it happened on a late Friday afternoon or some Tuesday morning. Charlie had become fixated with the body count and Steve urged her to detach herself from the irrelevant data. A single plane hitting even the roof of the North Tower would kill hundreds, maybe even 1,700 by their models. Twenty floors lower, the number went up to 4,000. He'd concocted it all, the numbers, to satisfy her. *Was she concerned that another 2,300 condolence cards would have to be sent out?* She called Steve an asshole and an unfeeling bastard.

It had been brewing for months. Between them. When they had that discussion about death, when Charlie realized that Steve really didn't care, she was finally reminded that they were different species.

That's when she realized he was a monster. She didn't let up. She couldn't accept.

Back in the office after the memorial, like an Army chaplain given the duty of knocking on the front door of the home of some fallen soldier, Steve had two other calls to make, Bowlen informing him that they had to tell Cheney.

"About what?" Steve at first growled at him.

"That the White House is going to be hit ..."

Steve had a ton of questions about who knew, and about what Bowlen's expectations were, but they didn't get into it. He and Bowlen didn't say a word to each other on the way to the vice president's house, not as they drove south on the BWI parkway, not as turned on to New York Avenue and into Washington traffic, not up Massachusetts Avenue, not as they rounded Observatory Circle where Cheney lived, not as they were carded at the gate to the Navy base.

They entered the grounds through the Secret Service subway-like turnstile, their IDs checked again inside the protected residence grounds.

A Navy steward in white uniform ushered them into the parlor of the grand old house.

"What can I do for you," Vice President Cheney asked, sitting down opposite them on an upholstered sofa, asking a question without a question mark.

"You told us to contact you if there was an emergency," Bowlen said. "I am here to tell you that the entire Project Sumner plan as briefed to you has been upended."

Cheney remained rigid and blank-faced.

"The White House itself will be a target of attack. We know that the FBI was predicting it for the 4th of July," Bowlen continued, "and now that that didn't happen, many are lowering their guard. But we are certain that it *will* be hit, some time, we think, in the next two months."

Cheney's cold stare urged him on.

Bowlen said their intelligence indicated that pilots were already in the United States, and that, short of airport security detecting them, or the still-unknown hijackers not being able to actually fly the commercial airliners, the White House would be struck.

Bowlen talked about options and consequences. Steve watched and waited to see what would happen. Cheney continued to stare.

"I appreciate your coming," Cheney finally replied.

"Colonel?" the vice president called. A military aide dressed in Army uniform came in. He'd obviously been standing just outside the door. "Could you escort our guests out?" asked the vice president. He got up and shook their hands, and again said it. "Thank you for coming."

Back in the SUV, they were silent. Steve asked Roy if he could drop him off at his Dupont Circle apartment.

There on his couch, he stared off into space. The vice president. Perfectly composed. Maybe one twitch of the eye as he received the news.

It was okay. He was okay.

Steve again reassured himself that everyone else sleepwalked through life, that they were all lucky that they had a leader who wasn't lost in the mist. Or constrained by the rules. And then, with a chill that seemed like a celestial missive transmitted quicker than he could erect a countermeasure, he pondered just the opposite—they were all lucky that he wasn't really in charge, that Steve was just an analyst and an operator.

Call number one completed, CTRL-INS, Steve contacted KSM to tell him that he would be the one meeting him in Spain. It made the most sense to just keep the venue. KSM was scheduled to meet there with Charlie anyhow on the 9th. Steve told their man that nothing was wrong, she was just held up doing something else.

They checked in to the Barcelona hotel, Tony saying that he wanted to scout the market before their meeting the next day, urging Steve to get some rest, to take a walk, that he'd meet him at eight the next morning in the lobby. The soldier would do his job, Steve thought, as he later stared at the four blank walls of his room and contemplated his absolute aloneness. Tony would do his job even if he didn't like it and even if the last thing he wanted was to hang out with Steve or confront him about what happened.

When Steve and Tony arrived at the *Boqueria*, the vendors were still setting up, colorful flowers being cut and arranged, fruits and vegetables mounting into vibrant pyramids. As they walked down the aisles, boxes of blood oranges and bananas and pears and mangoes were scattered everywhere, the fruit sellers busy unpacking and arranging their wares. All around, men and women were trimming their bounty to visual perfection, laying out skewers and cups of their perfect goods for the arriving customers.

At a small table in front of the Bar Pinotxo, two empty chairs waited. In a third was KSM. He'd cut off his sideburns, Steve noticed. And he was dressed in simple khaki pants and a button-down shirt, looking little different than the two of them.

"Mr. Tony!" KSM greeted, shaking his hand. "And Professor! How are you? I trust your flight was good."

He had a cup of espresso in front of him and had been reading the *International Herald Tribune*, calling over the waiter and playing host, asking them what they wanted and ordering in Spanish. They all settled on the omelet of the day.

"So? Professor? Where is Miss Landry?"

"I have bad news, Khalid," Steve said. "She was in a car accident."

"Is she okay?"

"I'm afraid she's dead."

KSM sat back and looked off to the side, swallowing deeply, his mouth opened slightly, his chin quivering. Tony was closely watching, his ever-vigilant eyes scanning the crowd at the same time.

"How?" KSM asked.

"She was driving home from work and either ran off the road or was hit by another car," said Steve.

KSM took a sip of a cup of his coffee.

"Assassinated?"

"Khalid," Steve said. "It's not the movies. She had a car accident."

"I know assassination, Professor. Doctor Azzam was assassinated. With a car bomb, but still. Yes, it is not the movies, Professor, but have you asked who would want her dead?"

"Khalid," Steve said again, calmly. "No one would."

Khalid asked questions about her Lebanese family, how they were taking it. And he asked after *Mr. Jones*. And he pushed his omelet plate to the side when it came, appetite apparently gone.

Steve felt his heart pounding as he ate, wondering how long it would be before they could get down to business, before KSM shook it off.

Tony continued to scan the growing crowd of morning shoppers, steel jawed. He barely touched his omelet either, nibbling around the edges.

Steve spoke up. "Everything is okay, Khalid. Mr. Jones wants you to know that we are still partners, wants to reassure you that there will be real changes in Saudi Arabia, wants you to know that your men haven't been detected by the CIA."

"And you, Professor?"

"What, Khalid?"

"You. What do *you* want me to know?"

Before Steve could answer, KSM continued: "Do you want me to know that you've outsmarted me, that the *Sheikh* is done, that the Taliban are finished, that Islam will—how do you say—shrivel into oblivion?"

"Khalid," Steve said again, a tiredness in his voice, a man at the ready with comforting words if that's what it took. He was ready with comforting words, good ones, ones befitting friends who also were not really friends, words that might not be satisfying but also wouldn't enflame. After all, KSM knew, Steve thought, that they couldn't really have the same objectives, and that the planes operation only worked if both of them got what they wanted.

KSM spoke again before Steve mustered a response. "You expect me to believe this, Professor? To accept that a valuable officer just dies. Like a movie, as you say?"

"Khalid," Steve again said, calmly trying to coax him back, suddenly nothing more to say.

"You are lying," KSM said. "I can see it in your eyes, hear it in your voice." He looked straight at Steve.

"Khalid."

"You people. You are nothing but cowards. Cowards and pure evil. And for what? Have you no humanity?"

EPILOGUE

Steve, Charlie, Bowlen, Hal Jones and the rest of the Apex Watch crew are fictional characters.

Mohammed Atta piloted American Airlines Flight 11 into the North Tower of the World Trade Center.

Marwan al-Shehhi piloted United Airlines Flight 175 into the South Tower of the World Trade Center, surprising KSM. His plane was destined for the U.S. Capitol building.[885]

Ziad Jarrah piloted United Airlines Flight 93, which KSM claims was destined for the White House. It crashed in Pennsylvania.

Hani Hanjour, the Saudi who was not a member of the Hamburg group, piloted American Airlines Flight 77 into the Pentagon.

Khalid al-Mihdhar ended up being a "muscleman" on board American Airlines Flight 77, the plane which fellow Saudi Hani Hanjour piloted into the Pentagon.[886]

Nawaf al-Hazmi, al-Mihdhar's partner in San Diego, was also a "muscleman" on board American Airlines Flight 77. His brother, Salem, was a muscleman, too—the only team of brothers to participate in the planes operation.

Khalid Sheikh Mohammed applied for a U.S.-entry visa in Jeddah, Saudi Arabia on July 23, 2001 using the name Abdulrahman A. A. Al-Ghamdi. It was his last known attempt at travel outside Pakistan before 9/11.[887] The application was only connected to the 9/11 mastermind after the attacks. KSM was subsequently captured by a U.S.-Pakistani team on March 1, 2003 in Rawalpindi, a suburb of Islamabad and the home of the headquarters of the powerful Pakistani intelligence service.[888] As of this book's publication, he is being held in Guantanamo, Cuba.[889]

Osama bin Laden was killed by Navy SEALs on May 2, 2011 in Abbottabad, Pakistan.

Abu Hafs, the *al Qaeda* alias for the Egyptian Muhammad Atef, and the operational head of *al Qaeda*,[890] was killed in a U.S. airstrike in Kabul on November 13, 2001. He was unable to evacuate the city with the rest of the *al Qaeda* leadership because of his chronic back problems.[891] He telephoned the newspaper *al-Quds al-Arabi* moments before the airstrike,[892] allowing Air Force targeters to pinpoint his location.

Ayman al-Zawahiri was appointed head of *al Qaeda* on June 16, 2011 following the death of Osama bin Laden.

Ramzi Binalshibh, the fourth of the Hamburg cell, left Germany on September 5, 2001, flying to Pakistan via Spain and the UAE, where he was met by Ali Abdul Aziz Ali ("al Baluchi"), KSM's cousin and the operations' money man.[893] They together traveled to Afghanistan on September 10. Binalshibh stayed at various camps, evading U.S. attacks until December 2001, when he infiltrated Iran.[894] Nine months later, he was captured in Karachi, Pakistan on September 11, 2002. As of this book's publication, he is being held in Guantanamo, Cuba.[895]

Khallad, the *al Qaeda* alias for Walid bin Attash, KSM's best friend,[896] was captured in Karachi, Pakistan on April 29, 2003, along with Ali Abdul Aziz Ali ("al Baluchi"), the 9/11 money man.[897] As of this book's publication, he is being held in Guantanamo, Cuba.

Ali Abdul Aziz Ali (Cousin Ali or "al Baluchi")[898] flew from the UAE to Pakistan with Ramzi Binalshibh. Together they went to Afghanistan on September 10. He was captured on April 29, 2003 in Karachi, Pakistan along with Khallad, as he waited for the delivery of explosives for an alleged plot to attack the U.S. consulate. He was in possession of a perfume spray bottle that contained a low concentration of cyanide. As of this book's publication, he is being held in Guantanamo, Cuba.[899]

Ahmad Mohammad al-Hada, father-in-law of Khalid al-Mihdhar and operator of the "Yemeni switchboard," was arrested in Yemen on February 14, 2002.[900]

Abu Zubaydah, the main trainer of the "musclemen" in Afghanistan and the planner behind the various Millennium plots, was captured on March 28, 2002 during a raid of a safe house in Faisalabad, Pakistan. Gunfire was exchanged during the raid and Abu Zubaydah received several gunshot wounds and was severely injured.[901] He was the first "high-value detainee" captured to be moved to a secret prison, precipitating the CIA's torture program, primarily because the CIA overstated his value based upon the fear that he was the *al Qaeda* man working on WMD.[902]

Vice President Dick Cheney telephoned Saudi Crown Prince Abdullah on July 5, 2001. There is no record of the subject of their conversation.[903]

Louis Freeh was fired as FBI director in June 2001 by President Bush, two years before completing his ten-year term.[904] He formed the Freeh Group International, a consulting firm, in 2007. In 2009, he was hired by Saudi Prince Bandar as his legal representative on issues surrounding bribes associated with the arms trade. Freeh acquired Italian citizenship on October 23, 2009.

CIA director George J. Tenet slam dunked one more time regarding weapons of mass destruction and Iraq in the run up to the 2003 war.

Former CIA director John Deutch's security clearance was "suspended" after he left the Agency, an unprecedented move against a former director. Security goons concluded that, while serving as director, Deutch "had improperly handled classified material on a home computer."

Richard Clarke, the White House staffer on counterterrorism who served in both the Clinton and Bush administrations, was appointed special advisor to the president for cyberspace security and chair of the Critical Infrastructure Protection Board a month after 9/11, the bureaucratic equivalence of being fired.[905] After he left government in 2003, he established Good Harbor Consulting LLC, writing two best-selling books about 9/11. Of the post-9/11 period, he wrote: "finally, all of our plans to destroy *al Qaeda* and its network would be implemented."[906]

The Saudi organization called Apex is fictional.

Crown Prince Abdullah became king on August 1, 2005 upon the death of his half-brother King Fahd. He then died on January 23, 2015.

Prince Bandar remained ambassador to the United States until 2005 when he became King Abdullah's national security adviser and head of the Saudi National Security Council, a newly created body. He served in that position until January 29, 2015.

Prince Turki resigned as head of the General Intelligence Directorate on August 31, 2001 after 34 years of service.[907] He succeeded Prince Bandar as Saudi ambassador to the United States, but served only 15 months, until December 11, 2006.

Prince Nayef became crown prince on October 28, 2011. He argued after 9/11 that the attacks were a Zionist conspiracy concocted to discredit Muslims, further arguing that al Qaeda and other terrorist groups had secret relations with Israeli intelligence.[908]

Prince Sultan, Saudi minister of defense and crown prince, the man that bin Laden originally reasoned with not to allow American military forces into Saudi Arabia, died on October 22, 2011.

Omar al-Bayoumi, the Saudi intelligence officer in San Diego, left the United States for London prior to 9/11.[909] Though he was later interviewed by the FBI, he was never charged with any crime. In Saudi Arabia, he became a directorate head in the General Intelligence Directorate. It was subsequently revealed that he was the subject of an FBI investigation in 1999, long before Mihdhar and Hazmi arrived in the United States.[910]

Ramzi Ahmed Yousef was sentenced to 240 years in prison for his participation in the 1993 World Trade Center attack and received a consecutive life sentence for participation in the various Philippines plots. As of this book's publication, he is being held at the high-security Supermax prison in Florence, Colorado.

Ahmed Mohammed Ajaj, the man who entered the United States with Ramzi Yousef, was released from detention in the United States in March 1993, but was rearrested almost immediately on conspiracy charges, and as of this book's publication is serving a 115-year sentence in the Marion Penitentiary in Illinois for his role in the 1993 WTC attack.

Jamal al-Fadl is settled in the United States under the U.S. Marshals Service witness protection program.[911]

Omar Abdel al-Rahman ("the Blind *Sheikh*") was arrested by the FBI on June 24, 1993 in New York as part of the first World Trade Center investigation. He was indicted with eleven others on August 25, 1993, accused of waging "a war of urban terrorism against the United States."

On October 1, 1995, he was convicted of seditious conspiracy, and in 1996 was sentenced to life in prison. He died February 18, 2017 at the Federal Medical Center in Butner, North Carolina, 66 miles from where KSM went to college.

Endnotes

Prologue

1 Mohammad al-Amir Awad al-Sayyid aka Mohammed Atta (aka Mehan Atta; Mohammad El Amir; Muhammad Atta; Mohamed El Sayed; Mohamed Elsayed; Muhammad Muhammad Al Amir Awag Al Sayyid Atta; Muhammad Muhammad Al-Amir Awad Al Sayad), Egyptian national; born in Kafr el-Sheikh, Egypt in 1968. See also Project Sumner, Name List Working Paper (U), n.d. (2000?) (TS-MU-00-16).

2 See FBI, Working Draft Chronology of Events for Hijackers and Associates.

3 Atta's smoking is referred to in *Der Spiegel, Inside 9-11: What Really Happened* (St. Martin's Paperbacks, 2002).

4 Sayyid Qutb ash-Shaheed (1906–1966), or in full Ibrāhīm Ḥusayn Shādhilī Sayyid Quṭb, Egyptian author, poet, literary critic and *Sunni* Islamic theorist, and a leading member of the Muslim Brotherhood in the 1950s and 1960s. Qutb visited America from 1948–1950, studying at Wilson Teachers College (now the University of the District of Columbia); the University of Northern Colorado; and Stanford University. He returned to Egypt even more radicalized, became the head of propaganda for the Brotherhood. In 1966, he was convicted of plotting to assassinate Egyptian president Gamal Abdel Nasser and was executed.

The thoughtful and level-headed U.S. Army Combating Terrorism Center opined that the entire *jihadi* movement could be labeled "Qutbism," as deriving its thinking from Sayyid Qutb more than any other author. Using the term, the Center notes, is also grating, for it suggests that the entire movement follows a human and thus are also deviant. See Combating Terrorism Center, U.S. Military Academy, *Military Ideology Atlas: Executive Report*, November 2006, p. 10.

5 Sayyid Qutb ash-Shaheed, "The America I Have Seen": In the Scale of Human Values, Kashful Shubuhat Publications, 1951 (originally published in the Egyptian magazine *Al-Risala*).

6 *Jihad* generally means "struggle" or "effort." In this sense it means a struggle to uphold the Islamic faith in Muslim communities or individuals where "bad habits" have set in. *Jihad* is used very loosely in common language and contemporary literature. In the strictly religious context, it is the inner spiritual struggle within oneself against sin. In the political context, if refers to a war in the service of religion and thus military struggle, conflict against the enemies of Islam or non-believers.

When used as a noun, "*Jihadis*, the holy warriors and today's most prominent terrorists, whose movement is part of the larger *Salafi* movement (but note that most *Salafis* are not *Jihadis*). Since *jihadi* thinkers draw their legitimacy from the same tradition as *Salafis*." See Combating Terrorism Center, U.S. Military Academy, *Military Ideology Atlas: Executive Report*, November 2006.

7 There is no god but god, Elvis Presley, 1972; © Sony/ATV Music Publishing LLC.

There is no God, but God

I know this is true

For God made everything,

He made me, He made you

There'd be no birds,

No planes to sail in the blue…

They say God made land

And He gave it all to man

This I know is mighty, good and true

There is no God, but God

8 *Mukhtar* is Arabic meaning "chosen" or "the brain" or even the "mayor" and a moniker generally used to refer to the informal head of a village. Within *al Qaeda*, it also meant the "authorized one." It was a name that was given to Khalid Sheikh Mohammed, the so-called mastermind behind 9/11. Few inside *al Qaeda* knew of his real name.

See, in particular, Project Sumner, Name List Working Paper (U), n.d. (2000?) (TS-MU-00-16) for an extended discussion of the nickname and various aliases used by KSM.

It is important to note that the U.S. intelligence community did not actually associate the man known as Khalid Sheikh Mohammed with the man known as *Mukhtar* until the capture and interrogation of Abu Zubaydah in March 2002, more than seven months after the events of 9/11. On April 10, 2002, Abu Zubaydah revealed to FBI officers that an individual named "*Mukhtar*" was the *al Qaeda* "mastermind" of the 9/11 attacks. Abu Zubaydah identified a picture of *Mukhtar*, whom the FBI only knew of as Khalid Sheik Mohammed. The moniker of "KSM" was not publicly known until the 911 Commission Report was published in July 2004.

According to former FBI agent Ali Soufan, "The U.S. intelligence community … had no idea that KSM was even a member of *al-Qaeda* (he was believed to be an independent terrorist), let alone the mastermind of the 9/11 attacks." *The Black Banners: The Inside Story of 9/22 and the War Against al-Qaeda* (W. W. Norton & Company, 2011), p. 387.

9 CIA analytic report, "The Plot and the Plotters (U)," June 1, 2003, p. 93.

10 The flights are taken from FBI, Working Draft Chronology of Events for Hijackers and Associates.

11 CIA analytic report, "The Plot and the Plotters (U)," June 1, 2003, p. 98.

12 The account was mohamedatta@hotmail.com, an account used from the Las Vegas Cyber Café to both access the Travelocity travel service and to communicate with *al Qaeda*. FBI, Working Draft Chronology of Events for Hijackers and Associates.

13 Yahoo! Games, launched on March 31, 1998, was closed down on March 31, 2014 and the balance was closed on February 9, 2016. The games on the website were typically Java applets or quick Flash games. Julie Muncy, "Yahoo Games Has Passed Away at Just 17," *Wired*, February 4, 2016.

14 KSM Debrief Papers, 2005.

15 Ali Abdul Aziz Ali ("Ali"), known as al-Baluchi (aka Ammar al Baluchi, Aliosh, Ali A, Isam Mansur, Hani [of Fawaz Trading UAE]); Pakistani, born in Kuwait August 29, 1977; nephew of KSM, planes operational financial middleman and logistics support based in the UAE.
　　See CIA Terrorist Biographic Note, Ali Abdul Aziz Ali (U), CTC-094-00, October 2000; CIA analytic report, Khalid Sheik Muhammad's Nephews, CTC 2003-300013, January 31, 2003.

16 *Surah al-Baqarah* [2:275], *Qur'an*; aka Verse 2:275 of the *Qur'an*, the 275th verse of chapter 2, Sūrat al-Baqarah, The Cow, containing the story of Abraham and the necessity of God-consciousness.

17 FBI, Working Draft Chronology of Events for Hijackers and Associates; CIA analytic report, "The Plot and the Plotters (U)," June 1, 2003.
　　Ali Soufan labels Mohammed Atta "an alcoholic" who "pounded shots in a bar prior to 9/11" and calls al Qaeda operatives "brainwashed." *The Black Banners*, pp. xx, xxiii.

Chapter 1

18 The *Masjid al Quds* (the *al-Quds* Mosque) was a mosque in Hamburg, between 1993 and 2010 when it was shut down by Germany security officials.
　　While in Hamburg, Atta, al-Shehhi, and Jarrah attended the *al Quds* mosque "where they met a group of radical Islamists, including Mohammed Haydar Zammar, Mamoun Darkazanli, Zakariya Essabar, Ramzi Bin al-Shibh, Said Bahaji, and Munir Mottasadeq." See Joint Inquiry, p. 183.

19 Mohammed Fazazi, born 1949, in Morocco. See Douglas Frantz and Desmond Butler, "Imam at German Mosque Preached Hate to 9/11 Pilots," *The New York*

Times, July 16, 2002, p. A3; Yassin Musharbash and Andreas Ulrich, "Infamous Islamic Imam Forswears terror," *Der Spiegel* Online, October 29, 2009.

20 The Salafi movements (from *al-salaf al-salih,* Arabic for righteous ancestors, referring to the two first generations of Islam), which emerged at the end of the nineteenth century, sought to respond to the political, cultural, and military challenge of the West. The Salafis seek the "purification" of Islam by returning to the uncorrupted form that they believed was practiced in the time of the prophet Muhammad and his companions. Salafi movements are found throughout the Muslim world. Some have a strictly religious, nonpolitical agenda. Others have evolved into or influenced the modernist tendency in Islam. Yet others have become radicalized and given sustenance to violent and terrorist groups." See Angel M. Rabasa, *The Muslim World after 9/11* (Rand Publishing, 2004), p. 15.

"The Salafiyaa [sic] are a wide spectrum of people under a Sunni theological outlook that see the *Qur'an* and teachings of the Prophet Muhammad as the only legitimate source of religious conduct and reasoning, anti-Islamic establishment of madhabs. An off-shoot of the *Wahabbi* movement which can also constitute reformers … Using the terms *Salafi* and *Wahhabi* interchangeably to refer to terrorists alienates a major part of the Islamic world and is understood by Muslims as Western ignorance or a systematic attempt to disparage conservative Islamic practices." See DOD PowerPoint Briefing, IO [Information Operations] Implications of Arabic Terminology and the GWOT, August 24, 2005.

See, also: "Sunni Muslims want to establish and govern Islamic states based solely on the *Qur'an* and the example of the Prophet as understood by the first generations of Muslims close to Muhammad. *Salafis* differ over the final form of these states and the proper means for achieving them. This movement is ideologically akin to the medieval Puritan movement in England and America." See Combating Terrorism Center, U.S. Military Academy, *Military Ideology Atlas: Executive Report,* November 2006.

21 The *Hajj* is an annual Islamic pilgrimage to Mecca, Saudi Arabia, the holiest city for Muslims, and takes place in the last month of the year. It is a mandatory religious duty for adult Muslims that must be carried out at least once during their lifetime. The hajj is the fifth of the fundamental Islamic practices and institutions known as the Five Pillars of Islam.

22 CIA analytic report, "The Plot and the Plotters (U)," June 1, 2003, p. 16.

23 On Atta's family background, see FBI report, "Hijackers Timeline," November 14, 2003 (citing FBI electronic communication from Cairo dated September 13, 2001); CIA Analytic Report, "The Plot and the Plotters," June 1, 2003, p. 23.

24 In the fall of 1991, Mohammed Atta Senior met the German family in Cairo and he arranged for his son to continue his education in Hamburg, where they eventually invited the young Atta to live with them.

25 Atta entered Cairo University in 1986. On July 1, 1990, he graduated from the Urban Development Center, Cairo University with a bachelor's degree in architectural engineering; FBI, Working Draft Chronology of Events for Hijackers and Associates.

26 Muhammad Hosni El Sayed Mubarak, born May 4, 1928, in Kfar El-Meselha, Egypt. A military officer who rose to be commander of the Air Force in 1972, he became the Vice President under Anwar Sadat in April 1975 and Prime Minister and then President in October 1981.

27 CIA analytic report, "The Plot and the Plotters (U)," June 1, 2003, p. 21.

28 Ayman al-Zawahiri (aka Aiman Muhammad Rabi Al-Zawahiri, Abu Muhammad (Abu Mohammed), Abu Fatima, Muhammad Ibrahim, Abu Abdallah, Abu al-Mu'iz, The Doctor, The Teacher, Nur, Ustadh, Abu Mohammed Nur al-Deen, `Abd al-Mu`izz (Abdel Muaz, Abdel Moez, Abdel Muez), Egyptian, born June 19, 1951 to a prominent middle class family in Maadi, Egypt, a suburb of Cairo.

His father was a pharmacologist. By fourteen he joined the Muslim Brotherhood and become a student and follower of Sayyid Qutb. Zawahiri studied behavior, psychology and pharmacology as part of his medical degree at Cairo University. By 1979 he moved on to the much more radical Egyptian Islamic Jihad (EIJ), where he became one of its leading organizers and recruiters.

See Project Sumner, Name List Working Paper (U), n.d. (2000?) (TS-MU-00-16).

29 The Egyptian Islamic Jihad (EIJ), formerly called the Islamic Jihad, was founded around 1980 with the goal of overthrowing the Egyptian government and establishing an Islamic state. On October 6, 1981, Egyptian president Anwar Sadat was assassinated by radical army troops loyal to the EIJ.

30 The Combating Terrorist Center says that Zawahiri, often portrayed by Western media as the main brain in the *Jihadi* Movement, "is totally insignificant in the Jihadi intellectual universe." See Combating Terrorism Center, U.S. Military Academy, *Military Ideology Atlas: Executive Report*, November 2006, p. 9.

31 Sayyid Qutb, *Milestones (Ma'alim fi al-Tariq)*, originally published in 1964 (Kazi Publications, 1964).

32 *Jahiliyyah*: paganism, against which the Prophet Mohammed successfully waged war "in the path of God." See *A Fury for God*, p. 86. The "Age of Ignorance", *Jahiliyyah* defines pre-Islamic Arabia. In modern Islamic fundamentalism, it refers to any nation or community that has turned its back on God from the fundamentalists point of view.

33 Sayyid Qutb ash-Shaheed, *The America I Have Seen: In the Scale of Human Values* (1951) (Kashf ul Shubuhat Publications).

34 CIA analytic report, "The Plot and the Plotters (U)," June 1, 2003, p. 20.

35 FBI, Working Draft Chronology of Events for Hijackers and Associates. "What is left of Islamic 'civilization,' the fabric of tradition one finds in the labyrinthine alleys of the Aleppo souks so admired by Atta in his thesis on the Islamic city or the glorious mudbrick streets of old 'Unaida in Saudi Arabia, are everywhere succumbing to the corrosive effects of modernity. But for the Islamist it is not 'our' modernity, it is 'theirs.'" Malise Ruthven, *A Fury for God* (Granta UK, 2004), pp. 21, 260.

36 The master's thesis is lost to history, or it has been destroyed. It was finished in 1994.

See discussion in Janet Ward, "Rebuilding Babel: Urban Regeneration in the Modern/Postmodern Age," in *Legacies of Modernism*, Studies in European Culture and History (Palgrave Macmillan, 2007).

37 "The high-rise tower block which stacks people vertically may have come to suit societies where freedom is experienced as personal privacy (freedom from being observed by one's neighbours, freedom not to make conversation in the elevators). But in societies conditioned by centuries of 'horizontal' living, where the rules of extended family living, including sexual segregation, were maintained less by draconian restrictions than by the customary zoning of male and female areas, living in a skyscraper becomes a kind of tyranny, in which males and females are imprisoned vertically into the discretely separated nuclear families that prevail in Western societies." *A Fury for God*, p. 261.

Osama bin Laden came to similar conclusions, favoring the Spartan rural life, which he thought made society stronger and better able to resist threats. "Ibn Khaldun adhered to the Prophet's position that without the martial spirit Muslims would lose the ability to 'help the truth become victorious.' Urbanized societies encourage effeminacy, tyrannical government, and societal decline; Michael Scheuer, *Osama bin Laden* (Oxford University Press, 2001), p. 37.

38 CIA analytic report, "The Plot and the Plotters (U)," June 1, 2003, pp. 20–21.

39 On Atta's attendance at the mosque and his views on religion, see FBI electronic communication (EC), Subject: Khaled A. Shoukry, June 17, 2002.

40 ADCI(SP), Saudi Payments to Mohammed Fazazi—Background and Adherents," April 2001, TS/SP/MU.

41 CIA analytic report, "The Plot and the Plotters (U)," June 1, 2003, p. 6.

42 The breakup of Yugoslavia began in 1989 and officially Yugoslavia ceased to exist on April 28, 1992. Slovenia and then Croatia were the first to break away. The war in Croatia led to hundreds of thousands of refugees. By 1992 a further conflict had broken out in Bosnia, which declared independence. The Christian Serbs who lived there were determined to remain within Yugoslavia and to help build a greater Serbia. Receiving backing from extremist groups in Belgrade, they undertook a campaign of "ethnic cleansing" that drove Muslims from their homes. By 1993 the Bosnian Muslim government was besieged in the capital Sarajevo, surrounded by Bosnian Serb forces who controlled around 70 percent of Bosnia.

43 Saddam Hussein Abd al-Majid al-Tikriti, fifth president of Iraq from July 1979 to April 2003. He was executed in Baghdad on December 31, 2006.

44 The southern Russian republic of Chechnya declared independence with the breakup of the Soviet Union. In 1994, Russian troops were sent to quash the movement, the start of now decades of brutal conflict.

Chapter 2

45 CIA analytic report, "The Plot and the Plotters (U)," June 1, 2003, p. 18.

46 Hizb'allah ("Hezbollah"), Party of God, was founded in Lebanon in 1980 as a militia of Shi'a followers of the Ayatollah Khomeini, initially trained, organized and funded by a contingent of Iranian Revolutionary Guards.

47 The author intentionally uses the spelling *Hizb'allah* since *Hizb* means party, either political or socio-religious, and *Allah* means God. Many other different spellings are used: Hizballah, Hizbollah, Hezbollah.

48 Qana (Kfar Qana), a village in southern Lebanon, is located 12 kms (7.5 miles) from the Israeli border, southeast of Tyre. On April 18, 1996, during Operation Grapes of Wrath, Israeli artillery hit a United Nations peacekeeping compound in the village, killing some 106 civilians. The Lebanese civilians had taken refuge in the compound to escape fighting in the village.

49 CIA analytic report, "The Plot and the Plotters (U)," June 1, 2003, p. 18.

50 Mohammed Atta, In the Name of God Almighty; Last Will and Testament, April 11, 1996, 2 pp.

51 Marwan Yousef Mohamed R. Lekrab Al-Shehhi (aka Marwan Yousef Mohamed R. Lekrab AlShehhi; Marwan Yusif Muhammad Rashid Lakrab Al-Shihhi; Abu Abdullah; al-Sharqi); born May 9, 1978; United Arab Emirates citizen, son of an Emirate prayer caller (pilot). *The Black Banners*, p. 317, also mentions the name al-Sharqi. See also Project Sumner, Name List Working Paper (U), n.d. (2000?) (TS-MU-00-16).

52 On April 28, 1996, Marwan al-Shehhi arrived in Germany. See FBI, Working Draft Chronology of Events for Hijackers and Associates; CIA analytic report, "The Plot and the Plotters (U)," June 1, 2003.

"We believe he lived in Bonn through early 1999, when he passed a German proficiency exam, but apparently was a visitor to Hamburg before 1999." Unclassified Version of Director of Central Intelligence George J. Tenet's Testimony Before the Joint Inquiry, 18 June 2002.

53 "Message from Usamah Bin-Muhammad Bin-Laden to His Muslim Brothers in the Whole World and Especially in the Arabian Peninsula: Declaration of Jihad Against the Americans Occupying the Land of the Two Holy Mosques; Expel the Heretics from the Arabian Peninsula." August 23, 1996. The declaration was published on September 2, 1996 in *al-Islah*, the newsletter of the Movement for Islamic Reform in Arabia. See Michael Scheuer ("Anonymous"), *Through our Enemies' Eyes* (Potomac Books Inc., 2002), p. xvi.

54 In his August 23, 1996 "message," his so-called *fatwa*, Osama bin Laden said to his supporters and to Muslim youth everywhere: "Your blood has been spilt in Palestine and Iraq, and the horrific image of the massacre in Qana in Lebanon are still fresh in people's minds."

In November 1996, bin Laden again mentioned Qana in an interview with the Australian journal *Nida'ul Islam*, saying that when the United States government accuses terrorists of killing innocents it is "accusing others of their own afflictions in order to fool the masses."

55 CIA analytic report, "The Plot and the Plotters (U)," June 1, 2003, p. 20.

56 For details on his study in Germany, see German *Bundeskriminalamt* (BKA) report, Investigative summary re Atta, June 24, 2002; Federal Prosecutor General (Germany), response to 911 Commission letter, June 25, 2004, pp. 3–4.

57 54 Marienstrasse 21073, Hamburg, Germany. In actuality, in November 1998, Atta, Binalshibh, and a third man named Said Bahaji moved into the 54 Marienstrasse apartment in Hamburg. See KSM Debrief Papers, 2005; Joint Inquiry, pp. 132–133.

58 See Brigitte Nacos, *Mass-Mediated Terrorism: The Central Role of the Media in Terrorism and Counterterrorism* (Rowman & Littlefield Publishers, 2007); and Anandam P. Kavoori and Todd Fraley, eds., *Media, Terrorism, and Theory: A Reader* (Rowman & Littlefield Publishers, 2006)

59 *Dajjal* (Al-Masih ad-Dajjal), "the deceiver", is an evil figure in Islamic myth. He is said to appear from the East, pretending to be the Messiah before the Day of Resurrection.

60 There are suggestions in the official documents that Marwan was in fact gravely ill. See 911 Commission Report (Official Report), p. 167; Joint Inquiry, p. 137.

Chapter 3

61 CIA analytic report, "The Plot and the Plotters (U)," June 1, 2003, pp. 12–19.

62 Ziad Samir Jarrah (aka Zaid Jarrah; Zaid Samr Jarrah; Ziad S. Jarrah; Ziad Jarrah Jarrah, Ziad Samir Jarrah); Lebanese national; born May 11, 1975, Beirut, Lebanon.

For background, see FBI letterhead memorandum, profile of Jarrah, March

20, 2002; Project Sumner, Name List Working Paper (U), n.d. (2000?) (TS-MU-00-16).

63 The author visited Qana and the UN camp there as part of his work for Human Rights Watch in 1996, observing the shrine and experiencing the symbolic significance that the location had already taken on.

64 *Ulema (Ulama)* (singular, *'alim*). The Arabic term refers to the body of scholars who are well versed in the *Qur'an* and in Islamic beliefs and practices who are informally the leaders of Islamic society, including teachers, judges and *imams*.

65 *Mufti*, the Arabic term referring to the religious leader recognized by the community as qualified to give reliable (usually orthodox) interpretations of Islamic law.

66 *Zakat* is one of the Five Pillars of Islam, a religious obligation, ordering all Muslims who can to donate a certain portion of wealth each year to charitable causes. In Saudi Arabia, it is obligatory, with the religious establishment saying that those who fail to pay will face God's punishment on Judgment Day.

67 King Fahd bin `Abd al-`Aziz Al Sa`ud. On June 13, 1982, King Khalid, sickly and ineffectual, unexpectedly died of a heart attack, and Crown Prince Fahd (11th son of the founder of the Saudi kingdom) took his place. Fahd eventually adopted the title "Guardian of Islam's Holy Shrines" originally coined for the 16th century Grand Sultan Selim I.

"Fahd was considered effective and decisive." His elevation to Crown Prince coincided with the rise of his "uterine" brothers: Sultan, Abd al-Rahman. Turki, Nayef, Salman and Ahmad. The group of brothers came to be known as the Sudairi (or Sudayri) seven or *Al Fahd*, all from the same mother. They were later to occupy all of the key ministry posts of the government.

68 On April 4, 1996, Ziad Jarrah entered Germany from Beirut via Amsterdam.

See FBI, Working Draft Chronology of Events for Hijackers and Associates; Unclassified Version of Director of Central Intelligence George J. Tenet's Testimony Before the Joint Inquiry, 18 June 2002; 911 Commission Report (Official Report), Staff Statement Number 16, pp 15–16.

69 A month before he arrived in the United States, Ziad Jarrah met his Turkish-German wife Aysel Senguen in Greece for a short vacation. See FBI, Working Draft Chronology of Events for Hijackers and Associates.

70 CIA analytic report, "The Plot and the Plotters (U)," June 1, 2003, p. 33.

71 The Committee for Advice and Reform, Important Telegram to Our Brothers in the Armed Forces, 14-4-1415 (September 19, 1994).

72 The Committee for Advice and Reform, Do Not Have Vile Actions in Your Religion, 11-04-1415 (September 16, 1994). The story of the arrest of reformist

Saudi scholars in 1994 is told in *Osama bin Laden*, pp. 80–81.

73 *Surah Ayah an-Nur* [24:2], *Qur'an*.

74 The *Sunnah* ("path" or "way") refers to the words and deeds of the Prophet Mohammed, who set the example that all Muslims are to follow. In pre-Islamic times, the Arab word *sunnah* referred to a body of established customs and beliefs that make up a tradition.

Chapter 4

75 Ramzi Muhammad Abdullah Binalshibh (aka Ramzi Bin al-Shibh, Omar, Ahad Sabet, Ramzi Mohamed Abdellah Omar, Ramzi Omar, Ramzi al Sheiba, Umar al-Yemeni, Abu Ubaydah al-Hadrami, Ahad Sabet, Abu Ubaydah, Abu Obadiah, Ahad Abdollahi Saber, Hasan Ali al Assiri), Yemeni; born on May 1, 1972, in Ghayl Bawazir, in the Hadramawt region, Yemen; resided in Hamburg, Germany from 1995 to 2001.

A German arrest warrant was issued for Ramzi Omar in May 1998, but Binalshibh was no longer using this alias and German authorities did not know until after 9/11 that Ramzi Omar and Ramzi Binalshibh were the same person.

For background, see also CIA, intelligence report, interrogation of Ramzi Binalshibh, October 1, 2002; CIA intelligence report, interrogation of Ramzi Binalshibh, October 2, 2002; Joint Task Force Guantanamo, Subject: Combatant Status Review Tribunal Input and Recommendation for Continued Detention Under DoD Control (CD) for Guantanamo Detainee ISN: US9YM-010013DP (S), Secret/NF, December 8, 2006; Internment Serial Number (ISN): US9YM-010013DP; CIA Terrorist Biographic Note, 'Ramzi Bin al-Shibh' (U), CTC-038-00, February 2000; Joint Inquiry, pp. 133–134; Project Sumner, Name List Working Paper (U), n.d. (2000?) (TS-MU-00-16).

76 CIA analytic report, "The Plot and the Plotters (U)," June 1, 2003, p. 21.

77 Osama bin Laden was born in 1957 to Mohammad bin Awdah bin Laden, who moved to Saudi Arabia from Yemen, for financial opportunities. The elder bin Laden eventually became a construction magnate and the bin Laden family became highly respected in Saudi Arabia for their work in renovating the holy cities of Mecca and Medina.

78 Hadramawt was an ancient southern Arabian Peninsula kingdom that occupied what are now southern and southeastern Yemen and the present-day Oman. It was politically independent until the 3rd Century AD, when it was conquered by the kingdom of Saba'. The society is still coherent and centered around ancient tribes, including the Sayyid aristocracy, families that claim descendancy from the Prophet Muhammad. The *Wahabbis* from Saudi Arabia invaded in the first decade of 1800, destroying many important temples and structures.

79 The British Empire came to Yemen in 1888, with a treaty of protection signed between the al-Qu'ayti tribe, followed by another treaty with the Kathiri tribe in 1918. Britain became "advisors" to the Hadramawt in 1934. The Aden protectorate claimed independence in 1967, forming the People's Republic of South Yemen, encompassing Hadramawt. The Sultan of Hadramawt went into exile in Saudi Arabia.

80 CIA analytic report, "The Plot and the Plotters (U)," June 1, 2003, p. 20.

81 FBI, Working Draft Chronology of Events for Hijackers and Associates.

82 CIA analytic report, "The Plot and the Plotters (U)," June 1, 2003, pp. 20–61.

83 911 Commission Report (Official Report), Staff Statement 16, p. 3; Joint Inquiry, pp. 189ff.

84 CIA, intelligence report, interrogation of Ramzi Binalshibh, October 1, 2002.

85 CIA analytic report, "The Plot and the Plotters (U)," June 1, 2003, p. 42.

86 Walid Muhammad Salih Mubarak Bin 'Attash (aka Khallad Bin 'Attash, but mostly referred to as Khallad). See CIA, intelligence report, interrogation of Khallad, January 14, 2004. See also Project Sumner, Name List Working Paper (U), n.d. (2000?) (TS-MU-00-16).

87 *Mullah* Mohammed Omar, born circa 1960 in Kandahar, Afghanistan; founded the Taliban in 1994, in Kandahar. The Taliban recognized him as the "Commander of the Faithful", the Supreme Leader of all Muslims.

88 Abdel Bari Atwan in *The Secret History of al Qaeda* (Saqi Books, 2006) p. 24, labels rape 'the worst possible crime in Afghan culture."

89 "The students at the medressas [sic] were known as *taliban*, a Persianized plural of an Arabic word meaning seekers of knowledge or students....The key to the growth was the huge funds that had flowed into the Deobandi medressas from the Gulf when governments and donors there had decided that the Deobandis were the closest local equivalent to the Wahhabis and thus should be sponsored as part of the global push to encourage the spread of hardline Salafi strands of Islam." See *Al Qaeda*, p. 93.

90 "The nineteenth-century *Deobandi* movement in India propagated *Wahhabi* fundamentalism and imitation of Arab cultural behavior; its ideological successors in Pakistan launched the Taliban in Afghanistan." See *The Muslim World After 9/11*, p. 33.

"It is easy to confuse political Islamism and the strand of Islamic thought derived from the early *Deobandis*, yet the two are very different. Where political Islamism is focused on the Islamicization of the state through what are effectively political channels, the *Deobandis* reject politics altogether. The emphasis placed by the *Deobandis* on a rigid observance of a literal reading of *Qur'anic* injunctions is very different from the relative flexibility of the political Islamists." hence the rigidness of the Taliban, who were to emerge from Deobandi schools." See Jason Burke, *Al Qaeda: The True Story of Radical Islam* (I.B. Tauris, 2004) pp. 92–93.

91 The term Wahhabi, Arabic *muwahiddun*, comes from the teachings of theologian Muhammad ibn Abdal-Wahhabin in 18th century Arabia (1703-1787). His original Wahhabi campaign was dedicated to purifying Islam of "innovations" that had corrupted it and returning to the ways and beliefs of the "pious forebears" (al-salaf al-salihin).

Wahhabism was embraced by the Saudi rulers of Najd, who promoted it before it was overtaken by domination of the Ottoman sultan, and then reemerged again as the Ottoman Empire collapsed. The conquest of Mecca and Medina, together with Wahhabism doctrine increased the prestige of the House of Saud in the Islamic world.

"Wahhabis actually consider the term pejorative and prefer to call themselves *al-Muwahhidun* or *Ahl al-Tawhid*, "those who uphold the unity of God." By these terms Wahhabis presume an exclusive claim on *tawhid*, the oneness of God, the fundamental principle of Islam. ... Wahhabi teachings incorporate the concepts of *hejira* (flight from non-Wahhabi traditions), *takfir* (excommunication of other Muslims as infidels), and armed *jihad* as not only permissible but obligatory against unbelievers and non-Wahhabi Muslims, who are stigmatized as *mushrikin* or idolators." See *The Muslim World After 9/11*, p. 16.

92 In the 18th Century, Wahhabin rejected virtually all adornment, art, music, and technology as blasphemy; Steve Coll, *The Bin Ladens: An Arabian Family in the American Century* (Penguin Press, 2008) p. 35.

"*Wahhabism* traditionally is suspicious of new technology, viewing modernity as an evil that takes people further away from the ideal way of life as practiced by the Prophet." *The Black Banners*, p. xxii.

93 "Text of World Islamic Front's Statement Urging Jihad Against Jews and Crusaders," *Al Quds al Arabi*, signed by Osama bin Laden, Ayman al Zawahiri (emir of the Egyptian Islamic Jihad), AbuYasir Rifa'i Ahmad Taha (leader of the Egyptian Islamic Group), Mir Hamzah (secretary of the Jamiat ul Ulema e Pakistan), and Fazlul Rahman (head of the Jihad Movement in Bangladesh), February 28, 1998.

In March 1998, a conference of Afghan clerics endorsed bin Laden's call for a *jihad* against the United States, giving his *fatwa* greater authority. In late April of that year, a group of Pakistani religious figures also backed bin Laden. See also Committee for Advice and Reform, Supporting the *Fatwa* by the Afghani Religious Scholars of Ejecting the American Forces Form the Land of the Two Holy Mosques, 1-1-1419 (May 7, 1998).

94 *Khorasan (Khurasan)* is the ancient Islamic names for the lands of Afghanistan and a name that became common in *jihadi* writings after 9/11. The so-called "end of days" referred to by many in the *Qur'an* and the *hadith* (the sayings of the Prophet Mohammed) originates in *Khorasan*, led by the armies of the black banners.

In his "Message from Usamah Bin-Muhammad Bin-Laden to His Muslim Brothers in the Whole World and Especially in the Arabian Peninsula: Declaration of Jihad Against the Americans Occupying the Land of the Two Holy Mosques; Expel the Heretics from the Arabian Peninsula." the declaration ends with the dateline: Friday, August 23, 1996, in the Hindu Kush, Khurasan.

95 CIA analytic report, "The Plot and the Plotters (U)," June 1, 2003, p. 69.

96 On February 23, 1998, Ayman Zawahiri signed on to the joint *fatwa* with Osama bin Laden under the title "World Islamic Front Against Jews and Crusaders". See also CIA, intelligence report, interrogation of Khallad, January 14, 2004.

97 *The Black Banners*, p. 69.

98 CIA, intelligence report, interrogation of Khallad, January 14, 2004.

99 CIA analytic report, "The Plot and the Plotters (U)," June 1, 2003, p. 41.

100 Muhammad Atef, the *al Qaeda* alias for Tayseer Abu Sitah (aka Abu Hafs al-Masri ("The Egyptian"), Abu Hafs, Abu Hafs al Masry, Abu Hafs al-Misri, Subhi Abu Sitta, Muhammad Atif), Egyptian, born 1944 in Egypt, former Egyptian police officer; original member of Egyptian Islamic *Jihad* (EIJ); set up training camps for Somalia in 1993 to help Somali tribes oppose the UN peacekeeping operations; deputy head of the *al Qaeda* military committee, he became head of the committee in 1996 after the death of Abu Ubaidah al-Banshiri; member *majlis al shura* (or consultation council) of *al Qaeda*; primary operational commander above KSM. See *Al Qaeda*, p. 108; *The Secret History of al Qaeda*, pp. 24–25; *The Black Banners*, p. 345.

101 CIA analytic report, "The Plot and the Plotters (U)," June 1, 2003, p. 42.

102 Hafez al-Assad, the dictator "President" of Syria from 1971 to 2000.

103 CIA, intelligence report, interrogation of Khallad, January 14, 2004.

Chapter 5

104 Lawrence Bowlen's official title was Associate Director for Special Purpose, with the common acronym ADSP (pronounced "add-spee"). The complete and official acronym for his office was ADCI(SP), for Associate Director of Central Intelligence for Special Purpose.

105 James Jesus Angleton, director of CIA counterintelligence from 1954-1975, was the true phantom, a creepy hermit who headed counterintelligence for three decades. He was obsessed with Soviet deceptions and KGB moles hidden in the CIA's ranks. He ruined operations and careers in his obsessive quest. And yet for whatever reasons, director after director tolerated his corrosive and tyrannical presence. Cold War supremacy meant that anyone and everyone was vulnerable.

Angleton was long gone but his legacy lived on. Some claim he himself was that never-found KGB mole. Others speculate that he was even the man behind the Kennedy assassination.

106 The CIA Counter-terrorism Center (CTC), established as the Counterterrorist Center in February 1986. Its defined mission is to "preempt, prevent, and disrupt terrorist activities and plans."

Many sources state that the CTC was established in January 1996 during the Clinton administration, but that was the date that an Osama Bin Laden cell was established (sometimes called "Alec Station") to track terrorist finances associated with the young Saudi.

According to former CIA director George Tenet: "The Center enables the fusion of all sources of information in a single, action-oriented unit. Not only does it fuse source reporting on international terrorism from US and foreign collectors, but it also integrates counterterrorism operational and analytical activity. The Center is also the CIA's single point of contact on counterterrorism issues for US policymakers. The Center's fused, integrated activities give us the speed that we must have to seize fleeting opportunities in the shadowy world of terrorism." See Written Statement for the Record of the Director of Central Intelligence, Before the National Commission on Terrorist Attacks Upon the United States, March 24, 2004.

The might of the CTC is in question. It had only 40 analysts to begin with, and many of them were detailed from other Bureaus and agencies on temporary assignments. "Before September 11, CTC had forty analysts to analyze terrorism issues worldwide, with only one of its five analytic branches focused on terrorist tactics. As a result, the only terrorist tactic on which CTC had performed strategic analysis was the use of chemical, biological, radiological and nuclear weapons because of the obvious potential for mass casualties." Joint Inquiry, p. 213.

In late 2000, DCI George Tenet appointed a senior manager, who briefed him in March 2001 on "creating a strategic assessment capability" to address the deficiency of strategic analysis against *al Qaeda*. The CTC established a new strategic assessments branch in July 2001; the plan was to add about ten analysts to this effort. The new chief of this branch reported for duty on September 10, 2001. See 911 Commission, p. 342; Written Statement for the Record of the Director of Central Intelligence, Before the National Commission on Terrorist Attacks Upon the United States, March 24, 2004.

107 Project Sumner Timeline, V38, n.d. (2008) (TS/SP/MU).

108 Peter Baker, "Clinton Settles with Paul Jones Lawsuit for $850,000," *The Washington Post*, November 14, 1998, p. A1; Peter Baker and Susan Schmidt, "Clinton Lawyers Seek Jones Settlement," *The Washington Post*, September 25, 1998, p. A1.

109 Robert Pear, "CIA Settles Suit on Sex Bias," *The New York Times*, March 30, 1995, p. A21.

110 CTC, the acronym for the CIA Counterterrorist Center and how most insiders referred to the CIA organization, and pronounced "see-tee-cee."

111 At 9:30 PM on June 25, 1996, terrorists detonated an explosives-laden fuel truck outside Building 131 of a U.S. Air Force barracks complex called Khobar Towers just outside King Abdul Aziz Air Base in Dhahran, Saudi Arabia. The bomb ripped the façade off of the front of the eight-story dormitory building, killing 19 Americans and wounding 515, including 240 U.S. personnel. Five other buildings housing U.S. military personnel were damaged by the blast, windows shattering up to a mile away. Twenty miles away in Bahrain, the blast was heard.

Less than a year earlier, at approximately 11:20 AM on November 13, 1995, a car bomb parked next to a building called the Saudi Arabia National Guard Office of Program Management (OPM-SANG) exploded, killing five and injuring 55 others. Three years later, on the anniversary of the bombing, a sixth employee died from wounds sustained during the bombing. The building housed U.S. and Saudi bureaucrats managing part of the U.S.-Saudi foreign military sales (FMS) program.

112 Liaison relationships generally mean official information exchanges with foreign intelligence services. To some degree, they increased in importance with the end of the Cold War, as the U.S. intelligence community struggled to understand a greater and greater number of diverse countries. They became particularly important in the field of counter-terrorism. To anti-Clinton operatives, they also represented risk aversion, in deferring to "host notion" and squelching unilateral American initiatives and collection.

The Joint Inquiry later concluded that liaison partnerships significantly harmed the ability of the U.S. to develop its own human intelligence sources. "Prior to September 11, 2001, the Intelligence Community did not effectively develop and use human sources to penetrate the al-Qa'ida inner circle. This lack of reliable and knowledgeable human sources significantly limited the Community's ability to [page xviii] acquire intelligence that could be acted upon before the September 11 attacks. In part, at least, the lack of unilateral (i.e., U.S.-recruited) counterterrorism sources was a product of an excessive reliance on foreign liaison services." See Joint Inquiry, pp. xvii, 90–91.

Ali Soufan also writes of the structural problem associated with dealing with foreign intelligence and security services: "Overlapping jurisdictions and blurred boundaries between security agencies are deliberate in some countries. Having one agency means that there's a potential power base that may dominate the country. The presence of many jurisdictions, however, comes with its own problems: agencies spend their time fighting turf wars with each other, with the president of the country serving as the arbitrator. While such a situation may prevent one group from launching a coup, it doesn't help outsiders trying to work with the different agencies. See *The Black Banners*, p. 164.

113 The attack on the Saudi Arabia National Guard Office of Program Management (OPM-SANG) in Riyadh occurred on November 13, 1995. The attack on the Egyptian Embassy in Islamabad, Pakistan occurred on November 19,

1995. The so-called "Srebrenica massacre" occurred during July 1995. The war in Bosnia-Herzegovina was brought to an end by the General Framework Agreement for Peace in Bosnia and Herzegovina, negotiated by the parties in Dayton, Ohio between November 1 and 21, 1995 and signed in Paris on December 14, 1995.

114 Actually Osama bin-Muhammad bin-Awad bin Laden (aka Usama Bin Muhammad Bin Awad Bin Ladin, Abu Abdallah Abd Al-Hakim, Abu Abdullah, the *Sheikh* (by peers), the *Emir* (by subordinates)); born March 10, 1957 in the al-Maz (al-Malazz) district of Riyadh, Saudi Arabia.

115 *Al Qaeda* (القاعدة) (sometimes spelled Qa'eda, Qa'ida, or Qida) is often simply defined as referring to an organization, with a name, "The Base."

Jason Burke, despite an elaborate thesis that *al Qaeda* per se does not exist, writes: "*Al Qaeda* comes from the Arabic root *qaf-ayn-dal*. It can mean a base, as in a camp or a home, a foundation, such is what is beneath a house or a pedestal that supports a column. It can mean the lowest, broadest layer of a large cumulonimbus-type cloud. And crucially, it can also mean a precept, rule, principle, maxim, formula, method, model or pattern." See *Al Qaeda*, p. 1.

Steve Coll writes of the 1988 founding: "The camps where this training would take place would be called *Al Qaeda Al-Askariya*, or 'The Military Base.' *Al Qaeda* would be 'basically an organized Islamic faction' and would develop 'statutes and instructions,' but it would also be a vehicle for more open-ended, nonhierarchical participation in jihad." *The Bin Ladens*, p. 337.

Some think that *al Qaeda* specifically refers to a "database." For instance, James Bamford writes: "As Arabs around the Middle East heard of his ... camps, more began joining him in the fight. In an effort to keep track of the mujahedeen as they transited from *Beit-al-Ansar* [their guest house in Peshawar] to camp, to the front, then back to *Beit-al-Ansar*, bin Laden set up a tracking system he called "The Base"—"*Al Qaeda*" in Arabic ..." See James Bamford, *A Pretext for War: 9/11, Iraq, and the Abuse of America's Intelligence Agencies* (Anchor, 2005), p. 14.

116 "After the creation of a 'virtual station' to examine bin Ladin, CIA identified a multi-national network of cells and of affiliated terrorist organizations. That network was attempting to wage *'jihad'* in Bosnia and planned to have a significant role in a new Bosnian government. US and Allied actions halted the war in Bosnia and caused most of the al Qida related jihadists to leave." See Testimony of Richard A. Clarke before the National Commission on Terrorist Attacks Upon the United States, March 24, 2004.

117 According to former White House staffer Richard Clarke, writing about that time: "Not only had the CIA not tried to put a CIA officer posing as an American (or Moroccan or anything else) inside *al Qaeda*, in 1999 the new director of the Counterterrorism Center (CTC), Cofer Black, told me he had been shocked to learn on taking the job that no attempts had been made by the CIA to develop useful sources inside *al Qaeda*." See Richard A. Clarke, *Your Government Failed You: Breaking the Cycle of National Security Disasters* (Ecco, 2008), p. 107.

The Top Secret Joint Inquiry, p. 93, affirms that the CIA did not have a source

HISTORY IN ONE ACT

inside *al Qaeda* at this time.

118 Khalid Sheikh Mohammed Ali Dustin al-Balushi (aka Khalid Shaykh Mohammad); Pakistani national, born in Kuwait; born April 14, 1965, raised in the Badawiya neighborhood of Fahaheel, south of Kuwait City; graduated from North Carolina A&T University in 1986; worked for the Kuwaiti run Committee for the Call to Islam in Peshawar, Pakistan run by his brother Zahid; taught engineering in Pakistan; moved to Karachi in 1992 and purchased a house.

See Terry McDermott and Josh Meyer, *The Hunt for KSM: Inside the Pursuit and Takedown of the Real 9/11 Mastermind, Khalid Sheikh Mohammed* (Little, Brown and Company, 2012), p. 25; Richard Miniter, *Mastermind: The Many Faces of the 9/11 Architect, Khalid Shaikh Mohammed* (Sentinel, 2011), pp. 14, 39, 81; *Al Qaeda*, pp. 112-113.

In *Losing Bin Laden: How Bill Clinton's Failures Unleashed Global Terror* (Regnery Publishing, 2003) p. 34, Richard Miniter incorrectly calls Khalid Sheikh Mohammed "a relative of bin Laden's."

Khalid Sheikh Mohammed is also often reported as being married to the sister of Ramzi Yousef's wife.

See also KSM et al Indictment, p. 25; Joint Task Force Guantanamo, Subject: Combatant Status Review Tribunal Input and Recommendation for Continued Detention under DOD Control (CD) for Guantanamo Detainee, ISN: US9KU-010024DP(S), December 8, 2006; and Joint Inquiry, p. 310.

"A report *in The Los Angeles Times* mentions that while in Karachi, Shaikh [KSM] 'told people he was a holy water salesman, an electronics importer and a Saudi oil sheikh.'" Quoted in *Al Qaeda*, p. 114.

119 This is substantiated in ADCI(SP) Contact Sheet, Khalid Sheikh Mohammed, n.d. (1986?), MU-80-4/6; Apex files, Cabinet 19, Drawer 3, Box 9.

120 In 1992, KSM spent some time fighting alongside the *mujahedeen* in Bosnia and supporting that effort with financial donations. See 911 Commission Report (Official Report), p. 148.

Later KSM claimed that he also took a 1995 trip to Bosnia, a trip never known to Apex Watch. See CIA, intelligence report, interrogation of KSM, July 23, 2003.

In FBI investigations, it turns out the KSM may have been involved in another attack in 1995 relating to the trip. KSM's presence in Bosnia coincided with a police station bombing in Zagreb where the timing device of the bomb (a modified Casio watch) resembled those manufactured by KSM and Ramzi Yousef in the Philippines for "Bojinka." See FBI report, Manila air investigation, May 23, 1999.

Chapter 6

121 Prior to 9/11, the CIA Counterterrorist Center sounded a lot more impressive in terms of resources than it actually was. The Joint Inquiry, pp. 62-63 reported: "At the CTC ... there were only three analysts assigned to work on al-Qa'ida full time between 1998 and 2000, and five between 2000 and September 11, 2001.

Including analysts from elsewhere in CIA who were in some part attentive to al-Qa'ida, the total was fewer than forty."

"In terms of 'work years,' the equivalent of nine analyst work years was expended on al-Qa'ida within CTC's Assessments and Information Group in September 1998. According to CIA, nine CTC analysts and eight analysts in the Directorate of Intelligence were assigned to UBL in 1999. This was only a fraction of the analytic effort that was to be devoted to al-Qa'ida in July 2002 ... At the FBI, there were fewer than ten tactical analysts and only one strategic analyst assigned to al-Qa'ida prior to September 11, 2001. The NSA had only a limited number of Arabic linguists, on whom analysis depends, and, prior to September 11, few were dedicated full-time to targeting al-Qa'ida." See Joint Inquiry, p. 59.

Chapter 7

122 Young Faisal and his entourage departed Karachi on the RIMS Lawrence on September 6, 1919 and arrived in October 13, 1919. He met with King George V and Queen Mary. He returned via Bombay and Bahrain, arriving back in Saudi Arabia February 9, 1920. See also Paul L. Montgomery, "Faisal, Rich and Powerful, Led Saudis into 20th Century and to Arab Forefront," *The New York Times*, March 26, 1975, p. A10.

123 The United Nations officially came into existence on October 24, 1945. A total of 51 founding members joined that year. Only Egypt, Iraq, Lebanon and Saudi Arabia joined from the Arab world, the rest of today's nations then colonial possessions.

124 The Soviet Union, with a population of some 30 million Muslims, was the first state to recognize Abdul Aziz Al Saud ("Ibn Saud") as the King of the Hijaz and the Sultan of Nejd in February 1926. His son Prince Faisal was later dispatched to the Soviet Union in 1932. There, he was extensively shown Soviet industry and while visiting Soviet Azerbaijan, which was going through an oil boom, the young Prince expressed a desire to employ similar technologies in the kingdom. See Yury Barmin, "How Moscow Lost Riyadh in 1938," *Al Jazeera*, October 15, 2017.

125 Mecca (Makkah), located in southwestern Saudi Arabia near the Red Sea coast, is the birthplace of Muhammed. It is home to the Kaaba, one of Islam's holiest sites and the direction of Muslim prayer. It was long ruled by Muhammed's descendants until it was conquered in 1925 and became part of modern-day Saudi Arabia.

Medina is the burial place of Muhammed, located north of Mecca. It was conquered by Ibn Saud in 1924.

126 Saud bin Abdul Aziz Al Saud was the King of Saudi Arabia from November 9, 1953-November 2, 1964. He was the second son of Ibn Saud, the modern founder of the country.

127 *Wahhabism.* The name is from the theologian *al-Wahhabin* and it is the specific

Saudi brand of Islam that dominates the country and the *Sunni* world. "Wahhabism not only enjoys official sanction: it functions as both the state religion and the ideology used to legitimize the tribal absolutism of the Al Sa'ud [sic]." *A Fury for God*, p. 148.

"Saudi religious imperialism finds expression in three related but critical areas, all of which flow from the state's official *Wahhabi* ideology: hostility to non-Islamic religions, including Judaism and Christianity; anti-Sufism and anti-Shi'ism; *A Fury for God*, p. 173.

Wahhabism, "by emphasizing the absolute primacy of the Quran, an Arabic text, and the Prophet's "Arabian" *sunna* [sic, *sunnah*], while ignoring the cumulative traditions that had grown up over the centuries under the umbrella of Sufism with its multiplicity of regional variations, was in effect attacking regional identities, subjecting non-Arabs to Arab linguistic and religious authority." *A Fury for God*, p. 175.

128 King Abdul Aziz Ibn Saud (1875–1953), founder of Saudi Arabia and father of King Faisal. The title Abdul Aziz (Abd al-Aziz) is a male Arabic theophoric name ("servant of God"), that is, containing the name of a god in whose care the individual is entrusted.

129 "*Wahhabis* placed particular emphasis on monotheism by rejecting all the Shiite rituals of worshiping the Prophet Muhammad's family members, including Ali, Fatimah, Hassan, and Hussain." See Syed Saleem Shahzad, *Inside Al-Qaeda and the Taliban: Beyond Bin Laden and 9/11* (Pluto Press, 2011), p. 130.

130 Man of the Year—King Faisal, *Time Magazine*, January 6, 1975.

131 The Ba'ath Party was founded in 1947 by Michel Aflaq, a Syrian, and became the Arab Socialist Ba'ath Party in 1953. The party's initial slogan "unity, freedom, socialism" attracted a generation of Arab political activists who sought to overthrow the European-backed governments and create a modern industrial (and secular) societies. The Syrian Ba'thists took power in 1963; and in Iraq briefly in 1963 and then in 1968, under Saddam Hussein.

132 Idris was a Libyan political leader who served as the Emir of Cyrenaica and then as the King of Libya from 1951 to 1969. On September 1, 1969, he was overthrown by a group of military officers led by Col. Muammar Gaddafi.

133 The assassin was Prince Faisal bin Musaid, the son of a half-brother. See BBC, "Saudi's King Faisal Assassinated," March 25, 1975.

134 The best refutation appears in Alexei Vassiliev, *King Faisal of Saudi Arabia: Personality, Faith and Times* (Saqi Books, Reprint Edition, 2016). When Faisal came to power, the CIA was in fact concerned that he wouldn't resist Nasser's support for the Soviet Union and socialism in the Arab World. A National Intelligence Estimate was prepared, concluding that Faisal might likely take a more "neutral" posture in inter-Arab affairs and avoid open disputes with Nasser, but also continue to support the U.S. military presence at Dhahran airfield. It predicted that Faisal would also practice "intense antagonism" towards Israel. See Bruce Reidel, "Ricochet: When A Covert Operations Goes Bad," *Studies in Intelligence* (CIA), December 2018.

135 William Egan Colby, CIA director from September 4, 1973–January 30, 1976.

136 Though "normal" interagency presidential directives of the Ford Administration were called National Security Decision Memoranda (NSDMs) and were numbered, the more sensitive Top Secret policy documents were generally in the form of a letter from the National Security Advisor to the President. See Letter, Establishment and Authority of ADCI(SP), Top Secret Sensitive (TS/S/MU), November 29, 1975. President Ford initialed his approval of Tab A, with the hand-written comment, "Please do not distribute this within the White House other than to my Counsel. I would like a monthly briefing on the progress of this activity."

137 See White House Counsel Letter to the President, Renewal of Special Purpose Mandate and Revision to Charter, January 23, 1977 (TS/S/MU).

138 The senator is rumored to be Republican John Tower, chairman of the Armed Services Committee, who was nominated by President-elect George H.W. Bush to be secretary of defense. After his nomination floundered over allegations of drinking and womanizing, Dick Cheney was nominated instead and became secretary of defense.

139 See Modification 1 to Letter, Establishment and Authority of ADCI(SP), Top Secret Sensitive (TS/S/MU), November 29, 1975 (August 17, 1991). The directive states: "The ADCI(SP) must have expeditious and unrestricted access to all records … , regardless of classification, medium (e.g., paper, electronic) or format (e.g., digitized images, data) and information available to or within any DOD or IC Component, and be able to obtain copies of all records and information as required for its official use, regardless of security clearance. The ADCI(SP) is also authorized to access all records of the Departments of Justice and Treasury and all records within the private sectors in pursuance of its mission, in the case of the private sector, with the approval of the appropriate White House Counsel or the President."

140 See Letter, ADCI(SP) support to Operation Cyclone, Top Secret Sensitive (TS/S/MU), January 9, 1982.

141 Spelled a variety of ways including *Mujahedeen*, Arabic transliteration *mujāhidūn*, "those who engage in *jihad*."

Chapter 8

142 Khalid Sheikh Mohammed Ali Dustin al-Balushi (aka Khalid Shaykh Mohammad, also *Mukhtar* or *Mukhtar* al-Baluchi or Al-Mukh ("the Brain" or "the chosen") and to some *le moch tar* ("the man whose brain flew away"); KSM in

American parlance, aka Salem Ali, aka Abdulrahman Abdullah Faqasi Al-Ghamdi, and aka Abdulrahman Abdullah Abdulrahman Al-Fak'asi Al-Ghamdi.

Pakistani national, born in Kuwait; born April 14, 1965, raised in the Badawiya neighborhood of Fahaheel, south of Kuwait City; graduated from North Carolina A&T University in 1986. See KSM Debrief Papers, 2005; Joint Task Force Guantanamo, Subject: Combatant Status Review Tribunal Input and Recommendation for Continued Detention Under DOD Control (CD) for Guantanamo Detainee, ISN: US9KU-010024DP(S), December 8, 2006; CIA analytic report, "The Plot and the Plotters (U)," June 1, 2003, pp. 1–6, 50–85.

143 Though Khalid Sheikh Mohammed had studied English all through elementary and high school, he still had to brush up on his fluency before matriculating at North Carolina, where he was accepted to study engineering. So he enrolled at a small Christian college located in bucolic hills just south of the Virginia border. Chowan College (later Chowan University) is located in Murfreesboro in northeastern North Carolina. It was founded in 1848 by Baptist families and named Chowan—which means "people of the south"—to honor the Native American Algonquin Chowanook tribe.

Chowan was "virtually unknown in the United States but advertised abroad by the Baptist missionaries it graduated." *The Hunt for KSM*, p. 29.

144 FBI Electronic Communication (EC), Requests for information on KSM colleges/universities, June 10, 2002.

145 CIA/HR to ADCI(SP), Forwarding IB/AMLET Spot Report, April 3, 1984 (TS/S/MU).

146 ADCI(SP) Contact Sheet, Khalid Sheikh Mohammed, n.d. (1986?), MU-80-4/6; Apex files, Cabinet 19, Drawer 3, Box 9.

147 William ("Bill") Joseph Casey, CIA director, January 28, 1981–January 29, 1987.

148 Committee for Islamic Appeal; see *Mastermind*, p. 48. See also CIA analytic report, "Islamic Terrorists: Using Nongovernmental Organizations Extensively," CTC 99-40007, April 9, 1999.

149 KSM Debrief Papers, 2005.

150 Baluchi is a city in Pakistan, on the Iranian border (some parts of the city are actually in Iran) on the Indian Ocean and located in the state of Balochistan. Approximately 10 million people are Baluchi, residing mostly in Pakistan and Iran but also in Oman and the UAE. They are ethnically Persian and not Arab.

151 *Gama'a*, the pooling of money by a mosque or Islamic community to meet individual needs.

152 *Haram*, Arabic for forbidden, or proscribed by Islamic law and custom.

153 KSM Debrief Papers, 2005.

154 ADCI(SP) Contact Sheet, Khalid Sheikh Mohammed, n.d. (1984?), MU-80-4/6; Apex files, Cabinet 19, Drawer 3, Box 9.

155 KSM also spoke Urdu and a dialect of Balochi more akin to Persian; see NSA, "Balochi (Eastern Dialect) (U)," World Languages Series, G07-9961, April 2007 (S-HVCCO).

156 Joint Inquiry, p. 310; *Mastermind*, p. 70.

157 Abdullah Azzam's popular monthly magazine *Al-Jihad* first appeared in the fall of 1984 and was the successor to an earlier magazine called *Al-Mujahid*. Azzam's service bureau, known as the MAK, would eventually print 70,000 copies a month; see *Osama bin Laden*, p. 55.

158 Abdullah Yusuf Azzam (formally `Abd Allah Yusuf `Azzam; aka Abdallah Azzam), Palestinian, born 1941 in the village of Seelet Al-Hartiyeh, in the province of Jenin in the West Bank. He attended Shari`a College at Damascus University, where he obtained a BA Degree in Islamic Law in 1966. After the 1967 War, Azzam immigrated to Jordan. There, in the late 1960s, he joined the *jihad* against the Israeli occupation. In 1971 he was awarded a scholarship to al-Azhar University in Cairo, and graduated with a master's degree in *Shari`ah* and a Ph.D. in Principles of Islamic Jurisprudence in 1973.

Azzam moved to Saudi Arabia in 1978, where he took up a university teaching position at King `Abd al-`Aziz University in Jedda. Azzam was subsequently appointed a lecturer at the International Islamic University in Islamabad in 1981. He resigned this position in 1986 in order to devote full time to the *jihad*.

See Project Sumner, Name List Working Paper (U), n.d. (2000?) (TS-MU-00-16).

159 Michael Scheuer writes that 52 of Azzam's MAK offices were established in the U.S. during this period. See *Osama bin Laden*, p. 55.

Chapter 9

160 Memorandum, Attachment of Translated KSM Letter, August 4, 1987, 87-03 (MU).

161 Pakistan achieved independence and was declared a sovereign state following the end of the British Raj on August 14, 1947.

162 East India Company, also called English East India Company, formed for the exploitation of trade with East and Southeast Asia and India and was incorporated by royal charter on December 31, 1600. Starting as a monopolistic trading body, the company became political ruler and acted as an agent of British imperialism South Asia from the early 18th century to the mid-19th century.

163 CIA analytic report, "The Plot and the Plotters (U)," June 1, 2003, pp. 50–51.

164 Memorandum, Attachment of translated KSM Postcard, September 15, 1987, 87-22P (TS/MU).

Abed, the brother of Khalid Sheikh Mohammed reportedly died in Afghanistan; *The Black Banners*, p. 54.

165 Memorandum, Attachment of Translated KSM Letter, November 9, 1987, 87-30L (TS/MU).

166 Memorandum, Attachment of Translated KSM Letter, March 1, 1988, 88-09L (TS/MU).

167 Ali Soufan writes about this, generally unmentioned in most conventional narratives: "The [Soviet] invasion, and the creation of a new enemy for radical Muslims, served Egypt and Saudi Arabia well; both countries saw a chance to offload their domestic extremists by supporting their traveling to Afghanistan to join the jihad. Together the two countries poured billions of dollars into Afghanistan…" See *The Black Banners*, p. 22.

168 KSM Debrief Papers, 2005.

169 See Frontline, Muslims, Transcript of Program #2020, Original airdate: May 9, 2002.

170 Ayman al-Zawahiri, *al-Hisad al-murr* [*The Bitter Harvest: Sixty Years of the Muslim Brotherhood*], n.d. (1987).

171 The Muslim Brotherhood (*Al-Ikhwan al-Muslimun*) was founded by Egyptian Hassan al-Banna in 1928, four years after Kemal Ataturk's abolition of the Caliphate, under which the political and religious life of the Muslim community had been nominally unified. It is dedicated to the creation of a state of Shari'ah, or Islamic law. The organization grew by focusing on sympathy and social services for the poor.

The Muslim Brotherhood fell afoul of the Egyptian king, leading to the banning of the organization in 1948. Al-Banna was killed in 1949 by government agents in retaliation for the Brotherhood's assassination of Prime Minister Mahmud Fahmi al-Nuqrashi. The Brotherhood's reinstatement as a legal organization in 1951 enabled it to provide assistance to the "Free Officers" movement of the Egyptian army, led by Gamal Abdel Nasser and Muhammad Naguib, who in 1952 overthrew the king. The Brotherhood sought an Islamic government, splitting with the secular-minded Nasser, and going further underground. Nasser cracked down after an assassination attempt and ever since then, the Brotherhood was committed to replacing the secular state. It is fundamentally though an organization that insists on bringing about change in their societies through democracy and elections.

"The Egyptian Muslim Brotherhood, which served as the prototype for similar organizations in other countries, developed a sophisticated organizational structure, with sections in charge of different social sectors (students, workers, professionals) and functions (propaganda, liaison with the Islamic world, finances, and legal affairs). Like the European fascist movements, the Brotherhood also featured a paramilitary wing modeled on Mussolini's Blackshirts and a clandestine armed group called "the secret apparatus" (*al-jihaz al-sirri*)." See *The Muslim World After 9/11*, pp. 17, 90–92.

"[T]he history of Islamic activism in Egypt harks back to the 1930s with the establishment of Hassan al-Banna's Ikhwan al Muslimun, or Muslim Brethren, in 1929. Going beyond advocates of reform or revival of Islam, the Ikhwan advocated its restoration at the heart of Egyptian society, including the establishment of sharia, or Islamic law." See Roland Jacquard, *In the Name of Osama Bin Laden: Global Terrorism and the Bin Laden Brotherhood* (Diane Pub Co: 2002), p. 5.

172 Memorandum, Attachment of Translated KSM Letter, December 2, 1987, 87-32L (TS/MU); KSM Debrief Papers, 2005.

In 1990, after the Soviet withdrawal, Zawahiri returned to Egypt, where he continued to push EIJ in more radical directions and attempted to merge *Gamaa al-Islamiyya* and the EIJ. The two were involved in assassination attempts on the Egyptian interior minister in 1993 and then President Mubarak in 1995, followed by the successful bombing of the Egyptian Embassy in Islamabad in November 1995.

In November 1997 Zawahiri was held responsible for the death of 62 foreign tourists in the Egyptian town of Luxor, for which he was sentenced to death in absentia in 1999 by an Egyptian military tribunal.

173 Project Sumner, Name List Working Paper (U), n.d. (2000?) (TS-MU-00-16).

174 Al-Azhar University is the world's chief center of Islamic and Arabic learning, founded in 970. Nationalized in the 1960s, faculties of medicine and engineering were added. Women were first admitted in 1962.

175 A *fatwa* (*fatwah*) is a religious command, formally a ruling on a point of Islamic law (*Shari'ah*) given by a recognized authority.

176 Memorandum, Attachment of Translated KSM Letter, June 12, 1988, 88-35 (TS/MU).

177 When the Soviet Union invaded Afghanistan, Azzam was among the first to issue a *fatwa*—"Defense of the Muslim Lands, the First Obligation after Faith"—in which he called it personal obligation for Muslims to defend against the "occupiers."

178 Abdullah Azzam was just one of a growing cadre of exiled scholars invited to the Kingdom to escape pan-Arab nationalism and the emergence of the secular state. See *The Bin Ladens*, p. 153, 156–157, 201. Mohammed Qutb, the brother of Sayyid Qutb, also taught at the same university at the time and was another outspoken scholar of radical Islam. See *Al Qaeda*, p. 47; *Osama bin Laden*, pp. 29–34.

179 CIA intelligence report, Usama Bin Ladin's Historical Links to 'Abdallah Azzam, April 18, 1997. See also *The Bin Ladens*, p. 198; *Osama bin Laden*, p. 33.

The FBI states in an intelligence report: "Prior to 1979, UBL attended the King Abd al-Aziz University's (KAAU) School of Economics and Management where he attended a class taught by Sheikh Abdullah Azzam, a Palestinian theologian who was regarded as the historical leader of HAMAS." See FBI Intelligence Assessment, "Al-Qa'ida," April 15, 2004, p. 1. Michael Scheuer on the other hand writes that "there is no conclusive proof" of a meeting between bin Laden and Azzam at the University; *Osama bin Laden*, p. 53.

180 It is believed that Abdullah Azzam moved to Pakistan in January 1980, just a month after the Soviet invasion of Afghanistan.

181 "It was Azzam's epic, mythic, fantastical language that was to become the standard mode of expression for '*jihadi*' radicals over the next decade." *Al Qaeda*, p. 75.

182 Memorandum, Attachment of Translated KSM Letter, November 12, 1987, 87-31L (TS/MU).

183 Memorandum, Attachment of Translated KSM Letter, December 19, 1988, 88-24L-supplement (TS/MU).
  "In 1984 ... Sayyaf opened the first formal training camp for Arab volunteers, called Sada, or 'Echo.' It was an appropriate name—it was a reverberation from the real war. The camp was near the Pakistan border, an easy day trip for Saudi and other wealthy Gulf Arab visitors." *The Bin Ladens*, p. 255.
  Abdul Rasul Sayyaf was an Arab speaking Afghani mujahidin leader, and head of *Ittihad-i-Islami*, a Saudi-funded *Wahhabi* organization; *A Fury for God*, p. 185; *Al Qaeda*, p. 70.
  KSM might have heard Sayyaf speak in Kuwait when he was a teen; *The Hunt for KSM*, p. 28.

184 CIA analytic report, "The Plot and the Plotters (U)," June 1, 2003, p. 53.

185 Memorandum, Attachment of Translated KSM Letter, November 9, 1988, 88-42 (TS/MU).

186 KSM Debrief Papers, 2005.

187 Memorandum, Attachment of Translated KSM Letter, January 2, 1989, 89-02L (TS/MU).

188 Lester Grau, *The Bear Went Over the Mountain* (Taylor & Francis, 2012); Alex Alexiev, *The War in Afghanistan: Soviet Strategy and the State of the Resistance*, Rand Paper, 1984; Gregory Feifer, *The Great Gamble: The Soviet War in Afghanistan* (HarperCollins, 2009).

189 Memorandum, Attachment of Translated KSM Letter, January 2, 1989, 89-01 (TS/MU).

190 The articles were both written under a pseudonym, "from the front." CIA analytic report, "The Plot and the Plotters (U)," June 1, 2003, p. 53.

191 Under interrogation, KSM said that he first met Osama bin Laden for the first time when the Sayyaf group and Bin Laden's group of Arab mujahedeen were next to each other along the front line in Afghanistan. KSM Debrief Papers, 2005.

192 Bin Laden's height is itself an interesting factor, "like Ibn Saud (an important asset in a tribal society when physical prowess still lingers in the social memory), he conveyed all the vigour and dignity that the ageing monarch, the obese and semi-invalid Fahd, lacked." See *A Fury for God*, p. 136.

193 Memorandum, Attachment of Translated KSM Letter, January 22, 1989, 89-15 (TS/MU).

194 On November 20, 1979, a large group of Sunni activists—from Saudi Arabia, Egypt, Kuwait, Yemen and Pakistan barricaded themselves inside the Masjid al-Haram, the Grand mosque in Mecca, holding thousands of pilgrims' hostage. They called for the overthrow of the House of Saud. After two weeks, Saudi armed forces and police stormed the mosque, leaving 27 Saudi soldiers, more than 100 rebels, and 150 civilians dead. Sixty-three more rebels were later publicly beheaded. See *Secrets of the Kingdom*, p. 95.

195 French special forces were quietly brought in to assist Saudi forces to retake the extensive buildings and grounds of the Grand mosque. They pumped some kind of incapacitating gas into the labyrinth of underground tunnels to allow the Saudi and French forces to gain entry.

196 "As for himself and al-Qaeda, bin Laden said, "the mountains are our natural place ... [our only] choice is between Afghanistan and Yemen. Yemen's topography is mountainous, and its people are tribal, armed and allow one to breathe the clear air unblemished by humiliation." *Osama bin Laden*, p. 37.

197 ADCI(SP) Memorandum, KSM and OBL [Osama bin Laden], February 1, 1989, TS/SP/MU.

198 Memorandum, Attachment of Translated KSM Letter, January 29, 1989, 89-22R (TS/MU).

199 Maktab al-Khadamat (MAK), the "office of services" or the services bureau, founded by Azzam ad bin Laden in 1986. Azzam was appointed a lecturer at the International Islamic University in Islamabad in 1981. He resigned this position in 1986 in order to devote full time to the jihad. He founded the MAK and became the most influential intellectual behind the non-Afghan fighters in Afghanistan. The US government later called MAK the "precursor organization to *al Qaeda*." See 911 Commission Report (Official Report), p. 89.

200 KSM Debrief Papers, 2005.

201 FBI Intelligence Assessment, "Al-Qa'ida," April 15, 2004, p. 1.

202 Abdullah Azzam, *"Al Qaeda al Sulbah"* (The solid foundation), *Al-Jihad* magazine, April 1988.

203 Memorandum, Attachment of Translated KSM Letter, January 29, 1989, 89-22R (TS/MU).

204 Ali Soufan writes about Egypt's role, which is generally unmentioned in most conventional narratives: ""The [Soviet] invasion, and the creation of a new enemy for radical Muslims, served Egypt and Saudi Arabia well; both countries saw a chance to offload their domestic extremists by supporting their traveling to Afghanistan to join the jihad...." *The Black Banners*, p. 22.

205 ADCI(SP) Annual Year End Review 1989, January 23, 1990, TS/SP/MU.

206 CIA analytic report, "The Plot and the Plotters (U)," June 1, 2003, p. 59.

Chapter 10

207 Background information on Omar Abdel Rahman comes from Pre-Incident Indicators of Terrorist Incidents: The Identification of Behavioral, Geographic, and Temporal Patterns of Preparatory Conduct, pp. 340–342; The Sociology and Psychology Of Terrorism: Who Becomes A Terrorist And Why?, A Report Prepared under an Interagency Agreement by the Federal Research Division, Library of Congress., pp. 78–79; 1000 Years For Revenge: International Terrorism and the FBI—the Untold Story, pp. 39ff.

208 The Iranian Revolution, or the Islamic Revolution, *Enqelāb-e Eslāmī* in Persian, was a widespread popular uprising that began in January 1978 and resulted in the toppling of the monarchy of the Shah of Iran on February 11, 1979.

209 The *Intifada* (Arabic for 'shake', 'shaking' or 'shake off') refers to a Palestinian uprising against the Israeli occupation of the West Bank and Gaza. The First Intifada is said to have lasted from December 1987 until the Madrid Conference in 1991.

210 *Hamas* is the acronym for *Harakat al-Muqawama al-Islamiyya* or the Islamic Resistance Movement. It was founded in 1987.

211 Sayyid Qutb was executed on August 29, 1966 for his role in a failed conspiracy against the Nasser regime.

212 Egyptian Islam ...

213 Charter of Islamic Action (*Mithaq al-'Amal al-Islami*), 1984.

214 Ibn Taymiyya (1263–1328) came from Damascus in modern-day Syria. His arguments that Islam had become divided and diluted by different schools had weakened the religion. His writings became the basis for the *Wahhabi* movement in Saudi Arabia.

"The teachings of Hanbali disciple Ibn Taymiyya (d. 1328) were a major influence on Muhammad ibn Abd al-Wahhab and continue to be a source of inspiration for fundamentalist and radical fundamentalist ideologies. Ibn Taymiyya espoused a literal interpretation of the Quran and sunna, rejected all forms of innovation or bid'a (such as cults of saints and pilgrimages to tombs), and developed Quranically based justifications for rebelling against corrupt rulers. Religion and state were inextricably linked; without religion, the state would become tyrannical, and without the state, the religion would have no protector and would be in danger. The state's most important mission was to prepare for a society wholly devoted to the service of God." *The Muslim World After 9/11*, p. 100.

"Aside from the *Qur'an* and the *hadith* (records of the Prophet's words and actions), the *fatwas* by this 13/14th cent. AD jurist are by far the most popular texts for modern *Jihadis*, ... These texts are important to the modern Jihadi movement because 1) Ibn Taymiyya is the most respected scholar among *Salafis*, 2) he crafted very good arguments to justify fighting a *jihad* against the foreign invaders, and 3) he argued that Mongol rulers who converted to Islam were not really Muslims. The last two arguments resonate well today with the global *Jihadi* agenda." See Combating Terrorism Center, U.S. Military Academy, *Military Ideology Atlas: Executive Report*, November 2006.

215 Gamal Abdel Nasser, the President of Egypt, died of a heart attack on September 28, 1970.

216 Muhammed Anwar el-Sadat was the third President of Egypt, serving from October 15, 1970 until his assassination.

217 On October 6, 1981, Egyptian president Anwar Sadat was assassinated by army troops associated with the Egyptian Islamic Jihad (EIJ) and other organizations.

218 The Blind *Sheikh's* American visa was issued in May 1990, by the U.S. consulate in Khartoum, Sudan.

219 On August 2, 1990, Iraqi military forces entered Kuwait from the north and quickly moved on Kuwait City, while Iraqi commandos attacks royal palaces and government buildings. Hundreds of thousands fled south into Saudi Arabia. Iraq occupied Kuwait for the next seven months, before it was ejected in Operation Desert Storm, which commenced on January 17, 1991 and ended on March 3, 1991.

Chapter 11

220 *CIA Support to the U.S. Military During the Persian Gulf War*, Report, June 16, 1997.

221 Dick Cheney wryly notes later: "Having missed Saddam's invasion of Kuwait, our intelligence analysts now seemed to see signs everywhere of his invading Saudi Arabia." Dick Cheney, *In My Time: A Personal and Political Memoir* (Threshold Editions, 2011), p. 188.

222 Saudi ARAMCO (officially the Saudi Arabian Oil Company) is the Saudi state-owned enterprise, headquartered in Dhahran, a suburb just south of Dammam.

223 Michael Wines, "Confrontation in the Gulf; U.S. Aid Helped Hussein's Climb; Now, Critics Say, the Bill is Due," *The New York Times*, August 13, 1990, p. A1; The State Department later stated that "the number of international terrorist incidents in the Middle East increased from 65 in 1990 to 79 in 1991, largely because of a spate of attacks in Lebanon." Department of State, *Patterns of Global Terrorism 1991*. On October 5, 1990, the U.S. intelligence community issued a combined terrorist threat update, calling the threat "high".

Despite the concern, and all the preparations, there was one act of international terrorism in Saudi Arabia from the Iraqi invasion of Kuwait in August 1990 and the ceasefire in March 1991. On February 3, 1991, two U.S. airmen and a Saudi guard were wounded in an attack on a military bus in Jeddah, where the United States "secretly" deployed B-52 bombers. Four Palestinians (one a naturalized Saudi) and two Yemenis were arrested; their disposition was never shared with the United States.

224 Dammam is the capital of the Eastern Province of Saudi Arabia and the largest city and port. The Port of Dammam, also known as the King Abdul Aziz Port, is the largest in the Gulf. It is the main link to land-locked Riyadh, connected by rail.

225 Iraq was described as having the "fourth largest Army in the world" (after the Soviet Union, China and the United States), which in manpower and heavy equipment, was accurate. Most of those troops were forcibly conscripted young men, and after the war, much of the equipment was also found to be derelict. The label was purely propagandistic, as was demonstrated by the bluster of Gen. Norman Schwarzkopf afterwards, when he stated—quite wrongly—that "yesterday Iraq had the fourth largest Army in the world. Today they have the second largest Army in Iraq."

226 Dick Cheney, though a proponent of rapid deployment and a believer in Iraq's threat to Saudi Arabia later writes in his autobiography: "Having missed Saddam's invasion of Kuwait, our intelligence analysts now seemed to see signs everywhere of his invading Saudi Arabia." *In My Time*, p. 188.

227 On August 6, Secretary of Defense Dick Cheney arrived at King Fahd's summer palace to push for a U.S. military counter to defend America's lifeblood. General Norman Schwarzkopf, wearing combat fatigues as if he were ready to march to the border himself, unveiled highly classified satellite photographs showing Saddam's Republican Guards mustering south of Basra to attack the Saudi oil fields. Iraqi commandos and armored units were already deep into Kuwait and there were intelligence indicators, the general said, of Iraqi preparations for a possible incursion further south. Although intelligence on Iraq's intentions was paper thin, the General told the room of white robes: "We judge from similar Iraqi actions during the Iran-Iraq war that they are in what we call a strategic pause, rearming and reequipping before continuing offensive operations." Norman Schwarzkopf, *It Doesn't Take a Hero* (Bantam Books, 1992), pp. 304ff.

The American delegation was completely taken by surprise by the rapid Saudi reaction to their request to come in. As Schwarzkopf and Cheney presented the American case, the Princes and advisors asked about the immediacy of the Iraqi threat and thus the timing of an American entry.

But King Fahd cut off the discussion and said Saddam needed to be taught a lesson, granting permission for immediate American deployments. More than anything else, he was angry that Saddam lied to him when he said he would not invade and then he blatantly told him in a post-invasion phone call that Kuwait was no more and that the Royal al-Sabah family would never return to power. Then Saddam made no attempt to assure the Saudis that he wouldn't move further south. In fact, Iraqi diplomats were fanning out in the region to flame opposition to American intervention, giving credibility to further plans for conquest, at least of the Saudi eastern oil fields.

Peninsula Shield, Gen. Schwarzkopf named it, but a savvy Defense Secretary Cheney thought such a name was both too frank and politically evocative. It was Kuwait and the sanctity of international law that was being defended, not Saudi oil. Operation Desert Shield would be the official name instead. See Note from Secdef, Peninsula Shield name, August 12, 1990.

228 Norman Schwarzkopf later wrote: that "while we didn't know whether the Iraqis intended to attack Saudi Arabia, we judged from their deployment and from similar Iraq actions during the Iran-Iraq war that they were in what we called a strategic pause, busy rearming and reequipping before continuing offensive operations." *It Doesn't Take a Hero*, p. 304.

On August 13, 1990, CENTCOM intelligence reported that Iraq has three infantry divisions, two armored divisions, and one mechanized infantry division in Kuwait, all of the Republican Guards. The infantry divisions are assessed by U.S. intelligence as relieving the heavy units from "occupation duties." The intelligence reports state that the "replacement was ominous for, while it allowed a possible return of RGFC [Republican Guard Forces Command heavy] units to Iraq, it also freed these formations for a subsequent attack into Saudi Arabia, should Saddam order it."

229 On June 13, 1982, King Khalid, sickly and ineffectual, unexpectedly died of a heart attack, and Crown Prince Fahd (11th son of the founder of the Saudi kingdom) took his place. In November 1986, King Fahd adopted the title "Guardian of Islam's Holy Shrines" originally coined for the 16th century Grand Sultan Selim I. The title is sometimes referred to as "Custodian of the Two Holy Mosques."

230 *Shi'a* constitute 10 percent of the Saudi population and make up about 40 percent of the population of the eastern province, where Dammam is located.

231 "Many foreign workers were expelled from Saudi Arabia, and others were transferred or fired from sensitive government positions." Department of State, *Patterns of Global Terrorism 1991.*

232 *The Human Rights Watch Global Report on Women's Human Rights*, August 1995.

233 Algeria, Jordan, Libya, Sudan, Tunisia and Yemen would ultimately align themselves with Iraq. Only Jordan was a real surprise, but the country was economically dependent on Iraq and there was a sizable Iraqi community in Jordan. Nonetheless, the Jordanian government allowed U.S. military forces to stage from Jordanian territory, play both sides.

"After years of paying billions of dollars to cultivate the friendship of neighboring countries, the royal family was stunned to discover how isolated it was in the Arab world. The Palestinians, Sudanese, Algerians, Libyans, Tunisians, Yemenis, and even the Jordanians openly supported Saddam Hussein." Lawrence Wright, *Looming Tower: Al-Qaeda and the Road to 9/11* (Knopf, 2006), p. 156.

On August 4, 1990, King Hussein of Jordan stated that many Arabs considered Saddam Hussein a patriot and were uncomfortable with criticizing Iraq's actions in Kuwait. On August 22, Jordan closed its border with Iraq to stop an inundation by refugees leaving the country. King Hussein tries to act as broker of a peace, meeting with Saddam Hussein on September 5. After the meeting, the CENTCOM intelligence directorate established a "warning problem for Jordan," gaming Iraqi military use of Jordanian territory, particularly the U.S. reaction if Iraqi aircraft used Jordanian airspace. Saudi Arabia cut off oil supplies to Jordan on September 20, and Prince Bandar pens an open letter in *The New York Times* on September 26 castigating King Hussein for sympathy with Iraq.

234 CIA intelligence information report, subject: *Sh'ia* in Eastern Saudi Arabia—the Domestic "Threat" as seen by the Ministry of Internal Affairs, September 21, 1990; TS/HCS/MU.

235 In the end, the government of Saudi Arabia quietly detained over 70,000 persons, most Saudi citizens, all of whom were considered security risks. See U.S. Army INSCOM, AFRD-DSS, Subject: Postmortem Report; Topic Area: Terrorism, March 14, 1991.

236 CIA, intelligence information report, Roundup of Foreign Workers in Eastern Saudi Arabia, August 15, 1990 (S/NF/MU).

237 The 2nd Brigade of the 82nd Airborne Division began deploying to Saudi Arabia on August 8, 1990. The early arriving paratroopers referred to themselves as "speed bumps," thinking Iraqi forces so powerful that they wouldn't be able to stop them. Over the next two months the entire division was deployed, as well as the 101st air assault division, two heavy divisions and an armored cavalry regiment, plus supporting troops and aircraft, under the command of XVIII Airborne Corps. See *U.S. Army, War in the Persian Gulf: Operations Desert Shield and Desert Storm*, August

1990–March 1991, p. 3.

238 Andrew Rosenthal, "Bush Sends U.S. Force to Saudi Arabia as Kingdom Agrees to Confront Iraq," *The New York Times*, August 8, 1990, p. A1; Richard G. Davis, *On Target: Organizing and Executing the Strategic Air Campaign Against Iraq*, (Air Force History and Museums Program, 2002).

239 It is a common refrain that more Lebanese live outside the country than within. The first waves of emigration began following the 1860 conflict in Ottoman Syria and largely consisted of Lebanese Christians, Jews, and Druze (an esoteric non-Muslim group who identify as something equivalent to unitarians).

240 A total of 697,000 U.S. troops would eventually take part in the first Iraq war; see U.S. Army, *War in the Persian Gulf: Operations Desert Shield and Desert Storm, August 1990–March 1991* (Center of Military History, 2010).

241 After the Iraq invasion, Secretary of State James Baker crisscrossed the globe cobbling together the unlikeliest of grand coalitions. This included British, French, Italian, Saudi, the Gulf states, Mubarak's forces from Egypt, an otherwise hostile Syria (Damascus hated the regime in Iraq just slightly more than it hated the United States); a Senegalese battalion; even hundreds of veteran Afghan *mujahidin*, all to enforce the rule of law but in actuality foot soldiers in a magnificent battle to preserve the status quo. Richard Clarke would later write, simplistically, that "George H. W. Bush created an improbable diplomatic and military coalition of more than sixty nations that liberated Kuwait and reestablished an international security system." *Your Government Failed You*, p. 7.

There were official dissenters: King Hussein of Jordan, the Marxist government in Yemen, Palestinians, Tunisia, and the Islamic radicals in Sudan.

"After years of paying billions of dollars to cultivate the friendship of neighboring countries, the royal family was stunned to discover how isolated it was in the Arab world." *The Looming Tower*, p. 156.

U.S. intelligence interpreted and even almost excused such opposition as the reality of dependence on Iraqi oil or the final stand of 'leftist' leaning governments breathing their last gasps of Soviet-supplied oxygen.

242 On December 22, 1990, Baghdad announced that it would never give up Kuwait and would use weapons of mass destruction if attack, threaten as well to attack Israel. "Were Saddam Hussein foolish enough to use weapons of mass destruction," Cheney said at a press conference the next day, "the U.S. response would be absolutely overwhelming and it would be devastating." See William M. Arkin, "Calculated Ambiguity: Nuclear Weapons and the Gulf War," *The Washington Quarterly*, 19:4, January 2010, pp. 2–18.

243 Most of the "intelligence" work in Saudi Arabia prior to the attack entailed screening and debriefing the tens of thousands of refugees (and increasingly deserters) who entered Saudi Arabia from Kuwait and Iraq following the invasion. The U.S. and Saudi Arabia set up debriefing centers to screen the human flow.

When a government employee or scientist (or later, when a high-ranking military officer) arrived, they were directed to military intelligence and CIA interrogation centers where they were pumped for information about Iraqi military organization and strengths and about facilities that might be associated with weapons of mass destruction.

244 Neither Norman Schwarzkopf (*It Doesn't Take a Hero*), Colin Powell (*My American Journey*), or Dick Cheney (*In My Time: A Personal and Political Memoir*) make mention of one Osama bin Laden in their post-Gulf War autobiographies.

245 *Through Our Enemies Eyes*, pp. 124–125; John Miller, *The Cell: Inside the 9/11 Plot, and Why the FBI and CIA Failed to Stop It* (Hachette Books, 2002), pp. 157–158; *Looming Tower*, p. 158.

246 Prince Sultan was designated Commander of Joint Forces, in theory the highest-ranking officer, but was only equivalent to Gen. Schwarzkopf, as U.S. Commander and commander of U.S. and the relevant British, French and Italian armed forces components. See, in particular, P. Mason Carpenter, "Joint Operations in the Gulf War: An Allison Analysis," A Thesis Presented to the Faculty of the School of Advanced Airpower Studies for Completion of Graduation Requirements, June 1994.

247 The story is told this way in Project Sumner, Report prepared for the Review Committee, Analysis of Terrorism Literature, Conspiracy Theories, and Deception Impact (TS/SCI), MU-08-457, January 2008.

248 The People's Democratic Republic of Yemen (or South Yemen) existed from 1967–1990, when after the fall of the Soviet Union, it merged with North Yemen (the Yemen Arab Republic) to form present-day Yemen. In mid-March 1991, bin Laden again approached Prince Turki with a proposal to wage holy war against the communist regime in South Yemen. "Of course, his proposal was turned down flat by the government," Turki says. *The Cell*, p. 158.

249 In October 1990, bin Laden is said to have visited Khartoum, a year after the National Islamic Front coup; *Through Our Enemies' Eyes*, p. 132. The Saudi Binladen Group had received a contract to build an airport in Port Sudan and Osama bin Laden was reportedly the overseer of the project. See George Tenet, *At the Center of the Storm: My Years at the CIA* (Harper Collins, 2007), p. 101; *The Cell*, p. 145.

250 *Through Our Enemies Eyes*, p. 128; Peter Lance, *Triple Cross: How bin Laden's Master Spy Penetrated the CIA, the Green Berets, and the FBI* (William Morrow, 2006), p. 76; *The Cell*, p. 158–159.

251 On April 3, 1991, the United Nations Security Council adopted the primary ceasefire resolution (UNSCR 687), requiring Iraq to end its weapons of mass destruction programs, recognize Kuwait, account for missing Kuwaitis, return Kuwaiti property and end support for international terrorism. Iraq was also required to end repression of its people, specifically the *Shi'a* majority and Kurdish peoples.

On April 5, 1991, the UNSC further adopted UNSCR 688, which called on Iraq to end attacks on the Kurds and allows the international community to establish "safe havens." Kurds in these areas were then protected by a multinational force and provided food, shelter, and medical care by nongovernmental organizations.

Chapter 12

252 In April 1991, Hassan al-Turabi hosted the first Popular Arab Islamic Conference in Sudan. The conference provided a forum for disparate forces in the Middle East who opposed the American military presence in the region to come together. Al Qaeda, Hizb'allah, Iraqi and Iranian representatives all attend the meeting.

253 Hassan 'Abd Allah al-Turabi, born February 1, 1932, in Kassala, Sudan. He was a *Sufi* Muslim Sheikh, and became the leader of the Islamic Charter Front in 1964, a Sudanese offshoot of Muslim Brotherhood. After spending time in exile in Libya, he became Minster of Justice in 1979 as part of the Sudanese Socialist Union. A member of Parliament, he took part in the 1989 coup and became leader of the National Islamic Front (NIF).

254 The year before Iraq invaded Kuwait, Colonel Omar al-Bashir led a bloodless military coup and overthrew the democratically-elected president after he had the temerity to initiate negotiations with Christian rebels in the south. Bashir banned political parties and an independent press, introducing *Shari'ah*, the Islamic legal code, on the national level. For the first time, Islamic rule extended to the remaining Christian areas as well. At that time, the Christian and animist south were left alone. This fundamental geographic, ethnic, religious and colonial conflict wouldn't be resolved until South Sudan earned independence in 2011.

255 It is unclear when exactly bin Laden left Saudi Arabia, but in April 1991, he left for either Pakistan or Sudan. See *Through Our Enemies' Eyes*, p. 128; *The Cell*, p. 158–159; *Triple Cross*, p. 76.

256 Memorandum, Attachment of Translated KSM Letter, March 30, 1991, 91-12 (TS/MU).

257 Project Sumner Timeline, V38, n.d. (2008) (TS/SP/MU).

258 "An authoritative report in the *Los Angeles Times* mentions that while in Karachi, Shaikh [KSM] 'told people he was a holy water salesman, an electronics importer and a Saudi oil sheikh.'" Quoted in *Al Qaeda*, p. 114.

259 The Ba'ath party paper *Al Thawra* said after the ceasefire: "Victory is not how many tanks or planes we or the enemy used ... Baghdad will not bow its head to any arrogant person, no matter how tyrannical and oppressive he might be," Iraqi radio announced. See "Claiming Victory, Iraq Holds its Fire," *The New York Times*, March 1, 1991, p. A6.

The official military communique announcing the end of fighting repeated the core belief about Iraqi strategy. Iraqi forces were put in a position "contrary to the military and manly values for which the men of the mother of battles are reputed...," it said. See "Text of Cease-Fire Order to Iraqi Troops," *The New York Times*, March 1, 1991, p. A6; "Order...Not to Open Fire," *The Washington Post*, March 1, 1991, p. A8.

Saddam then said in an interview less than two weeks later, at a ceremony where he awarded medals to his commanders: "Gain and loss should assume their traditional meaning—that is, their inherited human criteria. ... And the inherited human criteria say: In order to attack a force, you need to have two to three times the size of that force. However, when you bring 15, 20, and 30 times the size of that force, you cannot claim that you are the winner." See "Saddam Says Allies `Lost" War Against Iraq," FBIS-NES-92-053, March 18, 1992, p. 15.

260 U.S. Ambassador to Iraq April Glaspie met with Saddam Hussein on July 25, 1990, less than a week before the Iraqi invasion of Kuwait and said that the United States "had no opinion" about the Iraqi border dispute with Kuwait. Iraq later released a transcript of the July meeting to substantiate that the U.S. had given it a "green light" to invade.

261 The mines referred were actually sub-munitions of larger cluster bombs used extensively in the first Gulf War. Both air-delivered and artillery-delivered cluster bombs were used, the technology dispersing a large number of smaller bomblets over a large area. No one particularly considered that even a small number of dud (unexploded bomblets) would cause havoc, not just to civilians later, but the friendly troops operating in territory where the bombs had been used. As it turns out, a large number of volatile duds resulted. The problem is described in Human Rights Watch, *U.S. Cluster Bombs for Turkey?*, December 1, 1994.

262 Patrick Sloyan, "Army Said to Plow Under Possibly Thousands of Iraqi Soldiers in Trenches," *The Washington Post*, September 12, 1991.

263 Steve Coll and William Branigin, "U.S. Scrambled to Shape View of Highway of Death," *The Washington Post*, March 11, 1991.

264 In the first Gulf War, the 24th Infantry Division (Mechanized) had the mission of blocking the Euphrates River valley to prevent the escape north of Iraqi forces in Kuwait, then attacking east in coordination with VII Corps to its south to assist in the defeat the armor-heavy divisions of the Republican Guard Forces Command. The division moved through the western desert, hooking east north of Nasiriyah. After 100 hours, it halted operations within 100 miles of the capital. See *The Whirlwind War: The United States Army in Operations Desert Shield and Desert Storm*; and HQ, 24th Infantry Division (Mech.), *Historical Reference Book* (Fort Stewart, Ga., 1992).

265 It is not without irony that decades later, the truth of King Fahd's rapid agreement to allow U.S. military forces into the kingdom was predicated on bad intelligence, both with regard to the strength of the Iraqi army, and Saddam Hussein's intentions.

266 Memorandum of TELCON, President Bush and King Fahd, March 9, 1991 (Top Secret). To the Saudis and the other Gulf states, the fall of Saddam Hussein and his Sunni-dominated military regime might unleash forces, particularly an internal *Shi'a* uprising, that would equally threaten them.

267 *Through Our Enemies Eyes*, pp. 124–125.

268 CIA Terrorist Biographic Note, Usama bin Ladin (U), CTC-005-00, January 2000. Prince Turki later denies any intelligence relationship with Osama bin Laden, but others see Saudi intelligence behind much of the Afghan *jihad*; see *The Bin Ladens*, p. 295.

269 Quoted in *A Fury for God*, pp. 204–205.

270 Notes are later found showing a meeting led by bin Laden discussing "the establishment of a new military group" on August 11, 1988. Bin Laden's plan was to have a multinational insurgent organization that would survive the Afghanistan jihad. See *Through Our Enemies' Eyes*, p. 110 and *Osama bin Laden*, pp. 71–74.

Michael Scheuer, who sometimes can sound like an adoring fan of *al Qaeda* because of the zeal with which he attempts to challenge conventional wisdom, writes: "A key point often lost on Western analysts is that neither bin Laden nor his colleagues ever intended to build a terrorist organization: they intended to construct an insurgent organization that could absorb substantial punishment from always far more powerful foes and endure." See *Osama bin Laden*, p. 72.

271 This view of the actors in Afghanistan is taken from KSM Debrief Papers, 2005.

272 CIA analytic report, "The Plot and the Plotters (U)," June 1, 2003, p. 93.

Chapter 13

273 Paul Lewis, "44 U.N. Inspectors Freed by Iraq With Secret Nuclear Documents," *The New York Times*, p. A1.

274 Ramzi Ahmed Yousef, an alias for Abdul Basit Mahmoud Abdul Karim (aka Abdul Basit Karim, Rashid al-Iraqi ("Rashid the Iraqi," Rashed), aka the Chemist, aka Kamal Ibraham, Al Baloch, Azan Mohammed/Mohammed Azan, Dr. Abel Sabah, Arnaldo Forlani, and Dr. Naji Owaida Haddad); Pakistani national of Baluchi origin, born April 27, 1968 in the United Arab Emirates (UAE). See CIA analytic report, Khalid Sheik Muhammad's Nephews, CTC 2003-300013, January 31, 2003; Project Sumner, Reconstruction of 'Bojinka Plot,' KSM vs. Official CIA/FBI Records (TS-MU-056-99); Project Sumner, Name List Working Paper (U), n.d. (2000?) (TS-MU-00-16).

275 The basic facts of Ramzi Yousef as known to the U.S. government comes from Brief of the United States of America, United States v. Ramzi Ahmed Yousef, No. 98-1041(L) (2nd Circuit, filed August 25, 2000).

Much of the narrative of the travel of Yousef and Ajaj comes from 9/11 and Terrorist Travel: Staff Report of the National Commission on Terrorist Attacks Upon the United States. A more descriptive—and maddening—narrative is contained in Mark S. Hamm, Crimes Committed by Terrorist Groups: Theory, Research, and Prevention, study for the DOJ Award #2003 DT CX 0002, pp. 38-48. See also CIA Terrorist Biographic Note, "Ramzi Yousef" (U), CTC-009-94, July 1994. See also Peter Lance, *1000 Years For Revenge: International Terrorism and the FBI—the Untold Story* (William Morrow, 2003), pp. 22, 80, 102, 109; *Al Qaeda*, p. 107ff; and Steve Coll, *Ghost Wars: The Secret History of the CIA, Afghanistan, and Bin Laden, from the Soviet Invasion to September 10, 2001* (Penguin Books, 2004), pp. 248ff.

276 The flight manifest for Pakistan International Airlines flight 703, Peshawar to Karachi to New York identified the passenger sitting in Seat 2C as one Mohammed Azan, a passport that Ajaj used to board the flight but not one that he presented to passport control at JFK airport. What happened to that passport is still a mystery.

277 There is actually no record of a Ramzi Yousef graduating from the West Gamorgan Institute of Higher Education in Swansea, Wales. But there is one Abdul Basit Karim, a Baluchistani who carries a Kuwaiti passport. See Project Sumner, Timeline of CIA Incompetence, July 1, 2001 (TS-MU-40-01).

278 There were two suitcases that had been initially checked in in Peshawar, one wrapped solidly in plastic Middle Eastern style and the other a cheap duffel. The two latex-gloved inspectors removed all of the contents and X-rayed the bags, checking for hidden materials and secret compartments. According to the Customs log from that day, there were various Arabic-language bomb-making manuals with diagrams and formulas, a half dozen VHS videotapes dealing with fighting in Afghanistan and other Islamic subjects relating to making violent *jihad*, anti-American and anti-Israeli pamphlets and posters, an instruction paper on document forgery, as well two devices that could be used to alter the seal on passports. Three of the papers made reference to an entity—Service Bureau—that could be translated at *al Qaeda*. The inventory also included various papers and letters written in Urdu or Dari. See Project Sumner, Timeline of CIA Incompetence, July 1, 2001 (TS-MU-40-01).

279 After midnight by this time on September 1, 1992, Ajaj is taken into custody. While in detention, Ajaj plead guilty to a charge of use of an altered passport and served six months. He was released on March 1, just a week after the February 1993 bombing of the World Trade Center. On March 9, he was taken into custody for a second time. A month later, while in custody, the FBI connected him to the WTC bombing by tracing telephone calls between him and Yousef.

Once Ajaj was arrested for involvement in the WTC bombing, he still did not give up on his political asylum claim. He petitioned for a new attorney and an exclusion hearing—held to determine whether someone is admissible into the United States—in Houston, where he had filed another political asylum claim in

February 1992. Ajaj's request was denied on April 24, 1993, on the grounds that a passport holder from a visa waiver country who uses a fraudulent passport—Ajaj used a fake Swedish passport to enter the United States—was not entitled to such a hearing. Not satisfied with that outcome, Ajaj asked to file a new political asylum claim and was given ten days by an immigration judge to do so. Thus, Ajaj was able to file a political asylum claim after his arrest for involvement in the bombing of the WTC.

280 911 Commission Report (Official Report), p. 89.

281 Rabbi Meir Kahane was assassinated on November 5, 1990 at the Marriott Hotel in midtown Manhattan while delivering a public speech. The driver of the getaway car was one Mohammed Salameh, who would subsequently become Ramzi Yousef's driver. See *The Cell*, p. 38ff, 55ff; *Triple Cross*, pp. 54–58.

Richard Miniter links KSM to the Kahane assassination; see *Mastermind*, pp. 48–49.

282 *The Cell*, pp. 49–50.

283 The head of the *al-Khifah* center in Brooklyn was actually assassinated as well in February 1991; see *The Cell*, pp. 64, 197.

284 *Case Studies in Terrorism-Related Cases (03/26/2008)*, First World Trade Center Bombing, pp. 3–5; See also *My FBI*, p. 281; *Triple Cross*, p. 112; *A Fury for God*, p. 221; *The Cell*, pp. 90–104; *1000 Years for Revenge*, p. 109; *Looming Tower*, p. 177; *Pretext for War*, pp. 100ff.

Chapter 14

285 Abdul in Arabic also means "servant of," and as such then, also had a particular connotation for Khalid Sheikh Mohammed when used out of context of any name. See KSM Debrief Papers, 2005.

286 The actual name is Abdullah Abdulrahman Al-Fak'asi Al-Ghamdi. Some sources refer to al-Ghamdi as Abdulrahman A. A. al-Ghamdi and some refer to an A. F. al-Ghamdi. A.A. al-Ghamdi is used throughout here, unless the source specified otherwise, as it did in the case of the Philippine immigration forms.

287 Pope John Paul II visited Asia from January 11–January 21, 1995, celebrating World Youth Day 1995 in Manila, and visiting Papua New Guinea, Australia, and Sri Lanka.

288 KSM Debrief Papers, 2005.

289 Project Sumner, Reconstruction of 'Bojinka Plot,' KSM vs. Official CIA/FBI Records, March 1999 (TS-MU-056-99).

290 Douglas Jehl, "Clinton Begins Pacific Visit in Manila," *The New York Times*,

November 13, 1994, p. A10.

291 Ministers from Australia, Brunei, Canada, Chile, China, Hong Kong, Indonesia, Japan, South Korea, Malaysia, Mexico, New Zealand, Papua New Guinea, Philippines, Singapore, Taiwan, Thailand, and the United States participated in the Sixth Asia-Pacific Economic Cooperation (APEC) Ministerial Meeting convened in Jakarta, Indonesia, November 11–12, 1994.

292 KSM entered the Philippines for the first time on a valid Pakistani passport in his own name on July 21, 1994.

293 Though KSM and Ramzi Yousef both discuss this explosion in their debriefings, there is no known news media report of its existence.

294 *The Cell*, p. 123.

295 The story of Bojinka and the three bombings is from *Triple Cross*, pp. 258–262; *The Cell*, p. 123ff; *Case Studies in Terrorism-Related Cases (03/26/2008)*, First World Trade Center Bombing, pp. 15–16.

296 *Case Studies in Terrorism-Related Cases (03/26/2008)*, First World Trade Center Bombing, pp. 15–16.

297 "Bojinka" is an intentional nonsense word, but one that KSM told Ramzi Yousef meant "big bang" in Serbo-Croatian. The plan, he told Ramzi Yousef, was for a series of explosions aboard a dozen commercial airliners while they were flying over the Pacific Ocean—American-flagged United, Northwest and Delta flights out of Manila, Tokyo, Singapore, Bangkok, Taipei, and Seoul. The event would take place nearly simultaneously with an assassination of Pope John Paul II in Manila. See KSM Debrief Papers, 2005.

    It is interesting to note that officially the U.S. government refers to Bojinka as "Bojinko," and that was the term used in the 1996 trial of Ramzi Yousef. See, e.g., Jeff Breinholt, "Air Bombings," *United States Attorney's Bulletin*, January 2004, p. 12.

Chapter 15

298 Much of the information on bin Laden's time in Sudan is taken from CIA, Terrorism: Historical Background of the Islamic Army and bin Ladin's Move from Afghanistan to Sudan (U), November 26, 1996; CIA Terrorist Biographic Note, Usama bin Ladin (U), CTC-005-00, January 2000.

299 The address and house description is from *Losing Bin Laden*, pp. 47ff.

300 FBI intelligence report, Bin Ladin's Activities in Somalia and Sudanese NIF Support, April 30, 1997; FBI intelligence report, Establishment of a Tripartite Agreement Among Usama Bin Ladin, Iran, and the NIF, Jan. 31, 1997; FBI intelligence report, Cooperation Among Usama Bin Ladin's Islamic Army, Iran, and the NIF, Jan. 31 1997.

301 Abu Hafs al-Masri, the *kunya* for Mohammed Atef, an Egyptian policeman before he fought in Afghanistan. He would rise to become the military *Emir* of *al Qaeda*. See CIA Terrorist Biographic Note, Mohammed Atef (U), CTC-943-01, November 2001; CIA, Biographical Information on Key UBL Associates in Afghanistan, June 11, 2001; Project Sumner, Name List Working Paper (U), n.d. (2000?) (TS-MU-00-16).

302 CIA analytic report, "The Plot and the Plotters (U)," June 1, 2003, p. 91.

303 U.S. relations with Sudan were strained in the 1990s after the country backed Iraq in its invasion of Kuwait and provided sanctuary and assistance to Islamic terrorist groups, including Osama bin Laden. After urging from Egypt and Saudi Arabia, and as a result of threats against U.S. diplomats, the Clinton administration designated Sudan a state sponsor of terrorism in 1993 and suspended U.S. Embassy operations in Khartoum in 1996. In October 1997, the U.S. imposed comprehensive economic, trade, and financial sanctions against the Sudan.

304 *Case Studies in Terrorism-Related Cases (03/26/2008)*, First World Trade Center Bombing.

305 Hassan al-Turabi, born February 1, 1932 in Kassala, Sudan. After attending the University of Khartoum, he attended King's College London and the University of Paris.

306 CIA intelligence report, Sudanese links to Egypt's Gama'at al-Islamiya and training of Egyptians, July 14, 1993; CIA intelligence report, Funding by Bin Ladin of Gama'at al-Islamiya and composition of its Sudanese wing, July 22, 1993.

307 On June 30, 1989, under the banner of The National Islamic Front (NIF), the elected coalition government in Sudan was overthrown by Brig. Gen. Omar Hassan al-Bashir and *Sheikh* Hassan al-Turabi. They impose strict Shari'ah law on the country including the Christian southern Sudan.

308 After Operation Desert Storm, Osama bin Laden began to invest in Sudan, buying numerous properties and businesses. The Saudi Binladin Group also received a government contract to build an airport in Port Sudan and Osama bin Laden was put in charge to oversee the project.

Ali Soufan later writes: "He established companies such as Ladin International, an investment company; Wadi al-Aqiq, a holding company; al-Hijra, a construction business; al-Themar al-Mubaraka, an agricultural company; Taba Investments, an investment company; Khartoum Tannery, a leather company; an Qudarat Transport Company, a transportation company, which all seemed to perform legitimate work. The construction company, for example, built a highway from Khartoum to Port Sudan." See *The Black Banners*, p. 40.

309 The Royal Family of modern Jordan, which has ruled since 1921. The same family previously held royal positions in Iraq and Syria before being overthrown by the Ba'ath Revolutionary Party. The Hashemite dynasty is named after the

Prophet Mohammed's great grandfather, Hashim.

310 CIA analytic report, "The Plot and the Plotters (U)," June 1, 2003, p. 92.

311 The Vinnell Corporation became famous in the 1970s when they took charge of the Saudi Arabian National Guard Modernization Program, flooding the country with civilian contractors. See "U.S. Company Will Train Saudi Troops to Guard Oil," *The New York Times*, February 9, 1975, p. A1; Jewish Telegraphic Agency, "Private U.S. Firm to Train Saudi Arabia's National Guard Under U.S. Defense Dep't, Contract," February 10, 1975.

   Executives of the Vinnell Corp. and some recruits are stressing that the program cannot be considered a "mercenary expedition." According to Robert Montgomery, Vinnell's general manager for special projects, "We are not creating a mercenary force. This is a one-time thing to do a specific job."

312 A final irony of the U.S. support for the Afghan people in their battle against the Soviets is that after the 1991 Gulf War (Operation Desert Storm), the CIA conducted an elaborate clandestine operation, with the cooperation of Saudi Arabia, Kuwait, and Pakistan, to ship captured Iraq military equipment and ammunition left in Kuwait to Afghan warlords that were still on the American payroll. This was long after the Soviets had withdrawn and before the Taliban were a factor. But it was still an operation to defeat "the communists." After 9/11, U.S. military forces would face some of those very same tanks, armored personnel carriers, and artillery guns in their Afghanistan fight. See *Ghost Wars*, p. 226.

313 Bill Clinton would later write: "As we pressed Turabi to expel bin Laden, we asked Saudi Arabia to take him. The Saudis didn't want him back, but bin Laden finally left Sudan in mid-1996, apparently still on good terms with Turabi." Bill Clinton, *My Life* (Knopf, 2004), p. 797.

314 Abu Abdullah was one of Osama bin Laden's aliases and an expression of respect often used by his closest advisors and personal assistants.

315 KSM Debrief Papers, 2005.

316 In August 1993, a bomb laden motorcycle exploded next to the car of Hasan al-Alfi, the Egyptian Interior Minister. The incident represented the introduction of what the West refers to as "suicide" bombers, the first such action by a Sunni group. See *The Looming Tower*, p. 185; *Al Qaeda*, p. 115.

317 This was basically true. See CIA intelligence report, Sudanese links to Egypt's Gama'at al-Islamiya and training of Egyptians, July 14, 1993; CIA intelligence report, Funding by Bin Ladin of Gama'at al-Islamiya and composition of its Sudanese wing, July 22, 1993.

318 "Unlike the kamikaze pilots who operated within a culture that sanctioned suicide, the Arab suicide bombers and pilots are bucking tradition by killing themselves. The religious legitimacy of these acts is, to say the least, highly questionable. The suicide bombings are referred to not as 'suicides' but as acts of 'self-martyrdom' ... " See *A Fury for God*, p. 101.

319 See Project Sumner, Name List, n.d. (2000?), no classification markings.

In Late June 1996, Jamal Ahmed Mohamed al-Fadl walked into the U.S. Embassy in Asmara, Eritrea. For a narrative of the al-Fadl story, see TD-314/00456-96, FBI report of investigation, interview of Jamal al-Fadl, November 10, 1996; FBI Form 302 (witness interview record), Subject: Interview of Al-Fadl, November 4, 1996; *United States of America v. Usama Bin Laden, et al.*, United States District Court, Southern District of New York, February 7, 2001, S(7) 98 Cr. 1023, particularly pp. 357–366; *The Black Banners*, pp. 42ff, 107; *Case Studies in Terrorism-Related Cases (03/26/2008)*, American Embassy Bombings in Kenya and Tanzania, pp. 30-31.

Al-Fadl had spent time in Brooklyn at the *al-Kifah* center before he decided to fight in Afghanistan. He arrived in Peshawar in 1988 and formally joined *al Qaeda* taking the battle name (*kunya*) Abu Bakr Sudani. He spent some time on the front lines in Afghanistan, participating in the battle at Jaji, and then running an al Qaeda training camp. He was then elevated to the business office when bin Laden moved to Sudan—al-Fadl's own homeland—and he further rose to be deputy, the natural go between with the Khartoum government.

Chapter 16

320 On November 19, 1995, the Egyptian Embassy in Islamabad was attacked in Islamabad. That occurred less than a week after Riyadh attack. See CIA/CTC, First Look: Attack on Egyptian Embassy, Islamabad, November 20, 1995.

321 Benazir Bhutto served as Prime Minister of Pakistan from 1988 to 1990 and again from 1993 to 1996. She was the first woman to head a democratic government in a Muslim majority nation.

322 CIA/CTC, First Look: Attack on Egyptian Embassy, Islamabad, November 20, 1995.

323 The source taught at *Dawa'a al-Jihad*, a "university" established during the height of the Soviet war in the 1980s, near the largest Afghan refugee camp, still a *jihadi* enclave and safe haven. See CIA Form 34, Source Identification, PD/TEACHOUT, October 2, 1993, TS/HCS/MU.

324 These insights are taken from the memoir of Melissa Boyle Mahle, a former CIA case officer, in *Denial and Deception: An Insider's View of the CIA from Iran-Contra to 9/11* (Nation Books, 2004).

"The discomforting effects of Western seduction are compounded by an obsession with sexual purity. According to the Moroccan feminist writer Fatima Mernissi, this may be due to the fact that the typical unmarried male's contact with his own sexuality is in a context deemed impure according to Islamic norms—sodomy and masturbation. 'It is no wonder,' she command, 'that women who have such tremendous power to maintain or destroy of man's position in society, are going to be the focus of his frustration and aggression.'; quoted in *A Fury for God*, p. 122.

Gilles Kepel also writes of sexual politics: "impoverished young men, humiliated and forced into abstinence or sexual misery by the crowded family conditions in which they lived ... [could] become heroes of chastity who sternly condemned the pleasures of which they had been so wretchedly deprived." See *Al Qaeda*, p. 133.

325 *Looming Tower*, p. 217; *Triple Cross*, p. 197.

326 On October 23, 1983, two truck bombs simultaneously struck barracks in Beirut housing U.S. and French military personnel assigned to the Multinational Force in Lebanon, a peacekeeping operation. A total of 241 Americans were killed, including 200 Marines.

327 The truth about *al Qaeda's* in Somalia in 1992–1994 is still not certain. There were Islamic terrorists, many of whom would later be associated with *al Qaeda*, on the ground, and the evidence seems to support a significant outside presence. Bin Laden associates also specifically went to Somalia to reconnoiter what was happening and to "train" people.

Ali Soufan later says that Zachariah al-Tunisi, who was killed with Mohammed Atef in Kabul in November 2001, "in fact fired the RPG that took down the U.S. helicopter in the episode that became known as Black Hawk Down; *The Black Banners*, p. 345. Lawrence Wright seems to be wrong when he writes definitively that *al Qaeda* has little to do with the incident and that bin Laden "simply appropriated such victories as his own." *The Looming Tower*, p. 188.

328 See David B. Ottaway and Steve Coll, "Retracing the Steps of a Terror Suspect," *The Washington Post*, June 5, 1995.

329 Robert M. Gates, CIA director from November 6, 1991–January 20, 1993.

330 In little more than a year after the end of Desert Storm, spending on Soviet issues went from 60 percent of the Agency budget to just 15 percent. For a general description of the Gates tenure, see CIA, "Directors of Central Intelligence as Leaders of the U.S. Intelligence Community 1946–2005" (Chapter 11).

331 The American Embassy compound was stormed and capture on November 4, 1979. The Iranian "students" originally took 90 hostages, and most were held until January 20, 1981, minutes before Reagan's inauguration as the nation's 40th president in Washington.

332 The group was the so-called Islamic Movement for Change, an organization that had never before appeared as such.

333 "We ask Allah to safeguard our country and guide the Muslim youth and all the nation to see what their enemies plot against them," the Statement read.

"The suspects cited three radical Islamists who had influenced them, one of whom was Usama bin Laden." Daniel Benjamin and Steven Simon, *The Age of Sacred Terror* (Floris Books, 2002), p. 132.

Ali Soufan later writes: "the perpetrators were led by Khalid al-Saeed, a close associate of bin Laden's." *The Black Banners*, p. 51. See also *The Cell*, p. 150.

334 Reuters, Saudi Arabia Beheads 4 in Riyadh Bombing, Friday, May 31, 1996.

Chapter 17

335 The information on the Clinton-Lewinsky sexual relationship comes from Referral to the United States House of Representatives pursuant to Title 28, United States Code, § 595(c), Submitted by The Office of the Independent Counsel, September 9, 1998 (the "Starr report").

The affair with Monica S. Lewinsky began two days after the first car bomb went off in Riyadh. Lewinsky began her White House unpaid internship in the office of Chief of Staff Leon Panetta in June 1995.

336 In February 1995, the Dow Jones Industrial Average broke 4,000, beginning a decade long rally. In November of that year, it broke 5,000. Chairman of the Federal Reserve Alan Greenspan warned of irrational exuberance when it broke 6,000 in October 1996.

337 On September 14, 1995, the leaders of the Bosnian Serbs agreed to end the siege of Sarajevo, laying the framework for final peace talks set to begin in Dayton, Ohio. On November 1, the conference began. The Bosnian, Serbian, and Croatian presidents attended, plus representatives from the United States, the United Kingdom, France, Germany, Italy, Russia, and the European Union (EU).

338 Pan Am Flight 103, a transatlantic flight from Frankfurt to Detroit, via London and New York, went down over Lockerbie, Scotland on December 21, 1988, the result of a bomb planted on the flight. A total of 270 people died, 269 on board the flight and 11 on the ground.

339 Israeli Prime Minister Yitzhak Rabin was assassinated in Tel Aviv on November 4, 1995.

340 CIA covert operations to depose Saddam Hussein began in 1994. They were largely dependent on access to Iraq afforded by U.N. inspectors assigned to the United Nations Special Commission (UNSCOM) verifying Iraq's disarmament. Much of the actual operations on the ground took place in Northern Iraq, in Kurdish areas that secured autonomy after the first Gulf War.

341 The U.S. and Saudi Arabia signed an agreement in 1973 to establish the Office of the Program Manager-Saudi Arabian National Guard Modernization Program (OPM-SANG).

342 For information about the Riyadh attack, see Department of Defense, The Protection of U.S. Forces Abroad: Executive summary of the Downing Task Force report on the Khobar Towers bombing and terrorism, part of Annex 1 in a secretary of defense report to the president, released September 16, 1996.

343 CNN correspondent Ralph Begleiter, reflecting conventional Washington wisdom and a great power paradigm, speculated that the attack might be retaliation for King Saud's support for the Oslo Accords, which set a path towards eventual peace with Israel, but he also mentioned continuing hostility between Saddam Hussein and Saudi Arabia and Saudi-Iranian rivalry for domination of the Gulf, as if that was what Saudi-Iranian enmity was about. He did mention that "some within Saudi Arabia strongly oppose the presence of U.S. military personnel," but even there he seemed to dismiss this by calling the American presence "small." CNN World Affairs Correspondent Ralph Begleiter, "Saudi Arabia dissension behind attack?," November 13, 1995, Web posted at: 11:25 a.m. EST (1625 GMT).

344 Three groups—the Islamic Movement for Change, the Tigers of the Gulf, and the Combatant Partisans of God—claimed responsibility for the Riyadh attack. See Department of State, 1995 Patterns of Global Terrorism, April 1996; *The Bin Ladens*, p. 432.

345 Ray Mabus served as Governor of Mississippi from 1988 to 1992, the youngest elected to that office in more than 150 years. Mabus was Ambassador to the Kingdom of Saudi Arabia from 1994–1996.

346 CIA Counterterrorist Center Commentary, Riyadh Bombing: Islamic Movement for Change Threatens Further Attacks, November 15, 1995 (S/NF).

347 CNN.com, From Correspondent Jamie McIntyre, "U.S. vows terrorist bomb won't affect Saudi relationship,"
November 13, 1995, Web posted at: 9:10 p.m. EST (0210 GMT).

348 At the time the United States operated mainly out of Prince Sultan Air Base, near Al Kharj, 50 miles southeast of Riyadh, and first occupied after the Iraqi invasion of Kuwait in 1990. The Combined Air Operations Center (CAOC) built there became the center of the enforcement of no-fly zones over Iraq, and then later, the attacks on Afghanistann.

349 The Saudi National Guard was established in 1963 under Prince (later Crown Prince and King) Abdullah's command. Abdullah was an ally of his half-brother, Prime Minister Faisal (who became king in November 1964), in the struggle to wrest control of the government from King Saud. See MOU, Governments of United States and Saudi Arabia, March 19, 1973, subject: Saudi Arabian National Guard Modernization Program.

350 CIA Counterterrorist Center Report, Riyadh Bombing: Sunni Radicals Behind Attacks, November 15, 1995 (S/N).

351 National Intelligence Council, National Intelligence Estimate (NIE), "The Foreign Terrorist Threat in the United States," July 1995. The NIE does discuss the plot to blow up twelve U.S. airliners and cited the consideration the Bojinka conspirators gave to attacking CIA Headquarters with an aircraft laden with explosives. The FAA worked with the Intelligence Community on this analysis and drafted the section addressing the threat to civil aviation, which said:

> Our review of the evidence ... suggests the conspirators were guided in their selection of the method and venue of attack by carefully studying security procedures in place in the region. If terrorists operating in [the United States] are similarly methodical, they will identify serious vulnerabilities in the security system for domestic flights.

The threat from established groups is assessed to be Hezbollah, *Gama'at al-Islamiya*, Hamas, and *Jama'a al-Fuqra*.

In 1997, the NIC did an update to 1995 National Intelligence Estimate. It concluded: "Civil aviation remains a particularly attractive target in light of the fear and publicity the downing of an airliner would evoke and the revelations last summer of the U.S. air transport sectors' vulnerabilities." See CIA analytic report, "Foreign Terrorist Threat in the U.S.: Revisiting our 1995 Estimate," April 1997.

352 King Fahd suffered a fully debilitating stroke on November 29, 1995 and decided to delegate the running of the Kingdom to Crown Prince Abdullah.

353 George Tenet would later defend the transient group theory and the 1995 NIE, saying that "It warned of the threat from radical Islamists and their enhanced ability 'to operate in the United States.' The Estimate judged that the most likely targets of a terrorist attack would be "national symbols such as the White House and the Capitol and symbols of U.S. capitalism such as Wall Street.' The report said that U.S. civil aviation was an especially vulnerable and attractive target." See *At the Center of the Storm*, p. 104.

The State Department also failed to mention *al Qaeda* in their 1995 report on global terrorism trumpeting "loosely organized" terrorists—"some representing groups"—but contrasting them with "members of the old established groups or those sponsored by states." See Department of State, Office of the Coordinator for Counterterrorism, *1995 Patterns of Global Terrorism*, April 1996.

354 Samuel Richard "Sandy" Berger, national security advisor to Bill Clinton, March 14, 1997–January 20, 2001.

355 Louis Joseph Freeh, director of the Federal Bureau of Investigation, September 1, 1993–June 25, 2001.

356 A classified Presidential Decision Directive 39 (PDD-39) of June 1995, signed by President Clinton, specifically gave the FBI "lead responsibility for investigating terrorist acts ... directed at U.S. citizens or institutions abroad." The FBI is a law enforcement agency, focused before 9/11 on apprehending terrorists after an attack, that is, investigations and indictments. The CIA, on the other hand, is an intelligence agency, focused on collecting information, even if their "covert action" goal is stopping a terrorist attack from occurring in the first place.

See also Statement of Louis J. Freeh, director, FBI, before the House Appropriations Subcommittee, May 16, 2001.

357 George Stephanopoulos, White House communications director, January 20, 1993–June 7, 1993 and senior advisor to the president, June 7, 1993–December 10, 1996.

358 President Clinton began his sexual relationship with Monica Lewinsky on November 15, 1995; the same date as the Islamabad attack.

359 According to two Clinton administration White House officials at the time, "he [Freeh] had a reputation for being fiercely honest and uncompromising, as straight an arrow as America produced." See *Age of Sacred Terror*, p. 299.

360 The Waco siege by the ATF and FBI, of the Branch Davidians compound, began on February 28, 1993 and end on April 19 with the storming of the compound, ultimately leaving 86 dead.

361 The question of "loose nukes" applied to the decrepit state of physical security found at nuclear weapons storage site in the former Soviet Union with the end of the Cold War, but also the under and unemployment of former Soviet scientists with nuclear knowledge, who might put their services on the open market. The problem of loose nukes would dominate the early 1990s.

Chapter 18

362 Project Sumner Timeline, V38, n.d. (2008) (TS/SP/MU).

363 According to KSM, starting in 1993, he traveled to Bosnia, Brazil, China, Iran, Kenya, Malaysia, Pakistan, the Philippines, Qatar, Russia, Spain, Sudan, Tajikistan, Turkey, Turkmenistan, the United Arab Emirates, Uzbekistan, and Yemen. He had previously been to Japan and lived in Kuwait. He traveled to or through a number of European countries in transit (often spending one night in transit), including Belgium, Germany, and the Netherlands. See KSM Debrief Papers, 2005.

364 Memorandum, Attachment of KSM Postcard Text, August 12, 1990, 90-65P (TS/MU).

365 ADCI(SP) Contact Sheet, Khalid Sheikh Mohammed, n.d. (1984?), MU-80-4/6; Apex files, Cabinet 19, Drawer 3, Box 9.

366 Israel invaded southern Lebanon on June 6, 1982 and laid siege to Beirut, the occupation taking place from June-September 1982.

367 DO, the directorate of operations: the common name for the clandestine service at this time.

368 The Farm is the nickname for the clandestine-service training facility on Camp Peary, Virginia. It is ostensibly a military base, and was once owned by the Army, but is now owned and operated by the CIA.

369 Col. Oliver North's famous testimony during the Iran-Contra investigation occurred on July 7–8, 1987.

370 Omar Abdel Rahman entered the US on a tourist visa in November 1990. The explanation for his entry has never been proven, various theories existing of his relationship with the CIA during the Afghanistan jihad and with the FBI thereafter. There was an official investigation: Department of State Inspector General Report, "Review of the Visa-Issuance Process Phase I—Circumstances Surrounding the Issuance of Visas to Sheikh Omar Ali Ahmed Abdel Rahman, March 1994. See also Department of State briefing materials, Presentation on Consular Systems Delivered to the Information Resources Management Program Board, April 26, 1995.

Chapter 19

371 KSM wrote to Apex Watch that he was starting a master's degree in Lahore. One Khalid Sheikh Mohammed actually enrolled in an MSc correspondence course at the University of the Punjab in Lahore in 1990. See KSM Debrief Papers, 2005.

372 Project Sumner Timeline, V38, n.d. (2008) (TS/SP/MU).

Chapter 20

373 Actual background information on Omar Abdel Rahman comes from Pre-Incident Indicators of Terrorist Incidents: The Identification of Behavioral, Geographic, and Temporal Patterns of Preparatory Conduct, pp. 340–342; The Sociology and Psychology Of Terrorism: Who Becomes A Terrorist And Why?, A Report Prepared under an Interagency Agreement by the Federal Research Division, Library of Congress., pp. 78–79; *1000 Years For Revenge*, pp. 39ff.

374 Abdullah Azzam, "Defense of the Muslim Lands: The First Obligations After Iman," English translation work done by Brothers in Ribatt, 1993.

375 George John Tenet, director of the CIA, December 16, 1996–July 11, 2004 (deputy director from July 3, 1995–July 11, 1997).

376 John M. Deutch, director of the CIA, May 10, 1995–December 15, 1996.

377 "They certainly are not as competent, or as understanding of what their relative role is and what their responsibilities are." See Tim Weiner, "The CIA's

HISTORY IN ONE ACT

most Important Mission: Itself," *The New York Times*, December 10, 1995.

378 The Joint Inquiry later said that though there were many impediments and failures associated with the Agency's lack of human sources inside al Qaeda, "CTC personnel said they did not view guidelines issued by former DCI John Deutch in 1996 concerning CIA recruitment of human sources with poor human rights records as an impediment to the pursuit of terrorist recruitments in al-Qa'ida, and none of the CTC officers interviewed by the Joint Inquiry attributed the lack of penetration of the al-Qa'ida inner circle to the Deutch guidelines. In fact, the effort to recruit such penetrations became increasingly aggressive with respect to Bin Ladin's network beginning in 1999." Joint Inquiry, p. 93.

379 George J. Tenet; deputy director of Central Intelligence, July 3, 1995–July 11, 1997 (under John Deutch); acting director of Central Intelligence, December 16, 1996–July 11, 1997; special assistant to the president and senior director for intelligence programs, National Security Council staff, January 1993–July 1995; President-elect Clinton's national security transition team, November 1992–January 1993; staff director for the Senate Select Committee on Intelligence, 1989–1992; staff, Senate Select Committee on Intelligence, 1985–1989; legislative assistant to Senator John Heinz (D-PA), 1982–1985.

380 See, e.g., Vernon Loeb, "At Hush-Hush CIA Unit, Talk of a Turnaround: Reforms Recharge Espionage Service." *The Washington Post*, September 7, 1999, p. A8. Loeb wrote: "The CIA's super-secret Directorate of Operations now seems on the mend ... . Money is pouring in from Congress, the CIA is engaged in the most significant recruiting drive in its history, morale is up and resignations by DO case officers are way, way down ..." How exactly does a reporter verify any of this?
 The Washington Post earlier reported: "So how's ... [DCI] George Tenet, doing? He's just finished two years on the job, and it's a good time for a fitness report ... . On paper, Tenet's record looks pretty good so far ... . [He] gets generally good marks from Congress ... . Tenet's biggest challenge will be to focus the agency's energies on the hard targets ... . Being CIA director may be the best job in Washington, but it's also the hardest. To do it right, Tenet will need to make more friends, yes—and also a lot more enemies." David Ignatius, "New Guy at the CIA," *The Washington Post*, August 22, 1999, p. B7.

381 With regard to Afghanistan after the Soviet withdrawal "the attitude of the USA (and to an extent the United Nations) could be characterized as uninterested rather than disinterested. The State Department was distracted by the Gulf War of 1991 and then by crises in east Africa and the Balkans and was simply not that concerned by events in Afghanistan. This abandonment, particularly given the intense involvement during the 1980s, must go down as one of the most ruthless and shortsighted policies of recent times." *Al Qaeda*, p. 129. See also *Ghost Wars*, pp. 231–235.

382 Memorandum, Attachment of Translated KSM Letter, May 4, 1989, 89-104 (TS/MU).

383 Abdul Hakim Murad; CIA Terrorist Biographic Note, Abdul Hakim Murad (U), CTC-156-95, November 1995.

Chapter 21

384 The date was January 7, 1995. Most news stories refer to it as the Josefa building. Steve Coll calls it Tiffany Mansion and says KSM owned the apartment; *Ghost Wars*, p. 274.

Richard Miniter says it was "a neighborhood of seedy nightclubs and cheap hotels that attracted a large, transient Arab population; the plotters knew that they could blend in." *Losing Bin Laden*, pp. 73, 78.

385 Apex Watch (ADCI(SP)) Memorandum for the Records, Reconstitution of Bojinka Timeline Based on KSM Reporting, November 1994 (TS/SP/MU).

386 Philippine authorities arrested Murad on January 7, 1995 and he was transported to the Southern District of New York on April 12. While *enroute*, he stated that the goal of the bombing plot was to punish the United States and its people for their support of Israel.

Philippine authorities also arrested accomplice Wali Khan Amin Shah on January 11, but he escaped. He was recaptured by Malaysian authorities in December 1995 and flown to New York on December 12, 1995.

387 FBI report of investigation, interview of Abdul Hakim Murad, April 13, 1995; intelligence report, 1996 ATEF Study on airplane hijacking operations, September 26, 2001.

388 From November 1991 to July 1992, Murad trained at U.S. flight schools in Texas, New York, North Carolina, and California and obtained his commercial pilot's license, surveying the World Trade Center as a possible target. See *Triple Cross* Timeline. See also United States Court of Appeals, Second Circuit (327 F.3d 56), UNITED STATES of America, Appellee, v. Ramzi Ahmed Yousef, Eyad Ismoil, also known as Eyad Ismail, and Abdul Hakim Murad, also known as Saeed Ahmed, Defendants; Appellants, Mohammed A. Salameh, Nidal Ayyad, Mahmud Abouhalima, also known as Mahmoud Abu Halima, Bilal Alkaisi, also known as Bilal Elqisi, Ahmad Mohammad Ajaj, also known as Khurram Khan, Abdul Rahman Yasin, also known as Aboud, and Wali Khan Amin Shah, also known as Grabi Ibrahim Hahsen, Defendants; Dockets No. 98-1041L; 98-1197; 98-1355; 99-1544; 99-1554; United States Court of Appeals, Second Circuit, argued: May 3, 2002; decided: April 4, 2003; and KSM Debrief Papers, 2005.

389 See *Triple Cross*, pp. 120, 184; *1000 Years for Revenge*, p. 198.

390 CIA analytic report, Khalid Sheik Muhammad's Nephews, CTC 2003-300013, January 31, 2003.

391 He actually flew under the Ghamdi alias; see CIA analytic report, "The Plot and the Plotters (U)," June 1, 2003, p. 103.

392 On February 6, 1995, based upon a tip-off from a walk in, U.S. diplomats learned that Ramzi Yousef was in Islamabad. Told that he was planning to go to Peshawar the next day, every American security person with a gun was mobilized for the capture, including DEA agents and State Department diplomatic security. See *Denial and Deception: An Insider's View of the CIA*, p. 160; *Age of Sacred Terror*, p. 25; *The Cell*, p. 134 ff; *Triple Cross*, p. 200. See also Samuel Katz, *Relentless Pursuit: The DSS and the Manhunt for Al Qaeda Terrorists* (Tom Doherty Associates, 2002).

Louis Freeh would later write: "I can't name the CEOs we approached for obvious reasons, but Ramzi Yousef … was flown out of Pakistan on a private corporate jet under very tight time constraints." *My FBI*, p. 179.

393 Project Sumner Timeline, V38, n.d. (2008) (TS/SP/MU).

394 KSM Debrief Papers, 2005.

395 CIA analytic report, Khalid Sheik Muhammad's Nephews, CTC 2003-300013, January 31, 2003.

396 *Case Studies in Terrorism-Related Cases (03/26/2008)*, First World Trade Center Bombing, pp. 7–9.

397 Under the alias "Khaled Shaykh" in Doha, Qatar, KSM wired $660 to Mohammad Salameh on November 3, 1992. Salameh was one of Ramzi Yousef's four co-conspirators in the World Trade Center attack; see Joint Inquiry, p. 310.

KSM was also involved in the statement regarding the attack. One of Yousef's last acts before leaving the United States was to deliver a letter to *The New York Times* announcing the bombing: "We are the fifth battalion in the Liberation Army," the letter said, declaring that the bombing was done in response to the American political, economic, and military support for Israel and the other dictator countries in the region … The American people must know, that their civilians who got killed are not better than those who are getting killed by the American weapons and support."

398 The real Ramzi Ahmed Yousef, a Pakistani national of Baluchi origin, was born April 27, 1968, possibly in Kuwait City. His mother was KSM's older sister Hameda. For background on this subject, see CIA analytic report, Khalid Sheik Muhammad's Nephews, CTC 2003-300013, January 31, 2003.

399 Robin Wright, "COLUMN ONE: Rewarding Terrorism Tipsters: A multimillion-dollar bounty program featuring a global hot line and matchbook ads has helped crack down on anti-U.S. violence. But paying people to turn in criminals makes some uneasy," *Los Angeles Times*, March 14, 1995; and Michael James, "Terrorism suspect meets his match," *The Baltimore Sun*, February 14, 1995.

400 KSM Debrief Papers, 2005.

Chapter 22

401 In February 1996, the U.S. trade embargo against the communist government was made permanent in response to Cuba's shooting down of two U.S. aircraft operated by Miami-based Cuban exiles. See Todd S. Purdum, "Clinton Seeking Wider Sanctions Against Cubans," *The New York Times*, February 27, 1996, p. A1.

402 The September 22, 1995 text is posted at "The Unabomber Trial: The Manifesto," *The Washington Post* website (as of 2020) at https://www.washingtonpost.com/wp-srv/national/longterm/unabomber/manifesto.text.htm.

403 Memorandum, Attachment of Translated KSM Letter, June 20, 1996, 86-09 (TS/MU).

404 On March 3, 1996, the Sudanese minister of state for defense Maj Gen. Elfatih Erwa met with Ambassador Timothy Carney and CIA officers in a hotel room in Rosslyn, Virginia. Erwa expressed Sudan's desire to get off the State Department list of state sponsors of terrorism and asks for a written checklist of measures that would satisfy the U.S. to list sanctions and restore relations. The CIA produced a memo, asking for the names of all bin Laden supporters, their passport numbers, and dates of travel; and information on bin Laden finances and training camps.

In later meetings, the U.S. pushed Sudan to expel bin Laden. Erwa argued that it is better for bin Laden to remain in Sudan, where the government can keep an eye on him. He also said that if the U.S. wants to bring charges against him, they wouldn't hand him over. Eventually the Americans insisted that the Sudanese government ask bin Laden to leave the country. Erwa warned that he would go to Afghanistan. According to Benjamin and Simon, Sudan suggested that it deport bin Laden to Saudi Arabia, but the Saudis told the U.S. that they would not accept him. See *Age of Sacred Terror*, pp. 246–247. George Tenet later writes "Press reports and the Internet rumor mill continue to contend that the Sudanese had offered to extradite UBL to the United States, but I am unaware of anything to substantiate that." *At the Center of the Storm*, p. 103. See also *The Looming Tower*, p. 220ff; *The Cell*, p. 151.

405 In mid-1995, Taliban forces settled in on the outskirts of the capital city and began a constant artillery and rocket attack on various neighborhoods. In November, they gave the government an ultimatum after which they would resume bombardment if the government did not leave the city. The city was besieged over the winter, an offensive beginning in 1996. The city was completely taken in September.

406 KSM Debrief Papers, 2005.

407 The Committee for Advice and Reform, Our Invitation to Give Advice and Reform To: King Fahd Bin 'Abd-al 'Aziz Al-Saud and the people of Saudi Arabian Peninsula 02-11-1414 (April 12, 1994). The Committee, also known as the Advice and Reformation Committee was established in London in 1994. Khaled al-

Fawwaz, a bin Laden friend, was the first head. Al-Fawwaz would later serve as the middleman between journalists seeking interviews with Bin Laden in Afghanistan. See *The Black Banners*, p. x; *The Cell*, p. 163.

408 *Osama bin Laden*, p. 45.

409 The Committee for Advice and Reform, Our Invitation to Give Advice and Reform To: King Fahd Bin 'Abd-al 'Aziz Al-Saud and the people of Saudi Arabian Peninsula 02-11-1414 (April 12, 1994).

410 The Committee for Advice and Reform, Saudi Arabia Supports the Communists in Yemen 27-12-1414 (7 June 1994). Also in The Committee for Advice and Reform, The Banishment of Communism from the Arabian Peninsula: The Episode and the Proof. 12-2-1415 (July 11, 1994), bin Laden attacks Prince Sultan for supporting communist factions in Yemen with money and weapons, noting that even "western powers were too smart to back the losing side … The defeat of the communists is a rejection of secular and atheist regimes across the region."

411 Bandar bin Sultan al Saud, Saudi Arabia Ambassador to the United States, October 24, 1983–September 8, 2005.

412 The Committee for Advice and Reform, Saudi Arabia Unveils its War Against Islam and its Scholars, 08-04-1415 (12 September 1994). See also The Committee for Advice and Reform, Quran Scholars in the Face of Despotism, 11-2-1415 (July 19, 1994); The Committee for Advice and Reform, Saudi Arabia Continues Its War Against Islam and Its Scholars, March 9, 1995; The Committee for Advice and Reform, Scholars are the Prophet's Successors, May 16, 1995. The story of King Fahd's decisions to arrest the scholars and his broader attack on Islamist dissenters is told in *The Bin Ladens*, pp. 404ff.

413 The Committee for Advice and Reform, Do Not Have Vile Actions in Your Religion, 11-04-1415 (September 16, 1994). The story of the arrest of reformist Saudi scholars in 1994 is told in *Osama bin Laden*, pp. 80–81.

414 The Committee for Advice and Reform, Urgent Letter to Security Officials, 11-04-1415 (September 16, 1994).

415 The Committee for Advice and Reform, Important Telegram to Our Brothers in the Armed Forces, 14-4-1415 (September 19, 1994).

416 The Committee for Advice and Reform, 10-05-1415 (October 15, 1994).

417 The Committee for Advice and Reform, Prince Salman and Ramadan Alms, February 12, 1995. "The timing of this initiative supports the U.S. presidents' decision to freeze the assets of groups that oppose the [Middle East] peace process, Osama Bin Laden wrote. He draws attention to the danger of depositing monies into official banks, as it may be frozen. Muslims are encouraged to avoid giving funds to the government agencies, but rather give them directly to the needy, or those "trusted individuals who will deliver them."

418 The Committee for Advice and Reform, Open Letter for Sheikh Bin Baz, 27-07-1415 (December 29, 1994); The Committee for Advice and Reform, The Second Letter to Sheikh 'Abd al'Aziz Bin Baz, January 29, 1995).

419 The Committee for Advice and Reform, The Second Letter to Sheikh 'Abd al'Aziz Bin Baz, January 29, 1995).

420 The Committee for Advice and Reform, Open Letter for Sheikh Bin Baz, 27-07-1415 (December 29, 1994).

421 The Committee for Advice and Reform, Important Telegram to Our Brothers in the Armed Forces, 14-4-1415 (September 19, 1994).

422 *Osama bin Laden*, p. 98.

423 The Committee for Advice and Reform, The Bosnia Tragedy and the Deception of the Servant of the Two Mosques, 15-3-1416 (August 11, 1995).

424 ADCI(SP), Translation of KSM Letter, May 30, 1996 (TS/SP/MU).

425 CIA/DI research paper, "Saudi Arabia's Islamic Awakening (U)," February 1995, SECRET/NOFORN.

426 For background on the attack, see Perry D. Jamison, *Khobar Towers: Tragedy and Response*, Air Force History and Museums Program, 2008; CIA analytic report, "Khobar Bombing: Saudi Shia, Iran, and Usama Bin Ladin All Suspects (U)," CTC 96-30015, July 5, 1996.

427 We will "hunt down" those responsible for the explosion, Secretary of State Warren Christopher said the same day, while on an official visit to Israel. See Philip Shenon, "23 U.S. Troops Die in Truck Bombing in Saudi Base," *The New York Times*, June 26, 1996, p. A1.

428 After bin Laden left Sudan, "the rulers of Sudan sat down to divvy up bin Laden's investments" and bin Laden reportedly lost more than $160 million in the liquidating of his assets. See *The Looming Tower*, p. 222; and *Losing bin Laden*, p. 125.

Michael Scheuer also writes about the fleecing of bin Laden as he was leaving Sudan in *Osama bin Laden*, pp. 102–103.

429 The *Hadith* is not the *Qur'an*; it is the sacred Islamic Traditions reputed to have been uttered by Mohammed or practices based on his actions and thus the product of an oral and written tradition distinguished from "the word."

430 KSM Debrief Papers, 2005.

431 The classified Presidential Decision Directive 39 (PDD-39) of June 1995 specifically gave the FBI "lead responsibility for investigating terrorist acts planned or carried out by foreign or domestic terrorist groups in the U.S. or which are directed at U.S. citizens or institutions abroad." See also Statement of Louis J. Freeh, Director, FBI, before the House Appropriations Subcommittee, May 16, 2001.

432 Abdullah bin Abdulaziz, Crown Prince, June 13, 1982–August 1, 2005.

433 The FBI files controversy ("File Gate") arose in June 1996 around improper White House access in 1993 and 1994 to FBI security-clearance documents.

434 "Saudi Arabia's able ambassador to the United States, Prince Bandar bin Sultan, had been quick to announce a reward of 10 million riyals (then about $3 million in U.S. dollars) for information leading to the arrest of the bombers." See *My FBI*, p. 5.

435 The O. J. Simpson case, held in Los Angeles County Superior Court, captivated the nation from January 25, 1995–October 2, 1995. Former National Football League player, broadcaster, and actor O. J. Simpson was tried on two counts of murder for the June 12, 1994 slashing deaths of his ex-wife, Nicole Brown Simpson, and her friend Ron Goldman. He was found not guilty.

436 CIA analytic report, "Khobar Bombing: Saudi Shia, Iran, and Usama Bin Ladin All Suspects (U)," CTC 96-30015, July 5, 1996, took a look at Bin Laden and other Islamic extremists as suspects in the Khobar Towers bombing, rejecting his involvement.

Later, in his 1997 interview with CNN, bin Laden praised the 'heroes' of Khobar Towers, but denied responsibility: "What they did is a big honour that I missed participating in." Osama bin Laden, quoted in *Al Qaeda*, p. 155.

437 *My FBI*, p. 9. See also FBI intelligence report, Establishment of a Tripartite Agreement Among Usama Bin Ladin, Iran, and the NIF [National Islamic Front], Jan. 31, 1997.

438 According to Freeh, in 2000, the FBI questioned Mustafa al-Qassab, a Saudi Shi'ite detainee implicated in the Khobar Towers attack. "In the late 1980s, al-Qassab had traveled from Saudi Arabia to Iran to meet with Ahmed al-Mughassil, the commander of the military wing of the Saudi Hezbollah. Now a decade later, al-Qassab laid out for us in detail the planning and logistics that had gone into the Khobar attack, traced the lineage irrefutably back to Tehran, and as far as I was concerned tied the whole package together for good. We still had to work our way around a wrong opinion from a prosecutor in the U.S. Attorney's Office for the District of Columbia, a civil lawyer who had little knowledge of criminal law. But she, too, passed, as did the Clinton-Gore administration and its apparent indifference to Khobar Towers." *My FBI*, p. 31.

Freeh later testified before the 911 Commission that, four days into the Bush administration, Rice "told me to pursue our investigation with the Attorney General and to bring whatever charges possible. Within weeks, a new prosecutor was put in charge of the case and, on June 21, 2001, an indictment was returned against fourteen Saudi Hizballah subjects who had been directed to bomb Khobar by senior officials of the Iranian government. I know that the families of the 19 murdered Khobar Airmen were deeply grateful to President Bush and Dr. Rice for their prompt response and focus on terrorism." Testimony of Louis J. Freeh Before the National Commission on Terrorist Attacks Upon the United States, April 13, 2004. See also *My FBI*, p. 32.

439 Prince Nayef bin Abd al-Aziz Al Saud, Minster of Interior (head of the Saudi national police) from October 11, 1975–June 16, 2012.

440 Samuel Richard "Sandy" Berger, national security advisor, March 14, 1997–January 20, 2001; deputy national security advisor, January 20, 1993–March 14, 1997.

441 Richard A. Clarke, *Against all Enemies: Inside America's War on Terror* (Free Press, 2004), pp. 118–119. See also Hugh Shelton, *Without Hesitation: The Odyssey of an American Warrior* (St. Martin's Press, 2010), pp. 342, 355.

Chapter 23

442 Turki bin Faisal al Saud; director general of the *Al Mukhabarat al A'amah* (General Intelligence Directorate), December 1979–September 2001.

443 APEC Philippines 1996 was a series of Asia-Pacific Economic Cooperation meetings focused on economic cooperation, held at the Subic Bay Freeport Zone in Subic, on November 24–25, 1996. It was the eighth APEC meeting in history and the first held in the Philippines.

444 "Pocket litter" is the intelligence community's name for the scraps that are found on the person of those who are captured or killed. It can include identification, tickets, photographs, notebooks, business cards, and in the age of thumb drives, often computer files.

445 Joint Inquiry, p. 310.

446 The actual name is Abdullah Abdulrahman Al-Fak'asi Al-Ghamdi. Some sources refer to al-Ghamdi as Abdulrahman A. A. al-Ghamdi and some refer to an A. F. al-Ghamdi. A.A. al-Ghamdi is used throughout here, unless the source specified otherwise, as it did in the case of the Philippine immigration forms.

447 On December 30, 1995, Khalid Sheikh Mohammed was identified from an FBI photograph, and he was subsequently indicted by a New York City grand jury in January 1996. The Joint Inquiry into Intelligence Community Activities before and after the Terrorist Attacks of September 11, 2001 reported that "He was indicted by a U.S. grand jury in January 1996. The indictment was kept under seal until 1998 while the FBI and CIA attempted to locate him and arrange to take him into custody." See Joint Inquiry, p. 30. Also *Denial and Deception: An Insider's View of the CIA*, p. 247.

448 John Brennan, CIA station chief in Saudi Arabia at the time. Brennan served on his first assignment in Saudi Arabia in 1982–1984 before moving to the Counterterrorist Center after it was established. He was daily intelligence briefer to President Clinton and then chief of station in Riyadh from 1996–1999, chief of staff to CIA Director George Tenet, and CIA executive and interim director of the National Counterterrorism Center, before retiring from the CIA in 2005. Brennan went on to become an advisor to Barack Obama, White House Counterterrorism chief, and director of the CIA from 2013–2017.

449 The "renditions branch" is one of the sub-elements of the Counterterrorist Center (CTC), involved primarily in cooperative renditions with a foreign government.

According to Michael Scheuer, in testimony before the Congress: "The CIA's Rendition Program began in late summer 1995. I authored it and then ran and managed it against al-Qaeda leaders and other Sunni Islamists from August 1995, until June 1999. There were only two goals for the program: First, to take men off the street who were planning or had been involved in attacks on the United States or its allies; second, to seize hard copy or electronic documents in their possession when arrested. Americans were never expected to read those, and they could provide options for follow-on operations." Joint Hearings, *Extraordinary Rendition in U.S. Counterterrorism Policy: The Impact on Transatlantic Relations*, April 17, 2007, p. 12.

Chapter 24

450 See Joint Inquiry, p. 328.

451 "In 1995 the United States also learned that Khalid Sheikh Mohammed, "KSM," was living in Doha, Qatar and was reportedly employed by a government agency there." See 911 Commission, Staff Statement No. 5, Diplomacy, n.d. (2004).

452 Project Sumner Timeline, V38, n.d. (2008) (TS/SP/MU).

453 In June 1992, Qatar signed a defense cooperation agreement with the United States, solidifying relations that blossom after the 1991 Gulf War. During that war, Qatar allowed U.S. military forces to operate from its territory; and a Qatari armored battalion also served with the Arab brigade as part of the coalition on the ground.

454 Crown Prince Hamad bin Khalifa al-Thani deposed his father in a bloodless palace coup on June 27, 1995.

455 "A rendition is the arrest and detention of terrorist operatives for return to the United States or another country for prosecution. Renditions often lead to confessions, and they disrupt terrorist plots by shattering cells and removing key individuals." See Joint Inquiry, p. 225.

Renditions of drug traffickers, criminals and fugitive government officials became increasingly routine in the Clinton years, a symbol at first of deeper cooperation internationally between law enforcement arms. Cooperation soon ceded to extraordinary, standard extradition merely a lot of paperwork while extraordinary meant flash and favors and the involvement of the top officials of the secret services and government, all bending the law. President Clinton took control himself of the authority to authorize forcible renditions if nuclear, biological or chemical materials were the subject. The Counterterrorist Center established a special renditions section just to select and go after terrorists who not only were directly connected to WMD but also those who might produce further intelligence leading to it.

On September 3, 1998, FBI Director Freeh testified before the Senate Judiciary Committee about the use of force to abduct suspects to bring them to trial, also known as a rendition. He says that the rendition process was controlled by Presidential Decision Directive 77 (PDD-77), "which sets explicit requirements for initiating this method for returning terrorists to stand trial in the United States." He said that over the past decade the United States had "successfully returned 13 suspected international terrorists to stand trial in the United States for acts or planned acts of terrorism against U.S. citizens." Under this procedure, whatever force was used in making the arrests should not have compromised evidence needed for trial; Senate Judiciary Committee, *U.S. Counter-Terrorism Policy*, Hearing Before the S. Comm. on the Judiciary, 105th Cong. 33 (1998).

PDD-77 was signed by President Clinton on February 24, 2000.

The best general discussion of the legality of renditions is Louis Fisher, "Extraordinary Rendition: The Price of Secrecy," *American University Law Review*, Vol. 57.

456 Ali Soufan later writes: "the perpetrators were led by Khalid al-Saeed, a close associate of bin Laden's." *The Black Banners*, p. 51.

Similarly, two former Clinton Administration counter-terrorism officials associate Riyadh with bin Laden. "The suspects cited three radical Islamists who had influenced them, one of whom was Usama bin Laden." *Age of Sacred Terror*, p. 132. See also *The Cell*, p. 150.

457 *Ghost Wars*, pp. 326–327; *Your Government Failed You*, p. 38.

458 Michael Scheuer, in his testimony before the Congress, refers to WMD intelligence in 1995 changing the rules regarding approval of renditions; see Joint Hearings, *Extraordinary Rendition in U.S. Counterterrorism Policy: The Impact on Transatlantic Relations*, April 17, 2007.

459 The interagency Counterterrorism Security Group (CSG) was established in 1992 to coordinate domestic and international matters that crossed department and agency jurisdictions.

460 Patrick Nickolas Theros served as the United States ambassador to Qatar from 1995–1998.

461 Janet Wood Reno, United States attorney general, March 11, 1993–January 20, 2001.

462 Justice Department approval occurred on March 5, 1996. See Memorandum for the CSG [Counterterrorism Security Group], Deputy Attorney General [name redacted], Subject: Approval for MON Action (U), March 5, 1996 (MU).

463 The FBI elite tactical unit is somewhat inaptly called the Hostage Rescue Team (HRT), even though it is involved in more than just hostage rescue. After the 1993 Waco disaster, in which 78 Branch Davidians lost their life, the Critical Incident Response Group (CIRG) was established. The HRT became just one of many paramilitary sub-elements of the CIRG.

464 "A close inspection of the register at the Su-Casa guesthouse reveals that one of the guests present when Ramzi was seized by the FBI was a Karachi-based businessman who had signed in under the name of Khalid Sheikh." See *Al Qaeda*, p. 114.

465 CIA analytic report, "The Plot and the Plotters (U)," June 1, 2003, p. 32.

466 Louis Freeh later wrote, "our agents and the CIA narrowly missed grabbing Khalid Sheikh Mohammed as he was about to travel from the Qatari capital of Doha to the United Arab Emirates. We believe he was tipped off, but however he got away, it was a slipup with tragic consequences." See *My FBI*, p. 281.

Losing Bin Laden says: "How did he get away? Qatar's minister of religious affairs had tipped off Mohammed and provided him and a traveling companion with false passports, according to Robert Baer, a former CIA official. That same book says that KSM, together with his traveling companion, are believed to have fled to Prague, where Mohammed assumed the identity of one Mustaf Nasir. See *Losing Bin Laden*, p. 86. This falsehood might be the origins of the Bush Administration's later belief that Mohammed Atta went to Prague to meet with Iraqi secret police agents.

The 911 Commission tells the story this way: "According to some unconfirmed information, KSM may have left Qatar in 1995 for an extended period after being warned by his nephew, Ramzi Yousef, that U.S. authorities were looking for him. According to this same information, he may have returned to Qatar later that year, but then became concerned again following the December 1995 capture of Wali Khan, another conspirator in the airliner bombing plot, and left Qatar for good in early 1996. The government of Qatar has not yet provided an account of this episode or its government's past relationship to KSM." See 911 Commission, Staff Statement No. 5—Diplomacy, 2004.

467 *Losing Bin Laden*, p. 86.

Chapter 25

468 ADCI(SP), Payments Associated with the F-15 Sale, May 1, 1978 (TS/MU). On February 14, 1978, Secretary of State Cyrus Vance announced that the Carter administration planned to sell 200 military aircraft to Saudi Arabia, Israel and Egypt, including 60 F-15's to Saudi Arabia. For background see Bernard Gwertzman, "U.S. Decides to Sell Equipment to Saudis to Bolster F-15 Jets," *The New York Times*, March 7, 1981, p. A1.

469 ADCI(SP), Additional Information on BAE Systems and RX-146, October 3, 1985 (TS/MU). Al Yamanah—the UK's largest export contract, signed in 1985 between the UK and Saudi Arabia governments, involved the provision of a complete defense package for the Kingdom of Saudi Arabia. BAE Systems was established as prime contractor, with overall responsibility for delivering the contract including aircraft, associated hardware, radar, communications, support, construction and manpower for the Royal Saudi Air Force, and the supply and support of mine hunters for the Royal Saudi Naval Forces.

The UK government's Serious Fraud Office (SFO) later uncovered commission payments totaling as much as $10 billion paid by BAE Systems. One recipient of these payments was established to be Prince Bandar. The investigation into bribery associated with the deal was prematurely ended in 2006 without any conclusions.

470 ADCI(SP), Improprieties associated with UARK "Gift," August 1, 1993 (TS/MU). Tim Weiner, "Clinton and His Ties to the Influential Saudis," *The New York Times*, August 23, 1993.

Chapter 26

471 Project Sumner Timeline, V38, n.d. (2008) (TS/SP/MU).

472 The port city of Karachi is the capital of the Pakistani province of Sindh. It is the most populous city in Pakistan, and fifth-most-populous city proper in the world.

473 A "tear sheet" is a specially prepared report that obscures the source of the intelligence information contained within and distributed widely. It originated in the days of telex. Below the tear in the paper, the source is discussed, as is other operational information.

474 Youssef M. Ibrahim, "Egyptian Military Blamed in Attack on Security Chief," *The New York Times*, August 19, 1993, p. A1.

Chapter 27

475 ADCI(SP), The Supreme Council of Charity—A History, May 1997 (TS/MU).

476 The history of the Saudis and bin Laden is still confused, but there is no doubt of Saudi leadership in opposing the Soviets in Afghanistan. To the Saudi clan, Afghanistan was a toehold and steppingstone to the vast reaches of Central Asia; there the royal family was intent on expanding *Wahhabist* Islam to the Caucasus. For background, see SMON Department 2, Special Intelligence Report, Threats to the Eastern Orthodox Church, Secret Paper, n.d. (1985).

" … in 1990, at the request of the Americans, the Saudis halted their subsidies and logistical aid to the Afghan Arabs, thus putting an end to Osama bin Laden's official mission." *In the Name of Osama Bin Laden*, p. 25.

477 The threats are described in CIA Terrorist Biographic Note, Usama bin Ladin (U), CTC-005-00, January 2000.

478 See *The Looming Tower*, pp. 153–154; *Through Our Enemies' Eyes*, p. 122; *Osama bin Laden*, p. 80; *The Bin Ladens*, p. 375.

479 On March 5, 1994, King Fahd personally revoked bin Laden's Saudi citizenship in punishment of his "irresponsible behavior that contradicts the interests of Saudi Arabia and harms sisterly countries." See Senator Bob Graham, *Intelligence Matters: The CIA, the FBI, Saudi Arabia, and the Failure of America's War on Terror* (Random House, 2004), p. 30.

480 On February 5, 1994, there was an assassination attempt on bin Laden's life in Khartoum, Sudan. Bin Laden actually believed it was Egyptian intelligence; the CIA believed it was the Saudis. See *The Looming Tower*, p. 192.

Richard Miniter writes: "Sometime in 1994, Prince Turki al-Faisal is believed to have ordered bin Laden's execution, a Sudanese intelligence source told the author. The details of the first Saudi assassination attempt on bin Laden's life in the summer of 1994 are hazy but undisputed." *Losing Bin Laden*, p. 107.

481 For the story of Prince Nayef's relationship with bin Laden, see CIA Terrorist Biographic Note, Usama bin Ladin (U), CTC-005-00, January 2000.

482 In fact, after the Soviets were defeated in 1989, the recruits continued to flow into Pakistan and Afghanistan, including Saudi boys, bin Laden continuing to provide a home. See *Al Qaeda*, p. 84.

483 *Takfir ("Takfeer")*: " … the declaration that someone is a *kafir* or infidel; excommunication." *A Fury for God*, p. xxii.

"the act of declaring a non-practicing Muslim an apostate." *Inside Al-Qaeda and the Taliban: Beyond Bin Laden and 9/11*, p. xvi.

The idea of *takfir*, Ali Soufan writes, "wherein Muslims who don't practice Islam the same way are labeled apostates and are considered to be deserving of death." *The Black Banners*, p. 12.

Osama bin Laden consistently rejected the *takfirs'* philosophy—"although Muslim and Western critics alike consistently try to hang the tag on him." See *Osama bin Laden*, p. 43.

484 "The Salafi movements (from *al-salaf al-salih*, Arabic for righteous ancestors, referring to the two first generations of Islam), which emerged at the end of the nineteenth century, sought to respond to the political, cultural, and military challenge of the West. The *Salafis* seek the "purification" of Islam by returning to the uncorrupted form that they believed was practiced in the time of the prophet Muhammad and his companions. Salafi movements are found throughout the Muslim world. Some have a strictly religious, nonpolitical agenda. Others have evolved into or influenced the modernist tendency in Islam. Yet others have become radicalized and given sustenance to violent and terrorist groups." See *The Muslim World after 9/11*, p. 15.

"The *Salafiyaa* are a wide spectrum of people under a Sunni theological outlook that see the *Qur'an* and teachings of the Prophet Muhammad as the only legitimate source of religious conduct and reasoning, anti-Islamic establishment of madhabs. An off-shoot of the *Wahabbi* movement which can also constitute reformers… Using the terms *Salafi* and *Wahhabi* interchangeably to refer to terrorists alienates a major part of the Islamic world and is understood by Muslims as Western ignorance or a systematic attempt to disparage conservative Islamic practices." See DOD PowerPoint Briefing, IO Implications of Arabic Terminology and the GWOT, August 24, 2005.

485 The al Sabah were and are the ruling family of Kuwait. See CIA/DI, Al Sabah Royal Family and Tribal Affiliations: A Reference Aid (U), Biographic Series 09-88/MU, n.d. (1988), Secret/NF.

486 Gary Lee, "Kuwait's Campaign on the PR Front," The Washington Post, November 29, 1990; Ted Rowse, "Kuwaitgate—killing of Kuwaiti babies by Iraqi soldiers exaggerated," Washington Monthly, September 1992; Arthur E. Rowse, "How to build support for a war," *Columbia Journalism Review*, September/October 1992; Michael Muller, "The polls—a review: American public opinion and the Gulf War: Some polling issues," *Public Opinion Quarterly*, 57 (1993), pp. 80–91.

487 Many terrorism analysts describe Osama bin Laden as having an alcohol-sodden whoring youth—no evidence. Sen. Bob Graham, former chairman of the Intelligence Committee, picked up the Saudi propaganda: "During his college years, he was spotted frequently in Beirut's nightclubs, drinking, fighting, and seeking the attention of women." *Intelligence Matters*, p. 27. See other examples of Saudi propaganda making their way into history in *The Looming Tower*, p. 151; *Age of Sacred Terror*, p. 165; *In the Name of Osama Bin Laden*, p. 14; *Al Qaeda*, p. 24; *Losing Bin Laden*, p. 71, 74–75; *Mastermind*, pp. 3, 88–89.

Ali Soufan equally labels Mohammed Atta "an alcoholic" who "pounded shots in a bar prior to 9/11" and calls *al Qaeda* operatives "brainwashed." *The Black Banners*, pp. xx, xxiii.

488 See, for example, *The Looming Tower*, p. 151. James Bamford also wrote that in 1982, a year after graduation from university (which is itself wrong), bin Laden decided to commit himself full-time to Abdullah Azzam's Services Bureau, arranging to ship scores of construction vehicles from Saudi Arabia into

Afghanistan; *A Pretext for War*, p. 139. The Service's Bureau (also known as MAK) probably wasn't founded until after 1984.

489 Many suggest that Osama bin Laden was a failure in Sudan and *al Qaeda* ran out of money partly as a result of his loss of his fortune in foolish investments, while the 911 Commission found that he left Sudan with several successful factories and corporations operating, his money having been stolen by the regime in Khartoum.

"When Bin Ladin left [Sudan] in 1996, it appears that the Sudanese government expropriated all his assets: he left Sudan with practically nothing." See 911 Commission Report (Official Report), p. 170; and DOS cable, Nairobi 11468, "Sudan: Major Usama Bin Ladin Asset Deregistered," August 6, 1996.

490 Most pre-9/11 sources state that bin Laden graduated with a degree in civil engineering earned from King Abdul Aziz University in Jeddah, Saudi Arabia in May 1979. The prestigious Combating Terrorism Center agrees; see Combating Terrorism Center, U.S. Military Academy, *Military Ideology Atlas: Research Compendium*, November 2006, p. 354.

But after 9/11, U.S. government and intelligence officials evidently took the Saudi bait. George Tenet later testified that: "At age 22, Bin Ladin dropped out of school in Saudi Arabia and joined the Afghan resistance almost immediately following the Soviet invasion in December 1979. See Written Statement for the Record of the Director of Central Intelligence, Before the National Commission on Terrorist Attacks Upon the United States, March 24, 2004.

Michael Scheuer writes: "In 1978, Osama entered King Abdul Aziz University in Jeddah to study economics, business administration, and management; he is said to have developed an enthusiasm for the latter. He did not finish his studies or earn a degree, and I have found no transcript of the course he took or the grades he achieved." *Osama bin Laden*, p. 33. Bin Laden, born in March 1957, would have more likely entered university around 1974–1975.

491 Michael Scheuer later writes about government, media, and intelligence fascination with bin Laden's health, a complete fabrication of the truth perpetrated by Apex; *Osama bin Laden*, p. 110. See also Response to Query, Subject: Bin Ladin's Health, SW-99-401(TS/MU), March 17, 1999.

492 Abdullah Azzam was assassinated by three bombs planted along the car route he regularly took to his mosque in Peshawar on November 24, 1989.

Triple Cross speculates bin Laden was responsible, saying that within months, with the support of the Egyptians, he takes over Azzam's Services Bureau, using it as a basis for *al Qaeda*. But that timing is slightly off and ignores bin Laden's earlier collaboration with Azzam. See also *Al Qaeda*, p. 82; *Osama bin Laden*, pp. 11–12.

Peter Lance writes, "The murders remain unsolved, and although he [bin Laden] expressed public grief at their deaths, some U.S. intelligence officials believe that Osama bin Laden himself gave the order for the hit. See *1000 Years for Revenge*, p. 41. *The Cell*, p. 64, also suggests bin Laden, or perhaps the Blind *Sheikh*.

Michael Scheuer writes, "Despite constant rumors, no evidence proves that bin Laden was in any way involved in the 1989 assassination of Azzam and his two sons." See *Osama bin Laden*, p. 59. He also discusses the actual disagreements between bin Laden and Azzam over support for the Afghan Northern Alliance, the only group Azzam thought capable of uniting the country into a pure Islamic nation. Bin Laden also supposedly wanted the Arabs concentrated, while Azzam supported their dispersal. But Scheuer writes, "Despite constant rumors, no evidence proves that bin Laden was in any way involved in the 1989 assassination of Azzam and his two sons." See *Osama bin Laden*, p. 59.

Steve Coll provides insight to Azzam's condescension towards bin Laden, perhaps even true, at *The Bin Ladens*, p. 336.

Ali Soufan suspects Dr. Zawahiri was responsible for Azzam's death: "While before Azzam's death Zawahiri had denounced him in public, after his death he pretended that they had been the best of friends." *The Black Banners*, p. 32.

A Fury for God, p. 211, doesn't even mention bin Laden among the suspects, saying that "the most likely candidate is an Afghani terror group controlled by the ISI."

493 Like all good propaganda, the inside details were there: Bin Laden's attraction to the Egyptians was that he could see that his inexperienced Arab martyrs were far overshadowed by Zawahiri's highly skilled cadre of former military and police officers, Mohammed Atef (Abu Hafs al-Masri), Sayd al-Adl and Abu Ubaydah al-Banshiri—all of whom 'took over' leadership position in *al Qaeda*—suggested a good movement gone awry for the political ends of 'radicals' and political men with objectives other than Islam.

494 *Through Our Enemies' Eyes*, p. 131.

495 George Tenet later wrote: "In 1991, the Saudis were thrilled to see him decamp for Sudan." *At the Center of the Storm*, p. 101.

496 "According to ex-CIA official Vince Cannistraro, who was advising the Saudi royal family on security issues at the time, the Saudis solved their dilemma by convincing bin Laden that the U.S. forces stationed in Saudi Arabia had been tasked by the CIA to kill him. The Saudis, Cannistraro says, then staged a dramatic midnight 'escape,' pretending to spirit bin Laden out of the country for his own safety." See *The Cell*, p. 159.

497 In April 2003, the Combined Air Operations Center (CAOC) would move from Prince Sultan Air Base in Saudi Arabia to Al Udeid, Qatar.

498 Madeleine Jana Korbel Albright was secretary of state from January 23, 1997–January 20, 2001.

499 On October 31, 1998, President Clinton signed into law the Iraq Liberation Act of 1998, making regime change formal American policy and authorizing $100 million to support the Iraq opposition.

The act provides significant new discretionary authorities to assist the opposition in its struggle against the Iraqi regime. It declares that "[i]t should be the policy of the United States to support efforts to remove the regime headed by Saddam Hussein from power in Iraq and to promote the emergence of a democratic government to replace that regime." In signing the Act, the president stated that the U.S. "looks forward to a democratically supported regime that would permit us to enter into a dialogue leading to the reintegration of Iraq into normal international life."

500 See Teresa Brawner Bevis, *A World History of Higher Education Exchange: The Legacy of American Scholarship* (Palgrave Macmillan, 2019), p. 178ff; Scott Carlson, "Mideast Unrest Reawakens Concern Over Taint of Foreign Money," *Chronicle of Higher Education*, March 20, 2011.

501 Princes Turki and Bandar, according to Steve Coll, did meet with Clinton in the White House to curry favor; and walked away "disconcerted, shaving their heads" about him. The Saudis though did write a check for $20 million to fund a Middle East studies program at the University of Arkansas, "a small housewarming gift for a new friend." *Ghost Wars*, pp. 262–263.

502 This refers to President George H. W. Bush, not President George W. Bush, his son.

Chapter 28

503 CIA analytic report, "The Plot and the Plotters (U)," June 1, 2003, p. 16.

504 The story of Ziad Jarrah and Aysel Senguen is told in Dirk Laabs and Terry McDermott, "Prelude to 9/11: A Hijacker's Love, Lies," *Los Angeles Times*, January 27, 2003; Fouad Ajami, "The Making of a Hijacker: The Banal Life and Barbarous Deed of a 9/11 Terrorist," *The New Republic*, September 15, 2011; and *Der Spiegel, Inside 9-11: What Really Happened* (St. Martin's Paperbacks, 2002).

505 *Surah an-Nahl* [16:89], *Qur'an.*

506 In Islamic law, *jizya* (جزية) "tax per head" is the per capita yearly taxation levied on non-Islamic residents. Jizya is mentioned in the *Qur'an*, and it is believed to have been adapted from systems of taxation and tribute that were established in the Byzantine (395–1453 AD) and Sasanian (224–651 AD) empires.

507 *Surah An-Nisa* [4:135], *Qur'an.*

508 Osama bin Laden, "Declaration of War against the Americans Occupying the Land of the Two Holy Places," August 1996.

509 Violence and separation in the Chechen Republic, an ethnic enclave and Autonomous Republic previously recognized by the Soviet Union, began soon after disintegration in 1991. Moscow clandestinely supplied separatist forces with financial and military support, and starting on December 1, 1994, openly began military operations to "restore constitutional order." The majority of ethnic Chechens are Muslims.

510 CIA, intelligence report, interrogation of Khallad, January 14, 2004.

511 Though Jarrah and Senguen married in an Islamic ceremony, it was not recognized under German law. After 9/11, Senguen only acknowledged to German authorities that she and Jarrah were engaged. See German *Bundeskriminalamt* (BKA) [Federal Criminal Police Office] Report, Investigative Summary re: Jarrah, July 18, 2002; and German BKA Report, Investigative Summary re: Shehhi, July 9, 2002.

512 The expression is said to refer to some mystical place in Yemen, near Hadramawt: "In it were castles of gold and silver and dwelling places under which flowed rivers ... three hundred thousand castles all made of jewels ..." See Dirk Laabs and Terry McDermott, "Prelude to 9/11: A Hijacker's Love, Lies," *Los Angeles Times*, January 27, 2003.

513 CIA analytic report, "The Plot and the Plotters (U)," June 1, 2003, pp. 91–92.

514 See FBI, Working Draft Chronology of Events for Hijackers and Associates; CIA, intelligence report, interrogation of Khallad, January 14, 2004; KSM et al Indictment, pp. 16–17.

515 CIA, intelligence report, interrogation of Khallad, January 14, 2004.

516 Mohammed Atef, See also Project Sumner, Name List Working Paper (U), n.d. (2000?) (TS-MU-00-16).

517 Osama bin Laden was added to the FBI's "Ten Most Wanted" list after the African Embassy bombings in 1998.

518 Ras Al Khaimah is one of the seven emirates that make up the United Arab Emirates (UAE), in the northeast, with a population of some 400,000.

519 CIA, intelligence report, interrogation of Ramzi Binalshibh, October 1, 2002.

520 *Surah An-Nur* [24:30], *Qur'an.*

521 Israel Prime Minister Yitzhak Rabin was assassinated on November 4, 1995 at the end of a Tel Aviv rally in support of the Oslo Accords (signed on September 13, 1993). The gunman Yigal Amir, a student, was apprehended within seconds by people in the crowd.

522 The World Trade Organization protests took place in Seattle in 1999, disrupting the Ministerial Conference from November 28–December 3, 1999.

523 CIA, intelligence report, interrogation of Khallad, January 14, 2004.

524 *Surah al-Baqarah* [2:190], *Qur'an.*

525 *Surah al-Mai'dah* [5:32], *Qur'an.*

526 CIA analytic report, "The Plot and the Plotters (U)," June 1, 2003, p. 93.

Chapter 29

527 Project Sumner Timeline, V38, n.d. (2008) (TS/SP/MU).

528 KSM Debrief Papers, 2005.

529 There was at least one public warning, if at the eleventh hour. The day before, Ali Soufan points out, the London-based *al-Hayat* newspaper published a message from Doctor Zawahiri and the Egyptian Islamic Jihad: "We wish to inform the Americans that their message has been received, and we are preparing our answer, with the help of God, in the only language they will understand." See *The Black Banners*, p. 100.

530 FFor background, see CIA intelligence report, *Al Qaeda* Targeting Study of U.S. Embassy Nairobi, prepared December 23, 1993, updated April 5, 1999; CIA Terrorist Biographic Note, Usama bin Ladin (U), CTC-005-00, January 2000; *Case Studies in Terrorism-Related Cases (03/26/2008)*, American Embassy Bombings in Kenya and Tanzania, pp. 20ff.

531 Testimony of DCI George J. Tenet, before the SSCI [Senate Select Committee on Intelligence] hearing on Current and Projected National Security Threats, January 28, 1998, as prepared for delivery.

532 On January 25, 1993, Pakistani national Mir Aimal Kansi killed two CIA employees and wounded three others in their cars as they were waiting at a stoplight to turn into the Agency headquarters in McLean, Virginia.

533 The misspellings here are reflected in George Tenet's written testimony on January 28, 1998. It was Kansi not Kasi; Kasi was the alias he used to get a visa in Karachi.

534 CIA memo, CTC Director Geoff O'Connell to DCI Tenet, "Information Paper on Usama Bin Ladin," February 12, 1998 (with attached paper, "Next Steps Against Usama Bin Ladin," prepared for the CIA director's meeting with NSA [National Security Advisor] [Samuel] Berger scheduled for February 13, 1998.

535 On June 17, 1997, the FBI arrested Mir Amal Kansi in Pakistan after a four-year hunt. See *My FBI*, p. 282; *At the Center of the Storm*, p. 43.

536 CIA intelligence report, *Al Qaeda* Targeting Study of U.S. Embassy Nairobi, prepared December 23, 1993, April 5, 1999; CIA Terrorist Biographic Note, Usama bin Ladin (U), CTC-005-00, January 2000; *Case Studies in Terrorism-Related Cases (03/26/2008)*, American Embassy Bombings in Kenya and Tanzania, pp. 20ff.

537 Department of State, "Report of the Accountability Review Boards, Bombings of the US Embassies in Nairobi, Kenya and Dar es Salaam, Tanzania, on August 7, 1998," January 1999; CIA briefing materials, "Bombings in Nairobi and Dar es

Salaam—An Update," August 14, 1998.

Chapter 30

538 George Tenet later wrote: "We believe that a dozen or more terrorists were killed ..." *At the Center of the Storm*, p. 117. Sandy Berger would later testify before the 911 Commission that "twenty to thirty *al Qaeda* lieutenants were killed." Former NSC staff aides Benjamin and Simon say that about 60 people were killed overall. See *Age of Sacred Terror*, p. 260.

539 The presence of Pakistan's military intelligence service and its *Harakat ul Ansar* trainees near Khost is discussed in 911 Commission Report (Official Report), p. 123. See also DOS memo, [Rick] Inderfurth to [Strobe] Talbott [deputy secretary of state], "Pakistani Links to Kashmiri Militants," August 23, 1998; *Against all Enemies*, p. 189; *Ghost Wars*, p. 439; *My Life*, p. 803

540 Project Sumner Timeline, V38, n.d. (2008) (TS/SP/MU).

541 KSM Debrief Papers, 2005.

542 Memorandum of email exchange with KSM, August 28, 1998 (TS/SP/MU).

543 Project Sumner Timeline, V38, n.d. (2008) (TS/SP/MU).

544 ADCI(SP), SP Analysis, Analysis and Translation of KSM Letter to AW, dated (?) August 21, 1998 (TS/SP/MU).

545 George Tenet later wrote: "as we were searching for ways to respond, we received a godsend: signals intelligence revealed that a meeting would be held by bin Laden. We were accustomed to getting intelligence about where UBL [Osama bin Laden] had been. This was a rarity: intelligence predicting where he was going." *At the Center of the Storm*, p. 115.

Richard Clarke, of course, takes credit; "*I* read a CIA report from a source in Afghanistan that bin Laden and his top staff were planning a meeting on August 20 to review the results of their attacks and plan the next wave... we had the opportunity not merely to stage a retaliatory bombing, but also a chance to get bin Laden and his top deputies ..." See *Against all Enemies*, p. 184 [emphasis added]. See also CIA memo, "Khowst and the Meeting of Islamic Extremist Leaders on 20 Aug.," August 17, 1998; 911 Commission Report (Official Report), p. 116; *Ghost Wars*, p. 409; *Without Hesitation*, p. 347.

546 George Tenet later wrote: "We never were able to determine if his departure was happenstance or if he was somehow tipped off." *At the Center of the Storm*, p. 117. See also *Ghost Wars*, p. 410. Berger later told the 911 Commission that "bin Laden was missed by a matter of hours." See Samual Berger testimony to 911 Commission. Former Joint Chiefs of Staff chairman Gen. Richard Myers later writes: "after the attacks on the Afghan camps we learned that Usama bin Laden and his senior associates had left the Zawhar Kili training center only hours before the cruise missile strike." *Eyes on the Horizon*, p. 129.

547 On May 28, 1998, John Miller of ABC News interviewed Osama bin Laden in Khost, Afghanistan. Not only are two of the embassy plotters in the background (Rashed Daoud Al-Owhali and Jihad Mohammed Ali (aka Azzam) and Osama bin Laden is in front of a map of Africa, his warning of attacks on American targets providing a clue about Africa.

548 Richard Clarke later writes that the "CIA knew there had been an al Qaeda cell in Kenya, but they had thought that, working with Kenyan police, the U.S. government had broken it up." See *Against all Enemies*, p. 183.

549 The U.S. received three warnings of possible attacks on the Nairobi embassy in the year leading up to the bombing. In August 1997, Wadih el-Hage was questioned by the FBI and his computer was examined. However, documents from a search of his house were not translated due to "resource constraints." It was later learned that El-Hage had established the Kenyan al Qaeda cell. In the summer of 1997, an informant told the CIA that al Haramein, a charity working with Somali refugees, was planning an attack on the embassy. According to the CIA, there has never been any evidence linking the charity to the bombing. In November 1997, Mustafa Mahmoud Saud Ahmed approached the embassy to report a truck bomb plot. He was discredited as a fabricator, although he was later implicated in the Dar es Salaam attack. See ISB Study on Educing Information, Intelligence Interviewing: Teaching Papers and Case Studies, p. 123.

The sealed indictment was dated June 10, 1998. Osama bin Laden and an unnamed co-conspirator are charged with conspiracy to destroy national defense utilities in the United States. (It is unsealed in November 1998). See Joint Inquiry, p. 129; *The Looming Tower*, p. 266.

On November 4, 1998, indictments for Osama Bin Laden, his military commander, Muhammad Atef, and al Qaeda members Wadith El Hage, Fazul Abdullah Mohhamed, Mohammed Sadeek Odeh, and Mohammed Rashed Daoud al-Owhali were returned before U.S. District Court for the Southern District of New York.

550 In November 1997, Mustafa Mahmoud Saud Ahmed approached the Tunisian embassy to report a truck bomb plot. He was dismissed as a fabricator, although he was later implicated in the Dar es Salaam attack. See ISB Study on Educing Information, Intelligence Interviewing: Teaching Papers and Case Studies, p. 123; CIA operational cable dated November 3, 1997.

"While the State Department focused on inadequate physical security, the Counterterrorism Center knew there had been an intelligence failure. There were so many indicators that an attack was in the works: the dismissed walk-in was only an important one of them." *Denial and Deception: An Insider's View of the CIA*, p. 279.

551 Richard Preston, *The Cobra Event* (Random House, 1997).

552 In April 1998, President Clinton hosted a roundtable at the White House with Dr. J. Craig Venter, head of the Institute for Genomic Research; Nobel Prize winning molecular biologist Joshua Lederberg; and Jerry Hauer, director of emergency services in New York, to discuss biological weapons. The three urged the President to start a crash program to improve U.S. public health capabilities and build a national vaccine stockpile. See *Age of Sacred Terror*, p. 254.

553 William Sebastian Cohen, secretary of defense, January 24, 1997–January 20, 2001.

554 See Maureen Down, "Liberties, Anthrax, Shmanthrax," *The New York Times*, November 19, 1997, p. A31.

555 On March 20, 1995, a Japanese doomsday cult unleashed sarin gas in the Tokyo subway system, killing 13 and seriously injuring more than 50.

556 On May 11, 1998, India conducted the first of three nuclear tests, not only a surprise to the CIA, but CIA analysts had explicitly reported that India would not conduct a nuclear test. Pakistan conducted five nuclear tests May 28–30 in response to India. George Tenet later writes: "We knew that both countries had nuclear desires, intent, and capabilities ... That said, the timing of the test caught us by surprise." *At the Center of the Storm*, p. 44. The official investigation is much less forgiving: CIA, The Jeremiah Report: Intelligence Community's Performance on the Indian Nuclear Tests, June 1, 1998.

The significance of India going nuclear seemed not to factor in the American assessments of bin Laden's WMD rhetoric even though his May 1998 announcement came when India tested nuclear weapons; see *Ghost Wars*, p. 394

557 International Front for Fight the Jews and the Crusaders, "The Nuclear Bomb of Islam," May 29, 1998.

558 On November 21, 1999, the FBI elevated counterterrorism to a standing division within FBI HQ separate from the national security division.

"In 1997, responsibility for managing and coordinating NSA's global SIGINT efforts against international terrorism was moved to a newly created operations analysis organization called the Global Issues and Weapons Systems Group, or W Group ... A unit within W Group, designated W9B, was the NSA Terrorism Customer Service Center, which served as the primary interface between NSA's collectors and analysts and the agency's intelligence consumers." Matthew M Aid, "All Glory is Fleeting: SIGINT and the Fight Against International Terrorism," *Intelligence and National Security*, Vol. 18, No. 4 (Winter 2003), pp. 72–120.

559 On November 4, 1998, the U.S. Attorney's Office for the Southern District of New York unsealed its indictment of Osama bin Laden, charging him with conspiracy to attack U.S. defense installations. Also indicted were the *al Qaeda* military chief Mohammed Atef (Abu Hafs al-Masri) and four others suspected of being involved in the African embassy bombings, including Mohamed Sadiq Odeh and Mohammed Rashed Daoud Al-Owhali.

560 Jamal al-Fadl told of his own supposed involvement in attempts to buy highly enriched uranium from South Africa. He provided chapter and verse regarding Sudanese and Iraqi cooperation to develop chemical weapons in Khartoum, as well as details of *al Qaeda* contacts with Iranian, Pakistani, former Soviet and North Korean chemical and nuclear experts and brokers.

Al Qaeda, he said, had not only attempted to acquire raw materials that could be used to develop these very chemical and biological weapons but also had worked on radiological, and nuclear weapons. Bin Laden had even hired scientific specialists to work on specific projects, an Egyptian physicist to work on nuclear and chemical weapons in Sudan, and a chemical and biological specialist to work in Southeast Asia. See *At the Center of the Storm*, p. 102.

See FBI TD-314/00456-96, FBI report of investigation, interview of Jamal al-Fadl, November 10, 1996; FBI Form 302 (witness interview record), Subject: Interview of Al-Fadl, November 4, 1996. and later, CIA intelligence report, Usama Bin Ladin's Attempts to Acquire Uranium, March 18, 1997; CIA intelligence report, Bin Ladin links to materials related to WMD, March 20, 1997.

Various reports lend veracity to the al-Fadl claims about WMD. Benjamin and Simon write: "By early 1994, if not before, [*Al Qaeda*] had begun work on acquiring weapons of mass destruction. Taking advantage of his close ties to the NIF [National Islamic Front in Sudan], bin Laden became involved in a Sudanese government operation to produce nerve gas." *Age of Sacred Terror*, p. 128. See also *Triple Cross*, p. 261; *Al Qaeda*, p. 84; *1000 Years for Revenge*, p. 51; *The Looming Tower*, p. 191.

Richard Clarke later writes that after the WMD intelligence came in from al-Fadl on *al Qaeda*, combined with the Tokyo nerve gas attack, and the attack in Oklahoma City (all by 1996), "I became increasingly concerned with our vulnerability to domestic terrorism and to terrorists using nerve gas or other weapons of mass destruction." *Your Government Failed You*, p. 158.

Michael Scheuer, in his post 9/11 testimony also refers to WMD intelligence in 1995 changing the rules (despite the fact that al-Fadl didn't walk in until June 1996). See Joint Hearings, *Extraordinary Rendition in U.S. Counterterrorism Policy: The Impact on Transatlantic Relations*, April 17, 2007.

561 George Tenet had the al-Fadl material prepared into highly detailed reports just for the President's eyes only. See CIA analytic report, "Usama Bin Ladin Trying to Develop WMD Capability?" CTC 97-30002, January 6, 1997.

562 George Tenet later writes: "On our list of potential targets were businesses in Sudan and elsewhere in which he had been involved. These businesses not only were part of the terrorist financial network but also had possible connections with *al-Qaeda* attempts to obtain chemical and biological weapons." *At the Center of the Storm*, p. 115.

The target was called al Shifa. On October 8, 1999, Tenet told a Georgetown University audience that "[e]vidence that a U.S.-destroyed Sudanese pharmaceutical plant was manufacturing chemical-weapons components remains 'compelling,' despite growing international skepticism over the 1998 bombing ... .

'We were not wrong.'"

"You can still get a debate within the intelligence community on how good a target al-Shifa was," Tenet later disingenuously wrote, even after the facts became apparent that the intelligence on al Shifa's connection to WMD was in error. See *At the Center of the Storm*, p. 117.

Richard Clarke also later writes: "Reports had been reaching us for several years that Sudan sought to make chemical weapons. The reports from several sources, including UNSCOM [the United Nations Special Commission on Iraq], indicated that Sudan was making chemical bombs and artillery shells. There were few places in Sudan where the needed chemicals could be created. One was a chemical plant at Shifa ..." He goes on to say that the "CIA sought to determine whether the Shifa plant might be spending some of its time making lethal gas for weapons. To do so, CIA sent an agent to Khartoum to collect trace material that would have floated away from the plants in the air or in liquid runoff ... [soil samples were taken] ... Their tests revealed a chemical substance known as EMPTA [a prime ingredient in Iraqi nerve gas] ..." See *Against all Enemies*, p. 145.

According to the 911 Commission, Clarke speculated to Sandy Berger that a large Iraqi presence at chemical facilities in Khartoum was "probably a direct result of the Iraq–Al Qida agreement." Clarke added that VX precursor traces found near al Shifa were the "exact formula used by Iraq." See 911 Commission Report (Official Report), p. 128.

Benjamin and Simon later wrote: "Only weeks before the embassy bombings, CIA briefers came to the White House to inform the National Security Council staff about intelligence reporting regarding *al Qaeda*'s efforts to acquire weapons of mass destruction ... . What made this news riveting was evidence that the group might already be preparing an attack with the chemical agent VX ... Proof came in the form of a clump of dirt—a soil sample collected near the al-Shifa chemical plant in Khartoum." *Age of Sacred Terror*, p. 259.

A former CIA case officer later wrote: "The CIA had sensitive reporting on a request by Usama bin Ladin to Sudanese officials to help him obtain chemical weapons that could be used against U.S. installations. The CIA began monitoring Sudanese procurement of dual-use equipment and raw materials. Suspected bin Ladin front companies managed large parts of the procurement chain ... . More than any other activity it was the chemical weapons threat that raised bin Ladin's profile with the CIA." *Denial and Deception: An Insider's View of the CIA*, p. 189.

President Clinton later wrote: "I still believe we did the right thing there. The CIA had soil samples taken at the plant site that contained the chemical used to produce VX. In a subsequent terrorist trial in New York City, one of the witnesses testified that bin Laden had a chemical weapons operation in Khartoum. Despite the plain evidence, some people in the media tried to push the possibility that the action was a real-life version of Wag the Dog, a move in which a fictional President starts a made-for-TV war to distract public attention from his personal problems." *My Life*, p. 805.

Former Joint Chiefs of Staff Chairman Gen. Henry "Hugh" Shelton sees the whole Sudanese episode as a CIA failure. He describes taking the CIA-nominated Sudan targets to the Tank [the secure JCS conference room] to solicit the Joint

Chief's opinions. "Not only did they concur with my trepidation, but they were perplexed as to how something with a case that weak could ever have made it that far up the ladder. (If they thought that case was weak, they should have stuck around for six more years to see the case that the same outfit gave Colin Powell to take before the United Nations)." *Without Hesitation*, p. 346. After the attack, Shelton write, "the intel started to fade on us ... and it turned out that this CIA intelligence had not really been collected at the pharmaceutical plant, but rather three hundred yards away from it. And now—by the way—the quarter teaspoon of soil sample turned out to have been collected two years earlier." *Without Hesitation*, p. 350.

563 *Age of Sacred Terror*, p. 260.

564 CIA memo, "Khowst and the Meeting of Islamic Extremist Leaders on 20 Aug.," August 17, 1998. 911 Commission Report (Official Report), p. 116; *Ghost Wars*, p. 409; *Without Hesitation*, p. 347.

Tenet later wrote in his autobiography: "as we were searching for ways to respond, we received a godsend: signals intelligence revealed that a meeting would be held by bin Laden. We were accustomed to getting intelligence about where UBL had been. This was a rarity: intelligence predicting where he was going." *At the Center of the Storm*, p. 115.

Richard Clarke takes credit; "*I* read a CIA report from a source in Afghanistan that bin Laden and his top staff were planning a meeting on August 20 to review the results of their attacks and plan the next wave ... we had the opportunity not merely to stage a retaliatory bombing, but also a chance to get bin Laden and his top deputies ..." See *Against all Enemies*, p. 184 (emphasis added).

565 It later turned out (after 9/11) that the intelligence community learned that more than one of the camps that was bombed wasn't even directly associated with al Qaeda, particularly Khalden camp. See CIA intelligence assessment, "Countering Misconceptions About Training Camps in Afghanistan, 1990–2001," August 16, 2006.

566 *Against all Enemies*, p. 184.

567 See NSC memo, Berger to President Clinton, terrorist threat at the millennium, December 18, 1999; DOS cable, Riyadh 003900, "Saudis on USG Warning to Taliban Concerning UBL Threats," December 14, 1999; CIA, SEIB, "Bin Ladin to Exploit Looser Security During Holidays," December 3, 1999.

568 Director of Central Intelligence (DCI) Memorandum, "We are at War (U)," December 4, 1998, Secret. See also *At the Center of the Storm*, p. 119; Joint Inquiry, pp. 40, 46-47.

The Joint Inquiry later observed (p. 40): "The Intelligence Community as a whole, however, had only a limited awareness of this declaration. For example, some senior managers in the National Security Agency and the Defense Intelligence Agency say they were aware of the declaration. However, it was apparently not well known within the Federal Bureau of Investigation. In fact, the assistant director of the FBI's Counterterrorism Division testified to the Joint Inquiry into Intelligence Community Activities before and after the Terrorist Attacks of September 11, 2001 that he "was not specifically aware of that declaration of war" … . Neither were the deputy secretary of defense or the chairman of the Joint Chiefs of Staff aware of the DCI's declaration.

A year later, after President Clinton signed a new presidential finding (memorandum of notification) authorizing covert action, Tenet sent out another message to all CIA personnel overseas, saying, "The threat could not be more real … . Do whatever is necessary to disrupt UBL's [sic, Osama bin Laden's] plans … . The American people are counting on you and me to take every appropriate step to protect them during this period." See 911 Commission Report (Official Report), p. 176.

A memorandum of notification (MON), more commonly known as a "presidential finding," is the legally-required authorization to the intelligence community to undertake a covert action. It is required to be briefed to the leadership in the Congress.

Chapter 31

569 Project Sumner Timeline, V38, n.d. (2008) (TS/SP/MU).

570 A gangplank recruitment refers to a "cold pitch" of a source, where the case officer has little or no opportunity to become acquainted with the target, to develop the target to see if he or she might be amenable to such an approach. See Frederick P. Hitz, *The Great Game: The Myths and Reality of Espionage* (Vintage edition, 2005), pp. 14–15.

571 Pat Robertson, *The New World Order* (CBN Partners Edition; W Pub Group, 1991).

572 Department of State, "Soviet Active Measures"—Forgery, Disinformation, Political Operations," Special Report No. 88, October 1981.

573 KSM Debrief Papers, 2005.

574 The article is William Kristol and Robert Kagan, "Toward a Neo-Reaganite Foreign Policy," *Foreign Affairs*, July/August 1996.

575 Trans World Airlines Flight 800 (TWA 800) exploded and crashed into the Atlantic Ocean off Long Island on July 17, 1996, 12 minutes after takeoff from John F. Kennedy International Airport. See Pat Milton, "Salinger Stands By Story About TWA Missile Strike," Associated Press, November 13, 1996.

576 It isn't. See Chairman, Joint Chiefs of Staff, Justification for US Military Intervention in Cuba, March 13, 1962; in the release of the National Security Archive, April 30, 2001.

The National Security Archive writes: "This document, titled 'Justification for U.S. Military Intervention in Cuba' was provided by the JCS to Secretary of Defense Robert McNamara on March 13, 1962, as the key component of Northwoods. Written in response to a request from the Chief of the Cuba Project, Col. Edward Lansdale, the Top Secret memorandum describes U.S. plans to covertly engineer various pretexts that would justify a U.S. invasion of Cuba. These proposals—part of a secret anti-Castro program known as Operation Mongoose—included staging the assassinations of Cubans living in the United States, developing a fake "Communist Cuban terror campaign in the Miami area, in other Florida cities and even in Washington," including "sink[ing] a boatload of Cuban refugees (real or simulated)," faking a Cuban airforce [sic] attack on a civilian jetliner, and concocting a "Remember the Maine" incident by blowing up a U.S. ship in Cuban waters and then blaming the incident on Cuban sabotage. Bamford himself writes that Operation Northwoods "may be the most corrupt plan ever created by the U.S. government."

577 KSM Debrief Papers, 2005.

578 Michael Butter and Maurus Reinkowski, eds., *Conspiracy Theories in the United States and the Middle East: A Comparative Approach* (De Gruyter).

579 KSM Debrief Papers, 2005.

Chapter 32

580 Project Sumner Timeline, V38, n.d. (2008) (TS/SP/MU).

581 The Alfred P. Murrah Federal Building in Oklahoma City, Oklahoma, was bombed on April 19, 1995. It was attacked by Timothy McVeigh, an American unconnected in any way to Middle Eastern terrorism.

582 P. R. Kumaraswamy, "Monica Lewinsky in Middle Eastern Eyes," *Middle East Quarterly*, Volume 6, Number 1, March 1999.

583 KSM Debrief Papers, 2005.

584 CIA, Demographic and Economic Material Factors of the Middle East and Arab World, DI/MENA, March 1999 (S/NF/MU).

585 KSM Debrief Papers, 2005.

586 Project Sumner Timeline, V38, n.d. (2008) (TS/SP/MU).

587 KSM Debrief Papers, 2005.

588 *Your Government Failed You*, p. 157. Steve Coll goes one step further, writing: "One of the [1996] defectors, Jamal al-Fadl, described the existence and history of *Al Qaeda*—it was the first time *anyone in the U.S. government* had heard the name." *The*

Bin Ladens, p. 472 (emphasis added).

589 Project Sumner Timeline, V38, n.d. (2008) (TS/SP/MU).

590 Project Sumner Timeline, V38, n.d. (2008) (TS/SP/MU).

591 The game was actually created later. See Daniel J. Wakin, "AFTEREFFECTS: BEIRUT; Video Game Created by Militant Group Mounts Simulated Attacks Against Israeli Targets," *The New York Times*, May 18, 2003, p. A24.

592 Project Sumner Timeline, V38, n.d. (2008) (TS/SP/MU).

593 Project Sumner Timeline, V38, n.d. (2008) (TS/SP/MU).

Chapter 33

594 KSM would give a near identical speech to the Military Commission at Guantanamo in 2007; see Verbatim Transcript of Combatant Status Review Tribunal Hearing for ISN 10024, March 10, 2007.

595 KSM Debrief Papers, 2005.

596 KSM Debrief Papers, 2005.

597 Al-Ghazi Madani al Tayyib (aka Abu Fadhl al-Makkee), Saudi national; lost a leg during the anti-Soviet *jihad*; former head of *al Qaeda* finance committee; traveled to Europe in 1997 and was reportedly taken into custody by Saudi authorities in May 1997.
  The Tayyib story is told in 911 Commission, p. 122; 911 Commission, Monograph on Terrorist Financing, pp. 39–40; 911 Commission, Staff Statement Number 5, p. 10; *Age of Sacred Terror*, p. 288; *The Bin Ladens*, pp. 482, 488–489; and *The Cell*, p. 200.

598 The efforts on the part of the U.S. government to gain access to Tayyib's secrets become Exhibit A for the White House in demonstrating Saudi intransigence and non-cooperation, far more so than anything to do with their stiff-arming investigators after the attacks in Riyadh or Khobar Towers. The higher the financial connections, the more freaked out the Saudis got about revealing facts to Washington. Hence, the matter of Tayyib became a year's long and tense standoff between the two governments, Washington wanting access, the Saudis negotiating impossible conditions. Apex Watch, of course, watched it closely, already understanding the financial trail.
  The Madani story is told in 911 Commission Report (Official Report), p. 122; and 911 Commission Report (Official Report), Monograph on Terrorist Financing, pp. 39–40; 911 Commission Report (Official Report), Staff Statement Number 5, p. 10; *Age of Sacred Terror*, p. 288; *The Bin Ladens*, pp. 482, 488–489; and *The Cell*, p. 200.
  See also CIA talking points, Vice President's Meeting with Crown Prince

Abdullah, September 24, 1998; CIA analytic report, "Usama Bin Ladin's Finances: Some Estimates of Wealth, Income, and Expenditures," CTC IR 98-40006, November 17, 1998; CIA analytic report, "Usama Bin Ladin: Some Saudi Financial Ties Probably Intact," OTI IR 99-005CX, January 11, 1999.

Richard Clarke later writes about learning that much of *al Qaeda's* financing came from Saudi Arabia, both from individuals and from quasi-governmental charities. "We decided that we needed to have a serious talk with the Saudis as well as with a few of the financial centers in the region. We recognized that the Saudi regime had been largely uncooperative on previous law enforcement-focused investigations of terrorism ... so we wanted a different approach ... . So we asked Vice President Gore to talk to the Crown Prince about the problem and about accepting a U.S. delegation that would meet to discuss only this subject [material assistance to the terrorists] with representatives of all relevant Saudi agencies together, so that there would be no run-around ... We wanted to avoid a typical pattern of Saudi behavior we had seen: achingly slow progress, broken promises, denial, and cooperation limited to specific answers to specific questions."

The Saudis agreed to a set of meetings in 1999. Behind the request for clandestine cooperation was a threat of public sanctions, which worried the State Department. Some at the FBI also didn't like the fact that a discussion of finances, which they saw strictly as a law enforcement issue, was going to take place outside their channel. The CIA Saudi desk also protested, jealously guarding "their" channel with Saudi intelligence. The Saudis protested the focus on continuing contacts between Osama bin Laden and his wealthy, influential family, who were supposed to have broken off all ties with him. "How can you tell a mother not to call her son," they asked. See *Against all Enemies*, pp. 194–195.

599 KSM Debrief Papers, 2005. "'Deception' ... refers to the effort to cause an adversary to believe something is not true, to believe a 'cover story' rather than the truth, with the goal of leading him to react in a way that serves one's own interests, rather than his." See Abram Shulsky, "Elements of strategic denial and deception," in *Trends in Organized Crime*, Vol. 6, Issue 1 (2000), pp. 17–31.

600 CIA analytic report, "Usama Bin Ladin's Finances: Some Estimates of Wealth, Income, and Expenditures," CTC IR 98-40006, November 17, 1998.

The question of bin Laden's finances returned again and again, picked up from Saudi propaganda. Later, many suggested that bin Laden was a failure as business, and particularly during his time in Sudan, and that *al Qaeda* ran out of money partly as a result of his loss of his fortune in foolish investments. The 911 Commission found that he left Sudan with several successful factories and corporations operating. "When Bin Ladin left in 1996, it appears that the Sudanese government expropriated all his assets: he left Sudan with practically nothing." See 911 Commission, p. 170.

See also DOS cable, Nairobi 11468, "Sudan: Major Usama Bin Ladin Asset Deregistered," August 6, 1996.

601 Steve Coll makes an important point about Osama bin Laden's fortunes, or in this case, what he calls his "exaggerated' personal fortune as characterized by many. "To some extent, their exaggerations are explained by Osama's fundraising achievements; his ability to attract outside donations and government support had made him appear wealthier to his comrades in Pakistan that he actually was. Still, the prosaic truth about his personal finances mattered greatly—because of misreporting about Osama's wealth, his adversaries, particularly those in the United States, would repeatedly misunderstand him." See *The Bin Ladens*, p. 348.

Later Steve Coll points out that in 2000, U.S. intelligence realized that: "Over his lifetime, Osama had received a total of about $27 million [from his family] ..." *The Bin Ladens*, p. 493.

602 Bidoon, meaning "without" and signifying without citizenship, are Arabs living without citizenship in the Gulf States, particularly in Kuwait, Bahrain, the UAE, and Qatar. See U.S. Census Bureau, National Security Unit, "(S) Bidoon Concentration and Affiliations (U)," report for the CIA/DI/NE, MU-90-07, September 1990.

Chapter 34

603 Project Sumner Timeline, V38, n.d. (2008) (TS/SP/MU).

604 There is no record of the thinking behind Project Sumner at this point in time, but here is one document that survives and lays out the plan from that time period; Project Sumner, PowerPoint Briefing, Strategic Outlook and Operational Scenario (S), TS/SI/P, June 1999 (TS-MU-99-146).

605 Project Sumner was the Apex Watch codename for assistance to KSM in his planes operation.

Chapter 35

606 Tawfiq Muhammad Salih bin Rashid al Atash, known as Khallad; aka Salah Saeed Mohammed Bin Yousaf, Tawfiq bin Attash, Tawfiq Attash Khallad, and Khallad bin Attash. See CIA, intelligence report, interrogation of Khallad, January 14, 2004; 911 Commission Report (Official Report), p. 192; *At the Center of the Storm*, p. 197.

607 CIA analytic report, "The Plot and the Plotters (U)," June 1, 2003, p. 13.

608 KSM Debrief Papers, 2005.

609 According to Ali Soufan, bin Laden selected Khalid al-Mihdhar to be Atta's "deputy." *The Black Banners*, p. 275. There is no particular evidence that he performed any special duties in this regard and KSM says he gave him no responsibilities in the United States. See KSM Debrief Papers, 2005.

610 Ahmed al-Hada, a Yemeni, was the operator of an *al Qaeda* "switchboard" discovered after the African embassy bombings. See FBI Form 302 (witness interview record), Subject: Interview of Mohammed al-Owhali, August 23, 1998; *The Black Banners*, p. 87; Joint Inquiry, pp. 155–156.

611 Khalid a-Mihdhar (aka Mihddar; Khalid Muhammad 'Abdallah Al-Mihdar; Sinan al-Maki; Sannan Al-Makki; Khalid Bin Muhammad; 'Addallah Al-Mihdar; Khalid Mohammad Al-Saqaf; the "fisherman"), Saudi national, born May 6, 1975. See, e.g., CIA (operational) cable, "UBL Associate Travel to Malaysia—Khalid Bin Muhammad bin 'Abdallah al-Mihdhar," January 5, 2000.

612 This is confirmed in Biographic Note, "'Khalid al-Mihdhar,' Saudi GID Agent," MU-04-99 (S/NF/A), July 1999; CIA (operational) cable, "UBL Associate Travel to Malaysia—Khalid Bin Muhammad bin 'Abdallah al-Mihdhar," January 5, 2000.

613 *Sayyid* is an honorific title denoting people accepted as descendants of the Prophet Muhammad and his cousin and son-in-law Imam Ali through his grandsons.

614 Steve Coll later describes the influence of the Wadi Doan in *The Bin Ladens*, pp. 22–23, and their son, Khalid, though he mistakenly says he piloted the plane that crashed into the Pentagon on 9/11. That was Hani Hanjour.

615 Nawaf M.S. al-Hazmi (aka Rabia al Makki, Nawaf al Harbi); Saudi; brother of Salem al-Hazmi.
    Salem Mohamed Salem al-Hazmi; Saudi national, born February 2, 1981 in Mecca; brother of Nawaf al-Hazmi.

616 On March 21, 1999, Nawaf al-Hazmi was issued Saudi passport #B673987 in Mecca, Saudi Arabia. On April 3, 1999, al-Hazmi obtained an American visa in Jeddah. On April 6, 1999, Khalid al-Mihdhar was issued Saudi passport #B721156. On April 7, 1999, al-Mihdhar received an American visa in Jeddah. See FBI, Working Draft Chronology of Events for Hijackers and Associates.
    According to the FBI, "On 4/9/99, Salem Mohamed Salem Al-Hazmi, date of birth, 2/2/81, place of birth, Mecca, Saudi Arabia, was issued a U.S. B1/B2 visa with Saudi passport #C562647. On 1/1/00, Salem Al-Hazmi departed Saudi Arabia to Yemen. On 1/24/00, Al-Hazmi departed Sana'a, Yemen to the UAE." FBI, Summary of Penttbom Investigation, p. 5; CIA (operational) cable, Mihdhar's visa application, January 5, 2000.

617 The supposed brother-in-law was Ahmed Mohammed Haza al-Darbi (aka Abdul Aziz al-Januoubi). See Substitution of the Testimony of Khalid Sheikh Mohammed, p. 15; *The Black Banners*, p. 79.

618 CIA, intelligence report, interrogation of Khallad, January 14, 2004.

619 KSM Debrief Papers, 2005.

620 The fiction of the fisherman persisted even long after 9/11, despite al-

Mihdhar's veteran *al Qaeda* status and family relationship with a senior *al Qaeda* administrator in Yemen, and his actual status working for Saudi intelligence. An article in *The Washington Post* on the one year anniversary of 9/11 said that when the Hamburg cell arrived in Kandahar, waiting were Khalid al-Mihdhar, a "former Red Sea fisherman who came from Mecca," and Nawaf al-Hazmi, a merchant also from Mecca, *according to interviews with officials at the Saudi Interior Ministry's offices in Jiddah* [Jeddah] (emphasis added). See Peter Finn, "Hamburg's Cauldron of Terror: Within Cell of 7, Hatred Toward U.S. Grew and Sept. 11 Plot Evolved," *The Washington Post*, September 11, 2002, p. A1.

Chapter 36

621 911 Commission Memorandum for the Record, Event: Interview of Caysan Bin Don, also known as Usama Dyson and Clayton Morgan, April 20, 2004; 911 Commission Memorandum for the Record, Subject: Location: Interview of Omar Al-Bayoumi Conference Palace, Riyadh, October 16–17, 2003.

622 The factual story of Nawaf al-Hazmi and Khalid al-Mihdhar is taken from 911 Commission Report (Official Report), p. 219; 911 Commission Report (Official Report), Staff Statement Number 16, pp. 4–16; and Joint Inquiry, pp. 131, 172ff. The report CIA analytic report, "The Plot and the Plotters (U)," June 1, 2003, contains nothing on Omar al-Bayoumi.

623 There is a GID report: Biographic Note, 'Khalid al-Mihdhar,' Saudi GID Agent MU-04-99 (S/NF/A), July 1999.

624 Memorandum for the Record, Subject: Location: Interview of Omar Al-Bayoumi Conference Palace, Riyadh, October 16–17, 2003.

625 GID National Security Department, Faisal Intelligence Academy Organization and Functions, Saudi Top Secret (MU), n.d. (1999); 911 Commission, Staff Statement 16, p. 4.

626 911 Commission Memorandum for the Record, Subject: Location: Interview of Omar Al-Bayoumi Conference Palace, Riyadh, October 16–17, 2003.

627 911 Commission Memorandum for the Record, Event: Interview of Caysan Bin Don, also known as Usama Dyson and Clayton Morgan, April 20, 2004.

628 See, in particular FBI classified letter report, "Omar al Bayoumi, Employed by Dallah al Baraka," San Diego, April 15, 2002, Secret; Project Sumner, Name List Working Paper (U), n.d. (2000?) (TS-MU-00-16).

Former Sen. Bob Graham of Florida, who was a member of the Senate Intelligence Committee, wrote about al-Bayoumi in his book *Intelligence Matters*. According to Sen. Graham, in 1993, Bayoumi began work for Ercan, which in turn contracted with Dallah Avco Aviation, "a Saudi government contractor owned by Saleh Kamel, a wealthy Saudi who belongs to what is known as 'the Golden

Chain,' which provides money to Osama bin Laden and *al Qaeda* on a regular basis." See *Intelligence Matters*, p. 167.

In 1999, al-Bayoumi was fired by Ercan, but the company was urged by the director general of Saudi Civil Aviation, that the government wanted Bayoumi's contract renewed "as quickly as possible."

"From his 'ghost job' al-Bayoumi was getting paid a monthly salary of about $2,800 with allowances of $465 a month." See *Intelligence Matters*, p. 167.

In March 2000, Bayoumi's monthly allowance from Ercan rose by a factor of eight, from $465 to $3,700. "They stayed at that level until December, when al-Hazmi left for Arizona. During that time al-Bayoumi got nearly $30,000 more than he would have normally." See *Intelligence Matters*, p. 167

629 Joint Inquiry, pp. 173–174.

630 GID National Security Department, Procedures for Contact Officer Responsibilities in Overseas Missions, Saudi Top Secret (MU), n.d. (1999); also FBI, TD-314/00459-99. For more reporting on Bayoumi's official intelligence connection, see Joint Inquiry, pp. 172ff; *Intelligence Matters*, pp. 19ff, 24–25ff; *The Looming Tower*, pp. 314ff; *Your Government Failed You*, p. 167.

The 911 Commission concluded that al-Bayoumi was not an intelligence agent or an extremist: "Bayoumi is a devout Muslim, obliging and gregarious. He spent much of his spare time involved in religious study and helping run a mosque in El Cajon, about 15 miles from San Diego. It is certainly possible that he has dissembled about some aspects of his story, perhaps to counter suspicion. On the other hand, we have seen no credible evidence that he believed in violent extremism or knowingly aided extremist groups. Our investigators who have dealt directly with him and studied his background find him to be an unlikely candidate for clandestine involvement with Islamist extremists." See 911 Commission Report (Official Report), pp. 217–218.

The Joint Inquiry on the other hand, in a heavily redacted section, speculates that al-Bayoumi was a Saudi intelligence officer; Joint Inquiry, p. 174.

631 Substitution of the Testimony of Khalid Sheikh Mohammed, pp. 8–9.

632 Masjid Ar-Ribat al-Islami is located at 7173 Saranac Street, La Mesa, California 92115.

The Joint Inquiry later reported (p. 27) that al-Hazmi and al-Mihdhar were in touch with "a local imam, who was the subject of an FBI counterterrorism inquiry for part of the time that the future hijackers were in San Diego, served as their spiritual advisor when they were living in San Diego." The man is evidently al-Bayoumi.

633 The Joint Inquiry reported: "Nawaf Al-Hazmi moved to San Diego at the suggestion of Omar al-Bayoumi, who had previously been the focus of an FBI counterterrorism [deleted] inquiry. In San Diego, they stayed at al-Bayoumi's apartment for several days until he was able to find them an apartment. He then co-signed their lease, paid [page 29] their security deposit and first month's rent, arranged a party to welcome them to the San Diego community, and tasked another individual to help them become acclimated to the United States." See Joint Inquiry, pp. 27, 172ff.

On February 4, 2000, al-Mihdhar opened a Bank of America account in San Diego with $9,900 and got a Visa debit card. Al-Mihdhar and al-Hazmi signed a four-month lease for apartment #150, Parkwood Apartments, 6401 Mount Ada Road, San Diego, the same apartment complex where Bayoumi lived. Bayoumi paid the deposit and the first month's rent because the two had not opened a bank account yet and the manager would not take cash. Shortly thereafter, Bayoumi threw a party for the two to introduce them to the Arab community in San Diego. See FBI, Working Draft Chronology of Events for Hijackers and Associates; 911 Commission Report (Official Report), Staff Statement Number 16, p. 4.

634 FBI, Working Draft Chronology of Events for Hijackers and Associates.

635 NSA/CSS Terrorist OPI, KL 2000-06 (TS/MU), San Diego Saudi cell, April 4, 2000 (TS/SI/49779).

636 FBI, Memorandum for the Record, Event: Interview of Caysan Bin Don, also known as Usama Dyson and Clayton Morgan, April 20, 2004; Memorandum for the Record, Subject: Location: Interview of Omar Al-Bayoumi Conference Palace, Riyadh, October 16–17, 2003.

637 FBI, Working Draft Chronology of Events for Hijackers and Associates.

638 They moved on May 10, 2001; FBI, Working Draft Chronology of Events for Hijackers and Associates.

639 CIA analytic report, "The Plot and the Plotters (U)," June 1, 2003, p. 101.

640 KSM Debrief Papers, 2005.

641 Hani Hanjour (aka Hani Saleh Hanjour; Hani Saleh; Hani Hanjour, Hani Saleh H. Hanjour), Saudi, born August 20, 1972 in Taif, Saudi Arabia; first received an American visa in 1991 in Phoenix, AZ.

For Hanjour's story, see 911 Commission, Staff Statement Number 16, p. 6; *The Black Banners*, p. 277.

The Joint Inquiry says that Hanjour went to Afghanistan in 1989 when he was 17 years old to participate in *jihad*; Joint Inquiry, p. 135.

On April 15, 1999, Hanjour earned an FAA commercial pilot certificate; *Intelligence Matters*, p. 41.

On April 28, 1999, Hanjour was also scheduled to leave JFK on a flight to Amman, Jordan; FBI, Working Draft Chronology of Events for Hijackers and Associates.

"INS records indicate that Hanjour departed the United States from New York on April 28, 1999. However, bank records indicate withdrawals in Arizona in the first two weeks of May 1999 from an account in his name." Statement for the Record, FBI Director Robert S. Mueller III, Joint Intelligence Committee Inquiry,

September 26, 2002.

642 911 Commission, Staff Statement Number 16, p. 6; *The Black Banners*, p. 277.

643 According to Sen. Graham, based on intelligence he received as a member of the Senate Intelligence Committee, between January–May 2000, al-Bayoumi also had an unusually large number of telephone conversations with Saudi government officials in both Los Angeles and Washington. See *Intelligence Matters*, p. 168.

Chapter 37

644 CIA analytic report, "The Plot and the Plotters (U)," June 1, 2003, p. 61.

645 KSM Debrief Papers, 2005.

646 KSM Debrief Papers, 2005.

647 While Atta was in Syria as part of his German-sponsored work, he met a young Syrian female archeologist and worked closely with her. She invited him to visit her family home and he grew close to her. But when she indicated romantic interest in Atta, he cut off all contact with her. See CIA analytic report, "The Plot and the Plotters (U)," June 1, 2003, p. 38.

648 CIA analytic report, "The Plot and the Plotters (U)," June 1, 2003, p. 93.

649 KSM Debrief Papers, 2005.

650 KSM Debrief Papers, 2005.

651 CIA analytic report, "The Plot and the Plotters (U)," June 1, 2003, p. 93.

652 CIA analytic report, "The Plot and the Plotters (U)," June 1, 2003, p. 93.

653 KSM Debrief Papers, 2005.

654 CIA analytic report, "The Plot and the Plotters (U)," June 1, 2003, p. 94.

655 None of this travel is mentioned in FBI intelligence report, Terrorism: Usama Bin Ladin's Intelligence Capabilities and Techniques, December 5, 1996.

656 KSM Debrief Papers, 2005.

657 Pakistan Air Force Museum, PAF Museum Road, Shahrah-e-Faisal Rd, Faisal Cantonment, Karachi, Karachi City, Sindh, Pakistan.

658 Marwan left Karachi at the end of December, flying to the UAE, where he met up with Ali Abdul Aziz Ali, the money man for the plane's operation. He was in the UAE for about a month, and while there, he acquired a Boeing 767-300 flight deck video and a Boeing 747 simulator program.

On January 2, 2000, Marwan was issued a new UAE Passport No. A0460773. He applied for a U.S. visa in the UAE and was issued one on January 18, 2000; FBI, Working Draft Chronology of Events for Hijackers and Associate; KSM et al Indictment, p. 16.

659 Ramzi Binalshibh applied for an American visa in Berlin on May 17, 2000. His application was denied. He applied again on June 15, 2000; his application was again denied; KSM et al Indictment, pp. 17–18; CIA, intelligence report, interrogation of Ramzi Binalshibh, October 1, 2002.

660 In the fall of 1999, Marwan al-Shehhi indeed stayed at Bin Laden's Kandahar guesthouse while awaiting transportation to Pakistan for medical treatment; Joint Inquiry, pp. 135, 137.

Ali Soufan writes, based upon interrogation of Ibraham al-Qosi, that, "It was during Ramadan, and Shehhi had apparently had some kind of stomach operation … so really it was dangerous for him to fast, but he decided to fast anyway. As a result he got very sick, and the emir of the guesthouse had to look after him." *The Black Banners*, p. 294.

661 Project Sumner Memo, Draper to Bowlen and Charbel, Subject: Intelligence on KSM's Pilot, MU-01-865, March 4, 2001. See also *Al Qaeda*, p. 239.

Chapter 38

662 On June 18, 2000, the two took up their first residence in Manhattan; FBI, Working Draft Chronology of Events for Hijackers and Associates.

663 FBI, Working Draft Chronology of Events for Hijackers and Associates.

664 On May 8, 2000, Atta was issued Egyptian Passport No. 1617066 at the Consulate in Hamburg, Germany. His old passport was still valid for five more years, but he reported it lost; FBI, Working Draft Chronology of Events for Hijackers and Associates.

665 Statement for the Record, FBI Director Robert S. Mueller III, Joint Intelligence Committee Inquiry, September 26, 2002.

Marwan arrived on Sabena Flight 537, landing at Newark International Airport in New Jersey. He was admitted by immigration authorities as a tourist for six months. However, he was pulled aside by a "roving" Customs inspector who conducted a secondary inspection. He was admitted after this two-minute examination, during which his bags were X-rayed but he was not personally searched. In theory, the Customs inspector was trained to look for drug couriers, not terrorists. See also 911 Commission; FBI, Working Draft Chronology of Events for Hijackers and Associates.

666 NYC Parks, Fort Tryon Park Pamphlet, n.d. (2002).

667 Gallery 460, Ottoman Art, Image of the Prophet Mohammed, The Prophet Muhammad and the Origins of Islam, n.d. (2001). See also Lorena Muñoz-Alonso, "Security Threats Force London's V&A to Remove Prophet Muhammad Artwork—Appropriate caution or self-censorship?," ArtNet News, January 26, 2015.

668 CIA analytic report, "The Plot and the Plotters (U)," June 1, 2003, pp. 106–108.

669 FBI, Working Draft Chronology of Events for Hijackers and Associates; Statement for the Record, FBI Director Robert S. Mueller III, Joint Intelligence Committee Inquiry, September 26, 2002.

670 FBI, Working Draft Chronology of Events for Hijackers and Associates.

Chapter 39

671 Project Sumner Timeline, V38, n.d. (2008) (TS/SP/MU).

672 Executive Order 13129, "Blocking Property and Prohibiting Transactions with the Taliban," July 4, 1999.

673 The White House, Presidential Memorandum of Notification, July 17, 1999, Top Secret.

674 Kenneth Winston Starr, best known for heading the investigation of members of the Clinton administration, served as a federal Court of Appeals judge and as solicitor general for George H. W. Bush. Starr faced criticism for his work as independent counsel, and in 1999 he resigned. Starr subsequently served as dean of Pepperdine University's law school before becoming president and chancellor of Baylor University.

675 This is discussed in more detail in Project Sumner, Report prepared for the Review Committee, Analysis of Terrorism Literature, Conspiracy Theories, and Deception Impact (TS/SCI), January 2003 (TS-MU-08-03).

676 See Project Sumner, Report prepared for the Review Committee, Analysis of Terrorism Literature, Conspiracy Theories, and Deception Impact (TS/SCI), January 2003 (TS-MU-08-03).

Chapter 40

677 On May 25, 2000, Jarrah applied for and received a five-year B-1/B-2 (tourist/business) visa in Berlin. Jarrah was a strong visa candidate, given his long residence in Germany (approximately four years), academic involvement in Germany (at two universities), and Lebanese nationality.

Ziad Jarrah entered the United States for the first time on a tourist visa on 27

June 2000, flying from Munich, Germany to Atlanta, Georgia. He then traveled to Venice, Florida to begin flight training and was enrolled through January 31, 2001. See Statement for the Record, FBI Director Robert S. Mueller III, Joint Intelligence Committee Inquiry, September 26, 2002.

678 On June 22, 2000, Mohammed Atta filled out an information sheet at the Century Flight Academy in Morristown, NJ. He and Marwan flew to Oklahoma City on July 4, 2000. On July 7, they registered at Huffman Aviation in Venice, FL. They also attended Jones Flying School in Venice for two weeks.

679 CIA analytic report, "The Plot and the Plotters (U)," June 1, 2003, p. 109.

680 Project Sumner Memo, Draper to Bowlen and Charbel, Subject: Intelligence on KSM's Pilot, MU-01-865, March 4, 2001.

681 Project Sumner Memo, Draper to Bowlen and Charbel, Subject: Intelligence on KSM's Pilot, MU-01-865, March 4, 2001.

682 516 West Laurel Road, Nokomis, FL 34275. See FBI, Working Draft Chronology of Events for Hijackers and Associates.

683 FBI, Working Draft Chronology of Events for Hijackers and Associates.

684 On July 7, 2000, Atta purchased a 1986 Pontiac Grand Prix from Cramer Toyota in Venice, Florida. He sold the car to Sun Auto Leasing (Elite Select Used Cars) of Ft. Lauderdale, FL, for $800.00 on September 7, 2001. See FBI, Working Draft Chronology of Events for Hijackers and Associates; Government Exhibit 0G00020.2 01-455A.

685 Project Sumner Memo, Draper to Bowlen and Charbel, Subject: Intelligence on KSM's Pilot, MU-01-865, March 4, 2001.

686 "LUṬI, also luti (pl. alvāṭ), has a variety of meanings. The term was first mentioned by the tenth-century poet Kesā'i, who equated the luṭis with catamites (tāz and mikyāz). For Jalāl- al-Din Rumi (13th century) and 'Obayd Zākāni (14th century) luṭis were pederasts, and the related word lavāṭi (sodomy) is still used as such. Not every text offers this negative sexual connotation. Nāṣer-e Ḵosrow (11th century) equated the luṭis with wine drinkers, thieves and whore-mongers." *Encyclopedia Iranica.*

687 "Mithli al-jins" ("homosexual"), sometime shortened to "mithli." See discussion in Brian Whitaker and Anna Wilson, *Unspeakable Love: Gay and Lesbian Life in the Middle East* (University of California Press; First edition 2006).

688 Abu Nuwas al-Hasan ibn Hani al-Hakami (ca. 756–813), born in Ahwaz on the Karun River in modern day Iran, was the most famous Arab poet of the Abbasid Caliphate, and one of the most revered poets of the secular Middle East. His poems reflected the licentious manners of the upper classes of his day. He died in Baghdad, and today Abu Nuwas Street runs along the east bank of the Tigris River. See W.H. Ingrams, *Abu Nuwas in Life and Legend* (Port-Louis, Mauritius: Typographie moderne, 1933).

689 Abu Nuwas' most famous poem is "In The Bath-House":

> In the bath-house, the mysteries hidden by trousers
> Are revealed to you.
> All becomes radiantly manifest.
> Feast your eyes without restraint!
> You see handsome buttocks, shapely trim torsos,
> You hear the guys whispering pious formulas
> to one another
> ('God is Great! ' 'Praise be to God! ')
> Ah, what a palace of pleasure is the bath-house!
> Even when the towel-bearers come in
> And spoil the fun a bit.

"In The Bath-House," in *Carousing with Gazelles: Homoerotic Songs of Old Baghdad*, Translated by Jaafar Abu Tarab (iUniverse, Inc., 2005).

690 *Surah an-Nisa* [4:147], *Qur'an.*

691 Project Sumner Memo, Draper to Bowlen and Charbel, Subject: Intelligence on KSM's Pilot, MU-01-865, March 4, 2001.

692 The five pillars of Islam, the essential religious duties required of every adult Muslim, are profession of faith (*shahada*), prayer (*salat*), almsgiving (*zakat*), fasting (*sawm*), and pilgrimage (*hajj*). The five pillars are the most central rituals of Islam and constitute the core practices of the Islamic faith.

693 *Surah al-A'raf* [7:31], *Qur'an.*

Chapter 41

694 FBI, Working Draft Chronology of Events for Hijackers and Associates.

695 On June 9, 2000, Nawaf al-Hazmi drove Mihdhar to Los Angeles. Mihdhar left the country the next day, boarding a Lufthansa flight to Frankfurt; 911 Commission Report (Official Report), pp. 220–222.

696 The 911 Commission says: "Mihdhar's mind seems to have been with his family back in Yemen, as evidenced by calls he made from the apartment telephone. When news of the birth of his first child arrived, he could stand life in California no longer." 911 Commission Report (Official Report), pp. 220–222.

697 CIA analytic report, "The Plot and the Plotters (U)," June 1, 2003, p. 110.

698 911 Commission Report (Official Report), p. 223.

699 On April 4, 2000, Nawaf al-Hazmi took his first flying lesson, a one-hour introductory session at the National Air College in San Diego. The next day, the two applied for driver's licenses; they received them on April 19. The two took a flying lesson at the Sorbi Flying Club in San Diego on May 5, followed by a second lesson at the same school five days later on May 10. They also took flying lessons at Gibbs Flying Services on May 8. But after that, they stopped taking lessons. See FBI, Working Draft Chronology of Events for Hijackers and Associates; 911 Commission Report (Official Report), pp. 221–222; *Intelligence Matters*, p. 26.

700 On May 30, 2000, al-Mihdhar closed his San Diego Bank of America account, withdrawing the balance of $4,888.69. The same day, al-Hazmi opened a new BAC account with a deposit of $100. On May 31, 2000, al-Hazmi deposited $4,800 in the account.

701 Ali Abdul Aziz Ali ("al Baluchi"), (aka al-Baluchi, Aliosh, Ali A, Isam Mansur, Hani [of Fawaz Trading UAE]); Pakistani, born in Kuwait August 29, 1977; nephew of KSM, planes operation communicator, financial middleman and logistics support based in UAE. See CIA analytic report, Khalid Sheik Muhammad's Nephews, CTC 2003-300013, January 31, 2003.

Ali left the UAE the day before 9/11 with Ramzi Binalshibh for the safety of Pakistan. He was captured on April 29, 2003 in Karachi, Pakistan with Khallad, as he waited for the delivery of explosives for an alleged plot to attack the U.S. consulate. He was in possession of a perfume spray bottle that contained a low concentration of cyanide. Internment Serial Number (ISN): US9PK-010018DP (PK-10018). See DOD, Office for the Administrative Review of the Detention of Enemy Combatants, Summary of Evidence for Combatant Status Review Tribunal—Al Baluchi, Ammar, March 28, 2007; Joint Task Force Guantanamo, Subject: Combatant Status Review Tribunal Input and Recommendation for Continued Detention Under DOD Control (CD) for Guantanamo Detainee ISN: US9YM-010013DP (S), Secret/NF. December 8, 2006; *The Black Banners*, p. 550.

702 It was later discovered that Khalid al-Mihdhar, Hani Hanjour, and Abdul Aziz al Omari (one of the Saudi muscle men) used credit cards drawn on Saudi Arabian banks to supplement their financing, the only hijackers to do so; Statement for the Record, FBI Director Robert S. Mueller III, Joint Intelligence Committee Inquiry, September 26, 2002.

703 On July 12, 2000, two days before the expiration of the six-month visa he had been granted on arriving in January, Nawaf al-Hazmi applied to the INS for an extension, using the address of the San Diego apartment he had shared with Khalid al-Mihdhar.

See Substitution of the Testimony of Khalid Sheikh Mohammed, p. 20.

704 Project Sumner Memo, Draper to Bowlen and Charbel, Subject: Intelligence on KSM's Pilot, MU-01-865, March 4, 2001.

705 KSM Debrief Papers, 2005.

706 Hani Hanjour joined up with Nawaf al-Hazmi and the two moved to Mesa, Arizona where Hanjour had previously lived. Al-Hazmi told his housemate that he and his friend "Hani" were headed for San Jose to take flying lessons and told his friends that he would stay in touch. Hanjour enrolled at Arizona Aviation for refresher flight training.

On January 10, 2001, Nawaf al-Hazmi and Hanjour move to apartment #2144, Indian Springs Village, 1031 South Stewart Street, Mesa, Arizona. See 911 Commission Report (Official Report), pp. 223–226; 911 Commission, Staff Statement Number 16, p. 6; *The Black Banners*, p. 277.

707 KSM Debrief Papers, 2005.

Chapter 42

708 Richard Bruce Cheney, born January 30, 1941, in Lincoln, Nebraska. White House chief of staff, November 1975–January 1977; House of Representatives for Wyoming at-large, January 1979–March 1989; secretary of defense, March 1989–January 1993; vice president of the United States, January 2001–January 2009.

709 James Mann, *Rise of the Vulcans: The History of Bush's War Cabinet* (Penguin Book, paperback edition, 2004).

710 Alison Mitchell, "The 2000 Campaign: The Running Mate; Bush is Reported Set to Name Cheney as Partner on Ticket," *The New York Times*, July 25, 2000, p. A21.

711 Albert Arnold Gore, Jr., born March 31, 1948, in Washington, DC. House of Representatives for Tennessee's 4th district, January 1977–January 1983; House of Representatives for Tennessee's 6th district, January 1983–January 1985; senator from Tennessee, January 1985–January 1993; vice president of the United States, January 1993–January 2001.

712 Project Sumner Timeline, V38, n.d. (2008) (TS/SP/MU).

713 Later at the first debate between Cheney and Lieberman on October 5, 2000, on a question regarding "taking out" Saddam Hussein, Cheney said:

> "We might have no other choice. We'll have to see if that happens. The thing about Iraq, of course, was at the end of the war we had pretty well decimated their military. We had put them back in the box, so to speak. We had a strong international coalition raid against them, effective economic sanctions, and an inspection regime was in place under the U.N. and it was able to do a good job of stripping out the capacity to build weapons of mass destruction, the work he had been doing that had not been destroyed during the war in biological and chemical agents, as well as a nuclear program.

Unfortunately now we find ourselves in a situation where that started to fray on us, where the coalition now no longer is tied tightly together. Recently the United Arab Emirates have reopened diplomatic relations with Baghdad. The Russians and French are flying commercial airliners back into Baghdad and thumbing their nose at the international sanction's regime. We're in a situation today where our posture with Iraq is weaker than it was at the end of the war. It's unfortunate.

I also think it's unfortunate we find ourselves in a position where we don't know for sure what might be transpiring inside Iraq. I certainly hope he's not regenerating that kind of capability, but if he were, if in fact Saddam Hussein were taking steps to try to rebuild nuclear capability or weapons of mass destruction, you would have to give very serious consideration to military action to—to stop that activity. I don't think you can afford to have a man like Saddam Hussein with nuclear weapons in the Middle East."

714 In August 1992, a no-fly zone is established in southern Iraq, prohibiting the flights of Iraqi planes south of latitude 32 degrees north. In September 1996, President Clinton ordered that the Southern no-fly zone extend to 33rd parallel (latitude 33 degrees north), one degree further north almost the suburbs of Baghdad.

715 Bin Laden believed that the "American soldier was a paper tiger and [would] after a few blows run in defeat ... dragging their corpses and shameful defeat." Quoted in *Osama bin Laden*, p. 90.

Bin Laden told Abdel Bari Atwan that *al Qaeda* was responsible for successful battle in Somalia and thought the U.S. "displayed a singular lack of courage by pulling out of Somalia immediately afterwards." See *The Secret History of al Qaeda*, p. 36.

"Bin Laden's analysis of the American character had been proven correct," proven by the Blackhawk Down incident. See *The Looming Tower*, p. 188.

716 Assaf Moghadam, *The Globalization of Martyrdom: Al Qaeda, Salafi Jihad, and the Diffusion of Suicide Attacks* (Johns Hopkins University Press, 2009), p. 109.

717 Condoleezza Rice; assistant to the president for national security affairs (aka "national security advisor") (2001–2005); Stanford University (1981–2000); director of Soviet and East European affairs/Soviet affairs, National Security Council (1989–1991).

718 Condoleezza Rice would later write: "At the start, there had even been one attempt to alter a long-standing tradition by having the Vice President chair the powerful Principals Committee, made up of the Cabinet secretaries, in place of the national security advisor. I went to the President and said, 'Mr. President, this is what the NSA [national security advisor] does: convene the national security principles [sic] to make recommendations for you.' He agreed, and that was the end of that." See Condoleezza Rice, *No Higher Honor: A Memoir of My Years in Washington* (Crown, 2011), p. 17.

Chapter 43

719 Associated Press, "Cheney: Swift Retaliation Needed," October 13, 2000. See also CNN broadcast, "CNN Ahead of the Curve," October 13, 2000.

720 "Dick Cheney Discusses the Final Days of Campaign 2000," Larry King Live, Aired October 27, 2000, 9:00 p.m. ET.

721 The Sultanate of Oman, located on the southeastern coast of the Arabian Peninsula on the Indian Ocean, was a powerful empire in the 17th Century, vying with Portugal and the UK for influence in the region. By the 20th century, the sultanate was under the influence of the United Kingdom, a de facto colony. The Dhofar rebellion led to a palace coup on July 23, 1970, when the Sultan was overthrown by his son, Qaboos bin Said. Qaboos, who had been trained in Britain at the Royal Military Academy in Sandhurst, reversed his father's policy of isolation and began to develop and modernize Oman.

722 According to the 911 Commission Report, bin Laden anticipated U.S. military retaliation. He ordered the evacuation of al Qaeda's Kandahar airport compound [Tarnak Farms] and fled—first to the desert area near Kabul, then to Khowst [Khost] and Jalalabad, and eventually back to Kandahar. In Kandahar, he rotated between five to six residences, spending one night at each residence. In addition, he sent his senior advisor, Mohammed Atef [Abu Hafs], to a different part of Kandahar and his deputy, Ayman al Zawahiri, to Kabul so that all three could not be killed in one attack. 911 Commission Report (Official Report), p. 191.

723 Ali Abdullah Saleh was the first President of Yemen, from Yemeni unification on May 22, 1990 to his resignation on February 25, 2012, following uprisings precipitated by the Arab Spring.

724 *The Black Banners*, pp. 176, 180.

725 KSM Debrief Papers, 2005.

726 Nasser Ahmad Nasser Al-Bahri, aka Abu Jandal. He was arrested after the attack on the *Cole*. In 2001, he was given amnesty by Yemen's President Ali Abdallah Saleh. See FBI report of investigation, interview of Nasser Ahmad Naser al Bahri, aka Abu Jandal, September 17–October 2, 2001.

727 Muhammed Abdu Al-Nashiri. In November 2002, after being captured and detained by a foreign country, Abd al Rahim al-Nashiri was transferred to CIA custody and transported to the same detention facility where Abu Zubaydah was located. Al-Nashiri was also subjected to the CIA's coercive techniques (torture), including waterboarding. Sometime between December 2002 and January 2003, while in detention, al-Nashiri was threatened with a handgun and a power drill during a CIA interrogation.

728 According to George Tenet: "In the spring of 1998 the Saudis foiled a plot by Abd al-Rahim al-Nashiri—head of Al Qaeda operations in the Arabian Peninsula and the mastermind of the attack against the USS *Cole*—to smuggle four Sagger antitank missiles from Yemen into Saudi Arabia." *At the Center of the Storm*, p. 105.

He writes: "We would have expected the Saudis to pass this information to us immediately.

"John Brennan, at the time our senior liaison to the Saudis, confronted the Saudi head of intelligence, Prince Turki, about the lapse, but Turki professed ignorance. Brennan suggested I make a quick trip to Saudi Arabia to underscore the importance of sharing such information."

George Tenet then travels to Saudi Arabia and meets with Prince Naif [sic, Nayef], the interior minister.

"Naif opened, as I recall, with an interminable soliloquy recounting the history of the U.S.-Saudi 'special' relationship ... After a while, I had had enough. [CIA Deputy Director] John McLaughlin and Brennan were by my side. I was struggling to be diplomatic, but they could see the frustration building ... ."

According to Tenet, he confronts the prince, putting his hand on his knee, and asks him what it would look like if he had to tell *The Washington Post* that the Saudi held out data that might have helped the U.S. to track down *al Qaeda*.

"I do remember Naif's reaction—what looked to be a prolonged state of shock, with his eyes continuously shifting back and forth between my face and my hand on his knee ... . Crown Prince Abdullah was decisive in breaking the log jam. Within a week of my visit, Brennan was given a comprehensive written report on the entire Sagger missile episode." See *At the Center of the Storm*, pp. 106ff.

729 Joint Inquiry, p. 130.

730 911 Commission Report (Official Report), p. 492.

731 On January 3, 2000, there was a failed attack on the USS *The Sullivans*, another U.S. Navy destroyer, when it visited Yemen. See 911 Commission Report (Official Report), pp. 195–196; CIA briefing materials, "Intelligence Assessment: The Attack on the USS Cole," December 21, 2000.

732 The Yemen switchboard was legendary, originally hinted at by the bin Laden defector al-Fadl, by al-Owhali, and by another senior operative.

Post 9/11 reports speak of al-Hada's home as a "safe house" and a "logistics center" and of the telephone number in Yemen being "wiretapped," with even bin Laden calling the number dozens of times. In some versions, the FBI is the hero in this tale. According to the account in *Looming Towers*, pp. 343ff and others, the New York office of the FBI used the phone records to map the entire *al Qaeda* global organization. In other versions, the CIA is an active and obstreperous culprit, withholding switchboard intelligence from the FBI, including information that Khalid al-Mihdhar and Nawaf al-Hazmi made calls to the switchboard. See 911

Commission Report (Official Report), p. 181; Moussaoui document DX-0471.pdf; Ron Suskind, *The One Percent Doctrine* (Simon & Schuster, 2006), p. 94; *A Pretext for War*, p. 174.

733 "FBI agents pursuing that case [the embassy bombings] came up with a telephone number of a suspected terrorist facility in the Middle East believed to be associated with al Qaeda or Egyptian Islamic Jihad terrorists. The suspicious phone number was shared with CIA, NSA, DIA, the State and Treasury departments, and others." *At the Center of the Storm*, p. 194.

734 Mohamed Rashed Daoud al-Owhali (aka Abdul Jabbar Ali Abdul Latif, Khaled Saleem bin Rasheed, Khalid Salim, Moath al-Balucci), Saudi; joined *al Qaeda* in 1996 as part of the Northern Group in Afghanistan.

735 FBI report of investigation, interview of Mohammad Rashed Daoud al Owhali, Sept. 9, 1998.

736 Fahd (Fahad) al-Quso was in Malaysia in January 2000, at the same time as Khallad and hijackers Nawaf al-Hazmi and Khalid al-Mihdhar. Ali Soufan wrote in 2011 that al-Quso is free in Yemen and remains on the FBI's most wanted list; *The Black Banners*, p. 565.

737 "The attack on the Cole demonstrated just how lightly the U.S. military had been taking the threat of terrorist violence. ... Equally culpable was the regional commander-in-chief, Anthony Zinni, who approved the decision to refuel in Yemen. A more telling display of the persistent disbelief concerning the threat from al Qaeda would be hard to imagine." *Age of Sacred Terror*, pp. 323–324. See also *The Cell*, p. 225.

738 Michael Sheehan later observes that even in the presidential debates, just five days after the USS *Cole* attack, the ship "still smoking in the harbor in Aden," the candidates were more focused on the death of Governor Mel Carnahan of Missouri the day before. "[Jim] Lehrer offered a moment of silence in Carnahan's honor. Nothing on the seven sailors, I thought with a twinge of dismay. Vice President Gore opened his prepared remarks by mentioning Governor Carnahan and 'the families' of those sailors who were killed on the USS Cole five days earlier. A little bit better, I thought, but what about al Qaeda? Gore quickly shifted his attention to the issue of health care. When Governor Bush's turn to speak came, Bush said something like 'God's blessing on the families whose lives were overturned ... last night.' He did not make a single mention of the Cole." See *Crush the Cell*, p. 19.

739 According to George Tenet: "neither our intelligence nor the FBI's criminal investigation could conclusively prove that Usama bin Ladin and his leadership had had authority, direction, and control over the attack. This is a high threshold to cross ... What's important from our perspective at CIA is that the FBI investigation had taken primacy in getting to the bottom of the matter." *At the Center of the Storm*, p. 128.

"Some investigators contend that within 48 hours of the bombing, the link to bin Laden was firm enough to justify a military response ..." See *The Cell*, p. 234.

740 Joint Inquiry, pp. 11, 129.

741 "Bin Ladin anticipated U.S. military retaliation. He ordered the evacuation of *al Qaeda*'s Kandahar airport compound and fled—first to the desert area near Kabul, then to Khowst and Jalalabad, and eventually back to Kandahar. In Kandahar, he rotated between five to six residences, spending one night at each residence. In addition, he sent his senior advisor, Mohammed Atef, to a different part of Kandahar and his deputy, Ayman al Zawahiri, to Kabul so that all three could not be killed in one attack." 911 Commission Report (Official Report), p. 191.

And not just Osama bin Laden. Ali Soufan, assigned to the FBI investigation in Yemen, later writes: "Everyone—the White House, the military, the CIA, CENTCOM—were all briefed on the fact that the bombing of the Cole had been an *al-Qaeda* operation. We waited for an official U.S. response against *al-Qaeda*. And we waited." *The Black Banners*, p. 194.

742 According to Richard Clarke's classified testimony, Berger upbraided Tenet so sharply after the Cole attack—repeatedly demanding to know why the United States had to put up with such attacks—that Tenet walked out of a meeting of the principals. See 911 Commission Report (Official Report), p. 193.

743 On October 16–17, 2000, Clinton was in Sharm el-Sheikh, Egypt to attend an Israeli-Palestinian summit meeting attended by Arafat and Barak, cosponsored by Egypt. George Tenet attended the summit in his role as handholder of the Palestinian intelligence; *At the Center of the Storm*, p. 78.

744 On October 17–18, 2000, Secretary of State Albright went to Riyadh, Saudi Arabia to discuss the Middle East peace process with King Fahd and senior officials; she also met with Syrian President Bashar Assad.

Chapter 45

745 In addition to Nawaf al-Hazmi and Khalid al-Mihdhar, there were 13 other so-called muscle hijackers, all but one from Saudi Arabia. They were Satam al Suqami, Wail and Waleed al Shehri (two brothers), Abdul Aziz al Omari, Fayez Banihammad (from the UAE), Ahmed al Ghamdi, Hamza al Ghamdi, Mohand al Shehri, Saeed al Ghamdi, Ahmad al Haznawi, Ahmed al Nami, Majed Moqed, and Salem al Hazmi (the brother of Nawaf al Hazmi).

746 Their main instructor was a Jordanian Abu Turab. Substitution of the Testimony of Khalid Sheikh Mohammed, p. 24.

The name Abu Turab (Father of the Soil) is taken from the fourth Sunni Caliph. The nickname was given to Ali by the Prophet Muhammad, when he found Ali sleeping while covered with soil. There is a verse in the *Qur'an* that says, "Indeed, we have warned you of a near punishment on the Day when a man will observe what his hands have put forth and the disbeliever will say, 'Oh, I wish that I were dust!'"

747 The al-Farooq (Faruq) camp, part of the Garmabak Ghar complex in the rough mountainous region near Kandahar, was one of *al Qaeda*'s most important training sites. The camp consisted of classrooms and prayer halls, bunkers, testing fields, and firing ranges, and concrete underground stores for weapons and chemicals from which complex tunnels led to concealed entrances.

748 The man was *al Qaeda* explosives expert Abu 'Abd al-Rahman al-Muhajir.

749 CIA analytic report, "The Plot and the Plotters (U)," June 1, 2003, pp. 34–52.

750 Substitution of the Testimony of Khalid Sheikh Mohammed, p. 24–26.

751 Saeed (Said) Abdalah Ali Sulayman al-Ghamdi, Saudi citizen, date of birth, November 21, 1979. The Saudi Arabian passport of al-Ghamdi #C573895 was later recovered from the Flight 93 crash site in Pennsylvania. Al-Ghamdi acquired this new Saudi passport, replacing one (#B516222) he used to acquire a visa on September 4, 2000, in Jeddah. He acquired the new passport because there was evidence of his travel to Afghanistan in his previous passport.

752 Ahmad Ibrahim Ali al-Haznawi, Saudi citizen, date of birth, October 11, 1980.

753 Abd al-Aziz Abd al-Rahman Muhammed al-Umari (often referred to as Alomari), Saudi citizen, date of birth, May 28, 1979.

754 Wail Muhammad Abdallah al-Shehri, Saudi citizen, date of birth July 31, 1973.

755 Hamza Salih Ahmad al-Hamid al-Ghamdi, Saudi citizen, date of birth November 18, 1980.

756 The *Salat al-Istikhara* is a prayer recited by Muslims when in need of guidance on an issue in their life.

757 911 Commission Report (Official Report), p. 231.

758 See *A Fury for God*, p. 37.

Chapter 46

759 The 911 Commission says: "Mihdhar left the United States against the wishes of the operational organizer of the plot, Khalid Sheikh Mohammed. ... Mihdhar's decision to strand Hazmi in San Diego enraged KSM, who had not authorized the departure and feared it would compromise the plan." See 911 Commission Report (Official Report), pp. 220–222.

760 KSM Debrief Papers, 2005.

761 CIA analytic report, "The Plot and the Plotters (U)," June 1, 2003, p. 121.

762 Years later, the 911 Commission would conclude that while in the United States, "Jarrah made hundreds of phone calls to her [Aysel Senguen, his wife] and communicated frequently by email." 911 Commission Report (Official Report), p. 224.

763 On October 7, 2000, Jarrah flew from Atlanta, Georgia to Frankfurt, Germany on Delta Flight 20. See 911 Commission, Staff Statement Number 16, p. 6; FBI, Working Draft Chronology of Events for Hijackers and Associates; Project Sumner Memo, Draper to Bowlen and Charbel, Subject: Intelligence on KSM's Pilot, MU-01-865, March 4, 2001.

764 On October 29, 2000, Ziad Jarrah arrived back in the United States, flying from Dusseldorf, Germany (Condor Flight 7178) to Frankfurt and on to Tampa, Florida (Lufthansa Flight 223). FBI, Working Draft Chronology of Events for Hijackers and Associates; Project Sumner Memo, Draper to Bowlen and Charbel, Subject: Intelligence on KSM's Pilot, MU-01-865, March 4, 2001.

765 For the travel of Jarrah and Senguen travel to Paris, see in particular, FBI letterhead memorandum, profile of Jarrah, March 20, 2002.

766 After passing this test, Atta and al-Shehhi were able to sign out planes for solo flights without an instructor. They did so on a number of occasions thereafter often returning at 2:00 and 3:00 a.m. after logging four or five hours of flying time.

767 By far, the best description of the 2000 presidential elections and the days that followed is Jeffrey Toobin, *Too Close to Call: The Thirty-Six-Day Battle to Decide the 2000 Election* (Random House, 2001).

Chapter 47

768 Though there are countless books on George W. Bush and the Bush administration, I have been most edified by Robert Draper's *Dead Certain: The Presidency of George W. Bush* (Free Press, 2008), from which the observation about George Bush and his band of "brothers" is borrowed.

769 Project Sumner Timeline, V38, n.d. (2008) (TS/SP/MU).

770 Donald Henry Rumsfeld, secretary of defense from 1975–1977 under President Gerald Ford and again secretary from January 2001 to December 2006.

771 *At the Center of the Storm*, p. 135.

772 President Bush later wrote of George Tenet in his autobiography: "He was the opposite of the stereotypical CIA director you read about in spy novels—the bow-tied, Ivy League, elite type. Tenet was a blue-collar guy, the son of Greek immigrants from New York City. He spoke bluntly, often colorfully, and obviously cared deeply about the Agency," George W. Bush, *Decision Points* (Crown Publishers, 2010), p. 84.

773 Paul Dundes Wolfowitz; deputy secretary of defense (January 2001–March 2005); Commission to Assess the Ballistic Missile Threat to the United States; dean of the Paul H. Nitze School of Advanced International Studies at Johns Hopkins University (1994–2001); Commission on the Roles and Capabilities of the United States Intelligence Community (1995–1995); under secretary of defense (policy) (May 1989–January 1993), ambassador to Indonesia (1986–1989); assistant secretary of state for East Asian and Pacific Affairs (1982–1986); director policy planning staff, Department of State (1981–1982).

Dick Cheney later writes about Wolfowitz, when he served as his under secretary of defense for policy in the first Bush administration: "Paul had the ability to offer new perspectives on old problems. He was also persistent. On more than one occasion, I sent him on his way after I had rejected a piece of advice or a policy suggestion, only to find him back in my office a half hour later continuing to press his point—and he was often right to do so." *In My Time*, p. 162.

Condoleezza Rice later wrote that "Paul was a cerebral, almost other worldly intellectual." *No Higher Honor*, p. 3.

774 Joint Inquiry, p. 217; *No Higher Honor*, p. 64. Rice later writes that: "When later there were claims of extensive briefings concerning *al Qaeda* during the transition, I recalled that North Korea, not terrorism, had been the Clinton administration's most pressing business with the incoming team." *No Higher Honor*, p. 34.

775 Condoleezza Rice, "Campaign 2000: Promoting the National Interest," *Foreign Affairs*, January/February 2000.

776 Richard Clarke writes that from his perspective, policymakers know more: "The experienced policy maker has probably spent more time working the issue, repeatedly been to the parts of the world in question, met privately with foreign officials involved in the issue, and acquired a network of academic or corporate experts who trust him and will tell him things they would never confide to an intelligence officer. Who is likely to know more ... the career Foreign Service officer who has led American negotiations on the subject for years, or a newly minted CIA analyst who has seen ... only through the lens of a satellite that flies by a hundred miles above?" See *Your Government Failed You*, p. 135.

Of course, there is a danger to *intelligence* being only shared at the top; maybe it can come in and go by without anyone having a chance to comment. Condoleezza Rice tells an interesting sub-story of President Bush's first meeting with Vladimir Putin, the one that is often dismissed when Bush later said that he had looked into Putin's soul.

Rice also writes that "After touching on some other issues, Putin suddenly raised the problem of Pakistan. He excoriated the Pervez Musharraf regime for its support of extremists and for the connections of the Pakistani army and intelligence services to the Taliban and al Qaeda. Those extremists were also being funded by Saudi Arabia, he said, and it was only a matter of time until it resulted in a major catastrophe." *No Higher Honor*, p. 62.

777 The Highway of Death refers to the road from Kuwait to Basra in southern Iraq, the main escape route for occupation authorities in Kuwait City. As they began to evacuate Kuwait at the end of February 1991, traffic jams on the two-lane road presented lucrative targets for U.S. aircraft. Since the traffic was all assumed to be Iraqi military, even though there were many civilian cars and trucks that had been commandeered, a very loose rule of engagement was issued, and the convoys were extensively bombed. When the first images of the highway were received in Washington, and then started to dribble out to the news media, decisions were made to constrain air attacks, and then stop the ground war. Kuwait had been won and the images of a bloodbath had the potential to stain the outcome. Only Saddam Hussein's blowing up of Kuwait's oil infrastructure and flooding the Gulf with oil knocked the Highway of Death out of the news.

778 George Tenet later wrote: "From the outset, it was obvious that Condi was very disciplined, tough, and smart, but she brought a much different approach to the job than her predecessor. Sandy [Berger] not only didn't mind rolling up his sleeves and wading into the thick of things; he seemed to relish it. Condi, by contrast, was more remote. She knew the president's mind well but tended to stay out of policy fights that Sandy would have come brawling into." *At the Center of the Storm*, p. 138.

Former Joint Chiefs of Staff Chairman Gen. Hugh Shelton says of Berger: "Picture a sharp little ball of energy running around in the National Security Council and that's Sandy," calling him a "feisty fireplug." *Without Hesitation*, pp. 296, 297.

779 Though Dick Cheney received a verbal briefing of the Presidential Daily Brief, accompanied by his chief of staff I. Lewis "Scooter" Libby, most days he joined Bush for his brief as well; *In My Time*, p. 314.

Condoleezza Rice later testified: "At the beginning of the administration, President Bush revived the practice of meeting with the director of Central Intelligence almost every day in the Oval Office—meetings which I attended, along with the vice president and the chief of staff. At these meetings, the president received up-to-date intelligence and asked questions of his most senior intelligence officials. From January 20 through September 10, the president received at these daily meetings more than 40 briefing items on al-Qaida, and 13 of these were in response to questions he or his top advisers had posed." National Security Advisor Dr. Condoleezza Rice, Opening Remarks, The National Commission On Terrorist Attacks Upon The United States, April 8, 2004.

780 Gen. Shelton later writes: "There are two kinds of relationships between a Chairman and a Secretary of Defense. There was the kind I had with Bill Cohen, where we worked together and protected each other's flanks. And there was the McNamara-Rumsfeld model, based on deception, deceit, working political agendas ... " *Without Hesitation*, p. 401.

781 Condoleezza Rice later writes that President Bush didn't want to be put in the position of cruise missile attacks and doing "nothing more," Rice wrote. "We needed a more comprehensive approach," she said. *No Higher Honor*, p. 65.

782 In the FBI's official annual budget goals memo date May 10, 2001, AG John Ashcroft does not mention counterterrorism in his "seven strategic goals." Likewise, Ashcroft's later internal draft of the strategic plan for the Department of Justice, dated August 9, 2001, does not include counterterrorism among DOJ's most important issues. This is a sharp departure from Janet Reno, who had listed it as her highest priority. See 911 Commission Report (Official Report), p. 209.

Former NSC staff aides Benjamin and Simon later wrote that John Ashcroft sought additional funding for 68 Justice programs, none of them related to counter-terrorism. Ashcroft also declined to support the FBI's request for $58 million for some 400 counterterrorism agents, analysts, and translators; *Age of Sacred Terror*, p. 340. See also Joint Inquiry, p. 47.

Louis Freeh also met with Bush and Cheney on January 26, 2001: "at 8:45 a.m., I had my first meeting with President Bush and Vice President Cheney. They had been in office four days. We discussed, among other things, terrorism and in particular al-Qaeda, the East African Embassy bombings, USS Cole attack and the June 1996 al Khobar bombing in Saudi Arabia. When I advised the President that Hizballah and Iran were responsible for the Khobar attack, he directed me to follow-up with National Security Advisor Dr. Condoleezza Rice." See Testimony of Louis J. Freeh Before the National Commission on Terrorist Attacks Upon the United States, April 13, 2004.

783 Louis Freeh later wrote: " ... early in the Bush administration, the acting deputy attorney general told me that the 'Department's' priorities would be guns, drugs, and juvenile crimes. My response was that terrorism, complex economic crimes, and just about everything else we were doing domestically and internationally was of more import. The response I got was 'those are our marching orders ... '" *My FBI*, p. 38.

784 According to Louis Freeh, in 2000, the FBI questioned Mustafa al-Qassab, a Saudi *Shi'a* detainee implicated in the Khobar Towers attack. "In the late 1980s, al-Qassab had traveled from Saudi Arabia to Iran to meet with Ahmed al-Mughassil, the commander of the military wing of the Saudi Hezbollah. Now a decade later, al-Qassab laid out for us in detail the planning and logistics that had gone into the Khobar attack, traced the lineage irrefutably back to Tehran, and as far as I was concerned tied the whole package together for good. We still had to work our way around a wrong opinion from a prosecutor in the U.S. Attorney's Office for the District of Columbia, a civil lawyer who had little knowledge of criminal law. But she, too, passed, as did the Clinton-Gore administration and its apparent indifference to Khobar Towers." *My FBI*, p. 31.

Freeh later told the 911 Commission that, four days into the Bush administration, Condoleezza Rice "told me to pursue our investigation with the

Attorney General and to bring whatever charges possible. Within weeks, a new prosecutor was put in charge of the case and, on June 21, 2001, an indictment was returned against fourteen Saudi Hizballah subjects who had been directed to bomb Khobar by senior officials of the Iranian government. I know that the families of the 19 murdered Khobar Airmen were deeply grateful to President Bush and Dr. Rice for their prompt response and focus on terrorism." Testimony of Louis J. Freeh Before The National Commission on Terrorist Attacks Upon the United States, April 13, 2004. See also *My FBI*, p. 32.

785 Ali Soufan later writes: "To this day what keeps me awake at night is the disgraceful way that so many in the U.S. government treated the memory of the sailors. I cannot understand the lack of support for our investigation. For reasons unknown, both Democrats and Republicans in the White House and in senior government positions tried to ignore what had happened to the USS *Cole*. Families of the murdered sailors told me with sadness that President George W. Bush refused to meet with them." *The Black Banners*, p. 253.

786 By early 2001, George Tenet basked in the now accepted conventional wisdom that he had turned the Agency around. Though Agency funding overall had stayed level throughout the late 1990s, counterterrorism funding went up more than 50 percent. Tenet is also credited with expanding the ranks of the clandestine service for the first time since the end of the Cold War. By September 2011, the CIA had some 2,500 case officers with almost half of them overseas at any one time.

Former CIA number three James L. Pavitt later says: "We trained roughly two dozen new officers in 1995. Even as our missions were expanding and changing, the number of intelligence positions throughout the government, especially overseas, dropped by almost a quarter in the mid-90s. At CIA, recruitment of both operations officers and analysts came to a virtual halt." Remarks by Deputy Director for Operations James L. Pavitt at the Foreign Policy Association, June 21, 2004 (as prepared for delivery).

Tenet wrote that by the time he took over the Agency in 1997, "the FBI had more special agents in New York City than CIA had clandestine officers covering the whole world." *At the Center of the Storm*, p. 15.

787 911 Commission Report (Official Report), p. 201; *The Black Banners*, p. 221.

George Tenet later wrote: "neither our intelligence nor the FBI's criminal investigation could conclusively prove that Usama bin Ladin and his leadership had had authority, direction, and control over the attack. This is a high threshold to cross ... What's important from our perspective at CIA is that the FBI investigation had taken primacy in getting to the bottom of the matter." *At the Center of the Storm*, p. 128.

Michael Sheehan writes that before he left the Clinton administration at the end of December 2000, the CIA and FBI "had still not formally attributed the attack to *al Qaeda* ... " He later was surprised to read in the 911 Commission Report that the two agencies had in fact "concluded the obvious" right around the time of the transition; Michael Sheehan, *Crush the Cell: How to Defeat Terrorism Without Terrorizing Ourselves* (Crown, 2008), p. 138.

According to former NSC staff aides Benjamin and Simon, on February 9, 2001, intelligence briefers met with Vice President Cheney and told him that the CIA had concluded that *al Qaeda* was responsible for the bombing of the USS *Cole*; *Age of Sacred Terror*, p. 336. Before Vice President Cheney visited the CIA in mid-February, Clarke sent him a memo suggesting that he ask CIA officials "what additional information is needed before CIA can definitively conclude that al-Qida was responsible" for the *Cole*; 911 Commission Report (Official Report), p. 202 based upon NSC memo, Clarke to Vice President Cheney, February 15, 2001.

On March 2, 2001, Roger Cressey, one of Richard Clarke's assistants at the NSC, wrote Rice and Hadley that, at a belated wedding reception at Tarnak Farms for one of Bin Laden's sons, the *al Qaeda* leader had read a new poem gloating about the attack on the *Cole*. See NSC email, Cressey to Rice and Hadley, "Bin Ladin on the USS Cole," March 2, 2001. Three weeks later, Cressey again wrote Hadley to say that while the law enforcement investigation went on regarding the USS *Cole*, "we know all we need to about who did the attack to make a policy decision." See NSC email, Cressey to Hadley, "Need for Terrorism DC [Deputies Committee] Next Week," March 22, 2001.

On March 24, 2001, Richard Clarke wrote Rice and Hadley saying that the Yemeni prime minister had told the State Department counterterrorism chief that while Yemen was not saying so publicly, Yemen was 99 percent certain that Bin Laden was responsible for the *Cole*. NSC email, Clarke to NSC Front Office, "Yemen's View on the USS Cole," March 24, 2001.

Chapter 48

788 Compromise initially almost came in August 1998 when the Agency received a list of individuals who had flown into Nairobi before the Embassy attack. One of the passenger's names was an alias KSM was using. Then another report to the CIA from the intelligence service of the UAE described this same man—under alias—as being close to Osama bin Laden. The CIA's CTC even disseminated an intelligence report to the FBI highlighting a lieutenant in bin Laden's organization who was possibly linked to the African attacks, but typical of the mass of information that swirled around, the dispatch was never linked to other reports nor ultimately to KSM. With the 1996 indictment, Khalid Sheikh Mohammed was also summarily added to the State Department's TIPOFF watch list of known and suspected international terrorists, but Sheikh Mohammed had long ago ceased using his real name. By 1997, the KSM file at the CIA was empty.

Even after 9/11, the Mukhtar name wasn't connected until a year later. The Joint Inquiry stated: "The Intelligence Community knew that KSM had attended college in the United States in the 1980s. Both the CIA and FBI tried to track this down, but they were unsuccessful until the Kuwaitis published information in the media." Joint Inquiry, p. 314.

789 Project Sumner Timeline, V38, n.d. (2008) (TS/SP/MU).

790 911 Commission, pp. 256, 277; Joint Inquiry, pp. 31, 171.

791 CIA, Biographical Information on Key UBL Associates in Afghanistan, June 12, 2001.

792 Joint Inquiry, p. 28.

793 Joint Inquiry, pp. 31–32, 314.

794 Israel Prime Minister Ariel Sharon visited Washington June 26–27, 2001 on a private visit to discuss the Israeli-Palestinian Conflict with President Bush and Secretary Powell.

795 When asked about the tape on June 20, 2001, Richard Boucher, State Department spokesman says: "We don't have any particular information on this videotape ... We don't know its origin. As far as the responsibility for the bombing of the USS *Cole*, that is a matter of an ongoing investigation, and so I don't have any conclusions to draw about that. I would just say that we have heard about this tape, we have seen the reports. The kind of exhortations in this videotape that we have heard about, exhortations to violence, deserve strong condemnation from everyone. Once again, we call on the Taliban to comply with UN Resolution 1333, shut down the terrorist training camps in Afghanistan and expel Osama bin Laden to a country where he can be brought to justice for his crimes."

796 In mid-June 2001, George Tenet later writes, the CIA picked up intelligence that Osama bin Laden told trainees that there would be an attack in the near future. *At the Center of the Storm*, p. 152.

797 The CTC chief at the time of 9/11, Cofer Black, argued against deploying the Predator for reconnaissance purposes. He recalled that the Taliban had spotted a Predator in the fall of 2000 and scrambled their MiG fighters. Black wanted to wait until the armed version was ready. "I do not believe the possible recon value out-weighs the risk of possible program termination when the stakes are raised by the Taliban parading a charred Predator in front of CNN," he wrote. Military officers in the Joint Staff shared this concern." 911 Commission Report (Official Report), p. 211. See also *At the Center of the Storm*, p. 158.

Chapter 49

798 Paul Dundes Wolfowitz, deputy secretary of defense, March 2, 2001–June 1, 2005.

Chapter 50

799 "On June 10, 2000, al-Mihdhar left the United States enroute to Kuwait transiting Frankfurt, Germany. Al-Mihdhar is then believed to have returned to Saudi Arabia ... ." Statement for the Record, FBI Director Robert S. Mueller III, Joint Intelligence Committee Inquiry, September 26, 2002.

800 "Known" here is a complex formulation that mirrors the language of the intelligence community. Though the Mihdhar name was mentioned in a variety of intelligence cables and reports from January–March 2000, the Saudi was never "known" to anyone inside the Agency or the FBI. See CIA (operational) cable, "UBL Associate Travel to Malaysia—Khalid Bin Muhammad bin 'Abdallah al-Mihdhar," January 5, 2000; CIA (operational) cable, "UBL Associates: Identification of Possible UBL Associates," March 5, 2000; CIA (operational) cable, Mihdhar's visa application, January 5, 2000; CIA (operational) cable, "Recent Influx of Suspected UBL Associates to Malaysia," January 5, 2000; 911 Commission Report (Official Report), pp. 181, 268; *At the Center of the Storm*, p. 197. See, in particular, Testimony of Michael E. Rolince, Special Agent in Charge, Washington Division, FBI; before the Select Committee on Intelligence, United States Senate, Permanent Select Committee on Intelligence, September 20, 2002.

801 CIA (operational) cable, "UBL Associates: Identification of Possible UBL Associates," March 5, 2000; 911 Commission Report (Official Report), p. 181.

802 Nurjaman Riduan Isamuddin (aka "Hambali"), served as the *al Qaeda* operations director for the East Asia region and head of *Jemaah Islamiyah* (JI) ("Islamic Congregation). See Statement by the Treasury Department Regarding Today's Designation of Two Leaders of *Jemaah Islamiyah*, January 24, 2003

803 The January 2000 meeting in Malaysia also included Yazid Sufaat, a Malaysian scientist and a member of JI who also owned a laboratory that U.S. intelligence suspected provided cover for *al Qaeda* chemical and biological weapons developments. See 911 Commission Report (Official Report), pp. 159, 226; *At the Center of the Storm*, p. 196; CIA (operational) cable, "UBL Associates Depart Malaysia," January 8, 2000.

804 Hazmi and Mihdhar both took an introductory lesson at the Sorbi Flying Club at Montgomery Field in San Diego on May 5, 2000, followed by a second lesson at the same school five days later on May 10. See FBI, Working Draft Chronology of Events for Hijackers and Associates; Statement for the Record, FBI Director Robert S. Mueller III, Joint Intelligence Committee Inquiry, September 26, 2002.

805 Mohammed Rashed Daoud Al-'Owhali. On June 12, 2001, a federal court sentenced Saudi citizen al-'Owhali to life in prison without parole for his role in the 1998 bombing of the U.S. Embassy in Kenya. See *The Cell*, p. 212; *Looming Tower*, pp. 276–278; *Age of Sacred Terror*, pp. 28ff.

806 FBI Form 302 (witness interview record), Subject: Interview of Mohammed al-Owhali, August 23, 1998 (obtained by the author). See also *The Black Banners*, pp. 87, 291; Joint Inquiry, pp. 155–156.

At the request of the FBI, the Kenyan Telephone company, which maintained paper records of international calls, pulled every call made from Kenya to Yemen, including al-Owhali's number. That call was made from a house the Bureau then raided with their Kenyan counterparts.

807 Joint Inquiry, p. 144.

808 Ali Soufan later writes: "At the same time, we traced the telephone number Rasheed [al-Owhali] [sic—the name is Mohammed] had written down to a man in Yemen named Ahmed al-Hada. By monitoring the number, we found that it appeared to be used as the main contact number for al-Qaeda in Yemen, and that calls placed from it went regularly to a satellite phone that U.S. authorities had already been monitoring because it belonged to Osama bin Laden." *The Black Banners*, p. 88. See also ISB Study on Educing Information, Intelligence Interviewing: Teaching Papers and Case Studies, pp. 107, 110, footnote 8.

809 See Moussaoui document DX-0471.pdf; Joint Inquiry, p. 11.
   James Bamford and Ali Soufan write that the NSA intercept indicated that Khalid, "Nawaf" and "Salem" (Salem al-Hazmi, Nawaf's brother) were traveling to Malaysia. See *A Pretext for War*, pp. 222ff; *The Black Banners*, p. 291. That in itself was evidently based upon the same information contained in 911 Commission Report (Official Report), p. 181. But it is not true; Salem stayed in Afghanistan until July 2001.
   Nawaf al-Hazmi also did not fly together with Khalid al-Mihdhar. He arrived in Kuala Lumpur from Karachi, Pakistan on January 4, 2000. See discussion in Joint Inquiry, pp. 143–145.
   Lawrence Wright's *The Looming Tower* (p. 310) also reports an inverted version of events: "At the end of 1999, Khallad telephoned Mihdhar and summoned him to a meeting in Kuala Lumpur. It was the only time that members of the two teams would be together. The NSA picked up a conversation from the phone of Mihdhar's father-in-law, Ahmad al-Hada, in Yemen—the one that *al Qaeda* used as a message board—in which the forthcoming meeting in Malaysia was mentioned, along with the full name of Khaled [sic] al-Mihdhar and the first names of two other participants: Nawaf and Salem. The NSA had information from the same phone that Nawaf's last name was Hazmi, although the agency did not check its own database. 'Something nefarious might be afoot,' the NSA reported, but it did not pursue the matter further."

810 CIA (operational) cable, "UBL Associate Travel to Malaysia—Khalid Bin Muhammad bin 'Abdallah al-Mihdhar," January 5, 2000; CIA (operational) cable, Mihdhar's visa application, January 5, 2000; CIA (operational) cable, "Recent Influx of Suspected UBL Associates to Malaysia," January 5, 2000.

811 *At the Center of the Storm*, pp. 194–195; Unclassified Version of Director of Central Intelligence George J. Tenet's Testimony Before the Joint Inquiry.

812 Khalid al-Mihdhar arrived at Dubai International on Yemeni Flight 802 from Sanaa, Yemen on January 4, 2000 and stayed for one night at the Nihaar Hotel; FBI, Working Draft Chronology of Events for Hijackers and Associates.
   George Tenet later wrote: "With the help of a local intelligence agency, on January 4, 2000, one person whom we initially knew only as 'Khalid' was identified as he passed through a third country en route to Malaysia. The local intelligence

service copied the man's passport, which identified him as Khalid al-Mihdhar." *At the Center of the Storm*, p. 194.

Ironically, KSM would later tell U.S. intelligence that al-Hazmi and al-Mihdhar were supposed to use Yemeni documents to fly to Malaysia, then proceed to the United States using their Saudi passports to conceal their prior travels to and from Pakistan, a statement that was either false or al-Hazmi and al-Mihdhar ignored his orders. See 911 Commission Report (Official Report), p. 158.

An example of how reporting can be incorrect or incomplete, obviously giving credit where it isn't due and based upon the self-interest of the source, is in *The Looming Tower*, p. 311, where the author says that the CIA broke into al-Mihdhar's hotel room in Dubai and photographed his passport, suggesting of course a greater decisiveness and sense of derring-do on the part of the Agency than is true. Wright's sources were primarily FBI though, and this version of events additionally shifts any blame for subsequent mistakes regarding identifying al-Mihdhar from the FBI to the CIA.

Bob Woodward also gets the story wrong in *Bush at War* (Simon & Schuster, 2002), pp. 23–24: "A paid CIA spy had placed him at an *al Qaeda* meeting. They had informed the FBI, who put him on a domestic watch list, but he had slipped into the United States over the summer and avoided detection by the bureau." This version absolves the CIA and place blame on the FBI.

See also Joint Inquiry, p. 144; CIA [operational] cable, "Activities of Bin Ladin Associate Khalid Revealed," January 4, 2000; CIA [operational] cable, "Identification of UBL Associate Khalid Transiting Dubai," January 4, 2000; CIA [operational] cable, "Transit of UBL Associate Khalid through Dubai," January 4, 2000; CIA [operational] cable, Khalid's passport, January 4, 2000.

Most important though, Ali Soufan writes that the CIA passed the information on al-Mihdhar to "foreign intelligence agencies but had not told the FBI, the Immigration and Naturalization Service, or the State Department" and he makes a pretty detailed case to back up his claim; see *The Black Banners*, p. 290.

813 The fiction that Khalid al-Mihdhar was a fisherman from Mecca persisted even long after 9/11, despite al-Mihdhar's veteran *al Qaeda* status and family relationship with a senior *al Qaeda* administrator (the Yemen switchboard operator), and his actual status working for Saudi intelligence, probably under *al Qaeda* cover under a false name. An article in *The Washington Post* on the one-year anniversary of 9/11, for instance, said that when the Hamburg cell arrived in Kandahar, waiting were Khalid al-Mihdhar, a "former Red Sea fisherman who came from Mecca," and Nawaf al-Hazmi, a merchant also from Mecca, *according to interviews with officials at the Saudi Interior Ministry's offices in Jiddah* [Jeddah] (emphasis added). See Peter Finn, "Hamburg's Cauldron of Terror: Within Cell of 7, Hatred Toward U.S. Grew and Sept. 11 Plot Evolved," *The Washington Post*, September 11, 2002, p. A1.

814 CIA [operational] cable, "UBL Associate Travel to Malaysia—Khalid Bin Muhammad bin 'Abdallah al-Mihdhar," January 5, 2000; CIA [operational] cable, "UBL Associates: Identification of Possible UBL Associates," January 5, 2000; CIA [operational] cable, Mihdhar's visa application, January 5, 2000; CIA [operational] cable, "Recent Influx of Suspected UBL Associates to Malaysia," January 5, 2000; CIA [operational] cable, Arrival of UBL Associate Khalid Bin Muhammad bin 'Abdallah al-Mihdhar," January 6, 2000; CIA [operational] cable, "UBL Associates Travel to Malaysia and Beyond—Khalid Bin Muhammad bin 'Abdallah al-Mihdhar," January 6, 2000; CIA [operational] email, Rob to John and others, "Malaysia—for the record," January 6, 2000.

The 911 Commission incorrectly concluded that the Malaysia meeting was preparation for a plane's operation in Southeast Asia and that bin Laden subsequently cancelled that part in the spring of 2000. "He evidently decided it would be too difficult to coordinate this attack with the operation in the United States." See 911 Commission Report (Official Report), p. 159; 911 Commission, Staff Statement Number 16, p. 3; Substitution of the Testimony of Khalid Sheikh Mohammed, p. 7.

815 *Jemaah Islamiyah* is a Southeast Asian extremist Islamist group dedicated to the establishment of an Islamic state. It was founded in January 1993.

816 The 911 Commission Report (Official Report), p. 181, says that the CIA and FBI directors, as well as national security advisor Samuel Berger were all briefed in real time during the January 2000 Malaysia meeting.

817 911 Commission Report (Official Report), p. 158.

818 FBI, Working Draft Chronology of Events for Hijackers and Associates.

819 CIA [operational] cable, "Efforts to Locate al-Mihdhar," January 13, 2000; CIA [operational] cable, "UBL Associates: Flight Manifest for MH072," January 9, 2000; CIA [operational] cable, "UBL Associates: Flight Manifest," January 9, 2000; CIA [operational] cable, "UBL Associates Depart Malaysia," January 8, 2000; cited in 911 Commission Report (Official Report), p. 181.

820 FBI, Working Draft Chronology of Events for Hijackers and Associates; 911 Commission Staff Statement Number 16, pp. 4, 13.

821 The 911 Commission concluded that on the basis of links associated with Khalid al-Mihdhar, the CIA's bin Laden cell speculated that Khallad and Khalid al Mihdhar might be one and the same; 911 Commission Report (Official Report), p. 266.

George Tenet later writes: "By December 2000, investigators began wondering whether Khallad bin Attash [Khallad] and Khalid al-Mihdhar ... might be one and the same. It turned out that both were at the [January 5–8 Malaysia] meeting, but they were two different individuals." *At the Center of the Storm*, p. 197.

According to the FBI IG report (Moussaoui document 952a.pdf): The CIA reported in a December 2000 cable it had learned that Fahd al Quso, who was in Yemeni custody for his participation in the USS Cole attack, had received $7,000 from someone named Ibrahim, which Quso had taken to Bangkok on January 6, 2000 to deliver to "Khallad," a friend of Ibrahim's. The cable notes that this is the same time al-Mihdhar had departed Kuala Lumpur for Bangkok, and that

Khalid al-Mihdhar was the "Khallad" mentioned by Quso. When a source is shown Malaysia pictures to confirm the CIA's supposition, he is unable to identify Mihdhar, but says that another individual in the photographs is "Khallad." The CIA then determined that its supposition that Mihdhar and Khallad are one and the same is wrong.

822 CIA [operational] cable, "UBL Associates: Identification of Possible UBL Associates," March 5, 2000.

Yousaf is the alias used by Khallad for his trip to Southeast Asia. He left Bangkok on January 20 for Karachi, Pakistan. CIA, intelligence report, interrogation of Khallad, January 14, 2004.

823 CIA [operational] cable, Hazmi entered U.S., March 6, 2000. See also Testimony of Michael E. Rolince, Special Agent in Charge, Washington Division, FBI; before the Select Committee on Intelligence, United States Senate, Permanent Select Committee on Intelligence, September 20, 2002; Unclassified Version of Director of Central Intelligence George J. Tenet's Testimony Before the Joint Inquiry.

824 Joint Inquiry, p. 147.

825 FBI, Working Draft Chronology of Events for Hijackers and Associates; Joint Inquiry, pp. 16–17.

826 After the October 2000 attack on the USS *Cole*, George Tenet says that "we discovered further intelligence linking Khallad to the phone number in Yemen that had been associated with the Kuala Lumpur [January 5–8] meeting. See *At the Center of the Storm*, p. 197.

827 Two family members from Yemen delivered their package to Khallad in Bangkok after the two Saudis had left for America. The $5,000 cash dowry was very much appreciated by her family, they told Khallad to convey to the *Sheikh*. Bin Laden married his fifth wife on July 25, 2000. See 911 Commission, Staff Statement Number 16, p. 3.

Chapter 51

828 Project Sumner Timeline, V38, n.d. (2008) (TS/SP/MU).

Chapter 52

829 Taif is a city in the Mecca Province of southwest Saudi Arabia on the slopes of the Sarawat Mountains at the elevation of 6,000 feet. It is the unofficial summer capital and retreat for royals from the heat of Riyadh.

830 "Taif Home to Magnificent Historical Palaces," *Saudi Gazette*, April 10, 2015.

831 The Sudairi (or Sudayri) seven or Al Fahd refers to the "uterine" brothers of Hussa Sudairi: Sultan, Abd al-Rahman. Turki, Nayef, Salman and Ahmad. See *A Fury for God*, pp. 155–156.

832 The Sudairi seven brothers came to occupy all of the key ministry posts of the government; see *The Bin Ladens*, p. 159.

833 In the August 7, 1990 meeting between Secretary of Defense Dick Cheney and King Fahd, which included a large entourage, the King sought the advice of the princes present. See *It Doesn't Take a Hero*, pp. 306ff; William T. Y'Blood, *The Eagle and the Scorpion: The USAF and Desert Shield First-Phase Deployment*, 7 August–8 November 1990 (Center for Air Force History, 1992); Richard A. Clarke, "Mission to Jeddah," Middle East Institute, August 7, 2015.

834 Condoleezza Rice stresses more than once in her autobiography the degree to which the June and July threat warnings were for an attack "on U.S. interests abroad." *No Higher Honor*, p. 69.

835 CNN, Rush Transcript, "Kuwait Celebrates 10th Anniversary of Iraqi Troop Withdrawal; Former President Bush, Schwarzkopf, Powell on Hand," February 26, 2001; 10:07 a.m. ET.

836 *No Higher Honor*, pp. xvii, 67.

837 The Khobar Towers indictment was unveiled on June 21, 2001. The Eastern District of Virginia files 46 charges against 14 suspects (13 Saudis and one Lebanese) arising from the June 25, 1996 truck bomb attack on the Khobar Towers military barracks in Dhahran, Saudi Arabia. All were indicted for conspiracy based on their connection to Saudi Hizb'allah.

Louis Freeh later writes: "Jim Comey had accomplished what an entire administration had failed to do over the course of four and a half years. ... The timing of the indictment was not by chance. Had we failed to bring the charges by June 26, a number of the counts would have been barred by the five-year statute of limitation." *My FBI*, p. 32.

838 Condoleezza Rice talks frankly about this pro-Israel bias and the split within the early administration. She explains that she was drawn to Ariel Sharon, the leader of the conservative Likud, who became Prime Minister on February 6, 2001. "He seemed to embody the Israeli experience because, in truth, without toughness, perseverance, and even ruthlessness, Israel would have ceased to exist in a neighborhood bent on its destruction." See *No Higher Honor*, pp. 50–56.

839 "The call, warm and familiar in tone, was, according to one Administration official, "designed to encourage Abdullah to think of the new President as having a grasp of the Middle East similar to that of his father." Editorial, "Review & Outlook: Bush's Mideast Box," *Wall Street Journal*, August 2, 2001.

On February 27, 2001, Crown Prince Abdullah also received former President Bush in Saudi Arabia. Bush was accompanied by former Secretary of Commerce

Robert Mosbach. See ADCI(SP) Apex Watch Memorandum, Travel of SX-183 (S/NF), February 25, 2001, TS/SP/MU.

840 Condoleezza Rice refers to "the Vice President's staff" in a pejorative way numerous times in her autobiography; see *No Higher Honor*, p. 17.

841 Condoleezza Rice later writes: "the intelligence assessment was that an attack would most likely come in Jordan, Saudi Arabia, Israel or in Europe." *No Higher Honor*, p. xvii.

842 Joint Inquiry, p. 111.

843 Joint Inquiry, p. 151.

Chapter 53

844 *Dead Certain*, pp. 130–131.

845 Tony Karon, "Bin Laden Rides Again: Myth vs. Reality," *Time Magazine*, June 20, 2001.

846 On June 19, 2001, Vice President Cheney refused to release records of energy task force meetings even to the General Accounting Office, a government agency.

847 John David Ashcroft, Attorney General of the United States, February 2, 2001-February 3, 2005.

848 Condoleezza Rice tells an interesting story as to how the announcement of abandonment of Kyoto originated in the vice president's office and went to Congress before she even had a chance to see the announcement; *No Higher Honor*, pp. 41–42.

849 On June 17, 2001, Secretary of State Colin Powell announced that the United States would withdraw from the ABM Treaty. Powell stated, "If there is no ABM Treaty tomorrow, there is no nation that's going to run out and start making nuclear weapons. We are going to move forward with missile defense." Powell also stated that the U.S. cannot allow the constraints of the treaty to bind American technology.

850 See Senator Jim Jeffords party affiliation announcement, May 24, 2001, from Republican to independent.

851 Deputy National Security Advisor Steven Hadley circulated the first draft of the new National Security Presidential Directive (NSPD) on June 7, describing it as "an admittedly ambitious" program for confronting *al Qaeda*. The draft goal was to "*eliminate* the al Qida network of terrorist groups as a threat to the United States and to friendly governments." It called for a multi-year effort involving diplomacy, covert action, economic measures, law enforcement, public diplomacy, and if necessary military efforts.

See National Security Advisor Dr. Condoleezza Rice, Opening Remarks, The National Commission On Terrorist Attacks Upon The United States, April 8, 2004; 911 Commission Report (Official Report), pp. 205, 208, 210; based upon NSC memo, Hadley to Armitage, Wolfowitz, McLaughlin, and O'Keefe, "Next Steps on al-Qida," June 7, 2001. See also *Age of Sacred Terror*, p. 343.

852 Project Sumner Timeline, V38, n.d. (2008) (TS/SP/MU).

853 911 Commission Report (Official Report), p. 255. See also NSC email, Clarke to Rice and Hadley, Terrorism Update, March 30, 2001; CIA (operational) cable, "Intelligence Community Terrorist Threat Advisory," March 30, 2001.

854 See NSC email, Clarke to Rice, Terrorist Threat Warning, April 10, 2001.

855 The call to the UAE was originally reported by the CIA on May 16. It came from an anonymous caller. Neither the CIA nor the FBI was able to corroborate the information in the call. See FBI report, Daily UBL/Radical Fundamentalist Threat Update, ITOS [International Terrorism Operations Section] Threat Update Webpage, May 16, 2001; 911 Commission Report (Official Report), p. 256, based on CIA intelligence report, Threat Report, May 16, 2001.

856 In the infamous Presidential Daily Brief of August 6, 2001, "Bin Laden determined to strike in U.S.," there is this entry:

> *"We have not been able to corroborate some of the more sensational threat reporting, such as that from a [deleted] service in 1998 saying that Bin Ladin wanted to hijack a US aircraft to gain the release of "Blind Shaykh" 'Umar 'Abd al-Rahman and other US-held extremists.*
>
> Nevertheless, FBI information since that time indicates patterns of suspicious activity in this country consistent with preparations for hijackings or other types of attacks, including recent surveillance of federal buildings in New York.
>
> The FBI is conducting approximately 70 full field investigations throughout the US that it considers Bin Ladin-related. CIA and the FBI are investigating a call to our Embassy in the UAE in May saying that a group of Bin Ladin supporters was in the US planning attacks with explosives."

857 911 Commission Report (Official Report), p. 256; based upon SEIB, "Terrorist Groups Said Cooperating on US Hostage Plot," May 23, 2001.

858 Joint Inquiry, pp. 202–204 describes the March through June 2001 warnings and alerts.

859 The 27th G8 Summit met in Genoa, Italy on July 21–22, 2001. See also *Age* *of Sacred Terror*, p. 342; *The Looming Tower*, p. 338.

860 Written Statement for the Record of the Director of Central Intelligence, Before the National Commission on Terrorist Attacks Upon the United States, March 24, 2004.

861 The meeting took place on April 19, 2001. 911 Commission Report (Official Report), p. 255, based upon NSC email, Cressey to Rice and Hadley, Threat Update, April 19, 2001. See also FBI electronic communication, Heightened Threat Advisory, April 13, 2001 (Moussaoui document 428.pdf); NSC email, Clarke to Rice, Terrorist Threat Warning, April 10, 2001.

862 Abu Zubaydah, the alias for Zein al Abideen Mohamed Hussein (aka Zayn al-Abidin Muhammad Husayn, Daud (Daood), Malik, Tareq (Tariq), Hamza Ibrahim Zuhayfa al-Abdi Asiri, Abd al-Aziz al-Numani, Takhi Obed Takhi al-Kantani, Simon the Palestinian); Palestinian born in Riyadh, Saudi Arabia on March 12, 1971, where his father worked as a teacher.

After growing up in Saudi Arabia, Abu Zubaydah attended computer school in India, although he considered studying in the United States before and after. He is suspected of having illegally entered Pakistan during the Afghan war against the Soviets and received militant training in the late 1980s. After the Soviet war he remained in Pakistan; in 1992 he moved to Peshawar, where he may have set up a honey trading business. Abu Zubaydah sustained a head wound from shrapnel while on the front lines. He had to relearn fundamentals such as walking, talking, and writing. In 1991 or 1992, he applied for membership in *al Qaeda* but was rejected (possibly because of his injury), and then later declined to join because of his desire to focus on Israel. He began work as an administrator, travel facilitator and documents expert, aiding mujahidin coming to and going from Afghanistan.

Many sources say Abu Zubaydah was head (*emir*) of Khalden and Darunta camps near Khost, Afghanistan; but this is confusion with the fact that he was head of administration for the camp and also head of the Khalden guesthouse in Islamabad (and other guest houses), where he handled young men arriving for *jihad* and assisted them to receive training in Afghanistan. During 1994, he was either emir or a trainer at the al Farooq camp in Afghanistan for seven to eight months, returning to Pakistan to continue his work as a travel facilitator, helping *al Qaeda* members move from Sudan to Afghanistan. From 1998–2001, Abu Zubaydah traveled between Afghanistan and Pakistan, mostly involved in travel facilitation, training, and plotting terrorist attacks on Israel.

Abu Zubaydah was involved in Ahmed Ressam's 1999 attempt to bomb Los Angeles International Airport and other Millennium plots in Jordan. "While he was not a member of al-Qaeda, his role as external emir of Khalden was of considerable importance." See *The Black Banners*, p. 373.

See also DOD, Office for the Administrative Review of the Detention of Enemy Combatants, Subject: Summary of Evidence for Combatant Status Review Tribunal—Husayn, Zayn Al Abidin Muhammad [Abu Zubaydah] March 19, 2007; and *The Black Banners*, p. 143.

863 CIA, Biographical Information on Key UBL Associates in Afghanistan, June 11, 2001. See also 911 Commission Report (Official Report), p. 277.

864 *No Higher Honor*, p. 66.

865 Egyptian intelligence reported a plot by *Jemaah Islamiya* to attack U.S. and Israeli interests to seek the release of the Blind Sheikh. "Four trucks filled with C-4 explosives had been brought to Kampala, in Uganda, and operatives there had begun casing the American embassy. We immediately contracted the Ugandans and also brought in the Tanzanians and Kenyans." *At the Center of the Storm*, p. 155.

866 "The Joint Inquiry reviewed SEIBs [Senior Executive Intelligence Briefs] distributed by the Intelligence Community in the spring and summer of 2001 and confirmed a rise in reporting on Bin Ladin between March and June. This increase was still only a relatively small portion of the array of intelligence subjects that the SEIBs brought to the attention of policymakers. For example, the peak in Bin Ladin–related reporting came in June 2001 when Islamic extremists, including Bin Ladin and al-Qa'ida, were referred to in eighteen of the 298 articles that appeared in the SEIBs that month." Joint Inquiry, pp. 206–207.
    Condoleezza Rice remembered the spring of 2001 differently: "The remainder of the spring was [other than dealing with the Chinese on the P-3 incident] for the most part, relatively straight-forward. Though the Balkans flared up, with violence in Macedonia that threatened stability in the region, it was not the kind of crisis that dominated the agenda of the White House every day." *No Higher Honor*, p. 49.

867 Condoleezza Rice later writes that after President Bush said in an interview that the sanctions against Saddam had become 'Swiss cheese,' the first NSC meeting "reviewed the state of the sanctions regime and also examined the problem of how to make the no-fly zones more effective." *No Higher Honor*, p. 31.

868 *State of War*, pp. 183–184. Interestingly when National Security Advisor Rice mentions the pre-9/11 no-fly zones in her autobiography for the first time, she says that U.S. aircraft were flying out of Turkey and Kuwait, omitting Saudi Arabia. Perhaps the secret detail hadn't reached her level, or more, the omission is emblematic of the way Saudi Arabia is treated differently, even in history, by just omitting them. See *No Higher Honor*, p. 32.

869 On April 10, 2001, the CIA published its first assessment of Iraqi importation of aluminum tubes (Senior Executive Intelligence Brief, 01-083 CHX), noting that they "have little use other than for a uranium enrichment program." The tubes, manufactured in China, were seized in Jordan and a sample was obtained by the U.S. government. On June 14, the CIA published a senior-publish-when-ready (SPWR) report which stated that the aluminum tubes being imported by Iraq from China are "controlled items under the Nuclear Suppliers Group and Chinese export laws, are suitable for uranium enrichment gas centrifuge rotors and, while less likely, could be used as rocket bodies for multiple rocket launchers (MRLs)." On June 30, the CIA published a SPWR report which noted that Iraq will likely claim that the aluminum tubes it is importing from China are intended for conventional or civilian use. The report acknowledges that such claims "cannot be discounted," but adds that the tubes' specifications "far exceed any known conventional weapons application, including rocket motor casings for 81mm" multiple rocket launchers. See also CIA, Iraq's Current Nuclear Capabilities (June 20, 2001) (noting that although the aluminum tubes are "more consistent" with a centrifuge application, "we are also considering nonnuclear applications for the tubes."); DOE Daily Intelligence Highlight, "Iraq: Aluminum Alloy Tube Purchase," May 9, 2001; DOE Daily Intelligence Highlight, "Iraq: High Strength Aluminum Tube Procurement," April 11, 2001.

870 See DOS cable, State 041824, "Secretary's 26 February Meeting with Saudi Crown Prince Abdullah," March 8, 2001; DOS cable, State 117132, "The Secretary's June 29 Meeting with Saudi Crown Prince Abdullah," July 5, 2001.

871 If there was any doubt that the Bush administration had no Middle East policy, just look at the testimony of Gen. Tommy Franks before the House Armed Services Committee on April 13, 2001. Franks says that American "vital interest" is to maintain uninterrupted access to energy resources. "The Persian Gulf region contains roughly 68 percent of the world's known oil and natural gas reserves—more than 40 percent of which pass through the Strait of Hormuz," Franks said. "And so, one of our responsibilities—in fact, one of our objectives—is to maintain access to these energy resources at the same time that we maintain access to markets in the region," he remarked.

872 George Tenet later wrote: "In early June 2001, I flew out to Amman, Cairo, and Tel Aviv. I don't think the Bush people expected much to come out of my trip—to them, it was more like a duty call—but after a week of intense negotiations and constant shuttling from capital to capital, we managed to produce what became known as the Tenet Security Work Plan, a very clear, very straightforward timetable that laid out the steps both sides had agreed to take to strengthen the security framework." *At the Center of the Storm*, p. 81.

He later writes that he "spent a good part of early June in the Middle East trying to come up with a work plan that would stabilize the security situation between the Israelis and Palestinians." *At the Center of the Storm*, p. 303.

873 There was internal criticism of the liaison system. Michael Scheuer, for instance, believed that "The CIA needed to break out of lazy dependence on liaisons with corrupt, Islamist-riddled intelligence services such as the ISI and the Saudi General Intelligence Department ... If it did not ... the CIA and the United States would pay a price." See *Ghost Wars*, p. 415.

874 *At the Center of the Storm*, p. 149; 911 Commission Report (Official Report), pp. 250, 258; "Planning for Bin Laden Attacks Continues, Despite Delays," the Senior Executive Intelligence Brief (SEIB) lead piece headlined on July 2, 2001.

875 According to the 911 Commission, Condoleezza Rice viewed the draft directive on counterterrorism as the embodiment of a comprehensive new strategy employing all instruments of national power to eliminate the *al Qaeda* threat. Richard Clarke, however, regarded the new draft as essentially similar to the proposal he had developed in December 2000 and put forward to the new administration in January 2001; see 911 Commission Report (Official Report), p. 205.

The distinction between roll-back and elimination is so inscrutable, the Deputy National Security Advisor Steven Hadley confusingly later told the Joint Inquiry that: "From the first days of the Bush Administration through September 2001, it conducted a comprehensive, senior-level review of policy for dealing with al-Qa'ida. The goal was to move beyond the policy of containment, criminal prosecution, and limited retaliation for specific attacks, toward attempting to 'roll back' al Qa'ida." Joint Inquiry, p. 218. See also *No Higher Honor*, p. 65.

876 911 Commission Report (Official Report), pp. 205–207, based upon NSC memo, Summary of Conclusions of June 29, 2001, Deputies Committee meeting, undated (attached to NSC memo, Biegun to executive secretaries, July 6, 2001).

Perhaps one of the reasons why the deputies meetings dragged on was that Rumsfeld disliked NSC principals meetings, according to Rice, "letting it be known that they were an unwelcome distraction from his day job of running the Pentagon ... " See *No Higher Honor*, p. 19. "The atmosphere in the Pentagon was one where nothing was really settled until the security had opined. That handicapped the Deputies Committee ... that Steve [Hadley] chaired and made necessary the very Principals meetings that Don detested." See *No Higher Honor*, p. 20. And then there was the animus between Rumsfeld and Powell. Rice writes: "The truth is that we would have had fewer Principals meetings had the distrust between Don [Rumsfeld] and Colin [Powell] not made the levels below the secretaries largely incapable of taking decisions." See *No Higher Honor*, p. 20.

877 As the draft presidential directive was circulated in July, the State Department sent the deputies a lengthy historical review of U.S. efforts to engage the Taliban about Bin Laden from 1996 on. "These talks have been fruitless," the State Department concluded; See 911 Commission Report (Official Report), p. 206.

878 Charles Krauthammer, "A Vacation Bush Deserves," *The Washington Post*, August 10, 2001; Howard Kurtz, "Bush, Mass Feel Washington," *The Washington Post*, August 7, 2001; Jim VandeHei and Peter Baker, "Vacationing Bush Poised to Set a Record," *The Washington Post*, August 3, 2001.

"By the summer of 2001, President Bush was being berated in the press for not being a particularly hard worker, a chorus that intensified when he announced in July that he would be taking a thirty-one day vacation because in August and lasting through Labor Day." See *Intelligence Matters*, p. 80.

Chapter 54

879 The 911 Commission says: "KSM attempted to drop Mihdhar from the planes operation and would have done so, he says, had he not been overruled by Bin Ladin." 911 Commission Report (Official Report), pp. 220–222.

880 KSM Debrief Papers, 2005.

Chapter 55

881 Project Sumner Timeline, V38, n.d. (2008) (TS/SP/MU).

882 KSM makes reference to each of these individuals in his debriefs as well, often with multiple names. See CIA analytic report, Khalid Sheik [sic] Muhammad's Nephews, CTC 2003-300013, January 31, 2003.

883 See White House Counterterrorism Security Group (CSG), Memorandum, Al Qai'da Warning for July 4th Weekend, June 29, 2001. "Clarke and others told us of a particular concern about possible attacks on the Fourth of July. After it passed uneventfully, the CSG decided to maintain the alert." 911 Commission Report (Official Report), p. 258.

"The head of counterterrorism at the FBI, Dale Watson, said … [t]hey had expected an attack on July 4. Watson said he felt deeply that something was going to happen. But he told us the threat information was "nebulous." He wished he had known more. He wished he had had "500 analysts looking at Usama Bin Ladin threat information instead of two." 911 Commission Report (Official Report), p. 265.

Bob Woodward later wrote: "Tenet had worried that there would be attacks during the July 4, 2001, celebration … there had been 34 specific communications intercepts among various bin Laden associates that summer making declarations such as 'Zero hour is tomorrow' or 'Something spectacular is coming.' There had been so many of these intercepts—often called chatter—picked up in the intelligence system and so many reports of threats that Tenet had gone to maximum alert. It seemed like an attack of some sort was imminent against U.S. embassies abroad or concentrations of American tourists, but the intelligence never pinpointed when or where or by what method." *Bush at War*, p. 3.

State Department spokesman Richard Boucher said on July 5th that there was a "Worldwide Caution" in effect until September 2: "The 4th of July was not cited in the Caution. We do continue to believe there is an increased risk of terrorist action from extremist groups and recommend that people exercise a high level of vigilance, take appropriate steps to increase their security. So no, nothing has changed in that. If it should change, we will revise the Caution."

" … the FBI's Executive Assistant Director for Counterterrorism testified that in 2001 he thought there was a high probability—'98 percent'—that the attack would be overseas. The latter was the clear majority view, despite the fact that the Intelligence Community had information suggesting that Bin Ladin had planned, and was capable of, conducting attacks within the domestic United States." Joint Inquiry, pp. 8, 208.

884 Mohammed Atta also traveled to Spain in January 2001.

George Tenet later says: "No details have yet emerged on the week he spent in Spain, although it may have been to meet with another al-Qa'ida operative to pass along an update on the pilots' training progress and receive information on the supporting hijackers who would begin arriving in the US in the spring. On 10 January, Atta returned to the US, flying from Madrid to Miami." See Unclassified Version of Director of Central Intelligence George J. Tenet's Testimony Before the Joint Inquiry.

Epilogue

885 KSM Debrief Papers, 2005.

886 A record of the call was captured in toll records maintained by the telephone companies and identified in a record's check after 9/11. See FBI, Working Draft Chronology of Events for Hijackers and Associates.

887 KSM et al Indictment, p. 25.

888 See in particular, Interagency Intelligence Committee on Terrorism (IICT), "Khalid Shaykh Muhammad's Threat Reporting—Precious Truths, Surrounded by a Bodyguard of Lies," April 3, 2003.

889 Joint Task Force Guantanamo, Subject: Combatant Status Review Tribunal Input and Recommendation for Continued Detention Under DoD Control (CD) for Guantanamo Detainee ISN: US9YM-010013DP (S), Secret/NF, December 8, 2006.

890 Project Sumner, Name List Working Paper (U), n.d. (2000?) (TS-MU-00-16).

891 *The Black Banners*, p. 345 says he was killed with seven other *al-Qaeda* members.

892 *The Secret History of al Qaeda*, p. 25.

893 Joint Task Force Guantanamo, Subject: Combatant Status Review Tribunal Input and Recommendation for Continued Detention Under DoD Control (CD) for Guantanamo Detainee ISN: US9YM-010013DP (S), Secret/NF. 8 December 2006.

894 CIA analytic report, "The Plot and the Plotters (U)," June 1, 2003, p. 185.

895 Joint Task Force Guantanamo, Subject: Combatant Status Review Tribunal Input and Recommendation for Continued Detention Under DoD Control (CD) for Guantanamo Detainee ISN: US9YM-010013DP (S), Secret/NF. 8 December 2006.

896 CIA, intelligence report, interrogation of Khallad, January 14, 2004.

897 *The Black Banners*, p. 550.

898 DOD, Office for the Administrative Review of the Detention of Enemy Combatants, Summary of Evidence for Combatant Status Review Tribunal—Al Baluchi, Ammar, March 28, 2007.

899 CIA analytic report, Khalid Sheik Muhammad's Nephews, CTC 2003-300013, January 31, 2003; Summary of Penttbom [Pentagon attack] Investigation, p. 65; *The Black Banners*, p. 550.

900 The sons of al-Hada, Najeeb al-Hada (Abu Jaffar al-Yemeni) and Sameer (Samir) Ahmad al-Hada (Abed al-Rahman), both were killed, Najeeb in an explosive accident in Afghanistan in 1997 or 1999; Sameer, an *al Qaeda* courier, died in a hand grenade suicide the day his father was being arrested. See Combating Terrorism Center at West Point, "A False Foundation? AQAP, Tribes and Ungoverned Spaces in Yemen," September 2011, p. 35; *The Black Banners*, pp. 318, 338.

901 DOD, Office for the Administrative Review of the Detention of Enemy Combatants, Subject: Summary of Evidence For Combatant Status Review Tribunal—Husayn, Zayn Al Abidin Muhammad [Abu Zubaydah] 19 March 2007; *The Black Banners*, p. 143.

902 The Abu Zubaydah story is told in detail in *The Black Banners*, pp. 373–435. It is also the most heavily censored part of former FBI Special Agent Ali Soufan's memoir, the deletions forced by the CIA to hide its behavior.

903 911 Commission Report (Official Report), p. 207.

904 Rumors started to circulate that FBI director Louis Freeh was going to be a sacrificial lamb almost the moment the arrest of Soviet spy (and FBI special agent) Robert Phillip Hanssen was announced on Tuesday, February 20, 2001.
On February 22, President Bush held his first full-fledged presidential news conference, in which he defended his tax-cutting and budget-tightening plans and gave FBI Director Freeh a vote of confidence, Washington's first kiss of death. On May 1, 2001, FBI Director Freeh informed President Bush that he would be resigning by the end of June; *My FBI*, p. 33.

905 Richard Clarke insists he resigned: "When, in June 2001, I became convinced that the Bush administration was hopelessly naïve and deaf on the terrorism issue, I resigned the senior U.S. counterterrorism job effective October 1." *Your Government Failed You*, p. 54.

906 *Your Government Failed You*, p. 2.

907 According to Lawrence Wright: "It was the first time in decades that a senior prince had been pushed aside, reputedly because of Crown Prince Abdullah's impatience with Turki's failure to get in Laden." *The Looming Tower*, p. 354.
Steve Coll writes that Saudi Arabia "adapted to a system of contracting that

American and British diplomats in the kingdom referred to as graft, but which the Saudis who benefited from it regarded as an entirely proper form of business in a country where all the land, all the natural resources, and all the power to dispose of them were vested in the estate of the royal family." *The Bin Ladens*, p. 47.

908 *The Bin Ladens*, p. 524; *The Muslim World After 9/11*, p. 126.

909 The San Diego office of the FBI closed a counterterrorism investigation of Omar al-Bayoumi on June 7, 1999; Joint, p. 174.

910 The 911 Commission staff interviewed Bayoumi in 2003. See Memorandum for the Record, Subject: Interview of Omar Al-Bayoumi Conference Palace, Riyadh, October 16–17, 2003.

911 *The Black Banners*, p. 554.

About the Author

William M. Arkin has been working in the field of national security for over 45 years: in U.S. Army intelligence, as an author, activist, journalist, academic and consultant to government. He provided on-air and behind-the-scenes analysis of 9/11 and its aftermath for NBC News. He is the author of two national bestsellers—*Top Secret America* and *Nuclear Battlefields*—as well as over a dozen other books.

Over the years, his award-winning reporting has appeared on the front pages of *The Washington Post*, *The New York Times*, and *The Los Angeles Times*. On behalf of Greenpeace International, Human Rights Watch, and the United Nations, he has visited Middle East and South Asia battle zones numerous times.

Arkin is weirdly proud to say that he spent the night in Saddam General Hospital in 1991 after being injured by an unexploded cluster bomb in Iraq, and that some of his fondest memories are picking through the rubble of Slobodan Milosevic's Belgrade villa and Taliban leader Mullah Omar's compound outside Kandahar in Afghanistan.

Over the course of his career, Arkin's specialty has been to conceive and implement large-scale and original data projects and public campaigns about the secret world. His 1980s research resulted in the first revelation ever of where all nuclear weapons in the world were located. He was one of the conceivers of the ground-breaking *Nuclear Weapons Databook* series for NRDC, ultimately a five-volume encyclopedia that challenged secrecy during the Reagan years. He conceived of and led the research for the Nuclear Free Seas campaign of Greenpeace International, which combined activism and information to eliminate all tactical nuclear weapons from the U.S. Navy. He conceived of and published the first authoritative dictionary of U.S. secret programs in *Codenames*. And he conceived of and co-wrote Top Secret America for *The Washington Post*, a three-year investigation into the shadows of the enormous system of military, intelligence and corporate interests created in the decade after 9/11.

Foreign Affairs, the bible of the foreign policy establishment, commented about Arkin in 1997: "The author is well known (and in some government quarters, cordially detested) as an indefatigable researcher in military affairs, whose cunning and persistence have uncovered many secrets ... " A 2003 *Washington Post* profile of Arkin commented: "William Arkin seems to have mastered one of the great juggling acts of the multimedia age—persuading news organizations, advocacy groups and the Pentagon, through sheer smarts and a bulldog personality, to take him on his own terms."

History in Oct Act is Arkin's debut novel. He lives in Encinitas, California. Contact at warkin@igc.org or follow on Twitter @warkin.

*f*eatherpr*oof* BOOKS

Publishing strange and beautiful fiction and nonfiction
and post-, trans-, and inter-genre tragicomedy.

Available at bookstores everywhere,
and direct from Chicago, Illinois at

www.*fe*atherproo*f*.com